EXPLORATIONS IN MUSIC, THE ARTS, AND IDEAS

Essays in Honor of
Leonard B. Meyer

Leonard B. Meyer

EXPLORATIONS IN MUSIC, THE ARTS, AND IDEAS

Essays in Honor of Leonard B. Meyer

Edited by Eugene Narmour
and Ruth A. Solie

FESTSCHRIFT SERIES No. 7

PENDRAGON PRESS
STUYVESANT

THE FESTSCHRIFT SERIES:

No. 1   *A Musical Offering: Essays in honor of Martin Bernstein* edited by
       E. Clinkscale and C. Brook (1977) ISBN
       0-918728-03-7   32.00

No. 2   *Aspects of Medieval and Renaissance Music: A birthday offering to Gustave*
       Reese edited by Jan LaRue (Pendragon Edition 1978) ISBN
       0-918728-07-X   64.00

No. 5   *Music in the Classic Period: Essays in honor of Barry S. Brook* edited by Allan
       A. Atlas (1985) ISBN 0-918728-37-1   48.00

No. 6   *Five Centuries of Choral Music: Essays in honor of Howard Swan* edited by
       Gordon Paine (1987) ISBN 0-918728-84-3   48.00

Library of Congress Cataloging-in-Publication Data

Explorations in music, the arts, and ideas.

(Festschrift series; no. 7)
1. Music–History and criticism: 2. Music–Theory. 3. Arts. 4. Meyer, Leonard B. I. Meyer
Leonard B. II. Narmour, Eugene III. Solie, Ruth A. IV. Series.
ML55.M46 1988   780'.9   87-32858
ISBN 0-918728-94-0 (lib. bdg.)

Table of Contents

Introduction

In the humanities great scholars tend to be either epistemologists or metaphysicians, realists or idealists, codifiers or innovators. Leonard B. Meyer stands as an anomaly in this company, for within the realm of musicology his work is at once pragmatic and imaginative. An astonishing blend of intellectual depth and breadth, his five books and numerous lengthy essays have covered all the major fields of the discipline—not only theory, analysis, criticism, and aesthetics, but also twentieth-century culture, psychology, the nature of science versus the study of the humanities, and, most recently, a refined historical theory explaining style change in the music of the nineteenth century.

It is hard to imagine a career launched more auspiciously than with *Emotion and Meaning in Music* in 1956—which served as Meyer's Ph.D. dissertation! One of the earliest and most innovative attempts to discuss in concrete terms the relevance of the Gestalt laws for music analysis and perception, the work explores as well how these laws might be used to construct a theory of perceptual aesthetics. (One finds parallels in Gombrich's *Art and Illusion*, Arnheim's *Art and Visual Perception*, and Smith's *Poetic Closure*—which latter, as its author acknowledged in 1968, owes a good deal to Meyer's influence.) Indeed, since its publication *Emotion and Meaning* has sold some 40,000 copies to date (surely a record of some sort for a music book with this type of intellectual content) and has remained a standard, seminal reference for all studies in musical aesthetics, musical ambiguity (as opposed to indeterminacy), psychology of music, and communications theory. Its reigning status is perhaps best summed up in a recent book on music cognition, which ranks it as one of the three most important books ever written in the psychology of music, along with Helmholtz's *On the Sensations of Tone* and Francès's *La Perception de la musique*.

In 1960, together with Grosvenor Cooper, Meyer published a second book, *The Rhythmic Structure of Music*, a theoretical study which continued to explore the relevance of the Gestalt laws to musical analysis and perception, but here specifically applied to rhythm as a summarized phenomenon. Ostensibly, the codificatory aspect of this book was concerned with the analytical application of the poetic-feet symbols to various hierarchical levels. Of course, this method of analyzing rhythm has a long tradition in music theory, from Mattheson, Riepel, and Koch in the eighteenth century and Reicha, Weber, and Westphal in the nineteenth to Riemann in our own, to name but a few. But excepting a very brief reference to Riemann, Cooper and Meyer discuss none of the work of these earlier theorists.

The omission was not an oversight, as some have suggested, but rather an indication that Cooper and Meyer's book was to extend beyond the usual historical ascription of poetic feet in analysis and point to something quite different, namely the identification of rhythmic groupings. (Even on the lowest level the accent/nonaccent symbols represented organizations of rhythmic groupings rather than meter: low-level trochees were *not* equivalent to the downbeat/upbeat stresses of $\frac{2}{4}$ meter, and as one moved to higher levels, the authors made it clear that each symbol stood for a multiplicity of parametric interactions: accent or nonaccent within any bracketed grouping indicated a *distribution* of varied parametric impingements.) To this day, the book remains the starting point for all twentieth-century studies of rhythmic theory and is routinely cited in psychological studies concerning temporal perception. In our view, in music theory it is still the best and most valuably suggestive book on the subject of musical grouping.

Meyer next brought out *Music, the Arts, and Ideas* (1967), a highly original work with wide-ranging essays on such diverse topics as information theory, aesthetics, and historiography. But the main thrust here was an attempt to make sense of the crazy-quilt of musical styles which had emerged in Western culture following World War II. From his penetrating analysis of twentieth-century culture, Meyer predicted that, unlike previous epochs, our own would continue to be dominated by a diverse stylistic multiplicity, a prognosis that remains true to this day. For example, in our roots-minded century, it is clear that every socio-politico-economic-intellectual class cultivates its own music. Thus, we not only have specialized audiences for Baroque and Classical music but also for transcendentalist, expressionist, and minimalist music, for jazz, early music, world music, and for academic-university-elitist music; moreover, we have large numbers of listeners devoted to rock, country, bluegrass, gospel, soul, pop, big band, "golden oldies," and no doubt many others identified by their own devotees.

There was another courageous prediction in *Music, the Arts, and Ideas* that appears to have been realized. Meyer argued that "total serialism" as a compositional technique was fatally perceptually flawed, lacking the psychological power to create a style with the built-in redundancy necessary for ordinary listeners to learn a syntax, and consequently that its pseudo-scientific basis (founded on no historical necessity whatever) would never achieve wide acceptance even among highly competent, music-loving audiences. And so it hasn't, much to the chagrin (and doubtless surprise) of the academic community that at the time so proudly touted it as the music of the future.

Leaving the heady world of contemporaneous cultural analysis to others, in 1973 Meyer returned once again, with the writing of *Explaining Music*, to the codification of certain analytical ideas. The book is cast in two parts, the first containing essays on criticism (a subject he later expanded into a monograph-size article on the Trio of Mozart's Symphony no. 40), performance, conformant structures, and hierarchies —a continuing preoccupation in all his books. The second part, a theory of melodic implication, presents a synthesis of various ideas discussed in *Emotion and Meaning* and *The Rhythmic Structure of Music*. For instance, the musical processes noted in the earlier work were now closely related to the rhythmic groupings from which they come. Objectifying the concept of expectation, Meyer used poetic-foot groupings as the criteria for generating and determining structures of melodic implication and realization. And he hypothesized the fundamental processes of gap-filling and continuation from which he was able to identify certain basic melodic schematic structures in tonal music—for example, axial, changing-note, neighboring-note, triadic, linear, complementary, and so forth. The conclusions of this book have had, and will continue to have, we believe, important ramifications for future theories of melody concerned with perception.

No discussion of Meyer would be complete without mentioning his role as a teacher. Any extended talk with the man invariably leads to at least three good book-sized ideas; indeed, it is doubtful whether any scholar has ever been more generous with his original ideas than Leonard Meyer. For unlike some other influential scholars of his day, Meyer has never tried to establish a ''school,'' and this is because, as his work clearly demonstrates, he is a pluralist at heart, with an abiding distrust for anything that masquerades as ''capital-T'' truth. As a devout empiricist Meyer is essentially a ''doer'' instead of a ''talker.'' Some years ago, several students and colleagues of his bemoaned in his presence the shortcomings of most recent music histories: the current books seemed to be more ''about'' music rather than ''of'' it, and offered too little in the way of real explanation why inherited Western music is the way it is—whereupon Meyer averred that if they were really concerned, they themselves should write a ''real'' history of music instead of complaining about the state of affairs. Now he himself has done just that in his fifth book, *Style and Music: Theory, History, and Ideology,* expected in the fall of 1988.

How might we sum up the Meyerian production to date—which in its seventieth year miraculously shows no signs of abating? It is in this: Meyer's theoretical-analytical works—the epistemological side of his personality—represent a search for the nomothetic unity of the humanistic experience. In complement, his historico-cultural books demonstrate why, in this great metaphysical quest for codification, we must not compromise or sacrifice the idiographic diversity of our subject matter. One searches in vain in this generation for a comparable figure who has so pragmatically and imaginatively, so realistically and idealistically, so searchingly and yet so broadly, assimilated, explicated, and interconnected so many nominally heterogeneous disciplines.

All of the essays in this celebratory volume reveal their affinity with, and the more or less direct influence of, Leonard Meyer's work; their widely variegated array bears witness to the catholicity of his thought and the ubiquity of its impact. Emblematic of this impact, and so of the volume, is the opening sentence of Rose Subotnik's essay: "Emotion and meaning are coming out of the musicological closet." Thus, certain issues familiar to readers of Meyer pervade the collection: meaning and meaningfulness; the centrality of experience—both of listener and composer, and of each both as individual and as historic construction; the delicate balance of often opposed demands of theoretical rigor and humanistic sweep; a certain salutary self-consciousness—the sense, one might say, of the implications of methodology. Above all, what these writers have learned from Meyer is the refusal to be defeated by or capitulate to the sometimes argumentative interplay between the historical persona of musicology and its more analytical moods.

The essays collected in the first section of the book inhabit the terrain where musical experience intersects with the phenomena of history, thus raising questions about the autonomy of musical compositions and of composers as independent actors on the historical scene. Ruth Solie looks at nineteenth-century discourse about music in order to illuminate the ways in which music was embedded in contemporaneous intellectual life; in turn, she suggests, that discourse vividly affects present-day experiences of the music in question. In like manner drawing evidence from a repertory of writing about music, John Platoff explores the problematic issue of musical influence. He asks why musicologists concern themselves with this issue, under what conditions influence may validly be asserted, and what this musicological habit tells us about our historiographic presuppositions. Margaret Murata confronts the notion of artistic autonomy directly, attempting a *rapprochement* between traditional formalism—with its disconcerting tendency to make history disappear—and the currently more fashionable contextualism, with its attendant threat, the disappearance of the individual work. Rose Rosengard Subotnik deconstructs the ideology of "structural listening," documenting its birth out of particular historical circumstances and political conditions. Her close comparative reading of Adorno, Schoenberg, and Stravinsky on this subject thus reveals history actively impinging upon our personal experience of music.

The next three essays constitute a multidisciplinary meditation on theorizing and what to make of it. Barbara Herrnstein Smith explores the role and force of theoretical activity within the mechanisms of academic discourse itself. Interested, like Subotnik, in the social responsibilities of the critic, she demonstrates the mutual entailment of the canon and the critical methodology surrounding it, and so invites a certain skepticism about the immanent properties of texts. Burton Rosner's paper provides a model for the interaction of theories originating in different disciplines in order to solve problems accessible to neither alone. He details three different epistemological relationships between psychology and music theory, in which psychology may provide explanations of music-theoretical concepts, psychological experiments may serve to evaluate the hypotheses of music theory, or music theory may serve psychology as a source for models of mental structures. Jan Herlinger's essay is "interdisciplinary" in another sense; he encourages students of *trecento* music to consider what can be learned from contemporary theorists that is not evident from the musical artifacts themselves, and he shows what has been misconstrued because of the failure to do so. Like many of these essays, Herlinger's harks back to issues raised by Murata about the meaning—and meaningfulness—of written musical scores originating in a given historical context.

The five essays collected in Part III may be said to explore the role of empirical studies in these post-positivist days. Together they provide an interesting commentary on the topography of today's intellectual landscape since, even at this extreme of theoretical rigor, they are by and large profoundly subversive of the presuppositions of academic formalism common only a decade or two ago. However much machinery or mathematics may be entailed by their methods, they insist on the centrality of the "beholder's share," and on the significance of music as a transaction between and among human beings. Robert Gjerdingen invokes the power and vividness of what he calls "concrete knowledge" as opposed to abstract conceptualization, exploring what happens if, contrary to much of our theorizing, musical knowledge is posited as beginning from the concrete and stylistically specific. In this essay he describes a computer program which improvises counterpoint in the same practical show-must-go-on way sixteenth-century singers did (that is, without benefit of electronic prescience), even acknowledging its occasional miscalculations with an engaging "oops." Somewhat in the same vein, Frank Tirro describes the use of a Markoff chain to model the process of successive melodic choices made by a composer of Gregorian hymn tunes. In neither of these cases, of course, is the goal mechanical additions to a long-standing human repertory; rather, both authors seek to learn how experienced musicians know what they're doing and how they go about doing it. Diana Deutsch's contribution also takes on problems of classification and abstraction, reminding us at the same time of one of the modes described by Rosner for the inter- action of psychology and music theory. Deutsch demonstrates that the evidence provided by experimental subjects (listeners) may sometimes be at odds with the outcomes our standard systematization of musical materials would predict; even more disconcertingly, the evidence she provides of unexpectedly great variation among individual listeners poses an interesting problem for many of our theoretical suppositions. In yet another challenge to our customary habits of abstraction, John Chesnut takes on the recently taboo subject of musical affect, proposing a net- work of semantic categories as the underpinning of a new technique of formal analysis. As a capstone to this group, Eugene Narmour's essay brings together issues of musical affect, the "tacit knowledge" of ex- perienced musicians, the meaning of musical relationships, and the rela- tion of theorizing to musical practice. Good theory, he says and demon- strates here, should help performers discover how their interpretations are heard and understood by listeners.

The essays in the final group address the experiences of listeners directly—always bearing in mind that composers and performers are also, at bottom, listeners—demonstrating how analytic and critical tools may be fashioned that are more respectful of those experiences than most methods we have heretofore had available. Patricia Carpenter reminds us that analytic activity comprehends both the creator's and the beholder's stance and that therefore the critic must take epistemo- logical responsibility for the convergences and divergences of the two. Her essay explores the interrelatedness of musical time and space, both notionally and experientially, especially by means of what she calls the exploitation of simultaneity. Her approach to these matters is through

Schoenberg's conceptions of musical idea and musical space, and her essay thus enters into a particularly provocative dialogue with Subotnik's earlier in the volume. James Kidd's contribution considers aspects of our "direct, bodily, and vivid knowing" of music that systematizing theory has overlooked, and might perhaps be thought of as a more essayistic version of Gjerdingen's counterpointing computer. He asks how melodic tonality is perceived—and in particular what the performer makes of it—and what "tonality" can be said to mean when it is not taken as an abstract system-description but as a set of quite distinct and personal aural experiences. Raising a similar question in the formal arena is Robert Hopkins's exploration of the meaning of "coda." Suggesting that eighteenth-century definitions are not appropriate for nineteenth-century pieces, particularly in that formal definitions do not help listeners construe codas that take on new and unexpected functions, his essay reveals the extent to which we may be hamstrung by our etymological allegiance to a word, in this case "coda." Finally, David Brodbeck proffers the notions of "compatibility, coherence, and closure" as strategies for critical understanding that resemble Kidd's and Hopkins's, dealing fundamentally with sense-making. As a sketch study, Brodbeck's essay focuses specifically on the composer's own sense-making process as he rethinks the ordering of a series of pieces.

The editors gratefully acknowledge financial support for this volume from the President, Provost, and Dean of the School of Arts and Sciences of the University of Pennsylvania. We also thank all the authors herein for their contributions and cooperation—no editors ever had better—in bringing this Festschrift to fruition.

E.N.
R.A.S.

Ruth A. Solie

Beethoven as Secular Humanist: Ideology and the Ninth Symphony in Nineteenth-Century Criticism

> This symphony is one of those intellectual watersheds which, visible from afar, and inaccessible, separate the currents of antagonistic beliefs.
>
> Eduard Hanslick[1]

> The spirit of Beethoven is as humanising as the spirit of Sophocles.
>
> Edward Dannreuther[2]

In recent years musicologists have been energetic in their efforts to demonstrate that the history of music in Europe has participated in the history of ideas more widely understood.[3] Although instinct suggests that this must be so, exploration of the relationship has been difficult because the attribution of intellectual or political meaning-content to musical compositions is a notoriously slippery business. In this essay I will address the question through a "side door," as it were: I will argue that the link between music and other aspects of European in-

---

[1] *The Beautiful in Music*, trans. Gustav Cohen (Indianapolis, 1957), p. 68
[2] "Beethoven and His Works: A Study," *Macmillan's Magazine* 34 (1876), p. 194.
[3] An elegant study making use of the same piece I deal with here is Leo Treitler's "History, Criticism, and Beethoven's Ninth Symphony," *19th Century Music* 3 (1980): 193-210.

Ruth A. Solie is Professor of Music at Smith College where she also participates in the Women's Studies program. She is the author of essays and reviews in music theory and its history, aesthetics, music in the history of ideas, and women's history.

1

tellectual life can be made visible by studying music's place in the general
cultural conversation. The critical language in which music is described
and evaluated, I will suggest, derives from a common pool applicable
to all subjects of discussion, and therefore reveals common concerns
and ideological presuppositions of the period.

There are reasons why the nineteenth century proves a particularly
revealing arena for this kind of study. As has frequently been observed
(and was recognized at the time), music played a central role in artistic
and cultural life during most of that century; especially in Germany
and German-dominated areas (including England) it was considered the
paradigmatic art, and its current events made headlines. As Peter Gay
has commented in a discussion of Hanslick, music criticism in his time
was "something like a boxing match, a political maneuver, or a military
campaign"[4]—controversial, contentious, and a matter of great public
interest. In the absence of a highly professionalized class of scholars
of music and, particularly, of an "analytic" tradition in the sense in
which we know it, music was a regular part of general cultural discourse;
serious discussions of it found their way not only into the general
literature—music criticism was as likely from George Eliot or Friedrich
Nietzsche as from Robert Schumann or George Grove—but even, as
we shall see, into works of popular fiction.

What made this broad cultural conversation possible was primarily
an underlying set of assumptions about music and its role in individual
and social life. It was taken for granted that, at least among the intelligent-
sia, people both enjoyed contemporary music and understood
it[5]—although that latter assertion requires some qualification, to which
I shall return below. Furthermore, it was expected that music had certain fundamental relationships to "real life," both as part of the social
fabric and in connection with individual experience. In the commentaries discussed throughout this essay these preconceptions are evident:
whatever the political, aesthetic, or other polemical position adopted
by a given writer, there is virtually always the assumption that personal
and social meanings are resident in whatever music is under scrutiny,
and that uncovering those meanings is one of the commentator's primary

[4]Peter Gay, *Freud, Jews and Other Germans: Masters and Victims in Modernist Culture* (Oxford, 1978), p. 258.
[5]William Weber has described the process by which, during the course of the century, bourgeois taste gradually fixated on "dead composers." (See his "Mass Culture and the Reshaping of European Musical Taste, 1770-1870," *International Review of the Aesthetics and Sociology of Music* 8 [1977]: 5-21.) Nonetheless, "men of letters" (as the English had it) retained their lively interest in current musical events and their right to comment upon them.

tasks. Despite Heinrich Schenker's assertion that he was among the first to discuss the "real content" of music, earlier writers—many of them part musician, part social critic—had an equally firm and equally distinct notion of "content," different as it was from Schenker's later vision.

This essay, then, is not "about" Beethoven, nor "about" the Ninth Symphony. Rather, it takes that piece and its attendant commentary as exemplary of the ways in which religious, philosophical, and political ideologies are reflected in the interpretation of music during the nineteenth century; these reflections, of course, come in turn to shape future perceptions of the piece and its place in the canon. That the Ninth Symphony yields a particularly rich harvest of such allusions will surprise no one: I have chosen it primarily because it is so very much discussed. It looms large during the three-quarters of the century after its composition, undergoing symbolic readings that vary enormously (often contradicting one another) but never slacken either in frequency or polemical force. One might imagine the piece as a reflecting glass or, better, something like the monolith of Stanley Kubrick's film *2001*—always present, hugely, at the center of discourse, inviting the attachment of meanings, almost as though it were a blank surface. In the nineteenth century only the music of Wagner was as central to conversation and as passionately argued over.[6]

THE IMAGE OF BEETHOVEN

First and foremost there is, of course, the legendary Beethoven, the composer above all others for whom the nineteenth century wrote what Roland Barthes has called a "bio-mythology." He was created, says Barthes, "a complete hero, granted a discourse (rare for a musician), a legend (a good score of anecdotes), an iconography, a race (that of the Titans of art: Michelangelo, Balzac), and a fatal flaw (deafness in one who created for the ear's pleasure)."[7] The names "Titan" and "Prometheus" are rampant in the literature about him, granting him mythic status early on; godlike images abound, in a confused hodgepodge of

[6]According to a recent NPR broadcast ("All Things Considered," 9 February 1987), the formation of "Number 9 choruses" is just now becoming a frenzy in Japan, complete with imported German-language teachers. Interestingly, some social critics are attributing the craze to Japan's World War II connection to Germany—now surfacing nostalgically in a neo-conservative world; others vehemently disagree. The Ninth, it seems, is still carrying disputed political/ideological messages.

[7]Roland Barthes, "Musica Practica," *L'Arc* 40 (1970) [Beethoven number], p. 16, my translation.

pagan and Christian references that represents Romanticism in distilled
form. A mere decade after the composer's death, Robert Schumann
heard in the Adagio of the Ninth the heavens opening "to receive Beethoven like a soaring saint" so that "it was impossible not to forget the
pettiness of this world and not to feel a presentiment of the Beyond thrilling the beholders ..." (223)[8] and his fellow *Davidsbündler* Feski heard
the *"Seid umschlungen"* passage in the finale as an irresistible invitation to throw himself into the composer's open arms (126). Nor, of
course, was the frenzy merely local. In 1856 a statue of Beethoven was
installed in the Boston Music Hall, and its inauguration marked by the
reading of a long poem by one William W. Story. Momentarily at a
loss for words, Story says:

> We can only say, Great Master, take the homage of our heart;
> Be the High Priest in our temple, dedicate to thee and Art.
> Stand before us, and enlarge us with thy presence and thy power,
> And o'er all Art's deeps and shallows light us like a beacon-tower.

Story's poem continues for forty-seven couplets and, it will be noted,
mimics the metric scheme of Schiller's "Ode to Joy."

There is more here than mere overheated rhetoric, else such fevered
quotes would be of little interest. What underlay the intense and ongoing fascination with the Ninth Symphony was the persistent belief—
apparently quite earnest—that Beethoven, like any other saint, had
messages to convey from beyond the grave. Wagner described the symphonies point-blank as "a revelation from another world" (1860, 77).
Edward Dannreuther, a serious writer in a serious journal, describes
the music of the late period as touching upon

> the domain of the seer and the prophet; when, in unison with all genuine
> mystics and ethical teachers, he delivers a message of religious love and
> resignation—of identification with the sufferings of all living creatures,
> deprecation of self, negation of personality, release from the world (197).

It is because the figure of Beethoven—his character and his life as well
as his music—was invested with religious and moral content that his
works were pored over so earnestly in search of oracles.

We learn something else about the popular view of Beethoven from
the fact that his name is so often coupled with those of Dante and

---

[8]Primary sources are listed alphabetically below, and are not hereafter footnoted in
the text.

Shakespeare, not merely as great creators but as definitively established avatars of national genius. This habit may in part account for Richard Wagner's problematic relationship to Beethoven, creating as it did the suspicion that there was room for only one permanent embodiment of the German spirit, or in any event only one in music. (When Beethoven shared this place of honor it was invariably with Goethe.) Many later arguments about Wagnerism were fought out on this battlefield—the personification of genuine German art—and at the same time the Beethoven myth helped to generate the perception, continent-wide by the end of the century, that serious music in a very real sense *was* German music.[9]

The ideology of genius has its own byways and ramifications, of course, and many of them participate in the creation here of an oracular symphony whose message had continually to be divined. The Romantic creator is one whose work "is initiated by the idea." That is, there is something transcendental at the core, underneath the eye's or ear's surface perception.

> And the purport of this idea, the dream picture of which [the artist] carries in his mind, determines the form in which it is to be realised... And if ever genius has demonstrated the truth of this fact, Beethoven is that one... Beethoven's most profound compositions [the last quartets and the first and third movements of the Ninth Symphony] ... serve to prove that the highest ideas cannot be adequately realised in the types mentioned. And upon the idea everything depends; for it is the Eternal, the Infinite (Elterlein 87).

This is pure idealism, Hegel out of Coleridge; it clearly invites exegesis, whose pursuit is not discouraged but rather spurred on by the concomitant realization that it can probably never be fully satisfactory.

> When any work of Beethoven's is called an organism, it is obvious that if the phrase is to convey any meaning, it must signify that in point of form and musical contents Beethoven's works are as perfect as any product of nature. That is to say, so far above any product of traditional or teachable art as to be only intuitively and not logically comprehensible (Dannreuther 197).

[9]When in 1874 George Eliot created her quintessential musician, Klesmer, her description of him as "a felicitous combination of the German, the Sclave, and the Semite" both recognized this tradition and responded provocatively to the racist Wagnerian polemics rampant at the time. (*Daniel Deronda*, ed. Barbara Hardy [Penguin English Library Edition, 1967], p. 77)

As we shall see further on, later and particularly American forms of idealism took a different view of the discoverability of nature's (and Beethoven's) secrets, as scientific advance gave credence to prevailing mores of social progressivism.

THE IMAGE OF THE NINTH

In addition to the aura that surrounded the name of Beethoven, there are features of this symphony itself that invited the development of a mystique of its own. From the beginning, its sheer size astonished critics. At first the length of the piece was routinely cited as a flaw; critics of the first London performance in March of 1825 complained that "the author has spun it out to so unusual a length, that he has drawn out the thread of his verbosity finer than the staple of his argument" ("C," 91) and, in another case, that "its length alone will be a never-failing cause of complaint to those who reject monopoly in sounds, as it takes up exactly one hour and twenty minutes in performance" (Anonymous 1825, 81). But this latter critic intuited as well the relationship between the piece's length and its sheer bigness of sound; he refers to "so much rambling and vociferous execution given to the violins," to the "deafning boisterous jollity" of the concluding section in which "all the known acoustical missile instruments I should conceive" are employed, and in general to "the obstreperous roarings of modern frenzy" that the symphony typified for him. In the long run, of course, his perception of the link between duration and size of musical conception proved more prophetic than, for example, the German critic Herrmann Hirschbach's opinion that the piece was *"zu lang ausgesponnen"* simply through sheer monotony and excessive repetition (32).

As later nineteenth-century compositions gradually became larger, as audiences became accustomed to concert-going as a mass social activity and to awed reverence as the appropriate mien in a concert hall,[10] the size of the Ninth took on a different connotation, giving it the lineaments of monumentality and making it appear prophetic. I would even argue that in a psychological sense the symphony continued to grow during the latter decades of the century. When Wagner writes in 1873 of the reorchestrations he used in his Leipzig performance of the work, his apologia rests upon the "opulence" of Beethoven's conception and suggests (reverently, of course) that the work is even larger than its composer realized it was, arguing that his deafness "led him

---

[10]See Weber, "Mass Culture..." *passim*.

at last to an almost naive disregard of the relation of the actual embodiment to the musical thought itself" (1873, 232, 241). The greater number of his changes in orchestration were made to enlarge the sound of the piece in what he saw as the correct proportion to its length and spiritual conception. It is well known that this tradition, once established, was continued with ever-increasing grandiosity by other conductors, including both von Bülow and Mahler.[11]

The many references to this symphony as a message from beyond the grave, like occurrences of the term "swan song," indicate that the Ninth's position as a late work in Beethoven's *oeuvre* is also important to its mystique. Again and again writers make casual reference to its status as a kind of last will and testament (although they must have been aware of the later origin of the last quartets),[12] and seem to be attempting to read it as we have recently seen Mozart's *Requiem* cinematically read, as the dramatic last utterance from a deathbed. There is a certain intrinsic quality to a late piece, perhaps based on what Janet Levy has described as the covert valuing of "maturity" in music criticism.[13] Certainly the idea is supported by Alexandre Oulibicheff's curious characterization of Beethoven as "old for his age" when he worked on the piece (269).

Since present-day audiences and scholars of music history have been bequeathed a traditional account of the Ninth Symphony dominated by incomprehension of its formal innovations and outrage at the appending of a choral movement to a symphony, it may come as a surprise that not all of its contemporary critics were troubled by these anomalies. Rather, such questions were themselves at the core of the debate about the deeper meaning of the piece, and the debating parties lined up in ways quite consistent with other aspects of their ideological posture. A characterization of those who found the piece unproblematic and clearly based on traditional classical forms—this is not to say that they agreed about what those forms were—reveals the lay of the land: they were French, or anti-Wagnerians, or orthodox religionists, or what we might call "proto-formalists"—explicators of notes instead of messages. The anti-Wagnerian Selmar Bagge characterizes Beethoven's forms as fairly

[11]See Walter Damrosch, "Hans von Bülow and the Ninth Symphony," *Musical Quarterly* 13 (1927): 280-93 and Denis McCaldin, "Mahler and Beethoven's Ninth Symphony," *Proceedings of the Royal Musical Association* 107 (1980-81): 101-10.
[12]This may suggest the exemption of the Ninth from the pervasive confusion and bafflement surrounding Beethoven's late works. See Robin Wallace, *Beethoven's Critics: Aesthetic Dilemmas and Resolutions during the Composer's Lifetime* (Cambridge, 1986).
[13]Janet M. Levy, "Covert and Casual Values in Recent Writings about Music," *The Journal of Musicology* 5 (1987): 3-27.

usual with some modifications, identifying the finale as a fantasy to which the composer has joined aspects of variation form. The primary category, fantasy, is of course significant since as a genre it has been marked by formal freedom from its beginning; thus the extreme irregularity of this movement is contained within a fixed historical tradition. Revealingly, Bagge bolsters his analysis with evidence that the symphony Beethoven left unfinished, the projected tenth, appeared from extant sketches to be purely instrumental. If this seems irrelevant, consider that the *Zukunftsmusik* line required the assumption that in the Ninth Beethoven had brought purely instrumental music to the limit of its possibilities, an apocalyptic arrival that in turn required the reading of the finale as innovative and entirely unprecedented, a new birth. True to form, Bagge reads the spiritual message of the piece in purely orthodox terms; Beethoven's message, he says, is that only religion can bring us from earthly pain into joy—indeed, the shape of the symphony as a whole makes it clear that only those who have seen extreme pain and suffering will be rewarded on this magnificent scale (71).

An exactly similar web of argumentation is presented by Vincent d'Indy as late as 1911. He discusses the Ninth together with the *Missa solemnis*, prefacing all with an account of the religious underpinnings of Beethoven's late style:

> ... wishing to have done with a wretched existence which no longer offers him a single exterior attraction, he turns his gaze inward, to that soul which he has ever striven to raise toward God, the Source of all that is good and beautiful ... And thus he comes to lead a purely introspective life, an almost monastic life, contemplative, intense, fruitful (92).

From this reading it seems naturally to follow that "... the entire aesthetics of his third manner are founded on ancient forms theretofore unemployed by him ... a solid ancestral basis ... These forms are the Fugue, the Suite, the Chorale with Variations" (97). There is perhaps a touch of overkill in d'Indy's subsequent easy classification of the first movement as "constructed after an impeccable sonata plan" (114), the third as "a prayer" (115), and the *"Seid umschlungen"* passage as "a liturgical chant, a psalm constructed on the eighth Gregorian mode (with—possibly—a trifle less delicacy in the use of the tritone than was observed by the monkish composers of the middle ages)" (116). The point, I need not stress further, is not who was "right" about the generic assignment of these movements, but that from a particular sort of orthodox religious commitment a particular kind of analysis follows, and that is because conversations about the Ninth Symphony had been going on for so long and in such a tangled but thoroughly familiar contextual web.

Among French commentators, Berlioz provides what at first appears to be a counterexample. His discussion of the piece begins with a different—though elsewhere familiar—trope of this discourse: "To analyze such a composition is a difficult and a dangerous task, and one we have long hesitated to undertake" (43). As one reads on, however, it becomes apparent that the sort of difficulty he has in mind is of the workshop variety. Beethoven's formal novelties, he argues, must occur here by "an intention as reasonable and as beautiful for the fervent Christian as for the pantheist or the atheist—in fact an intention purely musical and poetical" (44), and he then proceeds to explore the formal, harmonic and melodic structures of the piece with a professional eye toward understanding its inner workings. This is a notion of "difficulty" and "innovation" quite distinct from that intended by the camp for whom these terms are philosophically value-laden.

In this latter group, deeply committed to the mystification of the symphony, are Wagnerians, Romantic idealists, American transcendentalists, and those inclined to radical politics—in general, and here is the core of the argument that I will expand upon below, they were apologists for a growing secular philosophy they referred to as "humanism." It is, among other things, an orientation toward a moralistic ideology of "art" as opposed to "entertainment," so that the difficulty of the piece is an important mark of distinction. In a famous passage on hearing this symphony, Schumann wrote "I am the blind man who is standing before the Strasbourg Cathedral, who hears its bells but cannot see the entrance..." (98). By its mysteriousness, the work is elevated to a status above or beyond the comprehension of mere mortals. Lowell Mason's 1862 review of a Birmingham performance begins in this manner— "We are entirely incompetent to give any description of this composition"—and goes on to detail the implications of his disclaimer:

> Who comprehends immensity and eternity? But does it follow that, therefore, these may not fill the mind with aspirations after the Infinite, the source of all perfection and happiness? We may not understand, and yet may derive great pleasure and good from the musical forms of truth, which Beethoven or others have discovered (13).

Difficulty is important, then, because it suggests that the piece has something to teach or convey that will repay effort, and it assures that one is not merely enjoying oneself. Perhaps the quintessential confessional statement in this mode comes from an anonymous London correspondent, "P," to *Dwight's* in 1852:

> Then came the last movement, about which I stay my pen. I did not understand it, and reverently stand in hope and faith, that its secrets may at some future day be revealed to me.

So entrenched was this position vis-à-vis music that it went beyond simple spiritual experience to develop its own Puritan work ethic. Thus the British clergyman and amateur musician, H. R. Haweis: "... German music is ... a truer expression, and a more disciplined expression, of the emotions. To follow a movement of Beethoven is, in the first place, a bracing exercise of the intellect" (59).

In some critical circles, however, where the complexities and formal innovations of the piece as a whole were not valued but viewed as flaws, a different tone was taken. The symphony was frequently dubbed a "monstrosity," and its critics were particularly fond of inventing clever metaphors of incongruity to describe it. David Friedrich Strauss's entire reading of the piece is focused on this issue, and in a single two-page article he develops some half-dozen such images to drive home the point. He compares the piece to the dog-headed gods and man-beast creatures of myth and antiquity; he likens Beethoven to a sculptor who places a colored head atop a white marble torso; he characterizes the choral finale as a "vocal *deus ex machina*" used to rescue the composer from a musical dilemma. Hanslick called the finale "the gigantic shadow of a gigantic body" (1957, 69), and Oulibicheff dismissed the whole as "two works joined only by a catalogue number" (287). These epithets are prompted, of course, by the ever-present ideology of organicism, which demanded a sort of biological trueness to nature that would naturally prohibit any appearance of arbitrary constructedness. But it is an organicism folded back upon itself, belying its idealist origins (and what Stackelberg has called idealism's "contempt for material evidence")[14] and producing a criticism redolent of formalism. These writers are talking about the music, not about its message; indeed, it is clear that the practice of quasi-biblical exegesis in connection with the Ninth enabled critics who indulged in it to construct narratives that accounted for the symphony's formal puzzlements and thus domesticated

[14]Roderick Stackelberg, *Idealism Debased: From* Völkisch *Ideology to National Socialism* (Kent OH, 1981), p. 2.

them. It was writers dealing only with the notes who had the problem, and they recognized it. David Strauss, who was a theologian and historian of religion, saw clearly that in invoking pagan images like dog-headed gods he was acknowledging ''monsters'' of undeniably powerful symbolic meaning to human beings; nonetheless, he says, what is symbolic and psychologically important is not necessarily artistically successful (col. 130).

For these essentially conservative writers Beethoven's mixed-media event violated not only organic principles but also tenets of the earlier (but still powerful) pure form of Romanticism. In 1810, well before the composition of the Ninth, E. T. A. Hoffmann claimed Beethoven for Romanticism in a gesture, Rosen and Zerner explain, designed

> first, to appropriate an already acknowledged classicism and assimilate it into Romantic art; and, second, to take pure, instrumental music, the most abstract of the arts, as a model of Romantic poetry, and to claim for poetry the ability of music to create an independent world of its own—a visionary world, whose relation to the real world is always ironic, as the absolute purity of instrumental music is finally unattainable for the poet.[15]

In the 1850s conservative critics could hardly help seeing at least partial failure in a symphony that Wagnerians were citing as proof of the expressive limitations of purely instrumental music.

The genre confusion into which the piece threw its commentators can often be spotted in the varying constellations of names with which Beethoven's was associated by different writers as they pondered to what tradition the piece belonged.[16] The association most natural to us— Haydn, Mozart, Beethoven—appears only infrequently, not, I think, because its historical force was unrecognized but because nineteenth-century critics were less interested than we in the bald ''facts'' of music history and stylistic evolution. Then too, they saw the classical proportions of the two earlier composers in sharp contrast to the gigantism that had become a regular feature of Beethoven hagiography. The pseudonymous Elterlein specifically contrasts Beethoven to his two great predecessors on the grounds that, while their symphonic messages can more or less be viewed collectively — Haydn's is ''pure, childlike ideali-

---

[15]Charles Rosen and Henri Zerner, *Romanticism and Realism: The Mythology of Nineteenth-Century Art* (New York, 1984), p. 34.
[16]Treitler's article discusses the ways in which Beethoven's extraordinary mix of genres in the symphony functions as a set of codes for the listener. For Beethoven's contemporaries, apparently, the signals were often crossed.

ty'' and Mozart's ''noble, harmonious humanity''—''each [of Beethoven's symphonies] represents a world in itself, with an ideal centre
of its own'' (ix). Haydn is frequently invoked in fictional accounts of
the symphony's genesis, as we shall see below, but there he appears
as ''Papa Haydn,'' clearly in the role not of professional precursor but
of spiritual guide and mentor. Mozart's name is infrequent except in
the most technical discussions of *thematische Arbeit*; in some circles
he was suspected of too great a love of sensuous beauty.[17] British writers,
not surprisingly, often couple Beethoven's name with Handel's (see,
for instance, Grove 396), suggesting that for them the symphony could
most easily be taken in in terms of the English oratorio tradition which
simultaneously accounted for the chorus, for the tone of moral uplift,
and for the grandiosity of the spectacle.[18] This same habit of categoriz-
ing by association provided a perhaps unexpected forum for working
out disputes as to the purpose and function of music. Among the most
provocative of links, for example, is Dannreuther's of ''Palestrina, Bach,
and Beethoven''—a genealogy clearly designed to fix the piece in a
religious or didactic framework.[19] The English late-century insistence
upon art as primarily an instrument of moral education comes strongly
to the fore here. K. R. Hennig adds a different polemical twist by speaking of ''Beethoven, Schumann, Wagner''—that is, by projecting
Beethoven's lineage into a specifically Wagnerian future (8).

Hennig thus reminds us that the Ninth not only has ancestors but,
in proper organic fashion, generates offspring. The monumentality and
prophetic status granted the piece made its place in history a matter
of serious import that was much argued over. Through the 1830s the
Ninth Symphony still passed for ''contemporary music,'' and contemporary music was still the principal concert fare, although partisan and
nationalist quarrels were the order of the day. As time went on, and
the shift in repertory began—becoming fixed at the classical masters—
language changed to reflect a set of values higher than ''cutting-edge''
contemporaneity: that is, Beethoven and his masterpiece gradually came
to represent not only German music as a whole, but the spirit of the

[17]A marked exception is presented by Bernard Shaw, who links Mozart and Beethoven
in a particular way, as writers of what he considered serious religious music (1981,
I, 356).
[18]However, the fact that the first London performances were sung in Italian perhaps
suggests an early attempt to hear it in the context of opera.
[19]Palestrina's name is invoked in a different, political, context by the notorious Houston
Stewart Chamberlain, who wanted to consider him a sort of honorary German.
''Palestrina follows closely in the footsteps of the men of the north'' and is thus ultimately
related to Beethoven (511 ff.).

nineteenth century as well. Teetgen says that "Beethoven ushered in the nineteenth century; he was the Napoleon of its better half…" (117), and Dannreuther makes clear some of the background and socially-based reasons why this matters:

> The whole distance of the revolution and the birth of the modern spirit in poetry and philosophy lies between him and his predecessors. He was the first among musicians who distinctly felt the influence of the literary and social fermentation of his time. He is the first to become conscious of the struggles and aims of mankind *en masse*, and he is the first musician, if not the first poet, who consciously offers himself as the singer of humanity. Essentially a man of the 19th century, his music reflects modern life quite as much, if not more, than Goethe's *Faust* does (195).

By the 70s, the formerly fluid repertory having begun to congeal in various ways around the Gibraltar that the Ninth by then presented, local disputes and stylistic shifts had themselves become part of history. Haweis writes that history shows us two kinds of music.

> Between the spirit of the musical Sentimentalist and the musical Realist there is eternal war. The contest may rage under different captains. At one time it is the mighty Gluck who opposes the ballad-mongering Piccini; at another it is the giant Handel versus the melodramatic Bononcini; or it is Mozart against all France and Italy; or Beethoven against Rossini, or Wagner against the world … [in each case the issues are] false emotion, or abused emotion, or frivolous emotion versus true feeling, disciplined feeling, or sublime feeling (57).[20]

Talented at capsulizing various but related ideological strands, Haweis here makes it clear that as of 1871 the canon is firmly in place, that its heroes are without exception German, and that the famous Beethoven-Rossini rivalry has become part of a consistent and intelligible teleology, one moreover that legitimizes Wagner's claim to the historical succession. Elsewhere he deftly brings together several of the threads of this rhetorical web—racial characterization, the moral purpose of art, the habit of reading extramusical content into musical compositions, and the need to work at it all—in one summary sentence: "It would not be difficult to show in great detail the essentially voluptuous character of Italian music, the essentially frivolous and sentimental character of

[20]On the sense of "realism" intended here, an essentially avant-garde aesthetic, see Rosen and Zerner.

French music, and the essentially moral, many-sided, and philosophical character of German music'' (61).

Because of Beethoven's formal innovations, and largely on the strength of the choral finale, it was very early predicted that the Ninth would play a decisive role in music history as the efficient cause of the demise of the instrumental symphony since it was thought to have outrun the artistic and expressive possibilities of the genre. Sometimes Wagner is credited with originating this notion because he harped so relentlessly on the piece as prophetic of his *Gesamtkunstwerk*, but indeed some version of this rhetorical trope had been around almost from the beginning, and it was often enough invoked by those who had little interest in seeing the music-drama as the symphony's natural successor. Schumann already had to contend with it in his 1835 review of Berlioz's *Symphonie fantastique*, remarking that ''after Beethoven's Ninth Symphony, outwardly the greatest instrumental work, limit and proportion appeared to be exhausted'' (165). Elterlein makes use of a convenient accident of history, arguing that ''there was no climax possible beyond this; the tenth symphony had, of necessity, to remain a myth'' (79). Echo after echo sounds this theme: ''Such was the Ninth Symphony ... *It had to be the last one....* Another symphony could have been only a retrogression to a previous standpoint'' (Marx, 413); the piece was ''*un chef-d'oeuvre qui a tué le genre*'' (Vimenal, 21). Even Debussy, who had little sympathy with ''Wagner's highly-spiced masterpieces,'' remarked that ''It seems to me that the proof of the futility of the symphony has been established since Beethoven'' (17). It was, of course, precisely this notion that Wagner capitalized upon in his claim that the instrumental symphony was but a way-station along the evolutionary road to his *Gesamtkunstwerk*, that the Ninth proved Beethoven's acquiescence to the claim that further artistic progress could only be achieved through a new union of music and poetry.

> The Last Symphony of Beethoven is the redemption of Music from out her own peculiar element into the realm of *universal Art* ... Beyond it no forward step is possible; for upon it the perfect Art-work of the Future alone can follow, the *universal Drama* to which Beethoven has forged for us the key (1849, 126).

Despite the irritable dismissal of this argument by stubbornly sensible critics like Edmund Gurney—who found the idea that ''Beethoven, tottering on the final Pisgah-peak of the Symphony, pointed on to the Wagnerian Opera ... a real curiosity in the way of finding a text for a theory'' (514)—nonetheless the vehemence of the controversies surrounding Wagner and the frequency with which his disciples took up this interpretation of the Ninth made this the most significant and most frequent historical assertion about the symphony's influence. It was, to a great degree, the argument that made the piece famous. Wagner's familiar call to arms is couched in the images of sexuality that were favorites of his. "Music is a woman," he said (1851, lll) and poetry the male begetter. Therefore Beethoven's

> most decisive message, at last given us by the master in his *magnum opus,* is the necessity he felt *as Musician* to throw himself into the arms of the Poet, in order to compass the act of *begetting* the true, the unfailingly real and redeeming Melody (107).

It is this generative act that produces universal "patriarchal" melody. Having thought this over for some years, Nietzsche—by now on the way to turning *contra* Wagner—responded strongly:

> What therefore shall we think of that awful aesthetic superstition that Beethoven himself made a solemn statement as to his belief in the limits of absolute music, in that fourth movement of the Ninth Symphony, yea that he as it were with it unlocked the portals of a new art...? And what does Beethoven himself tell us when he has choir-song introduced by a recitative? "Alas, friends, let us intone not these tones but more pleasing and joyous ones!" More pleasing and joyous ones! For that he needed the convincing tone of the human voice, for that he needed the music of innocence in the folk-song. Not the word, but the "more pleasing" sound ...(1871, 38).

An occasional more pedestrian-minded critic objected to both these views that the double exposition of the finale—a feature, by the way, seldom mentioned by Wagnerian exegetes—rendered the whole debate moot since it was perfectly clear that the "joy" tune, the object of the elaborate introductory search process, was arrived at quite successfully by instruments alone. This observation, of course, had the drawback of providing no explanation whatever for the appearance of the chorus.

WAYS OF READING THE NINTH AS IDEOLOGICAL TEXT

Throughout the century, writers continually commented on the fact that exegesis of the Ninth was the standard procedure; those more inclined to "analysis" (there were some, although they were relatively rare compared to readers of "ideal content") naturally abhorred it, and it is clear from their bitter complaints that they heard a lot of it. In 1835 Schumann satirized the practice—already rampant—in the well-known "Mardi-Gras Speech by Florestan":

> ...these Beethovenians ... said 'That was written by our Beethoven, it is a German work—the finale contains a double fugue...' Another chorus joined in: 'The work seems to contain the different genres of poetry, the first movement being epic, the second comedy, the third lyric, the fourth (combining all), the dramatic.' Still another bluntly began to praise the work as being gigantic, colossal, comparable to the Egyptian pyramids. And others painted word pictures: the symphony expresses the story of mankind—first the chaos—then the call of God 'there shall be light'—then the sunrise over the first human being, ravished by such splendor—in one word, the whole first chapter of the Pentateuch is in this symphony.
>
> I became angrier and quieter ...(100)

A few years later, Berlioz insisted upon attempting to discuss the piece "without prying" into the composer's mind (143). As might be expected, the ever-growing exegetic literature provided a natural target for the acid-tongued Hanslick, who described one such account as giving

> an exhaustive description of the significance of the 'subject' of each of the four parts and their profound symbolism—but about the *music itself* not a syllable is said. This is highly characteristic of a whole school of musical criticism, which, to the question whether the music is beautiful, replies with a learned dissertation on its profound meaning (1957, 70).

By Debussy's time it was no exaggeration to say, as he did, that the piece "has been subjected to such transcendental interpretations, that even such a powerful and straightforward work as this has become a universal nightmare" (62). It is only too easy for us, with our positivist training and scrupulous avoidance of intentional and other fallacies, to sympathize with these sentiments and dismiss somewhat contemptuously the more fanciful discussions of the piece. This seems to me mistaken, however, since it ignores the overwhelming evidence they present about the central role music played in the formation and articulation of spiritual, political, and social thought.

Exegeses or "programs" of the Ninth fall roughly into four categories: search narratives, creation myths, accounts that interpret the piece as autobiographical on Beethoven's part, and those that content themselves with more general assessments of moral instruction. There are several features, though, that all have in common. For one thing, they assume a phenomenal stance: all are focused tightly on the experience of hearing the piece, not on "score study." Second, it can be argued, as I will below, that all of them finally belong to that last category—that is, all reflect ideological commitments of one sort or another, and these are overwhelmingly of a moral or religious nature.

The most familiar type are generally psychological narratives of varying degrees of sophistication; this bent seems fitting to the depth and seriousness of the piece, and accords with the belief that the composer is the bearer of an important message for the listener. Most of them resemble literary "quest" narratives, and appear to be retrospectively prompted by the opening of the last movement.[21] That is, Beethoven's search for "more pleasing and joyous tones" was generalized backward to the symphony as a whole, as Dwight somewhat ingenuously explains:

> It is in this first movement that one feels the pledge and prophecy of something grand, extraordinary, that is yet to come. We know no music which seems so pregnant with a future as this, teeming with more than it has means to utter, and foreshadowing a solution, such as came to Beethoven in that fourth or Choral movement. It is this first Movement that requires and justifies the last and finds its explanation there (414).

Because of this feature, the narrative format could usually serve to explain many of the symphony's formal anomalies. The technique, however, cut both ways. Berlioz's refusal to engage in such interpretation enabled him to see—though not to solve—the problem of the finale's double exposition, a mystery that remains opaque in most programs because it seemed to make no sense in terms of a psychological or spiritual quest. Consequently it was usually ignored altogether except, ironically, by the universally-recognized father of the entire genre. It was Wagner's absolute confidence in his own theory of the *Gesamtkunstwerk* that enabled him to describe that first successful arrival at the "Ode to Joy" tune as

> the ultimate attempt to phrase by instrumental means alone a stable, sure, unruffled joy: but the rebel rout appears incapable of that restriction;

[21]But in a recent article Anthony Newcomb has identified such a plot archetype as common in discussions of nineteenth-century symphonies. See his "Once More 'Between Absolute and Program Music': Schumann's Second Symphony," *19th Century Music* 7 (1984): 233-250.

like a raging sea it heaps its waves, sinks back, and once again, yet louder than before, the wild chaotic yell of unslaked passion storms our ear (1846, 252).

While all the narrative accounts are profoundly moralistic in tone, sharp religious and political differences turn up in the definition of *what* joy is found at the end of the search. Wagner's 1846 program is unquestionably the prototype, and often acknowledged as such by subsequent writers (it was widely translated, available in English and French fairly soon after publication, and even in Italian by the '90s). His story— the bulk of whose content, interestingly, is contained in quotations from *Faust*—is of the "Titanic struggle" of a heroic soul. In the first movement the soul wrestles defiantly against fate; in the second, momentarily fleeing from despair, it participates in an orgy of ultimately futile earthly jollities. In the slow movement the soul muses on the innocent joys of early childhood, and is gradually able to move from melancholy to a new resolve to continue the struggle. Finally, urged on by the instrumental hint of what prize might be won, the soul determines to join battle afresh and is ultimately rewarded with the attainment of ecstasy "with God to consecrate our universal love."

Elterlein provides a very close paraphrase of this program, though his is even more combative in tone. His stubborn "soul" is throughout hungry for fresh battle; in the finale he hears "stalwart youths .. eager to perform heroic deeds," and their reward is "sublime ecstasy in the beatitude of God's presence" (74). In these accounts we hear the Romantic cult of personal suffering along with a markedly militaristic tone, but they are religiously traditional, interpreting Schiller's text as though with a singular God instead of plural gods, beatitude instead of dithyrambic celebration. G. A. Schmitt, however, follows the familiar path to a different, quintessentially secular, conclusion. He makes the pattern of his narrative explicit, describing each middle movement as not satisfying the problems raised by the first, because "not devotion alone can make us happy ... but more is wanted. An active religion of good works to all men being the leading idea of all the subsequent parts, the motive of the Hymn to Joy is now stated." The governing idea of the piece, Schmitt says, is "an idea which is the polar star of all human aspirations: HUMANITY; human happiness, brotherly love to all men," and the choral finale thus represents "the apotheosis of Humanity by an invocation of its tutelar deity: JOY" (411, 410).

What is particularly interesting about Schmitt's discussion of the piece, which extended over several issues of *Dwight's Journal*, is that these programmatic and hortatory assertions appear freely interwoven among purely technical sentences whose purpose is the dissection of theme from motive, phrase from section; to Schmitt, as apparently to his audience, there was no distinction between the two modes of approach that would accord superior explanatory status or validity to one over the other. Willy Pastor's 1890 account—more purely programmatic—is particularly detailed, matching individual themes, phrases, and modulations to individual lines in the interior monologue; a psychodrama with a pungent *fin-de-siècle* flavor. Pastor's program could almost pass for a subtext to Schoenberg's *Erwartung*, except of course for the transcendence of its conclusion.

> Various fates befall [the] hero. That eternally unsolved, painful riddle of creation, doubt in God and longing after inner peace, lead him to seek solitude. But there he finds only despair. In order to deaden his pain, he throws himself into the maelstrom of life. But that too cannot satisfy him. Disconsolate, he turns again to solitude and now, finally, he finds what he sought ...

The name of this psychological drama, Pastor says, is *Der Mensch unter den Menschen*, and its hero is the human spirit (26).

Sir George Grove's book on the Beethoven symphonies, which is still widely read by students and music-lovers, focuses on thematic analysis; but like Schmitt, Grove is perfectly comfortable supporting and explaining his technical description with programmatic evidence.

> ...a remarkable passage occurs in which Beethoven passes in review each of the preceding three movements, as if to see whether either [sic] of them will suit for his *Finale*. ... Hitherto, in the three orchestral movements, Beethoven has been depicting 'Joy' in his own proper character: first, as part of the complex life of the individual man; secondly, for the world at large; thirdly, in all the ideal hues that art can throw over it. He has now to illustrate what Schiller intended in his Ode... (372)

Continuing on, he describes the so-called *Schreckensfanfare* as

> an impersonation of the opposite to all that is embodied in the 'Ode to Joy.' But this time the rebuke of the prophet finds an articulate voice, and Beethoven addresses us in his own words... (377)

It is as though the elaborately worked-out midcentury narratives have been distilled into a set of capsule associations so taken for granted that they serve as synonyms for structural description.

In the catalog of exegetic excess mentioned by Schumann in connection with the Ninth Symphony, the creation myth is a prominent one. Although at times its language turns up in other narrative accounts, still it forms a distinct type in the literature searching for the meaning of the piece. Thayer first heard it in Berlin in 1854,[22] first the three instrumental movements in two separate performances and, shortly thereafter, the whole. From the beginning, he described the opening movement as a void, a "strange, empty humming" across which electrical sparks shoot, "awakening life in the mass." His program, as it develops, follows the life cycle of a kind of homunculus or created being that, starting as a clod of earth, reaches full manhood by Beethoven's creative genius. Like other critics, Thayer uses the structure of his narrative to account for certain formal aspects of the piece, in particular the sequence of emotional states that seems to him appropriate for the development of the newly-vivified being:

> Poor humanized clod! Beaten back in all quarters, he may well despair of finding that Joy which he seeks. The trouble however is in himself. He must pass through still another state before he attains the goal (124).

At the arrival of the finale, Thayer exults: "This clod is now capable of Joy. Is this not Beethoven's philosophy? Could Kant desire a better?" Thayer here develops at full length a metaphor casually introduced by A. B. Marx, who likened the opening of the symphony to "lightning-flashes of a new birth" (394). A similar story is tartly reported by Chrysander in his description—part of a review—of a program published in 1870.

> In the first movement Hr. Hoffman is led down a primeval path. The second and third movements "represent the destinies of the world" which, of course, ultimately represents a dying one.
> ... we enter "the region of the beyond"
> ... the author seeks a speculative philosophy of life in Beethoven, and in taking that path he confuses metaphysics with fantasy.

Another school of thought considered the work to represent the reflection, more or less unmediated, of the composer's biography or psychic

---

[22]This unsigned article in *Dwight's Journal* is identified by Michael Ochs as being the work of Thayer; see his "A.W. Thayer, the Diarist, and the Late Mr. Brown: A Bibliography of Writings in *Dwight's Journal of Music*," in *Beethoven Essays: Studies in Honor of Elliot Forbes*, ed. Lewis Lockwood and Phyllis Benjamin (Cambridge MA, 1984): 78-95.

experience—as Ambros put it, Beethoven's works were seen as "types of the powerful life of his soul" (417). This is a pattern of thought into which the more guarded assessments of the piece naturally fell, since biographical facts could be used to explain or account for idiosyncrasies of compositional strategy. Oulibicheff, although he appreciated the magnitude of Beethoven's torments and remarked that the late works show him engaged in a "constant tortured self-interrogation," like Hamlet, ultimately judged that the tortures overcame the musical genius. Not all agreed, however. It was also possible to read Beethoven's message itself as autobiographical: that is, the symphony became his way of acting as a spiritual model for his admirers. Here is Vimenal's account:

> It is not surprising that the idea of joy should stir in Beethoven's mind at this time, if one imagines how little of it was his to savor... Deafness, isolation, family troubles, lack of money, artistic deceptions, the indignation of a genius if not unrecognized at least abandoned, anger at the crowds who enthusiastically pursued Italian music, preferring *Tancred* to *Fidelio*, such were Beethoven's joys at this date... Thence, doubtless, the joyous finale which crowns a symphony where melancholy dominates; thence these three first parts darkened in design and anticipating only blackness, not only to give by contrast more intensity to the joy of the finale, but also to oppose to this ideal tableau the aspirations of the unhappy poet ... the real tableau of his life (21).

I include one lengthy quotation from Marx, in order to make clear the seriousness of this interpretive pursuit. The artistic and moral role Beethoven played during the later nineteenth century, coupled with the secularization of society and the ubiquity of religious skepticism, made the great symphony as obvious and significant a source of moral instruction as the lives of the saints had once been.

> The first movement of every Symphony is decisive as to the thought of the whole work; it is particularly so decisive in the Ninth. And what has it uttered? The endless complaint of everlasting dissatisfaction, which accompanies in his own realm of the world of instruments Him, who filled and invigorated it with his mighty soul! Even though those voices of the instruments charm all nature together, even though they whisper into our ears sweet spirit tones, or sweep down from heaven like the greeting of angels to men: still man always needs, above all, Man; and the voice of man is to man the most dear, most deeply felt, most comprehensible music. This is universal truth; and this truth arose to the

consciousness of Beethoven in the world of instruments that he had so mightily peopled.

Then came the time to separate. And if, mayhap—as we cannot know—a presentiment of his death touched the noble man, it must have helped to awaken that consciousness and united with it. Was not he solitary in the loud world of man as he was solitary in the world of his instruments and musical visions? And his open, loving, altogether harmless soul so yearned for the dear companionship of man! This sense of brotherhood and love of men, how it penetrates all his works, his letters, and even shines through his attacks of suspicion, jealousy and injustice!

Thus the external resolve to give to his Symphony a new formation by appending to it a final chorus, became an internal necessity. That which was a general truth and a particular life experience of Beethoven, became now the ruling idea of the Ninth Symphony (395).

Somewhat in this same vein, the Ninth gave rise to an apparently unique fictional genre, a collection of originary myths focusing on that work itself. What is remarkable about these stories—apart from the fact that they were written for adult readers and published in journals specific to the musically literate—is their reliance upon fictions of divine intervention to explain the genesis of the symphony. In one, Beethoven is visited in his room by a procession of "good and evil spirits," at one extreme Satan, who offers to aid in the composition for his usual fee—Beethoven marks crosses in his manuscript to ward him off—and at the other a benign father who "bears a remarkable resemblance to Papa Haydn" and does finally prove helpful (Anonymous 1885). Another (also featuring Haydn prominently) hangs upon Beethoven's temptation to the sin of despair and his rescue by the brief, miraculous restoration of his hearing; as the sounds of spring momentarily surround him, a shepherd's pipe plays the chorale *"Freu' dich sehr,"* and the idea for the great symphony is born (Anonymous 1889).[23] A third tale symbolizes Beethoven's compositional genius with an apparently withered rosebush that miraculously flowers when the composer's hand touches it, thus reassuring him that his great gift still lives. A year later, says the author, the symphony was performed (Frey).

The reader will have observed that all of these programmatic accounts, despite their varying narrative types and the varying degree of particularity of imagery, all ultimately concern themselves with moral polemics

---

[23]This story appears in a separate "women's section" of the journal, a regular feature titled *Mildwida*; the name is of unclear reference although it may, as my colleague Philipp Naegele has suggested, be intended as reminiscent of the -*friedes*, -*lindes*, and -*hildes* of the Wagnerian cosmos.

of one sort or another. There seem to be, among these writers, both the assumption and the deep-seated hope that the great soul of Beethoven had lessons to teach that modern man ignored at his peril. The programs may have served to "coat the pill" or make the moral message apparently inarguable through coordinated musical analysis, but some writers preferred to go right to the heart of the matter, moral instruction undiluted by fable. These discussions tend to come late in the century and have a slight air of desperation. By the 1870s, it was impossible to ignore the serious crisis in which orthodox religious practice found itself, or the pervasive feeling of moral rootlessness it left behind. Conservative critics by and large gave up efforts at subtlety, straightforwardly marching Beethoven into the pulpit. Niecks is said to have characterized the symphony as "a musical exposition of Beethoven's philosophy;"[24] Bagge in 1876 offers a rather detailed reading of the pictures painted by the symphony, in the traditional programmatic mode, but concludes that the piece is not merely or fundamentally a musical experience but a spiritual one; Beethoven demonstrates, he says, that religion lifts us from pain to joy (71). K. R. Hennig, whose aesthetic approach involves the discovery and explication of a *Gesamtidee* for each musical work, expresses the core idea of the Ninth as a set of commandments or "precepts," one provided in each movement:

> I. Man's life should be a noble struggle for virtue, despite all the powers of fate.
> II. Man can with discretion enjoy the delights of life but not become too caught up in them.
> III. Man should be submissive even before the loss of whatever love he finds on earth.
> IV. Above the stars lives a loving father who calls us his children and who wants us all to reach out the hand of reconciliation to one another in brotherly love. This is the greatest happiness (88).

As late as 1911 Vincent d'Indy still expresses his certainty that the piece is not "a revolutionary apology for liberty," as some were claiming, but that religious faith and the presence of God in one's life are "what one must see in the Choral Symphony, if it be considered with the eyes of the soul" (116). What matters is what the alternatives were, as seen by one who was a professional composer himself. Politics or religion, an orthodox or a secular moral message, but never merely music.

---

[24]Quoted without reference by Edith A. H. Crashaw in "Wagner and the Ninth Symphony," *Musical Times* 66 (1925): 1090-91.

THE NINETEENTH-CENTURY SITUATION AND THE
CONFLICTING MESSAGES OF THE NINTH

Interpretive traditions such as these grew up during the nineteenth century because the pervasive spirit of Romantic and idealist aesthetic philosophies suggested that works of art bore hidden meanings behind their surfaces and carried important messages for the conduct of human life. They grew up in particularly luxuriant proliferation around the Ninth Symphony because, as we have seen, it had certain formal properties that confirmed its oracular status and because it occupied a particularly portentous place in the *oeuvre* of the composer who came to be both saint and hero to the century as a whole. I would like now to elaborate upon the issues that were debated within the criticism of the piece; that is, the ideological principles, often at great variance with one another, to which Beethoven was called as witness. As is well known, the century was one of enormous and continual upheaval in all the arenas in which humans customarily act according to received beliefs and common assumptions—politics, social relations, religion, standards of ethical behavior. For my present purposes, I will argue that all ultimately boiled down to religious faith and matters of morality; this is so because the arts themselves tended during the nineteenth century to be viewed religiously and became, for some, a substitute for religious orthodoxies they considered outworn. Houston Chamberlain wrote that "music alone has made possible the natural religion of the soul, and that in the highest degree by the development which culminated at the beginning of the nineteenth century in Beethoven" (561).

1. The Challenge from Science

In many respects the intellectual challenges of the period focused on religious traditions. The discoveries of science seemed to conspire in destabilizing the authority of scripture; the names of Darwin and Lyell are those most frequently mentioned, but evolutionary explanations gradually appeared in all disciplines, perhaps most strikingly in the social sciences. Herbert Spencer and August Comte, beginning from different contexts, both ended by asserting that human societies were evolving even as the biological species, and predicated their views of the future on the eventual, inevitable transformation of theistic religion into a new "religion of humanity." Thus belief in social "progress" came to imply atheism. One of George Eliot's critics, defending her against charges of immorality provoked by her expressed atheism, explains this connection quite clearly:

> She is perhaps the first great *godless* writer of fiction that has appeared in England; perhaps, in the sense in which we use the expression, the first that has appeared in Europe ... Now among the vast changes that human thought has been undergoing, the sun that we once all walked by has for many eyes become extinguished; and every energy has been bent upon supplying man with a substitute ... The new object of our duty is not our Father which is in Heaven, but our brothers and our children who are on earth.[25]

For a while, it was possible to retain a relatively orthodox religious stance in the face of scientific challenge, seeing "natural philosophy" as working in the service of religious revelation, but the posture was a tenuous one. An anonymous correspondent to *Dwight's Journal* in October of 1852 complained of German bias in the publication and demanded that the editor purge the journal of "German mysticism and Boston transcendentalism"—a highly intriguing juxtaposition, and right on the mark, of course, since both were offspring of the same idealist philosophical tradition.[26] (Nor is it insignificant that the letter was signed "Giustizia," written no doubt by a disgruntled Rossini fan playing out in yet another forum the fanatic rivalry between north and south that pervaded musical conversations everywhere at mid-century.)

Dwight answered, somewhat huffily, that these charges were mere "vulgar catchwords" and that the paper espoused no metaphysical position, a rather disingenuous response given his own connection with Brook Farm and his writings for its journal, *The Harbinger*.[27] Indeed, a year later *Dwight's* carried an account of the Ninth Symphony by Lowell Mason that goes far to substantiate "Giustizia's" charge. Judging the piece to be as yet inexplicable, Mason invokes other similarly imponderable entities—the sun and moon, electricity, the ocean, a tempest—that nonetheless "have great moral power over man," and he manages to work truth, beauty and goodness all into the next two

---

[25]Unsigned review in the *Edinburgh Review* 150 (1879): 557-86; quoted in *George Eliot: The Critical Heritage*, ed. David Carroll (London, 1971), p. 453.

[26]Leo Marx comments that "Germanic" was a common epithet in America during this period, "calculated to evoke memories of Goethe and other vaguely disreputable poets with curious manners and an unrealistic, freewheeling, metaphysical turn of mind." See his *The Machine in the Garden: Technology and the Pastoral Ideal in America* (New York, 1964), p. 218.

[27]In this connection, see Christopher Hatch, "The Education of A.W. Thayer," *Musical Quarterly* 42 (1956): 355-65.

sentences. That inclusion of "electricity," one notes, gives a typically American flavor to this discussion; Mason three times invokes the benevolent face of science in the course of his essay, once as the force that will eventually reveal God to us and once, by analogy, as that which Beethoven had discovered in the realm of music. This is the language that Leo Marx has called "the rhetoric of the technological sublime," as it occurs in the writings of Whitman and Emerson. Like Mason, Emerson believed, according to an 1843 entry in his journal, that "Machinery and Transcendentalism agree well."[28]

It was Mason's contemporary, the great American Beethoven apologist Alexander Wheelock Thayer, who fixed this imagery in its most vivid form in the course of the creation scenario we have encountered above— though as so often in this literature using a similar argument to come to the opposite philosophical stance, abandoning Mason's theistic conclusion. It is in the mysterious opening of the first movement, "like the humming of a wheel in a room full of machinery," that the miracle happens:

> Mark how the animal becomes vivified, how passion arises, how troubles encompass him, and he finds himself surrounded with difficulties against which he must struggle. The clod is a man! (124)

Is there a reader of English anywhere for whom these words are not redolent of another, more familiar text, one in its way as canonic in our culture as the Ninth itself?

> It was on a dreary night of November, that I beheld the accomplishment of my toils. With an anxiety that almost amounted to agony, I collected the instruments of life around me, that I might infuse a spark of being into the lifeless thing that lay at my feet. It was already one in the morning; the rain pattered dismally against the panes, and my candle was nearly burnt out, when, by the glimmer of the half-extinguished light, I saw the dull yellow eye of the creature open; it breathed hard, and a convulsive motion agitated its limbs.[29]

For this "modern Prometheus," as for *his* hapless clod, we know that there was no final transcendence into joy. The change in tone is created by both geographical and temporal distance, as well as by a pronounced shift in religious commitment. Mary Shelley's is a cautionary tale about

[28]Leo Marx, p. 222, 232.
[29]Mary Wollstonecraft Shelley, *Frankenstein, or The Modern Prometheus*, [the 1818 text] (New York, 1976), pp. 58-9.

scientific over-reaching, a "tower of Babel" story of human hubris, written in 1818 and reflecting conventional Christian values as well as early-Romantic unease about the darkly secret activities behind laboratory doors. By 1854, and particularly across the Atlantic, scientific advance had been comfortably accommodated into current visions of a universal social and spiritual progress based upon human learning and accomplishment. Thayer does not use this imagery disparagingly—for him it does not render the piece "artificial" nor "monstrous," as other commentators so pertinently had it. Rather, the imagery excites him, and he is filled with the same salvific optimism in whose grip Lowell Mason assures us that science will one day reveal to us the face of God. Beethoven, one gathers, had already acquired this understanding.

2. The Challenge from Politics

Not only scientific progress and social evolutionary theories but political developments had religious implications, as various socialisms and communal living experiments arose at least partially in response to the perceived failure of orthodox Christianity to solve social ills. Again, Beethoven faithfully continued to provide the necessary moral perspective. Berlioz noticed a new feature appearing in French attitudes toward Beethoven in the 1840s:

> A certain religious element appears [in Beethoven criticism], dimly indicated, but of so special a kind that it seems to point to new implications. This strain of thought appears to be influenced by ideas originating in the circle of Saint-Simon.[30]

That the connection of music to political commitment and activism was taken quite seriously is revealed in Ford Madox Ford's comment about Wagnerian music, that in some circles it was suspect as "atheistic, sexually immoral, and tending to further socialism and the throwing of bombs."[31]

The ideology of "difficulty," a feature of late-Romantic aesthetic philosophy about which I have spoken above, presents some complications in a school of thought that at the same time bore a commitment

[30]Quoted in Leo Schrade, *Beethoven in France: The Growth of an Idea* (New Haven, 1942), p. 89.
[31]Quoted in Anne Dzamba Sessa, "At Wagner's Shrine: British and American Wagnerians," in *Wagnerism in European Culture and Politics*, ed. David C. Large and William Weber (Ithaca, 1984), p. 246.

to democratic or even socialist values. How could the writer with such values avoid the charge of elitism, of creating a priestly inner circle uniquely capable of penetrating music's mysteries? To put it the other way round, how could one attribute high artistic value to a piece of music that anybody could understand and enjoy? Richard Wagner prefaced his programmatic description of the piece by explaining that he would not even try to help the audience to a real understanding of the piece "since that could come from nothing save an inner intuition" but that he would offer some hints since its scheme "might easily escape the less-prepared and therefore readily-bewildered hearer" (1846, 247). When the New York correspondent for *Dwight's Journal* reported on a performance by Theodore Thomas in 1866, his pleasure in the piece seems to have been genuinely disturbed by thoughts of "how many among the audience were capable of really comprehending the work they had just heard?" (Ritter 358). The priestly ideology of Romanticism is summed up in a comment of Leo Schrade expressing a view largely, but by no means exclusively, French:

> The French romantics never attributed to Beethoven's work an appeal to the masses, precisely because of their view of music and what constituted the power to be moved by it. Such appeal was reserved for the political interpretations to come. [32]

Even so, as late as 1893 so politically-inclined a figure as George Bernard Shaw still had trouble reconciling the exalting of difficulty with democratic social commitments. "Mass taste" was not yet quite so easily dismissed as it is today. Shaw wrote

> How far the work has become really popular it would be hard to determine, because ... so many people come whenever it is in the bills, not to enjoy themselves, but to improve themselves. To them the culmination of its boredom in an Ode to Joy must seem a wanton mockery, since they always hear it for the first time; for a man does not sacrifice himself in that way twice, just as he does not read Daniel Deronda twice; and consequently ... he never becomes sufficiently familiar with it to delight in it (1981, II, 825-6).

His observation, while sounding the familiar theme of the piece's difficulty, at the same time acknowledges the social grounding of bourgeois concert-going and the regnant ideology of self-improvement through

[32]Schrade, p. 43.

art. Simply complaining about philistinism did not acknowledge the complexity of the situation. His reference to *Daniel Deronda* is telling. Not only is Eliot's last novel intimately concerned with fashions and polemics in music, but it was received with language remarkably like that addressed to the Ninth. Also a late work, a particularly large one, and one instantly tagged as formally incoherent and difficult, it served as a locus for the same arguments we have been encountering. (Is its religious vision orthodox or humanistic? Does it rely on traditional formal types or on radical innovation? What is its message, its moral lesson?) It is not unusual, among late-century English critics, to find Eliot's name linked to Beethoven's just on the same grounds that Shaw invokes, as in this representative passage from an 1877 review:

> The manner of few great artists—if any—becomes simpler as they advance in their career, that is, as their ideas multiply, as their emotions receive more numerous affluents from other parts of their being, and as the vital play of their faculties with one another becomes swifter and more intricate. The later sonatas of Beethoven still perplex facile and superficial musicians. The later landscapes of Turner still bewilder and amaze the profane ... when the sustained *largo* of the sentences of *Daniel Deronda* is felt after the crude epigrammatic smartness of much of the writing in *Scenes of Clerical Life* we perceive as great a difference and as decided a preponderance of gain over loss.[33]

Ironically, the Ninth Symphony contains within itself an exemplary case of the elite/philistine conflict, in the "Ode to Joy" theme of its finale. Early in the century, that melody's anomalous character—deliberately archaic in style, closed, symmetrical, simpler than anything in its environment—proved problematic to the critics, who heard it as stylistically inappropriate. An early English writer called it "one of the most extraordinary instances I have ever witnessed, of great powers of mind and wonderful science, wasted upon subjects infinitely beneath its strength" (Anonymous 1825, 81). Writing satirically about critical reaction to a different piece, Robert Schumann indicates that he has heard this many times before: "You will think it common, unworthy of a Beethoven, like the melody to *Freude, schöner Götterfunken* in the D minor symphony ..." (105). Later, the "political interpretations" mentioned by Schrade began to come to the fore and lent the tune's simplicity a different social meaning. After midcentury, idealist

[33]Edward Dowden in *Contemporary Review 39* (1877): 348-69; quoted in Carroll, p. 444.

philosophy began to appear in quasi-populist form in so-called *völkisch* political ideology (a particularly although not exclusively German phenomenon, as was idealism itself) that Roderick Stackelberg has described as "the marriage of idealism and nationalism," one of "diverse movements of cultural revitalization whose goal it was to eliminate foreign influence and revive traditional values."[34] We are perhaps only too familiar with this phenomenon, not only for its eventual political ramifications in Germany but for its ravages in our own society; in the history of music, though, what seems to matter is that the currency of this ideology fed into a set of nationalistic musical controversies already long ongoing. They were not particularly sinister, but they were vociferous and easily heated to the boiling point. During and shortly after his lifetime Beethoven had been the standard-bearer in the struggle against the popularity of Italian music, especially the operas of Rossini and Bellini. George Eliot precisely captures the atmosphere of argumentation when she puts this polemic into the mouth of her musician, Klesmer:

> ...that music you sing [Bellini] is beneath you. It is a form of melody which expresses a puerile state of culture—a dangling, canting, see-saw kind of stuff—the passion and thought of people without any breadth of horizon. There is a sort of self-satisfied folly about every phrase of such melody: no cries of deep, mysterious passion—no conflict—no sense of the universal. It makes men small as they listen to it.

and she goes on with gentle satire to describe Klesmer's own composition as "a fantasia called *Freudvoll, Leidvoll, Gedankenvoll*—an extensive commentary on some melodic ideas not too grossly evident" (*Daniel Deronda*, 79).

The search for the national roots of a culture, in which its traditional values were presumably to be found, lent Beethoven's simple tune a newly prophetic and oracular aura. Wagner, whose politics with regard to populist values were unclear at best, led the way:

> That patriarchal melody—as I shall continue to call it, in token of its historic bearings ... shows itself wholly confined to the tone-family ties which rule the movements of the old national *Volkslied*. It contains as good as *no* modulation, and appears in so marked a simplicity of key, that in it the aim of the musician, to go back upon the historic fount of Music, is spoken out without disguise...(1851, 289).

[34]Stackelberg, p. 6, 9.

The same *völkisch* values are expressed in 1854 by Thayer,

> Again the simplicity of the tune which follows, and its perfectly popular
> character, was most striking and astonishing. But then as one reflects
> upon it, it is just what it should be, for it is the outpouring of the JOY
> of all the brotherhood of Man. Highly wrought, artistic (in the common
> acceptation) music, would be out of place; but this, so popular in its
> form, may well be the expression of the universal feeling (124)

and by A. B. Marx in 1859, who calls it "that simple people's melody.
For that which is most profound and grand finds at all times its last
sanctification and confirmation in the heart and mouth of the people"
(412). And so, turn by turn, the tune and the politics provide support
and context for each other.

The frequent invocation of The People brings to mind, of course,
the nationalist strains so common in both aesthetics and politics during
the century. As is well known, the argument sometimes turned vicious,
particularly in its Wagnerian form. Beethoven, said Wagner, had been
crucial in the struggle to rescue German music from Jewish and
ultramontane corruption. He

> again raised music, that had been degraded to a merely diverting art,
> to the height of its sublime calling, he has led us to understand the nature
> of that art, from which the world explains itself to every consciousness
> as distinctly as the most profound philosophy could explain it to a thinker
> well versed in abstract conceptions. *And the relation of the great
> Beethoven to the German nation is based upon this alone...* (1870, 41)

In its classic form, the response to this polemic is that of Nietzsche,
who thought little of what passed for German culture in his lifetime
and was far more concerned to make of Beethoven a type of the universal
human spirit.

> Beethoven is the intermediate event between an old mellow soul that is
> constantly breaking down, and a future over-young soul that is always
> coming; there is spread over his music the twilight of eternal loss and
> eternal extravagant hope—the same light in which Europe was bathed
> when it dreamed with Rousseau, when it danced round the Tree of Liberty
> of the Revolution, and finally almost fell down in adoration before
> Napoleon (1886, 200-01).

3. The Challenge from Theology

Another challenge to religious orthodoxy in the nineteenth century came, ironically enough, from theology itself. Biblical scholars began to study scripture "scientifically," in keeping with modern historical and philological methods. When their investigations did not yield the sorts of authenticity that literal-minded religious faith required, some responded by taking an evolutionary view quite in keeping with Spencer's or Comte's. They began to view traditional religion as a phase through which humanity passed on its way to a more comprehensive, non-sectarian religion of moral probity. The works of Feuerbach and of David Friedrich Strauss—especially the latter's *Das Leben Jesu kritisch bearbeitet*, which appeared in 1836—created storms of controversy. This is the same Strauss whose characterization of the Ninth as "monstrous" we have encountered earlier; his critique of the piece first appeared anonymously in 1853 in the *Augsburger Allgemeine Zeitung*. His assessment of it rests on an extremely subtle connection between religion and aesthetics. Strauss objects to the symphony's formal flaws precisely because, to his ear, they interfere with the communication of Beethoven's real message, which is humanistic at heart. The choral finale, he says, is deeply symbolic of the composer's understanding that "only in men and with men does the solution to man's torments lie" (col.130); he fears that the sensationalistic aspects of the composition will obscure this important recognition, rendering the piece overpopular and trivial. As his metaphors make clear, Strauss insisted on distinguishing religious meaningfulness from aesthetic value, a distinction with which the orthodox-minded were uncomfortable.

Strauss's odd little foray into music criticism had astonishing repercussions: it simply infuriated people. It was reprinted often, with editors often providing rejoinders and commentaries, as Chrysander did in 1877 in the *Allgemeine Musikalische Zeitung*. For the rest of the century it was repeatedly suggested, none too politely, that the great theologian stick to his own field.[35] The degree of furor is revealing, perhaps having less to do with the content of his article than to the intellectual posi-

---

[35]Strauss's "incompetence" was one of the last subjects on which Wagner and Nietzsche continued to agree, although their accord was not in turn based on common arguments. In his 1869 appendix to "Judaism in Music" Wagner refers sarcastically, and in the context of a vicious racial slur, to "genuine" German artistic values as "a subject the famous bible-student, David Strauss, might presumably expound with just as great discernment as Beethoven's Ninth Symphony" (Works Vol. III, p.114), and Nietzsche published a notorious full-scale demolition of him in the first of his *Thoughts Out of Season* [sometimes translated as *Untimely Meditations*], "David Strauss, the Confessor and the Writer," published in 1873.

tion he stood for, one every bit as threatening as Darwin's or Karl Marx's. The critique as it stands seems a harmless enough mix of pedestrian formal puzzlement (although his language is more than usually vivid) and utopian social commentary. He took the eventual triumph of "secular humanism" for granted, and he took for granted as well Beethoven's espousal of it, though suggesting that the latter lacked sufficient fervor. This, I suspect, is what caused the difficulty. As Hanslick pointed out, polemicists for the symphony were more likely to talk about Beethoven's greatness of soul than about the music itself. Strauss, apparently rather knowledgeable about music, found both soul and symphony wanting.

The uncertainties and ambiguities of exegetic interpretation were compounded by the absolute requirement that the message being discerned here must be Beethoven's, not Schiller's—which is as much as to say that such secure verbal reference as was available was cheerfully ignored. A. B. Marx put it quite bluntly, arguing that thematic material bears the meaning of the piece and "precludes all supposition that the meaning of the Symphony might have a connection with the meaning of Schiller's Ode" (394). This viewpoint, or at least its echo by scores of later commentators, may actually be a byproduct of the great *Zukunfts-musik* controversy because the futurist debate was whether it was the presence of words or the introduction of human voices as such that constituted Beethoven's revolutionary move; the conservative argument, on the other hand, had merely to do with whether the piece could properly be called a symphony. None of the discussants seemed much concerned with what words were used.

But for purposes of religious argumentation, the text was inextricably part of the experience of the work, and there were circumstances in which it was not simply ignored, but deliberately misread, turned into something more convincing as "Beethoven's own" text. Many critics suggested with greater or lesser degrees of subtlety that Beethoven had improved upon or clarified Schiller's meaning, or had compensated for the poet's lapses of taste. There seems to be consensus now that the poetry is slight;[36] Nietzsche buttressed his own argument with that same judgment: "To the dithyrambic world-redeeming exultation of this music Schiller's poem ... is wholly incongruous, yea, like cold moonlight,

---

[36]Maynard Solomon points out that Schiller himself did not think much of it. (See his "Beethoven and Schiller" in *Beethoven, Performers, and Critics* [The International Beethoven Congress, Detroit 1977], ed. Robert Winter and Bruce Carr [Detroit, 1980]. p. 166). That this assessment is still current is suggested by Robert Winter in "The Sketches for the 'Ode to Joy'" in the same volume, p. 200.

pales beside that sea of flame..." (1871, 38). Bagge used its weaknesses in support of an ingenious apologia for the hybrid form of the whole; the poem, he said, omits all of the human sorrows and struggles that must precede genuine joy, so Beethoven composed those in the first three movements (51). The acerbic Teetgen expostulated, "What made him in his grand old age (old for him) so harp upon Schiller's crude performance, we know not" (104); it was precisely the same "crudity" that provoked George Grove's account of why Beethoven chose the portions of the text that he did:

> In making his selection Beethoven has omitted, either by chance or intention, some of the passages which strike an English mind as most *risqués* in Schiller's Ode ... and the omissions furnish an example of the taste by which his colossal powers were, with few exceptions, guided (325).

Later, Grove worries at this topic some more, apparently feeling that those "few exceptions" needed to be accounted for.

> ...and if in the Finale a restless, boisterous spirit occasionally manifests itself, not in keeping with the English feeling of the solemnity, even the sanctity, of the subject, this is only the reflection, and by no means an exaggerated reflection, of the bad taste which is manifested in parts of the lines adopted from Schiller's Ode, and which Beethoven, no doubt, thought it was his duty to carry out in his music. That he did not entirely approve of such extravagance may be inferred from the fact that, in his selection of the words, he has omitted some of the more flagrant escapades ... (389).

It is important, I think, that Grove's sense of taste here was based on "the solemnity, even the sanctity" of the event that the Ninth had become, that is, on the ways in which audiences had learned to hear the piece. In England, by Grove's and many other accounts, Natalia Macfarren's singing translation of the finale text was used in most performances. I want to argue that its extensive and imaginative misrenderings of Schiller's original are not merely inept but in fact symptomatic of certain predominant readings of the piece already in place. That is, she projected into her text a number of responses to the symphony that had become commonplace, readings that had by virtue of cultural and ideological trends overwhelmed the actual text of the original.

To begin with, "joy" is not an entity really up to the level of religious solemnity people wished to hear in Beethoven's finale—not, at least, within an orthodox Christian tradition; a close reading of Grove's comments reveals this unease. It has rather a pagan air about it, something of what Nietzsche called the Dionysian. Religious exegesis of the piece had long played down its selfish pursuit of "joy" in favor of the poem's emphasis on "brotherhood," and in many cases entirely supplanted it with nobler virtues like "love" and "hope." In Lady Macfarren's version, these mainstays of a more muscular Christianity become real.[37] From the opening stanza she removes both Elysium and the plural "gods;" the third line, *"Wir betreten feuertrunken,"* is forcefully replaced with "Joy by love and hope attended." In one of the piece's most dramatic passages, she replaces Schiller's gnomic and somewhat threatening interrogatives

Ihr stürzt nieder, Millionen?
Ahnest du den Schöpfer, Welt?

with hortatory statements direct from the pulpit:

O ye millions, kneel before Him,
Tremble, earth, before thy Lord

and goes on to replace the *Sternenzelt* that Beethoven so gorgeously set with the Lord's sword of vengeance stayed by "mercy"—another familiar virtue helping to defend against hints of paganism.

English audiences apparently did not object to this bowdlerization because it accurately represented the way they already interpreted the piece. Grove does not comment upon it, and even the purist Tovey suggests only that Macfarren has reversed the poetic conception by urging prostration rather than rising to look upwards to the stars,[38] as

Brüder—überm Sternenzelt
Muss ein lieber Vater wohnen.

is replaced by

To the power that here doth place ye,
Brothers, let us prostrate fall.

Whereas German audiences, of course, continued to hear the poetry

[37]My source for Macfarren's translation is Grove, confirmed however by the many other sources in which it is quoted.
[38]Donald Tovey, *Essays in Musical Analysis*, vol. 2 (London, 1935), p. 42.

in its original language, there is considerable evidence in their narrative accounts of it to suggest that they read the music's message much as Macfarren did, or in other equally skewed ways. What such readings represent is a sort of middle stage in the evolution of the Ninth's meaning. As if in obedience to Comte's scheme of the spiritual evolution of mankind, the poet's text appeared first as rather "pagan," in keeping with the classicism of its eighteenth-century origin, and then it was Christianized. Finally, however, by the last decades of the century, the text was put to the service of the new religion of mankind. The tide, as we know, was not to be stemmed.

Traditional religionists, ironically enough, continued to derive support from Wagner's poetic and ultimately orthodox reading, and for several generations they elaborated upon it. K. R. Hennig, facing up to what was by 1888 a familiar charge, stoutly insisted that "Beethoven maintained throughout his life the pure dogmatic position of his church" (94); the symphony, he argued, could be read straightforwardly as a statement of the composer's religious faith. As d'Indy was to do later, Hennig projected his vision of orthodoxy onto his formal reading of the work, explaining the puzzling fourth movement as a rondo: with this formal design, it becomes clear, the recurrence of material aptly symbolizes doctrinal stability. Though this simple and usually rather clear-cut form bears little resemblance to the fantasy that Bagge heard in the same movement, both designations served to quiet their authors' anxiety about stability and orthodoxy.

CONCLUSION

In 1849, the revolutionary Michael Bakunin is reported to have said to Wagner, "All, all ... will pass away; nothing will remain; not only music, the other arts as well ... but one thing will endure for ever, the Ninth Symphony."[39] In a disturbed world, with political, social, and religious mores constantly shifting beneath one's feet like sand, Beethoven's masterpiece stood firm as a source of secure knowledge, despite the evident fact that every commentator divined from the piece whatever message was necessary to his own inner quietude.

In his 1876 article, drawing upon the vivid sense of history that characterized the nineteenth century, Edward Dannreuther "thinks out

[39]William Ashton Ellis, *Life of Richard Wagner: Being an Authorised English Version of C.F. Glasenapp's "Das Leben Richard Wagners"* (London, 1902), 2:321-2.

loud," as it were, about the developing relationship between spirituality, scientific discovery, and culture.

> As the culture of ancient Greece was based upon a mythical creed and a religious embodiment thereof in art, so in all likelihood the culture of the distant future will be based upon science and music... in our century the antipoetical spirit of positive science and the flat prose of productive industrialism is balanced by the music of Beethoven and his disciples... To read a string quartet, even taken merely in the light of a bracing intellectual exercise, seems on a par with the reading of a Platonic dialogue. Nay, one may affirm more than this—Beethoven is, in the best sense of the word, an ethical, a religious teacher (193-4).

We recognize, of course, that even as early as 1838 discussion of this piece commonly took place in the context of religious debate, as Berlioz insisted that the symphony was "as beautiful for the fervent Christian as for the pantheist or the atheist." Brendel, as quoted in Elterlein (78), could feel the tension, or rather the coexistence in the piece of things that might have been thought mutually exclusive: "By the side of a pronounced secularism," he says, "there are contained in this music all the elements of deepest religiousness."

The late century's awareness of itself as a period of change and uncertainty becomes more and more evident. In effect, after more than fifty years of struggle, the reading of the Ninth as an apologia for Christian orthodoxy is finally forced to give way. Alexander Teetgen couched his entire 1879 discussion of the symphony in terms of the conflict between Pessimistic and Optimistic philosophy. He heard in the piece a confusion, a paralysis of action he called "Hamletism," an appropriate frame of mind for the period and one that confirmed Beethoven's role as spokesman for the entire century. "The other centuries were centuries of belief or unbelief; this is one of doubt, with a soul—belief, groping after a new one" (100). Although Teetgen does not finally judge the symphony successful, for formal reasons, he is clear enough about its ultimate message.

> ...the voice of peace—in modern dialect the voice of man; in the light of which reading, this entry of the human voice becomes portentous, as though it said, let the elements rage, let the arts stutter, the human voice alone can bring relief (102).

Willy Pastor points in 1890 to a similar existential uncertainty, verging on despair. His entire discussion of the piece revolves around the question where spiritual consolation is to be found; it is a kind of epigrammatic remnant of the traditional "search narrative" program, of course, but its focus is interior, serious, and somewhat grim. The persistent "problem" of the finale's meaning he explains this way:

> The reconciliation of man with a world which, in its ideals, appears alien and repugnant to him, but which nonetheless draws near him if only he will not flee from it, that is the essential content of the last movement of the D minor symphony (314).

He is clear, as these critics tend to be, that "joy" is to be taken purely as itself: " 'Freude—Freude!' Dies Zauberwort löst alle Fesseln."

George Bernard Shaw wrote often about the Ninth in his days as a music critic, and often in the context of the spiritual pilgrimage of his century through its tangled web of religion, science, and social theory. In 1885 he observed that, "About the religious music of the xix century there is a desperate triviality" (1981, I, 345) and declared his own response to the musical situation:

> The Zauberflöte was the first oratorio of the religion of humanity. Beethoven's setting of Schiller's Ode to Joy was the second. The inextinguishable vital spark which in Handel's day still dwelt in Lutheranism has passed into Positivism and Socialism... (356)

But it was much later and in quite another context that its full implications became clear. In a 1911 speech to the Heretics Society, pointedly titled "The Religion of the Future," Shaw cast his lot firmly with the moral framework provided by socialism, at the same time invoking the name of the composer who had become its timeless spokesman. "In democracy we are trying to get human nature up to a point where idolatry no longer appeals to us" (32). In this new world, he explained in answer to a questioner, "For its external expression the religion of the future might have the symphonies of Beethoven and the plays of GBS. They need not bother about the past."

APPENDIX: PRIMARY SOURCES

Ambros, August Wilhelm.
"The Ethical and Religious Force in Beethoven," translated by KGW. *Dwight's Journal of Music*, vol. 30, no. 27 (1871): 417-18.

Anonymous.

1825
"Beethoven's New Symphony," *The Quarterly Musical Magazine and Review* 7 (1825): 80-84.

1870
"Beethoven's Choral Symphony," *Dwight's Journal of Music* 30 (1870): 361-2. Reprinted from the Analytical and Historical Programme of the London Philharmonic Concert, July 11, 1870.

1885
"Die 'Neunte Sinfonie' von Beethoven: eine phantastische Definition," *Neue Musik-Zeitung* 6 (1885): 105.

1889
"Die Neunte: eine Phantasie," *Deutsche Musiker-Zeitung* 20 (1889): 35-6, 47-8.

Bagge, Selmar.
"L. van Beethoven's Neunte Symphonie. (Eine Öffentliche Vorlesung, gehalten in Basel am 29. Novbr. 1876, bei Gelegenheit einer Aufführung zur Einweihung des neuen Concertsaales)," *Allgemeine Musikalische Zeitung*, 3rd ser. 12 (1877) col. 49-53; 65-74.

Berlioz, Hector.
Beethoven by Berlioz: A Critical Appreciation of Beethoven's Nine Symphonies and His Only Opera—Fidelio—with Its Four Overtures, comp. and trans. Ralph De Sola (Boston, 1975).

"C."
"Some Contemporary English Criticism of Beethoven," *Monthly Musical Record* 42 (1912): 89-91.

Chamberlain, Houston Stewart.
The Foundations of the Nineteenth Century, 2 vols., trans. John Lees (London, 1912).

[Chrysander, Friedrich].
Review of L. Hoffmann, "Ein Programm zu Beethovens Neunter Symphonie" (Berlin, 1870), *Allgemeine Musikalische Zeitung*, 3rd ser. 6 (1871): 72-3.

Dannreuther, Edward.
"Beethoven and His Works: A Study," *Macmillan's Magazine* 34 (1876): 193-209.

Debussy, Claude.
Monsieur Croche the Dilettante-Hater, trans. B.N. Langdon Davies, in *Three Classics in the Aesthetic of Music* (New York, 1962).

d'Indy, Vincent.
Beethoven: A Critical Biography, trans. Theodore Baker (Boston, 1911).

[Dwight, John Sullivan?] "Mr. Zerrahn's Beethoven Night," unsigned article in *Dwight's Journal of Music* 14 (1859): 414-15.

Elterlein (pseud. Ernst Gottschald). *Beethoven's Symphonies in their Ideal Significance* [orig. pub. 1853], trans. Francis Weber (London: 1893).

Feski, J. "Gedanken unter die neunte Symphonie von Beethoven," *Neue Zeitschrift für Musik* 4 (1836): 125-6.

Frey, M. "Zur Vorgeschichte von Beethovens neunter Sinfonie," *Bär: Berlinische Blätter für vaterländische Geschichte und Alterthumskunde* 24 (1898): 31-4.

Grove, George. *Beethoven and his Nine Symphonies* (London, 1896).

Gurney, Edmund. *The Power of Sound* [orig. pub. 1880] (New York, 1966).

Hanslick, Eduard.
1950 *Music Criticisms 1846-99*, trans. and ed. Henry Pleasants (Baltimore, 1950).
1957 *The Beautiful in Music* [orig. pub. 1854], trans. Gustav Cohen, ed. Morris Weitz (Indianapolis, 1957).

Haweis, Rev. H. R. *Music and Morals* [orig. pub. 1871] (New York and London, 1904).

Hennig, Karl Rafael. *Beethoven's neunte Symphonie: eine Analyse* (Leipzig, 1888). My translation.

Hirschbach, Herrmann. "Beethoven's neunte Symphonie: eine Ansicht," *Neue Zeitschrift für Musik* 9 (1838): 19-21, 27-8, 31-2.

Linke, Oskar. "Ueber das Finale der Neunten," *Neue Musik-Zeitung* 13 (1892): 158-9.

Marx, Adolph Bernhard. *Ludwig van Beethoven: Leben und Schaffen*, excerpt on the Ninth Symphony in A.E. Kroeger, "Marx's Characterization of Beethoven's Ninth Symphony," *Dwight's Journal of Music* 30 (1871): 386-7, 394-5, 401-2, 412-13; originally published 1859.

Mason, Lowell. "Beethoven's Ninth Symphony," *Dwight's Journal of Music* 20 (1862): 12-13; reprinted from *Musical World and Times*.

Nietzsche, Friedrich.

1871   "On Music and Words," *The Complete Works of Friedrich Nietzsche* (New York, 1909-13) II, trans. M.A. Mügge, 29-47.

1872   *The Birth of Tragedy*, trans. Walter Kaufmann (New York, 1967).

1873   *Thoughts Out of Season, I, Complete Works* IV, trans. Anthony M. Ludovici.

1879   *Human, All Too Human: A Book for Free Spirits*, trans. Marion Faber, with Stephen Lehmann (Lincoln NB, 1984).

1886   *Beyond Good and Evil, Complete Works* XII, trans. Helen Zimmern.

1888   *The Case of Wagner*, trans. Walter Kaufmann (New York, 1967).

Oulibicheff,   *Beethoven, ses Critiques et ses Glossateurs* (Leipzig
Alexandre.   and Paris, 1857). My translations.

"P."   Report from London, on a performance of the Ninth conducted by Berlioz, *Dwight's Journal of Music* 1 (1852): 109.

Pastor, Willy.   "Beethoven's 'Neunte': Versuch einer Deutung," *Musikalisches Wochenblatt* 21 (1890): 313-14. I am grateful to Philipp Naegele for assistance with the translation.

Ritter, F.L.   Untitled concert review in *Dwight's Journal of Music* 25 (1866): 358.

Schmitt, G.A.   "The Motives and Themes of Beethoven's Ninth Symphony," *Dwight's Journal of Music* 14 (1859): 403-4, 410-12.

Schumann, Robert.   *On Music and Musicians*, ed. Konrad Wolff, trans. Paul Rosenfeld (New York, 1969).

Shaw, George Bernard.

1963   "The Religion of the Future," in *The Religious Speeches of Bernard Shaw*, ed. Warren Sylvester Smith (University Park PA, 1963) 29-37.

1981   *Shaw's Music: The Complete Musical Criticism in Three Volumes*, ed. Dan H. Laurence (New York, 1981).

Story, William W.   "Beethoven" [poem], *Dwight's Journal of Music* 30 (1870): 361.

Strauss, David   "Beethoven's Neunte Symphonie und ihre Bewunder;
Friedrich.   Musikalischer Brief eines beschränkten Kopfes,"
                       Allgemeine Musikalische Zeitung 12 (1877) col.
                       129-33; appeared originally in 1853 in *Augsburger
                       Allgemeine Zeitung*, anonymously.

Teetgen, Alexander.   *Beethoven's Symphonies Critically Discussed* (London,
                       1879).

[Thayer, Alexander   "Diary Abroad, No. 8," *Dwight's Journal of Music*
Wheelock].   6 (1855): 123-4.

Vimenal, Charles.   "La Neuvième symphonie de Beethoven," *L'Art* 1
                       (1875): 19-22. My translation.

Wagner, Richard.
  1846   "Report on the Performance of Beethoven's Ninth
                       Symphony at Dresden" [includes Programme],
                       Richard Wagner's Prose Works, trans. William Ashton
                       Ellis (New York, 1966; rpt. 1892), vol. VII.
  1849   "The Artwork of the Future," *Prose Works*, vol. I.
  1851   *Opera and Drama*, *Prose Works*, vol. II.
  1860   "Music of the Future," in *Three Wagner Essays*, trans.
                       Robert L. Jacobs (London, 1979).
  1870   *Beethoven. With a Supplement from the Philosophical
                       Works of Arthur Schopenhauer*, trans. Edward Dann-
                       reuther (London, 1880).
  1873   "The Rendering of Beethoven's Ninth Symphony"
                       Prose Works, vol. V, 231-53.

John Platoff

Writing About Influences:
Idomeneo, A Case Study

Discussions of the influence of one composer or work on another form an integral part of the writings of music historians. Yet it is by no means always clear what purpose the mention of a given influence is intended to serve, or how it relates to any larger argument. Nor, for that matter, can the reader invariably discern the logical basis on which an influence is asserted.

There are several questions to be answered about the use of influences in a historical narrative or stylistic analysis. Why are the influences cited—what do they contribute to the broader issues being raised? Why is an influence statement seen as a useful tool, and why is it employed in some discussions and not others? What conditions must be fulfilled to demonstrate the existence of an influence, and how explicitly do music historians acknowledge and meet these conditions? And finally, how does our widespread interest in influences reflect certain widely-held views about the process of stylistic change and the nature of music history?

We can attempt to answer these questions by examining writings on a single subject, focusing on the circumstances in which influences are invoked and the ways they are presented rather than on the validity of any particular viewpoints. This approach helps to reveal the assumptions about influence that underlie particular historical accounts. The writings considered in this study concern the composition of Mozart's opera seria *Idomeneo, re di Creta* (1780). I have chosen *Idomeneo* both

John Platoff is Assistant Professor of Music at Trinity College in Connecticut. He is currently working on a study entitled "Mozart and the opera buffa *in Vienna."*

because of the substantial literature on this work, which is commonly
held to be a turning point in Mozart's career as an operatic composer,
and because of the frequent references to influence in that literature.
The picture that emerges is a surprising one. In part because explanations for musical decisions are so hard to come by, influences have been
a great deal more attractive to historians than their actual value seems
to warrant. In many cases the explanatory power of a proposed influence
is exaggerated, and the influence is presented as a more complete solution to a problem than it actually is. Conversely, the limitations of influences are frequently overlooked or minimized. And few writers have
come to grips with the fact that influences may leave us with as many
questions as they answer.

I. INFLUENCES AS EXPLANATIONS

Historians assert the existence of influences primarily because influence statements are seen as causal or quasi-causal reasons to be used
in a historical or stylistic explanation.[1] Göran Hermerén has written:

> Consider a sentence of the following kind:
>
>> X influenced Y with respect to a (choice of motifs, style, expres-
>> sion, technique, symbolism, meter, rhythm, rhymes, and so forth).
>
> Such sentences can be used to answer questions like: "Why has Y this
> or that particular property?" and "How is it possible that—or how could
> it happen that—Y was created with this or that particular property?" These
> questions are clearly requests for explanations.[2]

That proposed influences frequently serve to explain certain features
of a work of art may be shown in the following examples.
In his discussion of the libretto of *Idomeneo*, Daniel Heartz describes
the changes made by Mozart and his librettist Varesco in the original
French play (*Idomenée* by Danchet), and he attempts to explain them:

> The additions of Mozart and Varesco to Act III are: a crowd scene before
> the palace, a High Priest's monologue, a chorus of mourning, a temple
> scene with March, an expiatory chorus of priests, a reconciliation scene,
> a heroic substitution, and an oracular pronouncement.

[1] There are profound problems with the view that an influence may be a "cause," as
I discuss below.
[2] Göran Hermerén, *Influence in Art and Literature* (Princeton, 1975), p. 120.

To seek a single work deploying all these dramatic opportunities we need go no further than *Alceste* by Calzabigi and Gluck....Mozart must have wanted to demonstrate what he could do with some of the stage situations so effectively treated by the older master.[3]

Here Heartz clearly presents both a "problem"—why were all these changes made?—and an explanation—the influence of Gluck's opera on Mozart.[4]

To explain what he views as not only a historical but an aesthetic "problem" in *Idomeneo*, Edward Dent suggests two sources of influence:

> Still more troublesome to a modern audience are the long instrumental introductions to many of Mozart's arias..., especially those which make a *concertante* display of individual instruments. One has to admit that Mozart sometimes committed errors of judgement in his desire to please his professional friends. In the operas of Gluck the introductions are often intensely expressive....Mozart is aiming at the same type of expression, but he was a much more accomplished composer for the orchestra..., and he had had far more practice in the composition of symphonies and concertos....[He is thus tempted] to combine the spontaneous and perhaps even crudely expressive instrumental solos of Gluck with the finished elegance of an instrumental concerto, especially as he was often on terms of personal friendship with the players and took a pleasure in showing them off.[5]

In this more complex quotation Dent offers several reasons for the long introductions to some of Mozart's arias, which he clearly feels need explaining. To begin with, Mozart is a talented instrumental composer. Further, he is trying to achieve the expressiveness of the instrumental introductions of Gluck, and he is trying as well to please his friends in the orchestra. Only the first of the two influences cited by Dent is artistic, namely that of Gluck. Mozart's "desire to please his professional friends" also affects his musical decisions, but this influence is "personal" rather than artistic.

---

[3]Daniel Heartz, "The Genesis of Mozart's *Idomeneo*," *Musical Quarterly* 55 (1969), pp. 12-13.

[4]Of course, one might reasonably ask *why* Mozart "wanted to demonstrate what he could do with some of the stage situations" taken from Gluck. This most important issue, the role of choice in influence, is considered below.

[5]Edward J. Dent, *Mozart's Operas: A Critical Study*, 2d ed. (London, 1947), p. 43.

II. CONDITIONS FOR INFLUENCE

In both of the above quotations, influences are asserted, treated as facts, and used as part of a larger explanation (in this case, of why certain features of *Idomeneo* are as they are). Notwithstanding the common use of this procedure, however, it is clear that an influence is not a fact but a hypothesis, a proposed relationship between one composer or work and another, and like any hypothesis it requires confirmation by means of appropriate evidence. Some discussions explicitly acknowledge the hypothetical nature of a proposed influence, and provide support for it by demonstrating (more or less successfully) that the conditions necessary for influence are met.

These conditions are three in number. The single external condition may be called Awareness, and the two internal conditions Similarity and Change.[6]

By Awareness I mean the following:

> If *X* influenced *Y* with respect to *a*, then the composer of *Y* had to have contact with *X* (with respect to *a*) before the completion of *Y*.[7]

In most cases this condition presents few difficulties for the historian: one either does or does not have the necessary biographical and documentary evidence to satisfy it. Thus, according to Otto Jahn, Mozart "had been present as a boy at the first representation of 'Alceste'."[8] And Heartz states that the composer "had just returned from witnessing Gluck's triumph at the Paris Opera, and both *Iphigénies* were well-known to him."[9] Neither statement is problematic, except that the evidence for Mozart's knowledge of Gluck's Iphigenia operas is not actually presented.

In his discussion of Mozart's ballet-music for *Idomeneo*, Georges de Saint-Foix acknowledges the need for Awareness, even though he cannot fulfill the condition.

> One will find in the rest of the dances (the gavotte for example) analogies with those of the score of *Amadis des Gaules* by Johann Christian Bach (1779), *but it is not possible for us to know positively if Mozart*, at the

---

[6]The following discussion draws in part on Hermerén, pp. 156-262, although I have conflated his three external conditions into one for present purposes.
[7]This is essentially equivalent to the requirement of contact in Hermerén, pp. 164-68.
[8]Otto Jahn, *Life of Mozart*, trans. Pauline D. Townsend, 3 vols. (1882; reprinted, New York [1968?]), 2:163.
[9]Heartz, p. 13.

end of his stay in Paris, *knew the work* which his teacher and friend from London was to have performed a year later on the stage of the opera in Paris.[10]

It is clear, then, that historians have respected the role of Awareness in demonstrating artistic influence. As noted above, the nature of the condition and the kind of evidence brought to bear on it make the problem one of objective data rather than more controversial interpretation.

The condition of Similarity threatens to leave all simplicity and clarity behind. It can be stated thus:

If X influenced Y with respect to a, then X and Y must be similar with respect to a.[11]

But just what does "similar" mean? Does it mean "similar in a way that any observer will notice," or "any expert will notice," or "any observer will assent to once it is pointed out"? The problem is enormously complex; and Hermerén's assertion that "we need to distinguish not only between the respects and levels of similarity, but also between the extensiveness, precision, and exclusiveness of the similarity" (followed by the definition of these terms) is admittedly only a framework for its consideration rather than any sort of solution.[12]

The degree to which historians specify the nature of a similarity varies widely, depending in part on the degree to which the proposed influence seems controversial. In presumably unequivocal instances, historians feel it sufficient merely to state the connection, relying on a similarity which may be only implied.

Above all it was in the organization of a large dramatic scene through the use of the chorus that Gluck could have provided the model. The choral scene with the high priest or the unison chorus of priests could hardly have been imagined without Gluck.[13]

To Schrade, the similarities between particular scenes of Gluck's operas and those of *Idomeneo* are so obvious that they need only be mentioned rather than demonstrated.

[10]Téodor de Wyzewa and Georges de Saint-Foix, *W.-A. Mozart: Sa vie musicale et son oeuvre*, 5 vols. (Paris, 1912-46), 3 (by Saint-Foix alone):238 (emphasis added). This and subsequent translations are my own.
[11]See Hermerén, p. 177.
[12]Ibid., p. 201.
[13]Leo Schrade, *W.A. Mozart* (Bern and Munich, 1964), p. 113.

But similarity relationships may be considerably more complex. Jahn
writes that the influence of *Alceste*

> is apparent in many details, such as the harmonic treatment of the oracle,
> and the use of sustained chords for the horns and trombones in the ac-
> companiment to the appeal of the High Priest. The march in "Alceste"
> has served as a model for the style, if not for the execution, of the last
> march in "Idomeneo." The High Priest's soliloquy is altogether
> analogous in plan and treatment to that of Gluck's High Priest; again,
> the recurring subject of the interlude—

> reminds us of the corresponding one in "Alceste"—

> and other similarities may be detected.[14]

Here the similarities mentioned are of different kinds and at different
levels. The comparison of themes in the interludes of comparable scenes
is very specific, whatever we may think of the *precision*, or exactness,
of their similarity. The "use of sustained chords for the horns and trombones" to accompany the High Priest is also quite specific, while the
"harmonic treatment of the oracle" and the "plan and treatment" of
the High Priest's scene are both more far-reaching and harder to pin
down. But Jahn is making a case for the *extensiveness* of the similarity
between the two works: roughly speaking the number of respects, at
different levels, in which they are similar.[15]

The requirement of precision plays an important role in demonstrating
similarity, as the following examples show.

> To seek a single work deploying all these dramatic opportunities [which
> Mozart and Varesco added] we need go no further than *Alceste* by
> Calzabigi and Gluck. Moreover musical reminiscences of *Alceste* such
> as those in the High Priest's monologue, the F-major March, and the
> Oracle's speech help to confirm this.[16]

[14]Jahn, 2:163. Jahn's quotation of Gluck's interlude contains an error; the D-flat in
the third measure is actually a D-natural.
[15]The terms *precision* and *extensiveness* are both defined by Hermerén, pp. 207-08.
[16]Heartz, p. 12.

The phrase "musical reminiscences" suggests similarities that are extremely close.

Another result of the new school of melodrama which had so struck Mozart is the recitative in which the orchestra of *Idomeneo* comments...on the sentiments expressed by the text. In the recitative no. 19 which introduces the aria of Arbace, for example, one finds procedures and even themes borrowed directly from *Ariadne auf Naxos* by Benda: Mozart...remembered these melodramas which had so much occupied him lately; and he wanted to incorporate the procedures and even the same rhythms in the recitative.[17]

The strength of Saint-Foix's assertion of similarity rests on Mozart's borrowing of "themes" and "the same rhythms" from Benda's work: these obviously imply that the two works sound very much alike.

But even when a precise similarity is made the basis for an asserted influence, the relationship may be vulnerable on other grounds. Dent writes that "following the example of Gluck, Mozart accompanies the oracle with trombones,"[18] and Schrade likewise observes that "the fact that Mozart accompanied the voice of the oracle with trombones demonstrates that he knew Gluck's *Alceste* very well."[19] But Stanley Sadie suggests another basis for this resemblance. As he remarks, historians have often pointed to "Gluck's influence, notable in Mozart's setting of the oracle scene with trombones (cf *Alceste*—though the idea, *in any case obvious in view of the association of trombones with ritual*, was put forward by Leopold)."[20] More important than the matter of Leopold's role is the idea that the association of trombones with the oracle scene was "obvious," and thus perhaps a choice made by Mozart independently of *Alceste* or any other particular work.

The issue raised here concerns the *exclusiveness* of a similarity.[21] Quite simply, a similarity between two works may be meaningless in a discussion of influence if the feature exists in many other works, or forms part of the common style of the period.[22] It follows from this that the

[17]Wyzewa and Saint-Foix, 3:230.
[18]Dent, p. 64.
[19]Schrade, p. 114.
[20]Stanley Sadie, "Wolfgang Amadeus Mozart," *The New Grove Dictionary of Music and Musicians*, 6th ed. by Stanley Sadie, 20 vols. (London, 1980), 12:700 (emphasis added).
[21]Hermerén, pp. 207-08.
[22]Jan LaRue makes this point very effectively in "Significant and Coincidental Resemblance between Classical Themes," *Journal of the American Musicological Society* 14 (1961): 224-34. He argues that in judging whether a thematic similarity is significant, one must rely both on the "structural similarity" (which encompasses extensiveness and, particularly, precision) and on the "statistical background," which measures the exclusiveness of the similarity.

use of conventions cannot be logically explained by reference to influences since by definition a convention is widely used by any number
of composers within a style.

> As to the great heroic appeals of the first measures [of the overture to
> *Idomeneo*], they are found on the threshold of a large number of similar
> dramas, and one could scarcely find, we believe, a single musical tragedy
> which did not have, as early as the first measures of the overture, a
> roulade ending on a unison *forte*.[23]

Here Saint-Foix argues against the assertion that Mozart's overture was
influenced by that of Gluck's *Iphigénie en Aulide*. Specifically, he
dismisses the similarity on which the assertion is based for its lack of
exclusiveness: the "heroic appeals" can be found in any number of
overtures, not merely these two.

Despite the crucial importance of exclusive similarity to any discussion of influence, historians often fail to deal with this condition. They
seem to invoke it more often in refuting a proposed influence, as in
the quotations from Sadie and Saint-Foix above, than in proposing one.
William Mann does not consider the question of exclusiveness in this
passage:

> Choral movements of this kind [with four soloists drawn from the chorus]
> were an importation from France. French too is the character of the music
> with its fizzing orchestral trills and busy string writing, as well as its
> solo episodes separated by choral refrains.[24]

Characterizing the music of a chorus as French by virtue of its "fizz-
ing orchestral trills and busy string writing" overlooks the many other
possible sources of these features: for instance, Viennese church music,
whose choruses are filled with busy string writing.[25]

Without claiming to have done more than touch upon the complex
problems of Similarity, let me proceed to the third condition, that of
Change:

> If *X* influenced *Y* with respect to *a*, then *Y* must be different (with respect
> to *a*) than it would have been, had there been no influence.[26]

[23]Wyzewa and Saint-Foix, 3:235.
[24]William Mann, *The Operas of Mozart* (London, 1977), pp. 264-65.
[25]To be fair, Mann's intention here is to establish influence by means of the extensiveness of the similarity; but this is one of many instances in which a historian considers similarity from only one point of view, without addressing other essential aspects
of the question.
[26]Compare Hermerén, p. 246.

This statement, which seems self-evident in the abstract, concisely defines what Leonard Meyer has called a deflecting influence, one that leads a composer to make choices other than those he would probably have made in the absence of the influence.[27] And it is almost exclusively deflecting influences that attract the interest of music historians.

Schrade acknowledges the condition of Change in discussing *Idomeneo* as a whole:

> In contrast to all previous operatic compositions, *Idomeneo* is *the first work which accomplished* that which becomes an inalienable characteristic—of course, to a greater degree—of later works: *a new individualizing of opera seria*. The model is in *Idomeneo* influenced, not unimportantly, by Gluck.[28]

For the reader to find Gluck's influence plausible, it must be at least claimed (if not demonstrated) that what Mozart has written is "different." Clearly, the simplest way to assert that Mozart did something different from what he *would have done* is to argue that he did something different from what *he has done* in the past. Here Schrade has gone further, by stating that what Mozart did is different from what any composer had done up to that time.

In the following pair of quotations Charles Osborne and William Mann both rely on Change, although they arrive at opposite conclusions.

> In Mozart's earlier *opere serie*, and in Italian eighteenth-century opera in general, very little use is made of the chorus....In Gluck and in French opera, however, the chorus played an important part in the dramatic structure of the work, and it is from what he saw and heard in Paris that Mozart derived his ideas for the choruses in *Idomeneo*.[29]

Osborne has invoked quite explicitly the new importance of the chorus in *Idomeneo*. Here are Mann's views on the subject:

> *Idomeneo* is full of marvellous choruses, some purely dynamic and theatrical, some gravely solemn with solo and duet episodes. These are

---

[27]Leonard B. Meyer, *Style, Music and History*, unpublished draft, Chapter 4, "Influence," pp. 50-51. Meyer also distinguishes two other types: a negative influence leads a composer to reject choices that he might otherwise have made—this is therefore a type of deflecting influence—while a reinforcing influence strengthens or encourages a composer's already probable pattern of choices. As may readily be seen, reinforcing influences are often difficult to detect.

[28]Schrade, p. 112 (emphasis added).

[29]Charles Osborne, *The Complete Operas of Mozart: A Critical Guide* (New York, 1978), p. 156.

attributed to Gluck's influence. But Mozart had included choruses of
this kind in *Apollo et Hyacinthus*..., in *Ascanio in Alba* and in *Lucio
Silla*, all powerfully effective. There were choruses in *Il sogno di Sci-
pione* and *La Betulia liberata*. The choruses in *Idomeneo* are not to be
underrated, and they owe their frequency to French opera, but Mozart
had been writing them assiduously into his operas before he was aware
of Gluck or French operatic style. Their superiority does not mean that
Mozart copied them from *Alceste*.[30]

Mann here distinguishes carefully between what is and is not new about
the choruses in *Idomeneo*. And he flatly disagrees with Osborne on the
facts: since choruses did play a part in Mozart's earlier *opere serie*,
their presence in *Idomeneo* cannot be attributed to outside influence.
It is the *frequency* of the choruses that is new, and that therefore can
be explained by recourse to Gluck and French opera.[31] The quotation,
then, shows another way of refuting a claim of influence: by showing
the condition of Change to be unfulfilled.

Depending on the evidence available, a historian may combine and
weight in different ways the essential conditions of Awareness, Similarity, and Change. A long passage from Jahn addresses all three (as indicated), though in differing degrees of detail:

> But, since in the improvements he made [Change] he was indebted to
> French opera, and especially to Gluck, the question arises how much,
> and in what way, Mozart had learnt from the great Parisian master. It
> is not merely unquestionable that Gluck exerted a general influence over
> Mozart's opinions and tendencies, but the traces of a close study of his
> works, and especially of "Alceste," may be easily discovered. He had
> been present as a boy at the first representation of "Alceste" [Aware-
> ness]. Its influence is apparent in many details. . .

The passage continues (as quoted on page 48 above) with a discussion
of different examples of Similarity, and concludes with a general
statement:

> More important is the similarity of dramatic style, which is especially
> evident in the treatment of the recitatives, and in the share taken by the
> orchestra in the characterisation.[32]

[30]Mann, p. 286.
[31]An alternative reading of the quotation might be that Mann is actually suggesting
Gluck and French opera as a *reinforcing* influence, which strengthens Mozart's predilec-
tion for the use of choruses.
[32]Jahn, 2:163.

By referring to Mozart's "improvements" upon the old forms of opera seria—improvements discussed in the preceding pages of his book—Jahn invokes the condition of Change to justify the assertion of influence that immediately follows. The influence is then explored in greater detail, with attention to Awareness and above all to Similarity.

Since every case is different, the degree to which Similarity, Awareness, and Change figure in the argument may vary widely. In considering a proposed influence between two works whose similarities may be debatable, Hermerén declares that the historian must begin by evaluating the similarities with respect to extensiveness, exclusiveness, and precision.

> Furthermore, he should...try to point out or describe the similarities he has noticed as clearly as possible, and...to weigh these similarities against the differences between the works and against other available evidence, including statements made by the artist or poet himself. The last point is essential, and it is obvious that this weighing is a very complex operation.

And in discussing the painter Mondrian, who claimed to be influenced by his mentor van der Leck even though no one can see the influence in Mondrian's work, Hermerén says that one can use

> the following rough rule of thumb: the more probable it is that the creator of *Y* was familiar with *X*, the less extensive, exclusive, and precise need the similarities between *X* and *Y* be.

In short, he advocates a kind of inverse relationship between the degrees to which the conditions of Similarity and Awareness need be established.[33]

III. LEVELS OF EXPLANATION

But what of the many discussions of influence that ignore these conditions, or that treat them incompletely or unconvincingly? The quotation from Osborne on page 51, for example, makes a flat statement about influence, without any attempt to demonstrate it. To understand why this kind of writing occurs so frequently, we need to return to a distinction

[33]Hermerén, pp. 233-34. In a fascinating example outside the scope of this paper—an attempt to relate Brahms's Scherzo, Opus 4, to the Scherzos of Chopin (in "Influence: Plagiarism and Inspiration," *19th Century Music* 4 [1980-81], pp. 93-94)—Charles Rosen fails to deal with the intuitively apparent obverse of this rule of thumb.

only hinted at above: the difference between statements that posit an influence as part of a larger explanation, and those that assert an influence which itself requires documentation and support.

The quotations with which we began do the former: they use a presumably non-controversial statement about an influence to explain why an aspect of *Idomeneo* is the way it is. Although actually just a hypothesis, the influence is presented as fact, to which the reader is likely to assent either by faith in the authority or because, based on his or her own knowledge, the asserted relationship seems plausible.

In other cases, the influence suggested is not one to which everyone will assent, or a previously claimed influence is being challenged. Under these circumstances the influence is explicitly treated as a hypothesis, and supporting or refuting evidence is called for. It is important, then, in reading music history to be aware of the distinction. Influences posited without evidence may at times frustrate the reader; but we must recognize that this practice belongs to a tradition in which influence statements are presented as facts, which serve the purpose of some other explanation. The difference is one of levels; at a lower, more detailed level, a proposed influence requires demonstration, while at a higher level the influence forms part of a larger explanation of a work's characteristics.[34] Nearly all discussions of influence either begin at the higher level or proceed rapidly to it from the lower level.[35] As this suggests, historians are most interested in the higher level of explanation, in using influences to make larger points about a work or a composer.

It is in such higher-level explanations that one finds those passages in which a historian directs attention to the *differences* between the influencing work and that which it influences:

> Mozart had a great admiration for Gluck's *Alceste*, and *Alceste* is obviously the model for many scenes in this opera; but for the recitatives and arias of Electra Gluck could provide no example—the wildest outbursts of Armide and the Furies seem almost childish in comparison with the utterances of Electra's savage jealousy. Mozart adopts Gluck's declamatory, almost barbarous and unvocal style of phrase, but whereas Gluck's rhythm nearly always becomes monotonous, and his management of purely musical technique often fumbling and helpless, Mozart's

[34]The distinction between the two types of statements is often far from clear. Most of the quotations presented thus far fall somewhere in between: they deal at least in part with one or more of the three conditions needed to show an influence, but without explicitly acknowledging its hypothetical nature. Most often a fairly clear similarity (perhaps with some evidence of awareness) is considered sufficient to "prove" the influence.

[35]The exceptions are cases in which an asserted influence is being refuted.

complete mastery of symphonic resources enables him to pile up his phrases to a well-defined climax, to contrast the brute force of diatonic harmony with the anguished wail of gliding chromatics.[36]

Here Dent uses an asserted influence to explain the matter that most interests him: why are Mozart's scenes for Electra so powerful? Because he does not doubt that the reader will accept the basic connection between *Idomeneo* and Gluck's works, Dent can pass quickly over the similarities—"Mozart adopts Gluck's declamatory, almost barbarous and unvocal style of phrase"—and emphasize the differences, which are further explained by reference to Mozart's "mastery of symphonic resources."

Many discussions of influence employ the concept of "the same means for different ends." Saint-Foix uses this similarity/difference juxtaposition to emphasize contrasts in dramatic conception:

> With all [the previously described similarities], Mozart...does not continue the theatre of Gluck. Mozart certainly "deepened and widened by the use of the chorus" the old *opera seria*; but, in spite of many considerable innovations, he remains bound to the old Italian ideal of the latter. Mozart does not think at all of modifying the old theatrical drama: he thinks above all of adapting his arias to the varying abilities of his protagonists....He states on the subject of *Ilia's* aria, *Se il padre perdei...*"that he does not want to be too restrained by the words." Impossible, in all this, to be further from Gluck.[37]

"Same means/different ends" is a useful notion, for at least two reasons. First, it provides a consistent framework for the description of a work of art. The statement that "*Y* resembles *X* in these respects, while differing from it in these other respects," somehow seems more cogent and organized than "*Y* resembles *X* in these respects, and also has these other features that do not have anything to do with *X*." Second, the concept provides a strong bastion of defense for the historian whose claim of influence may be attacked for reasons of insufficient similarity. "Of course!" the threatened historian may reply, "there are many differences between *Idomeneo* and *Alceste*. I made that very point myself when I showed that Mozart used some of Gluck's procedures, but for his own ends." Clearly, such an argument—that the influenced artist was "inspired" by the earlier work, but that his inspiration led him

---

[36]Dent, p. 51.
[37]Wyzewa and Saint-Foix, 3:227-28; the first quoted phrase within the passage is apparently from Hermann Abert, *W.A. Mozart: Neubearbeitete und erweiterte Ausgabe von Otto Jahns Mozart*, 5th ed., 2 vols. (Leipzig, 1919-21).

far away from its source—can make it very difficult to construct a convincing refutation of a proposed influence.[38]

IV. INFLUENCE, CHOICE AND CAUSALITY

The following excerpt from a "same means, different ends" argument calls attention to another issue of fundamental importance: the matter of choice in artistic influence.

> But that Mozart learnt from Gluck only as one master learns from another,...it needs but a closer consideration of these details, as well as of the whole work, to make plain....We must also remember that Mozart received these impressions and this instruction [from Gluck's operas] into a nature self-dependent and productive, and that his artistic cultivation enabled him to appropriate only what was in accordance with his nature.[39]

According to Jahn, Mozart used only those aspects of Gluck's works which were "in accordance with his nature"; otherwise, he followed his own instincts. As the quotation reminds us, the process of influence merely begins when Mozart becomes aware of the operas of Gluck. It is Mozart's choosing of certain options from among the many made available by Gluck's works that actually constitutes the influence;[40] and it is the explanation of the choices that is, or should be, of greatest interest. We seek to know *why* Mozart adopted certain features of Gluck's operas and not others.

Of course, this is at least as complex a matter for the historian as any of those discussed so far. Jahn grapples with it without throwing any notable light on the problem. Indeed, to assert that Mozart borrowed only what was "in accordance with his nature" borders on the tautological, even if we infer that by "nature" Jahn means Mozart's own established musical style. Jahn has raised the question of choice without being able to do much with it.

Schrade is able to go a little further:

> But it was not Gluck the reformer who had an influence on *Idomeneo*.
> Mozart had not the least to do with the highly rationalistic operatic reform

---

[38]In this connection see Rosen, pp. 87-88, 100.
[39]Jahn, 2:163-64.
[40]Leonard B. Meyer, "Innovation, Choice, and the History of Music," *Critical Inquiry* 9 (1983), p. 530.

which Gluck carried out in his *Orfeo* and *Alceste*; and he wanted nothing to do with it....Mozart was not interested in reforms and by no means in any theories, be they musical or literary. He was highly interested in anything entirely new in operatic composition, even if it seemed to be only an experiment.

Schrade goes on to describe Mozart's excitement at hearing the melodramas of Benda, and then adds:

In novelty his spirit could catch fire, so that he even wanted to write a melodrama in the style of Benda; he accordingly planned to compose a *Semiramis*.[41]

This is a picture of Mozart that makes plausible the combination of similarities and differences from Gluck's operas that Schrade finds in *Idomeneo*. He argues that Mozart was interested not in theories or reform but in new methods and techniques for operatic writing. It is thus understandable that Mozart would take from Gluck such elements as a greater use of the chorus, or a newly important expressive role for the orchestra, while ignoring those innovations which threatened the basic structure of Italian opera seria. Schrade has provided a hypothesis that explains some of Mozart's choices, given the options made available by Gluck's operas and Benda's melodramas.

The nature of choice requires more consideration in discussions of influence than most writers on *Idomeneo* have given it. One can infer from some of the writings surveyed above the following sort of thought process:

1. Here is a feature I have not seen in Mozart's previous operas. [Change]
2. Where does it "come from"?
3. It can be found in Gluck's *Iphigénie en Aulide*. [Similarity]
4. Was Mozart familiar with this opera before the time of the composition of *Idomeneo*? Yes. [Awareness]
5. Mozart therefore "got" this feature from Gluck's opera.

The implicit assumption that Mozart heard something new, liked it, and borrowed from it begs the question of why he liked it, and whether he was influenced by everything he liked. Even the typical formulation of influence statements—"Mozart was influenced by *Alceste*"—suggests

---

[41]Schrade, pp. 112-13.

that the active role in the influence process is taken by the model, rather than by the composer of the "influenced" work.[42] But it is the composer who must of necessity choose from among the many possibilities presented by the model.

The crucial role played by choice in the influence process casts doubt upon the view of influence statements with which we began: that they are used to give reasons, of a causal or quasi-causal nature, in historical explanations. Meyer explicitly denies that influences are causal: "Influence is not a kind of causation....Influence allows for choice, causation does not."[43] On the other hand, Hermerén makes the following claims:

> Influence statements provide us with explanations; they indicate *why* works of art have certain definite properties, and they provide us with causal explanations, since they indicate the cause or at least a cause of the fact that the works of art in question have these properties.[44]

This disagreement may be resolved by distinguishing carefully between *influences* and the *influence statements* to which Hermerén is referring. Consider the following explanatory statement:

> *Idomeneo* has many choral scenes because Mozart was influenced by Gluck's operas.

The problem is not that the statement is not causal, but that it is so incomplete. It is really a kind of shorthand version of the following:

> *Idomeneo* has many choral scenes because Mozart modelled *Idomeneo* after Gluck's operas in this respect.

Here attention is drawn to Mozart's active role in the process, and to his *decision* to model his opera (in this respect) after those of Gluck. This may be restated as follows:

> *Idomeneo* has many choral scenes because Mozart chose to write many choral scenes, following the example of Gluck's operas.

In this formulation the causal portion of the explanation (up to the comma) is reduced to a virtual tautology. The sole interest resides in the dependent clause, which raises the question *why* Mozart followed Gluck's example.

We may, then, agree with Hermerén that an influence statement can be a causal explanation, while going on to insist that the causal portion

[42]Meyer,"Innovation," p. 530.
[43]Ibid.
[44]Hermerén, pp. 122-23.

of the explanation is so incomplete as to be trivial. What surely matters is the next level of explanation—in Hermerén's words "why the person who created *Y* was influenced by *X* on this occasion, or why he was influenced by *X* rather than by *Z.*"[45] Another way of putting the matter is that influence statements may be causal explanations—though not, as we have seen, in a particularly useful way—but that the element of choice implicit in the influence statement is not causal and remains to be explained.

The implications of this stance for the practice of music history are substantial. For once one strips influences of the causal status they have long been implicitly granted, their usefulness in historical explanation is drastically diminished. It no longer suffices to show that a particular characteristic of *Idomeneo* occurs earlier in an opera by Gluck, or in French music; any satisfactory explanation must deal with the question of why Mozart adopted it. And the answer must be grounded in a whole host of issues, including Mozart's personality and artistic goals, the circumstances for which the work was written, current stylistic trends both generally and in *opera seria,* and so on.

Why then do so many discussions of influence stop short of this point? Why do historians assert an influence as an explanation for a work's characteristics, while ducking the further questions that the influence statement itself generates? The answer seems to lie in the great difficulty of explaining artistic decisions. In contrast to a number of shared hypotheses about human action in most other realms, as Meyer points out,

> we have few viable hypotheses about artistic behavior....Ironically, we can explain Beethoven's actions (choices) vis-à-vis his nephew (an area in which he was scarcely competent) more easily than we can his choice of E major for the second key area of the first movement of the *Waldstein* Sonata (an area in which he was supremely skillful).[46]

And influences, if one overlooks the problem of choice and sees them as causal explanations, hold out the promise of providing answers to otherwise extremely difficult questions. If, for example, an 1802 piano sonata by Dussek were discovered, in which the second key area of the first movement were in the mediant, the discovery would no doubt lead to studies asserting that Beethoven's use of E in the "Waldstein" occurred because of the influence of this newly found work. Only an

---

[45]Ibid., pp. 123-24.
[46]Meyer,"Innovation," p. 543.

exceptional commentator would go on to ask why Dussek might have
used the mediant for the second key area, or why Beethoven might have
borrowed this procedure from Dussek.

V. INFLUENCES AND VIEWS OF HISTORY

We began by asking why influences are so often cited in historical
or analytic discussions. Another, closely related question remains: Why
are influences cited in connection with some works and not others? Why,
for example, are discussions of *Idomeneo* full of references to influences
on Mozart, while such references occur far more rarely in discussions
of the great piano concertos of 1784?

The principal answer seems to be that influences are posited to explain anomalies, to deal with features of a work that seem unexpected
to the historian in the light of a composer's other, or perhaps previous,
compositions.[47] The following quotation provides an example:

> How can we explain the almost revolutionary fervor of Mozart's storm
> music? Scarcely intimated before in his art, and for lack of an occasion,
> rarely to be called upon again, it is quite peculiar to *Idomeneo*.[48]

Heartz finds it necessary to search for an explanation for the character
of Mozart's storm music not simply because of its "almost revolutionary
fervor," but because this fervor is virtually unique in Mozart's operas:
nothing in his previous works would have led one to expect it. And
the explanation Heartz subsequently arrives at is an external one: the
influence of Munich's *maître de ballet*, Pierre Legrand, and the stage
designer and engineer, Lorenzo Quaglio.

To perceive anomalies or discontinuities of style, historians must inevitably rely on some rule (or set of rules) with which they can make
predictions about what a particular work "should" be like, given the
characteristics of the group of works to which it belongs. (By this I
mean *Idomeneo* in the context of Mozart's other operas, or of *opere
serie* of the period around 1780, or some similar group.) The rule that

---

[47]I am aware that claims of influence may also arise from a perceived similarity, as
for example between the Funeral March of Beethoven's "Eroica" Symphony and the
public *marches funèbres* of post-Revolutionary Paris. Yet in cases like this as well,
the significance of the relationship depends on the fact that the Funeral March is
anomalous as a symphonic slow movement; if many such slow movements existed in
Viennese symphonies of the period, the connection between Beethoven's symphony
and the French marches would be neither a convincing nor a necessary explanation.
[48]Heartz, p. 11.

underlies most writing about influence may be called the "axiom of inertia,"[49] under which constancy is the norm and it is change that must be explained. (Leo Treitler characterizes diachronic music history by its "tendencies to represent the past in continuous narratives, and to make *change* and *novelty* the principal subjects of history.")[50]

In its simplest form the axiom of intertia might postulate stasis, so that any new work by a composer, or a given genre, should be like all previous ones. It follows that any new or different characteristics would be anomalous and require explanation. Most historical writing, however, is based on a more sophisticated version of the axiom, in which a limited degree of orderly and gradual change is to be expected from one work to the next. As a result, some kinds of changes are not seen as anomalous and need not be explained in terms of influence. This approach accounts for the use of concepts like "improved compositional technique," "greater maturity," or "an increased awareness of the possibilities of the style," which can be employed to explain less dramatic, more predictable stylistic changes. Here for example is a passage in which Alfred Einstein discusses Mozart's early symphonies:

> In general the signs of increasing depth grow from year to year, as does the change towards greater freedom and individuality in the use of the instruments, the development of figuration in the direction of more singing character, and the perfection of the technique of imitation.[51]

The same attitude informs Einstein's comparison of Mozart's *Il re pastore*, which is not normally discussed in terms of influence, with the earlier *Ascanio in Alba*:

> The invention in *Il Re pastore* is of a quite new order—warmer, more full-blooded, more personal, less stereotyped. Everything is richer and more concentrated—not simply shorter.[52]

The differences Einstein cites, such as "warmer" and "more personal" invention, can presumably be understood as the result of Mozart's natural development in the four years between the two works. On the other hand, of *Idomeneo* Einstein says: "*Idomeneo* hardly preserves anything

---

[49]Meyer, "Innovation," p. 521.
[50]Leo Treitler, "History, Criticism, and Beethoven's Ninth Symphony," *19th Century Music* 3 (1979-80), p. 204.
[51]Alfred Einstein, *Mozart: His Character, His Work*, trans. Arthur Mendel and Nathan Broder (1945; reprint ed., New York, 1979), p. 221.
[52]Ibid., p. 403.

in common with the earlier *opere serie* or *feste teatrali* of Mozart.''[53]
And it is no surprise that in this instance he goes on to discuss the relationship of the work to Gluck and French opera—the many new features
of *Idomeneo* exceed the limits of novelty predicted under the axiom
of inertia, and therefore require external explanations of this sort.

The view of history characterized by the axiom of inertia is not the
only prevalent model, but it is the only one in which influence statements
are usefully employed. The concept of inertia clearly cannot explain
the larger changes of musical style that have occurred in the history
of European art music, such as the transition from Renaissance music
to the music of the Baroque. What is needed in such cases are more
broadly conceived general hypotheses about the nature of stylistic change.

> Successive changes in musical style may be explained by placing them
> in the framework of larger patterns of change (for example, ''evolution''
> either within a limited period or through the history of a civilization);
> or by showing them as instances of a recurrent pattern of change (for
> example, alternations of ''ethic'' and ''pathic'' styles); or by showing
> that style changes regularly occur in a certain way (for example, by pro-
> cesses analogous to those of ''adaptation'' in biology). More strictly linear
> are explanations which assume certain kinds of change (for example,
> in the social structure as determined by methods of production) as basic
> and attempt to show how changes in musical style are related to these.[54]

One reason why influences do not figure in these accounts of stylistic
change is the scale on which such accounts operate. Any particular influence is unimportant, because any individual compositional decision
is essentially trivial. Measured against the grand stylistic march from,
say, the birth of opera to the tragic masterpieces of Verdi, Mozart's
enriching and deepening of the emotional possibilities of opera seria

---

[53]Ibid., p. 405.

[54]Donald Jay Grout, ''Current Historiography and Music History,'' in *Studies in Music
History: Essays for Oliver Strunk*, ed. Harold Powers (Princeton, 1968), p. 36. The
various evolutionary models (and their problems) are amply documented by Warren
Dwight Allen, *Philosophies of Music History* (New York, 1939), Chapters 7, 10, 11,
and *passim*. Gerald Abraham, *The Tradition of Western Music* (Berkeley, 1974), p. 17,
posits a particular kind of evolutionary process that operates ''by the successive ex-
haustion of techniques and styles and their replacement by new ones.'' The chief pro-
ponent of cycles of ''ethos'' and ''pathos'' in the arts is Curt Sachs, *The Commonwealth
of Art: Style in the Fine Arts, Music, and the Dance* (New York, 1946). An early presentation of the organicist, biological analogy for style change (which is related to the
evolutionary approaches) may be found in August Wilhelm Ambros, *Geschichte der
Musik* (1862-82); see Hans Heinrich Eggebrecht, ''Historiography,'' *The New Grove
Dictionary*, 8:597.

under the influence of Gluck are reduced to a matter of mere coincidence. If Mozart had not, following Gluck's lead, brought certain elements into the genre, this development might have occurred at a slightly later date but it would have occurred nonetheless.

But the problem is not only one of scale. Whenever a specific hypothesis or model is advanced to explain changes in musical style, influence statements are of negligible value. This is because each model is fundamentally deterministic, positing one or more general principles to account for the stylistic changes it discusses; and any specific cases of influence, were they mentioned at all, would have to be subordinated to these general principles. It follows that even limited accounts of stylistic change, those that focus on one era from a diachronic perspective, tend to exclude influence statements.

In an interesting example of such an account, David Burrows has drawn attention to analogies of stylistic development in the works of the composer Vivaldi, the librettist Apostolo Zeno, and the painter Marco Ricci.[55] By applying general analytical categories to the three artists' different spheres, Burrows traces ''stylistic synchronism'' in the way their works changed over time. The governing hypothesis is one of ''cultural style,'' defined as ''perceptual habits shared by members of a group, which are manifested in their activities as shared consistencies in the handling of scope and structure.''[56]

At one point Burrows shows that between 1712 and 1730 Vivaldi published concertos that increasingly contained just three movements, rather than four or five. ''This is evidence of a trend from complexity toward standardization and simplicity'' that is also found in other features of Vivaldi's concertos, and in the works of Zeno and Ricci.[57] Now let us imagine that in 1720 an enormously successful set of concertos was published, all containing three movements and the other features that Burrows cites. Even if one could prove that Vivaldi was influenced by the success of the set, the information would have no fundamental bearing on the study, for the following reason. The influence of the imaginary set of concertos might explain (at least in part) Vivaldi's move towards three-movement concertos. But to account for the existence of, and the success of, the imaginary set, we would have to return to the theory of stylistic change with which the study is concerned. In the terms of Burrows's hypothesis, the importance of the imaginary concerto set

---

[55]David Burrows, ''Style in Culture: Vivaldi, Zeno, and Ricci,'' *Journal of Interdisciplinary History* 4 (1973): 1-23.
[56]Ibid., p. 1.
[57]Ibid., p. 6.

would not be its influence on Vivaldi but its further demonstration of the asserted "trend...toward standardization and simplicity."

In short, influence statements may serve as (partial) explanations of choices made by individual composers. But since the hypotheses advanced to explain changes in style operate at levels transcending the particular decisions of individuals, matters of influence are fundamentally irrelevant to such accounts of stylistic change. (This might not be the case for "great man" accounts of history, those claiming that historical developments result purely or largely from the decisions of particular individuals, such as Napoleon or Beethoven. But such views of history are no longer taken very seriously, if indeed they ever were.)

While the present study is not intended to be prescriptive, many of the foregoing observations suggest that influence, and influence statements, need to be viewed in a new light. In several respects the value of influence statements is more circumscribed than is generally acknowledged. To begin with, such statements are applicable only within the kind of historical framework in which the axiom of inertia obtains. Such a framework is necessarily limited: it encompasses studies of a single work or a group of works, but excludes investigations that attempt to explain changes of musical style over time. This is because such investigations involve general hypotheses about the reasons for stylistic change—hypotheses to which any particular influence is inevitably subordinate.

Second, influence statements are hypothetical. In practice, their status as hypotheses is recognized only at times; but in many cases (perhaps all of those in which the relationship is potentially controversial) scholarly responsibility requires that the hypotheses be proved, by explicitly addressing the conditions of Awareness, Similarity, and Change. A proposed influence may therefore call for appropriate evidence before it can be used as part of some other discussion.

As we have seen, a thorough consideration of a proposed influence must encompass the role of choice. Because choice is invariably involved, any use of an influence statement to explain why a work has certain features raises new questions about the influence itself: specifically, questions about the choices made by the composer being influenced. An influence statement, then, can never be an explanation without also being a statement that itself requires explanation.

In sum, the preceding suggests that an influence statement should not be seen as an easy explanation, or a way of avoiding more complex problems of interpretation. Proposed influences are at once less powerful and more limited in their scope than has been fully understood. Influence statements are attractive in large part because they seem to offer explanations in an area where few are available. This will ensure that influences continue to play an important role in historical and analytic writing; but their attractiveness must not blind us to their limitations, nor to the additional responsibilities of demonstration and explanation placed on historians who propose them.

Margaret Murata

Scylla and Charybdis, or Steering Between Form and Social Context in the Seventeenth Century

> To feel close to things past is
> to misconstrue them, while to
> understand them is to sense
> their remoteness.
>
> Carl Dahlhaus[1]

I

Here is Dr. Burney in 1789, presenting the music of Giulio Caccini:

> Those who are acquainted with the operas of Lulli, will find a great
> similarity between his style and that of Caccini... We must ascribe some
> of its success to simplicity, poetry, and expression... Though we are
> now inclined to wonder how pleasing effects could be produced by such
> simple, unadorned, and almost unaccompanied melodies... The expres-
> sion of the music of this period in Italy is so entirely lost, that, like a
> dead language, no one is certain how it was pronounced.[2]

---

[1]*Foundations of Music History,* trans. J.B. Robinson (Cambridge, 1983), p. 63.
[2]Charles Burney, *A General History of Music from the Earliest Ages to the Present
Period* (1935; reprint ed. New York, 1957), 2: 603-605. Burney's history is among
the most important eighteenth-century comprehensive historical treatments of Western
music. Here Burney is discussing Caccini's song collection *Le nuove musiche* (Florence,
1602).

*Margaret Murata is Professor of Music at the University of Califor-
nia, Irvine. She is currently preparing a documentary chronology of
seventeenth-century operatic performances in Rome, a catalogue of the
music manuscripts in the Barberini Library in the Vatican, and a study
of the Roman cantata.*

One-hundred twenty-three years later, Hugo Riemann began his history
of seventeenth-century monody with an analysis of eight lines from the
messenger scene in Rinuccini's opera *Euridice*. He established the meter
and rhyme scheme of the text and then compared Peri's musical setting
with Caccini's.

> The sustained bass alone reminds us here—and in many such places in
> Peri and Caccini—of later recitative, also especially in the general direc-
> tion of the line: the rise at the beginning, the half-cadence in the middle
> register at the mid-point, at the end of the first part (cadence at b^2); and
> the extension downwards in the closing passage with the complete cadence
> at the end of the first section, given complete here (c^1). These are already
> natural tendencies [*Direktiven*], not ones that distinguish recitative from
> aria, but rather ones that characterize all logical construction of musical
> forms [*allen vernünftigen musikalischen Formgebung*].[3]

These two passages symbolize great differences in approach to the music
of the past and in the notion of what is the material of the history of

[3]Hugo Riemann, *Handbuch der Musikgeschichte* (Leipzig, 1904-1912), 2: part 2, pp.
4-6. *Euridice* (Florence, 1600), to a libretto by Ottavio Rinuccini, is the earliest opera
to have survived in complete score. One setting by Jacopo Peri and another by Caccini
are contemporaneous. The excerpt Riemann discusses is:

music. Burney's history is untouched by Hegelian theories. Riemann's is on its way to the New Criticism. This is to say that Burney's interest in music is archaeological. Riemann, using a Hegelian metaphor, is tracking the spirit of music through history by its "forms" and is well on the high road to a scientific compilation of universal musical principles. Burney saw musical change partly as the passing of fashion. Still of Caccini he says, "The passages of taste and embellishment, which are now antiquated and vulgar were then new and elegant..."[4] Later nineteenth-century music historiography instead moved toward the view that such change was part of the internal progress of musical style and technique, a view which has not yet disappeared from our current music histories.[5] Burney seemed to recognize that the past is past. The nineteenth century has given us a legacy of a past unprecedentedly always alive in the present.

We have inherited a jumble of approaches to Western music: they represent the search for theoretical handles that could order, make sense of, and valorize music both past and present. The Hegelian model traces a continuing "spirit" in successive historical epochs.[6] The scientific model seeks universal principles, for example, the generation of musical elements from the overtone series or the operation of technical devices that produce "form."[7] A more critical approach establishes standards for aesthetic evaluation that cross style periods. This task, however,

---

[4]Burney, 2: 605.

[5]An illustration of this point of view is Eugen Schmitz's treatment of the term *cantata,* which appears in the 1620s: ". . . so ist dieser Name, selbst sofern er noch keinen individuellen formlichen Hintergrund hat, doch immerhin ein Dokument des Erstrebens und Wollens einer neuen besonderen Form, mag deren tatsächliche Erreichung auch noch ferne liegen. Diese neue Form der Kantate . . . lässt sich nach Vollendung ihres historischen Werdeprozesses . . . als ein aus einer Reihe irgendwie . . . kontrastierter Einzelsätze zusammengesetztes Gesangsstück für eine Singstimme mit Begleitung definieren." *Geschichte der Kantate und des geistlichen Konzerts* (1914; reprint ed. Hildesheim, 1966), 1: 51.

See Dahlhaus, pp. 13-17. The notion of musical progress also re-valorized the various technical elements of music; see Ruth A. Solie, "Melody and the Historiography of Music," *Journal of the History of Ideas* 43 (1982): 297-308.

[6]E.H. Gombrich points out Carl Schnaase's *Geschichte der bildenden Künste* of 1843 as an early appearance of a Hegelian history of art. See his *In Search of Cultural History* (Oxford, 1969), pp. 13-14.,

[7]See the illustration by Riemann, note 3 above. The analytical procedures derived from the writings of Heinrich Schenker provide another example. An attempt to find more universal universals is Jay Rahn, *A Theory for All Music: Problems and Solutions in the Analysis of Non-Western Forms* (Toronto, 1983), which expresses itself in appropriately scientific language, for example: "If a referential construct for pitches or moments is invoked, it will be based on bisection" (p. 225).

of discerning superior works from just legitimate or just competent ones
was a major challenge to music critics after about 1850;[8] it proved to
be not easy. Increasingly apparent in these approaches is the tendency
to regard music as an active object rather than as a medium for an active performer or listener. Music that served as a medium for another
activity—functional music—was condemned to a subsidiary status. More
and more importance was given to "aesthetic autonomy," which in one
passage Carl Dahlhaus has characterized as "extreme complexity of
structure with intensity of expression."[9] The ideal, in short, came to
be more and more absolute; that is, compositions could be regarded
as special realizations of the eternal and ineffable, or as free-standing
sonic designs, or as exemplars of tonal organisms or mechanically functioning structures, to list attitudes from the sublime to the systematic.

If the nineteenth century, however, elevated some music of the past
to a new plane (sometimes re-interpreting history to do so), then the
isolationist aesthetics of twentieth-century formalism and New Criticism
liberated old music from history. Close analysis revealed inner structures and self-reflexive coherences. It is on this model that the American
textbook *Sonic Design* can present rhythmic modules in Machaut
alongside metric modulations by Elliott Carter, or Lewis Rowell's *Thinking about Music* can offer "Guidelines for Excellence in Music" that
do not mention subject or expression.[10] The problem is that structural

[8]Dahlhaus, *Esthetics of Music,* trans. William W. Austin (Cambridge, 1982). On the
formation of the "canonic" repertory at this time, see Joseph Kerman, "A Few Canonic
Variations," in *Canons,* ed. Robert von Hallberg (Chicago, 1984), pp. 177-195. Music
criticism blossomed late, as serious discourse on music became the province of non-
professional musicians only well after the seventeenth century. Charles Avison's *Essay
on Musical Expression* of 1753 stated that "musical composition is known to very few
besides the professors and composers of music themselves . . ." Quoted in Peter le
Huray and James Day, *Music and Aesthetics in the Eighteenth and Early-Nineteenth
Centuries* (Cambridge, 1981), p. 61.

[9]Dahlhaus, *Foundations,* p. 111: "Having been abstracted from its set purposes, this
music [of J.S. Bach] became the paradigm and *locus classicus* of one of the pivotal
thoughts behind absolute music: the perfect dovetailing of extreme complexity of structure with intensity of expression." Dahlhaus has here described the replacement of
a lost cultural context by a new one, re-invented by the nineteenth century. He has
postulated, "In the course of historical reconstruction, anything that happens to survive the past in the form of an aesthetic presence will automatically receive an emphasis that it did not have at the time of its origin . . ." (p. 112). The implication
is that one is constrained to perceive and discuss formal elements, *however they be
interpreted,* because for music of the past that is almost all there is. See also his *Die
Idee der absoluten Musik* (Kassel, 1978).

[10]Robert Cogan and Pozzi Escot, *Sonic Design: The Nature of Sound and Music*

autonomy, what might be termed competent syntax, is not necessarily *aesthetic autonomy* in the nineteenth-century sense of a demand for structural "complexity . . . with intensity of expression." For most twentieth-century listeners, a musical composition should be more than just a representative—of a *Geist,* a *Zeit,* a set of formal principles, or a genre. Each composition has to speak for itself and speak intersubjectively. Music that was not created to be self-contained, to meet the expectations of saturation, structure, and novelty, often fails to stand up to the double burden of twentieth-century standards and residual nineteenth-century ones. Are such pieces unfairly destined to the cabinets for generic and conventional specimens, about which only chronicles of music composition are written?

Reactions against the primacy of the ideal of autonomy have also proliferated in the twentieth century, the result of the domination of various formalist aesthetics. Marxist criticism must reject autonomy in principle.[11] Adorno scrutinized avowedly absolute modern creations, determined to reveal their contextuality.[12] Modern ethnomusicology refuses to consider music apart from the social rituals for which music is performed.[13] In this spirit, "social context" has become *de rigueur* in any discussion of pre-classical music, although sometimes this "context" amounts only to knowing the names of performers, how much they were paid, and who paid them. Postwar reception theory allowed for several contexts, and relativized single works into a historical series of autonomous states.[14] Moreover, the more specialists in nineteenth-century music reveal to us the diversity of the trends in nineteenth-century

---

(Englewood Cliffs, NJ, 1976), chapter 3. Lewis Rowell, *Thinking about Music: An Introduction to the Philosophy of Music* (Amherst, MA, 1983), pp. 188-189.

[11]See Dahlhaus, *Foundations,* pp. 121-126, and his *Realism in Nineteenth-Century Music,* trans. Mary Whittall (Cambridge, 1985), pp. 2-9.

[12]For a recent survey of Adorno on music, see Martin Jay, *Adorno* (Cambridge, MA, 1984). pp. 131-154.

[13]". . . A further social object for musicology is the need to consider the relation between all the circumstances of music making and the styles and forms of musical composition, rather than to regard musical forms as autonomous growths that come and go according to the inclinations of composers and the tastes of audiences." Frank Ll. Harrison in *Musicology,* ed. Frank Ll. Harrison, Mantle Hood, and Claude Palisca (Englewood Cliffs, NJ, 1983), pp. 79-80. Christopher Small gives a list of assumptions about musical autonomy that need to be rejected in order to receive non-Western music with open ears in his *Music, Society, Education* (London, 1980), p. 36.

[14]Dahlhaus responded to reception theory (historical and German) in *Foundations,* chapter 10. See also his later "Philologie und Rezeptionsgeschichte: Bemerkungen zur

musical thought—the critical contexts in which old and new music was heard and in which it survived—the more it appears that the ideal of aesthetic autonomy will be itself de-consecrated as it is reinserted into *its* original context.

With such wide-angle vision, the danger is that individual works disappear from view. "The artist," as Leonard Meyer has said, becomes "little more than an automaton for the transcription of culture into art."[15] In practice, the loss is often greater than just that of the creative artist and his creation, because often the notion "culture" is itself reduced to a few unconnected, unsatisfactorily simplified characteristics,[16] or the "facts" of social context cannot be placed at a level where they help to form a coherent idea of a culture. Sometimes in a typical synoptical illusion a symbolic image of the music is held up to cast light on its context in one moment, and in the next a catchphrase standing for the context is applied to explain the music. A well-intentioned book such as Henry Raynor's *A Social History of Music*[17] applies snippets of social interest to musical monuments already established as canonical on grounds having little to do with society. Thus it is incoherent both as a history of music in society and as a social history of musicians. A 1984 book on Western liberalism mentions Mozart, Haydn, and Berlioz, and discusses Beethoven, Verdi, and Puccini in a sub-chapter about "Revolutionary Culture and Liberal Nationalism."[18] Aside from

---

Theorie der Edition," in *Festschrift Georg von Dadelsen zum 60. Geburtstag,* ed. Thomas Kohlhase and Volker Scherliess (Neuhausen-Stuttgart, 1978), pp. 45-58: "Varianten . . . sind *'Bestandteile eines anderen Textes,'* einer Fassung, die neben dem Original eine selbständige Existenz und Bedeutung behauptet," (p. 52), quoting Herbert Kraft, *Die Geschichtlichkeit literarischer Texte* (Bebenhausen, 1973). Reception theories have since branched out in opposing directions, some more sociological (assuming reception according to the norms of definable social groups) and some more personal (based on "reception" by discrete individuals whose autonomy is mediated by cultural formation). See Robert C. Holub, *Reception Theory: A Critical Introduction* (London, 1984).

[15]Leonard B. Meyer, "Innovation, Choice, and the History of Music," *Critical Inquiry* 9 (1983), p. 531.

[16]The notion of "culture as a common denominator already contains in embryo that schematization and process of cataloguing and classification which brings culture within the sphere of administration," Max Horkheimer and Theodor W. Adorno in *Dialectic of Enlightenment* (1947), trans. John Cumming; quoted in Jay, p. 113.

[17]Henry Raynor, *A Social History of Music from the Middle Ages to Beethoven* (London, 1972).

[18]Anthony Arblaster, *The Rise and Decline of Western Liberalism* (Oxford, 1984), pp. 215-223.

the fact that the music cited is entirely from the "classical" canon, the works mentioned are for the most part operas or oratorios. The musical scores are not evoked at all; the points the author makes would be the same if he everywhere substituted the names of the librettists for those of the composers.

In his *Introduction to the Sociology of Music* of 1978 Peter Rummenhöller asks, "Exactly which specific (musical) details have what meaning at which time, and how does this meaning change with the progressive alterations in society?"[19] The question is a good one, but the "details" brought forward are not specific to individual compositions. Rather, Rummenhöller describes the changing use of subdominant-function chords in general, which he then interprets as corresponding to four stages in the condition of the European bourgeoisie.[20] In this kind of argument, too, the individual musical work has disappeared, and has done so without really commenting on society. A much more conscientious inquiry, focused on form, is Jonathan Beck's 1984 study of Franco-Burgundian poetry, music, and visual arts between 1470 and 1520.[21] Beck asked, "What are the functions of form in works of art produced in an age . . . of semantic collapse?" He asked this with the implication that "a language ceases to mean" when it no longer provides "the spiritual scaffolding undergirding the community's values." (The underlying assumption is that structuring itself had at the time a semantic value.) Despite the analogies he found among the three arts, however, Beck concluded that musicians were more independent than

[19]Peter Rummenhöller, *Einführung in die Musiksoziologie* (Wilhelmshaven, 1978), p. 56.
[20]Ibid., pp. 59-61: "Verfolgen wir die Spurlinien dieser musiktheoretischen Ueberlegungen zu den musikgeschichtlichen-geistesgeschichtlichen Etappen, so entspräche die erste Phase, die mit der relativen Selbstgenügsamkeit der Dominante [before 1660], dem, was man mit der feudal-absolutistischen Bedeutung des Barock in der Musik verbindet . . . Es ist bereits Musik des Bürgertums . . . jedoch noch ganz im Dienst oder eingebunden in die feudal-absolutistische Ordnung. Was wir hier mit der zweiten Phase bezeichen wollen, die Generationsgenossenschaft J.S. Bachs . . . zeigt vor allem eine Konsolidierung des Bürgertums innerhalb der feudalen Gesellschaftsordnung . . . In der dritten Phase [in which the subdominant is often replaced by a substitute chord] die wir ansprachen, die der sog. 'Vorklassik' . . . bildet die bürgerliche Kultur selbstbewusst bereits Opposition zu höfischen am Vorabend der bürgerlichen Revolution. Die vierten Phase schliesslich ist die des Aufstiegs und der Etablierung des Bürgertums in der Macht [exx. given are references to subdominants in Beethoven and Schubert]. In allen beschriebenen Phasen nun zeigt sich, dass immer, wenn von Entwicklung der Tonalität die Rede ist, auch zugleich der Fortschritt, der Aufschwung, der Stillstand oder die Opposition der bürgerlichen Klasse zur Diskussion steht."
[21]Jonathan Beck, "Formalism and Virtuosity: Franco-Burgundian Poetry, Music, and Visual Art, 1470-1520," *Critical Inquiry* 10 (1984): 644-667.

poets, that music was "more autonomous, less programmatic" as an art, and that "the technical artifices in the music of the time were . . . more discreet, even hidden." Beck's findings indicate that formal structure is not of equal semiotic importance in the different arts. The music which is considered the epitome of the High Renaissance achievement can hardly be construed to stand for "semantic collapse" (not without some Adorno-esque dialectics).

The examples adduced above, beginning with Burney's reaction to Caccini, demonstrate at the least that the relation of musical compositions to society has been different at different—historical—times. To try to determine a specific relation between the two, one must try not to confuse the relative autonomy of a single work, in terms of its singularity in structural or expressive form, with the autonomy of music as an art of sounds that can be relatively independent from the other arts and from culture. If we question both positions with regard to music of the seventeenth century, we find that music is autonomous and pieces are not, because of the way music was produced in seventeenth-century society.

II

A rigid autonomist would say that a musical entity lies within the boundaries of a single composition, for example, within a Beethoven string quartet. We know, however, that a composer like Beethoven might work on a complex of musical ideas for years, producing a number of inter-related yet independent compositions from this complex:[22] a group of pieces—the late string quartets—is the "tip of the iceberg." The part under water includes the complex of sketches, Beethoven's own methods as a composer, his intentions, and his musical culture at the base.

Analogously, any group of musicians passes around complexes of musical ideas. These "ideas" constitute a performance culture out of which compositions become notated, what we call composed. Unwritten is the whole auditory formation and experience of each generation of musicians, just as behind every writing is the linguistic formation and experience, in speaking and writing, of each writer. Joseph Kerman has noted that "once [music] is written down it yields up an object (a

---

[22]See Robert Winter, *The Compositional Origin of Beethoven's Op. 131* (Ann Arbor, 1982) and Douglas Johnson, Alan Tyson, and Robert Winter, eds., *The Beethoven Sketchbooks: History, Reconstruction, Inventory* (Berkeley and Los Angeles, 1985).

score) and is itself on the way to becoming objectified."[23] In the seventeenth century, however, the score is not yet identical to the notion "music." In manuscript, the score is still very much part of an artisan's kit. It can be a short-hand for obtaining a performance, or it can be an *exemplum* of a class of performance possibilities. The score is either a disposable part of the musical culture, or it is a sign of it. (Scores of modern pop music might be an equivalent.) In print, the score is quite as often a counter or token in patron-artist relations as it is a functional tool for making music. Scores in the seventeenth century are by no means co-extensive with the repertory, actual or potential.[24] They are the tip of another iceberg.

Bianconi and Walker, in their 1977 study of the "Production and Consumption of Seventeenth-Century Opera," describe the building of the seventeenth-century operatic repertory as the "continual rotation of essentially similar materials."[25] Those materials that cross from aria to aria or move from opera to opera are the oral, or aural, elements of musical style and performance. Being "oral," they are relatively immune to drastic change, while at the same time any oral system is eminently open to modification by means of "permutation and recombination of more or less discrete separable traits or clusters of traits."[26] This interchangeability is often revealed by the lack of "authority" we perceive in the extant sources. Dahlhaus describes the different performing versions of eighteenth-century operas as sets of "variations without a theme." Confronted with the sources for seventeenth-century variation cycles, he questions whether one should

---

[23]Kerman, "Variations," p. 178.

[24]Recent studies have shown this to be surprisingly so. For example, Tim Carter (in an unpublished paper of 1986, "Music Printing in Late Sixteenth-Century and Early Seventeenth-Century Florence") has shown how circumstantial were the conditions of music printing in early seventeenth-century Florence. Claudio Annibaldi's work in the Doria-Pamfili archive in Rome and the author's with the music manuscripts of the Barberini library in the Vatican have revealed how casual are the contents of the "collections," in comparison to the known extent of the Pamfili and Barberini patronage of musical performances. See Annibaldi, "L'Archivio musicale Doria Pamphilj: Saggio sulla cultura aristocratica a Roma fra 16° e 19° secolo," *Studi Musicali* 11 (1982): 91-120 and 277-344; and the author's unpublished paper "The Barberini Manuscripts of Music," given at the joint California chapters' meeting of the American Musicological Society, Stanford University, May 1984.

[25]Published as Lorenzo Bianconi and Thomas Walker, "Production, Consumption and Political Function of Seventeenth-Century Italian Opera, *Early Music History* 4 (1984): 209-296.

[26]Meyer, "Innovation," p. 534.

consider even the hypothetical existence of an "authentic," closed version for any one of them.[27] Any serious evaluation of these repertories has to ask, then, why Beethoven's scores are so much more different from each other than are Pallavicino's from Pollarolo's from Perti's. Any answer to this rhetorical question must refer to the historical, qualitative differences in the functions of artistic production at different periods, differences that are perhaps most marked before and after 1800. Dahlhaus hinted at the nature of this difference when he observed:

> It is one of the commonplaces of music history that the representation of affections in baroque music is not so much a matter of giving a musical expression to the inner stirring of an emotion as of attempting to "paint" its exterior characteristics and manifestations.[28]

Roland Barthes gave a telling and sympathetic presentation of this difference in his 1953 essay "Is there any Poetic Writing?" He contrasted classic and modern sets of expectations from art and interpreted the "rotation of similar materials" in classic art as signs of *oral* culture.

> In classical art, a ready-made thought generates an utterance which "expresses" or "translates" it. . . . In modern poetics, on the contrary, words produce a kind of formal continuum from which there gradually emanates an intellectual or emotional density which would have been impossible without them; . . . The classical flow is a succession of elements whose density is even; . . . The poetic vocabulary itself is one of usage, not of invention . . . Classical conceits involve relations, not words: they belong to an art of expression, not of invention. The words, here, do not, as they later do, thanks to a kind of violent and unexpected abruptness, reproduce the depth and singularity of an individual experience; they are spread out to form a surface, according to the exigencies of an elegant or decorative purpose. . . . Classical language is a bringer of euphoria because it is immediately social. . . . It is a product conceived for oral transmission, for a consumption regulated by the contingencies of society: it is essentially a spoken language, in spite of its strict codification.[29]

---

[27] Dahlhaus, "Philologie und Rezeptionsgeschichte," p. 51.

[28] Dahlhaus, *Realism*, p. 98.

[29] Roland Barthes, *Writing Degree Zero*, trans. Annette Lavers and Colin Smith (New York, 1968), pp. 43, 45, 49. Barthes's aim in this section is to characterize the demands made on language by "modern poetics," which he achieves by contrasting it with "classic art," classic understood as the French *classique*. In the passage, Barthes opposes "classical usage" to "invention" where, in a turnabout of meaning, *modern*

Barthes's masterful characterization stands for the similar degree to which seventeenth-century music is regulated by such "classical" expectation, that of "expression, not invention," based on "usage," not "invention." It is a given condition, one parallel to the dynamics of today's popular music scene, and one that was still the context for Burney's remarks.

But it is not enough to say that a seventeenth-century musical culture represents a socially conservative exchange of aesthetic experience—namely transmission and reception entirely within consensual, homogeneous social groups. We need to distinguish any concept of an oral, performance-based musical culture *in Europe* from other oral musical cultures (as in Bali or south Africa) wherein making music is a communal undertaking that signifies social cohesion, co-operation and stability, and often where music-making is a sacred activity. Under these latter conditions, *tradition* in materials and performance is of paramount importance. This seems not to be the case in the West. Rather, in Europe the rate of style change and the rapid dissemination of new musical styles argue against comparative interpretations of the relationships of musical language to an oral society.

The standard "explanation" for this noticeable changeability in Western music has typically been the invention of musical notation. But this explanation, even if it be valid to explain the emergence of a form as tightly structured as the fourteenth-century isorhythmic motet, does not and cannot apply generally to the changes in the sounds and rhythms of Western music as a whole, nor can notation alone account for the poor fit between musical change and what we know of the "social contexts" of music. Notation does not account for Baroque monody; practice does. One could argue that notation, being a method of preservation—its original Frankish function?[30]—would have tended to retard change and innovation. Instead it became a tool of a dynamic musical culture. The

---

invention is the opposite of the classical rhetorical term *inventio: "L'inventio* renvoie moins à une invention (des arguments) qu'à une découverte: tout existe déjà, il faut seulement le retrouver: c'est une notion plus 'extractive' que 'créative.'" (Barthes, "L'ancienne rhétorique" [1970], published in *L'aventure sémiologique* [Paris, 1985], p. 125.) In the old system, novelty of expression lay in finding a new way to realize a common trope (ibid., "Les couleurs," p. 156).

[30]See Leo Treitler, "Reading and Singing: On the Genesis of Occidental Music-Writing," *Early Music History* 4 (1984): 135-208. Treitler examines early music notations for cues for the non-professional singer (priests and deacons) as well as music writing for professionals: "The neumes in their original multiplex functions represent the entrance of a writing practice into the domain of an oral tradition" (p. 175).

existence of notation does not necessarily diminish the ''classic'' or oral character of earlier Western musical culture; it probably tends to hide it.

Nevertheless, even allowing for ''oral'' time before and after major periods in musical style, music seems to change and diversify more rapidly than would have been necessary! If the social and aesthetic functions of musical performances are the same in churches as in palaces in seventeenth-century Rome—namely, to aggrandize the aristocratic prestige of a cardinal-prince or duke—and if music does this in the same manner as did splendid carriages and a liveried retinue, then distinctions between church style and chamber style are semiotically irrelevant. Irrelevant also, in the face of luxury consumption, are evaluations of the quality or expressiveness of the music. Similarly, the differences between fifteenth-century Parisian motets and seventeenth-century Roman cantatas are irrelevant to the constancy of such a social function. Dahlhaus on this point has acidulously written that

> . . . it is by no means an established fact that those social factors which are most clearly at work in music history necessarily rank among what social historians would regard as the essential features of the age.[31]

The social historian H.G. Koenigsberger has examined two fundamentally distinct forms of civic organization—the early modern republics and the courts. Their ideological and social differences should have expressed themselves concretely in the spheres of culture, either in terms of production or content. But among his ten conclusions, Koenigsberger observed that

> The political, social and religious changes of the sixteenth century which had such profound effects on the visual arts, political thought and drama had far less effect on two other fields of creative activity, namely music and the natural sciences. . . . Churches, courts, town halls and the houses of private persons could all be, in their own way, excellent patrons of music. In Italy and in Germany music developed in all of them.[32]

In the seventeenth century, the outstanding situation in this regard is the rapid spread and adoption of contemporary music by all levels of society in both Catholic and Protestant areas. Although we lack a com-

---

[31]Dahlhaus, *Foundations,* p. 121.
[32]H.G. Koenigsberger, ''Republics and Courts in Italian and European Culture in the Sixteenth and Seventeenth Centuries,'' *Past and Present* No. 83 (1979), p. 55, summarizing pp. 45-49.

prehensive picture, we can easily see that there were traditional functions for music in all the Christian liturgies, but not necessarily permanent, traditional musical styles associated with those functions.

Counter-Reformation Rome immortalized and preserved the music
and the style of the late sixteenth-century composer Palestrina. This
has typically been interpreted as the desire of an arteriosclerotic institution to mummify a retardataire style. But after Palestrina's death, St.
Peter's and the other Roman churches did not rely on his *oeuvre*, which
was "preserved" in the repertory of the Sistine Chapel. Modern
music—if any music at all—was sung in other Roman basilicas, in the
parish churches, and in the devotional services of the lay confraternities,
often by the same Sistine singers. "Modernization" was even an issue
with respect to post-Tridentine plainchant. As late as 1657 a treatise
by Giovanni d'Avella devotes a whole section to plainsong composition, averring that its difficulty lay in the perfection of Gregorian chant,
but not discouraging new compositon.[33] In 1664 a Franciscan, Gioseppe
Maria Stella, published monophonic *melodies* in a modern style to traditional *recitation* texts of the Mass and Divine Office.[34] Stella mentions
some other modern interventions, such as melismas added to all parts
of the music for the Passion. Another chant treatise of 1671 tries to
correct the use of false *musica ficta* that destroys the modes.[35] The author
bewails singers who sing the Sanctus of the Requiem Mass with the
tones A-A-G-sharp instead of A-A-G-natural! Gino Stefani, who has
studied these chant manuals, has concluded that the situation with regard
to chant was "unintelligible and chaotic."[36] A historicist purist in the
nineteenth-century mold would deplore these signs of "corruption."
They are signs, however, that musical performance in the Catholic liturgy
was alive and contemporary. More important, these "corruptions" indicate that the music itself was of little doctrinal import.[37] Such modifica-

[33]Giovanni d'Avella, *Regole di musica . . . con le quali s'insegna il canto fermo e
figurato* (Rome, 1657), trattato quarto. Other instances are cited in Gino Stefani, *Musica
e religione nell'Italia barocca* (Palermo, 1975), p. 176.

[34]Gioseppe Maria Stella della Mirandola, *Breve instruttione alli giovani per imparare
con ogni faciltà il canto fermo* (Rome, 1665), part II.

[35]Guilio Cesare Marinelli, *Via retta della voce corale* (Bologna, 1671), p. 225. Under
certain conditions pertaining to pitch intervals, singers sang tones (*musica ficta*) other
than those notated. These adjustments were made not from memory but according to
the musical situation. In the example cited, the application of "rules" that modernized
the style over-rode the tradition. See also Stefani, pp. 165-167.

[36]Stefani, p. 154.

[37]This is so despite the attention given music by the Council of Trent. A telling incident is reported by Jean Lionnet, "Una svolta nella storia del Collegio dei cantori pon-

tion and continual replacement of elements in a cultic rite suggest that on a broad plane specific musical styles *per se* were non-essential to meaning, that the music was decorative and ideologically neutral, however much it may have contributed to the perceived efficacy of the rite. Those who wished to reform the confusion of practices had conflicting motives. Stefani has pointed out that some wished to restore the symbolic purity of ancient tradition, but were stopped by the scholarly task; others wished to impose uniformly the perfection of modern music; others would have accepted *any* authoritative practice so long as it could be imposed from above to create uniformity in the hierarchy, from the cathedrals to the provinces, from Rome to the world.[38]

What we seem to have, then, is an oral culture for which ideology controls signs on a broad social level, in the rationalization of institutions or in the value given fashion. At this level, the use of music can be semiotic, as part of a structure removed from either musical form or musical content. Given the dissemination of change through more slowly-moving social forms, one can only ask, using one of Meyer's theorems, "What is the operating ideology with the impetus and energy to encourage the *replication of change* and to override the maintenance of tradition," traditions as inimical as the Reformation and Counter-Reformation?[39] This is a question outside the focus of this essay, but the answer may lie, as it did in the ninth century, in the policies of political and cultural rationalization of expanding administrations in the south and in the development of new social cohesiveness in the north. In somewhat different ways in the two different political situations in Germany and in Italy, conformity to the new eliminates or suppresses the untidiness and divisiveness of local traditions.[40] The history of music

tifici: il decreto del 22 guigno 1665 contro Orazio Benevolo; origine e conseguenze," *Nuova Rivista Musicale Italiana* 17 (1983): 72-103. The pope makes a rare plea to his personal choir to return to the music of the golden days of his youth, namely that of Agazzari, Anerio and Monteverdi (p. 77); Tridentine composers are nowhere mentioned. An edict is designed to extend the "reform" to the Roman basilicas, including St. Peter's. The other *maestri di cappella* resist, especially as their music is by implication unsuitable (music by Benevolo, Corsi, Stamegna, Carissimi). Even the vice-protector of the Sistine Chapel declines to enter the controversy—it has so little importance. A year and a half later the original edict is annulled.
[38]Stefani, pp. 178-183.
[39]Meyer, "Innovation," p. 523: "What is required for replication is the impetus and energy of ideology . . . because replication requires continuity that transcends idiosyncratic circumstance and particular occasion."
[40]Koenigsberger relies on a Victorian aesthetic notion of music to explain the "efflorescence of music" (the production of new music?) in German and Italy: "The rela-

is more than the history of scores. It can concern itself with trying to establish the significance of musical activities, knowing well that such inquiry may not directly illuminate a specific score, stylistic recurrence, or "idiolect." One can assume that all the grand seventeenth-century Roman choral music served to instruct, delight, and persuade, and that it also made a political statement. But that statement, from composition to composition, is always the same and, to paraphrase Barthes, it expressed something already understood.

Similarly, we know a lot about the different reasons for and ways of putting on operas[41]—but there is as yet no overwhelming evidence that the aesthetic value of the score that gets mounted is a major consideration in the decision to stage a work. Often the score is the last thing completed or assembled; it can be the unknown quantity in the undertaking.

III

This view—of the relative separability of the single score and its function—does not further diminish the importance of individual compositions; rather it suggests the relative independence of musical culture within the greater context of seventeenth-century society: not the autonomy of the single composition, which it was and is impossible to experience, and not the subjectivist autonomy of the composer speaking personal or universal mysteries from his heart. Without going back to the schemata of early twentieth-century histories of style such as cycles of primitive to classic to degenerate stages, or "classic" alternating with Baroque/Romantic styles, we need to re-consider the relative autonomy of the language(s) of music.[42]

Music is a syntax among sounds that is most attentively listened to

tionship between religion and music was a complex and subtle one. In the long run . . . it depended on the decline of religious sensibilities among the educated classes of Europe and the ability of music to fill the resulting emotional void," "Republics and Courts," p. 46, which refers to his "Music and Religion in Modern European History," in *The Diversity of History*, ed. J.H. Elliott and H.G. Koenigsberger (London, 1970), pp. 35-78.

[41]Bianconi and Walker, especially part 5; Margaret Murata, "Formal Entertainment and Opera for the Aristocracy in 17th-Century Rome," unpublished paper given at the meeting of the International Musicological Society, Strasbourg, August 1982.

[42]As suggested by Beck, note 21 above, and argued (with limited proof) by Émile Benveniste in reference to the order of sounds in music, *Problèmes de linguistique*

by musicians who reproduce it and transmit it through performance. The continuity of the history of music in the West has always been intermediated by professional musicians, whether guild pipers, clerics, or rock stars. Music is created in the social context, therefore, of a *double* oral culture. The first is the social one that determines the demand for music; it conditions what is expected and what is expressed, but not in great detail. The second consists of the transmission of music by and among musicians, through performances. The language of this second oral culture is musically specific, and it is syntactical. For example, the second note of a descending second gets an ornament under certain rhythmic conditions; anyone who plays enough Baroque music begins to do this naturally without having the ''rule'' spelled out for him, but this syntactical detail is not of itself semiotic or ideological. Both oral cultures are historical, of course, but scores and society should not be expected to speak reciprocal languages. Lionel Sawkins recently recounted how the king of England sent the composer Pelham Humfrey to France to learn the French grand motet style.[43] The incident bears witness to the necessity for *oral* transmission—Charles II did not have French scores copied and sent over for the composer to study. Moreover, the king was probably not interested in any particular motet, but in the motets as a class of beauteous (and prestigious) enhancements to acts of monarchical piety. The king seems to have assumed that like motets could be crafted. The motet *style* is autonomous, transferable and socially desirable, all questions of craft and expression aside. Both oral cultures are represented by Humfrey's trips across the channel. Two kinds of listeners are as well: professionals such as Humfrey and the ''receivers,'' who are lay listeners with differing levels of musical acuteness.

Carl Dahlhaus's dissatisfaction with ''reception history'' is precisely its neglect of the acute listener, the one who hypothetically was interested in musical syntax, whether it was Palestrina's or Frescobaldi's.

---

générale (Paris, 1966-1974), 2: 56: ''Si la musique est considérée comme une 'langue,' que c'est une langue qui a une syntaxe, mais pas de sémiotique.'' John Blacking has put it this way: ''In music, code and message are inseparable: the code is the message, and when the message is analyzed apart from the code, music is abandoned for sociology, politics, economics, religion and so forth,'' ''The Problem of 'Ethnic' Perceptions in the Semiotics of Music,'' in *The Sign in Music and Literature,* ed. Wendy Steiner (Austin, 1981), p. 185.

[43]Lionel Sawkins, ''The French *grand motet:* Evidence for a More Vital Performing Style for a Neglected Genre,'' unpublished paper given at the Conference on Late Renaissance and Early Baroque Music, Birmingham, England, July 1986.

Domenico Morgante has asserted that the more important "receivers" of Frescobaldi's scores are keyboard players, not listeners.

> I believe that Frescobaldi . . . wanted above all to make manifest the expressive forms of his own variegated affective baggage, . . . and specifically for those who directly experience the act of performing his compositions. For this reason Frescobaldi's keyboard music should be imagined in a . . . dimension which is found only in the realization of its original purpose, that is what we may call a kind of "affectionate syntonization [or being in tune]" between composer and performer, made possible by the artistic product. [This is] the real and more authentic significance of its existence.[44]

Morgante is talking about neither delayed kinesthesia nor emotional transference, but purely about the "syntonic" transmittal of new musical figures from musician to musician.

The historical acute listener, moreover, in all probability saw no reason to "translate" these musical figures into any other language. And if he had, he would have disposed of the syntactical parts into the classic categories of *topoi* and paradigmatic forms, which are not "explanations" that satisfy our modern conceptions of aesthetic success. Perhaps the most convincing representation of the importance of the oral/aural transmission of seventeenth-century music has been the development of modern, historically-based playing styles for this repertory. Music that was difficult to make sense of—such as the violin repertory before Corelli—now is played with animation, subtlety, and an expressive rhetoric of virtuosity that modern "early" violinists have "discovered" and passed around among themselves. The essential techniques, such as fluctuating tempos, rhythmic articulations, a wide range of bowstrokes and pressures, subtle intonation, are all absent from the musical notation.[45] Sound recordings, in this respect, have done much more to transmit a musical pronunciation than any library of clean critical editions could have.

The rough map of this seascape of perils seems to show that the uses of music are tied to society's values and ideals, as are the resources

---

[44]Domenico Morgante, "Gli affetti sonori. Prassi musicale ed esteticità tra Cinque- e Seicento," in *Modernità e Coscienza Estetica,* ed. F. Fanizza (Bari, [1986]), pp. 286-287.

[45]The "authenticity" of this phenomenon is the subject of Richard Taruskin's essay "On Letting the Music Speak for Itself: Some Reflections on Musicology and Performance," *Journal of Musicology* 1 (1982): 338-349.

of its expression. The dissemination of music, likewise, depends on
specifics of social infrastructures. These aspects ought to be capable
of semiotic analysis. The materials and language of music, however,
are to a high degree autonomous and presumably not easily subject to
semantic interpretation.[46] Individual pieces draw on both oral cultures,
the social and the musical.

This structuring of seventeenth-century musical culture is neither
special nor novel. It is an attempt to maintain and evaluate the importance of its unwritten aspects in terms of both transmission and performance. Between the mass of music that is made up of individual compositions and the mass of statements that we use to characterize Baroque Rome or Louis XIV's Paris or seventeenth-century Europe lies
the sub-culture of seventeenth-century musicians. Moving from the musicians to the music, we can restore a degree of autonomy to the pieces,
according each one the perennial musicians' detailed interest in composition and performance techniques. Granting a degree of autonomy
to the music as a syntax of sounds (maintained by this expert sub-culture),
we can avoid the fallacies of cultural determinism, the extreme types
of which reduce artists to permeable membranes or mirrors, and thus
directly connect chromatic half-steps to the Thirty Years' War.

> Culture is not a compelling force that determines what artists must create.
> Rather it is a richly variegated presence providing possibilities from which
> artists choose.[47]

The specific fascination of the period lies in the intersection where society
offered the musician a range of *topoi* or "ready-made thoughts" which
it was his profession to "realize" in composition or performance, improvising with the figures he had learned and could develop within his
musical sub-culture. It was this vocabulary of figures as well as the
context of rhetorical procedure that Burney could not perceive from

[46]Rose Rosengard Subotnik credits Beethoven with the transformation of this natural,
"classical" social order: ". . . Beethoven probably did more than any composer has
since to destroy autonomous music as a socially viable concept, that is, to destroy the
possibility that a precise coincidence between individually intended and generally perceived meanings would ever be established through the medium of music alone," "The
Cultural Message of Musical Semiology: Some Thoughts on Music, Language, and
Criticism since the Enlightenment," *Critical Inquiry* 4 (1978), pp. 756-757. The notion of the autonomy of single works, then (discussed in section one of this essay),
arose to contain the increasing *heteronomy* of musical language after Beethoven.
[47]Meyer, "Innovation," p. 531.

Caccini's scores. It is an aspect of "social context" that is not signified by any specific musical activities or economic relationships. But it is the recognition of this kind of creative premise which lies both outside of and within the musical composition that will re-awaken the speech of seventeenth-century music through its sources.[48]

[48]This essay germinated as a presentation for the eighth annual Irvine Seminar on Social History and Theory (University of California, Irvine, March 1985) in a session titled "The *Zeitgeist* Fallacy in Music, Culture and Society." In substance now, as well as in argument, it is an elaboration of a paper given at the Conference on Late Renaissance and Baroque Music held at the University of Birmingham, England, July 1986.

Rose Rosengard Subotnik

Toward a Deconstruction of Structural Listening: A Critique of Schoenberg, Adorno, and Stravinsky

> The highest criticism is that which leaves an impression identical with the one called forth by the thing criticized.
>
> Robert Schumann[1]

We have always two universes of discourse—call them "physical" and "phenomenal," or what you will—one dealing with questions of quantitative and formal structure, the other with those qualities that constitute a "world"... Computational representations... could never, of themselves, constitute "iconic" representations, those representations which are the very thread and stuff of life... Experience is not *possible* until it is organised iconically; action is not *possible* unless it is organised iconically... The final form of cerebral representation must be, or allow, "art"—the artful scenery and melody of experience and action.

> Oliver Sacks[2]

---

[1]Quoted in Oliver Strunk, ed., *Source Readings in Music History* (New York, 1950), p. 743. The passage continues, "In this sense Jean Paul, with a poetic companion-piece, can perhaps contribute more to the understanding of a symphony or fantasy by Beethoven, without even speaking of the music, than a dozen of those little critics of the arts who lean their ladders against the Colossus and take its exact measurements."
[2]Oliver Sacks, *The Man Who Mistook His Wife for a Hat and Other Clinical Tales* (New York, 1985), pp. 120, 140-1.

Rose Rosengard Subotnik is a musicologist who has written extensively about the philosophy of music, especially of the nineteenth and twentieth centuries, and about problems of historical and critical methodology.

Emotion and meaning are coming out of the musicological closet. The underground passages out of uncritical formalism, which Leonard Meyer began to chart more than thirty years ago, are in the process of being discovered by American musicology at large. This developing critique of musical formalism would be facilitated by a reexamination of what I would like to call "structural listening," a method which concentrates attention primarily on the formal relationships established over the course of a single composition.

The general principle of structural listening has become so well established as a norm in the advanced study and teaching of music, at least in this country, that it is all too easy for us to assume its value as self-evident and universal and to overlook its birth out of particular historical circumstances and ideological conflicts. Likewise it has become easy to "forget," in Nietzsche's sense, that the object of structural listening, a structure that is in some sense abstract, constitutes only one pole of a more general, dialectical framework in which modern Western conceptions of music have been developed.[3] The other pole, medium, is in its character a historical parameter of music, signifying the ongoing relationship of any composition to a public domain of sound and culture, from the time of its initial appearance up to the present. This pole is defined principally through the presentation of sounds, organized by conventional or characteristic usages, into particular configurations called styles, as objects of a physical yet culturally conditioned perception. The precise nature of the relationship between sound and style is an interesting problem which cannot be given attention here. In the discussion that follows, the terms "sound" and "style," as intertwined aspects of a common parameter, medium, will often be treated as more or less interchangeable.

This discussion, which developed from a much shorter critique in an earlier article, has resulted unintentionally in something very close to a deconstruction.[4] Recognizing a hierarchical opposition between structure and medium as fundamental to the concept of structural listening, I have in effect tried to reverse the conventionally assumed priorities in this hierarchy, to undercut the distinction between its poles by presenting the mode and object of structural listening as a function of (or in Derrida's sense as a "supplement" to) those of non-structural listening,

---

[3]On Nietzsche see Gayatri C. Spivak's preface to her translation of Jacques Derrida, *Of Grammatology* (Baltimore, 1976), pp. xxix-xxxiii.
[4]The article is "The Challenge to Contemporary Music," in Philip Alperson, ed., *What is Music?*, forthcoming from Haven press.

and to expose some of the concealed ideological assumptions which the concept of structural listening reflects.[5]

THE CASE FOR STRUCTURAL LISTENING

The variant of structural listening on which I wish to focus my primary attention is the one developed by Schoenberg and Adorno over the course of their writings. For I know of no variant that offers on the one hand a stronger or more broadly applicable defense of structural listening and on the other hand a more explicit basis for its own analysis as a cultural construct. To be sure, the concepts worked out by Schoenberg and by Adorno are not identical to each other. Schoenberg's concept is more narrowly focused on the practical concerns of the composer; Adorno's on the theoretical concerns of the critic. Schoenberg's philosophy is far more naive, and he by no means shared all of Adorno's emphases or opinions any more than Adorno witnessed without reservations all of Schoenberg's compositional decisions. Nevertheless, the two men were in very close agreement as to the specifics of structural listening; moreover, Adorno's concept of structural listening, like all of his music criticism, was not only developed in a full and informed sympathy with Schoenberg's enterprise but can in fact be read as a defense of Schoenberg. Thus, the limited philosophical justification that Schoenberg provided for structural listening is consistently and persuasively grounded by Adorno's more ample account, and for present purposes the two concepts will be considered as one here. Schenkerian conceptions of structure and perception, such as Felix Salzer's "structural hearing," will not be considered here; hence the "Toward" of my title.

This concept of structural listening, as Schoenberg and Adorno presented it, was intended to describe a process wherein the listener follows and comprehends the unfolding realization, with all of its detailed inner relationships, of a generating musical conception, or what Schoenberg calls an "idea."[6] Based on an assumption that valid structural logic

---

[5]On "supplement" see Derrida, *Of Grammatology*, pp. 141-64, and Jonathan Culler, *On Deconstruction: Theory and Criticism after Structuralism* (Ithaca, 1982), pp. 102-106.
[6]See especially Arnold Schoenberg, *Style and Idea*, ed. Leonard Stein (Berkeley, 1984), pp. 120-21 and 377-82, and Theodor W. Adorno, *Introduction to the Sociology of Music*, trans. E. B. Ashton (New York, 1976), pp. 4-5. Schoenberg's reference to "idea" is on pp. 122-23 of his book.

is accessible to any reasoning person, such structural listening discourages kinds of understanding that require culturally specific knowledge of things external to the compositional structure, such as conventional associations or theoretical systems. This includes the twelve-tone system and the constitution of any particular "row," though it does not, and indeed cannot, exclude a cultural familiarity with the dynamic of tonality.[7] In Adorno's formulation, knowing even the name of the composer or the composition in question could muddy the purity of the desired process.[8] Structural listening is an active mode of listening that, when successful, gives the listener the sense of composing the piece as it actualizes itself in time.

The concept of structural listening has complex roots in German musical, cultural, and philosophical traditions, with which both Schoenberg and Adorno felt a strong sense of historical continuity. The origins of the concept can usefully be traced to the final phase of the Enlightenment. Kant himself remained faithful to a mimetic notion of art and never drew the full range of aesthetic conclusions to which his own work pointed. Nevertheless, his *Critique of Judgment,* with its conception of disinterested aesthetic pleasure and especially its presentation of aesthetic judgment as a conceptless process involving the metaphor of a structural congruence between faculties, marks a crucial step toward the idealization that took place during the next century, in Germany, of both structural autonomy in art and of music as the highest art. A comparable shift was initiated in the musical domain by the instrumental works of Haydn and Mozart, which served as a powerful catalyst for the rich and paradoxical development of formalistic attitudes toward music in nineteenth-century Germany.

I say "rich and paradoxical" because this formalistic movement was from the start marked by a dialectical opposition and intertwining of values that can be associated with musical autonomy on the one hand and with critical, often even verbal, ways of thinking on the other. Beethoven's music itself can be construed as a self-conscious critique of earlier Classical musical conceptions. Arguing musically for autonomous structural values, sometimes through a physically thick and tonally extrinsic rhetorical emphasis, sometimes through a revisionist treatment

[7]On the row see, for example, the letter from Schoenberg quoted in Arnold Whittall, *Schoenberg Chamber Music* (London, 1972), p. 46; T. W. Adorno, *Prisms,* trans. Samuel and Shierry Weber (London, 1967), p. 167; and Charles Rosen, *Arnold Schoenberg* (New York, 1975), p. 78.

[8]See especially T. W. Adorno, "The Radio Symphony," *Radio Research, 1941,* ed. Paul F. Lazarsfeld and Frank N. Stanton (New York, 1941), pp. 128-33.

of inherited structural conventions, Beethoven succeeded in undermining the abstract security of the very condition of autonomy he sought to establish, and suggested musical structure as at bottom a contingent construct, subject to concrete cultural limitations on its character and significance.

Likewise, the notions of absolute music as developed by such early Romantic figures as Wackenroder and Tieck, and as treated in the music criticism of Hoffmann, Weber, and Schumann, are of a rich and concrete sort. Attending (in the case of the three music critics) with considerable detail to structural relationships within music, and at the same time affirming the inseparability of the musical structure from the poetic and spiritual associations and imagery which that structure evoked in the imagination, Romantic writing encouraged a kind of listening that was at once structurally abstract and full of content. The critic Edward Rothstein has suggested to me that we call this mode of listening "metaphorical;" Leo Treitler has called the quality to which it directed attention "narrativity."[9] The word I would use to characterize the Romantic conception of musical structure is "replete."

This twofold conception of musical form underwent something of a crisis in Hanslick's landmark work, *The Beautiful in Music,* published in 1854. Often construed as a bracing antidote to Wagner's expressive or rhetorical "excesses," Hanslick's restriction of the problem of musical understanding to the purely technical parameters of musical structure can indeed be read as a manifesto for formalistic values of a sort that, in time, reached beyond Germany and, by way of what Adorno calls Stravinsky's "phenomenology," right up to the present.[10] For a work that is deeply conservative in spirit—and not just because its concept of aesthetic value points directly back to Kant's third critique—*The Beautiful in Music* proved remarkably prescient.

Yet it should not be supposed that Hanslick renounced altogether the full-bodied or replete character of the ideal of autonomy which had been developed between Kant's time and his own. Asserting that "the domain of aesthetics . . . begins only where . . . elementary [mathematical] relations cease to be of importance," Hanslick argues that what "raises a series of musical sounds into the region of music proper and above the range of physical experiment is something free from external con-

[9]In "Mozart and the Idea of Absolute Music," a lecture delivered at the City University of New York Graduate Center, December 1, 1986.
[10]On phenomenology see T. W. Adorno, *Philosophy of Modern Music,* trans. Anne G. Mitchell and Wesley V. Blomster (New York, 1973), pp. 136, 139-142.

straint, a spiritualized and therefore incalculable something.''[11] This is not so far removed from Schumann's assertion that ''if we are to hear a convincing form, music must act as freely as poetry on our conceptual capacities''—or, for that matter, from his praise of Berlioz as similar to ''Jean Paul, whom someone called a bad logician and a great philosopher.''[12] If Hanslick proposes reducing the musical object of criticism to its phenomenological essentials, he arrives at this point through concepts of the aesthetic and of structure that idealize human cultural and spiritual capacities. If Hanslick encouraged a reinterpretation of the musically formal as connoting something essentially negative—say, ''mere'' or empty form, form as precisely that in music which does not express—the metaphysical spirit of the German traditions which formed his cultural context can and should still be discerned in his argument as what, in Derridean terms, could be called an important absent presence or ''trace.''[13]

This intertwining of German intellectual tradition with purely structural values continues to characterize the formalism of Schoenberg and Adorno.[14] It marks an important difference between their aesthetic theories and Stravinsky's, as set forth in his *Poetics of Music,* which otherwise converge on a number of more or less characteristic twentieth-century Western musical positions, including a common insistence on the need for some sort of structural listening. Both Schoenberg and Stravinsky, for example, define music as a field for the mastery of nature by culture, the latter of which is valued for its scientific and speculative capacities.[15] Both wish to subject music to a governing, objective, and

[11]Eduard Hanslick, *The Beautiful in Music,* ed. Morris Weitz, trans. Gustav Cohen (Indianapolis, 1957), p. 66. See also pp. 50, 122, etc. for the term ''replete'' form.
[12]Robert Schumann, ''A Symphony by Berlioz,'' in Hector Berlioz, *Fantastic Symphony,* ed. Edward Cone (New York, 1971), pp. 232 (quoting Ernst Wagner), 233.
[13]On ''trace'' see Spivak, pp. xv-xviii, and Culler, pp. 94-96 and 99. On Hanslick see Carl Dahlhaus, *Esthetics of Music,* trans. William W. Austin (Cambridge, 1982), pp. 52-57.
[14]Schoenberg's writings, to be sure, invoke the intellectual tradition far less explicitly than Adorno's do, and his notion of the potential relationships between music and politics is considerably less sophisticated than Adorno's (see especially Schoenberg, pp. 249-50). On the other hand his exclusion of cultural associations (ibid., pp. 377-78) as well as semantic content (pp. 126-27) from musical autonomy does not differ from Adorno's *ideal* of autonomy, and he considers structure implicitly expressive (see ibid., pp. 257 and 415-16). See also below, notes 34 and 47.
[15]See Schoenberg, pp. 253 and 220; and Igor Stravinsky, *Poetics of Music* (New York, 1960), chapter 2, pp. 23-24 and 28, chapter 3, p. 50, and chapter 6, p. 124. Because a more recent edition of the *Poetics* regrettably alters the earlier pagination, I will note here the page numbers on which the chapters in my edition start: 1) p. 3; 2) p. 23; 3) p. 47; 4) p. 70; 5) p. 95; 6) p. 125; Epilogue) p. 143. In subsequent references, chapter as well as page will be given.

essentially universal principle of rational necessity, which would counteract the capriciousness of personal self-gratification, prejudice, and taste.[16] Both would (theoretically) support an open-ended variety of musical works, which, so long as they were formally coherent, would have no need to justify their "kind" or existence;[17] the internal "necessity" of the work, so to speak, would sufficiently guarantee for both men the outward "necessity" for it.

Both Schoenberg and Stravinsky celebrate the activity of musical construction and would confine musical meaning within the boundaries of the individual composition, exclusive of contextual relationships and (at least in theory) of intent.[18] Both consider reception and effect extrinsic to the concept of composition—the functionalist craftsman Stravinsky no less than the endlessly explaining Schoenberg.[19] Adorno's position on these matters is similar, though always more complicated. Although he sees no actual way of extricating musical structure from its embodiment of social values, and recoils from the hypostatizing of objects as a symptom of ideological dishonesty, he nevertheless maintains the achievement of a totally autonomous musical structure as a Utopian ideal.[20] All three men end by locating musical value wholly within some formal sort of parameter, to which it is the listener's business to attend.

There is a difference, however, in the kinds of formal parameters chosen, which one of my students has characterized rather aptly as the contrast between Platonic and Aristotelian enterprises.[21] It is a difference which weakens to the point of undermining Stravinsky's case for structural listening. Allowing for a civilizing speculative capacity, but disallowing all connection between music and philosophy, and recoiling far more successfully than Adorno from any taint of systematic thought, Stravinsky gives himself over to a spirit of empirical discovery which subordinates logical, or even quasi-logical, necessity to useful-

[16]On taste see Schoenberg, p. 247, and Stravinsky, 3:66, and 4:75. On necessity and objectivity, see Schoenberg, pp. 53, 133, 220, 244, 256, 407, 432, and 439; and Stravinsky, 2:33 and 37, 3:47, 64, and 67-68. For Stravinsky on structural processes of listening see 2:24 and 6:140.

[17]For example, Schoenberg, pp. 257 and 285, and Stravinsky, 3:48-50 and 4:90.

[18]See Schoenberg, pp. 127 and 254 (see also below, note 44); and Stravinsky, 3:48 and 4:90.

[19]See Schoenberg, pp. 50, 104, and 135, despite, for example,215 on comprehensibility; and Stravinsky, 5:106 and 6:137-38, despite 4:78 on usefulness.

[20]See my article "Adorno's Diagnosis of Beethoven's Late Style: Early Symptom of a Fatal Condition," *Journal of the American Musicological Society* 29 (1976), pp. 270 ff.; also Martin Jay, *The Dialectical Imagination: A History of the Frankfurt School and the Institute of Social Research, 1923-1950* (Boston, 1973), p. 179.

[21]Elliot Hurwitt, a candidate for the M.A. in music at Hunter.

ness.[22] Indeed, everything about Stravinsky's musical career, including his relationship to past musical history, the progression of his styles, and the inner ordering of his works, points to the same essentially negative pattern of throwing overboard whatever does not serve an immediate purpose.[23] At none of these levels do we sense any interest in demonstrating that steady continuity through which rational processes, least of all those pertaining to logical (as opposed to dogmatic or arbitrarily imposed) necessity, might confirm their presence in the concrete world.[24] Nor does the *Poetics,* outside of a single evocative paragraph, offer any concrete, positive guidelines for the achievement of an unmistakably perceptible rationality in music.[25] The formal parameter of music for Stravinsky is simply sound as opposed to expression, that is, sound stripped of meaning;[26] and formal value, as characterized in the *Poetics,* amounts to nothing more than a persuasive impression that a particular combination of sounds "works."

By resting the case for a formalistic conception of music on such persuasiveness, Stravinsky, the arch-foe of Wagnerian rhetoric, forfeits the claim of music to validation by any universal principle of rational necessity. At most he allows the composition to project a plausible rationale, which suggests no necessary basis for its own validity. For all his talk of "necessity," what the Stravinsky of the *Poetics* values in music is not the conceptual but the qualitative or the stylistic attributes of objectivity.[27] For this Stravinsky, and arguably for Stravinsky in a good deal of his composition, music succeeds by attaining an appearance

[22]For example, Stravinsky, 1:8 and 3:51-57; also 4:78 (on craft).

[23]See especially Stravinsky, 4:87-88, on the use of various sources and materials as needed.

[24]This is so despite Stravinsky's shared preference with Schoenberg for "evolution" over "revolution" (see Schoenberg, pp. 91, 270, 409, and *passim,* and Stravinsky, 1:11-13). The "beautiful continuity" of history as Stravinsky describes it (4:73-74) is actually characterized by considerable discontinuity (and not just because, unlike Schoenberg's concept of history, it rejects the notion of progress). Compare also Stravinsky on post-tonal chords which "throw off all constraint to become new entities free of all ties" (3:40), and 3:36-37 (which accepts dissonance "because it's there," so to speak) to Schoenberg on his own relation to tonality (pp. 256 and 283-84). See also below, note 66. On Stravinsky's open dogmatism see 1:9, 18, and 2:25 ("Instinct is infallible"), though see also below, note 78, on Schoenberg's dogmatic certainty.

[25]The single paragraph appears in Stravinsky, 2:39-40, despite a constant emphasis on rightness and on rules which are never specified (for example, 2:25 and 3:68-69).

[26]For example, Stravinsky, 2:46, 4:79, and 6:130.

[27]It is interesting to note that Stravinsky's famous description of the "realm of necessity" which delivers him from the "abyss of freedom" gives to "solid and concrete elements" of sound and rhythm a priority over rules (3:66-69).

of elegance, moderation, and "cool" non-expressiveness. This condition, though in itself not beyond the reach of disciplined criticism, appeals not to the rational faculties, at least as Kant defined them, but simply to what in elitist circles of the modern West—and the *Poetics* is unabashed in its elitism—is considered good taste.[28] The patrician British description of an embarrassing social error as not being "good form" captures the spirit of Stravinsky's formalism precisely. The casual ease with which Stravinsky can cite the "tone" of his own work is in striking contrast to Schoenberg's attitude towards such matters.[29] In effect, Stravinsky redefines musical form to mean style, or even "high style" in the currently fashionable "Yuppie" sense. In so doing he transforms music from a potentially universal symbol of integrity into a culturally specialized pleasure, leaving its fate to exactly those arbitrary standards of taste that his formalistic principles of appreciation were designed to escape.[30]

Schoenberg and Adorno try to effect precisely this escape by distinguishing the formal parameter of music from mere sound or style.[31] Instead, Schoenberg and Adorno define the formal parameter of music as an interconnectedness of structure which is at once temporally established, and thus concrete in character, and also objectively determinable. Consequently, they define structural listening not as a sensibility to chic but as attentiveness to a concretely unfolding logic which can vouch for the value of the music. Practiced in the way prescribed by Schoenberg and Adorno, structural listening plunges us into the middle of what could be called the musical argument, allowing us to understand, from the position of an insider, not just the lines but the totality

---

[28]For his elitism see, for instance, Stravinsky, 3:57-58, and 6:139-40. Interestingly, whereas metaphors of taste are usually employed in a derogatory sense by Schoenberg ("spicy" as opposed to functional dissonances, p. 247) and Adorno ("culinary listening," *Prisms*, p. 154), Stravinsky revels in such imagery ("appetite," "flow of saliva," "kneading the dough," 3:51-52). This difference is consistent with Adorno's denigration of music as a "consumer" good. See also Pierre Boulez, *Notes of An Apprenticeship*, trans. Hebert Weinstock (New York, 1968), pp. 249-250, on Stravinsky's "hedonism," and below, notes 31 and 68.

[29]See Stravinsky, 1:12.

[30]See Adorno, *Philosophy*, p. 140 and *passim* on Stravinsky and "specialization"; also Schoenberg, pp. 387-88.

[31]"The tradition of German music—as it includes Schoenberg—has been characterized since Beethoven, both in the positive and the negative sense, by the absence of taste" (Adorno, *Philosophy*, pp. 153-54). (The term "positive" here, like Adorno's criticism of Schoenberg's lack of discrimination in his choice of texts, as in *Prisms*, pp. 162-63, points rather uncharacteristically to the stylistic limitations of Adorno's own culture. See below, notes 61 and 68). See also Schoenberg, p. 247, on the "dictatorship of taste."

of the argument as it unfolds. Confronting at every moment the rationale of the composition from its own point of view, so to speak, the listener is ideally to be precluded from exercising negative prejudices or forming adverse judgments on the basis of stylistic uncongeniality or, in a sense, even on that of philosophical difference.

Adorno, to be sure, who is in most respects far more preoccupied than Schoenberg with the philosophical and ideological implications of musical structure, is not only prepared but determined to reject music he finds morally offensive, including that of Stravinsky's *bête noire,* Wagner, and of course that of Stravinsky himself. Significantly, however, Adorno never sees himself as having to choose between structural and moral value, precisely because for Adorno the two are essentially synonymous; "no music has the slightest esthetic worth," he asserts, "if it is not socially true."[32] From Adorno's standpoint, the virtues of the rationality which structural autonomy represents, and which render autonomy the highest condition of art, are not just logically abstract but historically concrete as well. The more a musical structure approximates the self-contained intelligibility characteristic of logic, the more it can and does free itself from what Adorno sees as the deceptions or falsehoods invariably fostered through social ideology in order to maintain the power of existing institutions.[33] Conversely, the greater the distance of music from the logical paradigm, the greater its entrapment in the special interests served by the conventions of social ideology and the smaller its claim to the essentially moral condition of aesthetic value. In other words, Adorno's characterization of a philosophical attitude in music as morally offensive is never separable from his perception of grave structural weaknesses in that music.

The concept of structural value offered by Schoenberg and Adorno, like their concept of the structural listening that can discern such value, is at once exacting and generous. Demanding an unflagging intelligent concentration on the part of the listener, these men require of the composer, and more generally of themselves, a no less stringent standard of discipline. Indeed, the self-conscious consistency, the sense of in-

---

[32]Adorno, *Sociology,* p. 197. Of interest is the related assertion by Mikhail M. Bakhtin that ". . . insight also involves a value judgment on the novel, one not only in the narrow sense but also ideological—for there is no artistic understanding without evaluation;" quoted in *The Dialogic Imagination,* ed. Michael Holquist, trans. Caryl Emerson and Michael Holquist (Austin, 1981), p. 416.

[33]Though Adorno regularly uses the term "ideology" in its negative Marxist sense, he does specify that "it is not ideology in itself which is untrue but rather its pretension to correspond to reality" (*Prisms,* p. 32).

tegrity, and the devotion to logic with which Schoenberg tried to regulate every relationship in his own compositional domain—the inner construction of his pieces, the unfolding of his own stylistic progress, and the preservation and development of past musical tradition as a kind of sacred trust—have probably never been equalled by another Western composer. As in Stravinsky's case, his entire musical career can be read as an enlargement of his own compositional principles, but in a sense that is far more "replete."

And correspondingly, Schoenberg's spirit of self-discipline results in a concept of musical structure, and of structural listening, that is far more positive and concrete in character than Stravinsky's formalism. Just as it is usually possible for any educated and reasonably sympathetic listener to perceive the retention of a capacity for individual expressiveness as a value in Schoenberg's music itself, so too, Schoenberg refuses in his writings to dehumanize either the individuals participating in musical life or music itself by separating structural rigor from an expressive capacity. For Schoenberg these last two are virtually synonymous: the deepest emotional satisfaction in music arises precisely through the achievement of an intensely expressive structural integrity (which is "independent of style and flourish" and communicable at least to those whose "artistic and ethical culture is on a high level").[34]

Nor does either Schoenberg or Adorno shrink from specifying the concrete musical components of a structure that allows structural listening to operate at full capacity. Although Adorno voices serious objections to the twelve-tone method, which Schoenberg explained so painstakingly and generously to his readers, both men are thoroughly dedicated to the goal of reducing music to a condition of what could be called pure structural substance, in which every element justifies its existence through its relation to a governing structural principle. Hence, both advocate the principle of "non-redundancy" in music, a principle with many compositional ramifications, including the rationale of chromaticism and dissonance, which they explore in detail; and both advocate the renunciation of pre-existing, externally determined conventions, such as symmetrical phrasing and refrains (which in fact often entail redundancy), as foreign to the generating idea of a composition.[35] Such renunciation, it should be stressed, is not to be confused with the simultaneous

---

[34]The quotations come from *Style and Idea,* pp. 454 and 450 (both on Mahler). See also ibid., pp. 75, 215, 254-57, 321, and 438; Rosen, p. 100; and below, notes 43 and 77.
[35]For example, Schoenberg, pp. 101, 102, 104, 114-17, 246, 257, 266-67, and 414-15; and Adorno, *Prisms,* p. 152 (Schoenberg's music is "structural down to the last tone"), and 168 ("the task of eliminating the apocryphal elements in twelve-tone technique").

acceptance and liquidation—or, in a word, *"Aufhebung"*—of artistically transmitted tradition, which both men demanded in their commitment to historical continuity and responsibility. Furthermore, as a way of distilling structural substance, both men place particular importance on the self-developing capacity of a motivic-thematic kernel, or on what they call "developing variation," a process they often though not exclusively associate with Brahms.[36]

The notion of development represents, of course, a continuation of structural concepts and values that originated in Viennese Classicism. (Schoenberg, somewhat idiosyncratically, locates its origins in Bach.)[37] This notion was likewise prized by Hanslick, who is cited, we should note, as a particularly adept practitioner of structural listening in one of the most detailed descriptions that Schoenberg gave of this method.[38] Although Adorno is clearly more sensitive than Schoenberg to the self-negating potentialities of development in post-tonal music, he is even more emphatic than Schoenberg in idealizing Beethoven for his developmental powers; and both men admire Brahms's tendency to transform composition into what Adorno calls "total development."[39]

At its best, Schoenberg's and Adorno's concept of structural listening makes a strong case, and certainly a more consistent case than Stravinsky's version does, for the values it wishes to sustain. Evoking as its ideal the possibility of reasoned musical discourse, and thus by extension the possibility of reasoned discourse itself, among differently situated individuals, their concept does not just hold musical form ac-

---

Non-redundancy indicates a need not only for avoiding repetition or reinforcement of a pitch, lest tonal hierarchy be evoked, but also for economy, variation, and musical "prose" as well as for historical originality. The analogy with computer imagery is obvious even though the informational value of redundancy is not highly valued. On the relation of art and information see the discussion of Yuri Lotman in Terry Eagleton, *Literary Theory; An Introduction* (Minneapolis, 1983), pp. 101-102; and Leonard B. Meyer, *Music, the Arts and Ideas: Patterns and Predictions in Twentieth-Century Culture* (Chicago, 1967), especially Chapter 11, Chapters 1-3, and p. 262.

[36]See Schoenberg, pp. 129, 279, 397, and *passim;* also Adorno, *Prisms,* p. 154. On Brahms see, for example, Schoenberg, pp. 80 and 129.

[37]See Schoenberg, especially p. 118.

[38]See Hanslick, p. 125, and Schoenberg, pp. 120-21.

[39]See Adorno, *Prisms,* p. 160-61; and Rosen, pp. 96-102; the great respect among musicologists for Schoenberg's *Erwartung* stems largely from its *musical* recognition of these negative potentialities. This seems to be music as self-negated logic or pure "trace," a condition which is no doubt related to its projection of extreme anxiety. On Beethoven, see Adorno, *Philosophy,* pp. 163-64; on total development see ibid., pp. 56-57.

countable for the connection of its own elements to a rationally governing principle. In addition, their concept ultimately demands that musical
form, through its uncompromising integrity and renunciation of sensuous distractions, contribute indirectly but concretely, as well as
metaphorically, to the betterment of society. In effect, Schoenberg and
Adorno offer structural listening as nothing less ambitious than a method
for defining and assessing the moral soundness of every relationship
that bears on music.

It is as a service to just some such ideal, I believe, that we in
musicology today would at bottom justify our firm and continuing commitment to various forms of structural listening. And yet, for all Adorno's self-conscious acuity, this concept is not without what Paul de Man
might call its areas of critical blindness to its own epistemological
weaknesses.[40]

THE CASE AGAINST STRUCTURAL LISTENING

A. Cultural Inappropriateness

The concept of structural listening imagines both composition and
listening to be governed by a quasi-Kantian structure of reason which,
by virtue of its universal validity, makes possible, at least ideally, the
ideological neutrality and, hence, something like the epistemological
transparency of music. This assumption of a congruence between the
underlying principles of composition and those of listening is what lends
force to the metaphor of listening to the musical structure "from within."
In actuality, however, in ways that I hope will become clear, the metaphorical listening position which structural listening encourages is less
that of Schoenberg's and Adorno's structural insider than that of the
externally situated, scientific observer. Indeed, it is very close to that
of the empirically oriented hero of Stravinsky's *Poetics*.

This shift in metaphorical position might at first glance seem too slight
to jeopardize the goals of structural listening. Scientific observation,
after all, is our cultural paradigm of methodological objectivity. Based
on concepts and values that are assumed universal, and thus presumably
exempt from subjective distortion, such observation seems to offer us
the power to focus intensely on a musical object entirely in its own terms.

---

[40]Paul de Man, *Blindness and Insight: Essays in the Rhetoric of Contemporary Criticism*,
2nd rev. ed. (Minneapolis, 1983), especially pp. 105 ff.

Thus a structural listening modelled on scientific observation might seem to offer us our best shot at a relativistic, ideologically neutral condition of tolerance in music, encouraging society to honor the music of all times and cultures equally, on terms set by the music itself.

But just as Western science has increasingly been criticized as a culturally limited and limiting construct, so, too, there is a strong argument to be made that the terms on which structural listening operates originate far less in universal conditions of music than in our own specific cultural predilections. Even at first glance it seems clear that this method does not lend itself with equal ease to all musical repertories, even in the West. Just as tonal theory has been more fully developed than any other Western system of theory, so, too, structural listening seems to work most smoothly when applied to the "common practice" repertory of Germany and Italy, say between Corelli and Mahler, which could be called the Western "canon."

This is hardly surprising, since structural listening is generally conceded to have "arisen" from the tonal canon. But why should this allegedly objective method of perception, which is supposed to concern itself with the structure of individual compositions, be used so regularly to confirm the aesthetic superiority of whole styles, and particularly Viennese Classicism, to other styles? (And how, for that matter, does the supposed objectivitiy of Stravinsky's formal perception, unless his very conception of structure is informed by stylistic prejudices, account for his denigration of Wagner's "symphonicism"?)[41] Why, if all music is equal in the ears of the structural listener, do some styles turn out to be more equal than others? And why (except perhaps to serve our own interests as masters of the specialized training and discourse which structural listening in practice nearly always requires) should we academics suppose such listening applicable to music that falls outside the canon?[42]

In fact, the concept of structural listening is considerably less widely applicable and objective a mode of perception than it seems. The very choice of this method, as well as the identity of the music it prefers, reflects our own culturally conditioned stylistic orientation as its users. Like Stravinsky's "good form," so to speak, what structural listening in all its variants offers us is less the conceptual attributes of objectivi-

---

[41]Stravinsky, 4:81
[42]On education as the mastery of a privileged discourse see Robert Scholes, "Is There a Fish in this Text?," in *On Signs,* ed. Marshall Blonsky (Baltimore, 1985), pp. 308-20; and Eagleton, p. 201.

ty than the stylistic impression of objectivity. For whereas it purports to examine music in terms of an intrinsic and potentially universal musical condition, structural autonomy, the notion itself of this condition is foreign to much, if not indeed most, music. One can of course decide to impose this condition as an ideal on any music one chooses. But before one claims the basis for this ideal as universal and intrinsic, one needs some evidence that the music in question is presenting its own structure as fundamentally autonomous, or as "fixed" in various senses.

A fixed structure is discrete and whole; it has clearly delineated boundaries, which would be violated by any conception of this structure as a fragment. A fixed structure is also unchangeable; its internal components and relationships are presumed to have attained something like a status of necessity which disallows alternative versions. Neither of these conditions can persuasively be called characteristic, even as a projected ideal, of Western art music up until the eighteenth century. It could even be argued that they did not obtain fully until that point in the nineteenth century when improvisation was decisively excluded from the concept of art composition and an ideal of precision was approached in composition. I mean here precision not just of pitch (which somewhat paradoxically the relativistic tonal notion of "key" had already established to the detriment of mode) but also of notation and instrumentation.

To be persuasively autonomous, moreover, a structure must show some evidence of trying to define itself wholly through some implicit and intelligible principle of unity. In music this requires that a composition has some technique for projecting itself as self-determining over time. Whether or not such a technique is suggested by Schenker's concept of linear organization, with its debatable audibility, its problematical ability to account for the particularities of a musical surface, and its reliance on archetypal musical structures as well as on non-temporal, visual schematics, is not a matter than can be analyzed here.

Development, on the other hand, is widely considered by Western musicologists to be capable of projecting the impression of such self-determination. Schoenberg and Adorno quite openly define structural listening as developmental listening. But as virtually all scholars would concede, very little music, even Western art music, makes use of the technique of development. (Schoenberg's perception of Bach's music as in some respects developmental is not widely shared. Indeed, Bach's achievement is probably better characterized as the synthesis of a great diversity of generic concepts—concerto, trio sonata, dance, fugue, and so forth—than as structural self-determination.)

In its pure state, moreover, the condition of self-determination, or even the projection of such a condition, would require the renunciation of premises, organizational principles, purposes, values, and meanings derived from outside of a musical structure. Almost no Western music outside of certain Classical and contemporary endeavors has come close to accepting such a condition of renunciation. Up until the end of the eighteenth century, for example, most music was shaped to serve an external social function; and in keeping with deep-rooted mimetic or rhetorical ideals, the dominating paradigm of music throughout this period was music with a text. Furthermore, Western music has been assumed in most periods to owe at least some of its significance to a larger cultural network of extra-musical ideas or stylistically related constructs.

Structural listening looks on the ability of a unifying principle to establish the internal "necessity" of a structure as tantamount to a guarantee of musical value. At the very least this assumption challenges the spirit of Gödel's theorems. In practice, however, the principle on which structural listening relies more than any other to authenticate value is not one of self-evident rationality but rather one of its own choosing, individuality. Both Schoenberg and Adorno emphasize the responsibility of the conscious individual, whether composing or listening, to clarify actively the internal intelligibility of a structure, a process which ideally frees the meaning of that structure from social distortion and manipulation. Even in those instances when Schoenberg and Adorno concede the possibility of an instantaneous intuition of musical value, they attribute such intuition at bottom to a structural integrity in the music; and this integrity can only be achieved through an individualistic "compositorial force" (Adorno's words), or through what Schoenberg terms an "originality [which] is inseparable from... profound personality."[43] In such respects, both men are deeply committed to the governing status of originating intention.[44]

---

[43]Adorno, *Sociology,* p. 74 (on Berg); Schoenberg, p. 133, also 454. See especially below, notes 44 and 77.

[44]Schoenberg in his writings and letters gave substantial recognition to the subconscious origins of composition. But he also stressed the discoverable structural logic in such origins and the need for conscious control (see, for example, Schoenberg, pp. 92, 217-18, 244, and 423-24). Schoenberg's description of his "mental tortures" in retaining a passage in the first Chamber Symphony which he was not able to justify structurally for another twenty years is remarkable (ibid., pp. 222-23). It is hard to imagine Stravinsky in such a position, or to overstate the intimidating effect of this passage on the would-be structural listener. See also Adorno, *Philosophy,* pp. 138-43, and below, note 77.

This is not the same as saying that advocates of even a "replete" structural listening ordinarily reserve their highest praise for the music that is most commonly characterized as individual in the sense of personally expressive, that is, Romantic music. Even the most ardent German advocates of a "replete" formalism are seldom prepared to idealize music that values personal expressiveness over developmental autonomy. Certainly Adorno does not; his greatest reverence is for that metaphorically powerful "moment" of individuality—Beethoven's middle-period style—in which the musical subject, determining its own action through uncompromising objective standards of developmental unity, turns itself into a locus of the universal.

Most of us in the Western musical world take for granted some related inseparability of musical greatness and individuality, which in turn we equate with musical value. Yet even excluding non-Western traditions, it would be difficult to characterize most art music before the common-practice period with any confidence through reference to ideals of individuality or even, perhaps, to a dialectic of individual and society. Even chromaticism, which we often interpret in effect as signifying resistance to prevailing social norms, does not seem characteristically to be used by earlier music to place the power of individuality at its own ideological center. We recognize as much when we relegate Gesualdo, who might well have been a cultural hero in Mahler's Vienna, to a pocket of historical eccentricity.

The apparent absence of an individualistic ideal of structural autonomy before the firm establishment of tonality as a cultural norm, together with our own commitment to such an ideal, helps account, in my judgment, for a certain lack of focus that can sometimes be sensed in our study and teaching of early music, and for a certain uneasiness that stems from the difficulty of distinguishing form from style in early music (see below, n. 73). On the one hand, given our reluctance to attribute the preservation of certain medieval and Renaissance music to either the overt power or the innate virtue of Christianity, much less to sheer happenstance, we want to assume the primarily structural value (and thereby the "greatness") of the early music we teach. But on the other hand, lacking any alternative to ideals of structural autonomy, we sometimes allow the teaching of medieval and Renaissance music, which does not strongly support our own structural biases, to disintegrate into the uncritical presentation of shifting stylistic hallmarks that can be named and dated on an exam.

The absence of a clear ideal of autonomy in early music may underlie the often noted failure of modern scholars to produce a persuasive theory of pre-tonal music (as, indeed, of any primarily texted music);[45] conceivably the very notion of such a theory, at least in any structural sense, is self-contradictory. This absence may also account for a certain hollowness palpable at the core of various encyclopedic surveys of Renaissance music, which seem to offer inclusiveness as a compensation for our lack of an aesthetic basis for selecting and evaluating works of this period.

Such problems indicate strongly that structural listening does not encourage the open-ended sensitivity to diverse sorts of music that it promises. Even as this concept urges us to judge a work in terms of the work's own chosen premises, it distances us from music that exhibits no interest in encompassing all of its own premises. In fact, there are ways in which structural listening can be construed as a cultural violation even of the one style, Viennese Classicism, which not only seems clearly predicated on some ideal of structural autonomy but also appears to have realized this ideal with some success. Not at least until Beethoven began to place rhetorical emphasis on many of his main structural junctures, in effect conceding the intrinsic intelligibility of structural relationships as a fiction, does the musical evidence suggest that composers valued active structural comprehension over the Enlightenment ideal, as articulated by Kant, of seemingly artless art.[46]

Even more important, perhaps, is the secondary status which such listening accords to the musical parameter of sound. The ideal of structural listening has made our perceptions and analytical concerns as musicologists almost completely dependent on scores, as if the latter were books. One is tempted to argue that structural listening makes more use of the eyes than of the ears. Certainly, to an important extent structural listening can take place in the mind through intelligent score-reading, without the physical presence of an external sound-source. But whereas the absence of concrete sound constitutes a debatable loss in the case of literature, it represents nothing less than a catastrophic sacrifice for music.

This is a sacrifice that Adorno, and even Schoenberg in certain respects, are actually prepared to make. Although their version of structural listening purports to account for every detail of a concrete musical logic, it depreciates the value of sound with unusual explicitness. Adorno identifies sound as that layer of music which, through its use of such

---

[45]See Joseph Kerman, *Contemplating Music: Challenges to Musicology* (Cambridge, Mass., 1985), pp. 71-72.
[46]Immanuel Kant, *The Critique of Judgment*, trans. James Creed Meredith (Oxford, 1952), Section 45, pp. 166-67.

historically conditioned resources as technology and conventions, bears the imprint of social ideology and allows the social "neutralization" of structural individuality. Thus the status Adorno accords this "manifest" (as opposed to "latent") layer is not privileged, to say the least. This explains his impatience with the archeological restoration of early musical sound to its original "purity."[47] It also helps explain his low estimation of Romantic music, which calls explicit attention to the opaqueness of its own sound and style. To Adorno this concreteness signifies not an honest admission by Romantic music of its own social and ideological concreteness but a capitulation to the power and modes of society—an abandonment of the effort, however quixotic, to define universal individuality in music.

By Adorno's account, in fact, "mature music," which concerns itself with that "subcutaneous" structure where individual integrity can hope to resist or even transcend social ideology, "becomes suspicious of real sound as such." Turning color into a function of total structural interrelatedness, such music makes color in itself essentially superfluous. Adorno praises Schoenberg's ascetic "negation of all facades," which he likens to that of late Beethoven, and projects a time when "the silent, imaginative reading of music could render actual playing as superfluous as . . . speaking is made by the reading of written material."[48]

Adorno's characterization of Schoenberg is echoed by Pierre Boulez's reference to Schoenberg and Webern as composers "for whom the idea of timbre is almost abstract, and who never cared at all about the physical conditions of sound emission."[49] In his writings, Schoenberg himself consistently subordinates the values of sound to those of structure, asserting in what may be the key passage of *Style and Idea* that the responsible composer "will never start from a preconceived image of a style; he will be ceaselessly occupied with doing justice to the idea. He is

[47]See Adorno, *Prisms,* pp. 142-46.
[48]For the entire quotation see Adorno, *Prisms,* p. 169. See also ibid., p. 157 (Schoenberg's "is music for the intellectual ear"); and Adorno, *Philosophy,* p. 15 ("Only in a society which had achieved satisfaction [i.e., for the free individual] would the death of art be possible"). For different views of silent reading see Roland Barthes, *The Responsibility of Forms: Critical Essays on Music, Art, and Representation,* trans. Richard Howard (New York, 1985), pp. 264-65; and Jacques Attali, *Noise: The Political Economy of Music,* trans. Brian Massumi (Minneapolis, 1985), p. 32.
[49]Boulez, p. 252. Such assertions do not deny Schoenberg's extraordinary coloristic achievements as a composer (often associated with, though by no means limited to, the third piece in the *Five Pieces for Orchestra,* op. 16, and *Pierrot Lunaire*) but rather emphasize that color *as such,* as opposed to color *as structure,* had no place in Schoenberg's theory of musical value. See also Rosen, p. 48.

sure that, everything done which the idea demands, the external appearance will be adequate."[50] This devaluing of medium has a direct musical counterpart in the naive certainty of Schoenberg's later works that the tonal conception of "developing variation" can sustain its intelligibility in a radically altered context of sound. This contradiction is often noted, but its implications with respect to the notion of "medium" have not so far been fully recognized.

The subordination of medium, toward which structural listening leads more strongly than most of us would happily admit, represents one logical resolution of the dialectical opposition between structure and sound that has for some time been discernible in Western music, and which has antecedents in a tension between essence and appearance that can be traced back in Western thought at least as far as Plato. In effect, Schoenberg and Adorno, that quintessential foe of ahistorical abstraction, take the same position as Derrida does when he interprets Aristotle's categories as evidence for the priority of abstract thought over concrete language.[51] Stravinsky, at bottom, draws the opposite conclusion, though in identifying essentially stylistic parameters of music as formal, he obscures the implications of his argument, and restricts its usefulness.

But however characteristic this tension may have become in Western music, it has seldom been resolved through depreciating sound. On the contrary, as the anti-corporeal bias of doctrinaire religion was left behind, Western composers, including the Viennese Classicists, came to place a high value on the sensuous actuality of their music. By the nineteenth century, as I have just indicated, specificities of instrumental color were considered normally constitutive of a musical configuration; they were among the components that "fixed" the piece as a distinctive, individual "organism."

Of course, Romantic music was typically contradictory in its attitude toward instrumental color. On the one hand integrating it into their notion of structure, the Romantics simultaneously emphasized color to a degree where it was bound to call attention to itself and, through the habit of associative listening, to things outside of music (the horns and the forest in Weber's *Freischütz*, for example). But this double-sidedness

---

[50]Schoenberg, p. 121. See also ibid., 56, 132, and 240, on sound, and compare Stravinsky, 2:27, on "the sensation of the music itself" as "an indispensable element of investigation"; and below, note 64.

[51]Jacques Derrida, "The Supplement of Copula: Philosophy *before* Linguistics," in *Textual Strategies: Perspectives in Post-Structuralist Criticism,* ed. Josué V. Harari (Ithaca, 1979): 82-120.

hardly supports the case for structural listening. On the contrary, to the extent that structural listening encourages concentration on the perception of formal relationships at the expense of maintaining an active (though less easily formalized)[52] sensitivity to sound itself, structural listening constitutes a cultural violation of this and many other styles.

This holds even in our own century if we make a clear distinction between the heirs of Schoenberg on the one hand and those of Debussy and, indeed, Stravinsky, on the other. In fact the only body of music for which we can be fairly confident that structural listening, in its most consistent sense, does not pose a violation of originating norms is Schoenberg's own. (One might, to be sure, extend this observation to Schoenberg's descendants, including Webern, especially in the sense that the latter "out-Schoenbergs" Schoenberg or, more precisely, that Schoenberg's ideals constitute an essential "trace" in Webern's music. Which means, of course, that in Webern's music the "self-negating potentialities of development" mentioned above are fully realized.) But despite its appropriateness to Schoenberg's compositional ideals, structural listening, in its devaluation of sound and style, involves another sort of epistemological limitation, which is nowhere more evident than in the application of this method to Schoenberg's own music.

B. The Need for Non-Structural Knowledge

> We attach too much and too little importance to sensations. We do not see that frequently they affect us not merely as sensations, but as signs or images, and that their moral effects also have moral causes.
>
> Jean-Jacques Rousseau[53]

Given Adorno's idealization of structural listening, the actual character of his musical writings might seem surprising. His entire output as a music critic can be viewed as illuminating the irreducibility of the concrete medium of music. Actually it was only through such criticism that Adorno could fulfill what he saw as the critic's principal obligation, to expose the destructive values of society as they manifest themselves

---

[52] A notable breakthrough in the formalizing of a technique characteristically associated with medium is the article by Janet M. Levy entitled "Texture as a Sign in Classic and Early Romantic Music," *Journal of the American Musicological Society* 35 (1982): 482-531.

[53] From the *Essay on the Origin of Languages,* quoted in Derrida, *Of Grammatology,* p. 206. Of interest also is the passage about music and poetry in ancient Greece that is quoted on p. 201: "In cultivating the art of convincing, that of arousing the emotions was lost."

in the public and conventional aspects of music, and to disentangle music from the corrupting power and effects of institutional ideology. This obligation required him to engage in continuous criticism of the musical medium (thereby performing much the same service that he praised in Schoenberg's and Webern's recasting of Bach's instrumentation).[54]

Adorno scorned the very notion of an actual non-ideological music. Insistence on the non-existence of ideology in music was radically different for him from a continuing sensitivity to ideology as a force to be resisted, a sensitivity which he discerned in the uncompromising structural integrity of the late Beethoven quartets and Schoenberg's music. Certainly he was no less adamant than Barthes has been in condemning as a lie any attempt by a musical "sign," so to speak, to hide its own cultural artificiality, and to present itself as either a socially and historically isolated object or an ideologically innocent or neutral construct, fit for "merely" formal analysis.[55] Such self-deceptively non-ideological analysis was far more consistent with the spirit of Stravinsky's *Poetics,* which can be shown to project a wide range of ideologically loaded, even anti-humanistic subtexts.[56] And, indeed, Adorno's own criticism of Stravinsky's music shows him every bit as sensitive as more recent, unmistakably anti-formalist critics, such as Eagleton, to the chasm that separates narrowly formal intentions from a purely formal character, effect, or significance, whether in art or in criticism itself.[57]

Adorno's constant preoccupation with social ideology, then, led him to a continuous engagement with that layer of music which he least valued, and to establish an ongoing, relatively explicit connection between his own values and those of the various cultures represented in the composition, performance, or reception of the music he discussed. As perhaps the premier practitioner in our century of concrete social and historical criticism, who deplored systems and abstractions, Adorno set an unexcelled example for those figures in current literary debate, such as Said, Jameson, Blonsky, and Eagleton, who likewise stress the concrete social and historical responsibilities of criticism.[58]

[54]See Adorno, *Prisms,* p. 146.

[55]On Barthes see Eagleton, p. 136, and also pp. 170 and 187.

[56]I have attempted to do precisely this in an unpublished paper delivered at Queens College, New York, November 5, 1986.

[57]See Eagleton, pp. 49, 207, and *passim.* My own response to Anthony Barone's paper "The Critical Reception of Verdi in Fascist Italy," at the annual meeting of the American Musicological Society in Cleveland (November 8, 1986) addressed the same theme.

[58]See, for example, Edward Said, "The Text, the World, the Critic," in Harari, pp. 161-88; Fredric Jameson, "The Realist Floor Plan," in Blonsky, pp. 373-83; Blonsky, "Introduction: The Agony of Semiotics," pp. xiii-li, and "Endword: Americans on the Move," pp. 507-509, in Blonsky; and Eagleton, especially pp. xix-1.

Furthermore, precisely because Adorno viewed music as part of an historically open-ended context of concrete social relationships, his principal focus as a practitioner of criticism was not the isolated work but the broader category of style. This, too, encouraged him to develop criticism as a mode of stylistic rather than structural analysis, even when dealing with elements of structure. In fact, what Adorno actually did in his musical writings was stylistic criticism of the highest caliber. By this I mean criticism of a kind that had nothing to do with the mere listing of characteristic musical devices but rather demonstrated the capacity of a rigorously fashioned critical language to analyze style incisively. Adorno's ability to find richly evocative yet succinct and precise metaphorical verbal equivalents for structural and non-structural elements in music, and thereby to characterize persuasively the cultural and historical significance of both individual works and styles, is masterful, even uncanny.

It is sometimes asked whether Adorno really "knew" music. Frequently he is taken to task for not doing the thing he seems most to require of the listener, structural analysis. Moreover, Schoenberg regularly used charts and diagrams as well as the specialized terminology of academic structural analysis; and Adorno himself identified the ability to "name the formal components" as a sign of competence in structural listening. Yet his criticism rarely offers such signs. Probably this was because at bottom such techniques smacked too much for Adorno of those anti-intellectual "proceedings in which general demonstrability of results matters more than their use to get to the heart of the matter."[59] But did Adorno get to the heart of the matter? I would argue that even if we reject vehemently the conclusions that pervade Adorno's metaphorical observations (a possibility which the unusually honest and explicit presentation of his own values allows), Adorno's thorough familiarity with the music he characterizes as well as the aptness and importance of his metaphors are virtually always confirmed by a reconsideration of the music in question. "The genuine experience of music," Adorno wrote, "like that of all art, is as one with criticism."[60] For Adorno, in fact, no less than for the German Romantics a century earlier, metaphorical criticism of the characteristics, choices, and relationships that embed music in one or another socio-historical context is not a "supplement," in Derrida's sense, to the possession of detailed structural knowledge but rather the very means of getting to the heart of such knowledge.

[59] Adorno, *Sociology,* p. 195; on "naming the formal components," see pg. 4.
[60] Ibid., p. 152.

Now in a way all of this amounts to saying that the kind of structural knowledge that interests Adorno and the German Romantics alike is culturally concrete, encompassing, or "replete." But here it must be explicitly acknowledged that the concept of replete structural listening is itself a concrete, metaphorical account of perception, not a logical principle. Not only does the concept of replete structure itself point to a condition which is characteristic only of music in certain styles, and thus first of all to a stylistic rather than to a structural condition. In addition, this concept depends no less than Stravinsky's chic formalism does for its intelligibility, persuasiveness, and usefulness on a culturally defined, stylistic sensibility in the listener. This stylistic particularity of replete structural listening as a principle helps explain how this concept can readily be misinterpreted by those of us from other cultures, not privy to its stylistic nuance, as justifying far narrower practices of structural listening. But the fundamental sense in which Adorno's concept of structural listening as well as Schoenberg's compositional choices were both governed by needs that were more stylistic than structural in character was something Adorno did not and probably could not recognize—any more than he could assess the degree to which his own aesthetic convictions represented cultural preferences.[61]

Nor was Adorno willing, therefore, any more than Schoenberg was, at bottom, to understand the widespread unresponsiveness to Schoenberg's music relativistically, as the reflection of something other than an immature unwillingness or intellectual incapacity to master the technical demands of structural listening. Grounding structural listening in a supposedly universal rational capacity, Adorno was utterly unable to criticize as "ideological" the elite social standing and the long years of education that were ordinarily required for the exercise of this capacity. He could not bring himself to characterize either Schoenberg's unpopularity or non-structural modes of listening as functions of legitimate differences among listeners in cultural or stylistic orientation.

This is not to say that Adorno was oblivious to actual characteristics and effects of his or Schoenberg's style.[62] On the contrary, Adorno explicitly considered irreducible stylistic "difficulty" necessary to the structuring and value of both men's work. From Adorno's standpoint, a "jagged physiognomy" not only signified the resistance of individual usage to the conventions of ideology. In addition it was needed to

---

[61]See especially Adorno, *Prisms,* pp. 152-53, on Schoenberg's compositional methods as an outgrowth of necessity rather than temperament; and also ibid., p. 154, on Adorno's characteristic equation, in effect, of non-structural listening with "musical stupidity."
[62]See notes 31 and 68.

preserve the integrity of "subcutaneous" argument from social "neutralization." Such integrity required a refusal by structure to compromise itself by "smoothing over," as Adorno accused Brahms of doing, or by allowing to be obscured a dehumanizing contradiction between the rational ideals of structure and the ongoing anti-rational force of society, as represented in the musical medium.[63]

Where Adorno's self-critical capacity failed him was both in his attribution of a universal necessity to the social analysis and the convictions that explained such stylistic choices and in his inability to imagine alternative, equally honest, stylistic definitions of, or solutions to, the social problems surrounding music. What drew Adorno to Schoenberg's music was not just its structural idealism but also the ugliness, by conventional standards, of its sound. But while it is true that Adorno valued this ugliness for its "negative" capacity to scorn the ideological blandishments of "affirmative culture," it is by no means clear that he would have been similarly drawn to the jagged qualities of punk rock or Laurie Anderson's music, much less that anything could have convinced him to view Leonard Bernstein's choice of the popular route as socially responsible. Adorno was sympathetic to Schoenberg's ugliness because he understood its cultural significance. And he understood this significance because he operated within the same set of concrete cultural assumptions, expectations, conventions, and values that Schoenberg did. He could listen to Schoenberg's music with the advantage of an insider's knowledge not of a universal structure but of a particular style.

Schoenberg, too, was inclined to dismiss objections to his style as signs of a "childish" preoccupation with pleasures of the senses rather than of differences in cultural orientation; just as form for Stravinsky is sound stripped of meaning, so style for Schoenberg is sound devoid of "idea."[64] In emphatically replacing the aesthetic notion of beauty with epistemological notions such as truth and knowledge as the central philosophical problem of music, Schoenberg revealed in his writings

[63]On "jagged physiognomy" see Adorno, *Philosophy*, p. 136; on Brahms see his *Prisms*, p. 156. See also ibid, pp. 144 and 153; and Adorno's *Philosophy*, p. 133: "Modern music... [has] all of its beauty in denying itself the illusion of beauty." Of the greatest interest in this connection is Lionel Trilling's characterization of "authenticity" in *Sincerity and Authenticity* (Cambridge, Mass., 1972). See, for example, p. 11 (on the "strenuous moral experience" of authenticity) and p. 94 ("Nowadays our sense of what authenticity means involves a degree of rough concreteness or of extremity.").
[64]On this whole topic see, for instance, Schoenberg, pp. 234, 401, and 408; on style *versus* idea see especially ibid., pp. 118 and 120. See also ibid., p. 378, where Schoenberg dismisses culturally associative modes of listening as directed only at "the perfume of a work."

the hope of weaning listeners away from sensuous preoccupation.[65] And yet instinctively he recognized the need to draw the listener inside his own stylistic world. Again and again in his writings he explains the numerous "lost" historical origins of his works, including the tonal system and earlier German compositional techniques, which although literally absent from his works, are nevertheless constituent elements in their conception and significance.[66] One would be hard pressed to find a composer whose work is more fully and clearly characterized by elements in Derrida's concept of the "trace"—or for that matter a critic whose intelligibility depends more than Adorno's does on a knowledge of absent "subtexts." In both cases, these traces and subtexts consist precisely in ideas and values defined in a surrounding cultural context. They are functions not of a literally present structure but of a more open-ended style.

Both Schoenberg's and Adorno's work provides massive evidence of the degree to which the communication of ideas depends on concrete cultural knowledge, and on the power of signs to convey a richly concrete open-endedness of meaning through a variety of cultural relationships.[67] Their work supports the thesis that style is not extrinsic to structure but rather defines the conditions for actual structural possibilities, and that structure is perceived as a function more than as a foundation of style. Even in a crude sense I would argue that if we are forced in musical analysis to grab hold of one end or the other of the dialectic between a style and a structure which are always affecting each other, it makes most sense to define the composer's starting point as his or her entrance into a pre-existing musical style. Certainly such a notion has large currency in our own culture, where its status as a cliché ("the medium is the message") no doubt accounts in large measure for our perception of Stravinsky as more modern than Schoenberg.[68] And certainly for those who begin interpreting either Schoenberg's or

[65]For examples of the shift in paradigm see Schoenberg, pp. 38, 101, 256, 283, 380, and 435. See also Carl Dahlhaus, *Realism in Nineteenth-Century Music,* trans. Mary Whittall (Cambridge, 1985), p. 11. On Adorno's derivation from Hegel of the view that truth is the vocation of art see, for example, the review of Adorno's *Aesthetic Theory* by Raymond Geuss in *The Journal of Philosophy* 83 (1986), p. 734 ff.

[66]For example, Schoenberg, pp. 49-51, 91, 284, and 288. Schoenberg's notion of "liquidation" (p. 288) is also suggestive in this connection.

[67]See especially Blonsky, pp. xvi-xvii.

[68]Adorno did indeed recognize this difference in general perception, and scorned it as a mark of intellectual (and moral) inferiority. See his *Prisms,* p. 152, on "Stravinsky and . . . all those who, having adjusted better to contemporary existence, fancy themselves more modern than Schoenberg." (See also Boulez, p. 252, where a similar distinc-

Adorno's work from the vantage point of a stylistic outsider, any relatively abstract, structurally rational argument is likely to constitute not the most but the least accessible parameter of meaning.

This is precisely the situation that confronts us with any culturally distant music. Did medieval music, for instance, once define structurally the value and power of individuality? Perhaps it would be most accurate to say that too much distance from the wealth of associations that once informed medieval usages prevents us from answering this question conclusively. To the extent that our perception of medieval culture and its signs remains what anthropologists call "etic" (that is, external and merely physical) rather than "emic" (that is, internal and literate), we are not in a position to view individualities of structure as signifying much more than a stylistic aberration.[69] (Why are we so much more inclined to apply the name "Mannerism" to early than to recent artistic styles?) Certainly the kinds of medieval musical "structure" that our culture allows us to perceive are nothing like the system of relationships that Adorno's structural listening would have us grasp from within.

Ever since the crystallization of the notion of "Art" in the early nineteenth century, it has become a truism of Western culture that the proper evaluation of any structure as "Art" requires the perspective of time. And in a culture that explicitly allows individuals, such as artists, to alter the conventional cultural meanings of signifiers, some time lapse undoubtedly is required for a full understanding of the altered medium. By this time, however, it has probably already (or more likely, as Derrida likes to say, "always already") become impossible to understand the full import of those changes at the time they were made, or, hence, to claim an insider's access to arguments structured within

---

tion is made between Wagner and Mussorgsky, though not on Adorno's grounds). Adorno might perhaps have linked Stravinsky more aptly to post-modern culture. See especially Trilling, p. 98, n. 1, on the end of the alienation and resistance which characterized modern art: in post-modern culture "the faculty of 'taste' has re-established itself at the centre of the experience of art."

[69]That perhaps there are grounds for developing a somewhat different definition of individuality from just such a perception, however, is suggested by this observation of Bruno Nettl's concerning (pre-Islamic) classical Persian music from the latter first millennium: "Similarly, individualism, another central cultural value, is reflected in the importance of the exceptional . . ." (*The Study of Ethnomusicology: Twenty-nine Issues and Concepts* [Urbana, 1983], p. 207). I am grateful to Ken Moore, a doctoral candidate in ethnomusicology at the City University of New York Graduate Center, for calling this discussion to my attention.

that medium.[70] By this point, as Hildesheimer suggests in his biography of Mozart, crucial aspects of an original significance have become unrecoverable.[71] The listener is already hearing overtones of intervening knowledge and experience which drown out or "erase" various responses that could have originally been intended or anticipated, while adding others. This condition of difference and delay, which Derrida has termed *"différance,"* calls increasing attention over time or distance to the irreducibility of style, both in its concrete physicality and in the ever-changing face it presents to new contexts of interpretation, as a source of signification.[72] In other words, the more culturally distant the music is, the more inescapably aware we become of its style—of its style as a barrier to understanding, and also as a condition of any structural perceptions we may form.[73]

The overtones of which I speak are in actuality so inseparable from all communication, even within a single culture, as to suggest themselves as essential to the very possibility of communication; without the possibility of misreading, as some post-structuralists have argued, reading itself becomes an inconceivable act. And such a situation seems nowhere more explicitly to obtain than when we are faced with interpreting an object that to most of us seems as directly dependent on the concreteness of a medium as music does, or as powerful in its ability to express, project, or evoke a good deal besides a commitment to its own logic. Thus, invoking our own cultural disposition to label certain music "Art" after a time-lapse is no proof of an acquired ability to hear musical structure in its original sense. If anything, the very use of this label probably signifies the degree to which we remain excluded as interpreters from the original inner dynamic of most music.

What limits the application of structural listening to Schoenberg's music is not the technical difficulty of this method but its misdirectedness. For most listeners, the barriers of Schoenberg's style, which in many ways seem to simulate a condition of great cultural distance, are simply too formidable to be penetrated and discounted as secondary by a focus on structure. Most listeners stand a chance of becoming engaged by Schoenberg's music only in the sense that by gaining sufficient access to the usages and characteristics of his style they might come to recognize its affinities with their own twentieth-century cultural ex-

[70]For "always already" see Derrida, *Of Grammatology,* p. 201.
[71]Wolfgang Hildesheimer, *Mozart,* trans. Marion Faber (New York, 1983), pp. 4, 11-12.
[72]On *"différance"* see Spivak, pp. xxix and xliii; and Culler, pp. 95-99.
[73]Strong support for this assertion is provided in Bakhtin, for example pp. 283-84, 289, 417, and 420-21.

perience (much as they recognize such affinities when contemporary music accompanies a film).

The Russian literary theorist Mikhail Bakhtin has argued that theories of literature which take into account only those aspects of style conditioned by fundamentally formal demands for comprehensibility and clarity, while ignoring the culturally interactive aspects of style, "take the listener for a person who passively understands but not for one who actively answers and reacts."[74] Applied to music generally, such an argument would suggest that structural listening reinforces not active engagement but passivity on the part of the listener, suppressing an inclination to participate in some sort of active dialogue with music. And applied specifically to twentieth-century music such as Schoenberg's, this argument suggests that only something akin to "stylistic listening" would permit contemporary listeners to exercise any prerogatives they might have as cultural insiders. Such an argument accords with my own observation that such prerogatives *can* be exercised in relation to twentieth-century art music, and with considerable insight. As I have noted elsewhere in some detail, I have found that college students almost invariably write more perceptively and articulately about the "difficult" contemporary music they hear at concerts than about any other style— once they have allowed themselves to focus on aspects of a contemporary composition besides its structural cohesiveness.[75]

But this is precisely the point. Of all methods, structural listening, even in its "replete" version, seems the least useful for entering the semiotic domain of sound and style. For carried to its logical conclusion, this method in all its versions, as an exclusive or even as the primary paradigm for listening, is not in a position to define much of a positive role for society, style, or ultimately even sound in the reception of music. Discounting metaphorical and affective responses based on cultural association, personal experience, and imaginative play as at best secondary not only in musical perception but also in the theoretical accounts we make of such perception, this method allows virtually no recognition to non-structural varieties of meaning or emotion in the act of listen-

---

[74]Bakhtin, p. 280.
[75]This discussion appears in my essay "The Challenge of Contemporary Music" (see note 4 above), as does an analysis of various difficulties connected with the mastery of structural listening. Of interest in this connection is Herbert Lindenberger's observation, in *Opera: The Extravagant Art* (Ithaca, 1984), pp. 226-27, that "modern ballet (even when accompanied by difficult musical scores)" may enjoy a large public today in part "because ballet is sufficiently abstract that audiences do not feel tempted to panic if they fail to understand the 'meaning.'" It would be interesting to compare Lindenberger's notion of abstraction here with the view taken throughout my own essay.

ing. Since these are of course precisely the varieties favored by the over-whelming majority of people, structural listening by itself turns out to be socially divisive, not only in what it demands but also in what it excludes or suppresses. And such divisiveness by no means necessari-ly serves the best interests of music. Indeed, to the extent that struc-tural listening brackets off the intuitive apprehensions of music that even specialists have, it unnecessarily limits the benefits of musical educa-tion, a point to which I shall return in my conclusion.

Stylistic knowledge *is* to some extent intuitive but this is by no means a fatal epistemological liability. To say this is only to admit the inarguable—that the very act of getting to know music begins with an extra-rational apprehension of sound—and also to argue that all of the musical knowledge we acquire is (or ought to be) a process of confirm-ing, modifying, or rejecting that apprehension through rational modes of thought. In other words, the rational substratum of musical knowledge rests finally on some act, choice, or principle which is not itself ra-tionally demonstrable.

It has been argued that this is the condition of all knowledge.[76] I find this argument persuasive; but even if one does not, there can be little question that in music, where we begin with a sound that can to some extent be analyzed into a style and structure, intuition is epistemologically valuable and, in many respects, indispensable. Certainly without such intuition there would be no hope of distinguishing responsibly between music which resists ideological deception and music which selfishly refuses to participate in the discourse of society. No amount of formal analysis by itself could ever arrive at a rational basis for making such a distinction. And yet the distinction is worth making, or at least attempting.

But this is not all. To place emphasis in listening and analysis on sound and style as prior to musical structure does not absolve the serious critic from a need for rigorous, self-critical discipline in the development of critical methods or of a critical language. Such an emphasis does not remove the historical responsibility of trying to sort out the meaning and values that may have been initially ''imprinted'' or subsequently imposed on a composition, even if, as I believe, this can only be done through some sort of dialectical interaction with the present, history

[76]See especially Stanley Rosen, *The Limits of Analysis* (New York, 1980), pp. 216-60. I am deeply indebted to David Bain, a doctoral candidate in music at the City Univer-sity of New York Graduate Center, for calling this book to my attention and, beyond this, for his clarifying insight into every aspect of this essay, especially those issues taken up in my concluding paragraphs.

being "now" as well as "then." Likewise, it does not remove the need for an exacting examination of one's response to the parameter of medium as a function of one's own tastes and prejudices—even though it is probably the case that the inescapable blindness of which Paul de Man has written is more than anything else a blindness to our own stylistic limitations and their effects on our knowledge. Nevertheless, although such an emphasis does entail the fullest possible recognition and analysis of one's own cultural predilections, it does not justify a capitulation to one's own biases, or a refusal to attempt sympathetic entry into an unfamiliar stylistic domain.

Nor, on the other hand, does such an emphasis absolve the serious critic from what I see as an ongoing obligation to seek carefully reasoned ways of investigating and assessing the social and moral significance of the values discerned in music. The desirability of cultural relativism ought not to condemn us, even in theory, to a positivistic tolerance for totalitarian musical styles and practices. It should not exclude us from confronting head-on the moral issues posed by Wagner's music or from giving thought to the overtones of prejudice in the Bach Passions and even *The Magic Flute*. Moreover, such an emphasis should not blind us to the wide-ranging implications of diverse compositional choices, whether these choices involve an uncritical acceptance of extant conventions and conditions or a total, even narcissistic disregard for either the needs of an audience or a public interest in music. It should not render us unwilling to analyze the implications, both literal and symbolic, of the metaphorical characterizations to which disciplined criticism leads us. And although such an emphasis does question an uncritical reverence for structural autonomy, or even complexity, as self-justifying virtues, it does not deny the importance of trying to understand as fully as possible the ongoing dialectical interaction between stylistic means and choices on the one hand and structural possibilities on the other.

Such an emphasis does require a constant effort to recognize and interpret relationships between the elements of a musical configuration and the history, conventions, technology, social conditions, characteristic patterns, responses, and values of the various cultures involved in that music. And such an effort almost invariably requires a willingness to recognize at least the possibility of some positive value in the kinds of immediate, though often diffuse and fragmented, sense that sound and style have for nearly all musical listeners. This is a recognition that Adorno and even Schoenberg, despite his wistful desire to be liked and even despite various efforts to defend his own intuitions, cannot at bottom permit.[77] In part this is because judgment on grounds of style, without attempts to understand associated particularities of argument, can be abused to justify an unlimited irrationalism in human interaction. Though I dispute the priority of structure in communication, I do not deny the very notion of structure or the value of efforts to give a rational account of the dialectic between medium and structure—if, that is, those efforts are morally as well as intellectually rigorous in the sense of being genuinely self-critical. For otherwise the possibility of another abuse arises, that stylistic biases which are denied rather than confronted smuggle their way into ostensibly rational objections to structural logic. This, too, is a form of irrationalism.

But there is also a second reason for the refusal of Schoenberg and Adorno to assign positive value to the musical medium. A medium, as the very word implies, tends to elude the possession, control, and to some extent even the conscious awareness of any single individual who makes use of it. Thus, valuing the medium of music tends to remove the individual from the center of music. Such a tendency in turn makes clear the vulnerability of music, and music criticism, to a condition of communicative contingency and, even worse for these men, of what I might call moral indeterminacy. And the inability to countenance such moral indeterminacy may be the greatest intellectual weakness of their position.

A willingness to entertain moral indeterminacy in music criticism involves not just a recognition of the incompleteness of any single interpretation, which Adorno, in his exquisite sensitivity to the dynamic character of history, surely has. It also involves acknowledging the possibility of limits on one's own moral certainties.[78] In music criticism

---

[77]Again, although Schoenberg's acknowledgment of the role played by intuition in music is not to be denied, neither is the uneasy relationship of this acknowledgment to his essentially discursive sense of musical value. See above, note 44, especially on the first Chamber Symphony, and note the exertion needed to defend his response to Mahler (pp. 449-60). Schoenberg justifies this response on grounds, such as Mahler's profound originality and his high level of culture, which for him confirm Mahler's structural greatness. See especially his remarks on page 454 concerning Mahler's mode of expression, material, and construction.

[78]See especially in this connection Schoenberg, p. 38, on the reasons for his unpopularity: "... An artist ... knowing that those parts which were found ugly could not be wrong because he would not have written them if he himself had not liked them, and remembering the judgement of some very understanding friends and experts in musical knowledge who have paid tribute to his work, ... becomes aware that he himself is not to blame." See also ibid., p. 218, on the artist's need to be "convinced of the infallibility of [his] own fantasy."

this means acknowledging the potentially positive as well as negative aspects of human experience which enable every listener, culture, and generation to interpret and even to perceive and identify differently the particular elements through which the metaphorical distinction is formulated between something called a "structure" and something called a "style." This means acknowledging the ability of any listener to regard as highlighted "foreground" elements of music that others have dismissed or ignored as inconsequential "background." And it therefore means acknowledging the possibility of legitimate differences in the ultimately moral values that can be ascribed to the same music. It is precisely this eternal indeterminacy that constitutes the post-structuralist concept of "text." (There may even be some cultural significance to the choice of opposing metaphors, in this connection, by Adorno—and, indeed, Schenker—on the one hand, and the post-structuralists on the other: whereas for the former the principal bearer of meaning is the "subcutaneous," not the "surface," layer of a construct, for the latter it is the "foreground," not the background.)

But in any event, it is precisely such indeterminacy that Schoenberg tries to forestall by marking certain musical voices *"Hauptstimme"* and others *"Nebenstimme."* Such a tactic is tellingly futile, for even such explicit stage directions cannot guarantee that the listener will be able, even with strenuous effort, to share the composer's own perception of a structure. The struggle of humans to live together is thoroughly pervaded by honest as well as dishonest differences in the perceptions on which interpretations are built.

The reluctance to acknowledge such indeterminacy characterizes and limits not only Schoenberg and Adorno's concept of structural listening but also the many versions of this concept that focus more narrowly on supposedly "fixed" musical structures. This limits the capacity of current formalistic educational methods to develop a new paradigm for the relationship between musical responsibility and society. As one counterbalance to such limitations, the post-structuralist perspective is surely useful, and it is interesting to note that Roland Barthes has given explicit attention to the reintroduction of affect into both musical listening and performance.[79] And it may well be a recognition of such limitations that has led an increasing number of Western composers in recent years to reject ideals of structural autonomy, and to concentrate

[79]See Barthes, *Responsibility*, pp. 252-60 (on listening) and 269 ff. (on performance); and also Louis Marin, "The 'Aesop' Fable-Animal," in Blonsky, p. 337 and *passim*. Such a rapprochement in the realm of neuorology is a principal theme of Oliver Sacks's book, which concerns itself extensively with music.

instead on a redefinition of the musical medium as replete with connections to many elements in the cultures of the twentieth century.[80]

In concluding, I would like to note a few of the ways in which my
own education in structural listening has convinced me of its limitations. My first second language was Roman numerals. In my college
harmony course, use of the piano was forbidden. Whereas scoreless
listening was unheard of in my university education, soundless keyboards
were fairly common.

As a music major I was required to take a course on Beethoven and
pressured to take the seminar on Bach; only non-majors were advised
to study Italian opera. Performance was never a matter for serious intellectual analysis in my education (except as it pertained to the authenticity of early performance practice). In numerous seminars on early
music I transcribed reams of manuscripts of which I never heard a note
or discussed the musical value. As a music major, and later as a teacher,
listening to scratched and otherwise dreadful monophonic recordings,
I developed a strategy of listening which I have never entirely shaken,
whereby I mentally "correct" for inadequacies of sound or performance
that distract from my structural concentration. These experiences, if
not universally shared by musicologists, are not, I believe, altogether
exceptional.

Yet I am not at all sure that any of this structural discipline has made
me a more competent listener than my brother, who travels eight hours
a week to the opera houses of New York to hum the tunes and listen
to certain sopranos. I'm not even sure that the composers whose works
I teach would necessarily prefer me as a listener.

I have heard it argued that structural listening is beneficial because
it requires repeated listenings to the same work. But even if repeated
listening is considered an unqualified good—in fact it may exact some
cost in terms of a living musical culture—does structural listening real-

---

[80]Compare also the following excerpt from a letter by a contemporary poet, Brooks
Haxton, to *The New York Times Book Review* (January 11, 1987, p. 37): "For various
reasons (including the obscure language of certain influential poets) intelligent, otherwise
literate people seldom look toward poetry for communication of any consequence. . . .
It is an important trend, which limits our access to the poetry of other ages, and thereby
weakens one of our deepest connections to past humanity, weakens our ability to imagine others in the present and, more frighteningly, diminishes our faith in the fullness
of a human future. The loss of such profound resources involves (together with literary
appreciation) the stewardship of all culture and ultimately of the now precarious natural
world."

ly produce the illusion of an ongoing active process of composition? Or does it rather confirm the passivity implicit in Barthes's sense that "'being modern' [is] but the full realization that one cannot begin to write the same works once again'"?[81] To this sad finality that Barthes associates with the analysis of closed "works," he opposes the "pleasure" of enjoying the open-ended "text."[82] And is it the "plot" or the sensuous moment that draws us back again and again to the same music? Are there not ambiguities and dynamics in music of which we structural listeners, as well as ordinary listeners, are in some fundamental sense aware, but to which we alone do not allow ourselves, at least in our professional mode, a full response?[83] And is it not significant that I, today, with all my specialized training, find myself virtually illiterate with respect to the principal musical mediums of my own culture, those of electronic audio and video?

If the Western dialectic of structure and medium is still with us, shouldn't we be trying in the classroom to develop intellectually rigorous ways of analyzing sound and style as well as structure? Is it not possible that encouraging less dependence on the score when we listen, and on ways of perceiving that the score itself suggests, might help us to develop new and richer ways of speaking about music? And might not such an expanded language enhance even our conception of how structure operates, and what it signifies, in music?

In the end, the concept of structural listening, despite the rigorous consistency with which Schoenberg and Adorno sought to define it, is deeply flawed by inconsistencies between what it promises and what it delivers. Designed to protect music as a preserve of individual integrity within society and thereby ultimately to contribute to the betterment of the individual's position within society, this concept in Schoenberg's and Adorno's version begs off its social responsibilities no less than the stylistic snobbishness of Stravinsky's formalism does. Because they make no effort to overcome the cultural narrowness of their own convictions, the distinctions Schoenberg and Adorno draw between "replete structure" and medium can be used to justify the same results that Stravinsky's doctrine encourages: the adherence to a positivistic and socially narrow concept of form by numerous practices of structural listening that fall between the extreme positions represented by these masters.

[81]Roland Barthes, "From Work to Text," in Harari, p. 80.
[82]Ibid.; see also Eagleton on pleasure in academia, p. 212.
[83]See especially in this connection Gregory Sandow, "Secret of the Silver Ticket," *Village Voice*, April 1, 1986, p. 86.

Only some music strives for autonomy. All music has sound and a style. Only some people listen structurally. Everyone has cultural and emotional responses to music. These characteristics and responses are not uniform or immutable but as diverse, unstable, and open-ended as the multitude of contexts in which music defines itself. And yet the world of knowledge opened up to us by acknowledging the bases of this indeterminacy as the foundation for our concept of music is far more encompassing than the domain which the supposedly universal principle of structural listening can hope to control without violating or exceeding itself. For whereas a restriction of knowledge to determinate structures provides no access to crucial aspects of music as it takes part in history and is actually experienced, an admission of those aspects as the starting point of musical knowledge precludes neither a concomitant analysis of structure nor an extension of rational thinking to an ever-greater area of that domain of experience where the significance and value of music are ultimately, and continuously, defined.

All of us who study music are caught in the Western dialectic. To an extent, all of us in the West who study anything are caught in that dialectic. Against the values we can protect by insulating abstract modes of thinking from the contingencies of concrete experience, we have to measure the risk, well symbolized by Schoenberg's paradoxical career, of coarsening through over-refinement our sensitivity to other responsibilities of knowledge. But music offers a special opportunity to learners, for it confronts us always with the actuality of a medium which remains stubbornly resistant to strategies of abstract reduction. In this respect it provides an ideal laboratory for testing the formalistic claims of any knowledge against the limits of history and experience. To ignore such an opportunity is to handicap musical study needlessly, and to consign music itself to a status of social irrelevancy that it does not deserve.

Barbara Herrnstein Smith

Masters and Servants:
Theory in the Literary Academy

The value and status of "theory"—or an assortment of relatively novel projects and practices assembled under that name—is currently an issue of some moment in the American literary academy. The energy that it attracts and generates suggests that something substantial is, or is seen to be, at stake, that the question is not merely, as we say, "academic"—or "theoretical." I will turn, a bit later on, to some aspects of the issue as currently posed. First, however, I would like to develop some quite general observations on theory or, rather, on what I shall be calling here, in a sense to be defined below, "theoretical activity," and also on the dynamics of its institutionalization.

It appears that human beings characteristically, though perhaps some more than others, are afflicted by a chronic cognitive irritability, an anxious need to bring their universe under the control of their intelligence. The desire for such control is understandable, for in making their universe more cognitively tractable, they are often able to make it more tractable in other ways as well: that is, to shape it more to their liking and to subordinate its operations more to their interests and purposes. The will to cognitive mastery, however, seems to exhibit itself even in the absence of any immediate goals or specific purposes: partly, no doubt, because we learn, through our individual life histories, the potential pragmatic power of such mastery, but also, it seems, because of the tendencies and mechanisms conditioned by our evolu-

Barbara Herrnstein Smith is Braxton Craven Professor of Comparative Literature and English at Duke University. Her works in literary theory include Poetic Closure, On the Margins of Discourse, *and* Contingencies of Value *(forthcoming).*

tionary history, particularly our evolution as creatures whose survival
has depended on, among other things, our capacity for symbolization:
that is, our ability and inclination to organize and govern our interactions with our environments through the production and manipulation
of verbal/conceptual constructs. In any case, it is clear that cognitive
mastery may be pursued, as we say, for its own sake, and even addic-
tively, not only without being directed toward the implementation of
particular pragmatic goals—individual or communal—but also with a
measure of personal obsessiveness and social irresponsibility.

   This pursuit is not, of course, confined to what we speak of as "intellectual" or "cerebral" activities, but is implicated in and dispersed
across a broad range—perhaps the entire range—of human behavior.
In speaking here of theoretical activity, however, I will be concerned
with a particular portion of that range or rather specialized form of that
pursuit, the mark of which is its production—that is, articulation, elaboration, analysis, and transformation—of relatively abstract verbal/con-
ceptual constructs: for example, explanatory models, causal ascriptions,
systems of classification, narrative representations, and various other
kinds of schemes, stories, and accounts. These products of theoretical
activity—which, it should be noted, are by no means clearly
distinguishable from the very process of that activity itself—may be
measured along a number of different dimensions. They may, for example, be more or less comprehensive (as opposed to *ad hoc*), more
or less highly articulated and richly elaborated, more or less explicitly
and systematically integrated with other currently available products
of theoretical activity, and more or less readily appropriable by other
people in connection with projects of current interest. The characteristics
of theoretical constructs in these respects are not, as I will discuss shortly,
necessarily a measure of their value—or only value—to those who produce and appropriate them, but they are a measure of what would usually
be seen as their social utility or communal value; and, it appears, they
are also the basis on which we commonly distinguish between, on the
one hand, those relatively fluid, ephemeral, and private (or covert) products of theoretical activity which we call "notions," "ideas," and
"beliefs" and, on the other hand, those relatively stable, publically issued
and institutionally circulated products which we sometimes call
"hypotheses" and "theories" or, when they have been communally
appropriated in relation to a broad range of specific problems and projects over some period of time, "facts" and "laws of nature."

   The products of theoretical activity may also, however, be measured
along other dimensions, including some rather different from those just

catalogued. For example, certainly for some of us and perhaps for all of us some of the time, the interest or value of a verbal/conceptual construct—say a cosmological model, or a system of biological taxonomy, or some historian's narrative of the rise and fall of an ancient Asian empire—may consist not in how well it functions to better articulate some domain of specific intellectual interest to us or in its instrumental utility in relation to some immediate project, but rather in how engaging it is as what we might call a cognitive toy: the extent, for example, to which it invites metaphoric elaboration or provides evocative material either for more or less desultory speculation or for relatively highly focused conceptual and imaginative exploration in relation to a variety of interests—including, perhaps, otherwise peripheral ones. These possibilities by no means exhaust the alternate functions that theoretical constructs may perform. They do suggest, however, that the range of those functions is quite extensive, that they include some that have been traditionally valorized in what we call "works of literature" (for example, poems and novels—which are, of course, also verbal/conceptual constructs) and, accordingly, that contrary to certain commonly drawn distinctions and oppositions, there are fundamental resemblances and perhaps continuities between, on the one hand, the motivation, operation, and gratifications of theoretical activity and, on the other, those of so-called "aesthetic" activity—or, we might say, between cognitive work and cognitive play.[1]

The latter point will be recalled later but, for the moment, I want to consider briefly another general aspect of theory, namely its institutionalization. Like all other forms of potentially productive human activity, theoretical activity may be subjected to the division of labor, lured or pressed into the service of specifically communal interests and purposes, and institutionally housed and organized. To the extent that this occurs, as in the disciplinary sciences or humanistic disciplines, theoretical activity will be constrained (or, precisely, "disciplined") by the operation of various institutionally developed structures and practices: for example, traditions of training, avenues of individual advancement, systems of incentives (which is to say, rewards and punishments), established routes and occasions of publication or performance and hence of public evaluation (or "peer review"), and innumerable routines and standard operating procedures, including more or less hallowed conceptual instruments and methodological practices. In addition to such explicit and acknowledged mechanisms of discipline, the institution will

---

[1] I discuss this concept more fully in *On the Margins of Discourse* (Chicago, 1978), pp. 116-124.

also develop more subtle forms of internal control that ensure that the activities pursued in its name are directed toward the particular communal missions that define the institution and are also directed toward the continued legitimation of its own authority to determine how those missions will be implemented. These include the repeated ceremonial narration of self-heroizing myths of the institution's history,[2] along with the repeated invocation of the spirits of its patron saints and exemplary heroes, whose names, engraved on the institution's gates, greet and inspire its latter-day practitioners every morning and whose portraits, hung on its corridor walls, accompany and chastise their every hour of work.

The conservative—that is, self-stabilizing and self-perpetuating—operation of disciplinary structures and practices is also reinforced by various well-known forces of institutional inertia: immediate convenience, long-standing habit, self-reproducing mechanisms of recruitment and certification, and the occupation of positions of power by persons of established status, linked to each other by networks of personal loyalty and ideological or temperamental affinity, at least some of whom, by virtue of the usual combination of increased vested interests and decreased capacity for personal transformation, will themselves have developed acutely conservative inclinations.

The institutional structures outlined here, and their tendency to operate conservatively, do not make innovative developments in a discipline impossible; nor, indeed, do they prevent the more or less continuous transformation of those structures themselves. If they did, the discipline would, of course, dissolve, since, in spite of some appearances to the contrary, no discipline can survive on inertia alone. If nothing else, it would sooner or later be unable to recruit new generations of productive practitioners or retain them in sufficient numbers to staff even the skeletal machinery of its own self-reproduction. Even more significantly, however (for a minimum number of recruits can perhaps always be shanghaied in various ways), if a discipline failed to transform itself in response to emergent social, cultural, and intellectual conditions, it would sooner or later be unable to perform effectively the broader communal functions that legitimated its existence and "justified" its continued maintenance. As we say, it would lose the "support" of the community—which, from the perspective of the community itself, it would certainly have deserved to lose.

[2]For an interesting discussion of narratives of self-legitimation in Western science (and an analysis of what he sees as their current crisis), see Jean-François Lyotard, *The Postmodern Condition: A Report on Knowledge*, trans. Geoff Bennington and Brian Massumi (Minneapolis, 1984).

Versions of the latter trajectory have, of course, been played out historically by a number of now extinct disciplines or, rather (for total extinction is actually rare), disciplines that have become peripheral to or altogether absorbed by other more intellectually responsive and productive ones. What we see more typically, however, is a history of self-transformation, itself the product not of any teleological propulsion (nor—which amounts to the same—the triumph of the forces of "progress" over the status quo) but, rather, of the more or less continuous interaction between, on the one hand, mechanisms of self-stabilization and self-perpetuation and, on the other hand, a wide variety of what prove to be destabilizing conditions and events. These latter range from the accumulated effect of numerous relatively minor adjustments in standard operating procedures (for example, hiring procedures or curriculum review procedures) made in response to also relatively minor conflicts among, breakdowns in, or external pressures on those procedures, to the uncontrollable—though perhaps not willfully—subversive consequences of the introduction into the discipline of various elements of novelty: for example, the changing character of its own recruits and new practitioners—their social origins, personal histories, prior training and, perhaps, the other institutions and communities to which they happen to have ideological allegiances. One might mention here the relatively recent entry into Anglo-American literary studies of a significant number of foreign—that is European-born and educated—scholars, plus the professional coming of age of a generation whose formative student years coincided with the political activism of the late sixties, whose formal education brought them into contact with contemporary intellectual transformations in other disciplines and who, moreover, were raised in a culture that was in many respects significantly different from that of their senior colleagues.

The outline of the dynamics of institutional transformation traced above suggests that when, in response to various emergent conditions, both internal and external, the practices and projects pursued in the name (and under the roof) of a particular discipline take especially innovative forms and move in what appear to be acutely subversive directions, and also when, as may happen, those activities are especially exercised by the very structures of the institution itself, then we may expect the forces of institutional conservatism to react aggressively to oppose and contain them.

This seems to be the case at present in the Anglo-American literary academy. (I would note, however, that, because the general dynamics just described prevail wherever theoretical activity is institutionalized and also because the emergent conditions that are relevant here have international scope, the situation I will be discussing no doubt has its European counterparts as well.) Specifically, it appears from the chatter in faculty clubs across America and from professorial contributions to the columns of the *Times Literary Supplement* and other journals, that certain relatively novel forms of theoretical activity in the literary academy are now widely seen as forces of treachery, channels of heresy, and agents of transgression and dissolution. That the transformative energies of literary theory have been cast in so specifically *satanic* a role is, I think, a measure of the strength of a lingering conception of the academy as a quasi-religious institution, and, at the same time, a measure of the extent to which the structures that support that particular conception are threatened and may indeed be crumbling.

What I refer to here may be called for convenience the Arnoldian/ humanist view of literary studies, in accord with which the defining communal mission of the academy is to preserve and honor a set of canonical texts, to make audible to the laity the profoundly instructive interior monologues which those texts speak and, through the exercise of the spirits of the young in encounters with those texts, to fortify them against the counter-humanistic forces of commerce, utilitarianism, relativism, and the barbarities of the mass media. (There are, needless to say, other less pious and confined ways to conceive of the communal functions of the literary academy, including its central role in the transmission of cultural competence.)[3] In any case, to those who conceive of the mission of literary studies along the lines just outlined, it seems obvious that there is only one legitimate—and, indeed, only one conceivable—function for literary theory, namely to implement that mission: specifically, to resanctify the canon, to sharpen the instruments of its exegesis, and to validate their own authority and the traditional practices in which that authority is made visible. The latter somewhat

---

[3]There are also, as I have detailed elsewhere (see "Contingencies of Value," *Critical Inquiry* 10 [1983]: 1-35) other traditions and ideologies besides Arnoldian humanism that have shaped the Anglo-American literary academy, most notably those of positivistic philology. Although the two traditions are in many ways mutually incompatible and the history of the academy has been marked by their struggles with each other for centrality, they have also achieved mutual accommodations—shared missions, distributions of territory, etc.—and now, especially since the foundations of the characteristic claims of positivism are being threatened by theoretical activity in the philosophy and sociology of science, are united in a common front against what is seen as the larger menace of "theory." It must also be added, however (for the plotline of intellectual history is never simple), that some of the energy, along with the classic ideology, of positivism has itself been engaged by a variety of theoretical projects—particularly, though not exclusively, those associated with structuralism and semiotics.

self-regarding aspect of this view of the role of literary theory is obscured by the characteristic language of self-abnegation that attends it; for, in accord with the Arnoldian/humanist conception of literary studies, to profess literature is to *serve* it: to minister to it, to be the mediator of its messages and vice-regent of its authority. It seems to be the conviction of selflessness among those who share this conception of literary studies that gives the familiar sanctimonious note to the efforts of the academy to control the consequences of its own theoretical projects. As I have already suggested, however, there are specific reasons why, given the general dynamics described earlier, those projects should now be the focus of so much antagonism and anxiety.

Before considering those reasons, I want to insert a few brief terminological remarks. The term "theory" is currently used with extraordinary inconsistency in the literary academy, both by those who associate themselves with it and those alienated by it. In some quarters of the academy, for example, it still primarily evokes—and is claimed by— an array of quasi-scientific projects: the construction of schemes, maps, models, taxonomies, grammars, and so forth, featuring diagrams with algebraic tables and vector arrows, and the technical language of various exotic disciplines. This is not the occasion to question the assumptions and claims of such projects but it may be noted in passing that, to the Arnoldian humanist, all of them are seen as bafflingly remote from the classical projects (or "proper business") of literary studies; and they *are,* of course, quite remote from the professional interests and intellectual competence of the humanistically trained scholar himself or herself. In other quarters of the academy, the term "theory" is narrowly equated with "critical theory," itself narrowly equated with a particular set of presumptively normative projects focused on the practices of what has come to be called "practical criticism"—that is, the close analysis and fine-grained interpretation of canonical texts in the classrooms and journals of the academy. And, to complicate the picture even further, "practical criticism" itself is often referred to as "theory," especially when it is seen as informed (or contaminated) by the concerns and conceptual instruments of contemporary—particularly continental—philosophy, and/or when it is practiced by Marxists, Freudians, feminists, and others with egregiously extra-curricular ideas on their minds.

Although much of this terminological disorder could be laid to hapless or militant ignorance (plus a measure of willful obfuscation), it would be pointless to call for a "clarification" of terms, much less etymological fidelity, logical precision, or any other supposed propriety of usage. For one thing, as already suggested here, the process and products of "theory" can always be seen as continuous along some dimension with any of the classic candidates that might be offered, for purposes of putatively precise definition or demarcation, as essentially distinct from or opposed to them: such as "fact" or "art" or, indeed, such as "criticism" or "practice." Also, by whatever label, the pursuits and projects that could be seen as exemplifying what I am calling here "theoretical activity" are always heterogeneous and asynchronic (that is, mutually "out of phase"), any apparent convergence or continuity among them or integration of their products being itself the product of institutionally contingent and otherwise local conditions and, at best, only temporarily stable. Indeed, it is clear that the current divergences of usage in the literary academy with respect to the term "theory" reflect a situation in which the institutional structures that would otherwise tend to standardize terminology are themselves in a state of unusual instability.

It is this situation that gives particular political force (that is, academic-political force) to that broad and high-flying anti-theoretical banner under which a group of neo-pragmatist theorists are currently pressing their critiques of a quite particular set of claims, notions, and practices currently exhibited on the literary scene.[4] For, given the conditions of embattlement noted earlier and the conditions of terminological diversity just traced, it is no surprise that any parade mounted under the colors of "Against Theory" will attract harrahs from a sizeable portion of the bystanders, many of whom will not pause to read the fine print. I would add here that, in view of the inevitable heterogeneity of theoretical activity in any discipline and also the variety of projects that, at present, bear that label in the literary academy, it would be as absurd to be "against" theory *per se* as to endorse all theories.

We may return now, however, to where I left off earlier, that is, to the observation that there are specific reasons why so much anxious self-reflection in literary studies is now attended by an antagonism toward "theory." To begin with, the various activities just mentioned have produced disruptions that are unquestionably radical: they have involved, at the least, a thoroughgoing skeptical scrutiny of the discipline's fundamental conceptual structures and instruments and also its most characteristic practices, objectives, and claims. One thinks immediately, of course, of the potential and, in some places, actual havoc wrought in such a classic project as "the establishment of an author's original

[4]See Stephen Knapp and Walter Benn Michaels, "Against Theory," *Critical Inquiry* 8 (1982): 723-742 [also reprinted in the volume cited below]; Richard Rorty, "Criticism without Theory," in *Against Theory*, ed. W.J.T. Mitchell (Chicago, 1985); Stanley Fish, "Consequences," and Richard Rorty, "Philosophy without Principles," both in *Critical Inquiry* 11 (1985): 433-458 and 459-465.

meaning" as each of these once taken-for-granted concepts—that is, "author," "meaning," "origin," and, indeed, "establishment"—has been subjected to theoretical analysis, as has also the syntax of their traditional discursive and conceptual manipulations: an analysis, moreover, that has not readily permitted their subsequent rehabilitation on slightly shifted ground. Even more fundamentally, however, at least in relation to the integrity of the discipline, the excursions of theory have threatened to undermine its self-defining claim to a specific domain of studies. Or, rather, what is now increasingly apparent is the signal failure of theory to underwrite that claim in spite of efforts devoted to that end over the past seventy-five years. For it has become clear that, although the term "literature" has idiomatic viability in a number of contexts of usage, those contexts have been historically mutable and are now irreducibly various, that there is no essential trait or quality, formal or functional, that marks the "literariness" of a text, and that there is therefore no particular self-evident set of texts that can be, or ever could be, assembled under that label and profitably explored as such.

Not only have the contents and structure of the traditional academic canon been substantially unsettled, but the very process of canon-formation has been subjected to revisionary account, an account that, among other things, undermines the traditional assumption of the location of canonical value in the immanent properties of certain texts and displaces it with a focus on the value-creating powers of the academy itself. Moreover, largely as the result of theoretical activity elsewhere but imported into literary study, the provinces of such related terms as "text" and "writing" have expanded monstrously, so that while it appears that nothing in particular falls within the domain of literary study naturally or inevitably, it also appears that just about everything in the universe falls within it potentially.

One consequence of these current scrutinies and novel accounts is that the domain of literary studies has been radically destabilized, its borders open to traffic to and from all directions: most obviously, perhaps, to and from other disciplines, among them linguistics, philosophy, folklore, and sociology—and also, as the borders of those disciplines have themselves dissolved (as the consequence of comparable theoretical activity within them), various newly emergent, hybrid and, to the Arnoldian humanist, barbarous or barbarous-sounding disciplines, such as ethnomethodology, communications, and semiotics. Thus professors of literature are distressed or appalled to observe some of their colleagues not only entering strange temples and returning from them with strange gods and ceremonies, but also inclined to perform their customary duties with non-canonical instruments and upon non-canonical objects: not merely upon such noble if still profane texts as works of history, philosophy, and science, but also upon such utterly taboo objects as popular and ephemeral writings, the verbal productions of children and other illiterates, and what is typically referred to as "pure trash."

Recent literary theory has not only thus opened the domain of the discipline to multiple transgression; it has also shown signs of altering or refusing to respect the master-servant relation that has traditionally been thought of as properly governing its practices. I observed earlier that theoretical activity could be seen generally as an aspect of our effort to make our universe more cognitively tractable. This characterization has particular significance for literary study, for it suggests, among other things, that the practice of theory is, in two fundamental respects, at cross-purposes with the mission of literary studies as conceived by Arnoldian humanism, and particularly with the latter's conception of the professorial role as one of service and submission. First, it suggests that the theorist (whose activities may, of course, be directed toward individual texts—often enough canonical ones—and may also issue in interpretive commentary as well as other kinds of analyses and accounts) characteristically seeks not to serve the object of study, but to master it, and to master it precisely in the sense of bringing it under his or her own cognitive control. And second, it suggests that the interests and purposes served by literary theory need not be, and inevitably will not be, confined to the specific custodial, exegetical, or pedagogic practices of the literary academy, but extend to other interests and purposes, indeed to *any* whatsoever: individual or communal, institutional or extracurricular, including not only what are seen as "practical" interests and purposes but also further *theoretical* ones.

We may recall here the familiar invocation of formulas to the effect that theory must "prove" or "justify" itself with respect to "practice." Since the literary humanist conceives of "practice" in this formula exclusively in terms of his or her own traditional practices within the literary academy, the pursuit by theory of any alternate ends—that is, extracurricular purposes (for example, explicitly political ones) or further theoretical interests (for example, broader questions of cultural theory or even more abstract questions of, say, epistemology)—will be found perplexing or, as it is said, "irrelevant" or "hermetic." And when—or to the extent that—the theorist's activities in pursuit of such alternate ends do issue in commentary on individual canonical texts, the humanist is likely to regard the failure of that commentary to exhibit the customary postures of service and submission to those texts as a mark of arrogance, an attempted displacement by "theory" of the specifically textual authority of "literature."

The setting aside or reversal of the traditional master-servant relation between the literary work and the literary commentary has been the occasion for perhaps the most energetic expressions of outrage directed at what are seen as the excesses of contemporary theory. Thus, in some recently published remarks, George Steiner writes as follows:

> I regard as pretentious absurdity current claims for the equivalence in importance or specific gravity of text and commentary. The existential-temporal dependence of the latter upon the former is not only a matter of elementary logic, but of moral perception.[5]

Earlier in the same piece, Steiner had written that, in his own critical and pedagogic practices, he seeks

> to bring to bear on the... text the "speculative instruments" (Coleridge) [sic] of linguistics, of philology, of hermeneutics ... The result is ... an *explication de texte* ... always and explicitly "at the service of" the poetic-creative act.

In a similar vein, Murray Krieger, in an essay titled "Literary Criticism: A Primary or Secondary Act?," writes as follows:

> The critics' instinct for arrogance is compelling enough without being encouraged by the suggestion that they need have no other motive, that their own work need never bow to the superior authority of a text proclaimed as primary by its every word ....
>   The conflict that the Anglo-American critical tradition still wages with the many dominant influences of continental "poststructuralism" has perhaps its most significant consequences ... in this question of the theoretical subservience of criticism to the elite literary text.[6]

As this passage suggests, Krieger's essay begs the question its title poses and also begs every other question presumably at issue. Most obviously, of course, it begs the question of the primacy of the elite text by making that primacy a matter of textual self-proclamation: absolute, immanent, and thus unquestionable. It also begs the question of whether

[5]George Steiner, contribution to "Literary Theory in the University: A Survey," *New Literary History* 14 (1983), p. 445.
[6]Murray Krieger, *Arts on the Level: The Fall of the Elite Object* (Knoxville, 1981), pp. 42-43.

the authority allegedly proclaimed by the elite text is of the same *kind* as that apparently claimed or proclaimed by the commentary, and thus whether the whole notion of a *competition* for primacy is a genuine issue at all. Most interestingly here, however, even if one grants that a particular commentary, by virtue of the functions it seems to perform, is comparable to—and in that sense competitive with—the literary text on which it comments, Krieger begs the question of whether the former cannot, in fact, ever match or even exceed the authority of the latter in those respects—or, to adopt Steiner's phrase here, whether a commentary cannot ever be comparable to a literary text in "importance and specific gravity." For it is difficult to see what in the nature of things (or in "elementary logic") could prevent that from ever occurring; and should it occur (which it surely sometimes does: one thinks of Plato's commentary on Homer in *The Republic*, or Aristotle's commentary on Greek drama in the *Poetics*, or Wordsworth's commentary on his own "lyrical ballads"), then, in Krieger's own terms, the commentary *is* an "elite text."

The remarks just quoted, and others of similar import and flavor published in recent years, suggest that the display of and demand for postures of subservience in literary studies are a matter of neither elementary nor advanced logic, but of something closer to what Steiner calls "moral perception": that is, they are institutional pieties. The sanctions that evoke the repeated affirmation of these particular pieties, however, are quite powerful, and appear to operate not only upon those whose antagonism toward theory is explicit, but also upon those who regard themselves as theorists or whose work is clearly informed by the products of theoretical activity. Their power reveals itself, for example, in the tendency of theoretical critics to perform last-minute rescues—salvaging and "savings"—of the texts that have engaged their otherwise irreverent attention. It also reveals itself in their related tendency to ascribe certain forms of agency and potency to those texts: the capacity for ideological self-criticism, for example, or for "self-deconstruction," which—at least in some of its usages—is not altogether different from that capacity for self-proclaiming self-authorization that Krieger ascribes to elite texts.[7] In all these ascriptions, the theoretical critic cedes ultimate power and authority to the literary text, making

[7] I allude here to, among others, Terry Eagleton (see his *Criticism and Ideology* [London, 1976]) and J. Hillis Miller (see esp. his "The Critic as Host," in *Deconstruction and Criticism*, ed. Harold Bloom *et al* [New York, 1979], p. 252, where, noting "the possibly self-subversive meanings" that deconstruction identifies in a given work, Miller also observes that "as a mode of criticism," deconstruction "attempts to resist its own tendencies to come to rest in some sense of mastery over the work.")

himself or herself once again its minister rather than, as it might have seemed, its master. Both tendencies appear to reflect the critic's internalization of institutional sanctions, an inhibition that repeatedly makes him or her stop short of what is intuitively sensed as an irreversibly transgressive—or, in effect, self-excommunicating—move.

A further point should, however, be added here. Krieger's conviction of the self-proclaiming primacy of canonical texts or, more generally, the conviction, widely shared by other members of the literary academy, of the self-evident disparity of value between works of literature and works of literary theory or criticism, is no doubt sincere: to say that it is a piety is not to say that it is an empty one. Indeed, it may be suspected that such convictions draw force—including rhetorical force—not only from a tradition at least two and a half thousand years old of valorizing literature over theory (or "poetry" over "philosophy," "history," and "science"), but also from what must be, for many—perhaps most—professors and students of literature, an undeniable fact of personal experience, reinforced daily in their professional lives: that is, the enormous disparity of *pleasure* afforded them by their engagement with canonical works of literature as compared with works of theory. This disparity of pleasure is understandable, given both the conceptual novelty and discursive rigor of much contemporary theory and also the nature of the academic training, personal histories and perhaps intellectual temperaments of many—or, again, perhaps most—of those who profess and study literature. It may be suspected, however, that the pleasure of the text here is not—for it never is—a simple one and that, along with whatever elements of more or less specifically "aesthetic" (or sensory/perceptual) excitements and gratifications it involves, it must, often enough, involve both the kinds of pleasurable engagement referred to earlier as "cognitive play" (which, as was noted, can also be occasioned by the verbal/conceptual constructs articulated in works of "theory"—for example, philosophy, history, and science) and also the kind of pleasure that can be produced—perhaps *especially* for professors and students of literature—by the sense of having grappled successfully with the elusive structural principles of a text, of having located it in some generic or historical series, and of having subdued its play of meanings to a stable and coherent unity: by the sense, in short, of *cognitive mastery*. The latter pleasure, then, is not, it appears, altogether alien or unwelcome to the votary servants of elite texts or altogether irrelevant to the motivations and gratifications of their own most characteristic engagements with those texts.

The latter point is bemusing and could be pursued further, but I want

to return now to some further general observations on theoretical activity and its institutionalization. As I suggested a bit earlier, there is
no self-evident principle, moral or logical, that puts literary theory—
or theory of any kind—at the service of any set of specific practices;
and, in fact, the products of theoretical activity can and do serve whatever
interests are at hand or come to hand. This is not to say, however, that
theoretical activity can be (or should be) pursued altogether without constraints. For one thing, the notion of an altogether unconstrained activity of any kind can hardly be entertained. Moreover, theoretical activity is rarely pursued without institutional constraints and never without,
at least, *social* constraints of some kind. For theorists, no matter how
solitary their pursuits or self-absorbed their interests, always operate
as social beings in two fundamental respects: first, in that the language
or symbolic mode of their conceptualizations, both its lexicon and
syntax—that is, the tokens, chains, routes, and networks of their conceptual moves—have necessarily been acquired and shaped, like that
of any other language, through their social interactions and through their
interactions, throughout their lives, with a socially mediated universe.
Second, in the very process of articulating and elaborating their
hypotheses, models, or constructs, they will be continuously testing and
evaluating the "rightness" or "adequacy" of their constructs in relation to their possible appropriation by some community: for the possibility of that appropriation will inevitably be part of the motive and reward
of the theorist's own activities. Due note may be taken here of the fact
that the "community" in question may consist of the theorist himself
or herself—which is to say, the *set* or, in effect, "society" of selves
(some of them quite demanding) constituted by the theorist in his or
her own alternate and subsequent roles and guises. In either case,
however (and they are not, of course, mutually exclusive), the process
and products of theoretical activity are continuously energized and shaped
by general social constraints as well as what may be specific institutional constraints. It may be added here that the effective operation of
the kinds of institutional constraints outlined earlier is by no means to
be regretted, for they are often theoretically productive—that is, productive *for* theory: motivating its energies, structuring its products, providing it with proximate goals as well as ultimate missions and, accordingly, both with ongoing measure of relevance and value and also with
occasions for local closure and provisional stability.

A further point may be noted here with regard to the always complex relation of theory to practice, namely that even where literary theory
does not "serve" the specific institutional practices of "practical

criticism,'' it will nevertheless inevitably interact with them and thereby have consequences—including quite "practical" ones—for those, and other, practices of the literary academy. To mention but one among innumerable examples, it is clear that the recent development of richer models of literary production has been of considerable significance for the contemporary generation and revision of "literary history" and that, even though such models may have been designed without reference to the specific projects of practical criticism, they have nevertheless figured centrally in the growing emergence of a neo-historicist trend in literary interpretation. Also, and more generally, it may be observed that, to the extent that theoretical activity orients the academy toward more intellectually responsive and productive projects, it thereby, by virtue of the potential instrumental power of cognitive mastery, orients it toward more *pragmatically*—for example, pedagogically and politically—responsive and productive projects as well. The consequences of feminist theory in this regard are, I think, especially notable.

Perhaps the major source of the value of theoretical activity to the literary academy, however, lies precisely in its addictive, compulsive will to cognitive mastery "for its own sake" and its consequent irrepressible drift toward institutional vagrancy. For it is thus—through its socially irresponsible intellectual adventurism, its nose for news, its irritation at conceptual and discursive incoherences, its impatience with disciplinary border patrols and rough disdain for such professional virtues as modesty, deference, and local patriotism—that it operates to subvert institutional structures and throw standard operating procedures off course (which is to say, off the course otherwise determined by institutional inertia) and thereby operates as a vehicle for the discipline's capacity for adaptive self-transformation or, as we say, its "vitality."

It must be acknowledged, of course, that neither everything currently named "theory" nor what I have specifically described as the will to cognitive mastery is inherently counter-establishment. For cognitive mastery, like any other type, seeks to maintain itself in power; and that very irritability at incoherence which, under one set of conditions, operates as a force for innovation and institutional subversion may also, when those conditions change, operate as a self-confirming, self-preserving, and distinctly conservative mechanism. As noted earlier, the difference between a theory and a fact may be largely a matter of how widely and over how long a period of time it has been appropriated; and, as is commonly observed in other terms, just as yesterday's challenging new approach is today's standard operating procedure, so also yesterday's disruptive theory is today's orthodoxy. Nevertheless, when approaches become mechanical and conceptual structures become dogmatic, what displaces them is not unreflective practice or submissive service but, of course, newly emergent theory.

One must also, however, be wary of reinscribing the value of theoretical activity in terms of an always benign service to its own institutional or disciplinary sponsors. None of us, including those who practice theory themselves, can determine in advance the nature and distributions of its ultimate profits: this, in part, is what distinguishes it from other more routine and calculable activities. Nor, of course, can we predict or limit in advance how disruptive its products will prove to be, or for whom. Theory is unquestionably a risky business: any institution or discipline that succeeded in banishing it altogether would condemn its own projects to repetitiveness, triviality, and inertness; but there is always the chance that it will—along the way, as it were—just happen to overturn the whole show.

This brings me to my concluding remarks, which consist of a brief speculative prediction. It is, I think, entirely possible that at some time in the future the discipline of literary studies—if it is, even now, a single discipline or ever has been one—will be effectively and undeniably undone: undone not in accord with the recipe for death by self-stultification outlined earlier, nor as a consequence of such more or less spectral threats as the shortsightedness of university administrators, the low motives of students, or the seduction and stupefaction of the entire culture by the mass media, but, indeed, as a consequence of the transformative energies of its own theoretical activities, including the radical implications of those activities in their role as mediator to the literary academy of more or less radical intellectual, cultural, and social transformations occurring outside its walls. Given both the power of institutional inertia and the no doubt continuing interest of the community at large in securing the academy's social services, particularly its services in transmitting textual competence to the children of the culturally dominant and economically ascending classes, I doubt that this will occur in the very near future—or at least I doubt that departments of English will soon disappear from the academies of Anglophone nations. But the kind of undoing I have in mind here—and it is, to a large extent, already underway—is not, in any case, an altogether entropic event; it is, rather, in Shakespeare's figure, an "interchange of state": "increasing store with loss and loss with store." Specifically, it seems likely that the "store" of literary studies (that is, the accumulated conceptual structures and technical practices of the discipline) will be appropriated by other now current disciplines, that it will thereby transform and be

MASTERS AND SERVANTS: THEORY IN THE LITERARY ACADEMY   139

transformed by them, and that it will also participate in the formation of a variety of newly emergent disciplines. In which case, I think it also likely that, in that process of interchange and transformation, much that we now call "literary theory" will be seen as having operated neither as the diabolic agent of an ultimate disintegration nor as the name or hope of any salvaging re-synthesis but, rather, as the most fertile site of an interim destiny.[8]

[8]An earlier version of this essay was delivered January 9, 1985 at a symposium on contemporary American literature, criticism and theory at the University of Würzburg, West Germany and appears, along with other papers of the symposium, in a volume entitled (relatively irrelevantly with respect to the concerns of this essay) *Making Sense: The Role of the Reader in Contemporary Fiction*, ed. Gerhard Hoffmann (München: forthcoming).

Burton S. Rosner

Music Perception, Music Theory, and Psychology

INTRODUCTION

Music theory and psychology jointly mold the study of the perception of music. My purpose here is to examine how they do so. I dedicate this essay to my friend and colleague, Leonard B. Meyer, whose widespread influence has strengthened the bond between these two disciplines.

Music theory often explicitly discusses listeners' perceptions. Theorists talk about the organization and general properties of the auditory experiences that music awakens. Psychologists in turn aim at specifying the mechanisms responsible for those experiences. Some of these mechanisms may be nonspecific, applying to all hearing. Auditory processes for localizing sounds in space are an example. Other mechanisms may operate under more restricted conditions. Some might even be confined exclusively to the perception of music. In all these cases, the psychologist can make an obvious argument: music theory may provide a topographical map of one particular (and often very appealing) region of our perceptual world; psychology, however, investigates the causes of that region's contours. Under this mode of relationship between music theory and psychology, the latter discipline would explain the former. The term ''explain,'' however, will need some examination.

This first mode apparently grants that the music theorist validly characterizes listeners' actual experiences. Furthermore, the psychologist may interpret conceptions from music theory in perceptual terms, even when the music theorist does not. One can ask in either event whether

Burton S. Rosner is Visiting Professor in Psychology at the University of Oxford. He is the author of numerous papers on perception.

music perception actually proceeds as claimed or suggested. Psychologists have developed experimental techniques for answering such questions. These methods can test the validity of proposals originating from music theory about the perception of music. Such tests define the second mode of relationship between psychology and music theory. This mode is another instance of investigating the ''psychological reality'' of mental structures which disciplines outside psychology may suggest. Many psychological experiments on music perception are of this genre. Positive results from this enterprise have obvious consequences. Proposals about perception arising from music theory are justified. This gives the psychologist some *bona fide* phenomena of music perception to explain. The consequences of negative results, however, are more complicated. I will return to this issue below.

So far, psychology seems to buttress music theory by ''explaining'' or ''evaluating'' it. But a third mode of relationship between the two disciplines runs in the opposite direction. Psychology may build music-theoretic concepts into its own theoretical edifice. For example, psychologists have adopted the notion of melodic contour as an explanatory device. Modern psychological theory is much concerned with ''mental structures.'' It sometimes freely imports suggested structures from other disciplines. Music theory is a potentially rich source of such suggestions and may thereby influence psychology considerably. Under this influence psychology may ultimately become more general and powerful—or perhaps more complicated and domain-specific.

Let us now examine selected examples of the three different modes of interaction between the two fields. The examples should bring out the implications for each discipline of the three different modes of interaction.

PSYCHOLOGY AS EXPLANATORY OF MUSIC THEORY

The Origins of Consonance

Helmholtz entitled his great work (1863) on hearing, *Die Lehre von den Tonempfindungen als physiologische Grundlage für die Theorie der Musik* (The Study of the Sensations of Tone as a Physiological Basis for the Theory of Music). Although this title promised a physiological treatise, Helmholtz's data were in fact mainly psychological. By the time of the book's publication, physiologists among others had been conducting psychological experiments. Experimental psychology had yet to become an independent discipline, with proper academic trappings of departments, journals, and societies. Helmholtz reported his own rich and ingenious program of psychological experiments. When he considered the ear, however, he could draw only on gross anatomical observations and on a few newly available microscopic studies. Microscopic examination of the ear (and the brain) was just developing in that period. Systematic physiological experiments on the ear were still decades away.

Helmholtz's main concerns included both establishing the role of upper harmonics in music perception and explaining their effects in terms of the action of the ear. The former is a psychological problem, the latter a physiological one. Helmholtz's treatment of the musical consonance or dissonance of two simultaneous notes affords a particularly revealing instance of his approach. He first drew his readers' attention to a well-known fact: two simultaneously sounded pure sinusoidal tones close together in frequency produce the perceptual effect designated "beats." Figure 1 depicts the *physical* result of adding two such pure tones. The tone in the top row on the left has a frequency of 15 Hz. The one in the middle row has both a lower frequency (12 Hz) and a lower amplitude. Each tone is represented as a function of time. To the right of each is its spectrum. This shows amplitude as a function of frequency. Each of the two spectra contains only a single line whose height indicates the amplitude of the tone. (The spectrum of a complex sound would have a line for each harmonic.) The bottom left part of figure 1 gives the result of adding the 12 and 15 Hz tones algebraically. The dashed lines trace the envelope of the combined waveform. Such a combined waveform *psychologically* produces beats. This is a percept whose loudness waxes and wanes. The *beat frequency* is the rate of fluctuation of loudness. It equals the frequency difference between the two tones. Beats are most noticeable when the two tones have equal amplitudes. (In actuality, both tones in the figure are below the audible frequency range. Therefore neither would be heard nor would their combination.)

Helmholtz pointed out, as had other observers, that beats have a rough, unpleasant attribute. Suppose we listen to two simultaneous pure tones who frequencies f^1 and f^2 are very close. We gradually increase their difference in frequency, keeping constant their average frequency $(f^1 + f^2)/2$. We would hear beats of increasing frequency and roughness. Roughness would become greatest at some particular frequency difference $f^2 - f^1$. Increasing that difference further would gradually weaken the beats and finally eliminate them. If we now raise the average fre-

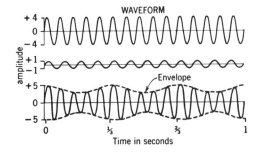 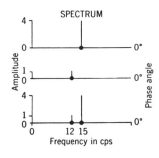

Figure 1. Left-hand panels: a 15-Hz sine wave, a 12-Herz sine wave, and their sum. Right-hand panels: Spectrum of the 15-Hz sinusoid, spectrum of the 12-Hz sinusoid, and spectrum of the summated sinusoids. From J.C.R. Licklider, "Basic Correlates of the Auditory Stimulus," *Handbook of Experimental Psychology,* ed. Stanley S. Stevens (New York, 1951), p. 988.

quency $(f^1 + f^2)/2$ and repeat our observations, the frequency difference producing the roughest beats may increase somewhat. Generally, frequency differences of around 25 to 50 Hz give the strongest beats; differences above some 100 to 125 Hz yield weak, irregular beats, if any.

Helmholtz identified dissonance with the presence of beats. He argued that the fundamentals of two musical notes separated by one to three semitones would generally produce beats. This accounted for the dissonance of chords in low or middle registers that include such intervals as a second. (A more complicated explanation involving combination tones was necessary for dissonances in upper registers. The frequency spacing there for one semitone may be several hundred Hz.)

The dissonance of large intervals such as a seventh would seem to challenge this theory. The fundamental frequencies simply are too far apart to generate beats. Helmholtz argued that dissonance over large intervals occurs because the *higher* harmonics of notes played by musical instruments produce beats. For two simultaneously sounded, consonant notes, the higher harmonics have either identical or well separated frequencies. In contrast, for two simultaneous dissonant notes spanning a large interval, some of their higher harmonics are close enough in frequency to produce beats. For example, compare two notes separated in just intonation by a fifth with two separated by a seventh. Let each note have six harmonics, including its fundamental. For the first pair, suppose that the fundamentals are 400 and 600 Hz. The two set of harmonics will be (400, 800, 1200, 1600, 2000, 2400) and (600, 1200, 1800, 2400, 3000, 3600) Hz respectively. All are easily audible. The third and sixth harmonics of the first set (1200, 2400) coincide with the second and fourth harmonics of the second set. Otherwise, no two harmonics in the combined set are closer than 200 Hz. But now play the first note with its fundamental of 400 Hz against another whose fundamental is 750 Hz. a seventh higher. The harmonic set for the latter will be (750, 1500, 2250, 3000, 3750, 4500) Hz. The 750 Hz fundamental is only 50 Hz away from the 800 Hz second harmonic of the partner note. These 750 and 800 Hz components will produce 50 beats per second. With this argument, Helmholtz could identify dissonance completely with the presence of audible beats. Their absence would produce consonance.

But why do we hear beats in the first place? To answer this question, Helmholtz invoked the properties of the ear, in effect contrasting it with an ideal frequency analyzer. When presented with the waveform at the bottom left of figure 1, an ideal analyzer would produce just two outputs. They would show respectively the amplitudes of the 15 and 12 Hz sinusoids illustrated in the top two panels of the figure. No output would occur at the difference frequency (3 Hz) of those sinusoids. On the bottom right of figure 1, the spectrum for the combined waveform demonstrates precisely this point: no line appears at 3 Hz. An ideal frequency analyzer therefore would never suffer from beats. Therefore, if the auditory system behaved in this way, we would never hear beats. A 750 Hz and an 800 Hz sine wave sounded together would yield a percept that simply added the subjective effects associated with hearing each tone individually. No additional sensory attribute would arise, apparently fluctuating 50 times per second. As Helmholtz realized, the phenomenon of beats necessarily implies imperfect frequency analysis by the auditory system. Beats are *not* in the acoustic wave itself, contrary to naive belief. Rather, beats reflect the response of the auditory system to certain acoustic waveforms. Helmholtz tried to explain that response in terms of specific properties of the inner ear. Those properties would cause it to fail as a perfect frequency analyzer.

Helmholtz's argument therefore "explains" in two steps how the intrinsic nature of the human listener creates a particular perceptual property of music. First, a *psychological* effect (beats) is offered to account for a musical phenomenon (dissonance between simultaneous notes). Second, a theory (in this case, biological) is proposed to explain the psychological effect. The first step treats the musical phenomenon as *a special case of a more general psychological effect.* The force of the second step depends on the power of the theory applied to that effect. Helmholtz realized that factors other than beats underlay many other musical effects categorized under consonance and dissonance. He was a gifted amateur musician and knew both the history and the theory of Western music.

More than a century has passed since Helmholtz published his treatment of dissonance. The current status of this problem is worth some attention. Plomp has summarized recent investigations of the dissonance of two pure tones.[1] He and Steeneken presented subjects with pairs of simultaneous sinusoids.[2] Within a presentation, the frequency of one tone was kept constant at f^1; the subject adjusted the frequency f^2 of the other tone so as to produce maximal roughness. The frequency f^1 was varied across presentations. Figure 2 shows the results. The horizontal axis is the average frequency $(f^1 + f^2)/2$ of a pair of stimuli after adjustment of f^2. The vertical axis is the frequency difference $(f^2 - f^1)$. The data (filled circles) show that in higher registers, maximal roughness requires larger frequency differences between the two tones. In a separate, somewhat earlier experiment, Plomp and Levelt had asked subjects to rate simultaneous pairs of tones on a seven-point scale of consonance.[3] Some pairs of tones had the same average frequency. Their difference in frequency was varied. As that difference moved away from a small value, the ratings of consonance dropped steadily, reached a minimum, and then increased. The open circles in figure 2 give the frequency differences evoking the lowest ratings of consonance for tone pairs whose average frequencies were 125, 250, 500, 1000, and 2000 Hz. The open triangles come from a similar study by Kameoka and Kuriyagawa on Japanese subjects.[4] The agreement between the three sets of findings shows that maximal dissonance tracks maximal roughness. Therefore, perceptual roughness is one (but not necessarily the *only*) basis for the experience of dissonance. Notice the large frequency differences, however, for maximal roughness of tone pairs whose average frequency exceeds 2000 Hz. These differences seem too large to produce beats. Roughness and beats therefore may not involve identical mechanisms.

These findings help to place some musical phenomena of consonance

[1]Reinier Plomp, *Aspects of Tone Sensation* (New York, 1976), pp. 68-74; fig. 2 derives from p. 69.
[2]Reinier Plomp and H.J.M. Steeneken, "Interference Between Two Simple Tones," *Journal of the Acoustical Society of America* 43 (1968): 883-884.
[3]Reinier Plomp and W.J.M. Levelt, "Tonal Consonance and the Critical Bandwidth," *Journal of the Acoustical Society of America* 38 (1965): 548-560.
[4]Akio Kameoka and Mamoru Kuriyagawa, "Consonance Theory Part I: Consonance of Dyads," *Journal of the Acoustical Society of America* 45 (1969): 1451-1459.

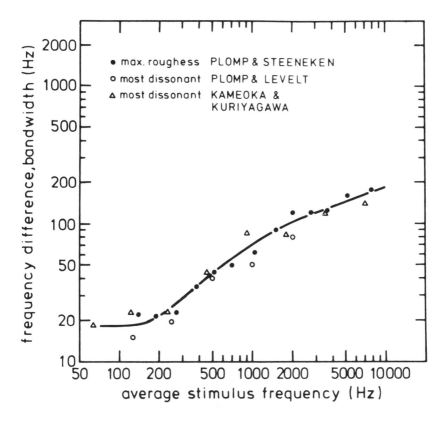

Figure 2. Frequency difference between two simultaneous sine waves which gives maximum roughness (filled circles) and maximum dissonance (open circles and triangles) as a function of average frequency of the two sinusoids. Modified from Plomp (1976).

and dissonance into more general psychological categories such as "roughness." But efforts to explain the roughness in terms of auditory mechanisms have not kept pace. Current views of the auditory system treat it as a set of filters tuned to various limited frequency ranges. Plomp noted that the findings in figure 2 did not exactly fit the prevailing version of those views. Subsuming dissonance under roughness apparently offered no further insights into dissonance itself. Further experiments on the properties of auditory filters, however, have appeared since Plomp's summary in 1976. The results have modified our ideas about auditory filtering. These changes may produce a new analysis of roughness and therefore of dissonance as consequences of fundamental properties of the auditory system.

Affect and Music

A second, rather different example of psychological explanations of musical phenomena is Leonard Meyer's own *Emotion and Meaning in Music*.[5] Meyer drew on two lines of psychological thought. The first sprang from theories of emotion, particularly that of Paulhan,[6] who had argued that affect arises when a psychological tendency is inhibited. Unblocking of the tendency allows its fulfillment and causes affective release. This argument gave Meyer a framework within which to treat music. He proposed that music activates tendencies, which he designated "expectations." Intrinsic affect arises because music then inhibits or frustrates those expectations. In due course it fulfills or resolves them, producing affective relief. Meyer next considered how expectations are formed. To answer this question, he exploited a second line of psychological thought, Gestalt psychology. Gestalt psychologists such as Koffka had argued that general mental laws of selection and organization determine our perception of all stimuli, including music.[7] These laws essentially favor maximal simplicity and continuity. Temporary violations of the laws would frustrate natural expectations and arouse affect. Reinstatement of the expected course of events would produce affective relief. Meyer also argued, however, that cultural and experiential influences together with Gestalt laws contribute to the formation of musical expectations.

An analysis of the "Liebestod" from Wagner's *Tristan und Isolde* illustrates Meyer's approach. Example 1 displays his analysis of the vocal line, which rises from A-flat in measure 1 through B-flat and C to C-sharp in measure 4. According to Gestalt views, good continuation would push this rising line beyond D-flat (in parentheses) in measure 5. After the actual D-natural in that measure, however, the ascending line is broken. This frustrates the expectation of a continuing rise and thereby arouses affect. Two upward skips in measure 7 finally lead back to the main rising line of the expected E-flat, F, G-flat, and (at last) A-flat in measure 8. This reinstatement and successful conclusion of the rising line in measure 7 and 8 discharges the previously aroused affect.

Meyer's theory once again treats aspects of musical experience under

---

[5]Leonard B. Meyer, *Emotion and Meaning in Music* (Chicago,1956); the example is from p. 98.
[6]Frédéric Paulhan, *The Laws of Feeling,* trans. C.K. Ogden (New York, 1930).
[7]Kurt Koffka, *Principles of Gestalt Psychology* (New York, 1935).

Example 1. Meyer's analysis of the vocal line of mm. 1-8 of Wagner's "Liebestod" from *Tristan und Isolde*. Note particularly the delay in the rising line at m. 5 and restoration of the line in m. 8.

more general psychological categories, this time in the areas of emotion and of perception. We must, however, consider the intellectual power of those categories. Let us turn first to affect. Since Paulhan's time, the psychology of emotion has developed slowly. More is now known about the conditions that evoke emotional responses and about the nature of the responses themselves. The few extant theories of emotion, however, do not offer many new insights. They largely try to explain how particular sets of momentary conditions produce particular emotional states. Among these theories is Schachter and Singer's. It is worth a small detour.[8]

Schachter and Singer propose that two main processes determine particular emotional states. The first is general arousal. The second is cognitive evaluation of the prevailing situation, based at least partly on past experience. According to their theory, a person interprets his general arousal, including such symptoms as a pounding heart and rapid breathing, in light of the circumstances that he faces and his knowledge about them. If the situation involves, say, an angry, clearly stronger opponent, the subjective result is fear. If it involves news of having won a rich lottery, a quite different subjective result, elation, accompanies the same symptoms of arousal. Well before Schachter and Singer, however, Meyer had argued that specific factors in past and present circumstances give particular emotional content to the generalized affect which music arouses. So far as I can tell, Schachter and Singer never read *Emotion and Meaning in Music*.

Coming next to Gestalt theory, two problems arise. First, its "laws" describe tendencies, so far unquantified, arising in stimulus situations

[8]Stanley Schachter and Jerome E. Singer, "Cognitive, Social, and Physiological Determinants of Emotional State," *Psychological Review* 69 (1962): 379-399.

which are not precisely characterized. Without appropriate specification of stimulus conditions and quantification of the resulting psychological processes, applications of the laws have often been *post hoc*. This looseness even allowed Meyer to invoke cultural and stylistic processes as major determinants of expectations, a position which Gestalt psychologists might have deprecated. The second problem with Gestalt psychology is that no current theories of perception try to explain why its laws should work. Some members of the Gestalt school attempted this through claims about the physiology of the cerebral cortex—claims which are now discredited.

The examples reviewed above do not support the strong position that psychology promises shortly to "explain" music theory, at least in any deep sense of the term "explain." A more modest view, however, is defensible. Psychology can subsume various aspects of music theory into broader categories. Insofar as psychology provides sytematic treatments of those categories, the music theorist can avail himself of a wider analytic framework than he might otherwise possess. This framework should integrate his concerns with observations and concepts which reach beyond music itself. If psychology should gain more searching insights into those observations and concepts, music theory would reap some of the benefits.

PSYCHOLOGICAL EXPERIMENTS AS EVALUATIONS OF MUSIC THEORY

The second mode of relationship between psychology and music theory revolves around psychological experiments designed to "test" music theory's import for perception. Music theorists may assume or assert that a listener's perceptions conform to their analyses. This claim is not always made, nor need it be. But music theory has long been concerned with the rules and conditions that determine what listeners perceive (or *should* perceive) when they hear music. Even when music theorists do not explicitly consider perception, the psychologist may still draw implications about the listener's experiences from their work.

Within the bounds of music theory itself, convincing tests of proposals about perception can become difficult. Acceptance or rejection of particular claims may turn on personal opinions. Polemics multiply in such soil. Furthermore, when the psychologist finds potential consequences for perception in a music-theoretic analysis, he tries to formulate appropriate empirical tests. In either case, psychology offers experimental procedures for assessing the validity, or "psychological reali-ty," of music theory's implications for perception. These techniques minimize the influence of personal opinion on the part of experimenter or theorist.

The psychological literature, however, contains some reports of ex-periments based on naive ideas about music and music theory. The stimuli (often composed by the experimenter) have been musically trivial or irrelevant. Happily, such naiveté has lessened in the last few decades. Psychologists working in the area have educated themselves about music theory, leading them to use stimuli which are relevant to music-theoretic assertions. Along with greater sophistication about music, a second development has enabled psychologists to conduct fruitful experiments on music perception. Multidimensional scaling techniques allow in-vestigators to work rigorously with complex stimulus materials.[9] These methods require that subjects merely rate pairs of stimuli for similarity. Multidimensional scaling places the stimuli in a geometric (Euclidean) space which reproduces the relationships among the ratings as com-pactly as possible. The number of stimuli used limits the number of meaningful dimensions in the space. Within this limit, the experimenter can select various numbers of dimensions; two to four are the usual choices. Dimensions are extracted in decreasing order of importance. The configuration of stimuli in the resulting psychological space often permits inferences about the main factors determining the judgments. With appropriate selection of stimuli, multidimensional scaling also offers a way to test hypotheses about perception. (Schiffmann et al. offer a good introduction to the entire methodology.)[10]

Musical Pitch and Harmony

Krumhansl's study on musical pitch is an excellent example of multi-dimensional scaling experiments.[11] The stimuli were the chromatic notes betwen C^4 and C^5 inclusive (C^4=middle C). The subjects heard all 156 possible ordered pairs of these 13 notes, played with the flute stop on an electric organ. For each pair, subjects rated the similarity of the first

[9]Roger N. Shepard, "The Analysis of Proximities: Multidimensional Scaling with an Unknown Distance Function," *Psychometrika* 27 (1962): 125-140 and 219-246.

[10]Susan Schiffman, M.L. Reynolds, and F.W. Young, *Introduction to Multidimensional Scaling* (New York, 1981).

[11]Carol L. Krumhansl, "The Psychological Representation of Musical Pitch in a Tonal Context," *Cognitive Psychology* 11(1979): 346-374; the left half of fig. 3 comes from p. 356; the right, from p. 357.

Table 1
Average Similarity Ratings for Pairs of Tones
(From Krumhansl, 1979)

	C	C#	D	D#	E	F	F#	G	G#	A	A#	B
C#	4.18											
D	5.66	3.68										
D#	3.47	3.76	3.92									
E	5.76	3.40	5.36	4.10								
F	4.70	3.38	4.10	3.62	4.85							
F#	3.10	3.44	3.82	3.82	3.83	3.86						
G	5.46	2.76	4.42	3.62	4.33	5.08	4.42					
G#	3.12	3.64	2.88	3.58	3.82	3.70	4.00	4.25				
A	4.22	2.92	3.86	2.99	4.12	4.49	3.84	5.24	4.27			
A#	2.98	3.01	3.08	3.54	3.06	3.72	3.66	3.82	3.74	4.22		
B	3.98	2.60	4.08	2.84	3.95	3.14	3.48	4.84	3.58	4.88	4.28	
C'	5.59	2.72	3.72	2.89	4.86	4.18	2.82	5.59	3.82	5.12	3.72	6.26

to the second note, using a seven-point scale. A rating of 1 was designated "Very Dissimilar," and a rating of 7 "Very Similar." On each trial, subjects heard a set of "context tones" immediately before the pair of notes to be rated. The context tones were intended to establish a C major tonal center. One context was simply the C major triad C^4, E^4, G^4, and C^5 played simultaneously. The other two contexts were respectively an ascending and descending C major scale. By design, all ten subjects had at least a certain amount of formal musical training. Table 1 is the matrix of similarity ratings averaged over subjects, contexts, and the two orders of presentation of each pair of test notes. Only the lower half of the matrix is shown; the upper half is symmetrical to it. These ratings underwent multidimensional scaling. For a two-dimensional space, the procedure yielded the configuration in figure 3a. In a three-dimensional space, the result became like the configuration in figure 3b.

The array in figure 3a looks like that of figure 3b viewed from above. The tones of the major triad fall on a tight arc, with the third, E, closest to the tonic, C. The other diatonic notes lie on another, larger arc, located farther from the vertex of the conical structure of figure 3b. In both diagrams, the subdominant F is clearly much farther psychologically from C than is the dominant G. In judgments of pitch made without any musical context, the opposite is true.[12] Finally, both solutions in figure 3 place the four chromatic notes farthest from the arc containing the major triad. Without a musical context, as previous experiments had shown, the frequency difference between two tones determines their psychological distance. Context-free judgments of pitch would place C-sharp, for example, much nearer to C than are any of the diatonic notes. Krumhansl's introduction of a musical context therefore markedly affects the perception of pitch relationships. Judgments now meet music theory's specificaton of the diatonic major scale with the major triad as the scale's backbone.

Effects of frequency difference do appear in figure 3. Notice that D, for example, is closer to C than is F. But frequency differences alone cannot explain all the relationships embodied in the figure. Furthermore, related notes lie on arcs rather than on some other type of geometric locus. Circles and their component arcs are familiar to music theorists.

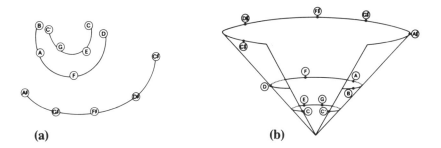

(a)   **(b)**

Figure 3. (a) Two-dimensional psychological configuration for judgments of similarity of tones within a C major context. Spatial array obtained by multi-dimensional scaling. (b) Idealized three-dimensional configuration for the same data. From Krumhansl (1979).

[12]See S.S. Stevens and J. Volkmann, "The Relation of Pitch to Frequency," *American Journal of Psychology* 53 (1940): 329-353; and Fred Attneave and Richard K. Olson, "Pitch as a Medium: A New Approach to Psychophysical Scaling," *American Journal of Psychology* 84 (1971): 147-166.

One could argue that figure 3 simply reproduces the contents of table 1 in geometric form. For example, B and C' comprise the highest rated pair and should be closest spatially as, indeed, they are in figure 3a. But C and C' received the same similarity rating (5.59) as C' and G. Yet G is closer to C' than is C in figure 4a. A third dimension therefore becomes necessary to represent the full details of table 1. Introduction of this dimension makes B and C', despite their higher rating, more distant than G and C'. This results from the *complete* structure of the ratings in the table. Geometric representations of perceived similarities therefore can reveal relationships which are hidden in a table of ratings. Multidimensional scaling does not merely summarize ratings. It can un-cover perceptual relationships which do not come through in the data themselves.

In a more recent experiment, Krumhansl et al. studied judgments of thirteen different triadic chords belonging to the keys of C major, G major, and A minor.[13] All possible root positions for each key were used. One chord, the A minor triad, belongs to all three keys; six others, such as the G major triad, belong to only two keys; the remaining six belong to just one key. On each trial, subjects first heard "context notes." These comprised an ascending scale, covering an octave, in one of the three keys. A pair of chords came thereafter. Subjects had to rate how well the second chord followed the first, given the preceding contextual scale. The chords were produced on a computer; each had fifteen sinusoidal components, providing a rich harmonic structure. The context notes came from the triangle wave output of a signal generator. They had a less complex harmonic structure.

Krumhansl et al. undertook various analyses of their data. The first one showed significant correlations across keys between the ratings of pairs of analogous chords. For example, the pair I-VI in C major received much the same rating as the pair I-VI in A minor. Krumhansl et al. applied multidimensional scaling to the ratings combined across analogous pairs of chords. A two-dimensional configuration (fig. 4a) accounted for much of the data. The tonic, dominant, and subdomi-nant triads bunch together in the center of the space. The chords with the other four roots are scattered peripherally. Another procedure, hierar-chical clustering, was also used on the data. This method produces a

[13]Carol L. Krumhansl, Jamshed J. Bharucha, and Edward J. Kessler, "Perceived Har-monic Structure of Chords in Three Related Musical Keys," *Journal of Experimental Psychology: Human Perception and Performance* 8 (1982): 24-36; fig. 4 comes from p. 32.

hierarchical tree structure.[14] Only a few nodes in the tree dominate close-ly related stimuli. The path between more distantly related stimuli must traverse a larger number of nodes. The tree which Krumhansl et al. found for the triadic chords (see fig. 4b) has a surprisingly regular struc-ture. Chords I and V are most closely akin, then IV joins them, then VI, and so forth. Both representations in figure 4 reproduce relation-ships important in the theory of harmony.

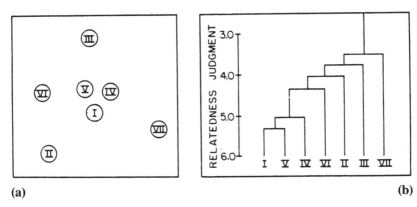

(a)   (b)

Figure 4. (a)Multidimensional scaling configuration for seven analogous chords in context keys of C major, G major, and A minor. (b) Hierarchical cluster-ing tree for the same data. From Krumhansl et al. (1982).

Comparison of figures 3 and 4 reveal some striking differences. As Krumhansl et al. point out, the first, third, and fifth scale tones cluster together most closely (fig. 3). Chords I, V, and IV, however, are the three nearest neighbors (fig. 4). The dominant plays a similar role in the two experiments. The subdominant is quite differently related to the tonic in the two cases. The mediant also has different psychological loci in the scale and the triadic root spaces. On the diatonic scale, the mediant is the tonic's closest psychological neighbor. This is a joint effect of musical relationships and of frequency difference in determining closeness of pitch. The influence of frequency difference, however, prac-tically vanishes in the domain of chords. Here, III is further from I than is, say, VI. Indeed, after VII, III is next farthest from I in the hierarchical clustering tree. Finally, the psychological distribution of scale tones follows circular paths. That of chords does not. This difference rein-forces the theoretical distinction between horizontal and vertical aspects of music.

[14]Stephen C. Johnson, "Hierarchical Clustering Schemes," *Psychometrika* 32 (1967): 241-254.

The findings in figure 4 lead back to the problem of consonance discussed earlier. According to the traditional classification by music theory, consonant chords contain only consonant intervals.[15] All triads and their inversions, except the diminished and augmented triads, meet this criterion. The exceptions are treated as dissonant. Krumhansl et al. had four dissonant triads in their study: B diminished, F-sharp diminished, G-sharp diminished, and C augmented. B diminished is VII in C major and II in A minor; the other two diminished chords are VII in G major and A minor respectively, whereas C augmented is III in A minor. So all the VII chords are dissonant. Precisely these chords lie in the rightmost region of the multidimensional space in figure 5a. They also are the last additions to the hierarchical structure in figure 4b. As was stated above, significant correlations appeared between judgments of pairs of *analogous* chords across the three scale contexts. Unfortunately, Krumhansl et al. do not say whether different ratings occurred when a pair in one scale contained a dissonant chord (e.g., II-IV in A minor) while the analogous pair in another scale (e.g., II-IV in C major) did not.

Melodic Processes

Recent work by Leonard Meyer and myself offers a final example of experimental psychological tests of proposals about perception drawn from music theory. In *Explaining Music* Meyer developed the concept of melodic process.[16] A melodic process describes the principal motions by which a melody leaves its main starting point and finally attains a point of resolution. At present, the concept applies only to Western tonal music, which seems to use a mere handful of processes. Meyer analyzed several of these devices and their variants. He argued that melodic processes are frameworks which organize the perception of music. Some initial tests of this position encouraged us to do a series of further experiments.[17]

The first three experiments followed the same basic plan. For each one, we chose six fully instrumented musical passages exemplifying

[15]*Harvard Dictionary of Music,* 2nd ed., s.v. "Consonance, Dissonance."

[16]Leonard B. Meyer, *Explaining Music* (Chicago, 1973), pp. 88-105.

[17]See Burton Rosner and Leonard B. Meyer, "Melodic Processes and the Perception of Music," in *The Psychology of Music,* ed. Diana Deutsch (New York, 1982), pp. 317-344; idem, "The Perceptual Roles of Melodic Process, Contour, and Form," *Music Perception* 4 (1986): 1-49; ex. 2 comes from p. 3; fig. 5 from p. 7; ex. 3 from p. 9; ex. 4, p. 3 (Haydn) and p. 19 (Beethoven, Handel).

one melodic process and six instantiating another. The excerpts were about four to ten measures long. Each was melodically complete, going from a clear beginning to a point of closure at its end. The selections came mainly from the Classical period. They included orchestral, operatic, and chamber works.

The subjects in each experiment heard all 132 possible pairs of the twelve stimuli. They rated each pair on a nine-point scale of dissimilarity, where "one" meant very similar and "nine" meant very dissimilar. Subjects were instructed to base their judgments entirely on the melodies of the stimuli, discounting other parameters such as tempo, dynamics, instrumentation, and texture. The data were analyzed by multidimensional scaling and hierarchical clustering.

In the first experiment, six melodies followed a changing-note process and the other six were linear. A changing-note melody (ex. 2) centers initially on the tonic, steps up to the second degree or down to the seventh degree, then down to the seventh or up to the second,

Example 2. (a) Melody from Mozart's Piano Quartet, K. 478, I, mm. 1-8. Changing-note process shown in lower staff. (b) Melody from Hadyn's String Quartet, op. 50 no. 6, III, m. 33 to m. 40. Linear processes indicated in lower staff. From Rosner and Meyer (1986).

and finally back to the tonic. In contrast, a linear melody may rise and descend in seconds and thirds. This pattern recurs one or more times before closure is achieved. Other linear melodies may move down then up, or purely upwards or purely downwards, in seconds or thirds. The melody in example 2b illustrates linearity on two different hierarchical levels. Two low-level descending patterns are marked "1" in the lower staff. A higher-level descending motion from A to G (marked "2") drops to F-sharp in the next phrase (not illustrated).

Table 2
Repertory of Excerpts for Melodic-Process Experiment
(From Rosner & Meyer, in press)

Code	Excerpt
	Changing-note melodies
2CN1	Mozart: Piano Sonata, K. 282, II, mm. 1-4
2CN2	Mozart: Fantasy, K. 397, mm. 12-15
2CN3	Beethoven: Piano Sonata, op. 10 no. 1, I, mm. 1-8
2CN4	Mozart: Symphony no. 39, K. 543, III, mm. 45-63
2CN5	Mozart: Piano Quartet, K. 478, I, mm. 1-8
2CN6	Haydn: Symphony no. 46, II, mm. 1-4
	Linear melodies
2LI1	Mozart: String Quartet, K. 428, IV, mm. 1-8
2LI2	Mozart: Symphony no. 41, K. 551, III, mm. 60-67
2LI3	Haydn: Symphony no. 104, IV, mm. 3-10
2LI4	Mozart: Symphony no. 35, K. 385, III, mm. 25-32
2LI5	Beethoven: Symphony no. 2, op. 36, III, mm. 85-92
2LI6	Haydn: String Quartet, op. 50 no. 6, III, mm. 33-40

Table 2 lists the passages used in this experiment. Figure 5a shows the results of two-dimensional multidimensional scaling. The dendrogram from hierarchical clustering appears in figure 5b. Linear melodies are coded "2LI" and changing-note selections are coded "2CN." (The initial "2" in these codes signifies a two-part form.) On the whole, both types of data analysis segregated excerpts according to their underlying melodic processes. In figure 5a, the linear melodies form a group in the central and right-hand regions of the space. The changing-note melodies lie to the left of this more central group. Separation of the examples of the two processes, however, is not perfect. Passage 2CN1 falls amidst the linear group, while 2LI4 verges toward the changing-note excerpts. Figure 5b confirms all these observations. Two changing-note clusters form below the third highest level of the tree. They are [2CN3 and 2CN5] and [2CN2, 2CN6, 2CN4, with (the deviant) 2LI4]. Linear clusters formed below this level are [2LI6, 2LI5, with (the deviant) 2CN1] and [2LI1, 2LI3, and 2LI2].

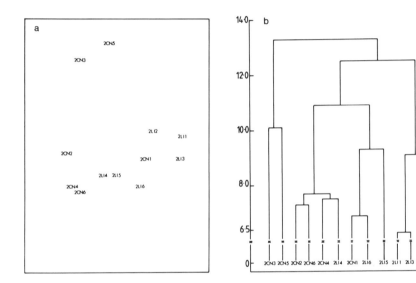

Figure 5. (a) Two-dimensional multidimensional scaling configuration for judgments of melodic similarity on six changing-note and six linear passages listed in Table 2. (b) Hierarchical clustering dendrogram for the same data. Scale at left indicates separation distance, normalized for number of subjects, at which clustering occurs. From Rosner and Meyer (1986).

Examination of the scores of various excerpts revealed plausible reasons for the behavior of stimuli 2CN1 and 2LI4. The melodic lines of those two selections appear in example 3. Passage 2CN1 was the only changing-note melody with upbeats. Its nearest neighbors 2LI2, 2LI5, and 2LI6 in figure 5 also had this feature. No other linear melody did. The changing-note pattern of 2CN1 also begins on the second beat of the first full measure (level 1). A higher-level linear motion (level 2) runs from the opening D to E-flat in measure 2 and continues on beyond the end of the example. These two factors give a briefly rising then falling contour to each half of 2CN1. Two up-down motions also mark stimuli 2LI5 and 2LI6, along with 2LI4. The deviant linear melody, 2LI4, shares with its neighbor 2CN6 a particular initial rhythmic structure (♩.♪♩ ≈ ♩.♪♪). This rhythm is embedded in a contour which rises and then falls.

Example 3. (a) Melody from Mozart's Piano Sonata, K. 282, II, mm. 1-4 (excerpt 2CN1 in Table 2). Analysis in lower staff indicates high-level linear motion (level 2) superimposed on changing-note pattern (level 1). (b) Melody from Mozart's Symphony no. 35, K. 385, III, mm. 25-32 (excerpt 2LI4 in Table 2). Analysis shows two rising and falling linear parts. From Rosner and Meyer (1986).

On the second, vertical dimension of figure 5a, excerpts 2CN4, 2CN6, and 2LI6 (see ex. 2b) are counterpoised against 2CN3 and 2CN5 (see ex. 2a). After discounting the influence of melodic process, no evidence of this dimension appears in the dendrogram in figure 5b. Inspection of the scores suggested that low-level aspects of contour had determined the second dimension of the configuration in figure 5a. Passages 2CN4, 2CN6, and 2LI6 have prominent scale structures. An upward followed by a downward movement occurs in each half of the AA′ form. Excerpts 2CN3 and 2CN5, however, begin with a downward movement which reverses with dramatic upward skips.

In another experiment, the difference between gap-fill and "Adeste Fideles" types of processes also influenced judgments of melodic similarity. A gap-fill melody (ex. 4a) starts with an early skip, usually upwards, of a fourth or more. It then returns in a step-wise fashion to a point of closure. The music in example 4a actually has two such processes. The main one (level 1) skips from E up to C and reaches closure at the end of the excerpt. Meanwhile, a subordinate process (level 2) skips from A to F and steps back to A. An "Adeste Fideles" melody (ex. 4b) behaves like the Christmas carol after which it is named. It always contains two characteristic skips. The first skip covers a fourth; the next spans a fifth. Usually, the initial half of the melody contains both skips. The second skip sets off an upward motion to the third or fourth of the scale, followed finally by downward resolution.

Multidimensional scaling and hierarchical clustering were applied to the ratings of melodic dissimilarity for gap-fill and "Adeste Fideles" excerpts. Both analyses placed the "Adeste Fideles" melodies in a compact group. The gap-fill melodies scattered around this group in the multidimensional scaling space. Two gap-fill passages, however, fell near the "Adeste Fideles" region. They also quickly joined the "Adeste Fideles" selections in the hierarchical clustering dendrogram. Low-level properties of contour, such as relatively late gaps and a prominent turn just before closure, explained the fate of those two gap-fill stimuli.

In yet another experiment we varied melodic form, using gap-fill passages exclusively. Six excerpts had a two-part and six a three-part form. Multidimensional scaling separated passages by form. This segregation, however, occurred primarily along the second dimension of the psychological space. Rhythmic differences seemed to determine the more important first dimension. We then varied process and form independently. Six gap-fill and six "Adeste Fideles" excerpts were chosen. Within each group, three passages had a two-part and three had a three-part form. Multidimensional scaling and hierarchical clustering pulled apart melodies based on different processes but uncovered no influence of form. In general, our results suggest that process, contour, and form control the perception of melody in a roughly but not strictly descending order of importance.

The Significance of Negative Results

One of our five experiments, however, clashed severely with our predictions. This experiment deserves more extensive discussion. We used

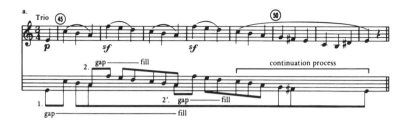

Example 4. (a) Melody from Beethoven's Piano Sonata op. 12 no. 3, III, mm. 45-52. Principal (level 1) and secondary (level 2) gap-fill processes shown in lower staff. (b) Melody from Handel's Flute Sonata op. 1 no. 5, V (Menuet), mm. 1-4. Adeste Fideles process indicated in lower staff. (c) Melody from Haydn's String Quartet op. 55 no. 3, I, mm. 1-8. Complementary process shown in lower staff. From Rosner and Meyer (1986).

six changing-note (ex. 2b) and six complementary melodies. In a complementary melody (see ex. 4c) the first part of the passage establishes a model. The second half replies with a complementary inversion of the model. Subjects rated the 132 possible pairs of melodies for dissimilarity. Neither multidimensional scaling nor hierarchical clustering gave any convincing evidence that melodic process had influenced the ratings. Instead, small subgroups emerged from the analyses. Each contained two to four melodies. The subgroups seemed organized around various simple properties of contour, such as an initially descending motion or early upward triadic skips.

Our findings on complementary and changing-note melodies lead back to a question posed earlier: what should we do when a psychological experiment *fails* to uphold a hypothesis from music theory about perception? One possible reaction is to blame the outcome on poor methodology or inadequate selection of stimuli. The methods in our experiment that failed, however, worked well in four other experiments. And our musical stimuli were chosen on straightforward theoretical grounds. So the first possible defense breaks down here. A second type of stratagem blames the subjects. They may have been too unsophisticated for the task at hand. Musical training and listening experience assuredly may influence the findings from experiments on the perception of music. Just this possibility led Krumhansl and others to select subjects who had some degree of formal musical training.[18] (Repeating those experiments with less sophisticated subjects would be worthwhile.) In all our experiments, however, Meyer and I recruited subjects without regard to training. Many subjects served in two or more of our experiments, including the one that failed. Furthermore, Meyer had argued in *Explaining Music* that melodic processes are cultural patterns absorbed through experience. Apparently, our sort of subject had nicely internalized the linear, changing-note, gap-fill, and "Adeste Fideles" frameworks without explicit training. Why then did our listeners disappoint us in one particular experiment which involved complementary and changing-note passages?

Quite a different approach is possible to an experiment which fails to support a hypothesis about music perception. This approach invokes general factors which inherently limit any subject's performance. In our case, for example, sensitivity to a complementary process places a burden on memory. The listener must detect a relationship of inversion between two halves of a melody. To do this, he may need to remember more detail than for the identification of other types of processes. The limitations of human memory may interfere with this requirement. This type of argument does not attribute an experimental failure to subjects' naiveté. Instead, the failure is seen as a consequence of finite human capacities which training could never improve. Ultimately, however, this position concedes that a wrong hypothesis inspired

---

[18]Krumhansl, "Psychological Representation," pp. 346-374; Krumhansl, Bharucha, and Kessler, "Perceived Harmonic Structure," pp. 24-36.

the experiment in the first place. Assertions which come from music theory about perception must concern human mental life and not that of superior creatures.

Before finally accepting that limited cognitive capacities explain a particular experimental failure, however, the investigator must try to overcome inadequate performance through appropriate training or through changes in the task. In our case, we cannot yet conclude that listeners are unable to exploit the distinction between complementary and other types of melodic processes. Our current evidence is insufficient for this purpose.

In some future instances, adequate empirical evidence might ultimately fail to support claims drawn from music theory about factors controlling music perception. Even highly sophisticated listeners might yield negative results. The psychologist then would explain the failure as due to irreversible limitations on human mental processes. Psychology would no longer care about those aspects of music theory which had generated the unsupportable position. In at least this sense, psychology may fail to support (and hence subsume) music theory. This should not cause alarm. The music theorist need not straightaway abandon the offending portions of his discipline. Parts of music theory which fail in characterizing perception may still serve quite different purposes, such as historical or stylistic analyses. The experimental psychologist has no license to decide *in toto* the form and content of music theory.

Reprise

Let me summarize the main features of psychological "evaluation" of music theory. The psychologist starts from some proposal about perception which music theory offers or inspires. He tries to design and execute experiments to test this proposal, using musically relevant stimuli. Systematic selection of subjects may be necessary. Appropriate experiments may yield positive results, as has happened with increasing frequency in recent years. Experimental findings, however, may contradict a particular hypothesis about music perception. Such an outcome is subject to various interpretations. Sometimes the interpretations can explain away the results. In other instances this effort may ultimately collapse. The music theorist, however, need not desert any analysis that psychological experimentation fails to support. He must only give up any attempt to represent human perception within that analysis. When music theory disclaims any relevance to perception, it should rightly go its own way. Psychology can be safely left to play with its own toys.

MUSIC THEORY AS A SOURCE OF MENTAL STRUCTURES

We come now to the third and last mode of relationship between music theory and psychology. Music theory may provide categories or theoretical concepts which enrich psychology. Over the last twenty years, psychologists have paid increasing attention to "mental structures." These are theoretical devices which attempt to embody the organization of human perception and knowledge. Psychology uses these devices to predict how subjects will deal with various types of stimuli under different experimental conditions.

Disciplines outside psychology itself may suggest mental structures. Linguistics has been a particularly prominent contributor. Recently, music theory has begun to play a similar role. Successful experimental tests of music-theoretic implications about perception may change psychological theory. The psychologist may integrate the relevant conceptions from music theory into his own field. He may even adopt ideas of great intuitive appeal from music theory, without any initial formal test. An example is Dowling's two-factor theory of music perception, which builds on music theory's concepts of scale and contour.[19] Sloboda has written an excellent review of contributions from music theory to psychology. In particular, he compares the relationships of linguistics and of music theory to psychology.[20]

Psychology's appropriation of mental structures originating from music theory raises two questions. First, do mental structures that operate in different domains, such as language or music, have common formal properties? If so, what is the significance of this fact? Second, how does the human perceiver coordinate the various mental structures that operate within a particular domain?

Music and Color

The possible significance of common formal properties is best addressed by examining particular cases. Some mental structures that derive

---

[19]W. Jay Dowling, "Scale and Contour: Two Components of a Theory of Memory for Melodies," *Psychological Review* 85 (1978): 341-354.
[20]John A. Sloboda, *The Musical Mind* (Oxford, 1985), pp. 11-66.

from music theory have the formal geometric property of circularity. Shepard has presented three-dimensional representations of musical pitch that include both its perceived circularity due to the octave and the well-known circular relationship among successive fifths.[21] The domain of color vision also has spawned representations that have circular properties. Shepard arrived at one such "color circle" (fig. 6) by multidimensional scaling of ratings of similarity on pairs of lights differing

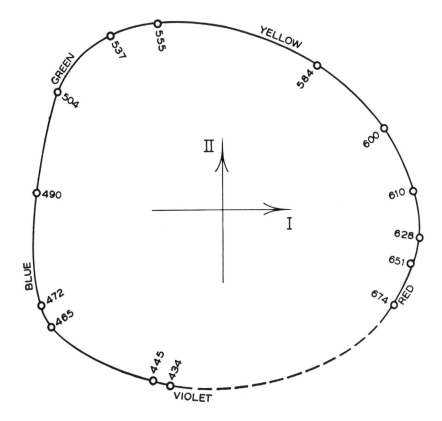

Figure 6. Two-dimensional configuration obtained from multidimensional scaling of Ekman's (1954) data on judged similarities of hues of visual stimuli differing in wavelength. Wave lengths appear inside, hue names outside the configuration. The axis labelled I accounts for the largest possible fraction of the variance. The axis labelled II accounts for the next largest possible fraction of the variance. From Shepard (1962).

[21]Roger N. Shepard, "Structural Representations of Musical Pitch," in *The Psychology of Music*, ed. Diana Deutsch (New York, 1982), pp. 344-390.

in wavelength.[22] The physical wavelengths (in nanometers) are inside the circle. The names of some corresponding perceived hues are on the outside. The dashed lines indicate that the color circle is not complete, unlike the pitch circle or the circle of fifths.

Does mere coincidence underlie this common property of (near-)circularity in mental structures for music and vision? Or has that property some deeper meaning? Possible relationships between pitch and color have exercised theorists for centuries. Many arguments have centered on attempts to link particular colors directly to particular pitches or keys. *The Oxford Companion to Music* gives a good review of the entire problem.[23] Cuddy has recently opened up a new and interesting path in this area.[24] She started from the fact that properly proportioned mixtures of two wavelengths that lie opposite one another on the color circle produce a neutral, gray hue. Mixtures of adjacent wavelengths on the color circle yield intermediate, desaturated hues. Cuddy next obtained some evidence that three successive, different notes which belong to a single major triad establish a strong tonal center perceptually. If the three notes were drawn from the major triads of two adjacent keys on the circle of fifths, the tonal center was weaker (read "desaturated"). Triads drawn from keys *diametrically opposite* on the circle of fifths hardly established any tonal center (read "neutral gray"). These sorts of results suggest an attractive general proposal: mental structures which share formal mathematical properties yield predictable, analogous interactions among corresponding constituents. If this proposal is correct, psychological theory should gain in abstractness and in power.

Tree Structures

The lure of this promise, however, must be tempered by careful theoretical analysis. Tree structures present a telling case of the need for caution. Some tree structures originally entered psychology from linguistics. The latter discipline had used them to represent the structure of a sentence. Figure 7 gives the phrase-structure tree for one of

---

[22]Shepard, "The Analysis of Proximities: Multidimensional Scaling with an Unknown Distance Function. II," *Psychometrika* 27 (1962): 235-237. The data are from Gosta Ekman, "Dimensions of Color Vision," *Journal of Psychology* 38 (1954): 467-474. Fig. 6 comes from 236 of Shepard's article.

[23]*The Oxford Companion to Music*, 10th ed., ed. J.O. Ward (London, 1970), pp. 202-210.

[24]Lola L. Cuddy, "The Color of Melody," *Music Perception* 2 (1985): 345-360.

the grammarian's favorite (if tiresome) sentences, "the boy hit the ball."
Figure 8 displays the phrase-structure tree for the sentence, "the ball
was hit by the boy."[25] Although the trees look different, everyone agrees
that the two sentences "mean the same thing." Modern linguistics has
sought formal, general grammars which yield all such equivalences.
This led Chomsky to the idea of a single "deep structure" underlying
diverse but related "surface structures" like those in figures 7 and 8.

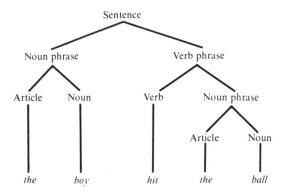

Figure 7. Grammatical phrase-structure description of the sentence, "the boy
hit the ball" given at the bottom of the tree. From Gleitman and Gleitman.

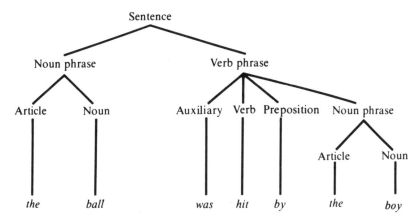

Figure 8. Grammatical phrase-structure description of the sentence, "the ball
was hit by the boy" given at the bottom of the tree. Notice the different appearances of the trees in figures 7 and 8, even though the sentences mean the
same thing. From Gleitman and Gleitman.

[25]Figures 7 and 8 come from Lila Gleitman and Henry Gleitman, "Language," in Henry
Gleitman, *Psychology* (New York, 1981), p. 372.

Sloboda suggests that Schenker's musical analyses may analogously depict the generation of many different (surface) compositions from a few (deep) structures.[26]

Lerdahl and Jackendoff carry matters farther.[27] They systematically introduce tree structures into musical analyses which supposedly describe perception. The analysis in example 5 covers the first two phrases of Bach's chorale, "O Haupt voll Blut und Wunden." Lerdahl and Jackendoff first establish a "time-span structure." Individual notes lie at the lowest level of this structure. Each note gets at least one meterical dot. The rectangular brackets that connect adjacent dots represent time spans on the lowest level. Additional rules of metrical analysis generate both the higher-level dots and the higher-level brackets. The latter brackets include several lower-level ones. The depth of metrical analysis, however, is limited. New rules of grouping analysis form still more extended time spans, indicated by the rounded brackets. The lowest level groups are then organized into groups at the next highest level. This process continues until a single group finally includes the entire piece.

Metrical and grouping analyses are strictly hierarchical. No superordinate region can partially overlap a subordinate one. Inclusion is always complete. Each superordinate region is subdivided exhaustively into subordinate regions at some lower level(s). Two nonadjacent subordinate regions belong to a superordinate one if and only if all in-

Example 5. Time-span organization of first two phrases of Bach's chorale, *O Haupt voll Blut und Wunden.* Dots indicate metrical structure; rectangular and rounded brackets indicate time spans due to metrical and grouping structure respectively. From Lerdahl and Jackendoff.

[26]Sloboda, pp. 14-17.
[27]Fred Lerdahl and Ray Jackendoff, *A Generative Theory of Tonal Music* (Cambridge, Mass., 1983); ex. 5 comes from p. 129; ex. 6, from p. 132; fig. 9, from pp. 315 (top half) and 317 (bottom half).

tervening subordinate regions also do. Recursive application of these principles produces a hierarchical structure like that of example 5.

Time-span reduction introduces a new set of rules. These rules select the most important pitch event in each lowest-level time-span. Metrical and grouping structures guarantee that the selected events must fall into superordinate spans at the next higher level. A further selection of the most important event now occurs within each superordinate span. Reduction proceeds upward. As example 6 shows, an event selected from a time span on the lowest level defines a node above that span. This starts the construction of a time-span reduction tree. A line ties each pitch event in that span to an appropriate node. The lines, however, behave differently for selected, compared to unselected, pitch events. Consider the two pairs of eighth notes in measure 1. The second member of each pair is taken as more important. An ascending, continuing line runs from each of these dominant events. The line from the other member of each span, however, ends when it meets the line from the dominant partner at a node marked ''c.'' The subordinate notes in a time span therefore have no further direct ties to any higher level of the evolving tree.

The time-span reduction tree is constructed recursively. The example shows nodes at two levels, marked ''b'' and ''c.'' When subordinate notes are reduced out at the lowest level, the analysis in example 6b results. The next cycle of reduction gives the analysis in example 6a. Lerdahl and Jackendoff's theory implies that the perceived similarity between two musical passages should increase with the similarity between their tree structures from time-span reduction.

The grammatical and musical trees illustrated respectively by figures 7 or 8 and by example 6 share very strong formal properties. One and only one branch arises immediately from each bottom, terminal item. Each terminal item or node in the tree is immediately subordinate to one and only one superior node. No branches of the tree cross. Finally, the tree develops recursively. These formal properties suggest that the perception of music and the perception of language may have much in common.

A closer examination of the trees in figures 7 and 8 and example 6, however, casts doubt on that suggestion. The trees of figures 7 and 8 show constituent structure. Imagine substituting into figure 7 ''the boy hit the ball'' for ''SENTENCE,'' ''the boy'' for ''NOUN PHRASE,'' and so forth. Those substitutions would demonstrate exactly how a grammatical tree functions. The tree breaks down its top node, an entire sentence, into constituents (e.g., ''the boy'' or NOUN PHRASE and ''hit

Example 6. Time-span reduction tree for first two phrases of Bach's chorale, *O Haupt voll Blut und Wunden*. Dots and rounded brackets as in example 5. Lowest part of tree appears above panel (c). Panels (b) and (a) show results of two successive cycles of reduction. In panel (b), notes marked *b* in tree remain; in panel (a), notes marked *a* in tree remain. From Lerdahl and Jackendoff.

the ball" or VERB PHRASE) at successively lower levels, stopping finally at individual words. The subordinate nodes of a grammatical tree represent *parts* of the event that is at the topmost level. The tree dissects that highest event in recursive, descending stages.

The reduction tree for music in example 6, however, does *not* show constituent structure. Instead, it portrays recursive *selection* from alternatives in an upward direction. The very forms of the two types of tree betray this difference. A line ties each bottom item in a grammatical tree directly to a superordinate node. None of those lines, however, continues upward. Nothing is "reduced out" of the grammatical tree. Just the opposite is true for the musical tree in example 6. Therefore, quite different *processes* form linguistic phrase-structure trees and musical time-span reduction trees. Furthermore, the problem of equivalence between different phrase-structure trees has no counterpart in the domain of time-span reduction trees.

Sundberg and Lindblom's "grammar" for Swedish nursery tunes presents another contrast to a time-span reduction tree.[28] These authors took an entire period as the top node of a tree common to all these pieces. The lower nodes represent constituents of that period, such as phrases or bars. The resulting tree arises by a process of subdivision from above. Just this process yields the phrase-structure trees of figures 7 and 8. It does not generate the time-span reduction tree of example 6.

Lerdahl and Jackendoff, however, give another argument for a close psychological relationship between time-span reduction trees and linguistic trees.[29] They consider structures which represent prosodic stress in speech. The upper half of figure 9 displays prosodic stress trees for the words "reconciliation" and "contractual." The top node of the tree for "reconciliation" splits into two parts with weak (w) and strong (s) stress respectively. Each of the latter gives rise to another w and another s branch, etc. Individual syllables of "reconciliation" are at the bottom of the tree. The stress for each is given by combining the markers at the nodes which dominate it. For example, two nodes marked w dominate "con." This syllable has the weakest stress of any. One node marked s and two marked w dominate "li." Three nodes marked s dominate "a." Therefore, "li" has slightly more stress than "con" and "a" has the highest stress of any syllable. The tree for "contractual" is read in the same way.

Using their notation for time-span reduction trees, Lerdahl and Jackendoff reformulated prosodic stress trees. The bottom half of figure 9 shows their new representation. On any given level, they replace the sequence [w s] reading from left to right with a left-branching structure. This happens, for example, on the first level below the top of the tree. A sequence [s w] turns into a right-branching framework. An example is the structure that ties "re" to "con" at the bottom of the tree. This establishes a one-to-one relationship between prosodic stress notation and time-span reduction notation.

This relationship helps Lerdahl and Jackendoff to argue for a psychological affinity between linguistic stress trees and musical time-span reduction trees. While making their argument, however, they notice

[28]Johan Sundberg and Björn Lindblom, "Generative Theories in Language and Music Descriptions," *Cognition* 4 (1976): 99-122.
[29]Lerdahl and Jackendoff, pp. 314-329.

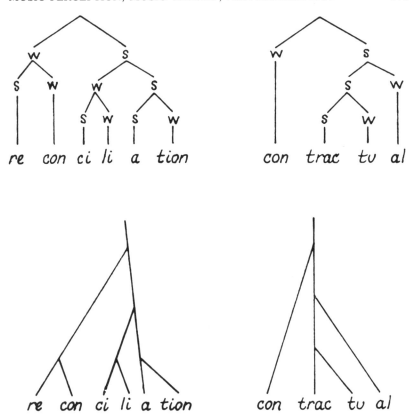

Figure 9. Tree structures which represent prosodic stress. From Lerdahl and Jackendoff.

that nothing is reduced out of a prosodic stress tree, in contrast to a time-span reduction tree. The top node of a stress tree represents an entire word, not a single syllable. The tree is formed by a process of subdivision from above. Time-span reduction trees arise by a process of elimination from below. These facts relieve Lerdahl and Jackendoff's notational isomorphism of any psychological significance. Work by Restle provides additional support for this conclusion.[30] He built trees by using the same kind of notation as Lerdahl and Jackendoff's. Restle even tried applying them to music. Restle's trees, however, represent stimulus sequences used in serial pattern learning. They display analyses of such patterns into constituents. Rules such as inversion and transposi-

[30]Frank Restle, "Theory of Serial Pattern Learning: Structural Trees," *Psychological Review* 77 (1970): 481-495.

tion relate subgroups of constituents. Quite clearly, his trees are formed downward and pick out subgroups built by rules. They do not reduce
a sequence to progressively smaller numbers of constituents. Indeed,
they are more like prosodic stress trees than are time-span reduction
trees. In short, quite different mental structures may have representations with identical formal properties and even identical notation.

This argument, however, leaves intact the implication that greater
similarity of time-span reduction trees should make musical passages
more alike perceptually. Lerdahl and Jackendoff present no data supporting this implication. They only assert that the tree structures represent their own musical intuitions. Empirical tests are obviously possible, using techniques described above. Such tests may well prove successful with short passages. With increasingly longer passages, however,
I believe that such tests will quickly fail, even with highly sophisticated
listeners. My reasons reflect a problem peculiar to music theory compared to linguistics. Grammarians have taken the sentence as their highest
unit of analysis. Listeners can easily hold most single sentences in
memory. Music theorists, however, work with sections, movements,
and even entire pieces. Listeners have grave difficulty in storing such
larger stretches of music faithfully in memory. Fortunately, written
scores compensate for the limitations of memory for auditory material.
Scores allow music theory to pursue many of its tasks. I suspect that
theorists, including Lerdahl and Jackendoff, often arrive at their intuitions by studying scores. If so, we leave the purely auditory territory
of what listeners hear. We enter instead a different psychological realm
where information preserved in the visual medium of scores guides hearing. The boundary between these two regions should not be crossed
with impunity. The penalty may be psychologically misleading
conclusions.

Coordination of Mental Structures

The experimental evidence reviewed in this essay supports the
"psychological reality" of structures such as the tonal circle, the circle of fifths, features of contour, harmonic relationships, and melodic
processes. Doubtless, future evidence will show that other mental structures derived from music theory affect the perception of music. This
prospect leads to a fundamental problem for both music theory and
psychology: how do these several structures collaborate during the unfolding act of hearing a particular passage? Music theory has already
broached this question through its distinction between "horizontal" and

"vertical" aspects of music. Analyses of specific works have demonstrated interrelationships between horizontal and vertical factors. Various rules have resulted—for example, the principles of part-writing. Although these rules codify "good" practice, they also deserve attention from the psychologist. They may point to general constraints on the coordination of mental structures during perception. Greater understanding of such psychological constraints may someday contribute in turn to aesthetic theory itself.[31]

[31]I owe special thanks to Nancy C. Waugh for many useful comments on an earlier version of this essay.

Jan Herlinger

What Trecento Music Theory Tells Us

Two commonly held beliefs plague students of medieval music theory.
The first of these is that "theory" and "practice" are antithetical terms.
The *Oxford English Dictionary* defines "theory" as follows:

> . . . abstract knowledge . . . , often used as implying more or less un-
> supported hypothesis: distinguished from or opposed to *practice*. . . .
> *In theory* . . . : according to theory . . . (opposed to *in practice* or *in fact*).

The second belief is that the Middle Ages were a period of great abstraction—a period when scientists based their conclusions more on authority
than on observation, when theologians debated how many angels could
dance on the point of a pin—and that consequently the testimony of
medieval writers on concrete matters is unreliable.[1]

These beliefs have infected modern writings on medieval music theory
to a singular degree. Listen, for instance, to the author of a textbook
on musical notation—a textbook that after more than forty years has
yet to be superseded—as he writes about the medieval theory of
accidentals:

> The danger of relying on theoretical writers is obvious. Theory always
> means generalization. There are cases where such generalizations are

---

[1]For a veritable catalogue of pejorative uses of the term *medieval*, see Fred C. Robinson, *"Medieval, the Middle Ages,"* *Speculum* 59 (1984): 745-756.

*Jan Herlinger is Associate Professor of musicology at Louisiana State
University. His publications have focussed on the music theory of the*
trecento *and include translated editions of treatises by Marchetto of
Padua and Prosdocimo de' Beldomandi.*

in accord with the facts, as with the rules of mensural notation, or with the simple and uniform system of major- and minor-tonalities in the 18th and 19th centuries. But it is very doubtful whether this is true in our case.[2]

Or listen to the author of the definitive history of medieval music responding to a scholar who had claimed that "the medieval composer was eminently practical":

If medieval man was, at times, "eminently practical"—which we doubt—he was more often eminently theoretical.[3]

And that scholar who called the medieval composer practical, a scholar who time and again drew the most brilliant and provocative conclusions from the writings of Renaissance theorists, pointed to a "gulf between theory and practice" that was "painfully obvious in medieval theory."[4]

These writers notwithstanding, attempts to show how medieval music theory is at variance with practice have foundered. Consider two of these attempts, one dealing with rhythmic theory, the other with melodic—and both involving the first great theorist of the Italian Trecento, Marchetto of Padua.

The rhythms of Trecento music typically unfold over the span of a tempus—that is, the value of a breve—and the value of a note in this music depends not only on its shape but on its position within the tempus. If a tempus contains fewer than the requisite number of semibreves, those at the end of the measure are lengthened, and the music is said to proceed *via naturae*—in the natural way. To make the semibreves at the beginning of the measure longer, the composer applied downward tails to them; to make the semibreves shorter, he applied upward tails. Then the music was said to proceed *via artis*—in the artificial way. the artificial way.

These principles account for a number of pieces in Italian Trecento

[2]Willi Apel, "The Partial Signatures in the Sources up to 1450," *Acta Musicologica* 10 (1938), pp. 1-2. Many readers of this volume will note with interest Apel's reference to "the simple and uniform system of major- and minor-tonalities in the 18th and 19th centuries."
[3]Richard H. Hoppin, "Partial Signatures and Musica Ficta in Some Early 15th-Century Sources," *Journal of the American Musicological Society* 6 (1953), p. 204; responding to Edward E. Lowinsky, "The Function of Conflicting Signatures in Early Polyphonic Music," *Musical Quarterly* 31 (1945), p. 241.
[4]Edward E. Lowinsky, "Music of the Renaissance as Viewed by Renaissance Musicians," in *The Renaissance Image of Man and the World*, ed. Bernard O'Kelly (Columbus, 1966), p. 130.

notation—but by no means all. Take the caccia *Or qua conpagni* from the Rossi Codex, the earliest major musical manuscript of the Trecento.[5] *Or qua conpagni* shows groups of two, three, four, and six plain semibreves; upward and downward tails are scattered, as it first seems, with gay abandon. Discussing this piece in the first edition of his *Notation of Polyphonic Music*, Willi Apel commented drily that "a rhythmic evaluation of the various combinations is not without its difficulties." He presented a table of tentative interpretations of the various groupings. "It is interesting to note," wrote Apel, "that the rhythms *via naturae* absolutely contradict the teaching of Marchettus and other fourteenth century theorists, according to which the longer values appear at the end of the group." Apel also called attention to the letters "sg" written between the top two staff lines at the beginning of each part. "S" patently means "senaria," that is, a meter characterized by six semibreves to the *tempus*. In that first edition of his textbook Apel had to confess ignorance of the meaning of the letter g.[6] But in the fifth edition he appended the following note:

> The sign *.sg.* means *senaria gallica*. Marchettus de Padua in his *Pomerium musicae* . . . comments in detail upon the difference of the French and the Italian interpretation of the smaller values . . . and suggests using the letters *g* (*gallice*) and *y* (*ytalice*) for the purpose of distinction.[7]

In his discussion of *senaria gallica* Marchetto, in fact, explains the meaning of five of the eight patterns Apel had included in the table; two more can easily be deduced from Marchetto's principles.[8] So much for the assertion that *Or qua conpagni* contradicts the teaching of the theorists; and so much, too, for the assertion that medieval theorists dealt exclusively in generalizations. Like the theorists of every period, they concerned themselves now with generalizations, now with particulars, as appropriate.

---

[5]Biblioteca Apostolica Vaticana, ms. Rossianus 215, ff. 19v-20r. *Il canzoniere musicale del codice vaticano Rossi 215*, ed. Giuseppe Vecchi, Monumenta Lyrica Medii Aevi Italica, ser. III: Mensurabilia, vol. 2 (Bologna, 1966), plates 20, 21. There is a facsimile of this piece also in Willi Apel, *The Notation of Polyphonic Music, 900-1600* [The Mediaeval Academy of America, Publication no. 38] 5th ed. (Cambridge, Mass., 1953), p. 383.
[6]Apel, *The Notation of Polyphonic Music, 900-1600* (Cambridge, Mass., 1942), pp. 382-384.
[7]Apel, *Notation*, 5th ed., p. 451.
[8]Marchetto, *Pomerium* 43(*Marcheti de Padua Pomerium*, ed. Giuseppe Vecchi, Corpus Scriptorum de Musica, no. 6 [n.p.: American Institute of Musicology, 1961], pp. 173-80).

For the second unsuccessful attempt to separate Marchetto from the practice of his time, consider the musical examples he presented in his *Lucidarium* of 1317 or 1318 (ex. 1).[9] Musicologists of the nineteenth century stood aghast at these examples. "The harmonic progressions . . . in these examples," wrote François-Joseph Fétis in the 1860s, "are of a boldness prodigious for the time when they were imagined. . . . Too premature, they were not understood by musicians, and remained meaningless until the end of the sixteenth century."[10] August Wilhelm Ambros described Marchetto's progressions thus in the 1890s: "These fruitful ideas were paid no attention. . . . It was a bold idea for that time; no one had the courage to follow him."[11]

Example 1. Progressions from Marchetto's *Lucidarium*

Those nineteenth-century musicologists, of course, were not familiar with most of the sources of Trecento music. They might have noticed, however, that even Marchetto's severest critics, Prosdocimo de' Beldomandi and Johannes Gallicus Carthusiensis, who attacked his tuning system with its heterodox mathematical underpinning, failed to raise a single objection to the progressions in his musical examples. But those musicologists certainly did know that all the evidence concerning Trecento music was not in. When the evidence of the so-called Paduan Dramatic Offices did come in, in the 1950s, these were found to contain progressions that matched two of Marchetto's (ex. 2).[12]

[9]Marchetto, *Lucidarium*, Examples 3, 5, 6, 7 (*The Lucidarium of Marchetto of Padua: A Critical Edition, Translation, and Commentary*, ed. Jan W. Herlinger [Chicago and London, 1985], pp. 142f., 150-155).
[10]"Les successions harmoniques présentées dans ces exemples sont des hardiesses prodigieuses pour le temps où elles ont été imaginées. . . . Trop prématurées, elles ne furent point comprises par les musiciens, et restèrent sans signification jusqu'à la fin du seizième siècle." François-Joseph Fétis, *Biographie universelle des musiciens et bibliographie générale de la musique*, 2d ed., 8 vols. (Paris, 1866-1868), 5:449.
[11]"Diese fruchtbaren Ideen blieben unbeachtet. . . . Es war ein für jene Zeiten kühner Gedanke, Niemand hatte den Muth zu folgen." August Wilhelm Ambros, *Geschichte der Musik*, 3rd ed., 5 vols. (Leipzig, 1887-1911), 2:431.
[12]*Uffici drammatici padovani*, ed. Giuseppe Vecchi, Biblioteca dell'*Archivum Romanicum*, serie 1, vol. 41 (Florence, 1954), pp. 108, 110. A more recent edition is *Italian Sacred Music*, ed. Kurt von Fischer and F. Alberto Gallo, Polyphonic Music of the Fourteenth Century (hereafter: PMFC) vol. 12 (Monaco, 1976), p. 114.

Not that these are isolated instances of chromaticism. Passages from Giovanni da Cascia's madrigal *Sedendo all'ombra* (ex. 3) and an anonymous *Benedicamus Domino* (ex. 4) match another two of Marchetto's progressions—and these are only two of many examples that could be given. Even Marchetto's descending chromatic progressions have their counterparts in the anonymous madrigal *L'antico dio Biber* (ex. 5) and Gherardello's *Intrando ad abitar* (ex. 6).[13]

Example 2. Passages from the Paduan Dramatic Offices

(a) Anon., *Quis est iste,* mm. 1–8

(b) Anon., *Iste formosus,* mm. 1–6

Chromatic progressions had lain outside the boundaries of melodic theory for centuries. A theorist as late as Jerome of Moravia, writing between 1272 and 1304, still regarded them as impossible. The Paduan Dramatic Offices date from early in the fourteenth century; F. Alberto Gallo has suggested that they were composed for the dedication of the Scrovegni Chapel in 1305 ("Marchetus in Padua und die 'franco-venetische' Musik des frühen Trecento," *Archiv für Musikwissenschaft* 31 [1974], p. 42). By 1318 Marchetto not only included these progressions in his treatise but had worked out a melodic theory to support them.

[13]Giovanni, *Sedendo all'ombra*, mm. 6-7 of the Squarcialupi version: *The Music of Fourteenth-Century Italy* (hereafter: *MFCI*), ed. Nino Pirrotta, Corpus Mensurabilis Musicae, no. 8, 5 vols. (Amsterdam, 1954-1964) 1:39-42; a version of the Panciatichi codex also is presented here. *Italian Secular Music by Magister Piero, Giovanni da Firenze, Jacopo da Bologna*, ed. W. Thomas Marrocco, PMFC, vol. 6 (Monaco, 1967), contains alternate versions of the same piece, pp. 74-77.

Benedicamus Domino, mm. 79-84: *Italian Sacred Music*, p. 103.

L'antico dio Biber, mm. 4-6: *MFCI*, 2:44; also in *Italian Secular Music: Anonymous Madrigals and Cacce and the Works of Niccolò da Perugia*, ed. W. Thomas Marrocco, PMFC, vol. 8 (Monaco, 1972), pp. 53-55.

Gherardello, *Intrando ad abitar*, mm. 26-29: *Italian Secular Music by Vincenzo da Rimini, Rosso de Chollegrana, Donato da Firenze, Gherardello da Firenze, Lorenzo da Firenze*, ed. W. Thomas Marrocco, PMFC, vol. 7 (Monaco, 1971), p. 89f. (editorial flats added by the present author); also in *MFCI* 1:62f.

Example 3. Giovanni da Cascia, *Sedendo all'ombra*

Example 4. *Benedicamus Domino*

Example 5. *L'antico dio Biber*

Example 6. Gherardello, *Intrando ad abitar*

Contrast Nino Pirrotta's characterization of the relationship of Marchetto's theory to the practice of his time with that of Fétis and Ambros:

> The special interest which Marchettus shows in chromatic alterations is the reflection in theory of the taste for chromaticism which is one of the most marked characteristics of Italian music of this time.[14]

[14] Nino Pirrotta, "Marchettus de Padua and the Italian Ars nova," *Musica Disciplina* 9 (1955), p. 64.

Having established that Trecento music theory does reflect Trecento musical practice, we can now begin to answer the question what that theory tells us about the music that we otherwise would not know.

First of all, everything we know about the rhythm of Trecento music (and of all medieval music, for that matter) we know from the writings of the theorists. For though the notation of Trecento music resembles modern notation superficially (some notes being solid and some void, some with tails and some without, for instance), it proceeds on different principles. One note can contain two, three, or even more notes of the next smaller value; notes can have tails that extend upward, downward, diagonally, or in some combination of these directions, each tail affecting the value of the note in its own way; notes can be ligated in any number of ways, each with its own rhythmic effect; the dot has several functions, only one of which corresponds to that of the modern dot; even the position of a note within the *tempus* affects its value, as has been pointed out. Without the theorists' rules and the detailed explanations that they give, the rhythm of medieval music could never have been deciphered.

One misconception about Italian Trecento notation that remains particularly vexing—and a misconception that the study of Trecento music theory ought to have cleared up—is the belief that the system does not accommodate syncopation from one tempus to the next. Willi Apel has asserted that Italian fourteenth-century composers were limited to rhythms that unfolded only within the tempus; Richard Hoppin has suggested that this limitation forced Italian composers to adopt the French system of notation.[15] In fact, Italian Trecento notation had a means of notating syncopation whether within the tempus or from one tempus to the next, the one-pitch ligature—that is, one in which two notes of the same pitch were written so as to be just touching. The existence of one-pitch ligatures was documented in the first major treatise on Italian mensural notation, the *Pomerium* of Marchetto of Padua (1319):

---

[15]Apel, *Notation of Polyphonic Music*, 5th ed. p. 385: ". . . There was no place in Italian notation, and consequently in Italian music of the fourteenth century, for syncopation from one measure [i.e., tempus] to another; the entire display of rhythmic imagination is an unfolding of the possibilities within a measure and nothing more." Richard H. Hoppin, *Medieval Music* (New York, 1978) p.435: ". . . Dots of division . . . severely limited, when they did not entirely eliminate, the possibility of tied notes or syncopation across the barline. It was undoubtedly such restraints that eventually led Italian composers to adopt the principles of French notation in a revolt against the tyranny of the barline. . . ."

If however it is necessary for the sake of the beauty of the harmony not to re-articulate several notes [of the same pitch] we say that they may be included in one figure *via artis* [i.e., through the addition of a tail]. If not by this method, they are drawn so close together as to be just barely touching, but yet so that one takes nothing of the space of the other, for the reason set forth above.[16]

One-pitch ligatures occur in a number of major Trecento manuscripts (notably the Rossi, Panciatichi, and Mancini codices and Paris 568). When the syncopation crosses from one tempus to the next, a dot of division is written between the two contiguous notes forming the ligature. Marchetto's description of the one-pitch ligature provided the impetus for fascinating accounts by Michael P. Long and John Nádas of the gradual replacement, in the course of the Trecento manuscript tradition, of syncopated one-pitch ligatures by unsyncopated figures or by syncopated figures notated by other means, as well as of their interpretation and misinterpretation by modern editors.[17]

Deciphering the pitches of Trecento music is not as difficult as deciphering its rhythms, for the notes are placed on staves with clefs like ours; but even that has its problems where chromatic inflections are concerned. It is well known that medieval and Renaissance scribes notated only a fraction of the chromatic signs that were appropriate; but even the chromatic signs that do appear in manuscripts cannot be interpreted correctly without reflection. The music of the early Trecento, for instance, shows many signs that resemble the modern sharp. A case in point is Giovanni da Cascia's madrigal *Naschoso'l viso* as it appears in the Panciatichi codex.[18] The second staff of the discant ends with an A-B-C-D progression with sharps applied to both B and C. But was B-sharp really a part of the musical vocabulary of the fourteenth century? And if not, why is the sharp there?

---

[16]"Si autem ad pulchriores armoniam sit necesse non repercutere plures notas, dicimus quod si in uno corpore possunt includi via artis, ut dictum est, includantur. Sin autem, propinquius figurentur etiam usque ad contactum, ita tamen quod una de spatio alterius nihil tollat, ratione superius allegata." Marchetto of Padua, *Pomerium* 50.33, as emended by Michael Paul Long, "Musical Tastes in Fourteenth-Century Italy: Notational Styles, Scholarly Traditions, and Historical Circumstances" (Ph. D. diss., Princeton University, 1981), p. 16. The translation is from Long's Appendix 5, p. 4. See also *Marcheti de Padua Pomerium*, p. 200.

[17]Long, pp. 15-20, 98-121. John Louis Nádas, "The Transmission of Trecento Secular Polyphony: Manuscript Production and Scribal Practices in Italy at the End of the Middle Ages" (Ph.D. diss., New York University, 1985), pp. 49, 99-101, 212-13, 262-64, 320-23, 449-58.

[18]*Il codice musicale Panciatichi 26 della Biblioteca Nazionale di Firenze*, ed. F. Alberto Gallo, Studi e Testi per la Storia di Musica, no. 3 (Florence, 1981), ff. 49v-50r.

To answer the question we need only consult a medieval theorist who wrote about accidentals. The last great theorist of the Trecento, Prosdocimo de' Beldomandi, defines musica ficta as follows:

> Musica ficta is the feigning of syllables or the placement of syllables in a location where they do not seem to be—to apply mi where there is no mi and fa where there is no fa, and so forth.[19]

Medieval melodic theory was based on the hexachord—a succession of six notes of which the central two are separated by a semitone, the others by whole tones. Hexachords normally were built only on Cs, Gs, and Fs. The syllable *mi* thus occurred only on Es, Bs, and As, *fa* only on Fs, Cs, and B-flats. Placing *mi* or *fa* anywhere else—placing them *where they do not seem to be*, in Prosdocimo's words—necessitated constructing hexachords on notes other than C, G, and F, and was called musica falsa or musica ficta. If we place *mi* on F-sharp, for instance, we construct a hexachord with *ut* on D; if we place *mi* on C-sharp, we construct a hexachord with *ut* on A.

What about the accidental signs? Prosdocimo, again:

> The signs of musica ficta are two, round or soft b and square or hard ♮ . . . . Wherever round or soft b is applied, we ought to sing the syllable fa, and wherever square or hard ♮ is applied, we ought to sing the syllable mi.[20]

Thus medieval music had but two chromatic signs, not three. One is the round b. Wherever it appears we are to sing *fa*. If a round b is applied to the note C, it tells us to sing the note as *fa*—as we do when it occurs in the hexachord that has *ut* on G; it would thus be transcribed in modern notation with a C-natural. When applied to the note B, it again tells us to sing the note as *fa*—as we do when it occurs in the hexachord that has *ut* on F; it would be transcribed in modern notation as B-flat. The other sign is the square ♮ . Wherever it appears we are to sing *mi*. If the square ♮ is applied to the note B, it tells us to sing the note as *mi*, as we do when it occurs in the hexachord that has *ut*

[19]"Ficta musica est vocum fictio sive vocum positio in loco ubi esse non videntur, sicut ponere mi ubi non est mi, et fa ubi non est fa, et sic ultra." Prosdocimo, *Contrapunctus* 5.1 (Prosdocimo de' Beldomandi, *Contrapunctus*, ed. and trans. Jan Herlinger, Greek and Latin Music Theory, vol. 1 [Lincoln and London, 1984], pp. 70f.).
[20]"Signa huius ficte musice sunt duo, scilicet b rotundum sive molle et ♮ quadrum sive durum, . . . unde ubicumque ponitur b rotundum sive molle dicere debemus hanc vocem fa, et ubicumque ponitur ♮ quadrum sive durum dicere debemus hanc vocem mi." Prosdocimo, *Contrapunctus* 5.3 (pp. 74-77).

on G; it is then transcribed as B-natural. If the square ♭ is applied to
the note C, it tells us to sing the note as *mi*, as we do when it occurs
in the hexachord that has *ut* on A; it is then transcribed as C-sharp.
The medieval round b is to be transcribed in modern notation
sometimes as a flat, sometimes as a natural, depending on what note
it is applied to, and medieval square ♭ is to be transcribed sometimes
as a natural, sometimes as a sharp, depending on what note it is applied to.

Medieval scribes, however, often wrote the square ♭ in the form
#. That is how it appears in the Panciatichi codex. In the progression
from *Naschoso'l viso* that appears to the (modern) eye as A – B-sharp–
C-sharp– D, the sharps are actually square ♭s, and the progression
would be transcribed in modern notation as A – B-natural– C-sharp– D.

But the real problem confronting those who edit or perform early music
is knowing where accidentals are to be added beyond those indicated
in the original sources. It is the theorists who tell us where these accidentals are to be placed. Prosdocimo, once more·

> These signs are to be applied to octaves, fifths, and similar intervals . . .
> to enlarge or diminish them in order to make them good consonances
> if they earlier were dissonant...[21]

Or, in other words, octaves, fifths, and their compounds are to be chromatically altered so that they are made perfect if they were diminished
or augmented. Quoting Prosdocimo further:

> But these signs are to be applied to imperfectly consonant intervals—the
> third, the sixth, the tenth, and the like— . . . to give them major or minor
> inflections as appropriate. . . . You should always choose that form,
> whether major or minor, that is less distant from that location which
> you intend immediately to reach.[22]

This explains why, in the transcription of the beginning of *Naschoso'l
viso* in the version of the Panciatichi codex (ex. 7; positions of the
chromatic signs in the manuscript are indicated in parentheses, and

[21]"Octavis, quintis, et hiis similibus ponenda sunt hec signa secundum quod oportet
addere vel diminuere ad ipsas reducendum ad bonas consonantias, si prius forent
dissonantes." Prosdocimo, *Contrapunctus* 5.6 (pp. 78f.).
[22]"Sed in vocum combinationibus imperfecte consonantibus, sicut sunt tercia, sexta,
decima, et huiusmodi, ponenda sunt etiam hec signa secundum quod oportet addere
vel diminuere in ipsas reducendo ad maioritatem vel minoritatem opportunas. . . . Il-
lam semper sumere debes que minus distat a loco ad quem immediate accedere inten-
dis." Prosdocimo, *Contrapunctus* 5.6 (pp. 80-83).

editorial accidentals are added above the notes to which they apply), the F in the sixth measure of the discant is sharped: the minor sixth A – F is made major so as to lie closer to the octave to which it moves.

Example 7. Giovanni da Cascia, *Naschoso'l viso*

Similarly, the C in the discant in measure 2 is sharped so that the minor sixth E – C is made major and lies closer to the octave to which it moves. Note that in this case the closest-approach principle, which dictates that the C in measure 2 be sharped, overrides the principle that the fifth F – C be perfect.[23]

These chromatic inflections were notated in the original source, but others were not. The same considerations concerning the closest approach from an imperfect consonance to the following consonance call for a sharp on the tenor's F in measure 3 and a sharp on the discant's C in measure 4.

Difficulties do of course appear from time to time. Francesco Landini's ballata *D'amor mi biasmo* (ex. 8) presents a particularly interesting problem.[24] The discant has a signature of one flat, the tenor a signature of two flats; twice a C sharp is indicated in the discant against an E in the tenor (mm. 48 and 53). If the sharps on the Cs are observed,

---

[23]The signs that we call chromatic signs were in medieval times not so much signs of chromatic inflection as solmization signs, indicating where changes were to be made from one hexachord to another. The sharp that applies to the first C in *Naschoso'l viso* is placed to the left of the first note (A) to tell the singer he must start with *ut* on A in order to have *mi* fall on C. Similarly, the sharp that applies to the F in m. 6 is placed not immediately before it but at the point where the singer ought to change hexachords and sing E as *re*.

[24]*The Works of Francesco Landini*, ed. Leo Schrade, PMFC, vol. 4, pp. 10f.

Example 8. Francesco Landini, *D'amor mi biasmo*

augmented sixths result unless the E-flat of the tenor's signature is cancelled. Carl Shachter argued in favor of retaining the augmented sixths:

> I am of the opinion . . . that the augmented interval ought to be retained. It results from convincing melodic motion in both parts; it occurs in a composition rather individual in other respects as well. This ballata contains the only use of A flat in Landini's works; the signature of two flats is also quite unusual.[25]

Despite Schachter's argument, the augmented sixth can be rejected on the basis of the theorists' testimony, and on two counts. First, no medieval theorist discusses the augmented sixth, from which we can infer that it was not part of the harmonic vocabulary of the time. Second, the augmented-sixth-to-octave progression can be shown to be

[25]Carl Schachter, "Landini's Treatment of Consonance and Dissonance: A Study in Fourteenth-Century Counterpoint," *The Music Forum* 2 (1970), pp. 180-81. Schrade let both augmented sixths stand; Ellinwood ignored the first, retained the second (*The Works of Francesco Landini*, ed. Leonard Ellinwood (Mediaeval Academy of America, Publication no. 36) [Cambridge, Mass., 1939], pp. 58f.).

The A-flat Schachter refers to occurs in m. 27 in two of the madrigal's three sources (in the Squarcialupi codex and Paris 568, but not in the Panciatichi codex) but was not adopted by Schrade. The sharps in measures 48 and 53 do not appear in Squarcialupi; the first is misplaced in Paris 568.

anomalous in light of a precept so common it can be regarded as a harmonic law of the fourteenth and fifteenth centuries. Here is Prosdocimo's formulation of the precept, which is given also by Antonio da Leno, Ugolino, Tinctoris, Hothby, and Guilielmus Monachus:

> In perfectly consonant intervals we ought never to place mi against fa or vice versa, because we would straightway make the perfectly consonant intervals minor [i.e., diminished] or augmented, which forms are discordant.[26]

The rule obviously prohibits B-natural, for instance, sounding against B-flat; but Margaret Bent developed an ingenious argument to show that it also excludes the augmented-sixth-to-octave progression.[27] If the tenor has an E-flat, that note is solmizated as *fa*, and the following D must be *mi*; if the discant has C-sharp, that note is solmizated as *mi*, and the following D must be *fa*. So *mi* will sound against *fa* in the perfectly consonant octave D – D. Prosdocimo's statement that an octave in which *mi* sounds against *fa* must be diminished or augmented shows that he could not conceive of a case in which *mi* against *fa* could produce a perfect consonance—and hence that he could not conceive of a perfect octave preceded by an augmented sixth.

Even in those cases where solutions to musica ficta problems are not clear cut, the writings of theorists help delimit the range of possibilities from which an editor may choose. Given a passage like that in example 9,[28] most editors, I think, would not entertain the notion of sharping the tenor's first C so as to make that sixth lie closer to the following sixth—because of the augmented fourth that would result between the C-sharp and the preceding G. Yet Prosdocimo sharped this C when he presented this example in his counterpoint treatise—and he did not consider the augmented fourth even worthy of mention. There is no reason why a modern editor should feel timid about following in Prosdocimo's footsteps.

---

[26]"In combinationibus perfecte consonantibus nunquam ponere debemus mi contra fa, nec e contra, quoniam statim ipsas vocum combinationes perfecte consonantes minores vel maximas constitueremus, que discordantes sunt." Prosdocimo, *Contrapunctus* 4.6 (pp. 62-65). For references to the other theorists, see Prosdocimo, *Contrapunctus*, pp. 63, 65 (note 6).

[27]Margaret Bent, "Musica Recta and Musica Ficta," *Musica Disciplina* 26 (1972), p. 74.

[28]Prosdocimo, *Contrapunctus* 5.6 (pp. 85f.), with the sharp on the tenor's first C deleted.

Example 9. Prosdocimo, *Contrapunctus* (modified)

Despite the profusion of chromatic signs in this example, by the way, Prosdocimo warned that musica ficta should be used *only where necessary*[29]—evidence that he considered it necessary much more often than most modern editors.[30]

Marchetto's chromatic progressions open the door to chromatic solutions to certain musica ficta problems in the Trecento repertory. The historical validity of these progressions having been established, why should we hesitate to introduce chromaticism where possible—as in the anonymous madrigal *Involta d'un bel velo* (ex. 10) or Piero's *Si com'al canto* (ex. 11)? On the other hand, the occasional occurrence of harmonic augmented fifths in the Trecento repertory (as at the opening of *Naschoso'l viso* (ex. 7) suggests alternative solutions to these problems (exx. 12, 13).[31]

Example 10. *Involta d'un bel velo*

[La] qual	spes- so	me	[fa cridar, "Oymei."]
[Dis-] si	"Ma- do-	na,	[cum vui sia pace."]
[Fe-] ce	ri- spo-	sta	[più che morte oscura.]

[La] qual	spes- so	me	[fa cridar, "Oymei."]
[Dis-] si,	"Ma- do-	na,	[cum vui sia pace."]
[Fe-] ce	ri- spo-	sta	[più che morte oscura.]

[29]Prosdocimo, *Contrapunctus* 5.1 (pp. 70-73).

[30]The exuberant profusion of editorial accidentals in *The Works of Johannes Ciconia*, ed. Margaret Bent and Anne Hallmark, PMFC, vol. 24 (Monaco, 1985), may serve as a bold example for other editors. In the introduction (p. xix) Bent writes, "It should be remembered that Prosdocimus is very close in place and time to Ciconia, and that if his well-known ficta examples . . . have application anywhere, it is surely here;" and the editors' choices concerning musica ficta amply bear out these words.

[31]*Involta d'un bel velo*, mm. 24-26: *Italian Secular Music: Anonymous Madrigals and Cacce*, pp. 39f. (editorial accidentals supplied by the present author). Also in *MFCI* 2:31f., where Pirrotta sharps both Cs, thus creating a harmonic augmented fifth.

Si com'al canto, mm. 27-28: *Italian Secular Music by Magister Piero*, pp. 18f. (editorial accidentals supplied by the present author). Also in MFCI 2:4f., where Pirrotta suggests a chromatic progression.

Example 11. Piero, *Si com'al canto*

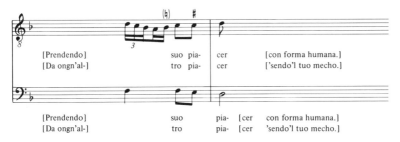

Example 12. *Involta d'un bel velo*

Example 13. *Si com'al canto*

Writings of the theorists also suggest precisely where in florid passages accidentals should be introduced. There is nothing absolutely wrong with the application of musica ficta Alberto Gallo and Kurt von Fischer suggest in a passage from Gherardello's *Gloria* (ex. 14); but Marchetto's progression in example 1c suggests that the sharp might well be introduced on the third beat of measure 49 rather than at the end of the measure (ex. 15).[32] And in Lorenzo's Sanctus, measures 18-19, there is no reason to delay the appearance of the F-sharp until the end of measure 18 (ex. 16); in the light of Marchetto's progression in example 1b the sharp probably ought to be introduced on the second beat of the measure (ex. 17)—which, incidentally, is what Pirrotta suggested in his edition of the piece.[33]

---

[32]Gherardello, Gloria, mm. 49-50: *Italian Sacred Music*, pp. 5-8; also in *MFCI* 1:53-55. Pirrotta's musica ficta agrees with that of Gallo and von Fischer.

[33]Lorenzo, Sanctus, mm. 18-19: *Italian Sacred Music*, pp. 73-75; also in *MFCI* 3:1-2.

The editors of the new Ciconia edition do not hesitate, by the way, to introduce chromaticism where appropriate. See for instance the Gloria *Suscipe, Trinitas*, mm. 206-8 (*The Works of Johannes Ciconia*, pp. 36-43), where, if the tenor and contratenor are played alone without ornamentation, they produce a transposition of Marchetto's progression given above as Example 1b.

Example 14. Gherardello, Gloria

Example 15. Gherardello, Gloria

Example 16. Lorenzo, Sanctus

Example 17. Lorenzo, Sanctus

Or consider a passage from Bartolo's Credo (ex. 18). The piece has a signature of B-flat. In measure 231 Gallo and von Fischer suggest an accidental B-natural to cancel the signature and make the diminished fifth perfect just as Prosdocimo told them to; they retain this natural in measure 232. Pirrotta's solution to this problem, again, was more daring: he suggested a natural on the first B, like Gallo and von Fischer, but changed to a flat on the second—thus creating a descending chromatic succession of three semitones (ex. 19).[34] Surely he would not have dared to propose such a solution without the precedent of another

[34]Bartolo, Credo, mm. 231-37: *Italian Sacred Music*, pp. 53-59; *MFCI* 1:1-6 (mm. 111-12).

of Marchetto's progressions (ex. 20).[35] But if we accept the B-flat in measure 232 of example 19, why not introduce an A-flat in measure 233 as well (ex. 21)?

Example 18. Bartolo, Credo

Example 19. Bartolo, Credo

Example 20. Marchetto, *Lucidarium*

Example 21. Bartolo, Credo

Just preceding this passage Gallo and von Fischer suggest the addition of a G-sharp even though that produces the unusual melodic progression B-flat – A – G-sharp (ex. 22).[36] A progression from Prosdocimo's monochord treatise would certainly grant them this small license

---

[35]Marchetto, *Lucidarium*, Example 4, variant from the majority of sources (Herlinger ed., p. 145).
[36]Bartolo, Credo, mm. 224-26; Pirrotta (m. 108) adds no accidental.

(ex. 23);[37] though for that matter similar progressions are not unknown in practical sources, for instance the anonymous motet *Ave corpus sanctum gloriosi Stefani* dating from the 1330s, Bartolo's time, but originating in the Veneto, Prosdocimo's domain; or Ciconia's madrigal *Una panthera*.[38]

Example 22. Bartolo, Credo

Example 23. Prosdocimo, *Monacordum*

Despite its instructive polyphonic examples, the *Lucidarium* is first and foremost a treatise on plainchant, and Marchetto has much to say on the use of accidentals there too. He specifies which modes use B-natural, which B-flat, and which both, and shows how to determine the appropriate inflection in specific melodic contexts. He suggests transpos-

---

[37]Prosdocimo, *Monacordum* 8 (Prosdocimo de' Beldomandi, *Brevis summula proportionum et Parvus tractatulus de modo monacordum dividendi*, ed. Jan Herlinger, Greek and Latin Music Theory, no. 4 [Lincoln and London, 1987], pp. 106-7). In Coussemaker's edition this example is incomplete (*Scriptorum de musica medii aevi nova series a Gerbertina altera*, 4 vols., ed. Edmond de Coussemaker [Paris, 1864-1876], 3:256).

[38]*Ave corpus sanctum gloriosi Stefani*, mm. 117-18: *Italian Sacred Music*, pp. 133-37; this motet, written for a ceremony in memory of the translation of the body of St. Stephen to Venice, mentions Francesco Dandolo, Doge 1329--1339. *Una panthera*, mm. 72-74: *The V orks of Johannes Ciconia*, pp. 126-29.

ing chants so as to avoid inflections outside the musica vera system,[39] or, failing that, so as to minimize them. It is precisely to minimize such inflections that he proposes that the Gradual *Salvum fac servum*, which begins with two ascending whole tones, should begin on a flatted low B even though that is not a musica vera note.[40] The only published sources of *Salvum fac* accommodate the two whole tones by beginning the chant on F or C and avoid unorthodox chromatic inflections through internal transposition. But Jeffrey Wasson has reported finding three unpublished Beneventan sources of *Salvum fac* in which the melody does indeed begin on the low B, as Marchetto says it should.[41]

Most intriguing, however, is Marchetto's assertion that the leading tones of musica ficta are used in chant in two circumstances: when the chant is taken over as the tenor of a motet or *when it is sung with color*.[42] Does anyone have the courage to emulate Fétis and Ambros by asserting that Marchetto was mistaken—that leading tones were never used in plainchant? Perhaps it would be wiser to wait until more evidence comes in.

There is one last aspect of musical practice about which we would know nothing whatever without the testimony of the theorists. That is tuning—for medieval musical manuscripts are as silent on that topic as the scores of Beethoven's symphonies.

Medieval theorists agree almost unanimously in describing the tuning system that has since come to be called "Pythagorean." The defining characteristic of this system is that all perfect fifths are pure. The theorists generally give tunings for the natural notes and B-flats. What about the other chromatically altered notes?

One would guess that F-sharp, C-sharp, G-sharp, and D-sharp ought to be tuned by successive pure fifths upward from B-natural; E-flat, A-flat, and D-flat by successive pure fifths downward from B-flat. Since each of these pure fifths is two cents (that is, two-hundredths of an equally tempered semitone) wider than the perfect fifths of equal temperament,

---

[39]The musica vera system comprises those notes which belong to hexachords that have *ut* on the Cs, Gs, and Fs between G and g' inclusive; that is, those notes in the range G—e♭' that are not musica ficta notes.

[40]Since the musica vera system does not comprise a hexachord with *ut* on the F below the bass clef staff, B-flat on the second line of that staff is not a musica vera note but a musica ficta note.

[41]Private communication; Benevento VI.38 (f. 12r); Benevento V.19 (f. 228v); Vatican, Ottoboni lat.576 (f. 71r). For Marchetto's discussion of *Salvum fac*, see *Lucidarium* 11.4.59-72 (Herlinger ed., pp. 420-27).

[42]Marchetto, *Lucidarium* 8.1.7 (Herlinger ed., pp. 274f.).

notes that would be enharmonically equivalent in equal temperament (C-sharp and D-flat, for instance), differ in Pythagorean tuning by 24 ($=12\times2$) cents—almost a quarter of a semitone—an interval called the "Pythagorean comma."

Better said, one would have to guess that these notes ought to be tuned thus were it not for the occasional explicit testimony of some theorist. Prosdocimo, for instance, described a scale tuned in just this way, and extended it as far as G-flat in one direction and A-sharp in the other, thus arriving at a scale with seven "natural" notes, five sharps, and five flats. He took pains to point out that the sharp and the flat lying between two adjacent natural notes did not have the same pitch, so that, for instance, D-flat could not serve in place of C-sharp nor A-sharp in place of B-flat.[43]

It is not just the perfect fifths that are different in Pythagorean tuning and equal temperament, of course. The Pythagorean minor semitone is ten cents narrower than the equally tempered semitone. The Pythagorean major third is eight cents wider than the equally tempered one, and twenty-two cents wider than the pure major third (twenty-two cents being more than one-fifth of a semitone)! Its large size makes the Pythagorean major third dissonant. Putting it together with a perfect fifth somehow exacerbates the dissonance so that the major triad is quite ugly. In the typical fourteenth-century cadence with double leading tone (ex. 24), the narrowness of the semitones by which the two leading tones progress emphasizes their tendency to resolve upward while the dissonance of the penultimate major triad impels the notes toward a resolution on the open fifth-and-octave. Whereas the major triad—the basis of eighteenth- and nineteenth-century harmony—is dissonant in Pythagorean tuning, the fifth-octave combination—which sounds bare in a context of equally tempered triads—is particularly resonant in Pythagorean tuning. No wonder fourteenth-century composers preferred to avoid full triads at the ends of their pieces.[44]

Example 24. Double-leading-tone cadence

---

[43]Prosdocimo, *Monacordum* 5-8 (pp. 90-111).

[44]It is possible to trace the increasingly frequent use, over the course of the fifteenth century, of triads in final positions; and during this same century theorists began to

In summary, it should be clear that medieval theorists did not deal exclusively in generalities; that they were, by and large, practical people; and that there was in fact no gulf separating the theory of Trecento music from its practice. The Latin *theoria*, after all, borrows a Greek word that signifies a looking at, a viewing, a spectating, a contemplation; and medieval theorists did look, and did look thoughtfully, at the music of their time. They reflected on it, and they reflected it in their writings. How fortunate for us that they did—because without their testimony, medieval music would have remained, for us, uncharted territory.[45]

describe meantone temperaments (with major thirds that are pure or nearly so, fifths that are tempered slightly, and triads that are quite euphonious) and just intonation (with triads that are pure). On meantone temperaments in the fifteenth and early sixteenth centuries, see Mark Lindley, "Pythagorean Intonation and the Rise of the Triad," *Royal Musical Association Research Chronicle* 16 (1980):4-61.

[45]This paper owes much to conversations with Professor Theodore Karp of Northwestern University and Professor John Nádas of the University of North Carolina at Chapel Hill. I thank both of them most gratefully.

Robert O. Gjerdingen

Concrete Musical Knowledge and a Computer Program for Species Counterpoint

> . . . knowledge of style is usually "tacit": it is a matter
> of habits properly acquired (internalized) and appropriate-
> ly brought into play. . . . the goal of music theorists and
> style analysts [is] to explain what the composer, performer
> and listener know in this tacit way. To do so, they must
> make explicit the nature of the constraints governing the
> style in question, devising and testing hypotheses about
> their function and their relationships to one another.
>
> L. B. Meyer

In the fourth and last part of *The Man Who Mistook His Wife for a Hat and Other Clinical Tales*, Dr. Oliver Sacks discusses several endear- ing patients who, though labeled by science and society as retarded, possess gifts of symbolic expression realized through drawing, poetry, theater, or music. In seeking to explain how these individuals with such severely restricted powers of abstraction or conceptualization could nonetheless function artistically, he focuses on the "concreteness" of their world—how it is "vivid, intense, detailed, yet simple, precisely because it *is* concrete: neither complicated, diluted, nor unified, by abstraction." He argues further that in exalting man's powers of abstrac- tion neurologists have grossly slighted the extraordinary role that con- crete images and memories play in defining what is "essential to per- sonality and identity and humanity."[1]

A similar slighting of the concrete can sometimes be detected in discus-

---

[1]Oliver Sacks, *The Man Who Mistook His Wife for a Hat and Other Clinical Tales* (New York, 1985), pp. 164-65.

Robert O. Gjerdingen is Assistant Professor of Music at Carleton College. He is the author of A Classic Turn of Phrase: Music and the Psychology of Convention.

sions of musical minds. For example, W. Jay Dowling's perceptive
analysis of four hierarchically organized levels of pitch material clearly leads from the abstract to the concrete. Dowling proposes that each
level "is formed by making a selection of pitches out of the next higher
level or by imposing some constraint on them." Thus the Western
chromatic scale is a selection from the continuum of the "psychophysical
pitch function," the diatonic scale is a selection from the chromatic
scale, and a "very concrete modal scale" such as the Dorian mode is
a selection from, or imposes constraints upon, the diatonic scale.[2]

Yet, at least in the history of Western music, just the reverse would
seem to be the case. Modes, in all their concreteness, were primary
with diatonic or chromatic scales being the later products of rationalization and abstraction.[3] Even cross-cultural evidence bears upon this point.
For example, of the three great Moslem musical traditions—the North
Indian *rāga*, the Arabian *maqām*, and the Persian *dastgāh*—that with
the least developed theoretical tradition (*dastgāh*) is most closely tied
to concrete, meaningful melodic cells (*gusheh-hāh*) with a typical am-
bitus much smaller than an octave. So in *dastgāh*, and to a lesser extent in *maqām*, an octave scale must often be conceptualized as the union
of other primary constituents. Constrast this with the clear octave
organization of the Indian *rāga*, product of one of the world's longest
and most distinguished traditions of theoretical speculation.[4]

Theories of musical structure also frequently view the concrete only
as the end product of abstract operations and transformations. Melodies
are thought to result from ornamenting or prolonging triads, triads from
prolonging higher-level harmonic functions, and those functions from
prolonging a central tonality. Yet what if concrete, stylistically specific
melodies are the very stuff of music? What if musical knowledge and
experience begins and is rooted in the concrete? The following discussion explores that possibility.

THE PRAENESTE COMPUTER PROGRAM

No doubt a professor lecturing on species counterpoint sometimes
reminds the befuddled student of an Old Testament patriarch calling

[2]W. Jay Dowling and Dane L. Harwood, *Music Cognition* (Orlando, 1986), pp. 113-21.
[3]A psychologist of music questions the primacy of scales and other products of rationalization in Mary L.Serafine, "Cognition in Music," *Cognition* 14 (1983): 119-83.
[4]A brilliant introduction to modal theory in general with specific sections on *dastgāh*,
maqām, and *rāga* has been written by Harold Powers in *The New Grove Dictionary
of Music and Musicians*, ed. Stanley Sadie, "Mode: §V, 2."

out the commandments: Thou shalt have no tritones; Thou shalt not leap to dissonance; Thou shalt not commit parallel fifths; and so on. The contrapuntal sins are set forth in a manner so precise and vivid that avoiding them can become the student's central concern. The good deeds of counterpoint, on the other hand, are vague. Much like New Testament exhortations to "Love thy neighbor as thyself," pleas for a good melodic contour or a sense of melodic logic and balance seem difficult to realize in practice.

Yet species counterpoint, or something like it, was once very much a practice concerned with contrapuntal good works. A sixteenth-century singer of any repute would have found the problems of two-part species a trifle and could improvise correct counterpoints on the spot. Unlike the modern student, the sixteenth-century singer would not have needed to pay great attention to averting errors; the use of concrete correct patterns would have been habitual as part of the singer's internalized knowledge. Instead, such a singer would concentrate on doing something aesthetically pleasing—avoiding sin would be overshadowed by the desire to do good works.

PRAENESTE (ancient name of the city Italians call Palestrina) is modeled on this latter view of species counterpoint as an active practice based on concrete knowledge. That is, just like a trained contrapuntist improvising, PRAENESTE works forward in time[5] without benefit of being able to back up and start over. In response to each new contrapuntal situation—the cantus firmus ascending a third, for example— PRAENESTE uses a small but powerful memory of various concrete musical schemata to provide for itself a selection of correct melodic patterns. Then, given what it has done up to that point, it selects a single melodic path that best satisfies a number of higher-level aesthetic constraints. For PRAENESTE, being correct is a matter of course; its main concern is with style.[6]

Let us first examine how PRAENESTE can automatically select correct melodic patterns through its CHOICES subroutine.

For each species, PRAENESTE has a memory of all the basic melodic

[5]The PRAENESTE program does not currently operate in real time, though in most cases perhaps it could. For instance, as implemented in the FORTH language on a small Macintosh computer, PRAENESTE writes a nine-measure first-species counterpoint in one second, a fifth-species counterpoint in nine seconds.
[6]For PRAENESTE, style is embodied in the elegant species counterpoint of Knud Jeppesen. Jeppesen's intimate knowledge of the style of Palestrina enriched species counterpoint and all who pursue the higher forms of this discipline today owe him a tremendous debt. There are extant, of course, truncated remnants of the work of J. J. Fux posing either as sixteenth-century counterpoint, as a type of medicinal musical geometry, or as a core of eternal musical verities. These poor tatters are not discussed.

patterns. For example, it knows sixteen melodic schemata for third species (i.e., for counterpoint in quarter notes against a cantus firmus in whole notes). These are quite specific, quite concrete, as the following list demonstrates:

Simple Intervals:

1. A second ascends from a weak beat to a consonant quarter note on a strong beat (terminal schema event).
2. A second descends from a strong beat to a consonant quarter note on a weak beat (terminal schema event).
3. A third ascends from a weak beat to a consonant quarter note on a strong beat (terminal schema event).
4. A third descends from a strong beat to a consonant quarter note on a weak beat (terminal schema event).
5. A fourth ascends from a weak beat to a consonant quarter note on a strong beat (terminal schema event).
6. A fourth descends from a strong beat to a consonant quarter note on a weak beat (terminal schema event).
7. A fifth ascends from a weak beat to a consonant quarter note on a strong beat (terminal schema event).
8. A fifth descends from a strong beat to a consonant quarter note on a weak beat (terminal schema event).
9. A sixth ascends from a weak beat to a consonant quarter note on a strong beat (terminal schema event).
10. An octave ascends from a weak beat to a consonant quarter note on a strong beat (terminal schema event).
11. An octave descends from a strong beat to a consonant quarter note on a weak beat (terminal schema event).

An Ascending Passing-Tone Figure:

12. A second ascends from a strong beat to either a consonant or a dissonant quarter note on a weak beat (initial schema event), and a second ascends from that weak beat to a consonant quarter note on a strong beat (terminal schema event).

A Descending Passing-Tone Figure:

13. A second descends from a strong beat to either a consonant or a dissonant quarter note on a weak beat (initial schema event), and a second descends from that weak beat to a consonant quarter note on a strong beat (terminal schema event).

A Lower Neighbor-Tone Figure:

14.   A second descends from a strong beat to either a consonant or a dissonant quarter note on a weak beat (initial schema event), and a second ascends from that weak beat to a consonant quarter note on a strong beat (terminal schema event).

A Cambiata:

15.   A second descends from a strong beat to either a consonant or a dissonant quarter note on a weak beat (initial schema event), a third descends from that weak beat to a consonant quarter note on a strong beat (medial schema event), a second ascends from that strong beat to either a consonant or a dissonant quarter note on a weak beat (medial schema event), and a second ascends from that weak beat to a consonant quarter note on a strong beat (terminal schema event).

Compensating Skips (i.e., a pattern like c´-a-d´):

16.   A third descends from a strong beat to a consonant quarter note on a weak beat (initial schema event), and a fourth ascends from that weak beat to a consonant quarter note on a strong beat (terminal schema event).

Of course it is not this prolix verbal listing that is kept in PRAENESTE's memory. Instead, for each schema event five small numbers are stored. The first tells the position of an event within the schema, initial, medial, or terminal (coded as 0, 2, and 1 respectively). The second tells the number of scale degrees up or down from the previous event (an ascending step is coded as $+1$, a descending third as -2, etc.). The third tells the event's duration (eighth note = 1, quarter note = 2, etc.). The fourth tells the ending metric position of the event, whether on a specific beat in a $4/4$ measure (0,1,2,3) or on a strong or weak beat (coded as 4 or 5). And the fifth number tells whether the event must be a consonance (coded as 1), either a consonance or a dissonance (0), or specifically an imperfect consonance (2). Thus, through a crude numerical cipher the verbal listing given above can be distilled into the compact form show below.

1.   {1,+1,2,4,1} [i.e., term. event, up 1 step, ¼ note, to str. beat, cons.]
2.   {1,-1,2,5,1}   3.   {1,+2,2,4,1}
4.   {1,-2,2,5,1}   5.   {1,+3,2,4,1}

6. {1,-3,2,5,1}   7. {1,+4,2,4,1}
8. {1,-4,2,5,1}   9. {1,+5,2,4,1}
10. {1,+7,2,4,1}   11. {1,-7,2,5,1}
12. {0,+1,2,5,0} — {1,+1,2,4,1}
13. {0,-1,2,5,0} — {1,-1,2,4,1}
14. {0,-1,2,5,0} — {1,+1,2,4,1}
15. {0,-1,2,5,0} — {2,-2,2,4,1} — {2,+1,2,5,0} — {1,+1,2,4,1}
16. {0,-2,2,5,1} — {1,+3,2 4,1}

And in PRAENESTE's own parsimonious representation all this concrete melodic knowledge takes less space in memory than would this
sentence.

The CHOICES subroutine is a loop that sequentially goes through
the melodic memory for a species and tests each melodic schema to
determine whether it is a correct pattern in the particular local environment. This local contrapuntal environment can vary in size depending
on the size of the melodic schema. For a small schema like a simple
interval the local environment consists only of the current metric position, the preceding two pitches in the counterpoint, and the preceding
and current pitches in the cantus firmus. For a long schema the local
environment may also include several future pitches of the cantus firmus and a series of progressive metric positions.

To check if a melodic schema is correct in the local environment,
the CHOICES subroutine compares the features called for by its memory
of each melodic event with those features allowable in that context. To
do this, CHOICES must monitor and update metric position, valid consonances, and local melodic contour. The simplest task is to monitor
the current metric position by means of a simple metric schema. Updated by the duration of the previous tone in the counterpoint, this schema
is in essence no more than a numerical representation of $^4/_4$ time with
the added knowledge that the odd and even numbered beats share an
affinity we call "strong" and "weak." If the coded metric position
required of a melodic event matches the current position within the metric
schema, then CHOICES goes on to check the allowable consonances.

Given the local environment, the consonant pitches that the counterpoint could employ are listed in an array that is updated by a subroutine
called CONS/DISS. This subroutine associates the tone in the cantus
firmus with specific memories of various classes of consonances: octaves, fifths, and thirds or sixths. For the purpose of illustration, let
us say that the tone A is in the cantus firmus. First, CONS/DISS would
automatically remember all the thirds and sixths that go with A in the

gamut from F to a ", that is, F-c-f-c '-f '-c "-f ". Then, before proceeding to either octaves or fifths, CONS/DISS would determine whether the cantus firmus had just changed tones and, if so, the direction of that change. With this knowledge CONS/DISS can limit its association of perfect consonances to those that do not result in parallel or direct intervals. That is, if we assume that our A in the cantus firmus was just approached from the G below and the preceding pitch in the counterpoint was e ', then only perfect consonances from e ' and below are considered. Thus, when CONS/DISS associates octaves (and unisons) with this context, only A and a are considered—a ' or a " would have resulted in direct motion to an octave, something quite beyond the pale of strict two-part species.

After remembering the proper thirds, sixths, and octaves, CONS/DISS proceeds to fifths. Whether an association is made with fifths above the tone in the cantus or with fifths below it depends on the relation of the cantus tone to the voice range of the counterpoint. If the cantus tone is below the voice range of the counterpoint, then only fifths above it are considered (e.g., e-e '-e " above A). If, on the other hand, the cantus tone is above the voice range of the counterpoint, then only fifths below it are considered (e.g., d "-d '-d below a "). In those cases where the cantus tone is in the middle of the voice range of the counterpoint, then fifths both above and below it are possible (e.g., d and e ' straddling a). CONS/DISS also takes special note of when the cantus tone falls upon B, a troublesome pitch in this style. When this occurs the upper fifth, F, is considered only when a permissible chromatic alteration of musica ficta would be available to prevent a diminished fifth (i.e., F-sharp in Mixolydian or Aeolian cadences, or B-flat in the Dorian mode).

CONS/DISS collates the three sets of consonances (in the hypothetical example above with the A in the cantus: the thirds and sixths F-c-f-c '-f '-c "-f ", the octaves or unisons A-a, and the fifths e-e '), eliminates from consideration any tones lying outside a particular voice range (say, the alto range from f to d "), and then checks whether the pitch called for in the melodic event under review is present in this array of pitches (i.e., whether a certain pitch is contained among f-a-c '-e '-f '-c "). If it is present, or if it is not but a dissonance is permissible, CHOICES then proceeds to check on the low-level melodic contour that will result if this pitch is eventually selected.

In keeping with the way we have seen it deal with the low-level features of meter and consonance, CHOICES examines a three-tone melodic contour not to see if it breaks any rules but to see if it matches any of the schemata it knows for such contours. The process of matching, carried out by a subroutine called NARMOUR (after Eugene Narmour, who has described these contours in detail),[7] affects only the first event of a melodic schema in relation to what immediately precedes it. Low-level contours within any of the longer melodic schemata do not need to be examined since the melodic patterns stored in memory are, a priori, all examples of good contour.

NARMOUR attempts to match the contour resulting from the previous two tones of the counterpoint and the first tone of a new melodic schema with one of four contour types: (1) return, (2) reversal, (3) uniform linear movement, and (4) unequal linear movement. "Return" and "reversal" are both broken contours. That is, the contour changes direction at the middle tone. In "return," however, the first and third tones are the same or just one step apart, whereas in "reversal" the first and third tones are at least a third apart. Thus the three pitches g-e-a would fit the "return" contour while the pitches g-e-c' would fit "reversal." It could be argued that the distinction made between these two broken contours is unnecessary inasmuch as both are allowed. Yet if these types of contour suggest different psychological processes—return suggesting a judgment of similarity, reversal a judgment of difference—then it is more in keeping with the spirit of the program to make the distinction. In addition, the ability to make the distinction is a resource the program could use at higher levels.

"Uniform linear process" and "unequal linear process" are likewise related contours differentiated by a judgment of similarity or difference. "Uniform linear process" is a straight contour of two like intervals in a row, either two seconds or two thirds (larger successive intervals, for example two fifths, are not allowed in species counterpoint). "Unequal linear process," as the name implies, is a straight contour of dissimilar intervals. For this contour the larger of the two intervals must always be on the bottom (one of several precepts in species counterpoint suggesting that knowledge of the style includes a psychological "law of gravity").[8] Thus NARMOUR recognizes contours such as c-d-e , c-g-a , and (descending) c'-g-c , but does not recognize con-

---

[7]See Eugene Narmour, *The Analysis and Perception of Basic Melodic Structures: The Implication-Realization Model*, Vol. I (forthcoming).

[8]"It is almost as though one had submitted himself involuntarily to the law of gravity and other natural laws." Knud Jeppesen, *Counterpoint: The Polyphonic Vocal Style of the Sixteenth Century*, trans. Glen Haydon (New York, 1939), p. 138n. In addition to unequal skips, strict species practice differentiates up from down in relation to the reversal of direction after large skips, the treatment of suspensions, the preferred metric locations of the beginnings of scalar quarter notes, the treatment of neighbor notes, the use of anticipations, and the allowance of accented stepwise dissonance.

tours such as c-f-b, c-d-a, and c'-g-f . A perverse contour like A-a-f',
recognized as an "unequal linear process," is disallowed because it
has too great a range. On the other hand, a fine contour like c-d-f-(e),
the first three tones of which do not match any of NARMOUR's contours, is itself a melodic schema in first and second species and thus
exempt from any check on its internal contour.

Having compared the features of every event in each melodic schema
to determine if they fit into the local environment of metric position,
consonance, and contour (two other minor checks are also made—one
to ensure that any melodic sixth will be minor and one to ensure that
any suspension will resolve to an imperfect consonance), CHOICES
then reports to PRAENESTE, listing the "good" schemata for that context. To understand better what such a list might be like, and to review
before moving on to discuss the higher levels of the program, let us
return to the local environment sketched above in relation to CONS/DISS
and trace the whole cycle of what CHOICES would do in third species.
Here is the case of the environment discussed:

counterpoint: | - - g' e' | ? . .
cantus firmus: | G | A

In this environment, only those third-species melodic schemata whose
initial (or only) events end on a strong beat will pass the test of metric
position. Thus, of the sixteen third-species melodic schemata listed
earlier, only numbers 1, 3, 5, 7, 9, and 10 could be inserted at the question mark. They are, respectively, the simple intervals of an ascending
second, third, fourth, fifth, sixth, and octave. CONS/DISS then determines which of these intervals taken from the reference point of e' matches a pitch in the array of allowable consonances associated with the A
in the cantus firmus (i.e., the array f-a-c'-e'-f'-c"). Since only ascending intervals are in question and since the counterpoint was last on e',
only the two pitches f' and c" match the intervals. Inasmuch as NAR-
MOUR recognizes both the contours g'-e'-f' and g'-e'-c" (as "return"
and "reversal," respectively), CHOICES reports that schemata numbers
1 and 9 (the ascending second and sixth) are "good."

In this instance, PRAENESTE would have just two schemata to choose
from for the counterpoint's immediate continuation. It might seem that
programming PRAENESTE to make such a decision would be simple,
but it is not. A single line of reasoning that leads to a clear choice between two simple intervals may well be hopelessly confounded by the
wealth of possibilities that arise in other situations. In the florid style

of fifth species it is quite possible that twenty or more diverse and complex schemata might fit a single environment. The problem then is not just to choose between intervals, but to choose between a cambiata and a suspension, between an ascending line of five quarter notes and a descending line with a dotted half note and three quarters, or between a single whole note and a florid pattern with eighths.

PRAENESTE's main goal is to make a good piece of music; and as the computer scientist Marvin Minsky has said, "The problem of making a good piece of music is the problem of finding a structure that satisfies a lot of constraints."[9] The CHOICES subroutine already provides PRAENESTE a method for satisfying the several low-level constraints known collectively as the "rules" of counterpoint. Low-level constraints do in fact resemble rules in their specificity. The matter, for instance, of whether a tone is consonant, on a strong beat, or part of a "return" contour is rarely in doubt. But mid-level constraints are less specific, and high-level constraints can be positively vague. If the force of a constraint is proportionate to its specificity, then constraints become weaker as they become broader. Whereas a low-level musical constraint can demand that a tone must be a consonance and nothing else, a mid-level constraint might only require that after a large ascending interval the melody should reverse direction and fill in the registral gap if possible, and a high-level constraint might be so feeble as only to suggest that, all things being equal, in the course of an entire counterpoint it would be better to use a wide variety of pitches.

To monitor diverse mid- and high-level constraints, rate their relative strengths in a particular context, and decide on an optimal melodic path, PRAENESTE makes use of a subroutine called PATH. Understanding how PATH operates requires an introduction to three things: its "scorecard" system of combining diverse constraints, its "topographic" method of selecting an optimal melodic schema, and the specifics of PATH's five mid- or high-level constraints. Let us first explore the "scorecard" system.

Imagine a hypothetical musical style with only three constraints—X, Y, and Z—and a ten-note gamut of scale degrees numbered one through ten. At a certain point within an imaginary counterpoint each constraint might have a different force and be satisfied in different ways. For example, constraint X might strongly urge that scale degrees 4, 5, or 6 be used; constraint Y might suggest that any scale degree above number five is good; and constraint Z might hint that, all things being equal,

[9]Quoted in Curtis Roads, "Interview with Marvin Minsky," *Computer Music Journal* 4 (1980), p. 29.

the odd-numbered scale degrees are preferable. Roughly translating the supposed strength of each constraint into a numerical score might result in the scale degrees satisfying constraint X being given four points each, the degrees satisfying constraint Y three points each, and the degrees satisfying constraint Z just two points each. Adding these individual scores together results in a general scorecard for that stage in the counterpoint. As shown below, degree 6 would have the highest score, followed by degrees 5, 7, and 9. Somewhat surprisingly, degree 4 receives only the fifth highest score, even though it is strongly urged by constraint X. This is because no other constraint corroborates degree 4; a scale degree that satisfies both of two weaker constraints may outscore a degree that satisfies one, but only one, strong constraint.

constraint X:				4	4	4				
constraint Y:						3	3	3	3	3
constraint Z:		2		2		2		2		2
scale degrees:		1—	2—	3—	4—	5—	6—	7—	8—	9—10
score totals:		2	0	2	4	6	7	5	3	5 3

In PATH itself there are five constraints of varying strength that contribute to a scorecard for the twenty-four scale degrees in PRAENESTE's gamut (F-a″). The type of numerical representation shown above is not good at visually conveying the highs and lows of the various scores, especially when twenty-four scale degrees are involved. A more tangible sense of the topography of constraint can be obtained by transforming a scorecard into a simple contour. Figure 1 shows such a transformation of the hypothetical scorecard just discussed.

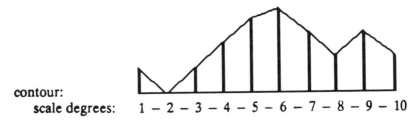

contour:
scale degrees: 1 – 2 – 3 – 4 – 5 – 6 – 7 – 8 – 9 – 10

Figure 1.

After determining the local topography of constraint, PATH takes the melodic schemata sent it by CHOICES, rates them on the basis of how they fit into the peaks and valleys of constraint, and then selects the single melodic schema that matches the highest peaks, that is to say, the schema that best satisfies all the constraints. In the example worked through for the CHOICES subroutine, the two melodic schemata approved were simple intervals—an ascending second and an ascending minor sixth. Were PATH evaluating these two intervals in the hypothetical environment of constraint shown in figure 1, its selection would depend on which scale degree was the reference point. If scale degree 2 were the reference point, the ascending sixth would be rated higher and therefore selected because scale degree 7 has a higher score than scale degree 3. But if these same ascending intervals were judged from the reference point of scale degree 4, then the ascending second would be rated higher.

In evaluating a more complex, longer melodic schema, PATH sums the ratings of all its constituent tones (not counting the reference tone). In many cases this procedure gives PATH a preference for the longest schema allowed at any point. It is still, however, quite possible for a single interval to rate higher than a longer schema. If, again in the context of figure 1 with scale degree 1 now as the reference point, the choice were between the simple interval of an ascending sixth and the longer pattern of an ascending passing-tone figure (i.e., scale degrees 2 and 3), the simple interval with its score of seven would nevertheless be selected over the longer pattern with its score of just two. Clearly those melodic patterns whose tones coincide with the peaks in this topography of constraint are the most likely to be selected.

Of the five main constraints that guide PATH, two might be termed mid-level constraints while three are more high-level. Let us first look at the mid-level constraints to see how they use a fading memory of the counterpoint's recent past to create implications for its future.

A subroutine called MEYER takes two important concepts developed by Leonard B. Meyer—the psychological implications of linear melodic processes and melodic gaps—and translates them into numerical form.[10] In Meyer's view of linear melodic process, the Gestalt law of good continuation dictates that unidirectional scalar or triadic melodic motion creates an implication for its own continuance. Put more simply, if we hear c followed by d, there is an implication that an e will follow. This implication can be greatly affected by rhythm. In particular, the perceived need to continue linear motion seems more vivid when the last duration heard is relatively short. No doubt this is why, for example, the

---

[10]See, for example, Leonard B. Meyer, "Toward a Theory of Style," in *The Concept of Style*, ed. Berel Lang (Philadelphia, 1979), pp. 3-44.

Palestrina style requires that two ascending eighth notes *must* have a linear, stepwise continuation but does not demand this of two ascending whole notes.

When asked by PATH to determine the constraint of "good continuation," MEYER checks the last two tones in the counterpoint to determine if they are a second or a third apart (larger intervals suggest a different category discussed below). If no more than a third, MEYER then projects a continuation of the interval and gives the implied scale degree (or degrees) a score based on several stylistic criteria. First, the duration of the last tone in the counterpoint is taken into consideration; the shorter the last duration, the higher the score. Second, movement by step and movement by third are treated differently. In this style, scalar motion is favored and engenders strong implications. When, for instance, the pitch c is followed by d, both e and f are given scores, though the score for the immediate implication, e, is higher than that for the somewhat more remote tone f. On the other hand, movement by third is less strongly implicative in the Palestrina style; only a single scale degree is projected, and it is given a low score. The third and final criterion distinguishes between ascending and descending motion. For scalar movement, only suspensions are affected. That is, a suspended tone cancels any possible upward melodic implication but can retain a modest downward implication. For movement by third, descending motion receives the higher score, though movement in either direction is only weakly implicative.

For comparison with the other constraints described later, it may be useful to cite instances of what, in varying situations, actual scores for "good continuation" are. As a first example, consider two ascending quarter notes, e and f. On a separate scorecard kept just for linear implications, MEYER will place a score of 13 in the slot for g, and a score of 10 in the slot for a. Were e and f half notes, the scores for g and a would be 7 and 4 respectively—a reduction in roughly inverse proportion to the doubling of the note values. The scores would be lower still for motion by thirds. If e were followed by g in half notes, MEYER would place a score of 1 in the slot for b; or were the motion descending, the score would have been no higher than 3 (triadic motion in quarters or eighths is not possible in this style).

Implications are not always realized immediately, so scores are retained on the linear-process scoreboard to encourage PATH to return to a previously implied pitch. For instance, if a counterpoint has the melodic progression c-d-e followed by a change of direction back down to d, the earlier implied f and g still retain a score and are thus attractive to PATH. Of course if every linear implication from each stage of the melody were still operative, one could imagine the confusion by the end of a counterpoint. Every pitch in the scale might be implied from both directions. To surmount this problem PATH treats linear implications as information in short-term memory. Every time it moves on to a new stage in a counterpoint, PATH "forgets" half the values of the scores from all previous linear implications. In practical terms this means that the strength of a linear implication begins to fade rapidly over time and effectively disappears after three or four new melodic schemata have been chosen.

In contrast to the sense of continuation that characterizes linear process, melodic gaps—the other of Leonard B. Meyer's concepts used here as a mid-level constraint—are distinguished by discontinuity. A large melodic leap seems to require that the intervening scale degrees subsequently be used to "fill in the gap." While this principle is surely at work to some degree in many musical styles, it is patently evident and especially compelling in the Palestrina style emulated in species counterpoint.[11] It would be out of the question, for instance, for a Palestrina-style melody to leap up an octave without then turning back and in some fashion touching upon many of the degrees leapt over. The force of this implied filling in of a melodic gap appears to be proportional to the size and direction of the gap. In relation to size, MEYER evaluates the leaps of a third, fourth, fifth, sixth, and octave by assigning to each of the intervening scale degrees a score of 5, 6, 8, 10, or 14 respectively (notice that thirds are ambiguous, being treated simultaneously both as gaps and as the beginnings of linear processes). And in relation to direction, MEYER gives a bonus of one extra point to all ascending scores, since it is widely held that ascending leaps are in greater need of a compensatory filling in.

Implications for filling in gaps fade, just as do the implications of linear processes. So PATH also experiences a progressive loss of memory for the implications of a past melodic gap. Nevertheless, it is quite possible that the scorecard recording this gap-filling constraint may at any one time reflect two or more gaps that overlap or are embedded one within another. For example, if a melody leapt up from c to c', the gap scorecard would show 15 points each for the intervening tones d-e-f-g-a-b. If conditions then prompted PATH to follow this up-

[11]"The skip of the fifth . . . is filled out in the following measures, as is the skip of the fourth. . . . It is thus normal in the Palestrina style that skips are compensated by stepwise progressions or—as is also somewhat common—by skips in the opposite direction." Jeppesen, *Counterpoint*, pp. 85-86.

ward octave leap with a downward leap to g, then the revised scorecard would show the tones d-e-f-g fading to 7 points each (roughly one half the previous score) while the tones a and b still would have 13 points each (the faded 7 points from the octave leap and 6 points from the descending fourth).

At a somewhat higher level than the dynamic mid-level constraint of a line or gap lies a constraint I call "variety." As an aesthetic constraint, "variety" is not concerned with a tone being right or wrong; instead it judges whether something contributes to the impression that diverse resources are being employed. At present, PATH only analyzes the variety of individual pitches, a rather low-level view of variety. Though it has, through its NARMOUR routines, the capability of also judging the variety of melodic contours, this potential has yet to be implemented.

In analyzing the variety of individual pitches that a counterpoint employs, PATH makes use of two additional scorecards. The first merely tallies the number of times each scale degree has been used. After each new melodic schema is selected, and before the next one is chosen, PATH reviews this tally to determine which scale degree has occurred most frequently, which has occurred least, and so forth. Scores reflecting the *opposite* ranking are then entered into the second scorecard. In the hypothetical case of four tones, c-d-e-f, where the first scorecard may tally c as having been used four times, d three times, e twice, and f once, the second scorecard will give a score of zero to c, one to d, two to e, and three to f. Thus, the least used scale degree will have the highest score for "variety" and be most attractive to PATH.

The magnitude of the scores given for "variety" is low compared to the scores given for lines or gaps. This is in keeping with the principle described earlier that as constraints become broader they become weaker and less specific. Broader still are the two high-level constraints of overall contour and mode. These constraints, in their present form within PATH, do not respond to note-by-note or even measure-by-measure changes that take place as a counterpoint is being constructed. Instead they can be thought of as a constant background, a fixed frame of reference.

The high-level constraint of overall contour recognizes that there are preferred general trajectories for counterpoints in the strict style. PATH takes one of the most common of these trajectories—an initial descent followed by a strong rise to a culminating peak and then a subsequent, more gradual descent to a cadence—and attempts to use it to weakly influence its choice of ascending or descending melodic schemata. To

create this influence, PATH first divides the voice range of the counterpoint into two regions: those tones at or below the modal finalis and
those tones at or above it. Then, using another scale-degree scorecard,
it gives points to all the scale degrees in the upper or lower region,
depending on which region its contour model suggests. As currently
programmed, PATH's contour model gives two points to all the tones
in the lower region during the first 15 percent of the counterpoint's
length, then it gives four points to all the tones in the upper region until
the counterpoint is 56 percent complete, after which it gives three points
to all the tones in the lower region until the counterpoint is finished.
In this manner, the choice of individual pitches is affected very little
while the general upward or downward movement of the counterpoint
is nevertheless subtly guided.

Recognizing that the meaning of "mode" with respect to polyphony
has been the subject of dispute since the Renaissance itself, PATH takes
a very cautious approach to making mode a constraint on a counterpoint's progress. In fact, all PATH does is to set up a "mode" scorecard
and award the modal finalis, its authentic dominant, and its plagal dominant one point each. This simple procedure, a far cry from a theory
of mode, nonetheless results in two desirable effects that may not be
self-evident. The first effect is felt at the very beginning of a counterpoint. In choosing its initial move, PATH can receive little guidance
from those of its constraints that react to past events—gaps, lines, and
to a lesser extent, variety. So the fixed framework of mode, weak though
it may be, can constrain a counterpoint to begin with, for example, a
leap from the finalis to its authentic dominant—an opening gambit well
established in the works of Palestrina. The second effect results in a
general avoidance of leaps to B or undue emphasis on that troublesome
degree. If we look at the modal tones that PATH favors—Dorian d-f-a;
Phrygian e-a-c; Mixolydian g-c-d; Aeolian a-c-e; Ionian c-e-g (Lydian
is treated as transposed Ionian)—we see that B is conspicuous by its
absence.

All the scorecards for the various constraints—lines, gaps, variety,
contour, and mode—are summed by PATH before it begins evaluating
the melodic schemata sent it by CHOICES. Thus PATH does not attempt to match each melodic schema to the peaks and valleys of five
separate constraints. Rather, it works with a single and summary
topography of constraint that, as a result of changes in its components,
varies considerably during the course of creating a counterpoint.

A more concrete feel for the way in which PRAENESTE molds its
memories of melodic schemata into patterns that satisfy multiple con-

straints may be gained by following step by step how it actually creates a counterpoint. For a cantus firmus, let us take one in the Mixolydian mode by Knud Jeppesen: g-d'-c'-a-b-c'-b-a-g. And since the third-species melodic schemata have already been introduced, let us direct PRAENESTE to work in that species in, say, the mezzo soprano range (a-f").

The first thing PRAENESTE must do is to select a starting pitch. For this purpose it calls upon a special subroutine called INITIALIZE that specifies how a counterpoint in each species ought to begin. In this case INITIALIZE finds that g' will work well, being in the center of the mezzo soprano range and forming a perfect consonance with the beginning of the cantus firmus. The same subroutine also places this pitch on the second beat of the first measure, as is shown below in example 1:

Example 1.

Having selected its first tone, PRAENESTE queries CHOICES as to the melodic schemata that can fit into this local environment. CHOICES checks all of its sixteen third-species melodic schemata and reports to PATH just two simple intervals, an ascending third and an ascending fifth. PATH updates its various scorecards, sums them, and comes up with the topography of constraint shown at the bottom of figure 2 (line 1). The relatively flat topography at this point reflects the lack of any preceding gaps, lines, or other pitches. Only the weak higher-level constraints are represented, the somewhat higher scores for tones in the lower half of the register reflecting the constraint of overall contour (an initial descent) and the slightly higher scores for C's and D's confirming a faint modal preference for these pitches.

PATH selects the ascending fifth over the ascending third on the basis of the aforementioned modal preference for d' over b and queries CHOICES again about what melodic schemata will fit into this new environment. This time CHOICES finds five different possibilities: a descending third, a descending fifth, a descending octave, an ascending passing-tone figure (d"-e"-f"), and a descending passing-tone figure

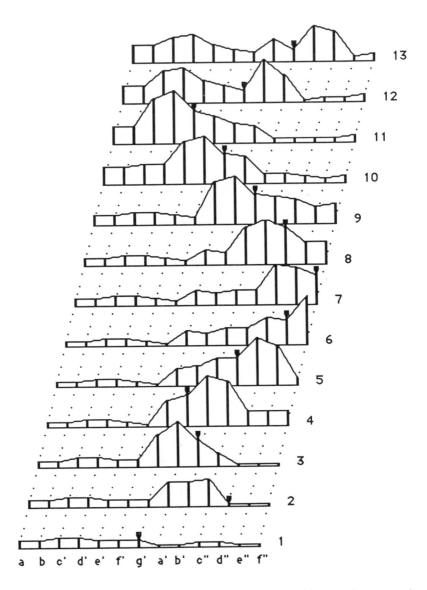

a b c' d' e' f' g' a' b' c" d" e" f"

Figure 2. Small black squares show melodic positions prior to each schema selection (cf. ex. 2).

(d″-c″-b′). When PATH now updates its scorecards it finds that the melodic gap from g′ to d″ has had a big effect (see fig. 2, line 2). Inasmuch as the descending passing-tone figure matches the highest and next highest peaks of this gap, it is the obvious schema to select.

As shown below in example 2, after the second melodic schema is selected the counterpoint has advanced to b′ at the beginning of the second measure. CHOICES reports another set of schemata, and PATH updates its scorecards to reflect the strong descending linear motion d″-c″-b′. The schema chosen that best matches the topography of line 3 in figure 2 is a cambiata—b′-a′-f′-g′-a′. It not only touches upon the two highest peaks (a′ and g′) but also touches the highest peak twice (a′).

Example 2.

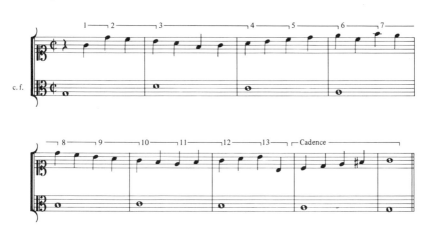

The cambiata turns the counterpoint upward, and a comparison of figure 2 with example 2 will show that this upward movement is sustained until the melody reaches the top of the voice range (f″) (line 7 of fig. 2, measure four of ex. 2). An upward shift in the scoring of overall contour and a stronger desire for variety contribute to the strength of this ascent in determining the course of the melody. That is, at the same time that the cambiata turned the counterpoint upward, the scorecard for overall contour shifted from giving two points to each scale degree in the lower region to giving four points to each degree in the upper region. And the repetition of the pitches g′ and a′ caused by the cambiata made the still unused pitches e″ and f″ more attractive to PATH.

After peaking at the top of its range, the counterpoint begins a linear descent that takes it all the way down to e' (line 11 of fig. 2, measure 6 of ex. 2). Again this motion is abetted by a second and downward shift in the scoring of overall contour (line 10 of fig. 2) reemphasizing the lower region of pitches. From this low e' CHOICES cannot approve yet another descending passing-tone figure, though it does allow a simple descending third and an ascending passing-tone figure. PATH selects the ascending passing-tone figure because the longer figure slightly outscores the simple interval. Had the simple interval matched the highest peak instead of the second highest (line 11 of fig. 2), it would have outscored the passing-tone figure.

Reversing direction at its low e', the counterpoint ascends first to g' and then to b' where, because of a similar inability to continue its implied stepwise motion, it makes a descending octave leap to b. At these last two stages (shown in lines 12 and 13 of fig. 2) the behavior of PATH begins to change. Instead of selecting from all the melodic schemata approved by CHOICES, PATH began limiting itself to only those schemata that would not extend beyond the end of measure 7. To understand why PATH behaves in this manner, it is first necessary to discuss how PRAENESTE deals with the problems of cadencing a counterpoint.

In programming PRAENESTE to cadence correctly, three strategies were considered. The first strategy was for CHOICES and PATH to continue their work to the end of the cantus firmus and then for a new subroutine to go back and see what sort of conventional cadence could be spliced into the just written counterpoint. The second strategy was for a new subroutine to write a conventional cadence first and then to constrain CHOICES and PATH in such a way that they would be forced to lead the counterpoint to the beginning of this cadence. The third strategy called for CHOICES and PATH to work normally until reaching an area just before a conventional cadence would begin and from that point to try to find a connection with any of several cadences.

In evaluating these strategies the guiding principle was that PRAENESTE should behave as much as possible like a knowledgeable practitioner, whether that meant a sixteenth-century chorister, a theorist like Knud Jeppesen, or even an active listener in the sense of one who can mentally participate in the performance of this style of music. Such a principle automatically disqualified the first strategy with its reliance on working backwards. Improvisers cannot improvise backwards, listeners may recall things from the past but cannot actively listen backwards, and even Knud Jeppesen, so concerned with stylistic perfection, never advocated working backwards. The second strategy was better in suggesting that a counterpoint progress toward a specific goal. But choosing a single cadence ahead of time and not letting the experience of the unfolding counterpoint affect that choice seemed too rigid a procedure. In the same light, the advance choice of a cadence would be largely an arbitrary act inasmuch as it would be unconstrained by any knowledge of what the cadence would follow.

The third strategy, with its human sense of ''trying to work something out on the go from lots of possibilities,'' was the most promising though the most difficult to effect in a step-by-step program. In the first place, it required more memory than the other strategies. PRAENESTE had to be given a precise memory of several conventional cadences appropriate to each species. And second, it required a new concept, that of a ''cadence point'' for each cadence. As defined in PRAENESTE, a ''cadence point'' is a marker in musical time and space containing the knowledge of exactly where, given a particular mode, voice range, and species, a conventional cadence would need to begin. For example, the common fourth-species cadence shown in example 3 has a cadence point defined as being at the pitch level of the finalis and two and one-half measures prior to the end of the cantus firmus. This is the type of knowledge that an improviser would need in order to determine whether he had gone beyond the point where a certain cadence would have begun.

Example 3.

For most species, PRAENESTE is provided with four conventional cadences arranged in its memory from the longest to the shortest. Thus the cadence point for the first cadence is the one furthest from the end of the cantus firmus and the one that CHOICES and PATH will encounter first. CHOICES and PATH work quite normally until the counterpoint begins to approach the first cadence point. Then PATH begins ignoring any melodic schema that would extend beyond this cadence point. This usually has the effect of bringing the counterpoint right up to the first cadence point. At that time a subroutine called

CADENCE takes over and, in the manner of CHOICES, checks to see if the first cadence and its connection to the counterpoint fit properly into the local environment.

If this first cadence fits, then it is adopted and the counterpoint is finished. If not, CHOICES and PATH continue and attempt to make a connection with the second cadence. Should that also fail, subsequent attempts are made at the third cadence and, if necessary, the fourth cadence. Thus PRAENESTE always tries first to use the longest cadence but proceeds to shorter and shorter cadences if its early attempts fail. In this way, much like an improviser, PRAENESTE allows the counterpoint at hand to dictate which cadence is selected. By the same token, also like a human improviser, it can run out of ideas and simply be unable to make a graceful cadence. In such cases, presently about one counterpoint in five, it is programmed to be silent and signal its embarrassment by the word *oops*. Its difficulties are, in general, not caused by its strategy but by the complexity of programming that strategy. That is, as it currently operates, PRAENESTE is not always aware of all the legal connections that it could make with cadences and overlooks some that a skilled contrapuntist would recognize.

In the case of the counterpoint shown above in example 2, PRAENESTE determines that the first cadence point it knows for third species (a location two measures from the end and a fifth below the finalis) does fit into the local environment. It also determines that the cadence marked by that cadence point—four ascending quarter notes leading up to a whole-note finalis—matches the requisite low-level constraints of consonance, meter, and so forth. So PRAENESTE then selects that cadence and finishes the counterpoint. As is clear from example 2, the cadence selected turns out to be especially well chosen, given the way in which it fills in the large descending gap of the octave b '- b. In part this complementarity is fortuitous—PRAENESTE does not yet judge cadences according to higher-level constraints. But at the same time some credit must be granted the program's strategy. That is, given the facts that the overall contour directs the counterpoint down toward the finalis, that the possible cadences are characterized by stepwise motion, and that the operation of PATH prior to the cadence favors single intervals (often leaps), then the occurrence of a pre-cadential leap away from the finalis with ensuing linear motion back toward the finalis becomes rather likely.

How good is PRAENESTE at writing species counterpoint? To answer this question it may be useful to conduct a side-by-side comparison of counterpoints written by both PRAENESTE and Knud Jeppesen over the same Mixolydian cantus firmus already introduced.[12] Example 4 shows two first-species counterpoints. In this simple case, PRAENESTE (P) and Jeppesen (J) write identical counterpoints, suggesting that in simple circumstances they "think" more or less alike.

Example 4.

Example 5 shows two second-species counterpoints. The extent to which the two counterpoints coincide is surprisingly high, though PRAENESTE and Jeppesen differ slightly in the way they begin and differ markedly in how they descend from the high d″ to the cadence. Jeppesen descends in a single leap of an octave, while PRAENESTE descends first by thirds and then by a fifth. By Jeppesen's precepts the two melodies are of like quality, his own work being vulnerable to criticism for lacking direction after the octave leap and PRAENESTE's for having too many consecutive leaps.

Example 5.

[12]The Jeppesen examples are all taken from his *Counterpoint*: ex. 4 (p. 113), ex. 5 (p. 118), ex. 6 (pp.127-128), ex. 7 (p. 135), ex. 8 (p. 150).

Example 6 shows the third-species counterpoint of PRAENESTE already discussed and a similar counterpoint by Jeppesen. As in the second-species example, these counterpoints begin differently. Jeppesen, in descending from the initial g', is taking advantage of a special situation unknown to PRAENESTE. That is, ordinarily one cannot make a descending leap from a weak beat in strict third species. But since the g' is not preceded by another pitch, the problems of contour usually associated with such a leap do not arise. The counterpoints also differ in how they cadence. Jeppesen's might be criticized for the consecutive downbeat octaves in the last two measures, though he specifically allows such patterns. PRAENESTE's might be criticized for the octave leap—not easy to sing at a brisk tempo—and for perhaps too much stepwise motion. Again, the two counterpoints are of similar quality.

Example 6.

In the absence of a fourth-species example by Jeppesen on this same Mixolydian cantus firmus, example 7 compares an Ionian counterpoint by Jeppesen with one by PRAENESTE. Two reasons would seem to explain why these counterpoints differ. First, Jeppesen and PRAENESTE have opposing strategies for the fourth species. Jeppesen feels that the purpose of this species is to practice suspensions. Therefore he allows melodic infelicities when they make possible the use of an additional suspension (see, for example, the awkward b'-c"-f" contour in measures 4-5 of ex. 7). PRAENESTE, on the other hand, does not vary its standards of good melody and in consequence uses fewer suspensions.

The second reason why these counterpoints differ is attributable to an inadequacy in the current state of PRAENESTE's program. As explained earlier, PRAENESTE uses a rich memory of concrete melodic schemata to enable it to expeditiously piece together a stylistically sound

Example 7.

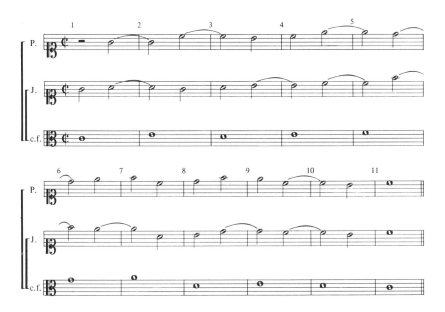

counterpoint. At present, however, PRAENESTE cannot make any associations between related schemata, something a human contrapuntist surely does all the time. For example, in the third and fourth measures of example 7 Jeppesen chose to ascend from a′ to c″. He was able to associate the simple three-half-note pattern a′-b′-c″ with the consonant suspensions of b′ and c″ in such a way as to produce the final pattern a′-b′-b′-c″-c″. That is something PRAENESTE cannot yet do because it currently treats melodic schemata as completely separate entities. The terminal event of one schema, for instance, cannot be considered as the medial event in a second, overlapping schema—a limitation that often unduly restricts the "good" schemata in a given contrapuntal environment.

The consecutive downbeat octaves that PRAENESTE allowed in example 7 (mm. 8-9) point up a rather surprising aspect of its program. Simply put, PRAENESTE knows nothing at all about avoiding melodic sequences. Furthermore, it knows nothing about avoiding too many consecutive similar consonances, or melodic tritones, or many other "sins." Though procedures to prevent these faults could surely have been written into PRAENESTE's program, they were not. The reason for these omissions was a desire to determine first to what extent such faults were likely, given the way PRAENESTE works. As it turns out, these problems arise only rarely. PRAENESTE, unlike a student contrapuntist, is not drawn to a sequence as a "quick" solution to a contrapuntal problem. So apart from those situations in which the cantus firmus itself is sequential, few melodic sequences result.

In those cases where certain sins nevertheless become frequent enough to be troubling, PRAENESTE can be taught to avoid them by altering the behavior of PATH with a special subroutine called GLOBALS. GLOBALS is, as its name implies, concerned with large issues of how the counterpoint is proceeding. For example, it is GLOBALS that monitors the approach to the cadence point in order to affect the selections of PATH. At present, the only special sin to which GLOBALS is alert is the occurrence of a downbeat unison between counterpoint and cantus firmus. When this would occur, GLOBALS forces PATH to give the offending schema a very low score, resulting in a general (but not guaranteed) avoidance of the problem.

Example 8 returns to the Mixolydian cantus firmus and demonstrates how the complexities of fifth species point up both Jeppesen's strengths and PRAENESTE's weaknesses. One might liken the difference between the two counterpoints to the difference between the play of a chess grandmaster and that of a simple chess-playing computer program. The grandmaster, like Jeppesen, will have a large-scale thematic unity to his or her play that a simple program, in spite of its internal library of good moves, cannot duplicate. PRAENESTE's counterpoint is, to be sure, not that bad; it does respond well to the movement of the cantus firmus and seems to build up nicely to the climax of high b' in measure 5. But its mid-level monitoring of pitch variety does not prevent it from choosing schemata that result in six rather too prominent appearances of g', the finalis. Jeppesen, on the other hand, in measure 3 moves dramatically away from the finalis by means of an octave leap (e'-e") motivated not by the immediate environment but by an overall strategy for making more satisfying the eventual return to the stable finalis.

PRAENESTE constitutes a model of a music based on, to paraphrase Dr. Sacks, "vivid, intense, detailed, yet simple" memories of concrete melodic fragments. In the sense that PRAENESTE then "knows" something of "real" music it is distinguished from most previous computer or theoretical models. The necessity of PRAENESTE's employing what is sometimes called "knowledge-based programming" became evident to me only after an initial, and in retrospect humorously misguided, attempt to program species counterpoint using only the "rules" of counterpoint.

Example 8.

I constructed a classic chain of if-then conditionals representing the standard commandments of simple species counterpoint. Random pitches were evaluated by, so to speak, having them run the gauntlet of these if-then conditions. The survivors then represented the tones of the counterpoint. As might be expected, the musical results were abysmal. The overt rules of counterpoint simply do not suffice to guarantee musical results. Even attempts to convert the covert precepts of good counterpoint into fixed rules were largely unsuccessful. One quickly can be forced to describe single special cases as general rules with the result that such supposed abstractions are often more complex than the situation or phenomenon on which they are based.

Rule-based grammars are, nonetheless, at the heart of most previous attempts to program musical knowledge. The first account of a species-counterpoint program must surely be that given by Lejaren Hiller and Leonard Isaacson in their 1959 classic *Experimental Music*,[13] a volume that still conveys the excitement of working with early computers. Their work, which stimulated newspaper headlines such as " 'Brain' Makes like Bach for Scientists,"[14] was based on a set of sixteen rules which, though powerful enough to give a rough impression of a type of strict style, were unable to prevent so awkward a melody as that shown below in example 9.[15]

More recently, David Lewin has turned his attention toward aspects of species counterpoint.[16] In a computer program written to demonstrate

[13]Lejaren A. Hiller, Jr., and Leonard M. Isaacson, *Experimental Music: Composition with an Electronic Computer* (New York, 1959). The programming of counterpoint rules is discussed in chapter five.
[14]I. Wilheim, *Washington Post*, Sept. 2, 1956.
[15]Hiller and Isaacson, p. 187, mm. 68-72.
[16]David Lewin, "An Interesting Global Rule for Species Counterpoint," *In Theory Only* 6 (1983): 19-44.

Example 9.

an algorithm for preventing unfilled melodic gaps, he also resorted to employing a chain of the rules of counterpoint. Using more rules than Hiller and Isaacson, and with a higher-level rule preventing unfilled gaps, Lewin's program writes far more stylistically and with few obvious mistakes.[17] Yet as a model of a style the Lewin program is unsatisfactory. It writes counterpoint backwards, viewing a melody as the solution of a problem rather than as an aesthetic act or utterance. And, as in Hiller and Isaacson's work, there is no obvious means for extending the methods applied in the "simple species" (the rhythmically uniform first, second, and third species) to the more musically real circumstances of fifth species.

In models of music outside the restricted domain of species counterpoint the exclusion of concrete musical knowledge is equally apparent. Recent overviews of such models[18] make it clear that the preferred representations of musical knowledge are often abstractions divorced from specific content or context. I suspect that this is not an approach native to specifically musical modes of thought but rather the result of influence from the field of linguistics. There, one may conveniently separate syntax from semantics, grammar from meaning. But whether this may be done in music is certainly open to debate.

In what might be thought an unexpected correspondence, of all the recent models of music the one most similar to PRAENESTE is a view of jazz improvisation propounded by Perlman and Greenblatt.[19] Jazz improvisation and species counterpoint are usually taken to be antithetical arenas, stylistically as remote as is the Papal Chapel in Rome from the

[17]What constitutes a mistake may depend on the style of species counterpoint in which one was trained. For example, Jeppesen allows voice crossing and melodic successions of two (or even more) thirds whereas many Fuxian versions of species counterpoint do not. Lewin's examples of first species might be faulted only for allowing consecutive fourths in the same direction, a construct neither tradition favors.

[18]See, for example, Robert West, Peter Howell, and Ian Cross, "Modelling Perceived Musical Structure," in *Musical Structure and Cognition* (London, 1985), pp. 21-51; and Curtis Roads, "Grammars as Representations for Music," *Computer Music Journal* 3 (1979): 48-55.

[19]Alan M. Perlman and Daniel Greenblatt, "Miles Davis Meets Noam Chomsky: Some Observations on Jazz Improvisation and Language Structure," in *The Sign in Music and Literature*, ed. Wendy Steiner (Austin, 1981): 169-83.

Latin Quarter in New Orleans. But when viewed as melodically sophisticated active musical practices they seem less distinct. Like a cantus firmus, the harmonic progressions of jazz dictate a succession of local musical environments, what Perlman and Greenblatt call the "deep structure" of jazz. And like the melodic schemata in PRAENESTE's memory that are fitted by CHOICES to the local environment, the "licks" in a jazz soloist's mind are concrete, meaningful patterns to be matched to changing harmonic environments. In their terms, this pre-PATH stage is the "shallow structure" of jazz, "the array of possibilities that the musician may choose from at a given point" (p. 172). The ultimate selections made by PATH or the actual licks played by the improviser then form what they call the "surface structure." When viewed in this way these sacred and profane musics are quite similar in the processes they employ to achieve stylistic unity and expression. They are multileveled, temporally directed areas of human thought intimately tied up with a rich lexicon of meaningful musical memories.

Robert Morris once related to me how in his student days he managed to be so successful at writing sixteenth-century counterpoint. He said that although he assiduously studied the rules of counterpoint, when it actually came time to write his assignments he fell back upon his knowledge of what sixteenth-century counterpoint sounded like. In the same light, a computer model of species counterpoint will be successful to the extent that it too knows what good counterpoint sounds like. This knowledge is grounded not in abstract transformations but in the concrete experience and memory of real art.

Frank Tirro

Melody and the Markoff-Chain Model:
A Gregorian Hymn Repertory

In 1967 Leonard B. Meyer wrote:

> The fact that music, like information, is an instance of a Markoff process has important practical and theoretical ramifications.
> If music is a Markoff process, it would appear that as a musical event (be it a phrase, a theme, or a whole work) unfolds and the probability of a particular conclusion increases, uncertainty, information, and meaning will necessarily decrease. And in a closed physical system where the Markoff process operates this is just what does occur—probability tends to increase.[1]

If the Markoff-chain model is valid for describing the successive events which constitute a musical performance, then the related analytical methods used by mathematicians and the physical scientists who employ Markoff-chain analyses to test, understand, and describe events in other fields can be borrowed by musicologists to develop additional or complementary theories of music. We must first describe musical events in a format compatible with the mathematical formulae and graphic techniques used to study the data of other stochastic processes, and then we can generate new theories of music based on the analysis of this data. Further, when we encode music to enable a computer to perform the millions of repetitive operations necessary in the analysis of com-

---

[1]Leonard B. Meyer, *Music, the Arts, and Ideas* (Chicago, 1967), p. 15.

Frank Tirro is Dean and Professor of Music at the Yale University School of Music. He is the author of Jazz: A History *and* Renaissance Music Sources in the Archive of San Petronio in Bologna *as well as coauthor of* The Humanities: Cultural Roots and Continuities.

229

plete pieces of music, we obtain results based on systematic, objective criteria and methods. Lastly, the formidable task of data reduction can be accomplished without the problems of arbitrary or subjective selection of data by different individuals performing the same experiment. In fact, as is common in the "hard sciences," well documented experiments, with their hypotheses and conclusions, can be duplicated and tested by interested colleagues, a rare occurrence in the humanities.

In a later publication, Meyer rightly points out that:

> There is at present virtually no viable conceptual framework for the analytic criticism of melody. Most analyses consist of an unilluminating amalgam of blatant description (the melody rises to a climactic F-sharp and descends to a cadence on B), of routine formal classification (the first phrase is an antecedent, the second a consequent), and of a naïve account of motivic similarity (the motive of the first measure is repeated in the third and is inverted in the seventh measure). One reason for this sorry state of affairs is that, at least of late, too many writers have attempted to discuss melody in general. But it is difficult, if not impossible, to construct a theory which will encompass the melodic styles of Machaut, Mozart, and Webern—not to mention Javanese and Japanese music, and so on.[2]

The present study is an attempt to capitalize on Meyer's first observation concerning the applicability of mathematical models to explain music. I should like to follow his suggestion about the importance of developing a theory of melody, and also to heed his warning against attempting to understand all melodies at once.[3] I explore a very limited

---

[2]Idem., *Explaining Music: Essays and Explorations* (Berkeley, 1973), p. 109.

[3]The seminal studies seem to be those which applied mathematical theory to the study of linguistics. Noam Chomsky, in *Aspects of the Theory of Syntax* (Cambridge, Mass., 1965) and his other writings, has left the greatest imprint upon researchers in his and other fields. Nicolas Ruwet, whose principal work deals with theories of syntax and grammar in language, attempted to bridge the gap to music in his *Langage, Musique, Poésie* (Paris, 1972), but his discussion, especially chapter 4, serves to point out complexities and underscores a need for a generative grammar rather than proposing or attempt solutions. Also, he deals with much complex music in little space. Therefore, the discussion, although interesting and perceptive, tends to be superficial. More useful, perhaps, is his *An Introduction to Generative Grammar*, trans. Norval S. H. Smith (Amsterdam, 1973), but this book does not discuss music. It presents, however, views which contrast with those of Chomsky.

Another interesting study is that of Bjorn Lindblom and Johan Sundberg, "Towards a Generative Theory of Melody," *Svensk tidskrift för musikforskning* 52 (1970): 71-88. They apply some fundamental rules of linguistic prosody to melodies of Swedish nursery songs. Although they and I are both striving toward a melodic theory with a generative grammar, our methods are quite dissimilar.

repertory of melodies, hymn tunes from the Gregorian tradition, and I do not admit any presumptions about archetypes, modal dominants, leaps upward and turns backward, or other considerations for composing melodies in Gregorian style.[4] This particular repertory seems appropriate for such an initial study because it is real music integrally tied to the beginnings of the western European art music tradition; because harmonic considerations are obviated; and because text-tone relationships can be ignored (since hymn tunes are not only strophic but frequently reused with other texts on different liturgical occasions, no claim of specificity of word to melodic formula can generate strong support). Moreover, the hymns' modest length, limited range, and few accidentals permit simple encoding (no octave "equivalents") and easy visual and aural confirmation. This is particularly important at both the input and computer simulation stages, for until more researchers use, confirm, and develop these techniques, the approach must be considered experimental.

A similar study was carried out by Mario Baroni and Carlo Jacoboni of the University of Bologna, resulting in the publication of their *Proposal for a Grammar of Melody* in 1978.[5] They also selected a limited repertory, the melodies of the Bach Chorales, and directed much attention to transitions within melodic lines, but did not strictly analyze the material as a stochastic process.[6] In addition, they did considerable amounts of pre-analysis of the music before submitting the material to the impersonal manipulations of the computer, and they applied many common-sense rules to prepare their samples and organize their work. Also, their melodies were complicated by modal/tonal mixtures as well as by the addition of rhythm, underlying harmony, and ornament. Their method was essentially different from mine. However, one important

---

[4]Typical examples of didactic materials with rules for composing Gregorian style melodies are Knud Jeppesen, *Counterpoint: The Polyphonic Vocal Style of the Sixteenth Century*, trans. Glen Haydon (New York, 1939), p. 54ff., and Gustave Fredric Soderlund, *Direct Approach to Counterpoint in 16th Century Style* (New York, 1947), pp. 9-19.

[5]Mario Baroni and Carlo Jacoboni, *Proposal for a Grammar of Melody: The Bach Chorales* (Montreal, 1978). Also see M. Baroni and L. Callegari, eds., *Musical Grammars and Computer Analysis* (Florence, 1984) and the review of this collection by Stephen W. Smoliar in *Journal of Music Theory* 30 (1986): 130-141.

[6]"We do not fully tackle the problem of the epistemological role which Chomsky ["Formal Properties of Grammars," in *Handbook of Mathematical Psychology*, 2 vols., ed. Robert Duncan Luce, Robert R. Bush, and Eugene Galanter (New York, 1963) 2: 323-418] attributed to automata in the formulation of a general theory of grammar. . . . if the essential condition for the existence of a grammar must be, for Chomsky, that of being able to supply a structural description of a sentence . . . then ours is only in a metaphorical sense, a grammar" (Baroni and Jacoboni, pp. 27-28.)

similarity exists: the generative phase of our experiments has much in common, for we both attempted to test our work in like manner.

Another similar study was published in 1982 by Wolfram Steinbeck.[7] The focus of his study was not on the development of melodic theories, however, but the presentation of a variety of methods for computer analysis, among them a Markoff-chain analysis. His work is sound and remarkably useful, but the corpus of melodies he submits to analysis is what might be termed German folk or popular tunes all in the key of G major. His mathematical prowess is impressive, and the similarity of his method and presentation of Markoff-process analysis to my own is reassuring. But he falls into the trap of extrapolating results far beyond the studied repertory, and he does not, in my opinion, solve the problem of the addition of rhythm and underlying harmony in the analysis of tonal melodies.

The specific method for melodic analysis employed here was developed by William W. K. Zung, of Duke University, in his own research on normal and abnormal sleep. To solve the problem of comparing the data of continuous electroencephalographic (EEG) recordings of all night sleep patterns of human subjects, he demonstrated that it was possible to treat the EEG tracings, sometimes one-third of a mile long, as a simple Markoff-chain process and thereby avoid the problems of analysis from an oversimplification of reduced results. The resultant transition matrices provided a description of sleep data which was concise yet rich in information.[8] Zung, an avid music lover, sensed that his method of viewing the events of sleep through a carefully defined window which moved from left to right on the horizontal time axis would produce similarly useful results in the analysis of music. And, after suggesting to me that I might pursue this project in his laboratory, he placed his programs, computer, and synthesizer at my disposal. The resulting study is very much indebted to his help and encouragement.

THE CONCEPT

Melody and the Representation of Transition Probabilities

We will assume that the compositional process from which a satisfy-

[7]Wolfram Steinbeck, *Struktur und Aehnlichkeit: Methoden automatisierter Melodienanalyse* (Kassel, 1982) especially pp. 197-242.
[8]William W. K. Zung et al., "Computer Simulation of Sleep EEG Patterns with a Markov Chain Model," *Recent Advances in Biological Psychiatry*, 8 (1966): 335-355.

ing and stylistically correct melody might be generated is that series of events in which a composer selects among the stylistic alternatives available to him at discrete points in the composition; that is, it is a series of decisions to select pitches (here we will exclude rhythms, dynamics, and timbres) and their order after the choice of an initial pitch is made. This process might also be considered as a sequence of experiments which, as in this study, corresponds to the selection of future pitches one at a time in sequence. Each decision creates a melodic interval, or transition, and the complete melody is a chained series of transitions which take place unidirectionally in time—an example of a stochastic process.

To illustrate, let us consider the intonation of the first verse of Psalm 110, *Confitebor tibi Domine*, on Tone 2 with a D final (*LU* 134). This melody has thirty-one notes, one per syllable, and thirty transitions on five different pitches (C, D, E, F, G). Similarly, the intonation of the first verse of Psalm 111, *Beatus vir*, on the same psalm tone (*LU* 141) is a melody of twenty notes and nineteen transitions with the same five pitches (see exs. 1a and 1b).

Example 1a. Psalm 110, tone 2.

Example 1b. Psalm 111, tone 2.

Associated with each melodic interval, or transition, is one of five possible outcomes: C, D, E, F, or G. To use the Markoff-chain model for
the analysis of melody, it is necessary to assume that the probability
of the subject (the melody) being at the j-th pitch level (j = C, D, E,
F, G) at some point in time is not independent of pitch-level transitions
in previous intervals of time and depends mostly upon the pitch level
of the immediately preceding pitch, that is, the i-th pitch level (i = C,
D, E, F, G). Expressed another way, we can assume that it is possible
to specify a set of conditional probabilities P_{ij} that a melody which was
in the i-th stage in the preceding interval of time will be in the j-th stage
after its next transition. Since the melody must be in one of the five
pitch levels of its pentatonic scale after its transition, then the following relationship must hold:

$$P_{iC} + P_{iD} + P_{iE} + P_{iF} + P_{iG} = 1$$

Since there is a possibility that the melody will remain in stage i (e.g.,
a cadence), this, P_{ii}, can be included:

$$0 \leq P_{ii} \leq 1 \quad [9]$$

The pitch levels are known as "states" of the system, and the P_{ij}
values are called the transition probabilities of the system. If we can
assume a melody enters the compositional process at a particular state,
we can calculate the probability that the melody will be in any one of
the five states of the system during some particular interval in the future.
In our specific example, we may consider both melodies, without their
accompanying words, as two similar but different musical examples
of a stochastic process. We might then ask what are the transition probabilities operative in each and, when combined, in both melodies
together, which is, for a repertory of two pieces, the style.

The transition probabilities of a Markoff-chain model of a melody
with five possible states may be presented in the form of a transition
matrix as follows:

[9]To account for this possibility in the experiment, a rest is encoded at the end of each
phrase.

Figure 1. Transition probabilities for a Markoff chain with five possible states.

$$
P = \begin{array}{c|ccccc}
G & P_{GC} & P_{GD} & P_{GE} & P_{GF} & P_{GG} \\
\hline
F & P_{FC} & P_{FD} & P_{FE} & P_{FF} & P_{FG} \\
\hline
E & P_{EC} & P_{ED} & P_{EE} & P_{EF} & P_{EG} \\
\hline
D & P_{DC} & P_{DD} & P_{DE} & P_{DF} & P_{DG} \\
\hline
C & P_{CC} & P_{CD} & P_{CE} & P_{CF} & P_{CG} \\
 & C & D & E & F & G
\end{array}
$$

The matrix represents transitions from one state (left side or vertical axis) to another (horizontal axis). Since the probability of a melody being in one of the five possible states at any time is one (or 100%), the sum of each horizontal row, which represents all the transitions from one pitch, must also equal one. Therefore, the occurrence of each transition from a given pitch to one of the five possibilities is but a fraction of the whole or one. Applying this method to our first music specimen, example 1a, we draw a matrix of the five possible pitches with "from" on the vertical axis and "to" on the horizontal axis. We count and mark the transitions in their appropriate squares. These are the motions or connections that take place between the first and second notes, between the second and third, the third and fourth, and so on. What results is a transition matrix derived from the melodic motion of *Confitebor tibi Domine*:

Figure 2. Transition matrices representing melodic pattern of Psalm 110, *Confitebor tibi Domine*, tone 2.

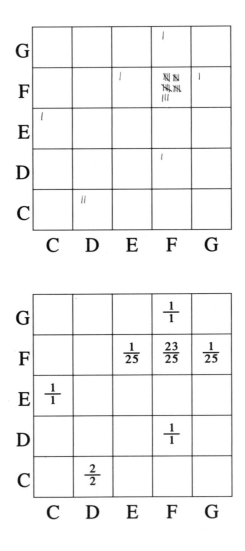

In figure 2 the first matrix illustrates a simple, handmade tally—thirty-one notes creates thirty transitions. The second matrix converts the tallies to fractions from which percentages can be determined, and from the second tally we draw the following conclusions:

C always moves to D;   (2/2 = 100% probability)
D always moves to F;   (1/1 = 100% probability)
E always moves to C;   (1/1 = 100% probability)
G always moves to F;   (1/1 = 100% probability)
F may move to E, F, or G, but it returns to itself (F) 92% of the time and to E or G only 4% of the time each.

By observation, we determine that in this style (with a repertory of one piece), melodies begin on C and end on D. We may also conclude that:

C never moves to E, F, G, nor does it return to itself;
D never moves to C, E, G, nor does it return to itself; and so on.

The results may also be summarized and illustrated in a transition diagram, thus:

Figure 3. Transition diagram illustrating the transition probabilities for change in the melody of Psalm 110, *Confitebor tibi Domine*, tone 2.

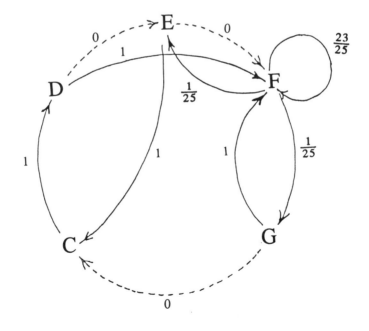

From the diagram it is clear that a composer, in this style, starting on C, must move to D and then to F. There are no other possibilities with a probability greater than zero. Upon arrival at F, he may move to E or G, but 92% of the time he will return to F. If he chooses to move to G, he must immediately return to F, where, 92% of the time, he will return to F. During the other 8% of the time, he will move to G or E. If he moves to G, we know what will happen—he will return to F. But if he moves to E, he must move to C and immediately end on D.

A similar analysis could be made for *Beatus vir* (ex. 1b), and the results would be the same except for the percentage of time returning to F or moving from F to E or G. These would have changed from 92%, 4%, and 4% respectively to 86%, 7%, and 7% respectively (12/14, 1/14, and 1/14). If these were all the compositions extant in the style, and we combined the tallies of both matrices, we would have a transition probability matrix for the compositional process of melodies for the style. Even with only five pitches, the style's pentatonic scale, the motion was far from random. We see that specific rules obtain for writing melodies, and from the results of a Markoff analysis, we see that we can specify not only the probabilities of motion from one note to the next but also the "forbidden" steps or intervals. Tallying by hand and constructing matrices with pen and paper is a laborious process, and this task is eminently suited to the computer.

HYPOTHESIS

Melody is an example of a Markoff chain, and each pitch is a variable of interest operating in a closed system. If one knows the note being played (the variable at time t, V_t), and if one can know what the note was before it (V_{t-1}), then one can predict what the next note will be (V_{t+1}).

COROLLARIES

If a large sample of melodies from a closed or well-defined repertory is analyzed using a Markoff-chain model as the structure for analysis, rules for the composition of melodies in the style of that repertory can be derived. With these results, a description of the melodic style can be formulated which will allow both the generation of new melodies in the style and the comparison of this repertory's melodic style with other melodic styles.

It would seem to follow that this method might be used to describe the melodic characteristics of individual composers within a style (and thereby allow a computer to identify anonymous melodies on the basis of statistical analyses), and it likewise should follow that more parameters of music might be added and analyzed within the context of the Markoff-chain model (additional pitches, rhythm, dynamics, timbres, and so on) by either using larger matrices or transition matrices of additional dimensions. The analysis of a complete symphony or a repertory of symphonies is not different from but only more complicated and difficult than the analysis of a melody or repertory of melodies. Through the application of this analytical method we arrive at a formulation of constraints imposed upon a composer by a particular style of music, and as Meyer more recently points out:

> As with knowledge of a language, what is involved is the acquisition of a skill, the internalization of the constraints as unconscious modes of perception, cognition, and response. The same is true of most performers, critics, and audiences. They, too, know the constraints of a style—the laws, rules, and strategies that limited the composer's choices—in this tacit way.
>   What composers, performers, critics, and listeners—and, yes, musicologists—*do* know consciously and explicitly are particular realizations (often grouped into types or classes) of more general stylistic principles. And from such realizations, music theorists attempt to infer the general principles that constrained, but did not determine, the choices made by composers. As constraints have changed over time, so have the patterns that are the basis for style classifications.[10]

THE EXPERIMENT

I. Recording and Classifying the Repertory

The entire repertory of Tone 1 and Tone 2 hymns of the *Antiphonale Monasticum (AM)*[11] was encoded first. This complete but limited group was used first for analysis to modify and test the computer programs that were originally developed for Markoff-chain analyses of all-night

[10]Leonard B. Meyer, "Exploiting Limits: Creation, Archetypes, and Style Change," *Daedalus* 109 (1980), p. 180.
[11]*Antiphonale monasticum pro diurnis horis* (Paris, 1934), pp. 1278f. [index].

sleep patterns.[12] Then, when a sampling method was applied to the complete repertory of hymn melodies, tones 1-8 and three unclassified hymns, the results of the analyses of all the hymns of tones 1 and 2 could be compared with the results of the Markoff-chain analyses of the sampled groups as another control process. Duplicate melodies were eliminated, and 37 tone-1 hymns with 162 lines of data (each phrase equals one line of data) and 34 tone-2 hymns with 156 additional lines of data were encoded. Classification by tone was that found in the *AM*. The formula for encoding the melodies was as follows:

Example 2. Numerical code for intabulating Gregorian hymns.

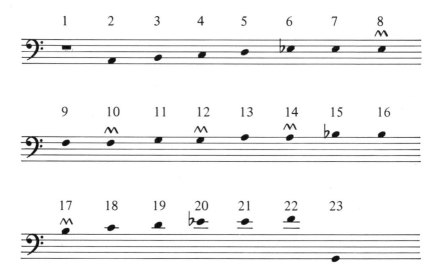

Every pitch employed by these hymns was given its own number, and chromatic pitches not found in the repertory were omitted. All pitches above e (e above middle c) as well as pitches below A (first space A, bass clef) were never used by the composers of this repertory, and one can see that the essential scale and compass of the music was the full range of the Guidonian hand.[13] Quilismas on E, F, G, a, and b were assigned numbers of their own so that no information would be lost

[12]Both Professor Zung, who had developed the Fortran programs for his own use, and Shiang Tai Tuan, of the Duke University Computation Center, were invaluable in helping me modify the programs for musical analysis. I gratefully acknowledge their expertise and generosity.
[13]In the hymns of tones 1 and 2, Gamma (first line G, bass clef) and f (f above middle c) were not used. The high f did occur elsewhere in the complete repertory of Gregorian

from the data by trying to interpret the specific notes of this ornament. All pitches of multiple-note neume groups were also considered as separate entities. (Plicas would have been considered as separate notes had they been found in the repertory.) The encoded repertory was checked for accuracy by digital synthesis of the melodies in the data files, and a comparison was made between the sound resulting from the synthesis of the encoded melodies and the original notation of the *AM* from which the encoded melodies were derived. Each initial, the first pitch of the first phrase of a hymn melody, was separately noted and counted, as was each final, the last pitch of the last phrase. Cadences were given a marker by inserting rests after the last note of each phrase.

The analyses of the hymns of tones 1, 2, 4, and 8 were based on a relatively large number of hymns; those of the other tones were not. The reason for this discrepancy derives from the sampling method and the fact that all tones are not equally represented among the hymn settings. After the work on tones 1 and 2 was completed, it was thought that an impartial method for selection would be an alphabetical (non-musical) choice from the index of the *Antiphonale*. This resulted in the following distribution:

Tone 1	—	21 Hymns
Tone 2	—	15 Hymns
Tone 3	—	4 Hymns
Tone 4	—	19 Hymns
Tone 5	—	2 Hymns
Tone 6	—	2 Hymns
Tone 7	—	1 Hymn
Tone 8	—	24 Hymns
Unclassified	—	3 Hymns (perhaps *Tonus Peregrinus*)

---

hymns, and the Gamma space in the probability matrix was used for other notes or ornaments when required (quilismas occasionally occurred on c, d, and f). These symbols were assigned codes of 22 and 23. The matrix was restricted to 23 variables because the 23 X 23 square matrix was already large for the storage capacity of the personal computer available to me. Also, the computer must run a full search for every possible variable in the program, and the 23-variable program proved to be relatively slow in its machine computation.

Lastly, I blush to admit that musica ficta raised its pernicious head even in a repertory as simple as this one. For example, see the first phrase of *Aeterna caeli gloria, Tonus in Hieme* (*AM* 72). Surely the b is flatted in the turning figure above the reciting tone, especially with the emphasized fs in the next two phrases. In situations as obvious as this, I added the ficta. *Eripe me de inimicis meis, Deus meus!*

By the sampling process, 91 complete hymns were studied. This number was increased to 126 complete hymns with the addition of the remainder of the hymns from tones 1 and 2.

A sample hymn melody, *Auctor beate saeculi*, (*AM* 1255) and its intabulation for digital manipulation, using the code from example 2, follows:

Example 3. *Auctor beate saeculi* (*AM* 1255).

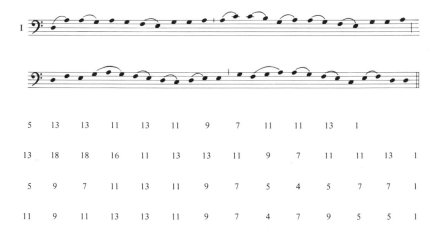

5	13	13	11	13	11	9	7	11	11	13	1	
13	18	18	16	11	13	13	11	9	7	11	11	13	1
5	9	7	11	13	11	9	7	5	4	5	7	7	1
11	9	11	13	13	11	9	7	4	7	9	5	5	1

II. Computer Analysis and Simulation of Melodic Patterns

The procedure for generating a Markoff chain process on a digital computer is not a new technique.[14] For input to the computer available to me at that time, a Processor Technology Sol Terminal Computer with extended disc Fortran compiler, numerical data was fed to a matrix composed of 529 digits (23 rows by 23 columns), each digit being the numeric equivalent of one of the 23 states of the melody. The 23 columns represented the 23 states, and the 23 rows represented the transition probabilities. To begin the analysis pattern, a window viewing two notes begins with the first and second notes, moves to the second and third, third and fourth, and so on, until completion. To begin the simulation pattern, the melodic process is started by randomly generating a possi-

[14]Herbert Parish Galliher, ''Simulation of Random Processes,'' in *Notes on Operations Research 1959* (Cambridge, Mass., 1959) Ronald A. Howard, *Dynamic Programming and Markov Processes* (Cambridge, Mass., 1960); and Keith Douglas Tocher, *The Art of Simulation* (Princeton, 1963) laid the groundwork almost three decades ago.

ble initial, a process which selects the row of the matrix on which the transition probabilities of that particular pitch are stored. A random number between 1 and 100 is generated, and the state of the melody stored at this N-th location becomes the state of the melody at time $T+1$. The process is repeated for the second stage and succeeding stages until the melody enters a pattern which moves to a rest. Each transition from note to note reflects the probabilities of the melody in that tone on that note, and the result is a new melody in the style, presumably of all the other melodies submitted for analysis from that same Tone. The process is repeated, and another melody is generated, a different melody from the same probabilities. The precision of the results is mathematically improved by generating a fairly large number of new melodies, and although this process could be carried out by hand, the computer aids us by generating these patterns quickly.

Figure 4. Block diagram illustrating steps in the computer generation of Gregorian hymn melodies.

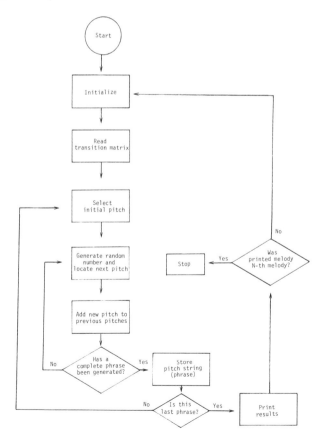

Figure 5. Computer program for analysis of Gregorian hymn melodies.

```
0001    $OPTIONS X, B, E
        C
        C        2ND ORDER MARKOV ANALYSIS
        C        FORTRAN PROGRAM I FOR TALLYING NOTE-TO-NOTE MUSIC
        C        DATA TO FORM 23x23x23 CONTINGENCY TABLES AND TRANSITION
        C        PROBABILITY MATRICES
        C        TYPED BY W.W.K. ZUNG, M.D. AND F.P. TIRRO
        C        INTERVALS = MAXIMUM NO. OF NOTES/DATA LINE MINUS ONE
0002             DIMENSION TALLY (23, 23, 23), x (50), SUM (23, 23)
        C        +, ITALL (23, 23, 23)
0003             CALL PLOT
0004             READ (0, 100) 'ENTER INPUT FILE:', FNAME
0005             READ (0, 100) 'ENTER OUTPUT FILE:', FLOUT
0006    100      FORMAT (5A6)
0007             TYPE ' '
0008             ACCEPT 'ENTER NUMBER OF INTERVALS:', LENTH
0009             TYPE ' '
0010             ACCEPT 'ENTER NUMBER OF LINES OF DATA:' IHYMN
0011             TYPE ' '
0012             WRITE (1,802)
0013    802      FORMAT ('WRITE 802')
0014             CALL OPEN (10, FNAME)
0015             LENT1 =LENTH +2
0016             WRITE (1,803)
0017    803      FORMAT ('WRITE 803')
0018             DO 4 I1 =1,23
0019             DO 4 I2 =1,23
0020             DO 4 I3 =1,23
0021    4        TALLY (I1, I2, I3)=0.
0022             WRITE (1,801)
0023    801      FORMAT ('WRITE 801')
0024             DO 5 M2=1, IHYMN
0025             READ (10,6) (X(J), J =1,LENT1)
0026             WRITE (1,6) (X(J), J =1,LENT1)
0027    6        FORMAT (6X,25I2)
0028             DO 8 J =1,LENTH
0029             I1 =X(J)
0030             I2 =X(J +1)
0031             I3 =X(J +2)
0032    8        TALLY (I1, I2, I3)=TALLY (I1, I2, I3)+1.
0033    5        CONTINUE
0034             DO 9 I1 =1, 23
0035             DO 9 I2 =1, 23
0036             SUM (I1, I2) =0
0037             DO 9 I3 =1, 23
0038    9        SUM (I1, I2) =SUM (I1, I2)+TALLY (I1, I2, I3)
0039             DO 10 I1 =1, 23
0040             DO 10 I2 =1, 23
0041             IF (SUM(I1, I2)) 11, 12, 11
0042    12       DO 13 I3 =1, 23
0043    13       TALLY (I1, I2, I3)=0.
0044             GO TO 10
0045    11       DO 14 I3 =1, 23
0046    14       TALLY (I1, I2, I3)=(TALLY (I1, I2, I3)/SUM (I1, I2)
0047    10       CONTINUE
        C        DO 15 I1 =1, 23
        C        DO 15 I2 =1, 23
        C        DO 15 I3 =1, 23
        C15      ITALL (I1, I2, I3)=TALLY (I1, I2, I3)
        C        CALL OPEN (9, FLOUT)
        C        WRITE (9,201) ((TALLX(I, J), J =1, 23), I =1, 23),
        C        +((ITALL(I, J), J =1, 23), I =1, 23
        C        WRITE (9,201)((ITALL(I1, I2, I3), I3 =1, 23), I2 =1, 23)
        C        +I1 =1, 23), (((TALLX(I1, I2, I3), I3 =1, 23), I2 =1, 23, I1 =1, 23)
        C201     FORMAT (23(23F7.3/)//23(23I5/))
        C201     FORMAT (23(23(23I5/))//23(23(23F7.3/)))
0048             CALL OPEN (11, 'PRNT1')
0049             WRITE (11,200) FNAME, NPHRAS, LENTH, IHYMN
0050    200      FORMAT (8X, 'MUZIC', 20X, A5, 5X, I2, 2X, I2, 2X, I3)
0051             WRITE (11, 16) M1, (((TALLY(I1, I2, I3), I3 =1, 23), I2 =1, 23),
                 + I1 =1, 23)
        C        +,(((ITALL(I1, I2, I3), I3 =1, 23), I2 =1, 23),
        C        +I1 =1, 23)
0052    16       FORMAT ('PHASE', I3//23(23(23F7.3/))//23(23(23I5/))////)
0053             CALL CLOSE (11)
0054             CALL EXIT
0055             END
        NO COMPILE ERRORS
```

Figure 6. Computer program for simulating Gregorian hymn melodies.

```
0001 $OPTIONS X, B, E
0002        REAL FIRST (23), PERC (23, 23), ACCUF (23), ACCUP (23,23)
0003        INTEGER N, ITAL (23, 23), IOUT (50)
0004        READ (0, 10) 'INFILE FOR FIRST NOTES:', FLFRS
0005        READ (0, 10) 'INFILE FOR PERCENTAGE:', FLPER
0006        READ (0, 11) 'RESET RAND, GIVE AN INTEGER:', N
0007 10     FORMAT (5A6)
0008 11     FORMAT (I3)
0009        CALL OPEN (8,FLFRS)
0010        CALL OPEN (9,FLPER)
0011        READ (8, 12) FIRST
0012 12     FORMAT (  F7.3)
     C      WRITE (1, 12) FIRST
0013        READ (9, 13) ITAL, PERC
     C      WRITE (1, 13) ITAL, PERC
0014 13     FORMAT (23(23I5/)//23(23F7.3/))
0015        ACCUF (1)=FIRST (1)
0016        DO 150 J = 2, 23
0017 150    ACCUF(J)=ACCUF(J-1)+FIRST(J)
0018        IF (ACCUF(23)-0.999) 159, 155, 155
0019 155    IF (ACCUF(23)-1.001) 160, 160, 159
0020 159    WRITE (1, 19)
0021 19     FORMAT ('WRONG SUM.')
0022        CALL EXIT
0023 160    CONTINUE
0024        DO 190 I=1, 23
0025        ACCUP(1, I)=PERC(1, I)
0026        DO 180 J=2, 23
0027        ACCUP(J, I)=ACCUP(J-1, I)+PREC (J, I)
0028 180    CONTINUE
     C      IF (ACCUP(23, I)-0.999) 188, 183, 183
     C183   IF (ACCUP(23, I)-1.001) 190, 190, 188
     C188   WRITE (1, 19)
     C      WRITE (1, 11) I
     C      STOP
0029 190    CONTINUE
0030        CALL OPEN (11, 'PRNT1')
0031        X=RAND(N)
0032        DO 500 LOOP=1, 10
0033        ICTR=0
0034        DO 250 J=1, 23
0035        IF (X-ACCUF(J))240, 240, 250
0036 240    K=J
0037        GO TO 260
0038 250    CONTINUE
0039        K=23
0040 260    CONTINUE
0041        WRITE (1, 21) K
0042        ICTR=ICTR+1
0043        IOUT(ICTR)=K
0044 21     FORMAT ('THE FIRST NOTE IS:', I3)
0045        DO 390 I=1, 50
0046 280    X=RAND(0)
0047        DO 300 J=1, 23
0048        IF (X-ACCUP(J,K)) 290, 290, 300
0049 290    K=J
0050        GO TO 350
0051 300    CONTINUE
0052        GO TO 280
0053 350    CONTINUE
0054        IF (K-1) 360, 410, 360
0055 360    WRITE (1, 22) K
0056        ICTR=ICTR+1
0057        IOUT(ICTR)=K
0058 22     FORMAT (I4)
0059 390    CONTINUE
0060 410    WRITE (1, 25)
0061 25     FORMAT ('END OF PHRASE.')
0062        WRITE (11, 31) (IOUT(J), J=1, ICTR)
0063 31     FORMAT ('THE NOTES ARE:', (50I3))
0064 500    CONTINUE
0065        CALL EXIT
0066        END
NO COMPILE ERRORS
```

III. Results

The transition matrices for tone-1 hymns follows in figure 7a. The tally is useful because it indicates the frequency of occurrence of a particular transition, while the transition probability matrix deals only in percentages (see fig. 7b).

Figure 7a. Transition matrices for tone-I hymns. Tally.

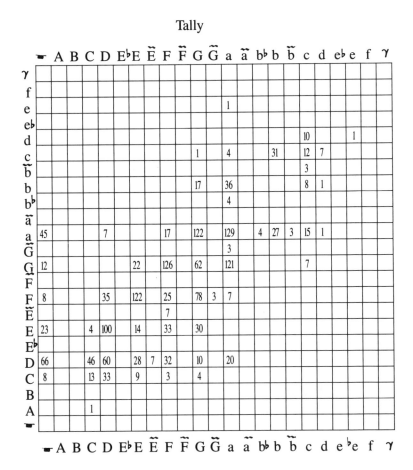

Figure 7b. Transition probability matrix for tone-I hymns (in percent).

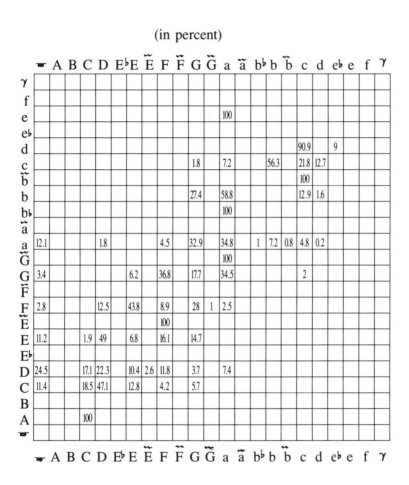

(in percent)

From these statistics, a transition probability diagram can be constructed, but unlike the diagram offered for Psalm 110, Psalm-tone 2, this figure now approaches a level of complexity that seriously hampers its usefulness (see fig. 8). Still, certain compositional features of the style are obvious: A never moves to B; E-flat is never used; quilismas always resolve upward; and so on.

Figure 8. Transition diagram for tone 1 hymns.

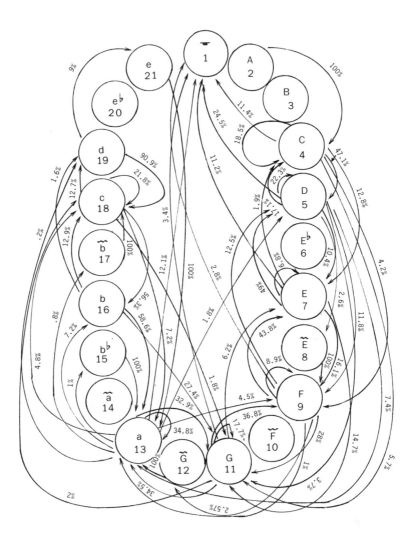

From these numerical analyses, other kinds of information can be derived that are both useful and informative (see fig. 9).

Figure 9. Frequency of occurrence (pitches) in tone-1 hymns (162 phrases).

$$
\left.
\begin{array}{r}
a \; - \; 370 \\
G \; - \; 350 \\
F \; - \; 278 \\
D \; - \; 269 \\
E \; - \; 204
\end{array}
\right\} \quad 87\%
$$

$$
\left.
\begin{array}{r}
C \; - \; \;\;70 \\
b \; - \; \;\;62 \\
c \; - \; \;\;55 \\
\tilde{d} \; - \; \;\;11 \\
b, \tilde{E} \; - \; \;\;\;\;7 \\
b^\flat \; - \; \;\;\;\;4 \\
\tilde{G} \; - \; \;\;\;\;3 \\
e, A \; - \; \;\;\;\;1 \\
\gamma, B, E^\flat \tilde{F}, a, e^\flat f \; - \; \;\;\;\;0
\end{array}
\right\} \quad 13\%
$$

It is clear that the hymn pattern varies markedly from the Psalm-Tone pattern discussed earlier (see fig. 10).

Figure 10. Possible destinations of tone 1 pitches.

$$
\begin{array}{l}
\text{e} - \text{a} \\
\text{d} - \text{c, e} \\
\underset{\sim}{\text{c}} - \text{G, a, b, c, d} \\
\tilde{\text{b}} - \text{c} \\
\text{b} - \text{G, a, c, d} \\
\text{b}^\flat - \text{a} \\
\text{a} - \mathbf{\text{,}} \text{ D, F, G, a, b}^\flat \text{, b, } \tilde{\text{b}}, \text{ c, d} \\
\tilde{\text{G}} - \text{a} \\
\text{G} - \mathbf{\text{,}} \text{ E, F, G, a, c} \\
\text{F} - \mathbf{\text{,}} \text{ D, E, F, G, } \tilde{\text{G}}, \text{ a} \\
\tilde{\text{E}} - \text{F} \\
\text{E} - \mathbf{\text{,}} \text{ C, D, E, F, G} \\
\text{D} - \mathbf{\text{,}} \text{ C, D, E, } \tilde{\text{E}}, \text{ F, G, a} \\
\text{C} - \mathbf{\text{,}} \text{ C, D, E, F, G} \\
\text{A} - \text{C}
\end{array}
$$

As can be seen, the possibilities (probabilities greater than zero) are severely limited for most notes, but the pitch a has the widest range of possibilities available for transitions within the style. Still, the pitch a cannot move to E! Another surprise: some notes cannot be repeated (*e.g.*, b or d).

Figure 11. Initial pitches of phrases.

a — 45
F — 35
D — 34
G — 26
E — 9
C — 6
b — 4
d — 2
A — 1

Figure 12. Favorite opening statements for tone-1 hymns (162 phrases).

a→a   26
D→a   14
G→F   13
F→E, F→F   11 each
a→G   9
G→G   8
F→a   7
D→D, D→Ẽ, E→G, a→c   6 each
D→F, F→G, G→a   4 each
C→D, C→E, D→G, a→b   3 each
E→F, F→G̃, b→G, b→c, c→c   2 each
A→C, D→E[!], E→D, G→E, a→d   1 each

Comparison of these data with similar data from other hymn tones reveals that striking differences exist not only among the four different authentic tones but also between each tone and its own plagal.

Finally a summary of all eight tones are given in the following transition probability matrices (figs. 13-20).

Figure 13. Transition probability matrix for tone-2 hymns (156 lines of data).

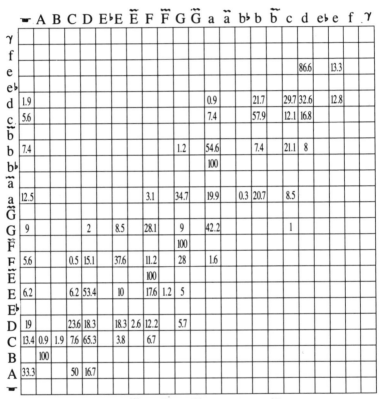

Figure 14. Transition-probability matrix for tone-3 hymns (19 lines of data).

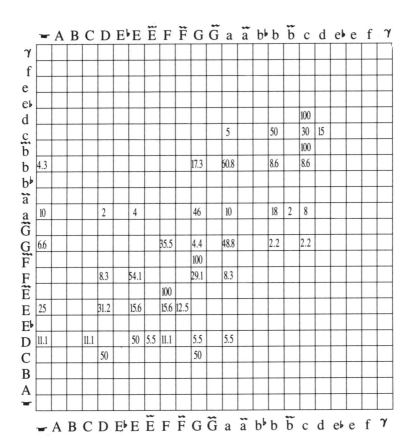

Figure 15. Transition-probability matrix for tone-4 hymns (95 lines of data).

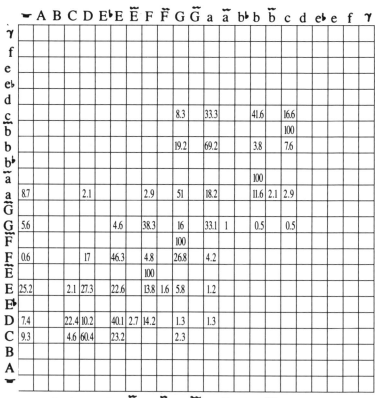

Figure 16. Transition-probability matrix for tone-5 hymns (10 lines of data).

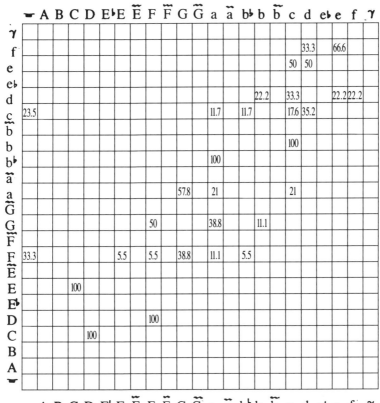

Figure 17. Transition-probability matrix for tone-6 hymns (8 lines of data).

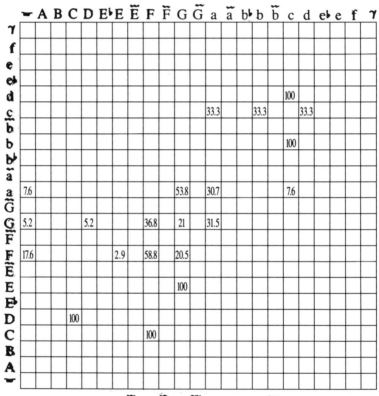

Figure 18. Transition-probability matrix for tone-7 hymns (7 lines of data).

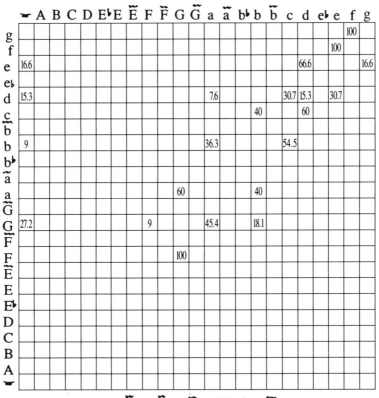

Figure 19. Transition-probability matrix for tone-8 hymns (104 lines of data).

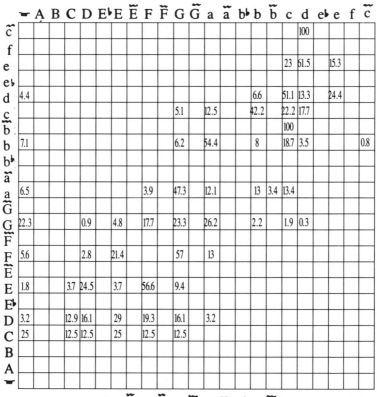

Figure 20. Transition-probability matrix for three hymns of similar but unclassified tones (*AM* 93, 184, 547) (14 lines of data).

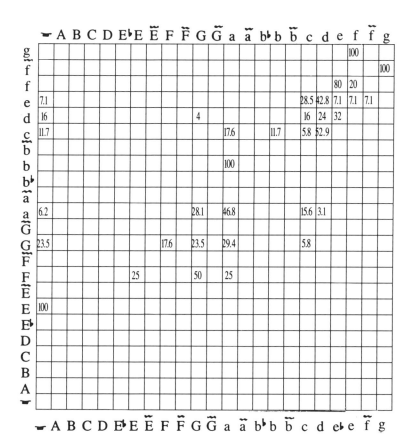

Lastly, to close this essay I submit the following hymn, music newly composed by the computer in Gregorian tone-1 style. The text, the familiar words of Venantius Fortunatus, *Vexilla regis prodeunt*, is a hymn with verses of four lines of eight syllables per line (8.8.8.8.):

Vexilla Regis prodeunt:
Fulget Crucis mysterium,
Quo carne carnis Conditor
Suspensus est patibulo.

In the version of the *Antiphonale monasticum* (*AM* 383), the music uses fourteen notes for the first line of text, twelve for the second, eleven for the third, and sixteen for the last, so I have selected phrases of those same lengths from my pool of randomly generated tone 1 phrases without any thought of matching. I grouped the notes, as in the original, to place melismas of the same number of notes under the same syllables of the text. The following, using the same code presented in example 2, is the result (see ex. 4):

Example 4. *Vexilla Regis prodeunt.*

11. 18. 16. 13. 16. 13. 11. 13. 13. 11. 13. 9. 7. 5
5. 11. 13. 13. 11. 7. 9. 5. 11. 13. 11. 13.
4. 5. 5. 4. 5. 4. 9. 7. 9. 7. 5.
4. 5. 4. 5. 9. 5. 4. 7. 11. 13. 11. 9. 7. 5. 4. 5.

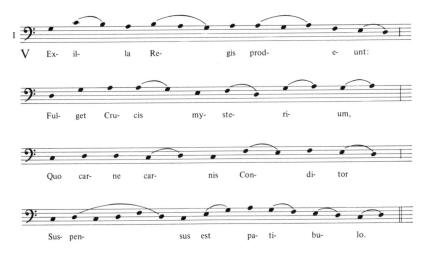

Diana Deutsch

Pitch Class and Perceived Height:
Some Paradoxes and Their Implications

Much lively debate exists concerning the framework within which musical materials should be considered as organized, classified, and abstracted. A number of concepts are, however, taken as axiomatic since they appear on common-sense grounds to be beyond dispute. One such is the concept of a musical note as having a pitch class and a register appropriate to its name (e.g., C_4, D_5, and so on). Another is the concept of invariance under transposition: Although one might argue about details, it is taken as generally self-evident that a musical passage retains its identity when played in different keys.

These two concepts are related to yet another which is also generally taken as axiomatic, namely the orthogonality of pitch class and perceived height. If a musician were faced with the question "Which note is higher, C-sharp or G?," he would probably reply that the question was nonsensical: one would have to know; *which* C-sharp and *which* G before a meaningful answer could be given. This essay presents some surprising findings showing that, at least under certain conditions, pitch class and height are not orthogonal; rather the perceived height of a tone can be shown to be related in an orderly fashion to its position along the pitch class circle. The theoretical and practical implications of these findings are discussed.

Diana Deutsch is Research Psychologist at the University of California, San Diego. She is editor of The Psychology of Music *and founding editor of the journal* Music Perception.

PITCH AS A GEOMETRICALLY REGULAR HELIX

The view that pitch class and height are orthogonal forms the basis of the model illustrated in figure 1. Pitch is here assumed to vary along both a circular dimension of pitch class and also a monotonic dimension of height. It can thus be represented as a geometrically regular helix, in which the entire structure maps into itself by transposition.[1] One can readily see that in this representation, any musical interval is represented by pairs of points that are separated by the same distance from each other. Further, the strong perceptual similarity between tones that are related by octaves is captured by their being depicted in relatively close spatial proximity.

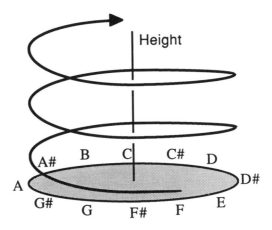

Figure 1. Pitch as a geometrically regular helix. (Adapted from Shepard, 1965.)

This helical model, as pointed out by Shepard,[2] leads to the intriguing possibility that, by suppressing the monotonic component of height, leaving only the circular component of pitch class, all tones that are an octave apart could be mapped onto the same tone, which would then

[1]See, for example, Roger N. Shepard, "Circularity in judgments of relative pitch," *Journal of the Acoustical Society of America*, 36 (1964): 2346-2353; "Approximation to Uniform Gradients of Generalization by Monotone Transformations of Scale," in *Stimulus Generalization*, ed. D. I. Mostofsky (Stanford, 1965): 94-110; and "Structural Representations of Musical Pitch," in *The Psychology of Music*, ed. Diana Deutsch (New York, 1982): 344-390; and also earlier work by M. W. Drobisch, "Über musikalische Tonbestimmung und Temperatur," *Abhandl. Math. Phys. Kl. Konigl. Sachs. Ges. Wiss*, 4 (1855): 1-120.
[2]Shepard, "Circularity."

have a clearly determined pitch class but an indeterminate height. The tonal helix would thus be collapsed into a circle, and judgments of pitch would be expected to be completely circular.

In order to test this prediction, Shepard performed an experiment in which he employed a specially contrived set of tones. Each tone consisted of ten sinusoidal components that were separated by octaves. The amplitudes of these components were scaled by a fixed, bell-shaped spectral envelope, so that those in the middle of the musical range were loudest, with the lowest and highest falling off below the threshold of audibility. Such tones are heard as well defined in terms of pitch class but somewhat ambiguously in terms of height.

Listeners were presented with ordered pairs of such tones and were asked to judge whether they formed ascending or descending series. When the tones within a pair were separated by a small distance along the pitch class circle, these judgments of relative height were found to be entirely dependent on proximity.[3] Thus, for example, the pattern C – C-sharp would always be heard as ascending, as would the patterns D – D-sharp, F – F-sharp, and B – C. Analogously, the pattern C-sharp – C would always be heard as descending; and so on.[4] When the tones within a pair were separated by a larger distance along the pitch-class circle, the tendency to follow by proximity gradually decreased. When the tones within a pair were separated by exactly a half-octave, ascending and descending judgments occurred equally often.

Shepard concluded that for such octave-related complexes, the monotonic dimension of height was indeed suppressed, leaving only

[3]Proximity is one of the principles of perceptual organization described by the Gestalt psychologists at the turn of the century. These principles have been shown to be prominently involved in the organization of tonal music. See particularly Leonard B. Meyer, *Emotion and Meaning in Music* (Chicago, 1956); and *Explaining Music: Essays and Explorations* (Berkeley, 1973).

[4]For other experimental work showing that proximity is invoked in making judgments of relative height, see Jean-Claude Risset, "Paradoxes de hauteur: Le concept de hauteur sonore n'est pas le meme pour tout le monde," paper presented at the *Seventh International Congress of Acoustics*, (Budapest,1971); Irwin Pollack, "Decoupling of Auditory Pitch and Stimulus Frequency: The Shepard Demonstration Revisited," *Journal of the Acoustical Society of America*, 63 (1978): 202-206; Edward Burns, "Circularity in Relative Pitch Judgments for Inharmonic Tones: The Shepard Demonstration Revisited, Again," *Perception and Psychophysics* 30 (1981): 467-472; Manfred R. Schroeder, "Auditory Paradox Based on Fractal Waveform," *Journal of the Acoustical Society of America*, 79 (1986): 186-188; Ryunen Teranishi, "Endlessly rising or falling chordal tones which can be played on the piano; another variation of the Shepard demonstration," paper presented at the *12th International Congress of Acoustics*, Toronto, 1986; and Kazuo Ueda and Kengo Ohgushi, "Perceptual components of pitch: Spatial representation using a multidimensional scaling technique," *Journal of the Acoustical Society of America*, 82 (1987): 1193-1200.

the circular dimension of pitch class. However, there are problems with this interpretation. In the case where the tones within a pair were related by close proximity, other factors that might have given rise to differences in perceived height would have been masked. Indeed, it has been shown in other contexts that proximity can override cues which would otherwise be operating to organize pitch materials.[5] Further, Shepard obtained his results by averaging over pitch classes, so that any relationship between pitch class and height would have been lost in the averaging process. The issue of orthogonality was thus left unresolved in his study.

THE PRESENT EXPERIMENTS

The present experiments were undertaken to explore the relationship between pitch class and perceived height where proximity could not be used as a cue. They examined the question of whether judgments of height would here be completely ambiguous, as predicted from the helical model, or whether some other principle might be invoked to resolve the ambiguity. A number of different types of pattern were explored, and in all cases, striking and paradoxical findings were obtained. The perceived heights of tones in such patterns were found to vary in an orderly fashion depending on their positions along the pitch class circle. As a result, when the patterns were transposed, entirely different configurations were perceived. These findings therefore constituted violations of the principle of invariance under transposition. As a further unexpected finding, the form of relationship between pitch class and perceived height varied substantially from one listener to another, so that any given pattern was perceived by different listeners in radically different ways.

[5]The scale illusion provides a particularly strong example of the overriding influnce of pitch proximity in the organization of musical materials. Here two series of tones emanate simultaneously from different regions of space. These are perceptually reorganized so as to create the illusion that tones in one pitch range are emanating from one region, and tones in a different pitch range from the other region. See Diana Deutsch, "Two-channel listening to musical scales," *Journal of the Acoustical Society of America* 157 (1975): 1156-1160; "Musical Illusions,", *Scientific American*, 233 (1975): 92-104. The principle underlying the scale illusion has been found to operate for a variety of musical patterns, and under a number of listening conditions. See David Butler, "A Further Study of Melodic Channeling," *Perception and Psychophysics* 25 (1979): 264-268; "Melodic Channeling in Musical Environment," paper presented at the *Research Symposium on the Psychology and Acoustics of Music*, Kansas (1979); and Diana Deutsch, "Dichotic Listening to Melodic Patterns and Its Relationship to Hemispheric Specialization of Function," *Music Perception* 3 (1985): 127-154.

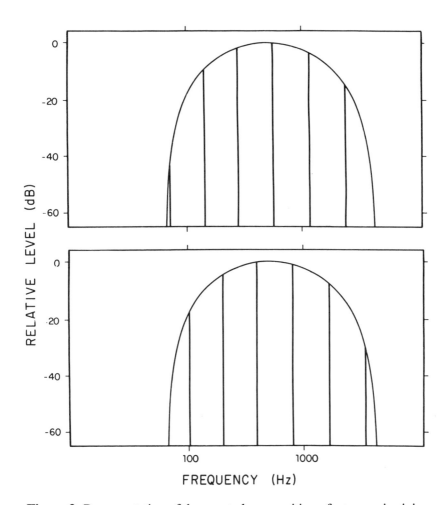

Figure 2. Representation of the spectral composition of a tone pair giving rise to the tritone paradox. In this case the spectral envelope is centered at C_5. Upper graph represents a tone of pitch class D, and lower graph a tone of pitch class G-sharp.

The Tritone Paradox

The first pattern to be described consisted of two successively presented tones which were related by a half-octave, and so were diametrically opposed along the pitch-class circle. Thus C-sharp might be presented followed by G, or A-sharp followed by E, and so on. Since the tones within a pair were separated by the same distance along the pitch-class circle in either direction, proximity could not here be used as a cue in making judgments of relative height.

In the first experiment on this phenomenon,[6] musically trained subjects were presented with just such tone pairs in random order, so that each of the twelve pitch classes served equally often as the first tone of a pair. The pitch class pairings employed were therefore C – F-sharp, C-sharp – G, D – G-sharp, D-sharp – A, E – A-sharp, F – B, F-sharp – C, G – C – G-sharp, G-sharp – D, A – D-sharp, A-sharp – E, and B – F. Subjects judged whether each pair formed an ascending or a descending series. All tones consisted of six octave-related sinusoids, the amplitudes of which were determined by a fixed, bell-shaped spectral envelope. A representation of the spectral composition of one such tone pair is given in figure 2.

In order to control for the possibility that judgments might be influenced by the relative amplitudes of the different sinusoidal components, tone pairs were generated under envelopes that were placed at six different positions along the spectrum. As shown in figure 3, the envelopes were spaced at half-octave intervals, centered at C_6, F-sharp$_5$, C_5, F-sharp$_4$, C_4, and F-sharp$_3$, so that the peaks varied over a two and one-half octave range.[7] Thus, for any given pitch class, the relative amplitudes of the components of tones that were generated under the envelopes shown on the left side of the illustration were identical to those for the pitch class a half octave removed that were generated under

[6]Diana Deutsch, "A musical paradox," *Music Perception* 3 (1986): 275-280.
[7]In this and the other experiments described in this chapter, tones were generated on a VAX 11/780 computer, interfaced with a DSC-200 Audio Data Conversion System, and using the music sound synthesis software (see F. Richard Moore, "The computer audio research laboratory at UCSD," *Computer Music Journal* 6 (1982): 18-29. The sounds were recorded and played back on a Sony PCM-F1 digital audio processor, the output of which was routed through a Crown amplifier and presented to subjects binaurally through headphones (Grason-Stadler TDH-49) at an approximate loudness level of 72 dB SPL. The convention in notation followed here is that C_4 corresponds to middle C, C_5 to the octave above middle C, and so on.

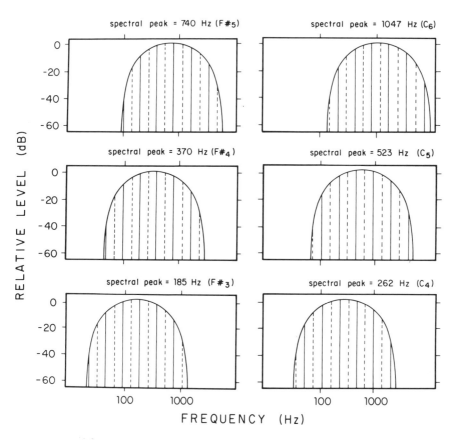

Figure 3. Representation of the spectral compositions of tones comprising the D – G-sharp pattern, generated under six spectral envelopes. Dashed lines indicate tones of pitch class D, and solid lines tones of pitch class G-sharp. The spectra of the two sets of tones are superimposed in the illustration, although the tones were presented in succession.

the envelopes shown on the right side. All twelve pitch-class pairings were generated under each of the six envelopes.[8]

At the phenomenological level, tones generated under the different envelopes sounded clearly diffferent in height. Roughly, the perceived height of one such tone corresponded to the center of the spectral envelope under which it was generated. Thus, for example, tones generated under an envelope centered on C_5 were perceived as approximating C_5 in height; tones generated under an envelope centered on F-sharp$_3$ were perceived as approximating F-sharp$_3$ in height; and so on. Thus, the experiment explored tones whose perceived heights varied quite broadly over the most salient musical range.

Figure 4 shows, for one subject, the percentage of judgments that a tone pair formed a descending series, plotted as a function of the pitch class of the first tone of the pair. Each graph plots judgments for tones generated under one of the envelopes, and averaged over two experimental sessions . As can be seen, patterns beginning with B, C, C-sharp, D, and D-sharp tended to be heard as descending, and those beginning with F-sharp, G, and G-sharp tended to be heard as ascending, for all positions of the spectral envelope. In other words, if we think of this two-tone pattern as successively transposed up in semitone steps, starting with C as the first tone of the pair, followed by C-sharp as the first tone, and so on, the pattern was first heard as descending, and then, when F-sharp was reached as the first tone, it was heard as ascending, and finally when B was reached it was heard as descending again.

Figure 5 shows the results for a different subject. It can be seen that they are virtually the mirror-image of those shown in figure 4. Patterns beginning with C-sharp, D, D-sharp, and E tended to be heard as ascending, and those beginning with F-sharp, G, G-sharp, A, A-sharp, and B tended to be heard as descending, again for all positions of the spectral envelope. So, thinking of the pattern as successively transposed up in semitone steps beginning with C-sharp as the first tone of a pair, the pattern was first heard as ascending, and then, when F-sharp was reached, it was heard as descending; and so on.

Figure 6 shows the results for these two subjects together, taking as an example judgments with the spectral envelope centered at F-sharp$_4$.1 It can be seen that as the pattern was transposed up in semitone steps, it was first heard one way and then it was heard as inverted. But for

[8]All tones were 500 msec in duration, and there were no pauses between tones within a pair. Tone pairs were presented in blocks of twelve, with five-second pauses between pairs within a block, and one-minute pauses between blocks. Each block consisted of tones generated under one of the six envelopesand contained one example of each of the pitch-class pairings.

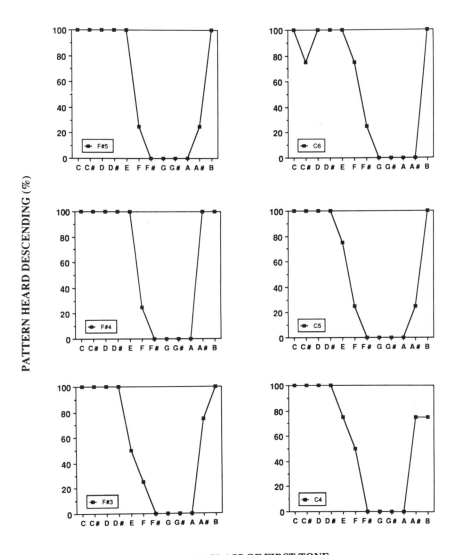

PITCH CLASS OF FIRST TONE

Figure 4. Percentages of judgments that a tone pair formed a descending series, plotted as a function of the pitch class of the first tone of the pair. Results from a first subject are here displayed, for tones generated under each of the six spectral envelopes shown in figure 3. Symbols in boxes indicate the peaks of the spectral envelopes. (Data from Deutsch, 1986.)

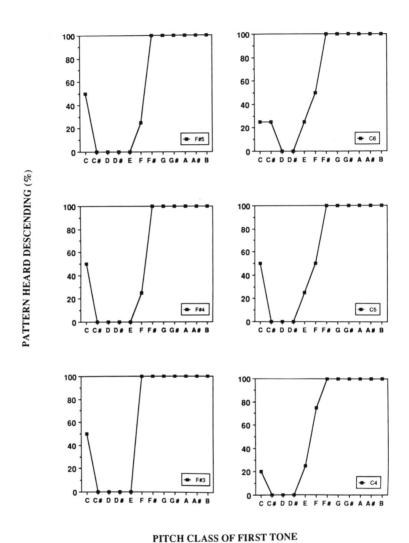

PITCH CLASS OF FIRST TONE

Figure 5. Percentages of judgments that a tone pair formed a descending series, plotted as a function of the pitch class of the first tone of the pair. Results from a second subject are here displayed, for tones generated under each of the six spectral envelopes shown in figure 3. Symbols in boxes indicate the peaks of the spectral envelopes. (Data from Deutsch, 1986.)

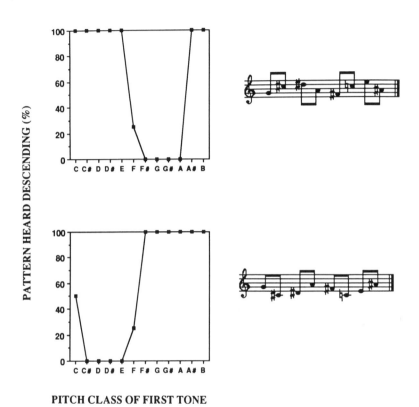

PITCH CLASS OF FIRST TONE

Figure 6. Graphs on left show percentages of judgments that a tone pair formed a descending series, plotted as a function of the pitch class of the first tone of the pair. Results are from the first and second subjects, for tones generated under the spectral envelope centered at F-sharp$_4$. Notations on right show how the two subjects perceived the identical series of tone pairs. (Data from Deutsch, 1986.)

the most part, when the first subject heard an ascending pattern the second subject heard a descending one, and vice versa. Thus, extended patterns composed of such tone pairs were heard by these listeners in radically different ways. An example is given on the right of the illustration, for the case of the series G– C-sharp, D-sharp– A, F-sharp–– C$_3$ and E– A-sharp.

Since this initial experiment was performed on a few musically trained subjects, the question may be raised concerning whether such findings would be confined to a specialized group of listeners, or whether they would also be produced in a general population. Accordingly, a further experiment was performed, using a much larger group of subjects.[9] These were selected using only the following criteria: that they should be university undergraduates, that they should have normal hearing, and that they should be able to judge without error whether pairs of sine-wave tones which were related by a half-octave formed ascending or descending series. Twenty-nine subjects were selected according to these criteria, and they each served in a single experimental session. None of the subjects had absolute pitch, in the sense of being able to attach verbal labels to notes played in isolation.

Again, in order to control for possible effects based on the relative amplitudes of the sinusoidal components, tones pairs were generated with envelopes that were placed at different positions along the spectrum, spaced at half-octave intervals. In this case, the twelve pitch-class pairings were all generated under the four spectral envelopes centered at F-sharp$_5$, C$_5$, F-sharp$_4$, and C$_4$.[10]

For each subject, the percentage of judgments that a tone pair formed a descending series was plotted as a function of the pitch class of the first tone of the pair. As can be seen from the three plots in figure 7, such individual judgments were again strongly influenced by the positions of the tones along the pitch-class circle. Further, as can also be seen, the direction of this influence varied considerably across subjects.

In order to obtain an estimate of the prevalence of the effect in the subject population as a whole, the following procedure was used. First, it was determined for the scores for each subject whether the pitch-class circle could be bisected in such a way that none of the scores in the upper half of the circle was lower than any of the scores in the lower half. This criterion was fulfilled by twenty-two of the twenty-nine sub-

[9]Diana Deutsch, William L. Kuyper and Yuval Fisher, "The Tritone Paradox: Its Presence and Form of Distribution in a General Population," *Music Perception* (in press).
[10]The other sound parameters were as stated in Deutsch, "A musical paradox."

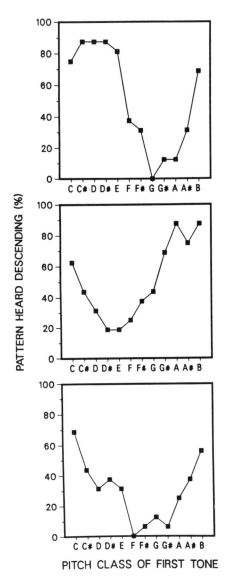

Figure 7. Percentages of judgments that a tone pair formed a descending series, plotted as a function of the pitch class of the first tone of the pair. Results from three different subjects are here displayed, averaged over four spectral envelopes. (From Deutsch, Kuyper, and Fisher, in press.)

jects. Next, in order to obtain a baseline estimate of the probability of obtaining such a result by chance, the proportion of random permutations of the scores (which could be so characterized) was determined by computer simulation. Averaged across subjects, this was found to be .027 per subject, thus yielding a vanishingly small probability of obtaining the combined result by chance. The effect was thus shown to exist to a very highly significant extent in this general population.

We may next enquire into the form of the relationship between pitch class and perceived height in this population as a whole. To examine this issue, the orientation of the pitch-class circle was normalized across subjects,[11] and the normalized data were then averaged. The resultant plot is shown in figure 8, and reveals a remarkably orderly relationship between pitch class and perceived height.

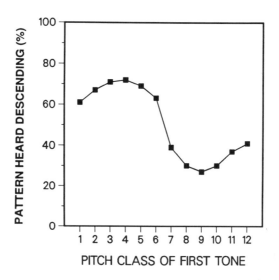

Figure 8. Percentages of judgments that a tone pair formed a descending series, averaged over a large group of subjects, with the orientation of the pitch-class circle normalized across subjects. Results were averaged over four spectral envelopes. (From Deutsch, Kuyper, and Fisher, in press.)

---

[11]For each subject, the pitch class circle was bisected so as to maximize the difference between the averaged scores within the two halves. The circle was then oriented so that the line of bisection was horizontal, and the data were retabulated with the leftmost pitch class of the upper half of the circle taking the first position, its clockwise neighbor taking the second position, and so on.

To examine whether the effect might be related to musical training, two analyses were performed. First, the absolute size of the effect was estimated for each subject separately by subtracting the averaged score for the lower half of the normalized circle from that for the upper half. Of the fifteen subjects who showed the larger difference on this measure, seven had had two years or less of musical training. Of the fourteen subjects who showed the smaller difference, seven also fell into this category. Indeed, the two who showed the largest difference on this measure had had no musical training whatever. For the second analysis, the proportions of "trained" and "untrained" subjects whose individual scores yielded statistically significant effects were calculated, and again no significant difference between the two groups emerged. Clearly, then, musical training is not responsible for the phenomenon.

A further study examined in detail the behavior of this phenomenon in face of variations in the position of the spectral envelope.[12] Such variations could, in principle, produce effects in two ways: first, through resultant differences in the overall heights of the patterns, and second through resultant differences in the relative amplitudes of the sinusoidal components of the tones. A further issue that was examined concerned the stability of the effect when subjects were tested over relatively long time periods.

Accordingly, twelve different spectral envelopes were employed, whose positions were spaced at intervals a quarter-octave apart, spanning altogether a three-octave range. The envelope peaks stood at A_5, F-sharp$_5$, D-sharp$_5$, C_5, A_4, F-sharp$_4$, D-sharp$_4$, C_4, A_3, F-sharp$_3$, D-sharp$_3$, and C_3. Thus, the effect of overall height could be examined by comparing the combined results from the four envelopes centered in each of the three octaves, and the effect of relative amplitude could be examined by comparing the combined results from the envelopes centered at each of the four different pitch classes.[13] Four subjects were employed in the study, and they each served in nine experimental sessions.

Figure 9 displays the results from the four subjects, in each case averaged over all twelve spectral envelopes, and over all nine experimental sessions. As can be seen, the data from each subject again revealed a highly systematic relationship between pitch class and perceived height; and again the form of this relationship varied considerably across subjects. Statistically, for some subjects the form of this relationship was

[12]Diana Deutsch, "The Tritone Paradox: Effects of Spectral Variables," *Perception and Psychophysics* 41 (1987): 563-575.
[13]The other sound parameters were as in Deutsch, "A musical paradox."

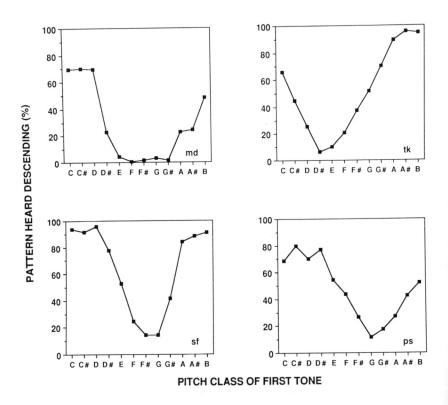

Figure 9. Percentages of judgments that a tone pair formed a descending series, plotted as a function of the pitch class of the first tone of the pair. Results from four different subjects are here displayed, averaged over twelve spectral envelopes and nine experimental sessions. (From Deutsch, 1987.)

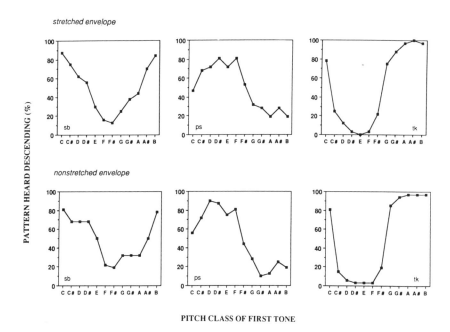

Figure 10. Percentages of judgments that a tone pair formed a descending series, plotted as a function of the pitch class of the first tone of the pair. Results from three different subjects are here displayed, for tones generated under both stretched and nonstretched envelopes, in each case centered at C₅.

influenced by the overall heights of the patterns, and for some subjects it was influenced by the relative amplitudes of the sinusoidal components of the tones; however, neither influence was necessarily present.

A further experiment considered the possible involvement of phase relationships in the effect. To examine this, tone complexes were generated whose envelopes were stretched slightly, so that the sinusoidal components stood in a ratio of 2.01:1. As a result, the phase relationships between these components were constantly varying. Figure 10 displays the results from three subjects when judging tone pairs generated under both stretched and nonstretched envelopes, both centered at C_5. It can be seen that the results under these two conditions were remarkably similar, showing that the phenomenon is not due to the processing of phase relationships.

A Two-Part Pattern

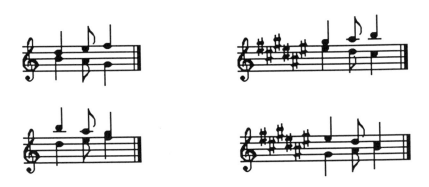

Figure 11. Configurations employed to examine the relationship between pitch class and perceived height in two-part patterns. The basic configuration was presented in both C major and F-sharp major, and is here notated in accordance with two alternative perceptual organizations. (From Deutsch, Moore, and Dolson, 1984.)

We may next ask what happens when more elaborate configurations are employed. One set of experiments[14] used the patterns shown in figure

[14]Diana Deutsch, F. Richard Moore, and Mark Dolson, "Pitch Classes Differ with Respect to Height," *Music Perception* 2 (1984): 265-271; and "The perceived height of octave-related complexes," *Journal of the Acoustical Society of Americal* 80 (1986): 1346-1353.

11. The first was in C major and consisted of the series D– E– F presented simultaneously with the series B– A –G. The second was a transposition of the first to F-sharp major, and so consisted of the series G-sharp – A-sharp– B presented simultaneously with the series E-sharp – D-sharp – C-sharp. The patterns were perceptually organized as two melodic lines in accordance with pitch proximity, so that the listener heard one line that ascended by a minor third, together with another line that descended by a major third. However, some listeners heard the ascending line as higher and the descending line as lower whereas other listeners heard the descending line as higher and the ascending line as lower. These two different perceptual organizations are shown in figure 11.

In one experiment,[15] the two patterns were each generated under envelopes that were placed at six different positions along the spectrum. These were spaced at half-octave intervals, so that their peaks spanned a two and one-half octave range. The envelopes were centered at C_6, F-sharp$_5$, C_5, F-sharp$_4$, C_4, and F-sharp$_3$. Figure 12 shows, as examples, the spectral compositions of the tones comprising the chord D/B, generated under each of these envelopes. On each trial, one of the patterns was presented, and subjects judged whether the higher of the two lines formed an ascending or a descending series; from these judgments it was inferred which tones were heard as higher and which as lower.[16]

Analogous effects were also found to occur with this type of pattern. When played in one key it was heard with the higher line ascending, yet when played in a different key it was heard with the higher line descending. When the pattern was transposed, the relative heights of the different pitch classes were preserved, so that a perceived interchange of voices resulted. Further, when the pattern was played in any one key, listeners differed radically in terms of which line they heard as higher and which as lower.

Table 1 shows, for both groups of subjects, the percentages of judgments where the higher line formed an ascending series, as a function both of key and also of position of the spectral envelope. It can be seen that for both groups of subjects, judgments depended almost entirely on the key in which the pattern was presented. Thus Type-A

[15]Deutsch, Moore, and Dolson, "The perceived height..."
[16]In all patterns, the first and third tones within a series were 500 msec in duration, and the second tone was 250 msec in duration. There were no pauses between tones within a pattern. On each trial, one of the patterns was presented three times in succession, the presentations being separated by 750 msec pauses. Trials were in blocks of twenty-four, with ten- second pauses between trials within a block, and five-minute pauses between blocks. The patterns within a block were presented in random order.

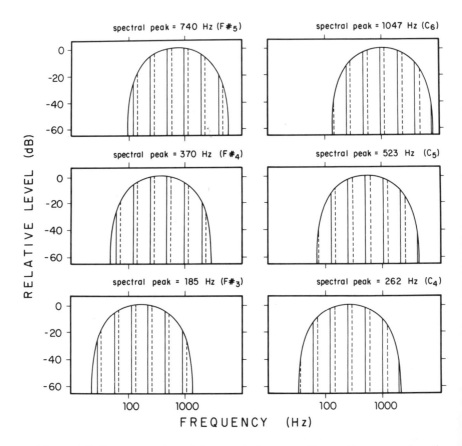

Figure 12. Representation of the spectral compositions of tones employed to examine the influence of pitch class on perceived height in two-part patterns. The chord B/D is here displayed, generated under six spectral envelopes. Solid lines indicate tones of pitch-class B, and dashed lines tones of pitch-class D. (From Deutsch, Moore, and Dolson, 1986.)

Table 1. Percentages of judgments that the higher line formed an ascending series. Tones were generated under nonstretched envelopes. (From Deutsch, Moore, and Dolson, 1986.)

	Spectral peak						
	F-sharp$_3$	C$_4$	F-sharp$_4$	C$_5$	F-sharp$_5$	C$_6$	
C major	100	100	100	97	94	100	
							Type-A subjects
F-sharp major	0	0	0	0	0	0	

	Spectral peak						
	F-sharp$_3$	C$_4$	F-sharp$_4$	C$_5$	F-sharp$_5$	C$_6$	
C major	3	9	0	3	6	0	
							Type-B subjects
F-sharp major	97	97	97	97	97	100	

C-major pattern: ascending line composed of pitch classes D, E, and F; descending line composed of pitch classes B, A, and G.
F-sharp major pattern: ascending line composed of pitch classes G-sharp, A-sharp, and B; descending line composed of pitch classes E-sharp, D-sharp, and C-sharp.

subjects heard the C major pattern with notes D, E, and F as higher and B, A, and G as lower, for all positions of the spectral envelope. They also they heard the F-sharp major pattern with notes E-sharp, D-sharp, and C-sharp as higher and notes G-sharp, A-sharp, and B as lower, for all positions of the spectral envelope. Figure 13 shows, on the left, the pitch-class circle oriented with respect to height so as to reflect this pattern of results. Type-B subjects, on the other hand, produced results which were the converse of those of Type-A. They consistently heard the C-major pattern with notes B, A, and G as higher and notes D, E, and F as lower, for all positions of the spectral envelope. They also heard the F-sharp-major pattern with notes G-sharp, A-sharp, and B as higher and notes E-sharp, D-sharp, and C-sharp as lower, for all positions of the spectral envelope. Figure 13 shows, on the right, the pitch-class circle oriented with respect to height so as to reflect these results.

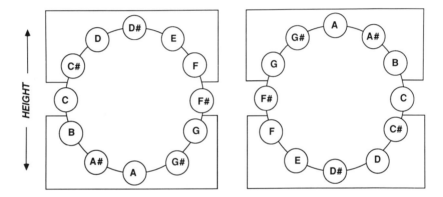

Figure 13. Two orientations of the pitch class circle with respect to height, as reflected in the judgments of Type-A subjects (shown on left), and Type-B subjects (shown on right). (From Deutsch, Moore, and Dolson, 1986.)

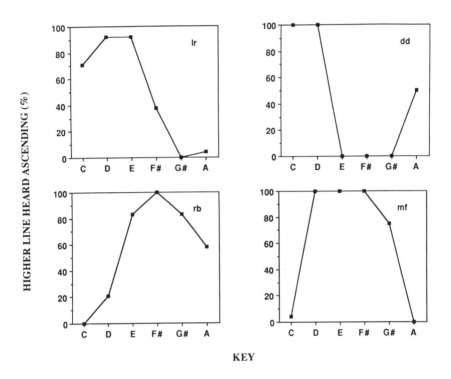

Figure 14. Percentages of judgments that the higher line of the two-part pattern formed an ascending series, as a function of the key in which the pattern was presented. The results from four different subjects are here displayed, averaged over three spectral envelopes.

In a further experiment,[17] tone complexes were generated under envelopes that were stretched slightly, so that the sinusoidal components stood in a ratio of 2.01:1. As a result, the phase relationships between these components were constantly varying. As shown in table 2, the influence of pitch class on perceived height was found to be unaffected by this manipulation.

Table 2. Percentages of judgments that the higher line formed an ascending series. Tones were generated under stretched envelopes. (From Deutsch, Moore, and Dolson, 1986.)

	Spectral peak						
	F-sharp$_3$	C$_4$	F-sharp$_4$	C$_5$	F-sharp$_5$	C$_6$	
C major	91	97	100	100	100	100	
							Type-A subjects
F-sharp major	3	3	3	0	0	0	

	Spectral peak						
	F-sharp$_3$	C$_4$	F-sharp$_4$	C$_5$	F-sharp$_5$	C$_6$	
C major	13	6	0	3	3	3	
							Type-B subjects
F-sharp major	97	97	100	94	97	100	

C-major pattern: ascending line composed of pitch classes D, E, and F; descending line composed of pitch classes B, A, and G.
F-sharp major pattern: ascending line composed of pitch classes G-sharp, A-sharp, and B; descending line composed of pitch classes E-sharp, D-sharp, and C-sharp.

In order to examine this phenomenon in greater detail, I generated the pattern in six different keys; namely C, D, E, F-sharp, G-sharp, and A-sharp. The results from four subjects are shown in figure 14, averaged over the spectral envelopes centered at F-sharp$_5$, C$_5$, and F-sharp$_4$. It can be seen that all subjects showed highly systematic effects of key, and they also differed considerably in terms of the direction in which key influenced their judgments.

Figure 15 illustrates these points more closely, by taking as an ex-

[17]Deutsch, Moore, and Dolson, "The perceived height...."

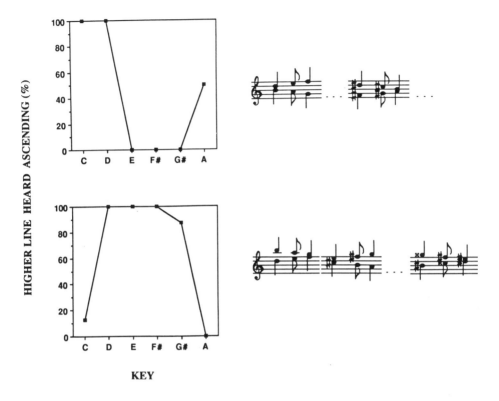

Figure 15. Graphs on left display the percentages of judgments that the higher line of the two-part pattern formed an ascending series, as a function of the key in which the pattern was presented. The results from two subjects are displayed, for patterns generated under the spectral envelope centered at C_5. Notations on right show how the identical patterns were perceived by the two subjects.

ample the judgments of two of the subjects for tones generated under the envelope centered at C_5. So taking the first subject and moving from left to right, the pattern in the key of C was heard with the higher line ascending, as it was in the key of D. But in the key of E it was heard with the higher line descending; and so on. It can be seen that the second subject produced judgments which were virtually the converse of the first. The perceived heights of tones in this pattern were therefore found to vary systematically with their positions along the pitch-class circle, in a fashion analogous to the tritone paradox.

The Semitone Paradox

Figure 16. Examples of patterns giving rise to the semitone paradox. Patterns A, B, C, and D are here notated in accordance with two alternative perceptual orgainizations.

The two-part pattern just described consisted of melodic lines which encompassed a relatively large region of the pitch-class circle. This could, in principle, give the subject freedom to focus on different parts of the pitch-class circle in making his judgments, which creates an ambiguity of interpretation. So in order to examine the phenomenon in a more fine-grained fashion, a different two-part pattern was devised.[18] As shown by the examples in figure 16, this pattern comprised two simultaneous tone pairs, one of which ascended by a semitone and the other of which descended. These tone pairs were diametrically opposed along the pitch class circle. The listener, following the principle of proximity, perceived these patterns as two stepwise lines which moved in contrary motion. However, as shown in figure 17, proximity could not here be used as a cue to determine which line would be perceived as higher and which as lower.

Subjects were presented with such patterns in random order, so that

[18]Diana Deutsch, "The semitone paradox," (in preparation).

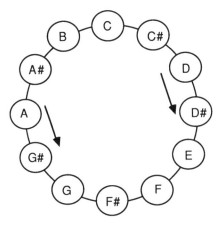

Figure 17. Representation of a pattern giving rise to the semitone paradox, in terms of relationships within the pitch-class circle. The pattern notated in figure 16C is here depicted.

each pitch class served equally often as the first tone of an ascending pair, and also as the first tone of a descending pair. The following pitch class combinations were therefore employed: C – C-sharp/G – F-sharp; C-sharp – D/G-sharp – G; D – D-sharp/A – G-sharp; D-sharp – E/A-sharp – A; E – F/ B – A-sharp; F – F-sharp/C – B; F-sharp – G/C-sharp – C; G – G-sharp/D – C-sharp; G-sharp – A/D-sharp – D; A – A-sharp/ E – D-sharp; A-sharp – B/F – E; and B – C/F-sharp – F. Subjects judged on each trial whether the higher line formed an ascending or a descending series; from these judgments it was inferred which tones were heard as higher and which as lower.[19]

The patterns were generated under envelopes which were placed at twelve different positions along the spectrum, which were spaced at quarter-octave intervals, spanning a three-octave range. The envelope peaks stood at A_5, F-sharp$_5$, D-sharp$_5$, C_5, A_4, F-sharp$_4$, D-sharp$_4$, C_4, A_3, F-sharp$_3$, D-sharp$_3$, and C_3. Four subjects were employed in the study, and each served in nine experimental sessions.

Figure 18 shows the results from the four subjects, in each case averaged over all twelve spectral envelopes and all nine experimental sessions. A strong influence of pitch class on perceived height was again

[19]All tones were 500 msec in duration, and there were no pauses between the tones within a pattern. Trials were presented in blocks of twelve, with five-second pauses between trials within a block, and one-minute pauses between blocks. Each block consisted of tones generated under one of the twelve envelopes and contained one example of each of the twelve pitch-class combinations.

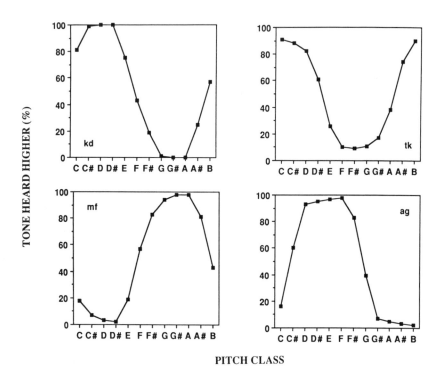

PITCH CLASS

Figure 18. The semitone paradox. Percentages of trials in which a tone was heard as part of the higher line, plotted as a function of the pitch class of the tone. Results from four subjects are here displayed, averaged over twelve spectral envelopes and nine experimental sessions.

apparent, and this was also found to be robust in face of variations in both the overall heights of the patterns and also with reference to the relative amplitudes of the sinusoidal components of the tones. Further, there were again striking differences between the subjects in the direction of the relationship between pitch class and perceived height.

Figure 19 illustrates these points more closely by taking as an example the judgments of two of the subjects, in this case with the spectral envelope centered on C_5. Here the series of pitch class combinations D-- D-sharp/A-- G-sharp, C-sharp-- C/F-sharp-- G and D-sharp-- E/A-sharp-- A were presented, and it can be seen that the subjects heard this extended pattern in ways that were radically different from each other. So the same perceptual principles were here manifest as for the other types of pattern.

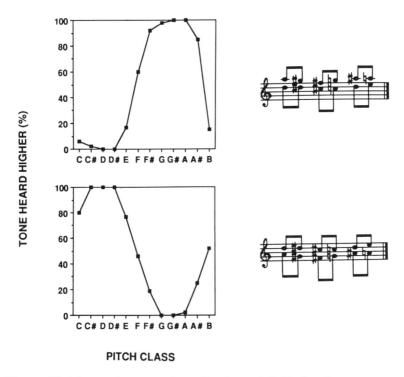

PITCH CLASS

Figure 19. The semitone paradox. Graphs on left display the percentages of trials in which a tone was heard as part of the higher line, plotted as a function of the pitch class of the tone. Results from two subjects are here displayed, for patterns generated under the spectral envelope centered at C_5. Notations on right show how the identical series of patterns was perceived by the two subjects.

DISCUSSION

The phenomena reported here are highly unexpected on a number of grounds. First, they provide clear counter-examples to the principle of invariance under transposition—a principle which has generally been regarded as self-evident. In the case of the tritone paradox, transposing the pattern resulted in a perceived inversion; in the case of the two-part patterns, transposition resulted in a perceived interchange of voices.

Particularly convincing demonstrations of these phenomena may be produced by tape-recording examples of such patterns and then playing the tape back at different speeds. This manipulation shifts the spectra of the patterns up or down in log frequency, so that different pitches are produced. One would assume that the patterns would, as a result, simply be heard as transposed; however, they are heard as having radically changed their shape as well.

Let us take as an example a particular instantiation of the tritone paradox—say the pitch-class combination D – G-sharp. Let us also take two listeners, one who hears this particular pattern as descending (as in figure 4) and another who hears it as ascending (as in figure 5). After playing the pattern at normal speed, we speed the tape up so that the entire spectrum is transposed up a half-octave, and the pitch pattern now becomes G-sharp – D instead. As a result solely of this manipulation, the listener who had heard the pattern as descending now hears it as ascending, and the listener who had heard the pattern as ascending now hears it as descending!

Similarly, let us take the D – E -- F/G– A – B pattern illustrated in figure 11. Let us also take a "Type-A" listener, who hears the pattern with the higher line ascending, and a "Type-B" listener, who hears it with the higher line descending. When the tape speed is increased so that the entire spectrum is transposed up a half-octave, and the pattern is thereby transposed from C major to F-sharp major, the "Type-A" listener now hears the pattern with the higher line descending, and the "Type-B" listener now hears it with the higher line ascending instead!

Since the relative heights of the different pitch classes remain invariant in face of overall shifts in the frequency spectrum, the findings demonstrate that pitch class and perceived height are not orthogonal dimensions, as had been supposed. The findings are therefore at variance with the helical model of pitch described at the beginning of the chapter. This point is illustrated with reference to figure 20. Take, for example, the listener who hears note A as higher and note D-sharp as lower,

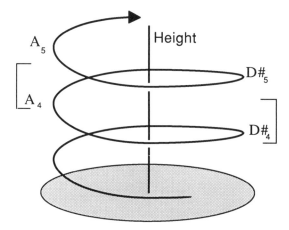

Figure 20. The relative heights of tones in different spectral regions, according to the model of pitch as a geometrically regular helix.

regardless of the position of the spectral envelope. The bracket on the right indicates a region of height which corresponds to a spectral envelope centered on F-sharp$_4$. Within this region, as shown in the diagram, the note A should indeed be heard as higher and the note D-sharp as lower. However, consider now the region of height indicated by the bracket on the left, and which corresponds to a spectral envelope centered on C$_5$. Here, according to the model, D-sharp should be heard as higher and A as lower instead. *However, the listener continues to hear A as higher and D-sharp as lower, regardless of the spectral region the tones are in.* We can see that the model of pitch as a geometrically regular helix cannot accommodate this phenomenon.

Another highly unexpected aspect of these findings concerns the pronounced differences between listeners in how such patterns are perceived. It is particularly striking that these differences occur as strongly among those who are musically proficient as among those who are musically naive. In general, it is assumed that while people differ in terms of how they might group or classify musical materials, or how accurately they can describe them, the issue of whether a simple two-note pattern forms an ascending or a descending series should not be a matter of dispute. These findings therefore lead us to wonder what other differences between listeners might exist that have not yet been uncovered. Such differences might give rise to disagreements about music which are at present considered to be aesthetic or otherwise evaluative in nature.

Variations between listeners have also been found to occur in the octave and scale illusions.[20] Here, proficient musicians may differ strikingly as to where notes appear to be coming from, and even how many and which notes are being played. In the case of these illusions, strong correlates have been found with the handedness of the listener, and even with his or her familial handedness background.[21] One might therefore assume that such variations reflect innate differences between listeners at the neurological level. In the case of the present set of paradoxes, no correlates have yet been obtained, though the highly orderly nature of the effects and their lack of association with musical training lead one to speculate that the individual differences found here are likely to be biological in origin.

The present findings also have implications for theories of absolute pitch, a faculty which is generally supposed to be confined to a few rare individuals. In the present experiments, where judgments of height were influenced by the positions of the tones along the pitch-class circle, listeners were, in effect, using absolute pitch in making these judgments. Yet, as described, this influence of pitch class was shown to exist to a highly significant extent in a general population.[22] Given this evident ability to employ absolute pitch indirectly,[23] it is puzzling that people do not in general possess this faculty, in the sense of being able to attach verbal labels to notes presented out of context. One is reminded here of the syndrome of color anomia,[24] in which people may perform normally on nonverbal color tasks but are unable to name colors when these are presented in isolation. Although color anomia is very rare, perhaps the majority of us (i.e., those who do not possess absolute pitch as conventionally defined) have an analogous syndrome with regard to pitch class.

The extent to which effects such as described here occur in other contexts remains to be investigated. However, recent work by the author

[20]Diana Deutsch, "An auditory illusion," *Nature* 251 (1974): 307-309; and also "Two-channel listening..." and "Musical illusions."
[21]Diana Deutsch, "The Octave Illusion in Relation to Handedness and Familial Handedness Background," *Neuropsychologia* 21 (1983): 289-293.
[22]Deutsch, Kuyper and Fisher, "The Tritone Paradox: Its Presence...."
[23]A related point has been made concerning key identification; see Ernst Terhardt and W. Dixon Ward, "Recognition of Musical Key: Exploratory Study," *Journal of the Acoustical Society of Americal* 72 (1982): 26-33; and Ernst Terhardt and Manfred Seewann, "Aural Key Identification and Its Relationship to Absolute Pitch," *Music Perception* 1 (1983): 63-83. These authors found that musicians could judge whether or not a passage was played in the correct key, even though most of the subjects claimed not to have absolute pitch. Such judgments were even made when differences as small as a semitone were at issue.
[24]Norman Geschwind and M. Fusillo, "Color-Naming Defects in Association with Alexia," *Archives of Neurology* 15 (1966): 137-146.

has shown that the influence of pitch class on perceived height persists when the tones are subjected to a number of time-varying manipulations, such as superimposing a vibrato, a tremolo, or a fast decay such as to produce the impression of a plucked string. The effect has also been found to persist when the sinusoidal components within each tone complex are all replaced with sawtooth waves, so that each component is replaced by a set of tones comprising a harmonic series. Similarly, the effect persists when the sinusoids are replaced with square waves, so that each component is replaced by the odd-numbered partials of a harmonic series. The spectra of these more elaborate tone complexes are quite similar to those produced by a group of natural instruments playing simultaneously, with their fundamental frequencies standing in octave relation. Therefore, good reason exists to expect that analogous effects should be obtainable from an ensemble of natural instruments playing at appropriate loudness levels relative to each other.

More generally, we may speculate that effects such as shown here might occur, at least to some extent, in listening to music played by natural instruments under conditions giving rise to registral ambiguities. Consider, for example, orchestral contexts in which instruments of different types play with multiple octave doublings. Under such conditions the perceived heights of tones are often not clearly defined. The question of how musical patterns are really heard under such circumstances has not yet been the subject of formal investigation.

At a strictly theoretical level, the phenomena described in this essay lead us to question the relationship between a musical note as it is written in a score, and as depicted in alphanumeric form, or as it is perceived. It is generally taken for granted that a clear correspondence between the two must surely exist.[25] However, the present work shows that under certain conditions at least the assumption is incorrect—if only because listeners disagree among themselves as to which notes they hear. It would appear that a symbolic description, which was originally developed as a practical convenience (for example, as instructions to the performer),

[25]It is often assumed that for single notes composed of harmonically related partials, the perceived pitch corresponds to that of the fundamental; see, for example, J. F. Schouten, "The Residue and the Mechanism of Hearing," *Proceedings of the Koninklgke Nederlandse Akademie van Wetenshappen* 43 (1940): 991-991. However, listeners may produce pitch matches to frequencies other than the fundamental even with strictly harmonic tone complexes (see, for example, Ernst Terhardt, "Gestalt principles and music perception," in *Auditory Processing of Complex Sounds*, ed. William A. Yost and Charles S. Watson (Hillsdale, 1987): 157-16⁷. In addition, compelling demonstrations of the failure of residue pitch have been presented by John R. Pierce, "What Do *We* Hear?" in a paper presented at the *81st Audio Engineering Society Convention*, Los Angeles, 1986.

has been elevated through common usage, and without logical or empirical support, to the status of a fundamental theoretical construct.[26]

In conclusion, the findings described in this essay cannot be readily accommodated within present theory, and raise considerably more questions than they answer. However, as Leonard B. Meyer, who has always argued so eloquently for the usefulness of the empirical approach to music, wrote: "Were complete information and incontrovertible theory a prerequisite for understanding, science, for example, would never have even begun."[27]

[26]Eugene Narmour, in *Beyond Schenkerism: The Need for Alternatives in Music Analysis* (Chicago, 1977) has advanced analogous arguments concerning the logical status of the *Ursatz*.

[27]Leonard B. Meyer, *Explaining Music*, p.14.

[28]I am indebted to a number of people for their collaboration and assistance in this research, specifically to F. Richard Moore and Mark Dolson for software used in synthesizing the tones, and to Lee Ray, Yuval Fisher, and William L. Kuyper for assistance and collaboration in various phases of the study. The work was supported by grants from the System Development Foundation, and from the UCSD Biomedical Research Support Program.

John Chesnut

Affective Design in Schubert's *Moment musical* op. 94 no. 6

INTRODUCTION

An important objective of modern theory is to identify functional relationships in music. This is difficult using traditional formal analysis, which suffers from several weaknesses. First, its nomenclature is so abstract that individual differences between compositions are obscured. After reduction to the standard categories, therefore, one sonata form looks much like any other, a motive is nothing but a letter of the alphabet, and successful compositons are barely distinguishable from failures. What does not fit into the standard forms is relegated to the catch-all category of unexplained "exceptions." Furthermore, because individual differences between compositions are obscured, it is difficult to evaluate the degrees of similarity and difference between the sections of a composition. This handicaps the effort to interpret any functional links between the sections that might be dependent on similarity relationships.

This paper is a pilot study testing the feasibility of analyzing music with a new technique of formal analysis that is not bound by the customary limitations. It proposes a method for characterizing similarity relationships and interpreting their functions. It categorizes textures and colors by their affective associations, according to a schema derived

John Chesnut, author of "Mozart's Teaching of Intonation," is a computer specialist interested in giving concrete meaning to the abstract, generalizable aesthetic and psychological foundations of music-compositional technique.

from Charles Osgood's semantic differential.[1] Schubert's *Moment musical* in A-flat op. 94 no. 6 will be analyzed to show the distribution of its affects and their organization in time.

The semantic differential outlines a dimensioned space within which we can conceptualize affective change through time.[2] Three principal semantic dimensions will be employed in this study: Forcefulness, Activity, and Brightness. Forcefulness is almost exclusively a matter of loudness.[3] Activity is based on a generalized impression of the rate of speed with which notes are played. Brightness is a rather complex concept. It has to do with what musicians call "tension," which is presumably a product of one or more different things, such as the minor mode, chromaticism, discord, and pungent timbre. In this nomenclature, high-tension music is *dark* and low-tension music is *bright*.[4]

[1]Charles Osgood, "On the Whys and Wherefores of E, P, and A," *Journal of Personality and Social Psychology* 12 (1969): 194-199; *Focus on Meaning*, v. I (The Hague, 1976). Charles E. Osgood, William H. May, and Murray S. Miron, *Cross-Cultural Universals of Affective Meaning* (Urbana, 1975); Charles Osgood, George J. Suci, and Percy H. Tannenbaum, *The Measurement of Meaning* (Urbana, 1957).

For a specific application of Osgood's theory to music, see L. Wedin, *Evaluation of a Three-Dimensional Model of Expression in Music*, Reports from the Psychological Laboratory, 349 (Stockholm, 1972).

These studies should be read against the background of Kate Hevner's earlier studies of musical affect. See Kate Hevner, "The Affective Character of the Major and Minor Modes in Music," *American Journal of Psychology* 47 (1935): 103-118; "The Affective Value of Pitch and Tempo in Music," *American Journal of Psychology* 48 (1936): 246-268; "Expression in Music: A Discussion of Experimental Studies and Theories," *Psychological Review* 42 (1935): 186-204; "Studies in Expressiveness of Music," *Music Teacher's National Association, Proceedings 1938 [33 (1939)]*: 199-217.

[2]The semantic differential tells us that people in our culture make associations between things that are affectively similar and that these associations fall principally into three independent dimensions of variability, which Osgood calls Potency, Activity, and Evaluation. For musical analysis, I have renamed these three dimensions of affect and added a fourth.

[3]Some small difference in our impression of the Forcefulness of music may depend on whether or not the performer plays the notes in a passage of music with accentuated attacks (I mean by "attack" the initiation of a note).

[4]In a very general sense, Forcefulness and Activity being considered equal, Brightness has to do with whether music is "happy" or "sad." For this reason, Brightness is also associated to some degree with the distinction between duple and triple meters. Triple meters and compound meters based on triple meters are *bright*. Purely duple meters are relatively *dark* or at least less *bright*. It is frequently pointed out that music in the minor mode is not always sad. That is because music in the minor mode can be written in triple meters with a minimum of chromaticism and discord. The fact remains that a passage in the minor mode has greater perceptual tension than an otherwise similar passage in the major mode.

A fourth, subsidiary, dimension of affect, Complexity,[5] will also be employed in this study. As a working definition of "complexity," I mean that which presents any degree whatever of perceptual difficulty, the sort of thing that requires some special acuity or mental concentration to construe, remember, sight-sing, or take in dictation. Presumably, variety and discontinuity in any element of musical construction, from pitch and rhythm to color and texture, are "complex" to most people. Some hypothetical measures of complexity will be presented here, and an attempt will be made to assay their relative importance; but this paper does not pretend to have exhausted the subject.

All of these dimensions of affect will be discussed more fully later.

Presumably, a passage of music can be rated as relatively "high" or "low" on any dimension of affective meaning, depending on whether it exhibits the quality in question to a greater or lesser degree of intensity or purity. A loud passage would be rated high on Forcefulness, for example, where a soft passage would be rated low on the same dimension of affect. A fast passage would be rated high on Activity, but a slow passage would be rated low; and diatonic, concordant music in the major mode would be rated high on Brightness, but music with the

---

[5]Some evidence from Watson's studies of musical affect suggests that Complexity is a factor. See K. Brantley Watson, *The Nature and Measurement of Musical Meanings*, Pscyhological Monographs, 54 (Evanston, 1942). For example, within the category of Cheerful music *(soft, fast, bright)*, we could also distinguish a subcategory called Humorous, which is similar but more complex. If this is valid, it is possible that there are not just three primary factors of affect, but four. The fourth factor, Complexity, might be weaker than the other three. My impression is that complexity in general is a more subtle concept than any of the three primary factors of affect. Complexity is certainly much harder to define; only the more sophisticated listeners may be sensitive to it. Perhaps, on the other hand, the Complexity factor is contained within the other three factors. As the reader will learn, this study found some evidence that Complexity may be associated negatively with Forcefulness and Brightness. I hope that experimental psychologists will help us sort this out one day.

However subtle they may be, complexity and simplicity, as I interpret them, contribute greatly to our understanding of the fantasy and logic of a musical composition and therefore figure strongly in our value judgments about music. The music we accept as our highest art can be considered a celebration of creative intellect. Fantasy and logic, according to this view, are formal aspects of imaginativeness and intellectuality, the two sides of creative intellect. Complexity and simplicity, therefore, which symbolize fantasy and logic, are essential to the vision of creative intellect; for the vision to be complete and satisfying, complexity and simplicity must be reconciled, most typically through hierarchic structure. Extreme manifestations of the primary dimensions of affect contribute as well to our understanding of the imaginativeness of music, by suggesting the passion of the creative impulse; but if these visceral elements are not integrated with both fantasy and logic, we dismiss them as merely blatant.

opposite characteristics would appear on the opposite end of the scale.

Since the three principal dimensions of affect (Forcefulness, Activity, and Brightness) are independent, however, we cannot fully characterize the affect of a passage of music without referring to all three. Dividing each of the three dimensions into two parts, high and low, gives us eight possible combinations. Roughly speaking, then, musical affect falls into eight basic categories, although infinitesimal distinctions can be made within them. The eight categories are these: Resigned *(soft, slow, dark)* vs. Exuberant *(loud, fast, bright);* Tragic *(loud, slow, dark)* vs. Cheerful *(soft, fast, bright);* Agitated *(soft, fast, dark)* vs. Masterful *(loud, slow, bright);* and Angry *(loud, fast, dark)* vs. Tranquil *(soft, slow, bright).* These eight categories define a "semantic space." Analyzing the affective design of a musical composition involves tracing a timeline through this semantic space.

METHOD

The affective complexity of Schubert's *Moment musical* catches our ear at first hearing. This is a challenging work, a good test case for any theory of affective design. If we can find an underlying order in the sequence of affects presented by this work, we should be well on our way toward construction of a useful theory.

There are two basic approaches we could follow in performing this analysis: the axiomatic and the empirical.

The axiomatic approach starts with the printed musical score, selecting the data it finds there on general principles. It uses slight variations on the traditional concepts and terminology of music theory and never has to make any direct reference to metaphors or descriptions of affect— although evaluating the more demanding dimensions of affective structure, Brightness and Complexity, does require judgment. No sophisticated mathematics is needed in the gathering of data, so the analysis gets off to a relatively quick start. The axiomatic approach is best suited to historical studies where a large number of compositons must be analyzed. Most musicians will probably find this approach more acceptable than the empirical approach. The disadvantages of the axiomatic approach are that it takes empirical verification for granted, and it may not reflect all the subtleties and ambiguities of the responses of actual audiences to music.

The empirical approach starts with subjective, metaphorical[6] audience reactions. It checks for statistical correspondences between these subjective judgments and objective data that can be found in the printed musical score, but the actual analysis is performed on ratings produced by the subjective evaluations. This method requires sophisticated statistical methods; it is not well suited for historical studies, and it will probably appeal more to experimental psychologists than to most musicians. Its chief advantage is that it provides scientific validation of theories of affect.

I have used both approaches, and I do not have an absolute preference for one over the other. In 1978, when I performed the analysis that will be described here, I was primarily concerned with validating the

---

[6]It is not customary in music theory to use metaphors explicity. Implicit metaphors, however, lie at the root of modern music theory. Some of our most important structural concepts (syntax, coherence, hierarchic structure, implication) are metaphors. All of these are interpretive, extramusical references to aspects of human reason. In fact, semantics, the science of meaning, is more fundamental to music than syntax, the science of structure, because the role of structure in music is largely symbolic.

One may argue that in the final analysis all human knowledge is metaphorical: see Christopher Butler, *Interpretation, Deconstruction, and Ideology* (Oxford, 1984). Taken to extremes, this idea can lead to an infinite regression; but the position taken here is simply that all human knowledge is theoretical and therefore tentative. We set up models to describe the world, and we accept those models as long as they accord reasonably well with our experience. Metaphors, in this view, are compact theoretical models, to be evaluated and tested like any other theoretical models.

We use metaphors to describe what music *is*. It depends on one's perspective whether or not we should say that we are describing by metaphors either what music *signifies* or what it *represents*. Confusion about this point must be resolved if the present study is to have a rigorous intellectual foundation in aesthetic theory.

Music comes close to having what semiologists call *iconic signs*, that is, signs like pictograms that establish their meaning by their resemblance to the thing signified. Normally, however, excluding associations like those engineered by Wagner for his leitmotivs, or private associations we may have formed between music and events in our own lives, it is not strictly correct to say that music *signifies* anything. Music is not an intermediary between ourselves and some external, third-party meaning. When we hear music, normally we respond to the music itself, not to something else that is suggested by the music itself. Music is a structured stimulus, not a sign.

On the other hand, music does bear perceptible if incomplete resemblances to certain psychological states and processes. For this reason, the musical stimulus falls on prepared ground; and we respond to it in somewhat the same way as we respond to the psychological qualities it resembles. It is fair to say, then, that music *represents* these psychological qualities, not in the sense that it points to them, but in the sense that it *stands in their place*. Because the resemblance between music and psychological qualities is only partial, however, their representation in music is semi-abstract.

300   JOHN CHESNUT

theory of affect, so I chose the empirical approach. For the benefit of a general musical audience, the procedure will be described informally.

Not having the resources of an experimental psychologist, I performed this experiment on an audience of one: myself. Clearly, since no-one participated in the endeavor but myself and some of my responses to music are undoubtedly unique, this study does not tell us anything specific about audiences in general. Presumably, however, I have enough in common with other listeners that my experience of music has some relevance to the experience of others. This experiment should suffice, then, as a pilot study that provides information that would be useful in setting up more formal studies in the future.

I listened to Alfred Brendel's recording of the Schubert *Moment musical*[7] registering my impression of the affect of each of its twenty-seven phrases as I listened (see example 1 and table 1). I rated the phrases from one to five (a customary range for psychological experiments) on four different metaphorically-defined scales. I did this on two separate occasions, to make sure that I was performing the ratings consistently. The results were quite similar both times.

Table 1. Beginnings of Phrases by First Full Measure

Allegretto

Phrase Nbr.	1	2	3	4	5	6	7	8	9	10
Measure Nbr.	1	5	9	13	17	21	25	29	34	37

Phrase Nbr.	11	12	13	14	15	16	17	18
Measure Nbr.	40	44	48	54	58	62	66	71

Trio

Phrase Nbr.	19	20	21	22	23	24	25	26	27
Measure Nbr.	1	5	9	13	17	21	27	31	35

The opposite ends of the four scales, Forcefulness, Activity, Brightness, and Complexity, were designated by the terms *gentle vs. assertive, slow vs. fast, bright vs. dark,* and *controlled vs. uncontrolled,* respectively. It was my intention to choose words that would suggest

[7]Philips SAL 6500 418.

approximately the four essential dimensions of affective meaning without actually specifying any objective characteristics of the music.

To discover the technical referents of the metaphorical ratings required statistical analysis. (It would be best to avoid calling the technical referents "purely musical." They were chosen for their potential extramusical significance.)

The ratings were compared with ten technical measures. Most of these measures were completely objective, in the sense that they were taken directly from the printed score; but loudness was judged intuitively from Brendel's performance. I wanted to study the effect of the dynamics as I was actually hearing them. My impression was that Brendel's performance followed the written dynamic markings rather closely; but there was still some variation, perhaps as much as half a dynamic level.

The *gentle vs. assertive* ratings were almost entirely explained by variations in loudness.

As one would expect, the *slow vs. fast* ratings were very strongly related to a simple measure of rhythmic activity. Unfortunately, I was not able to take Brendel's tempo changes into account. For the sake of reliability, I averaged together the ratings for all parallel passages in the piece; but this obscured Brendel's tempo variations. Rhythmic activity was calculated directly from the printed score. First I counted the number of discrete attacks (notes initiated) in each phrase. By "discrete," I mean one attack per simultaneity. An attack was counted in any voice; but when two or more notes were attacked at the same time, they were counted as one. The duration of each phrase was timed, and from that the number of attacks per minute was calculated.

One more step was necessary to create a measure of rhythmic activity that models our subjective responses to music. We think of rhythm in terms of hierarchic metric levels; there is a whole-note level, a half-note level, a quarter-note level, an eighth-note level, and so on. In a duple meter, for example, each of these levels represents a doubling of rhythmic activity. There is some evidence that our subjective response is influenced by this concept of levels. If the reader will think back to his high-school mathematics, he will recall that we can convert a series of doublings into a series of equal steps by applying logarithms. The measure of rhythmic activity finally employed here, therefore, is the logarithm of the number of discrete attacks per minute.

Because of an overlapping between the Brightness and Complexity scales, we should now turn directly to Complexity and save the discussion of Brightness for last.

By far the most important contributor to the Complexity ratings was dynamic range (not simple loudness, but the difference between the loudest and softest dynamic in each phrase). The smaller the dynamic range, the more *controlled* the mood of the music seemed to be.

Three other variables also added to the *control* ratings. Two of these, like dynamic range, are measures of complexity in general; and low scores on these measures were associated with *control*. One was the average number of chromatic alterations per measure.[8] The other was a statistical measure of rhythmic contrast within each phrase: using a measure of dispersion called the "variance" (the formula can be found in introductory statistics text books), I calculated the variability of the durations between discrete attacks in each phrase (actually, I calculated the variance of the logarithms of the durations, and I measured the durations in beats, not seconds or minutes). I was surprised to learn, however, that my ratings of *control* were partially correlated with simple loudness, the principal component of the *gentle vs. assertive* scale. Loud passages were perceived as somewhat more *controlled* than soft passages.

To be sure, in real life physical power is an element of the control that some people exert over others; so the association between the two concepts is perfectly reasonable, and the scale can be justified on empirical grounds. From a more theoretical standpoint, however, it would be desirable to have completely pure scales. Perhaps it would have been better to have called the *control* scale "simplicity vs. complexity." Fortunately, the overlap between the *control* and *assertiveness* scales is small.

I had thought that a couple of other measures of complexity might have added to the impression of *control,* but they did not. It did not make a significant difference whether or not the phrases were the standard four bars in length; and an alternative measure of rhythmic variety, described under Brightness below, also failed to influence the ratings of *control.* Perhaps these variables were too subtle to compete against the others. In another, less dramatic, context I believe they would have made a significant contribution.

Turning to the last rating scale, Brightness, four variables accounted for most of the perceived *darkness.* The first of these, in order of importance, was the average number of beats per measure having at least

---

[8]The correct count cannot be obtained simply by checking off written signs, because musical notation can include both redundancy and implicit cancellation of signs. To anyone who is familiar with the technique of the harp, which is fundamentally a diatonic instrument in conception, the easiest way to figure out what is an actual chromatic alteration is to think about whether changes would have to be made in the pedal settings to realize the alterations on a harp.

one discord lasting at least a full beat. The second was the average mode (counting 0 for the major mode and 1 for the minor). The third was dynamic range (there is some overlapping here with the rating for *control*, but dynamic range has a much stronger association with *control* than with *darkness*). The fourth was the alternative measure of rhythmic variety mentioned above. This was the average number per phrase of different one-bar-long rhythmic patterns. I was surprised to find that chromatic alteration had no important effect on *darkness*. Again, it probably does have some effect; but perhaps the effect was masked by stronger variables.

I was also surprised that irregularity of some kind seemed to have had almost as strong an effect on my judgment of *darkness* as tonal qualities did. Two of the four variables accounting for my evaluations of *darkness* were measures also correlating with Complexity: both dynamic range and variety of rhythmic patterning. I apparently take these irregularities as symbols of "rough sailing," symbols of the vicissitudes of life. That is reasonable as far as it goes; but if we want to have a rating scale that corresponds strictly to the concept of objective color tensions, it appears that we might do better in the future to choose other descriptive words. Perhaps *happy vs. sad, positive vs. negative, pleasurable vs. painful*, or *sweet vs. pungent* might be improvements.

If we are going to use these ratings in formal analysis, we have to be concerned about change in musical character over time; and we want to know which dimensions of affect make the strongest contributions to change in character. In addition to the ratings that have already been discussed, therefore, I also rated the degree of contrast between succeeding sections of the composition. Statistical analysis was performed to determine the relative contributions made to change in character by changes in the four rating scales. The most important conclusion to be derived from this part of the study is that differences in *control* had a very minor impact on the perceived changes in affective character.

In summary, my ratings of Forcefulness, Activity, and Brightness seemed to be quite independent of each other. Complexity, however, was a more ambiguous concept, overlapping to some degree with both Forcefulness and Brightness. If this experiment were to be done over again, it would be preferable to develop scales that are more conceptually pure.

So far as I understand the terms that were used, it appears that the scales I employed do have concrete musical meanings which are comprehensive and substantially, though not perfectly, independent from one another. Pragmatically speaking, that is as much as I wanted to show. It means that we are ready to go on to the next step, writing a model analysis.

Once the ratings have been established for each dimension of affect, the axiomatic and empirical methods converge. They differ only in the way they gather data. Analyzing the data presents the same problems for both methods.

SEMANTIC SPACE

We cannot use climax theory to analyze Schubert's *Moment musical* because its semantic structure is too complex. Climax theory reduces affective meaning to one dimension of variability, arousal. We have seen, however, that affect potentially varies in at least three or four dimensions. This means that it is not always possible to carry out a consistent analysis of climax structure. For example, in this piece, Activity and Darkness (negative Brightness) tend to work against each other; they are used in such a way that one tends to decrease arousal while the other increases it.

Now, as it happens, Schubert's *Moment musical* does not make use of the full range of variability in affect that might theoretically be possible. (This in itself is a kind of unity.) Not every possible combination of ratings actually appears, as changes in affect measured by the four scales described above are somewhat correlated with each other. We learn this by applying a statistical technique called "factor analysis."[9] Factor analysis shows that for all practical purposes we can collapse the variation in character of Schubert's *Moment musical* to two dimensions, one more than climax theory can handle.

The two dimensions isolated by factor analysis are composites of the four scales derived from Osgood's semantic differential. Factor I is a

---

[9]Andrew L. Comrey, *A First Course in Factor Analysis* (New York, 1973). It is not strictly necessary to use factor analysis. More intuitive, *ad hoc* methods can often be applied. However, preprogrammed statistical packages that include factor analysis are available for microcomputers; and they are available on mainframes at most well-equipped university computer service centers. The mathematical technique of factor analysis is complicated in itself, but the preprogrammed packages should be relatively easy to use. Granted, the older packages written to run on mainframes were intended to be used by specialists but the more recent microcomputer software is reputed to be accessible to the general user. For this reason, factor analysis would be the most practical technique to choose for any large historical study of affective design.

composite of Forcefulness, Complexity, and Darkness but has no important association with Activity. Factor II is a composite of Activity and Brightness. Brightness appears about equally in both of these factors, but with opposite signs.

It is difficult to give names to such combinations; but a positive Factor I score—*assertive, uncontrolled,* and *dark*—could be described as "distraught;" and its opposite—*gentle, controlled,* and *bright*—could be described as "calm." Similarly, a positive score on Factor II—*active* and *bright*—could be described as "elated;" and the opposite—*inactive* and *dark*—could be described as "depressed."

A journey through time in Schubert's *Moment musical* follows a path extending over a two-dimensional semantic space defined by a pair of oppositions: *calm vs. distraught* and *depressed vs. elated.* It is possible to calculate factor scores showing where every phrase of the composition lies in this semantic space.

The factor scores that were calculated are *relative* scores. A factor score of zero simply indicates the average on that factor for this particular composition. This is especially important for Factor II, because this factor is influenced by Activity, which, for all its variability in this piece, is never really fast, but only more or less slow.[10] A positive score on Factor II only indicates that the piece has moved in the direction of "elation," not that it exhibits this trait to any high degree.

UNITY OF SUBSTANCE

Unity of affect in the Schubert *Moment musical* will be examined here in three different aspects: unity of substance, unity of pattern, and uni-

---

[10]It is commonly accepted that the "neutral" tempo, neither fast nor slow, is about 80 beats per minute. There is probably a neutral rate of attack as well, around 200 attacks per minute. At 80 beats per minute, there are 160 eighth notes per minute; so an average rate of 200 attacks per minute corresponds at that tempo to a rhythm of mostly eighth notes with a few sixteenth notes. Brendel's average tempo was 101 beats per minute, which is faster than the neutral tempo; but the fastest rate of attack in his performance, averaged by phrase, was 127 attacks per minute, well below the neutral rate for attacks. The rate of attack seems to be more important than the tempo. My subjective reaction is that the piece is always "slow," even though it is played at a relatively fast tempo.

ty of connection.[11] We will start with unity of substance; repetition and contrast of the factor scores will be investigated by telescoping the passage of time. What is left when we do that is a picture of the overall distribution of the elements of the composition.

Figure 1 shows where the phrases of Schubert's *Moment musical* fall in their semantic space, irrespective of time. Phrases tend to fall into three clusters. Each cluster occupies one quadrant of the semantic space. One quadrant, strong on both factors, is nearly empty, however. To fall into this quadrant, a phrase would have to be relatively fast, loud, and complex; it might be only average in color tension, but even so, the combination of attributes would probably be a bit hysterical. It is characteristic of this composition, then, that for all the variety of affect it contains, Schubert has studiously avoided one particularly disturbing area of human experience.

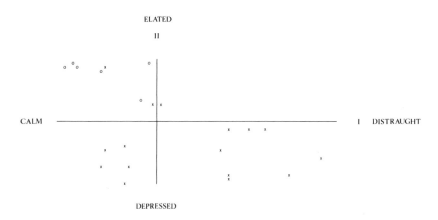

Figure 1. The distribution of character traits found in Schubert's *Moment musical* op. 94 no. 6. Estimated factor scores for the twenty-seven phrases plotted against Factor I *(calm-distraught)* in the horizontal dimension and Factor II *(depressed-elated)* in the vertical. Phrases from the Allegretto are plotted with X, phrases from the Trio with O. Some repetitions of points are not indicated.

[11]It is a mistake to confuse unity with simple uniformity. Unity is that which creates order out of diverse elements. What is considered an acceptable order varies with different musical styles. Unity is not a simple descriptive term; it is an honorific. A composition can be too uniform, but it cannot be too unified!

To the historian, this paper bears on a question raised by Enlightenment music critics that has never received a proper answer: did Unity of Affect cease to be a valid critical standard with the passing of the Baroque style, or did it live on in some new guise?

The clusters in the two lower quadrants belong to the largest formal division of the compositon, an Allegretto in rounded binary form. This Allegretto (whose phrases are marked with X's in the graph) tends to divide its time between two states, one relatively *calm,* though *depressed,* and the other more *distraught.* The remaining cluster in the upper left-hand quadrant belongs primarily to the complementary formal division of the piece, a Trio, also in rounded binary form. The Trio (phrases marked with O's) tends to be somewhat *elated* and *calm;* but there is some blurring of the distinction in character between the Allegretto and Trio. X's can be found in or near the cluster of O's. There are phrases in the Allegretto and Trio that resemble each other in character. This is an element of unity in the composition. The Allegretto and Trio modify the contrast between them by making references to each other. As we shall see, however, in these two sections the phrases which are similar to each other do not occur near to one another in time. They are not transitional and therefore do not satisfy one of the simplest criteria of cohesiveness.

Is clustering a typical phenomenon? It does appear, at least in this case, to be functional. Clustering assimilates diverse textures and colors in such a way that the mind can regard them as divided into units that are internally equivalent. Within the clusters there is similarity and cohesiveness. The gaps between clusters, however, create diversity and discontinuity. Clustering means that major changes of affect are traversed without smooth, gradual transitions. Moreover, the gaps between clusters are left as permanent features, never filled in, somewhat like the quarter-tones that one never hears in traditional Western art music. Affect is presented as falling into broad categories that, by giving affect a kind

The Enlightenment critics had a rather simple conception of unity, amounting to lit-tle more than redundancy. They opposed the frequent shifts of highly contrasting moods found in the Classical style. When it was recognized that artistically satisfying works could be composed in the Classical style by such respected composers as Haydn, Mozart, and Beethoven, the doctrine of Unity of Affect was discredited; but did that doctrine really have no merit at all, or is it possible to understand the doctrine in terms of a more sophisticated concept of unity, somewhat analogous to our concept of tonal unity? See Georgia Cowart, *The Origins of Modern Musical Criticism: French and Italian Music, 1600-1750* (Ann Arbor, 1981); Bellamy Hosler, *Changing Aesthetic Views of Instrumental Music in 18th-Century Germany* (Ann Arbor, 1981); Leonard Ratner, *Classic Music: Expression, Form, and Style* (New York, 1980).

of *metric*,[12] perhaps add to the comprehensibility of the music. The mere fact of categorization gives the music a logic of sorts, but it leaves one question unanswered. What, if anything, ties the categories together?

UNITY OF PATTERN

The answer to that question requires that we look for another kind of unity, pattern repetition. We will look at the time-sequence of the factor scores of the phrases in the same factor space we have just been discussing. As it happens, the time line of the affects tends to move in clockwise cycles through the semantic space of this composition. To show that clearly will require us to break up the time line into segments (fig. 2).

The first of these segments (segment *a*, fig. 2a) corresponds to the beginning of the Allegretto, up to the repeat sign (phrases 1-4). This segment approximates a closed circle, beginning in the lower left-hand quadrant of the semantic space and circulating clockwise.

The next segment (segment *b*, fig. 2b), corresponding to the beginning of the second half of the Allegretto up to the second double bar (phrases 5-10), begins in the same quadrant as the first segment (though lower on Factor II), and, like the first segment, makes its first move away from the beginning upward and to the right. Unlike the first segment, the second segment returns to its opening material; but from that point onward, it continues in a clockwise circulation like the first segment. In the course of that clockwise circulation, it is of interest that the second segment makes a deep incursion (phrase 8) into territory that is far more typical of the Trio. The last phrase of the second segment is a repetition of the preceding phrase; it only appears as a separate point on the graph because Brendel, in the recording that was analyzed, played the repetition somewhat more softly. Even though the second segment begins with the same rhythms as the first, it would not be apparent using

[12]An element of musical construction will be said to fall into a *metric* if its range of possible values is limited to a specific set of more or less regularly arranged, fixed values. Time and pitch are metricized in traditional tonal music; but loudness, rhythmic activity, harmonic color, and timbre are not, at least on the surface. (Loudness markings do not, appearances to the contrary, designate well-defined levels of volume.) Metricized elements of construction tend to be associated with intellect; non-metricized elements, with affect. Schubert, in this composition, creates a structural metric for elements that are not otherwise metricized: he puts affect into an intellectual framework, so to speak. A statistical model was necessary to bring that out.

traditional analytical techniques that the two segments have so much in common; for the second segment not only uses substantially different thematic material, on the whole, but also modulates much more freely, ultimately to the flat submediant major (written by Schubert for convenience in sharps instead of flats).

The third segment (segment *c,* fig. 2c) is a retransition to the tonic key (phrases 11-13). Like the first segment, this segment begins in the lower left-hand quadrant, makes its first move from that point upward and to the right, and continues in a clockwise direction. Again, using traditional analytic techniques it would not be so clear that we are observing an abstract variation on the opening of the Allegretto.

The last segment of the Allegretto (segment *d,* fig. 2d) is a partial recapitulation of the opening followed by a coda (phrases 14-18). The third phrase of this segment is an affectively equivalent variation on the corresponding phrase of the opening; or at least it averages out to be in terms of our composite factor scores, though it differs in particulars. The last two phrases of the Allegretto, forming its coda, are affectively a departure from the previous cyclic process, ending the Allegretto by breaking the links that held it together. Even though the coda ends with an ordinary cadence in the tonic, this is the tonic minor rather than the major in which the piece began; and the coda is in other respects a turbulent and centrifugal ending, with remote modulations to the Neapolitan key and dramatic contrasts of loudness.

The Trio (segment *e,* fig. 2e, phrases 19-22; and segment *f,* fig. 2f, phrases 23-27) is very different from the Allegretto in character. Nevertheless, the semantic time line for the Trio as a whole, taking segments *e* and *f* together, still exhibits the clockwise circulation we found earlier (after allowing for repeats). Its closest approach to the character of the Allegretto is found in the soft, chromatic, second phrase of its second half (segment *f,* phrase 24). This phrase, after its leading-tone pickup, descends from high F in a manner that recollects the last phrase of the retransition of the Allegretto (segment *c,* phrase 13); although it is more similar affectively to the preceding phrase (phrase 12) as well as to the second phrase of segment *b* (phrase 6).

The last phrase of the Trio (segment *f,* phrase 27) is a repetition an octave higher of the phrase before it. The register shift actually makes this phrase a bit *brighter* than the preceding phrase, but this slight difference in *brightness* seems to have been lost in the process of mathematically rounding off the ratings (other subtle effects may have been lost in the same way).

JOHN CHESNUT

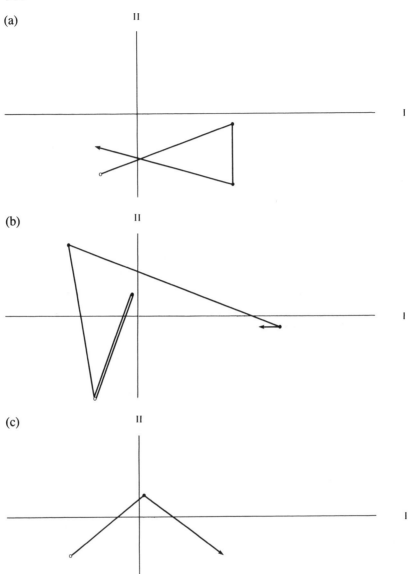

Figure 2. The semantic time-line of Schubert's *Moment musical* op. 94 no. 6. Factor scores for each phrase, grouped into six segments. Scores for each segment plotted against Factor I *(calm-distraught)* in the horizontal dimension and Factor II *(depressed-elated)* in the vertical. The beginning of each segment is indicated with an open circle, the end with an arrowhead.

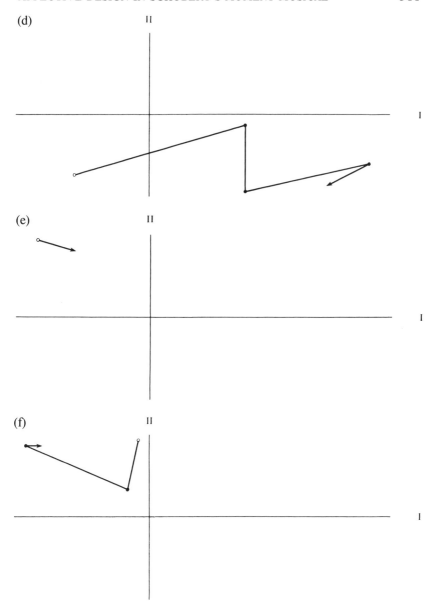

Start with the Allegretto: play segment *a* (phrases 1-4) and repeat; then play segments *b-d* (phrases 5-18) and repeat them. Proceed to the Trio: play segment *e* (phrases 19-20); play segment *e* again one octave higher (phrases 21-22); then play segment *f* (phrases 23-27) and repeat (the last phrase of segment *f* is a repetition of the preceding phrase an octave higher and is not given a separate point in the graph). Finally, repeat the entire Allegretto, segments *a-d*.

In general, the observations made here about patterns of change in character should be taken as approximate; but the patterns are quite hearable and aesthetically satisfying.

UNITY OF CONNECTION

Now we will look for yet another type of unity, continuity. Figure 3 is a graph of the degree of change in character from one phrase to the next, together with a summary of the formal analysis.[13] Since change in character involves a comparison between two successive phrases, the total number of phrases, counting all repeats, is one more than the number of ratings. Furthermore, phrase numbers do not take repeats into consideration, so one must exercise some care in linking phrase numbers to item numbers of ratings.

The Trio seems to be generally more continuous in character than the Allegretto. It is unusual for successive phrases in the Allegretto to have the same or even similar characters; but this is common in the Trio. Also, even the most discontinuous contrasts of the Trio are rather conservative for the Allegretto. To be sure, both the Allegretto and the Trio become more discontinuous at their middle repeat signs. Unlike the Trio, however, the Allegretto maintains that high level of discontinuity throughout its second part. It is noteworthy that the discontinuity in character between the phrases at the end of the Allegretto reinforces the distinctive turbulence of the phrases themselves.

The greatest discontinuity is found between the end of the Allegretto (fig. 2d) and the beginning of the Trio (fig. 2e). This discontinuity is large enough to constitute what Leonard Meyer calls a "structural gap." A structural gap is a discontinuity so significant that coherence demands that it eventually be filled in. The filling of this gap, if it is long delayed, becomes a fundamental structural event defining the larger coherence of a work. In this case, the gap is filled by the return of the Allegretto (fig. 2a); for the beginning of the Allegretto, unlike the ending, is comparatively close to the Trio in character.

The structural gap, in other words, is partly responsible for our sensation that we have "returned home" at the reprise of the Allegretto. The "return home" in this case is more than just the restatement of

---

[13]All of these were estimated from a direct hearing of the record, except item 22 (the change from phrase 18 back to phrase 1), which was calculated by a formula derived from the statistical analysis, because Brendel did not repeat the second part of the Allegretto as indicated in the score.

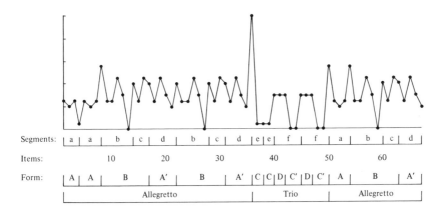

Figure 3. Change of character between phrases of Schubert's *Moment musical* op. 94 no. 6. Subjective ratings, ranged from 0 to 5. Each rating counts as one item; so the total number of items is one less than the total number of phrases, counting all repeats. Item count marked by tens. Item 22 (the change from phrase 18 to phrase 1 on the repeat of the second part of the Allegretto) calculated from a regression equation. Segments designated *a-f*. The formal analysis is also indicated.

Allegretto da capo

a musical idea. This event is aesthetically required by special circumstances that preceded it.

The affective leap from the world of the coda to the world of the Trio is an excursion into a foreign land. It is the fundamental challenge to our perception of coherence in the work, a vision of the imaginative thinker deliberately seeking the challenge of incommensurability. The "return home," on the other hand, the re-establishment of coherence, is the fundamental confirmation, traditionally given by our culture, that reason ultimately prevails.

EPILOGUE

In a paper of limited scope, such as this, not everything can be discussed as fully as it should be. For example, I have not explicitly reviewed the specific derivations of my interpretive work from the psychological literature on affect. I hope I will have an opportunity to explain this elsewhere.

Furthermore, the theory offered here is experimental; and it raises some difficult problems that are still unsolved. What is a useful definition of complexity, for example? Can the concept of brightness be pinned down more exactly? Can the theory presented here be applied to studies of musical style? Does it work better for some styles than others? Are there any archetypal forms or procedures waiting to be discovered?

The fact that some questions are left unresolved is not all bad, however. Theories are intended to do more than just explain what we already know. Theories are also supposed to raise questions that stimulate thought. I hope that the theory of affect presented here will suggest possibilities of musical construction to composers, that it will extend the boundaries of musical scholarship, and that it will encourage deeper inquiries into the fundamental assumptions we make about music.[14]

---

[14]I wish to thank my wife, Jerri, not only for her devoted editing, but also for her unfailing encouragement and support.

Eugene Narmour

On the Relationship of Analytical Theory to Performance and Interpretation

INTRODUCTION

For most performing musicians, analytical theory is largely a study of the grammar of music. As a utilitarian subject, analysis—whether of melody, harmony, rhythm, counterpoint, or musical form—presumably makes it possible for performers to learn the various languages of musical styles, thereby increasing the liklihood of their producing an informed and aesthetically satisfying interpretation. Theoretical skills like clef reading, score reading, solfège, and ear training on the other hand obviously enable performers to translate musical symbols into musical sounds efficiently and accurately. To musicians there is thus no question of the pragmatic usefulness of what is called theory in the curricula of the music school.

Music theory, however, has a nobler goal than just teaching musicians how to acquire a knowledge of musical style or instructing them in the ways of reading music better. For the ultimate aim of any theory is not utilitarian or didactic but explanatory: good theories of music illuminate the various syntactic meanings inherent in a given musical relationship. They do not just classify musical materials for the practitioner's ease of consumption. Indeed, the study of music theory should enable performers to determine not only how individual musical artworks are structured and how they fit into some stylistic scheme of history but should also endow performers with the means to discover how different interpretations alter the listener's perception and understanding of living works of art.

Eugene Narmour is Professor of Music at the University of Pennsylvania. He is the author of Beyond Schenkerism: The Need for Alternatives in Music Analysis, The Analysis and Perception of Basic Melodic Structures, *and* The Analysis and Perception of Melodic Complexity.

It is this topic I wish to explore in this paper. I will discuss both why from an analytical point of view a given performance may be heard as being either good or bad, and why performing a given passage one way or another makes a significant difference to the listener's experience. To accomplish this, I will frequently refer to commercial recordings, which to scholars are, after all, not just convenient products for home entertainment but also primary source documents for the study of performance in our century.

Traditionally performers have envisioned their obligations almost wholly in terms of their responsibilities to the composer—doubtless a holdover of nineteenth-century Romantic beliefs about composers being both priests and prophets, the saints of culture leading their supplicants (performers and listeners alike) to ever-new realms of self-awareness. But this is myopic. For as cognitive psychology has taught us, the temporal materialization of a musical artwork emanates not from the composer alone or from the performer alone but from a triarchical interrelationship among composer, performer, *and* listener. The composer produces a score, a kind of syntactical roadmap based on a highly efficient but therefore limited symbol system whose interpretation even in the relatively highly specified notation of Western culture is indisputably still partly dependent on oral tradition. The performer attempts to bring that score to life, in the process modifying it to fit with his or her own aesthetic beliefs, stylistic experiences, and tradition of learning. And listeners complete the interpretation by *actively* bringing to bear their own peculiar cognitive expectations based on their own idiosyncratic learning of the style. It is the fusion of these three active mind-forces—composer, performer, listener—that literally creates the musical artwork out of the thin air through which sound waves travel. Consequently, for performers to discharge faithfully their aesthetic responsibilities, they must give considerable attention not only to their understanding of the composer's demands and desires but also to the sensibilities of the audience for whom they make music.

The easiest way to cast oneself as performer in the role of the listener is to think of music at any given temporal point in terms of the syntactic consequences. Faced with a musical decision, the performer as listener says to himself: what are the implications of this passage *for the listener* if I perform the music like this? What perceptually follows from my presenting these notes in this particular way as opposed to another special way?

FORM

It is in this connection that analysis enters into the interpretive process. Take the matter of form. It is obvious that if formal relations are not properly analyzed by the performer, as well as carefully delineated in the performance itself, then many negative consequences follow. In Brahms's *Intermezzo* op. 118 no. 1 (ex. 1a), for instance, it is important to recognize that the overtly manifested melodic motive of C-B-flat-A in measure 1 is at the same time also a subset of another equally important motive, namely, the C-B-flat-A-E that goes into the left hand of measure 2 (see the analysis under the music in ex. 1a). The same thing can be said about the A-G-F and the A-G-F-C of measures 3-4. This is so because the "resolution" of the seventh (B-flat, m. 1; G, m. 3) in each appoggiatura occurs on a weak sixth (A, m. 1; F, m. 3) whose unclosed quarter-note setting takes the melody directly into the downbeats of the succeeding bars.

That is, even though in measure 1 Brahms's phrasing (assuming it is his and not just some editor's) spans only the C-B-flat-A melodic line, visually setting it apart from the leap down to the E in the left hand in measure 2, the C-B-flat-A-E connection encompassing measures 1-2 is nonetheless also clearly indicated both by the accented E in the left hand and by the cumulative dotted half note on the octave (note, for example, how the A of the arpeggio is tied across the bar to facilitate the sounding of the accented octave). Likewise for the octave C of the A-G-F-C pattern. Further, if we look ahead analytically, the precedence of the C-B-flat-A-E and A-G-F-C motives is unequivocally confirmed by the D-C-B-E augmentation at the end of the piece (ex. 1b). Thus, making clear the C-B-flat-A-E motivic gesture of the very opening—the C-B-flat-A integrated into the C-B-flat-A-E—is important to the perception of the piece's structure.

Yet pianists, in their technical anxiety to make the transfer of the arpeggio from left to right hand between measures 1 and 2 sound unbroken, frequently miss the C-B-flat-A-E relationship, treating the left-hand octaves of measure 2 as merely the fifth of the first-inversion A-minor chord, like a written-out part for the damper pedal, as it were. In Julius Katchen's performance, for instance, one does not hear a clear presentation of the C-B-flat-A-E motive in measures 1-2 (though the same figure in measures 3-4 perhaps fares slightly better).[1] Inexplicably, in the repetition of the phrase Katchen's performance of the C-B-flat-A-E motive is somewhat more audible, whereas this time around the mimicking A-G-F-C fares slightly worse. In short, Katchen's performance lacks analytical insight and therefore perceptual consistency.

[1]Katchen's performance of the Brahms may be found on the London album CSP5 (the individual record number is CS6396).

Example 1a. Brahms, *Intermezzo* op. 118 no. 1, mm. 1-7

Example 1b. Brahms, *Intermezzo* op. 118 no. 1, mm. 37-40.

How important is a clear performance of the opening C-B-flat-A-E? Well, a reading that fails to make clear the connection of the descending linear pattern down to the leap has strange syntactic consequences for the listener. For if the C-B-flat-A-E motivic relation of measure 1-2 is obscured, then to the listener what follows after the double bar (ex. 1c) seems to be only an elongated transformation of the opening three-note line rather than what it really is: namely, both a varied inversion of the four-note motive in the outside voice and simultaneously a variation of the original four-note motive in the inside voice (ex. 1d). Moreover, in an inconsistent performance like Katchen's the augmentation of the step-step-skip motive at the very end (ex. 1b) would seem to the listener to function as a kind of varied inversion of the motive in the middle part after the double bar rather than what *it* really is, namely, a cadential augmentation of the initial formal gesture of the first two bars of the piece.

Example 1c. Brahms *Intermezzo* op. 118 no. 1, mm. 8-12.

Example 1d. Brahms *Intermezzo* op. 118 no. 1, soprano ("varied original"), **mm. 11-12.**

Thus, an uncareful performance of the melody of the opening bars of Brahms's intermezzo ramifies negatively throughout. It is like making a mistake in a mathematical equation; the syntactic errors multiply.[2] Clearly, a careful analysis by the performer of motivic-formal relationships is important if the intended sense of the composer's score is to be conveyed to the listener.

FUNCTION

Let us not make the mistake, however, of conceptualizing form in music as a static element, as a symbolic configuration for the eye, represented on the score page like a geometric drawing in a math book. For we cannot understand the true importance of interpreting form properly unless we also take into account its structural function in time. Nowhere is this more true than in the matter of repetition.

---

[2]A correct interpretation, where one hears measures 1-2 and 3-4 as two very similar melodic motives of step-step-leap, is found in Glenn Gould's performance on Columbia MS6237. But then Gould ruins the form in other ways: by ignoring the repetition of the phrase he throws the form all out of proportion.

Consider, for example, the matter of repetition in sonata-allegro and rondo form in Classical style. As everyone knows, a major structural event in both sonata and rondo form is the recapitulation or the return of the theme in the tonic. As the development section in the sonata or the digression in the rondo winds down, the commencement of the retransition, most often over a dominant pedal, signals to the audience that a recapitulation or a return in the tonic key is imminent. In some sonata-allegro forms, like the first movement of Haydn's "London" Symphony (no. 104), the climactic retransition on the dominant is given its own definite ending—a silencing halt in the music—so that the listener knows almost absolutely that the next event to occur will be the return of the main material.

But in other sonata or rondo forms, though the beginning of the retransition working back to the tonic is clear, the ending of the retransition is written so that it dovetails completely with the return of the principal theme on the tonic. In these cases the listener knows through the onset of the retransition that the arrival of the recapitulation is imminent but at the same time is kept in the dark as to exactly where the overlaying return will occur—until it actually has happened.

Repetition plays an important function in such cases. Though *harmonically* in these cases the typical retransition prolongs the dominant, putting part of the listener's cognitive apparatus "on hold"—in a mode of waiting to see when the recapitulating tonic will arrive—*motivically* such dovetailing retransitions involving repetition lead the listener to project replicating continuation, thus heightening the sense of expectation.[3] The two functions together—the prolongation of the dominant and the propelling motivic repetition—combine to produce tension and suspense in that although, at the beginning of the retransition, the final "score" of the "game" is given away by the dominant pedal, the continuing motivic repetition prevents our knowing exactly when the return will come about. It is like being aware that a firecracker has been lit in your presence without knowing the length of the fuse. And it is precisely in such dovetailed retransitions that the performer must ensure that the repetition be allowed to serve its rightful aesthetic-perceptual function.

To be more specific, since in a dovetailed retransition the repetition leads the listener on, keeping him or her from knowing exactly when the recapitulation will occur, it follows that the performer must do nothing to let the cat out of the bag. That is, the performer must not telegraph musical clues to the listener allowing him or her to predict the exact arrival of the end of the retransition and the beginning of the recapitulation. In a passage like the retransition of the last movement of Haydn's "Surprise" Symphony (no. 94), for instance (ex. 2), the

[3]No one has written more perceptively about the role of repetition in expectation than Leonard B. Meyer.

orchestra must maintain a ''poker face'' so that the dovetailing between the end of the retransition and beginning of the recapitulation is seamless. An unannounced occurrence of the return, of course, results in a delightful denouement of the built-up tension, the sort of thing a conductor like Sir Thomas Beecham understood so well.[4]

Example 2. Haydn, Symphony No. 94, I, mm. 177-182.

DYNAMICS

If an analysis of the relationship between repetition and the prolongation of the dominant in dovetailing retransitions of these kinds of sonata-allegro and rondo forms seems obvious with respect to performance, it is surprising how often conductors fail to recognize it. For conductors frequently attach a little, or even a big, crescendo toward the end of the motivic repetition, letting the listener know that the tension is about to end and thereby giving the game away.

Consider, for instance, how the drama of the forte recapitulation in the first movement of Haydn's Symphony no. 83 (ex. 3) can be spoiled by a crescendo at the end of the retransition. In this symphony the G-minor theme of the first movement, with its sforzando, dissonant, non-diatonic appoggiaturas, is full of *Sturm und Drang*—features the development section is not reluctant to exploit. Indeed, the charged, pent-up energy of this theme is never exhausted in the development despite the manifold working-out which takes place. At the end of the development Haydn affords the listener relief by abruptly halting the forte music with seven beats of silence (mm. 116-117), after which, in a quiescent, reflective mood, the retransition begins (m. 118). This is followed by a recapitulated, subito fortissimo explosion of the strident *Sturm und Drang* theme (m. 130).

---

[4]Listen, for instance, to his recording of this symphony on Angel 36242 (with the Royal Philharmonic).

Example 3. Haydn, Symphony No. 83, I, mm. 111-135.

But by asking for a crescendo on the rising A-C-E-flat-F-sharp at the end of the retransition (mm. 128-129), a conductor somewhat saps the recapitulation of its dynamic and thematic shock, thereby depriving listeners of their cognitive pleasure (not to mention violating the directions of Haydn's score). Such is Leslie Jones's performance. If, however, attaching a crescendo to the A-C-E-flat-F-sharp is an obvious mistake, and I believe there is no denying it, it is also a common one: I found the same error in two other readings (Bernstein's and Heiler's).[5] Of course, it is possible to spoil the recapitulation in other ways as well. For instance, although Antal Dorati's recording of this symphony wisely maintains the piano dynamic, the conductor nevertheless allows a tiny ritardando to creep in at the very end of the retransition—which has exactly the same deflating negative effect as if the orchestra had played a crescendo.[6]

The point is, performers must add crescendos (and tempo alterations) very judiciously in order to fulfill their responsibilities to the composer and to the listener. As we see, this can be done only if the performer understands theoretically and analytically how function relates to form.

STRUCTURE AND DURATIONAL PATTERNING

Let us now consider how performance affects structure in the mind of the listener. Lack of space naturally prevents me from exploring in detail any theory of musical structure here, but the following are a few of the salient theoretical assertions necessary to understand how performance influences musical structure:

1. For the listener, structure is a result of closure.

2. Closure occurs in various degrees and thus on all levels of music, from low-level motives to the highest levels of musical form. (In-

[5]Jones's recording may be found on Nonesuch HC-3011-B (The Little Orchestra of London); Bernstein's is on Columbia ML 6009 (New York Philharmonic); and Heiler's on Haydn Society HSLP 1015 (Vienna Collegium Musicum).

[6]Dorati's performance is on London STS 15229 (Philharmonia Hungarica). Such incorrect tempo changes at strategic points like this are fairly rare, however. The main mistake conductors make in retransitions, it seems to me, is the dynamic one. Listen, for example, to Beecham's performance of the first movement of Haydn's Symphony no. 99 (Angel 36254, The Royal Philharmonic) or Scherchen's (Westminister WM-6601, Vienna State Opera Orchestra). In both of these performances the conductors at the last possible moment tip their hand with a tell-tale crescendo, betraying the intent of the score and allowing the listener to predict with complete assurance, much to his or her annoyance, that the recapitulation is the next immediate event. A somewhat better interpretation in this regard can be found in Dorati's performance (London STS 15322, Philharmonia Hungarica).

deed, closure is responsible for the emergence of hierarchical levels.)

3. Each parameter of music—melody, harmony, rhythm, dynamics, tessitura, timbre, tempo, meter, texture, perhaps others—carries with it its own internal means of closure.

4. Since at any given moment many different parameters are simultaneously operative in music, the closure in one may or may not coincide with the closure in another.

Though all this perhaps sounds quite abstract, these four theoretical statements can be put to work in the service of analysis and performance rather easily. We need only to recognize a few principles of closure in order to understand better how performance affects structure. Let us consider just harmony and rhythm for the time being—defining harmony as the syntactic (horizontal) progression of vertical intervallic relationships and rhythm strictly as durational patterning. Now closure—and therefore some degree of structure—occurs in harmony when, quite simply, dissonance moves to consonance. For instance, a dominant seventh chord, which vertically contains both a tritone and a minor seventh, creates closure at the point of the resolution of those intervals when they move to, say, the octaves, fifths, and thirds of a tonic chord. The reverse of this progression, I to V⁷, of course, creates nonclosure or the prevention of harmonic structure on the dissonant dominant.

As to durational patterning, closure—and therefore some degree of structure—occurs when a relatively short duration moves to one that is relatively longer, as, for instance, when a quarter note goes to a dotted half note. The reverse of this (half to quarter) creates nonclosure or prevention—or at least the weakening—of structure. Terminologically, all durational patterns that move from short note to long note may be called cumulative; patterns that move from long to short, counter-cumulative. Example 4 shows a sampling of these patterns.

Example 4.

cumulative rhythms   counter-cumulative rhythms
(closed)   (open)

Putting both parametric principles together, we can understand that a high degree of closure and thus strong structural stability occur when a V⁷-I progression is set congruently in a cumulative rhythm. And vice versa: closure and thus structure are prevented when a I-V^7 progression is set congruently in a counter-cumulative rhythm.

As it turns out, the most interesting cases (and probably the most common instances) in music are the noncongruent ones where, say, a V^7-I closed progression is set in a nonclosed, counter-cumulative rhythm, or where, say, an unclosed I-V^7 progression is set in a closed cumulative rhythm. One quickly grasps in such parametric noncongruence why music theory is such a difficult field since the degree of structure or nonstructure in such cases is exceedingly difficult to measure. For example, is a cumulative rhythm of a quarter note to a dotted half note in a I-V^7 progression strong enough to cause the V^7 to function structurally? Or does the strength of the dissonance in the V^7 chord so weaken the cumulative rhythm that, despite the noncongruent durational configuration, the pattern sounds open on the low level?

Since whole schools of music theory have attempted—and are attempting—to discover what is or is not structural, I cannot broach these issues here. Suffice it to say for our purposes that the manipulation of rhythm, of durational patterning, is one of the chief means performers have at their disposal to alter the meaning of parametric interrelationships. For by making certain notes slightly longer or shorter, thereby increasing or decreasing their cumulative or counter-cumulative effect, an entire universe of musical aesthetic is possible. For example, performers often stretch out the last chord in so-called feminine cadences, where, though the dissonant chord is resolved on an ostensibly counter-cumulative weak beat, the perceived rhythmic relationship is considerably less counter-cumulative than the written notation has it.

A more subtle noncongruence is the effect of rhythm on harmony in a case like the ritornello of the finale of Mozart's Piano Concerto No. 21 K. 467 (ex. 5). Here, it is unthinkable that a conductor would not insist that the eighth notes be played off the string since the saucy effect of this passage depends on the noncongruence between rhythm and harmony on the downbeats of measures 2 and 4. That is, despite the notational appearance in the beginning of this example that rhythmically nothing but eighth notes are present, off-the-string playing actually creates within the overall additive durational progression a slight rhythmic cumulation at the point of the slur in measure 2—a rhythmic closural motion conflicting with the nonclosural instability of the six-four harmony. The same, though more so, is true of the cumulative dissonance in measure 4. In short, a correct performance of Mozart's durational patterning attempts rhythmically to make structural tones out of appoggiaturas that are inherently nonstructural.

Example 5. Mozart, Piano Concerto, K. 467, III, mm. 1-4.

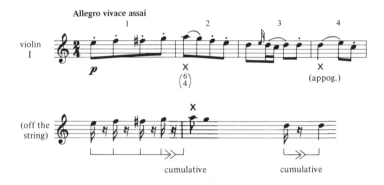

STRUCTURE AND MELODY

We see then that an analysis of the interrelationship between harmony and rhythm is crucial toward understanding not only the effect of a passage, but also why it must be played a certain way. Let us now add to these parameters a brief consideration of the parameter of melody.[7] I have avoided melody thus far because it is the least theoretically understood element of music. Moreover, its inherent factors of closure are more various than those of either harmony or rhythm, and thus more complex to sort out. The implicative, *nonclosural* aspect of melody, however, is a more manageable subject. With respect to performance and interpretation, let us therefore concentrate on that in relation to harmony and rhythm. Now by melody, or the parameter of melody if you will, I mean something very specific and narrow, namely, just the sequential "horizontal" relationships of pitch, shorn of their durational context and of their harmonic setting.

Since quite a bit is known about melodic nonclosure or implication—largely due to Leonard B. Meyer's work—the first hypothesis we need in order to analyze the performance of melody is this: with the possible exception of the leap of an octave, the larger a melodic interval is, the more implicative it is; and the smaller a melodic interval is, the less implicative it is. Thus, a single interval of a major sixth is more "open" than a minor second. This principle, naturally, is true if and only if all other parametric things are equal. Harmonic and rhythmic context, of course, will play an important part in determining exactly what is implied from any given melodic interval.

[7]The ideas of reversal and process mentioned here are explored in my book, *The Analysis and Perception of Basic Melodic Structures: The Implication-Realization Model*, Vol. I (forthcoming).

A second hypothesis is that small intervals tend to imply a continuation in the same direction in which they begin—after the Gestalt law of continuation—whereas large intervals tend to imply a reversal of direction. In other words, a string of ascending seconds, like a scale, suggests to a listener that the line will continue upward at the same relative intervallic rate, whereas a large ascending leap like a major sixth suggests that the melody will change direction.

Now with a little imagination, this melodic theory will take us a considerable distance. For as before, harmony and rhythm, separately or together, can act to reinforce melodic implication and thus the nonclosure of a melodic line. Or else they can act to create, or attempt to create, a structural tone out of a pitch that is melodically implicative. Either way, noncongruence offers an infinite wealth of different aesthetic experiences.

Consider a few synthetic examples. In example 6a the upward leap of a major sixth will imply a reversal only weakly since cumulative rhythm and harmonic resolution conspire, as it were, to close the leap on the high E. In example 6b the tendency of the high E to turn around is slightly stronger since in this case the rhythmic counter-cumulation supports the implication of the reversal despite the harmonic closure of the V^7-I. In example 6c all of the parameters are congruently open and ongoing: the melodic leap of G down to B is a reversal implication, the harmony moves toward dissonance, and the rhythm is counter-cumulative. In example 6d the context is similar except that here the rhythmic cumulation from quarter note to half note adds a modicum of noncongruent closure to the V^7 chord and to the downward leap. We have, then, four very narrowly constructed examples with the potential for four measurably different analytical explanations and four distinctively different experiences of structural-aesthetic effect.

Example 6.

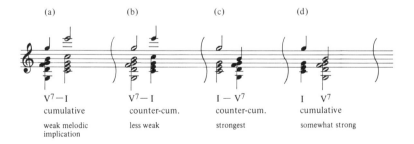

(a)	(b)	(c)	(d)
V^7-I	V^7-I	$I-V^7$	$I \quad V^7$
cumulative	counter-cum.	counter-cum.	cumulative
weak melodic implication	less weak	strongest	somewhat strong

PARAMETRIC NONCONGRUENCE AND PERFORMANCE

Armed with this small but potent conceptual theory, let us now see again how performance affects parametric interaction in two examples from the musical literature. Consider, for instance, that during the past thirty years we have witnessed a revolution in the performance of Baroque music. All kinds of new and important things have been discovered about ornamentation, instrumentation, tuning, and tempo—and also about the stylistically correct rendition of rhythm. Concerning the latter, for example, it now seems certain, as all musicians know, that the *Grave* of the overture to Handel's *Messiah* should be played in the double-dotted fashion of a French overture (ex. 7b), the actual notation to the contrary notwithstanding (ex. 7a).

Example 7. Handel, Overture to *Messiah*, mm. 1-2.

Musicological considerations aside, however, we might irreverently ask the question: does it make any aesthetic or structural difference to the listener whether the rhythm is played in the "correct" double-dotted fashion? The answer in terms of the theory I have outlined is decidedly yes. For even though in example 7b the melodic intervals and the harmony remain the same in terms of the overall pitch content, double-dotting the rhythms considerably alters the strength of melodic implication. The opening interval (a minor sixth), for instance, becomes much more implicative of reversal of direction in a counter-cumulative performance with a 7:1 rhythmic ratio (ex. 7b) rather than in one with a 3:1 ratio (ex. 7a). Likewise, the long notes themselves take on an aura of greater structuralness since in double-dotted rhythm they become part of a much greater cumulation—to be exact, 1:7 rather than 1:3. This has the not inconsiderable effect of making the realization of the melodic reversal on the B extremely stable. And it makes the dissonance on the third beat of measure 2 (an F-sharp lies in the bass) sound much more dramatic, more strident. To put it differently, the last G of measure 2 (over a tonic E) functions as much *less* of a resolution of the F-sharp-

G ninth when played in double-dotted rhythms than when played in single-dotted ones.

The reader may test this out by comparing, say, Sir Malcolm Sargent's old-fashioned recording with, say, Sir Colin Davis's newer one.[8] One notices, for example, how much less implicative, less ongoing the opening sixth is in the former recording (single-dotted, with a very slow tempo) as opposed to the latter (double-dotted). And one also observes how much less the dissonance in measure 3 (over the pedal point) sticks out in Sargent's version (single-dotted) than in Davis's (double-dotted). Finally, one hears how much more stable and therefore structural the long notes sound in Davis's version as opposed to Sargent's.

Clearly, the change from the counter-cumulative/cumulative relationship of 3:1:3 to the historically justified relationship of 7:1:7 makes a significant structural difference to the listener. Performing the overture with the "correct" double-dotted rhythms endows the music with an implicative and structural vitality unmatched in the unmusicological, spurious version.

To sum up: we saw in the Brahms intermezzo how important the analytical identification of motivic form was in enabling the listener to make the correct interconnections between melodic events; we saw in several Haydn retransitions how incorrect dynamics (and tempo change) were used deleteriously to detract from the dramatic or surprising function of the recapitulation in both sonata-allegro and rondo forms; and we see here in the Handel overture how a performance change of the written rhythmic relationships affects the realization of melodic and harmonic implication. In short, the interpretation of form, function, dynamics, tempo, and rhythm significantly alter the listener's perceptions and expectations and thus his or her aesthetic experiences.

THE SCIENCE OF UNIQUE SUBTLETY

The differentiating musical effects of one interpretation as opposed to another can be extremely subtle. Let us thus conclude by examining several subtly different performances of the same passage, specifically a short phrase from the second act of Strauss's *Der Rosenkavalier*. The passage I wish to concentrate on—Sophie's response on meeting Octavian for the first time—is among the most exquisite in the whole kingdom of musical artworks. I want to focus on the melodic setting of the words "wie himmlische, nicht irdische" (how heavenly, not earthly), which Sophie sings as she accepts the silver rose from Octavian and simultaneously falls truly in love for the first time in her life. The musical

[8]Sargent's recording exists on Angel 3598-C; that by Davis (who performs the Mozart orchestration) is on Philips SC71AX300.

setting of these words creates a moment of incandescent beauty wherein the listener is transported out of a mundane world of physical sensation to a transcendental plane of pure emotion. The passage in question may be seen in example 8.

Example 8. Strauss, *Der Rosenkavalier,* Act II, Sc. 1.

Strauss's setting of these words achieves its other-worldly aesthetic effect because practically every melodic event is in some way unexpected and in some way unclosed. The opening C-sharp to A-sharp is a reversal implication; that is, what is implied, what listeners expect, is that the leap will turn immediately around and descend in some fashion, within the intervallic area outlined by the leap (see the analysis underneath the music in ex. 8). Of course, the leap itself is certainly a surprise, given the written crescendo enveloping the initial C-sharp, but the high tessitura of the A-sharp makes the reversal implication all the more strong since from C-sharp to A-sharp the soprano skips nearly to the top of her range, with whose sheer physical energy the listener will viscerally empathize with. What is more, by indicating a crescendo from piano to subito pianissimo, Strauss commands the large interval to be sung *opposite* the natural mode. That is, there is natural tendency for an ascending motion to be performed with a slight crescendo and for a descending motion to be sung with a slight decrescendo. Thus, the large leap, directly ascending to the high tessitura as well as set in its "unnatural" dynamic configuration of piano to subito pianissimo, is, in a very concrete sense, not of this world but, as the libretto says, "heavenly."

But there is more. For the rhythm of the leap to the high A-sharp is cumulative, from quarter to dotted quarter, and the tempo instruction "un poco allargando" increases this closural effect so that, as the prolongation of the high note comes to be perceived in the mind's ear, the listener begins to wonder if and when the high A-sharp will reverse direction. That is, given the already tense state of this high note—owing to tessitura, pianissimo dynamic, and size of melodic leap—the increased cumulative duration stipulated by Strauss's tempo modification heightens for the listener an unworldly quality of uncertainty. In short, the listener's cognitive apparatus is sensitized as to what will happen to the high A-sharp.[9]

Yet there is still more. For in a master stroke of compositional inspiration Strauss elevates Sophie's state of bliss by surprisingly taking the melody *upward*, not downward as the leap of the major sixth implied. Moreover, the state of tension present is increased in that this high B is metrically unexpected as well, making its appearance as a syncopation and thereby momentarily suspending the beat. Finally, the unexpected high B is in fact a dissonant tone, clashing with the fifth of the F-sharp major chord (the C-sharp) in the orchestra.

Now to the performer the question arises: in a phrase as carefully composed as this one, are there other things a performer could or should do that would add to the aesthetic structure of the music? Aside from trying to adhere to Strauss's instructions as faithfully as possible, can the performer contribute anything more toward a convincing *recreation* of the music? It seems to me, given the theory advocated in this paper, that there are several compelling interpretive decisions to be made.

First, if the subito pianissimo on the high A-sharp is effective for the reasons discussed, namely, that (1) it is a totally unexpected tone, that (2) it initiates a strong reversal implication, that (3) its setting in a cumulative (closural) rhythm raises questions as to its continuation, and (4) that its dynamic setting goes against the natural mode, then it also follows that a *further* reduction in dynamic on the unexpected step up to the dissonant, syncopated, high B will also be extremely affective in an aesthetic sense (see ex. 9). Second, we could argue that the duration of the syncopated B should be slightly stretched out so that its rhythmic relation with the A-sharp will become somewhat less

[9]Sometimes conductors do utterly inexplicable things that make no sense at all. In Andre Previn's recording of the *Rosenkavalier Suite* (RCA AGL1-2940), for example, the conductor allows a break between the two notes of the skip, which, of course, has the effect of *weakening* the reversal implication when, obviously, exactly the opposite is called for.

counter-cumulative, therefore suspending the 4/4 meter all the more and enhancing the displacement of the beat (again see ex. 9). Third, we could make an argument for singing the descending A-sharp-G-sharp-F-sharp triplet on beat 3 more or less rhythmically "straight" since by this time the listener needs, for the sake of relieving the tension, to have some expectations fulfilled through an unadorned filling in of the opening C-sharp-A-sharp leap (via A-sharp-G-sharp to the F-sharp). It can also be argued that these triplets should be sung rhythmically unembellished because the unexpected leap of the major third which follows immediately on beat 4 (F-sharp to A-sharp) interrupts the continuation of the descent and restores the initial tension by renewing the high tessitura. Thus, and fourth, a slight lengthening of, and a decrescendo on, the high A-sharp in the triplet would appear to be an analytically justifiable recreative interpretation (again see ex. 9).

Example 9.

CRITICISM AND EVALUATION OF PERFORMANCE

After reading this relatively extended discussion of what amounts to only a few seconds of music—only eleven notes, after all—let us now critically compare five performances of this passage—those of Karl Böhm (soprano: Rita Streich), Sir George Solti (soprano: Helen Donath), Clemens Krauss (soprano: Adele Kern), Erich Kleiber (soprano: Hilde Gueden), and Herbert von Karajan (soprano: Teresa Stich-Randall).[10] It is fascinating to hear how different conductors and different sopranos interpret Strauss's music. All of these performances by major artists are, needless to say, highly competent, and all are stirringly musical. Of course, in an art like music there can never be any such thing as *the* definitive performance. The point, however, is that, given the analytical theory applied in example 9, we can say more or less objec-

---

[10]Böhm: Deutsche Grammaphon Gesellschaft 138040/3 (Sachsische Staatskapelle Dresden); Solti: London 1435 (Vienna Philharmonic); Krauss: Vox PL 7774 (Munich State Opera); Kleiber: London 22 (Vienna Philharmonic); von Karajan: Angel 3563D/L (Philharmonia Orchestra).

tively that, of these five highly competent interpretations, certain performances are subtly though demonstrably better than others. (Additionally, we may learn in undertaking such a critical comparison something about what kinds of principles are constant to the art of performance vis-à-vis the notation of the score.)

The chart of figure 1 compares the constancy or change of dynamics, the addition of accent or tenuto, and the relative durational relationships of the first three notes, as well as certain other properties found in the five performances of the passage in question. Along with the pitch names of the soprano part at the top of the chart are Strauss's dynamic indications and tempo markings together with the actual durational ratio of the first three notes.

Figure 1.

STRAUSS									
Notes:	C-sharp	A-sharp	B	A-sharp	G-sharp	F-sharp	A-sharp	G-sharp	A-sharp
Tempo			un poco allargando, *Etwas breit*						
Dynamics	p	pp							
Note length (ratios)	2:	3:	1.66						
Increment/ decrement		+50%	-44%						
BÖHM Dynamics	p, non cresc.	p	p< >	mp	mp	mp	>	mp	
Note length (hundredths of seconds)	1.536	2.196	1.895			poco ten.			
Note length (sec. approx.)	1 1/2	2 1/5	1 9/10						
Increment/ decrement		+43%	-13.7%						
SOLTI Dynamics	p, non cresc.	p	p	p	p	p	p	p	>
Note length (hundredths of seconds)	2.005	2.568	1.745			poco ten.			
Note length (sec. approx.)	2	2 1/2	1 3/4						
Increment/ decrement		+28%	-32%						

KRAUSS Notes:	C-sharp	A-sharp	B	A-sharp	G-sharp	F-sharp	A-sharp	G-sharp	A-sharp
Tempo			un poco allargando, *Etwas breit*						
Dynamics	p, non cresc.	pp	< >	pp	pp	pp	>	pp	>
Note length (hundredths of seconds)	1.770	2.482	3.004				poco ten.		
Note length (sec. approx.)	1 3/4	2 1/2	3						
Increment/ decrement		+40%	+21.7%						
KLEIBER Dynamics	p<	pp< >	ppp< >	pp	pp	<	>	>	
Note length (hundredths of seconds)	1.688	2.388	1.612				pochiss. ten.		
Note length (sec. approx.)	1 7/10	2 2/5	1 6/10						
Increment/ decrement		+41%	-32.49%						
VON KARAJAN Dynamics	p<	pp	ppp< >	pp	pp	pp	ppp	porta- mento	
Note length (hundredths of seconds)	2.261	2.980	2.234				pochiss. ten.		
Note length (sec. approx.)	2 1/4	3	2 1/4						
Increment/ decrement		+32%	-25%						

The dynamics attached to the individual notes of the five performances below the indications of Strauss's represent my own perceptions of the various recordings (after dozens of hearings). To arrive at the lengths of the durations of the first three notes, I used a digital stopwatch (listening via headphones), and timed each note individually five to ten times, depending on the variability of my perceptions: the note lengths expressed in hundredths of seconds are the averages of the several trials for each of the three pitches. For ease of reading, the decimals are also shown in simple fractions of a second along with the durational increment or decrement (expressed in percentages) of the second and third pitch—the A-sharp of the leap and the surprising ascent to the higher B. (Averaging note-length timings was necessary since perceptual deviation can result either from false anticipation of the onset of the note, from false anticipation of the termination of the note, or from the time lag resulting from the stimulus perception to the activation of the nerve in the finger muscle to hit the button on the timer. Doubtless, the measurements are not absolutely perfect, but they are sufficient for our purposes. More accurate measurements of either duration or dynamic require elaborate digital equipment with sophisticated filtering capabilities for identifying fundamentals from among the myriad acoustical signals emanating from what is, after all, an extremely complex orchestral-vocal tapestry.)

A quick comparison of the dynamics among the five examples shows considerable differentiation. Rita Streich's performance in Böhm's recording is perhaps the least imaginative and least faithful to Strauss's score. There is, for example, no piano-crescendo-subito pianissimo on the C-sharp-A-sharp leap, and the singing of the five notes of the triplet (A-sharp-G-sharp-F-sharp-A-sharp-G-sharp) at a dynamic louder (approximately mezzo piano) seems not only superfluous to but also unwarranted concerning an already animated and contrasting rhythm. Helen Donath's version in Solti's recording is similar to Streich's in that the dynamics specified by Strauss concerning the opening leap are more observed in the breach than in the practice.

Adele Kern's rendition in Krauss's performance is an improvement over both Böhm's and Solti's recordings in that, with the exception of the lack of a crescendo to the high A-sharp, Strauss's dynamics are followed. Moreover, the pochissimo crescendo-diminuendo on the high B is an effective expressive device—which, incidentally, as may be seen in the chart, is added by all the sopranos with the exception of Donath in Solti's performance. Our earlier analysis of the passage argues that such a treatment of the high B is analytically justified in that such a dynamic change internally intensifies further the registral surprise of the high B.

Hilda Gueden's version of the dynamics in Kleiber's recording is wonderfully expressive. Strauss's dynamic directions are followed to perfection. Furthermore, Gueden's diminuendo to the high B can only be called thrilling—an interpretation which followed from our analysis of the passage (recall ex. 9). One can quibble only about the slight crescendo to the last high A-sharp of the phrase, which, just as in our discussion of retransition in sonata and rondo, mistakenly anticipates the return and renewal of the high tessitura.

Lastly, we arrive at Stich-Randall's performance in von Karajan's recording of 1957. It has all the virtues of the Kleiber/Gueden rendition—the C-sharp-A-sharp-B is sung piano-crescendo-pianissimo-pianississimo according to our analysis—and Stich-Randall includes a pianississimo (*ppp*) on the last high A-sharp of the triplet as well. In all the other recordings the sopranos emphasize this pitch—which renews the high tessitura that initiates the opening leap—by first accenting the A-sharp in the triplet and then holding it slightly longer than the notation indicates (see the chart). As emphasized, however, since accenting a leap to a high note is a natural norm, that is not justified at this point in the passage since both the text and the music continue to stress what is supposed to be an other-worldly experience in the drama (the heavenly recognition of love upon the presentation of the rose). Thus, Stich-Randall's avoidance of stress on the high A-sharp of the triplet is a masterful interpretation: the transportation back to the transcendental realm of the A-sharp is prolonged with the tenuto, as in all the performances, but not at the expense of following the natural mode of singing the ascending leap louder.

Moreover, in a flash of inspiration, Stich-Randall sings the whole phrase from the beginning virtually in pure tone, without vibrato. The strange placidity immeasurably increases the heavenly quality denoted in the text. Furthermore, her pochissimo portamento from the last note in the bar to the downbeat in the next measure—the high G-sharp to the low A-sharp on the words "nicht irdische"—creates an especially tender moment since the downward leap and the dissonance on both of these tones is unexpected—in effect a kind of breathless sigh sung after the ecstasy of the "heavenly tessitura."

Von Karajan himself significantly contributes to the other-worldly quality of Strauss's music by virtually suspending the tempo: as can be seen in figure 1, the high A-sharp—the point at which the poco allargando starts—is held for a full three seconds, which is to say, three times as long as Strauss's specified tempo of the *Etwas breit* music of the allargando (where quarter=60). None of the other four conductors stretches out the phrase to the extent von Karajan does. But it is instructive to observe that to all five of them "un poco allargando" and *Etwas breit* mean *more* than a 100% increase in the length of the note specified by the change of tempo: in each performance the tenuto on the high A-sharp exceeds two seconds—from the 2 and 1/5 seconds of Böhm's performance to the 2 and 2/5 seconds of Kleiber's to the 2 and 1/2 seconds of Solti's and Krauss's to the 3 seconds of von Karajan's.[11]

Of course, it is not the sheer length of any individual note that matters in musical performance but rather the relationship among adjacent notes which determines the relative sense of tempo change. All five

---

[11]A film exists of the composer conducting music from the *Rosenkavalier Suite* in which the passage discussed in this article is given a very perfunctory reading—Strauss more or less ignores the poco allargando. Composers are rarely the best performers of their own music. (Stravinsky is something, but only something, of an exception in this regard.) Strauss's performances of his own music have always had the reputation of seeming somewhat insensitive—a peculiar state of affairs given the polish, craft, and originality of his music.

conductors play out the poco allargando more at the beginning than at the end of the phrase. The actual notated durations of the C-sharp-A-sharp-B reversal in the music are set in a 2:3:1.66 ratio (from the quarter-note C-sharp to the dotted-quarter A-sharp is an increase of 50%, whereas from the dotted-quarter A-sharp to the tied B is a decrease of 44%). As can be seen from the chart, no conductor maintains this ratio exactly for the obvious reason that the "un poco allargando" must accrue time gradually. Hence, the third note will be proportionately longer than that specified in the actual notation. By the same token, since all five conductors stretch somewhat the initial note (C-sharp), prior to the actual placement of the allargando direction on the score page, the cumulation on the high A-sharp never reaches an increment of 50%.

Nevertheless, one expects something of the durational ratio of the original notation to remain intact throughout the poco allargando, which is to say, one expects the notes C-sharp and B flanking the A-sharp to remain somewhat shorter in duration than the high A-sharp itself. In this respect, Krauss's performance would seem to err in that the high B in his rendition is *longer* (3 sec.) than the preceding C-sharp and A-sharp. That is, instead of a decrease in note length on the tied B, on the third note, we find an increase (of approximately 21%). Böhm's performance, where the tied high B is somewhat longer than the initial C-sharp (1 and 9/10 sec. vs. 1 and 1/2 sec.), would also seem slightly distorted: although the change to poco allargando will tend to accumulate durationally, it should not overly warp the durational contextual setting specified in the score. In contrast, by maintaining a semblance of the durational ratio specified in the actual notation, the other three conductors (Solti, Kleiber, and von Karajan) see to it that the the high B is not longer than the initial C-sharp.

CONCLUSION

So, then, can we say of the five that one performance of this magical moment in the opera is the best? If the analytical theory is correct both about the step up to the high B being a denial of a reversal implication and about the effect of the durational cumulation on that note, it would appear on the basis of our discussion about dynamics, note lengths, and tempo that Kleiber's and von Karajan's performances are indeed superior to the other three. Laying aside personal preferences for quality of voice (Gueden vs. Stich-Randall), which are anything but inconsiderable criteria to opera buffs, my own view is that von Karajan's stretched-out, time-suspended performance with Stich-Randall's use of non-vibrato throughout the passage, her triple piano on the last A-sharp, and her descending portamento into bar 2 is the most imaginative of the five.

Analytical theory is crucial in the planning, executing, and evaluation of musical performances. We see that what performers do crucially affects structure, not to mention the perceived aesthetic of the score. In order to fulfill their artistic responsibilities both to the composer and to the listener, performers, as co-creators, thus must acquire theoretical and analytical competence so as not only to know how to interpret, but what difference one interpretation versus another makes. To be sure, analysis is an intellectual assault on an artwork. But performers can never plumb the aesthetic depth of a great work without an intense scrutiny of its parametric elements. In this enterprise, analytical theory is not only central in the education of performers but indispensable.

Patricia Carpenter

Aspects of Musical Space

A work of art can be seen from two sides: that of the creator, the poet, as pouioumenon, and that of the beholder, as phenomenon. For the composer the musical work is a "made thing"; for the listener, a comprehended object. It is crucial in an analytic situation to distinguish where one stands in regard to the work and equally crucial not to lose sight of its unity.

Certain terms in our analytic language present some difficulty in regard to music, terms having to do with the musical object—how it is constructed, how it is apprehended, how it exists. 'Form' is such a word; it denotes that which the composer constructs, or the listener grasps, or perhaps the concrete work itself. Some terms can present indifferently different views of the work. 'Gestalt,' for example, is both the configuration the composer shapes and the shape the listener apprehends; 'texture' is the basic level of structure within which the composer works and the background against which the listener's comprehension unfolds. 'Articulation' is such a two-sided word. Arnold Schoenberg, from the composer's point of view, considers form to be the way in which the musical idea is articulated so that it is comprehensible to the listener. An idea is thought all at once and said a little at a time. It comes to the composer, he says, whole and clear; his effort to articulate it is solely for the sake of the listener. It is only in order to make the idea comprehensible that he must divide the whole into surveyable parts and then add them together again, so that the listener grasps a whole that is now conceivable in spite of its details.[1]

---

[1]Arnold Shoenberg, *Style and Idea* (hereafter *SI*), ed. Leonard Stein (New York, 1975), p. 285

Patricia Carpenter is Professor of Music at Barnard College and Director of the Graduate Program in Music Theory at Columbia University.

341

On occasion, if I have made an observation about compositional procedure and the response is, "But I don't hear it that way," I draw an analogy between a piece of music and a tapestry. I may be looking at the back side, at the way it is made, describing threads, knots, warp and woof, whereas the listener, in front, sees a wonderful world—flora, fauna, hunting party, mythical beasts. The philosopher Merleau-Ponty describes the difference between and unity of these two aspects of the work—meaningless details and meaningful whole—in a comparison between the use of language by a writer and the use of the "indirect language" of painting by a painter:

> Like the weaver, the writer works on the wrong side of his material. He has to do only with language, and it is thus that he suddenly finds himself surrounded by meaning.
> If this account is true, the writer's act of expression is not very different from the painter's....There are two sides to the act of painting: the spot or line of color put on a point of the canvas, and its effect in the whole, which is incommensurable with it, since it is almost nothing yet suffices to change a portrait or a landscape. One who, with his nose against the painter's brush, observed the painter from too close would see only the wrong side of his work. The wrong side is a feeble movement of the brush or pen of Poussin; the right side is the sunlit glade which that movement releases.[2]

Like the weaver, the writer, and the painter, the composer also works on the wrong side of his work. Having to do only with sounds and silences, he too suddenly finds himself surrounded by meaning. Composer and listener "see" two different aspects of the same musical image.

In this paper I shall develop a notion of musical space as the constructed and perceived continuum of a musical work. I take the musical space of a work to be that space intrinsic to it—analogous, for example, to that of a painting. In music it is the background against which both the coherence and the unity of the work unfold and which constitutes in a certain way the common ground for composer and listener.

I

'Space' has been said to be the form of the external world. Can that which is heard—call it the acoustic surface or field—be said to be spatial in any real way? Can spatial properties be attributed to the intangible,

[2] Maurice Merleau-Ponty, *Signs*, trans Richard McCleary (Evanston, IL, 1964), p. 45.

invisible, and immaterial musical object? We are accustomed to a division of the arts based on a notion of a divided sensorium which traces back to Kant, particularly to his contrast between the external senses, to which the form of space is inherent, and the internal sense whose form is time. In a tradition that has so dichotomized the world into static and dynamic, corporeal and mental, external and internal realms, music has taken a place on the side of time. Hegel, for example, has denied any objectivity at all to music. Art cannot remain an idea, he says, but must come into actual existence as object for the senses. But music is one with subjectivity, for its medium is tone and the tone does not spatially remain. Music thus abstracts from space altogether and subsists in time only. It is the most inward of the arts, for there is no separation of the spirit, interwoven as it is with the musical object itself.[3]

I believe this division of experience is no longer fruitful. Space and time are categories invented by the human mind for the apprehension of facts, but are inseparable in experience. In experience we are given a world which both extends and endures and is filled with meaning.[4] Problems concerning musical space are entangled with traditional conceptions of space in general, and as our understanding of experience has become more unified our notions of space have broadened. Serious concern with questions of auditory and musical space arose in the first decades of this century, as distinctions were made between experienced space and the objectified space of conception, and as stages in the development of spatial experience were explored. Music itself— particularly the gestalt-quality of a melody, its striking character as perceptual figure—has thrown new light on the visual perception of things and consequently on the conception of space in general.

Space has to do with the external world, but it is better understood as a kind of activity than a being of some sort. It is the name we give to the gradual differentiation of the world of the not-I from that of the I, the room we make for things to be, and the way we articulate and order those things as they become part of the external world. In its most primitive sense, it has to do with place, situation, where things are.

[3]Hegel, *Ästhetik* (Berlin, 1965), esp. pp. 153f.
[4]Rudolf Arnheim, *New Essays on the Psychology of Art* (Berkeley, 1986), pp. 80-81. "...Categories such as space and time are created by the human mind for the apprehension of facts in the physical and psychological realms, and...therefore they become pertinent only when such categories are needed for the description and interpretation of those facts....Things in action are what is primarily given in spontaneous perception. Perception is neither able nor willing to analyze behavior by differentiating the four dimensions....Visual dynamics is an indivisible unity, not broken down into space and time." This conception of perception as dynamic and unified forms a constant theme throughout Arnheim's work.

Space is the continuant against which things stand out, solidify, gather to themselves body, quality and texture, shape, location and distance. It is as well a container in which bodily things collect, an otherwise empty place. Thus space is that which holds things both apart and together in some sort of order.

As our experience develops, so does our sense of 'space.' Space may be concretely experienced as immediate, personal, dynamic—place in relation to me, extension as matter of things I can touch or as background for things I see or a motion I make. As it is differentiated from me and my own bodily orientation, it becomes more abstractly conceived—mediate, impersonal, static—hypostasized into a unified space of places. Ultimately, it is the abstract possibility of extension itself—continuous, boundless, homogeneous, a continuum in which all things have a place.

Music, in contrast to spatial things, seems to be the temporal art par excellence—the most interior of the arts, of all of them furthest removed from matter, body, distance, location and closest to my own mood, activity, or thought. Music is eminently immediate: unlike the image of a painting, for example, the memory of a melody *is* that melody, immediately present in the imagination, always retrievable. But even the actually sounding melody is only successively given, never wholly there, relying for its very existence upon the effort and skill of the listener who effects its synthesis above the sounding tones. A musical event has been said to be a piece of time, discontinuous and fragmentary in its mode of being, more like the subjective flow of consciousness than a thing, an analogue of the internal life. But a piece of music is not sheer time. It is not made *ex nihilo*. A composer, like any other artist, wrestles with the given intransigent stuff of his art in order to make manifest, as outer and other, a musical idea. A melody is not a fusion of undifferentiated moments, like our interior experience of unspatialized time, cradling the listener into a hypnotic or dreamlike state. It is a gesture, an entity, something there, which the listener must encounter, articulate, collect, and synthesize, that is, which he must objectify. I have maintained that this particular kind of form in Western music exploits factors that heighten wholeness and unity, distance and contemplation, and both perceptual and aesthetic isolation.[5]

In this paper I shall explore one way such form has been achieved, that is, by the exploitation of simultaneity in two senses: the juxtaposition, in an increasingly dense way, of musical events occurring at the same time, and the increasing extension of the amount of time to be

[5]"The Musical Object," *Current Musicology* 5 (1967): 56-87 and 6 (1968): 116-125 and "Musical Form Regained," *Journal of Philosophy* 62 (1965): 36-48.

grasped as "now." The consequent field of co-presence of events in time is the ground for the intrinsic space of the musical work. Shoenberg conceives of what I call an expansion of the present as a function of the musical idea, which unifies both the "two-or-more-dimensional" moment and the total span:

> The two-or-more-dimensional space in which musical ideas are presented is a unit. Though the elements of these ideas appear separate and independent to the eye and the ear, they reveal their true meaning only through their co-operation, even as no single word alone can express a thought without relation to other words. All that happens at any point of this musical space has more than a local effect. It functions not only in its own plane, but also in all other directions and planes, and is not without influence event at remote points.[6]

Schoenberg's conception of musical space is central to his concern for coherence and unity in music. He explicitly describes that concept in his lectures on twelve-tone method, but it is implicit as well in his writing on tonal theory. I believe musical space to be a representation of his concept of tonality. There is only a gradual difference, he maintains, between the tonality of yesterday and that of today. Any piece of music is tonal, he says, in so far as a relation must exist from tone to tone by virtue of which the tones, placed next to or above one another, yield a perceptible continuity.

> I believe...that this interrelationship of all tones exists not only because of their derivation from the first thirteen overtones of the three fundamental tones, as I have shown, but that, should this proof be inadequate, it would be possible to find another. For it is indisputable that we can join twelve tones with one another and this can only follow from the already existing relations between the twelve tones (*SI* 284).

Such a network of *a priori* relations among the tones constitutes, I maintain, the structure of his musical space.

Here I shall consider some aspects of musical space, especially in the light of Schoenberg's concepts, and demonstrate how a musical idea both extends and unifies such a space in a felicitous example by Schubert, his Impromptu op. 90 no.3.

---

[6]*SI*, p. 220. See also "Vortrag/12 T K/Princeton," ed. Claudio Spies, *Perspectives of New Music* 13 (1974): 58-136, esp. pp. 83-87.

II

Let me begin with a basic sense of musical space as ''spread-outness.''
Anything perceived requires extension of some sort; musical space is
first of all a span, sonorous extension.

Example 1. Schubert: Impromptu op. 90 no. 3. Opening statement (A-a)

Consider the opening statement of Schubert's Impromptu (ex. 1). If
I turn my attention to its sheer ongoing continuity and try to describe
simply its sound quality, I would say that I hear a piano sound, articulated
as what I might call ''piano homophony,'' a certain texture, an arpeg-

giated chordal progression defined by a two-voice structure, bearing a melody on the surface, supported by a bass. This is a quality of the whole, pervading the piece and constituting its basic unity. If Schoenberg is correct in taking form as the articulation (in the service of comprehensibility) of an ongoing musical continuity, this piece presents an interesting formal problem. There is no silence in the entire span, only continuity. Even at the fermata that marks its two halves there is no break in the sound. This space is above all a continuant.

Schoenberg refers to musical continuity at this basic level as "cohesion"; musical space is a unit because it coheres. And it coheres because it is tonal: with tones, he says, only that which is tonal can be produced; at least that connection based on the tonal must exist between any two tones if they are to form a progression that is at all logical and comprehensible (*SI* 210).

I would say, then, that what I hear first in the Impromptu is not only a certain tone quality but also a certain tonal unity. Now tonality refers to the relation of tones with one another, but especially with the fundamental. "If, however, we wish to investigate what the relation of tones to each other really is, the first question that arises is: what makes it possible that a second tone should follow a first, a beginning tone? How is this logically possible?" This question, Schoenberg says, is more important than it seems at first, and to his knowledge it has not been previously raised. His answer is: two tones can be joined only because a relation already exists between them (*SI* 270). The primitive and *a priori* source of tonal relations is thus the material.

The property of cohesion derives not only from the nature of the musical material, but also from the needs of the human mind. He concedes that the origin of tonality is found, and rightly so, in the laws of sound, but points out that other laws, laws governing the working of our minds—which force us to find a particular kind of layout for elements that make for cohesion—must also be obeyed (*SI* 259). Tonality, by exploiting certain features of good gestalt such as centricity and closure, is the easiest means of achieving form in music. Its function begins to exist if the phenomena that appear can, without exception, be related immediately to a tonic and if they are arranged so that their accessibility is a matter of sensory perception, or if one uses methods that allow those farther away to become accessible. In a piece so constructed the internal relationships acquire such cohesion that it is guaranteed in advance a certain formal effectiveness. The listener of a certain degree of comprehension, through the unity of relationships, must inevitably perceive a work so composed to be a unity.

The unity of the whole which tonality effects pervades the concrete work, from smallest element to tonal plan.[7] Figure 1 is a schema of the plan of the Impromptu, which shows at a glance the nexus of tonal relations at work here—tonic, submediant, subdominant—and the connection of submediant and subdominant involving F-flat. This complex of relations is the ground from which the tonality of the piece expands. (I shall use these sectional tags for orientation in my discussion of the piece.)

Figure 1. Schema of Schubert's Impromptu op. 90 no. 3

		Part I			Part II (varied repetition)	
		A Tonic statement				
a	1-8	opening statement	T	a	55-62	T
b	9-16	model/sequence,	to SD	b	63-71	to SD
b'	17-24	varied repetition,	to T	b'	72-74	T
		B Contrast section			(reduction)	
a	25-27		sm			
a'	28-31	varied repetition and extension (with F-flat)	sm			
b	32-34		to SD	c'	75-78	T
c	35-36,	37-38	SD		(variant 32, 35)	
	39	link to	sm	c''		T
		B'			(varied rep)	
d	40-43		sm			
d'	44-47	varied repetition (with F-flat)	sm			
b'	48-51		SM			
c'	51-54	transition	SM to V/T		83-87 coda	T

(I have used Schoenberg's names for the related key areas: T, tonic; SD, subdominant; sm, submediant; SM, submediant major.)

[7]I have attempted to illustrate this tonal unity in a sonata of Beethoven in "*Grundgestalt as Tonal Function,*" *Music Theory Spectrum* 5 (1983): 15-38.

III

In Schoenberg's view tonality provides for organization on (at least) two levels: cohesion, how one tone follows another; and comprehensibility, how tones are gathered into a whole. 'Organization,' like 'articulation,' is a dual-sided word, in that both creator and beholder organize a work. John Cage, speaking of his compositional activity, distinguishes two such levels of organizing. At one time, he says, he termed these "structure"—"the division of a whole into parts" and "method"—"the note-to-note procedure." He contrasts the two in terms of "one's ideas of order...and one's spontaneous actions."[8] The listener also organizes on different levels. He who follows "with his nose against the brush" only the moment-to-moment course of an unfolding musical process, may find that his "distance" from a work may be a matter of subjective factors, such as the level of form to which he attends or his capacity for comprehension; or it may be a matter of the structure of the work—perhaps the work itself does not invite him toward large-scale apprehension, toward the "sunlit glade."

The classic analysis of levels of organization in a temporal construct is that of Aristotle in regard to rhetoric. He distinguishes two levels similar to those of Cage: *lexis*, the diction, the movement in detail; and *taxis*, the arrangement, or movement in the large. Further, he contrasts both to *schema*, the outline or plan.[9] Although 'schema' ordinarily connotes visual form, Aristotle uses images for it drawn from modes of movement. It is the relatively fixed level in a continuing process of apprehension, the means by which we check and sustain the movement of the mind in order to hold something in thought or imagination. Specifically, as it applies to the art of rhetoric, it is the subject for speculation, the question or idea.

In regard to music a similar distinction is fundamental to Tovey's discussions of musical forms. These, he says, may be considered in two aspects: the texture of music from moment to moment and the shape of the musical design as a whole. He contrasts the procedures of "fitting together" and "composition" according as the elements arranged are small or large, and he identifies form, as an extended event or motion, with the techniques of tonality that have so effectively achieved this. Form or shape thus becomes the arrangement of sections in tonal relations, that is, a matter of "harmony," and is somehow spatial. Tex-

[8]John Cage, *Silence: Lectures and Writings* (Middletown, CT, 1961), p. 18.
[9]Aristotle, *The "Art" of Rhetoric*, trans. John Henry Freese (Cambridge, MA, 1959), for example 1401a2 and 1403b1 (pp. 324/25, 382/83).

ture, the elements of which are simple (in the sense that those of mathematics are simple) he takes to be "counterpoint." The laws of texture, he maintains, were mastered before those of form.[10]

In his early book, *Emotion and Meaning in Music*, Leonard Meyer has turned around the approach to levels of form in music by beginning with the unity of perceptual experience. Generally speaking, he says, his study is not concerned with the creative act but rather with the experience which the art work brings into being. By applying gestalt principles to the musical field, he cuts across the separation of visual and auditory modes. He interprets 'texture' in an illuminating way, translating traditional classifications into figure/ground relationships: texture, he says, has to do with the ways in which the mind groups concurrent musical stimuli—into simultaneous figures, for example, or a figure and accompaniment (ground), or several equally well-shaped figures without a ground, and so forth.[11]

In a sense, Meyer's notion of musical textures extends Koffka's theory of field to music. According to Koffka, at least in visual perception texture and shape are dynamic stages in a continuum of increasing articulation of the field; even a surface is a function of texture (by which Koffka means a primary variability or disequilibrium in the field). Analyzing the visual organization of the environmental field, he states that the simplest condition is one in which the distribution of forces on the sense surface is absolutely homogeneous—for example, a homogeneous distribution of neutral light. The observer, in the face of such light, will "feel himself swimming in a mist of light." Only as the "grain" or microstructure of the illuminated surface becomes less homogeneous (that is, only as the situation becomes more complex) does the space-filling fog condense into the appearance of surface for the observer. The segregation of a unity with a shape from the rest of the field is a further complex act of organization.[12] Koffka believes that figure and ground arise together. Meyer uses "texture" to denote organization at the level of figure and ground, but the important point here is that the organization of a field, from texture to surface to shape, is a single dynamic continuity. Meyer overcomes the opposition of shape and texture and establishes that in music, as in all perception, we grasp not moments or points but concrete forms, sounding and in motion.

[10]Donald Francis Tovey, "Contrapuntal Forms," in his *The Forms of Music* [orig. pub. 1906-29] (New York, 1956), pp. 19-29.
[11](Chicago, 1956), p. 185.
[12]Kurt Koffka, *Principles of Gestalt Psychology* (New York, 1963), especially pp. 110ff.

   In general, form as shape or configuration refers to the organization of wholes. If form be taken as the total web of relations among elements, a distinction generally can be made between relatively small- and large-scale elements or relatively near- or far-reaching relations. These levels of form can be distinguished in different perceptual modes. It is possible to construct for vision only a figure, a circle for example, or only small-scale texture. For touch these probably cannot be separated; can one grasp the roundness of a ball without also feeling its rubberness? Hearing incorporates temporality into the structure of its field. The perceived present is not a point, but a bit of time; its upper limit is ordinarily taken to be about five or six seconds. In music a pattern or well-articulated shape can extend that bit and we continually collect into larger and larger wholes.[13] Accordingly, in music at least two distinct levels of organization can be distinguished: at the level of the smallest unit are those musical events that can be grasped in a single mental act—a figure, for example, or a phrase; and these in turn are gathered up into larger wholes—a melody or a part.

   Minimally, comprehensible music requires phenomena that are clear to the ear and return at perceivable distances—that is, some kind of figure and some kind of repetition. Although figures can be shaped from any parameter of sound, the simplest are rhythmic and intervallic and the easiest kinds of collection are rhythmic and thematic recall. A child, once he grasps a figure, tends to repeat it unchanged for a while, then to vary it little by little, simplifying as he goes, spinning out a string of levelled, homogeneous parts.

   In the Schubert Impromptu a similar procedure forms the homogeneous, unified background. Against that background the closed shape of the melody unfolds (ex. 1). The first collecting point in this line is the half-phrase, which articulates the first figure, the initial interval of the melody, B-flat/G-flat. The "now" has been remarkably extended, to about fourteen or sixteen seconds. Notice how the melody then extends this simple figure into a closed shape in very specific ways. For example, the entire statement (a period) spans, in the large, the interval of the opening figure, B-flat/G-flat. Further, the symmetrical phrases of the period articulate the linear descent of that interval in the tonic: B-flat to A-flat at the half-cadence of the antecedent phrase; and B-flat, through A-flat, closing to G-flat at the end of the consequent phrase. Connections are built into the ongoing line by repetition, for example,

[13]Fred Lerdahl and Ray Jackendoff explicate principles of grouping applied to the several parameters of musical organization in *A Generative Theory of Tonal Music* (Cambridge, MA, 1983).

by rhythmic grouping and by scalar progression, which provides for strong linear continuity.

A melody is not only a paradigm for a perceptual figure but also a particular kind of motion. The Impromptu as a whole can be heard through as if it were a melody. It collects moments in its course but is as well a single action in pursuit of its goal. Koffka compares an instinctive action to a melody—he calls it a "movement-melody." A melody, he says, is something quite different from mere succession. Just as the beginning of a melody pushes forward in the direction of its continuation and completion, so an instinctive activity arises from organic needs and is directed from the very outset. A true movement requires forces, and a force is always in a certain direction. Such a movement "seeks" a goal; the ultimate causes of the forces that produce it are the needs of the organism.[14] At this basic level, because of the pervading texture of the Impromptu and the single unfolding melodic action, as well as its tonal unity, the musical space of this piece is a unit.

Schoenberg maintains that the deviations from the tonal center easiest to grasp are those that can be related back to it most readily, whose resemblances to it are maximal. More remote deviations, less immediately grasped, must be made to be accessible from the tonic by special methods. As I follow the course of this piece, I reach a point near the end where the tonal balance has been pushed very far, to a minor chord on the lowered second degree. The resemblance to the tonic is minimal; there are no pitches in common. In example 2 I have sketched two corresponding segments from the last section of the piece. The descending bass-line takes the motion first to a minor subdominant chord and then, in the varied repetition, to a C-double-flat, the lowered third of a Neapolitan sixth chord. The melody clarifies the difference between the two progressions: in both it moves to the crucial pitches in an inner voice, leaping a diminished fifth in the first statement, a diminished sixth in the variant (ex. 2c). This passage represents what I will call the "tonal problem." How can the tonality have been pushed so far in such an apparently simple way? My answer is: by a systematic exploitation on the large scale of the inherent possibilities of the initial figure.

[14]Kurt Koffka, *The Growth of the Mind: An Introduction to Child-Psychology*, trans. Robert Morris Ogden (New York and London, 1925), p. 108.

Example 2. The limit to which this tonality is pushed (1)

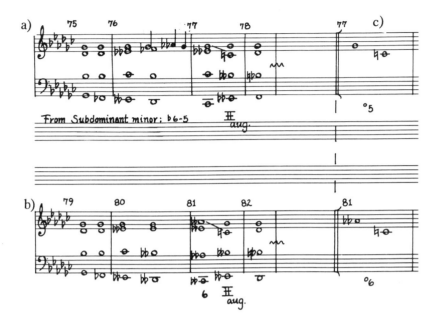

IV

Music as motion implies a space within which that motion takes place, a space which has been likened to an energy-space or a feeling-space or a field of action. Schoenberg considers movement to be latent in the tone itself: although the primitive ear hears the tone as irreducible, physics recognizes it as complex. Musicians discovered that it is capable of continuation, hearing in it and extracting from it the octave, fifth, and third.[15] The musical space in which a melody unfolds is a unit because it is a projection of the tone. For this reason as well its two (or more) dimensions are unified. Schoenberg takes 'dimension' in the traditional sense of harmony and melody (or strictly, scale), suggesting that each is an ''imitation of the tone'' in the vertical and horizontal planes, respectively. However, he develops this meaning into a more precise formulation of tonality as a projection of the fundamental:

---

[15]Arnold Shoenberg, *Theory of Harmony* (hereafter *HL*), trans. Roy E. Carter (Berkeley, 1978), p. 313.

Whenever all chords of a complete piece of music appear in progressions that can be related to a common fundamental tone, one can then
say that the idea of the musical sound (which is conceived as vertical)
is extended to the horizontal plane. Everything following it [the fun-
damental] springs from this fundamental postulate, refers back to it, even
when antithetical to it, elaborates and complements it, and finally leads
back to it, so that this fundamental is treated in every respect as central,
as embryonic (*HL* 26, 28).

This passage, which adumbrates his formulation of musical space in
the twelve-tone lectures, represents Schoenberg's conception of tonal
unity in spatial terms. The unified motion that takes place in the tonal
space is not merely a melody, but rather the tonal (harmonic) progression as a concrete whole. If we are short-sighted enough, he says, to
regard only the momentary result as the goal, considering now the chord,
now the melody as the Motor that produces musical movement, then
the possibility of perceiving and comprehending the whole vanishes,
and we are not able to see that both dimensions serve only one purpose, the penetration into what is given in nature.

Thus, although we can abstract from the concrete whole the course
of the harmony, the melodic motion, or motivic events, they are different aspects of the same process. The melody vitalizes the line, rendering the harmony comprehensible; the harmony defines the meaning of
the melody; the motivic course highlights crucial relations. The unity
of vertical and horizontal dimensions is a commonplace. For example,
those of us who do strict voice leading know how the change in
one structural line of a progression effects a change in another.
Example 3a is a sketch of the opening progression of the Impromptu.
Whereas a root progression from I (with $\hat{3}$ in the soprano) to II generates
an ascending third, a motion to a first inversion reverses the direction.
Schubert uses a chordal skip in the intervening VI to produce the opening figure from an otherwise stationary voice (ex. 3a, iii).

This opening figure is what Schoenberg calls the *Grundgestalt*, or
basic shape, which represents the musical idea at a certain level and
from which all subsequent events in the work derive. It is a concrete
shape, constructed by the composer, grasped by the listener. The
theoretical basis for its concrete unity is the unity of the two-dimensional
space; in this sense the musical idea is neither melody nor harmony
nor rhythm, but a concrete entity consisting of all three. The abstract
elements can be conceived separately, as I have sketched them in example
3b, but

Example 3. Unity of the dimensions of the musical space

a. The interdependence of vertical and horizontal dimensions

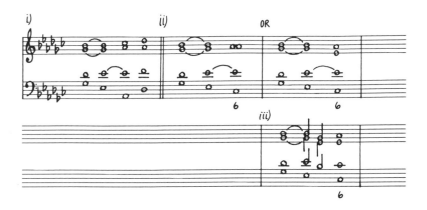

b. The basic shape as a concrete entity of interval, rhythm, and harmony

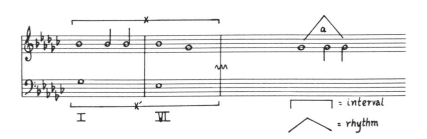

a musical idea, accordingly [because of the unity of the space], though consisting of melody, rhythm, and harmony, is neither the one nor the other alone, but all three together. The elements of a musical idea are partly incorporated in the horizontal plane as successive sounds, and partly in the vertical plane as simultaneous sounds. The mutual relation of tones regulates the succession of intervals as well as their association into harmonies; the rhythm regulates the succession of tones as well as the succession of harmonies and organizes phrasing (*SI* 220).

The effect of the idea within the space of a musical work is the result of its unity. For example, in the technique of model and sequence, melodic pattern and harmonic function work together to expand the tonal space. In the Impromptu the principal motion away from the tonic is to the subdominant side, one fifth counterclockwise (C-flat major/a-flat minor), acquiring the non-diatonic pitch F-flat. Example 3c shows the beginning of this motion in the first contrast section (A-b). The model is an inversion and variant of the opening figure; the sequence reaches the F-flat in both melody and harmony. This F-flat has a double meaning: as $\hat{4}$ in C-flat major or flat $\hat{6}$ in a-flat minor; the motion pivots on these two meanings but does not distinguish them here. In the varied repetition the function of F-flat as flat $\hat{6}$ is defined (ex. 3d). The bass line of the first statement is levelled to an ambiguous scalar descent (m. 18f.); but an inner voice, in the context of a diminished-seventh chord, spells out the characteristic leading-tones of a-flat minor (mm. 17-18). A diminished-seventh chord is defined by the resolution of its leading-tones; flat $\hat{6}$ (resolving to $\hat{5}$) is one of them.

The expansion of a tonal space is achieved because of the unity of pitch and function, but I will separate these two in order to explain the process of a tonal expansion by their interplay, by what I call "analogy." Consider, for example, the two aspects of this F-flat: its specific pitch and its function as flat $\hat{6}$ of a-flat minor. F-flat next appears as flat $\hat{2}$ in the submediant in measure 31, the link between submediant and subdominant (ex. 3e); the pitch takes on a new function. The function flat $\hat{6}$, as we shall see, provides for the acquisition "by analogy" of A-double-flat in the subdominant and E-double-flat in the tonic; and the A-double-flat ultimately appears as flat $\hat{2}$ in the tonic. Schubert reaches his remote goal in a systematic way, extending this tonality by relating remarkably few similar musical phenomena.

This two-dimensional musical space both contains the motion and is the continuant against which that motion unfolds. Like our concretely experienced space, it takes its shape from the motion it contains; but it is also abstractly structured by a network of relations generated by the tone.

c. Model and sequence expand the tonality (A-b)

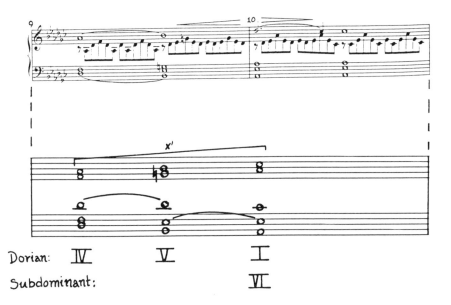

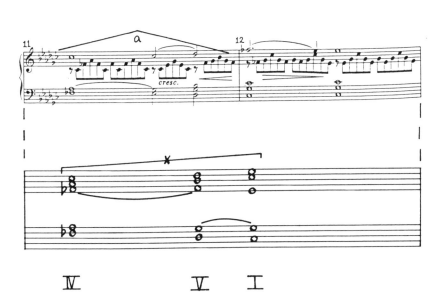

d. F-flat defined as flat $\hat{6}$ in a region on a-flat (Dorian) (A-b′)

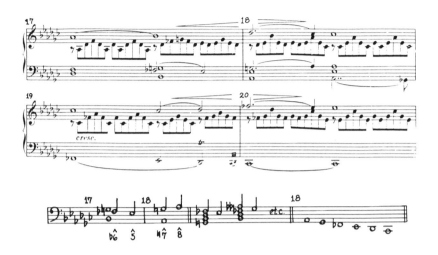

e. F-flat incorporated as flat $\hat{2}$ in a region on e-flat (submediant minor) (B-b)

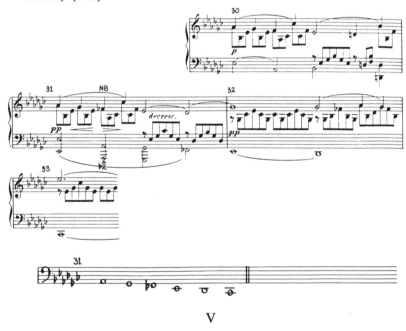

V

Meyer contrasts the organization of a background in aural and visual fields and attributes the several musical textures he describes to this contrast. He takes issue with an observation of Koffka's, that if th segregation of larger and smaller units is produced in a field, the smaller units will become figure, the larger, ground. Meyer believes this is not the case in music, in which several well-articulated, juxtaposed figures can coexist. The characteristic articulation of the Impromptu is such an example: the long notes of the melody are figure against the short figures of the ground. It is difficult, if not impossible, Meyer says, to imagine a visual figure without the more continuous, homogeneous ground against which it appears. "But in 'aural space,' in music, there is no given ground; there is no necessary, continuous stimulation, against which all figures must be perceived. The only thing that is continuous in aural experience is unorganized, timeless silence."[16]

A piece of music surely takes place against the silence of the external world (which is probably not true silence), but it creates its own intrinsic silence. The gaps within a musical work, for example, are not the same silence as that of the outside world. A work unfolds against a silence of its own. This intrinsic silence, however, does not seem to be unorganized. Aural space has indeed been described as indifferent to background; as a sphere without fixed boundaries, in contrast to a field or surface; and as a space made by the thing itself, not containing the thing.[17] But musical space has been framed and solidified by the material properties of tone, which not only give body to the musical work, but also make possible an inherent background structure. I believe the effect of "framed-ness" shapes the background in a fundamental way.

A framed visual field is not unstructured. In visual perception a frame creates a specific field of forces. Meyer Schapiro once remarked that a monkey's scribble on a sheet of paper is closer to a modern painting than are the cave paintings because the sheet becomes in effect a framed field. That field is described by Rudolf Arnheim:

A visual figure such as the square is empty and not empty at the same time. The center is part of a complex hidden structure, which can be explored by means of a disk, somewhat as iron filings will reveal the lines of force in a magnetic field. If the disk is put in various places within the square, it may be found that at some points it looks solidly at rest; at others it exhibits a pull in some definite direction, or its situa-

[16]Meyer, p. 186. Meyer observes, however, that within the context of a piece of music silence may appear to form a continuous ground, for certain attributes already established as given in the work, such as meter or repeated pattern, are continued subjectively in the mind of the listener, even in the absence of any objective stimulation.
[17]Edmund Carpenter and Marshall McLuhan, "Acoustic Space," in *Explorations in Communication* (Boston, 1960), p. 67f.

tion may be unclear and wavering....Investigation reveals that the disk is influenced also by the diagonals of the square as well as by the cross formed by the central vertical and horizontal axes. The center is established by the crossing of these four main structural lines.[18]

In temporal constructs the phenomenon analogous to the visual centricity described by Arnheim would seem to be a heightened sense of beginning, middle, and end. In modern Western music this has been achieved to a remarkable degree by triadic tonality. Schoenberg's theory of tonality conveys a precise analysis of the dynamic forces implicit in the background of tonal music as he conceived it. His notion of "monotonality" represents the network of relations among tones which I take to constitute the structure of his musical space.

I want to begin a discussion of Schoenberg's tonality with a distinction that is not always clear in his writings: between "key" and "tonality." In the early decades of this century the two were still used more or less interchangeably, but Schoenberg had a broader vision of the relationship between tones than that traditionally meant by key, a sense of extended tonality, monotonality, pantonality. In a footnote added to the revised edition of his *Harmonielehre* (1922) Schoenberg distinguishes between the "incorrect, exclusive" and "correct, inclusive" use of 'tonal': "Everything implied by a series of tones constitutes tonality, whether it be brought together by means of direct reference to a single fundamental or by more complicated connections" (*HL* 432). The concept of tonality is not to be identified with pitch-collection. "It coincides to a certain extent with that of the key, insofar as it refers not merely to the relation of the tones with one another, but especially to the particular way in which all tones relate to the fundamental tone of the scale" (*SI* 270). On the other hand, the harmonic sense of the key in all its ramifications is comprehensible only in relation to the idea of tonality.

> Tonality is a formal possibility that emerges from the nature of the tonal material, a possibility of attaining a certain completeness or closure by means of a certain uniformity. To realize this possibility it is necessary to use in the course of a piece only those sounds and successions of sounds... whose relations to the fundamental tone of the key...can be grasped without difficulty (*HL* 27).

---

[18]Rudolf Arnheim, *Art and Visual Perception: A Psychology of the Creative Eye* (Berkeley, 1957), p. 2f. The consequences of this field of forces in painting is further explored in his *The Power of the Center: A Study of Composition in the Visual Arts* (Berkeley, 1982).

Tonality, then, is centricity. It is not an end in itself, but only one of the means that facilitate the comprehension of a thought and satisfy the feeling for form.

Schoenberg denies that tonality is a natural law. Firm measures of art are required to establish it. A triad, he says, is entirely indefinite. Every major triad can of itself express a key, but every succeeding chord contests that feeling and pleads for others. Only a few very special kinds of chord-succession establish a particular chord, chiefly the last one, as fundamental of a key, and even this is final only if nothing contradictory follows the last chord. "Without application of very definite art-means a key cannot be unequivocally expressed" (*SI* 275).

Thus tonality is conflict and tonal space is a field of forces, indeed, a battleground. Even the traditional model for the derivation of the system, the two fifths around C, becomes a representation of struggle. Schoenberg likens the dependence of G on C to

> the force of a man hanging by his hands from a beam and exerting his own force against the force of gravity. He pulls on the beam just as gravity pulls him, and in the same direction. But the effect is that his force works against the force of gravity, and so in this way one is justified in speaking of the two opposing forces (*HL* 23-24).

Ultimately the conflicting forces in tonality are "centripetal" and "centrifugal," those which support the tonality and those which challenge it. "If life, if a work of art is to emerge, then we must engage in this movement-generating conflict. The tonality must be placed in danger" (*HL* 151).

The dynamic quality of tonality, and its unifying force, is generated by the power of the center. That center of gravity can permit harmonies with strong centrifugal tendencies to go astray if it also has the power to control them. In the *Harmonielehre* Schoenberg develops a concept of extended tonality that expands from those relations immediately accessible to the tonic to those at a border-line where he says, "This far, no farther," indicating that harmonic theory had reached a barrier it could not yet cross. Schoenberg's concept of extended tonality depends upon the strength of the tonal center. When a tone is the power center of the harmonic events, it is a prototype rich enough to include even the most complicated phenomena under its name. Under the pretense of modulation almost any property of other, quite distant keys, can be introduced. But to speak of modulation presupposes tonality.

Hence it is more to the point to regard tonality as the large region in whose outlying districts less dependent forces resist domination by the central power. If this central power endures, however...it then forces the rebels to stay within the circle of its sovereignty, and all activity is for its benefit....All activity, all movement leads back to it; everything turns within the circle (*HL* 369ff.).

(Tonal) musical space is a space of places, for which conflicting forces compete.

As Schoenberg sketches a path to an "inclusive" tonality, he indicates the main technical features of his theory of extended tonality. In the last hundred years, he says, the concept of harmony has changed tremendously through the development of chromaticism. From the beginning major and minor tonalties were interspersed with non-diatonic elements tending to form opposition to the fundamental tone yet compelling the application of strong means in order to verify the tonality, to paralyze eccentric effects. Imitation of modulatory processes permitted the introduction into every key of almost any property of other, quite distant, keys. Finally,

the appearance of vagrant chords—phenomena whose greatest value lies in their ambiguity—so greatly widened the field of events accessible from a tonic, that to an ever increasing extent the tonic could merely be proved, intellectually, to be in command, while it became steadily harder to hear....It is clear that all these tendencies, which exert an eccentric pull, worked against the desire to fix, make sensorily perceptible, and keep effective an harmonic central point (*SI* 259f.).

Three underlying assumptions of Schoenberg should be emphasized in discussing his theory of extended tonality: tonality is a conflict; the lines of force are defined by root progression, which expresses scale degree, that is, the relation to the tonic; the incorporation of a non-diatonic tone into a tonality is justified only by the comprehensibility of its relation to the tonic.

Tonality is a conflict of forces, those which challenge the tonality, creating imbalance, and those which foster tonality, restoring balance. One cannot think of tonality as I-IV-V-I without remembering the man hanging from the beam. The centripetal function of a progression is exerted by stopping its centrifugal tendencies; that is, a tonality is established through the conquest of its contradictory elements. Such elements are twofold in nature: undefined diatonic elements and non-diatonic elements.

What are "undefined" diatonic elements? An element—single pitch or chord—is defined only if its relationship to the tonic is unambiguous. That relationship is expressed by its scale degree, which is its function, its characteristic force. Root progression is the foundation for Schoenberg's explanation of all harmonic progressions, involving simple triads, transformations or vagrant harmonies. The power of the root is able to overcome great changes in the constitution of chords. The three classes of root progressions in traditional theory become themselves dynamic—"strong," "weak," and "superstrong"—and these (generally) function as such, regardless of transformation of their chordal members.

The function of a non-diatonic element incorporated into the tonality—single pitch, chordal transformation, or key area—is also defined by its relation to the fundamental, its scale degree. Such elements, however, are "borrowed" from the regions in which they originate and are "substituted" for diatonic elements. They also carry the force of their original region; thus elements borrowed from the subdominant minor, for example (in C) D-flat, are opposed to those originating on the dominant side of the tonality, for example F-sharp.

The point to be made here is that such borrowed tones do not entail modulation or tonicalization. Rather, this theory assumes a nexus of *a priori*, abstract relations at work, by virtue of which even a single borrowed pitch carries with it its context of function/force. Schoenberg's tonal space coheres as a field of abstract forces. One does not find one's way through it by tracking an explicit pitch line, nor is it contained by outer voices; its boundaries are drawn only where the force of the center no longer prevails.

Two examples may illustrate this point. The first (ex. 4) shows two corresponding segments of the B section of the Impromptu (B-b, B-d), the first in the submediant, the second in the submediant major. The formal analogy of these two sections in the Impromptu elegantly emphasizes the modal relation, major/minor interchange, which is one of the two relations used to expand this tonality (the other is tonic/subdominant). The second section carries out E-flat major as if it were a key, thereby elaborating it as a region in the tonality.

The second example (ex. 5) shows the use of elements of related keys that are not expressed as regions. Example 5a summarizes the process of "transformation." Schoenberg's model is a chord on the second degree, presenting the various possibilities of triad, seventh, or ninth chord, with or without its root. Pitches are borrowed from near-related regions and substituted for their diatonic counterparts (in any combina-

Example 4. Modal interchange

B-b

B-d

tion): the raised third from the dominant; the lowered ninth and lowered fifth from the tonic minor or subdominant minor. The root function supports these transformations; all continue to function as II (dominant preparation). Such transformations can be constructed on any degree.

In example 5b two passages trace the emergence of E-double-flat. It occurs first very briefly in the first contrast section (A-b) in the course of the melody, in the context of a diminished seventh chord that is ultimately revealed as V in the tonic (m. 21). Such a chord borrows for its lowered ninth the flat $\hat{6}$ from the tonic minor. E-double-flat next appears at the end of the first half of the piece (m. 54); here its resolution (flat $\hat{6}$ - $\hat{5}$) clearly defines the diminished seventh as V. This little

Example 5. Borrowing, substitution, and transformation

coda/transition summarizes in its bass-line descent, in a tonal context that deviates by only one pitch (F-flat) from the tonic, what will happen at the end of the piece. There the E-double-flat (analogous to C-flat here) will become the means by which the motion is carried to an A-double-flat minor chord.

Example 5c shows the passage (B-c) that is analogous to the codetta above. It consists of two phrases in the subdominant. The first borrows elements from the subdominant minor (especially its flat 6̂, A-double-flat); the second returns to the subdominant major. Compare the two forms of II which move to V: the first is an augmented six-five, the second a diminished seventh. The difference between these two transformations is the lowered fifth of the chord (see ex. 5a), here flat 6̂, A-double-flat, emphasized by the motif in the bass. The augmented six-five is a "vagrant" chord with "multiple meanings." By reinterpretation it functions both as a form of II and as V⁷ of the Neapolitan region. It is by means of this chord, at the end of the piece, that balance will be restored.

There are two traditional ways of representing the concept of extended tonality: the circle of fifths and a gridlike chart of key relations. Schoenberg uses both: the circle of fifths in the *Harmonielehre* and the "chart of regions" in *Structural Functions*. Both express two fundamental tonal relations: by fifth (vertical relations in the chart) and by third (horizontal relations in the chart). A motion by fifth expands the tonality by one new pitch; a major/minor interchange takes the motion a quarter of the distance around the circle. The chart of regions lays out the relationships to a single degree; it does not include, for instance, a motion to the dominant of the dominant. Therefore I will use the circle of fifths here to represent the possibilities of an extended tonality.

The circle of fifths is a representation of the network of tonal relations that constitutes the structure of tonal space. A particular tonal work is a framed segment of that space; its particular tonality can be represented as a segment of the circle. The particular way in which it makes manifest that tonality and utilizes its forces may be said to constitute, in one sense, what it is "about." The Impromptu, for example, makes manifest in a particular way a certain kind of "G-flatness," and in a particular way challenges that tonic, stretches its control to a far point, and finally, in an elegant stroke, restores its sovereignty. Figure 2 is my representation of the tonal space of this piece. Two tonal relationships are used: one fifth counterclockwise and modal interchange. A "static" tonal contrast (which articulates the two parts of the B section) is set up between submediant minor and submediant major, a motion a quarter of the circle to the dominant side (perhaps this serves as dominant contrast). A set of "dynamic" contrasts moves along the subdominant side: major/minor interchanges from the subdominant and the tonic carry the motion to the fifth place from the tonic on the circle; the introduction of an element from the subdominant's flat VI (D-, double-flat) involves the sixth place; a further exploitation of major/ minor interchange (introducing C-double-flat) extends the motion to the ninth place, almost closing the circle.

Schoenberg ultimately conceives of tonality as a "monotonality" that derives from the possibility of a fundamental tone "which in its vertical aspect alone makes available to the analyzing ear an unbelievable body of apparently foreign harmonies" (*HL* 385-6). Every digression, whether directly or indirectly, closely or remotely related, is still within the tonality. Every segment formerly considered as another tonality is only a region, a harmonic contrast within that tonality. This monotonality is a network of relationships embracing all pitches in the system, based on the fundamental premise that any pitch can be included in a tonality so long as its relationship to the fundamental is made comprehensible to the ear.

Figure 2. A representation of the tonality of the Impromptu

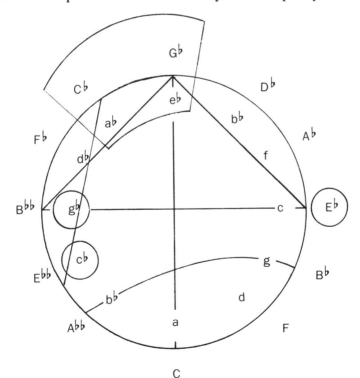

VI

I began this exploration of musical space with Merleau-Ponty's observation of the two sides of the acts of expression and apprehension: the
element, contrasted to the whole or the meaning. The great importance
of Schoenberg's concept of musical space is that it provides a theoretical
ground for the unity of these two sides: it is a metaphor both for gestalt
in music and for coherence. "Comprehensibility" embraces both. For
Schoenberg, music is the representation of a musical poet's or thinker's
ideas; musical space is that space in which such ideas are represented.
Thus his musical space is ultimately a conceptual space, the space in
which a thought takes shape, gathers body to itself, unfolds. The space
of a musical idea is a unity because we fully comprehend the thought
only after the last word is spoken.

The traditional sense of an "idea" in music is theme or melody;
Hanslick, for example, uses it in this sense.[19] For Schoenberg an idea
in music consists principally in the relation of tones to one another.

> In its most common meaning, the term idea is used as a synonym for
> theme, melody, phrase or motive. I myself consider the totality of a piece
> as the *idea:* the idea which its creator wanted to present. But because
> of the lack of better terms I am forced to define the term idea in the
> following manner: Every tone which is added to a beginning tone makes
> the meaning of that tone doubtful... The addition of other tones may
> or may not clarify this problem. In this manner there is produced a state
> of unrest, of imbalance which grows throughout most of the piece...The
> method by which balance is restored seems to me the real *idea* of the
> composition (*SI* 122f).

A melody is both idea and gestalt. Schoenberg maintains that the unity
of the musical space demands a unitary perception. It is an absolute
space, in which there is no up or down. Just as we recognize a hat or
bottle by any one of its aspects, so we recognize a musical idea in its
various appearances. Just as the constancy of an object in perception
is associated with our concept of it, so our recognition of the idea in
music in its many aspects depends upon our understanding of it as a
musical concept. I take Schoenberg's *Grundgestalt*, or basic shape, to
be the idea in its concrete form, as gestalt.

[19]I have explored one line of this sense of "idea" in "Musical Form and Musical Idea:
Reflections on a Theme of Schoenberg, Hanslick, and Kant," in *Music and Civiliza-
tion: Essays in Honor of Paul Henry Lang*, ed. Edmond Strainchamps and Maria Rika
Maniates, with Christopher Hatch (New York, 1984), pp. 394-427.

Finally, because the musical space is a unit, the idea has consequences on all planes and at all points of that space. In the Impromptu what is the idea? What are its consequences? How do its inherent forces operate to make manifest the structure of its space? Example 6 summarizes the essential tonal features of the *Grundgestalt*, its possibilities for expansion, expressed as variants of the root progression, and its projection through Part I of the Impromptu. The *Grundgestalt* (ex. 6a) consists essentially of a descending major third (x), supported by a "weak" root progression of a descending minor third (x'). There are four tonal contrasts which Schubert extracts from this figure (ex. 6b):

Example 6. The *Grundgestalt*

1. Notice the "undefined" character of the B-flat/G-flat: it can function as $\hat{3}$ $\hat{2}$ $\hat{1}$ in the tonic or $\hat{5}$ $\hat{4}$ $\hat{3}$ in the submediant. This relation, T/sm, is the first tonal contrast.

2. The second tonal contrast, T/SD, is a motion one fifth counter-clockwise, to C-flat major/a-flat minor, which adds the non-diatonic

pitch F-flat. The variant in the repetition of the first period (A-a') shows C-flat to be not only the subdominant, but also the flat VI of the submediant.

3. The third tonal contrast, sm/SM, results from a modal interchange.

4. The fourth tonal contrast is never carried out as a region: the lowered sixth degree (flat $\hat{6}$/flat VI) is borrowed from the minor. It is used by analogy in all three contrasting regions: c-flat in the submediant, A-double-flat in the subdominant, and E-double-flat in the tonic.

(I have emphasized that a "borrowed" form of a scale degree may be substituted in a diatonic key as a single pitch or applied to a transformation of a chord, or carried out as a region.) Example 6c is a sketch of the projection of the tonal forces of the *Grundgestalt* in the first part of the Impromptu. The first contrast section (A-b) moves one fifth counterclockwise by model and sequence. Notice how the descending bass line conflates a-flat minor and C-flat major, allowing F-flat to function as both flat $\hat{6}$ and $\hat{4}$. The tonal contrast in section B is the submediant. Notice how the bass line here conflates the submediant and subdominant, acquiring the function flat $\hat{2}$ for F-flat. In the segment B-c (a little codetta to the first part of B), A-double-flat is acquired as flat $\hat{6}$ of the subdominant, by analogy to F-flat. The second part of B confirms the procedure of modal interchange. It articulates two corresponding formal segments in the contrasting regions, submediant minor and submediant major. This latter region (a quarter of the circle clockwise) is as far in the tonality as the first part ventures.

Turn now to the "tonal problem"—its statement and resolution. Example 7 shows the variant of B' in Part II of the Impromptu and the earlier passage to which it refers. Example 7a is from B, part I: measure 31 links the two segments B-a and B-b (mm. 32-34); measures 35-36 are the first of the two phrases of B-c. Notice the three elements that are projected to the end of the piece (ex. 7c): the bass-line descent, the borrowed flat $\hat{6}$ (A-double-flat), and the use of that pitch to effect the transformation of II, the augmented six-five chord.

Now compare the later passage. Example 7b shows the two corresponding phrases in Part II. The first (mm. 75-78), referring to measure 32, conflates the tonic minor and subdominant minor; the differing pitch between them is A-double-flat, which functions as flat $\hat{2}$ and flat $\hat{6}$. Notice the descending bass line. Although it is configured as if it were a transposition of measure 32 to the upper third, it in fact encompasses the entire span, G-flat-C-flat, now incorporating E-double-flat. It supports the motion to the subdominant minor, which returns to the tonic by means of an augmented six-five chord.

Example 7. The limit to which this tonality is pushed (2)

The melody of the second phrase (mm. 79-82) extends that of the first; the upper neighbor A-double-flat is delayed until measure 81. The descending bass line of this phrase pushes the motion to D-double-flat (the differing pitch in a conflation of c-flat minor and its flat VI, A-double-flat major), and ultimately to C-double-flat, the effect of a major/minor interchange on the Neapolitan, A-double-flat.

Again, the tonic is regained by means of an augmented six-five chord. Thus the means by which balance is restored is an *a priori* relation: the vagrant chord, the augmented six-five on II, functions as both a preparation for the dominant in the tonic and a dominant seventh chord in the region of the Neapolitan.

I have not attempted here a motivic analysis of Schubert's Impromptu, which according to Schoenberg would explicate the interplay between interval and rhythm, as well as their tonal course. Rather I have tried to project a sense of the concrete unity of the melodic and harmonic dimensions, how they work together as functions, that is, forces, in the expression of a particular segment of tonality in its broad sense. I have used as a basis for my analysis a conception of musical space, of which tonality is the background structure, in the hope that this model of musical space might serve as a common ground for the two aspects of the aesthetic situation, expression and comprehension.

James C. Kidd

Tonality in a New Key

Donald Francis Tovey was undoubtedly correct when he remarked that defining tonality was as difficult as describing the taste of a peach. Although his cautionary remark asserts tonality as all-inclusive, his wonderful choice of simile, involving the sense of taste ("how does it taste?" and "sense" as in "do you sense it?" come immediately to mind), a mode of direct, bodily and vivid "knowing" ("sensing") that does not require conscious thought, suggests a useful line of inquiry. To describe and explain tonality fully may lie beyond the reach of words, but the mode by which one perceives tonality ("senses" its "flavor") may not. Tovey's implication that tonality is perceived with the directness and vividness of the sense of taste seems to presume an equally vivid and direct "sense of tonality." This implication in Tovey's remark, that tonality in its perception is more a "sense" than a consciously and cognitively understood "system," touches on several concerns worth pursuing.

Definitions of tonality as an ordering of tones that creates a "loyalty to the tonic" are technically correct, but they convey little of the sense of a performer's or a sensitive listener's experience of tonality. Second, tonality as it functions in melody, without regard to harmony, is an area of inquiry that has never received the amount of attention that it deserves. Third, analytical discussions about or involving tonality almost always concentrate on the long-range features of the tonal-structural hierarchy.

In the following discussion (looking through the other end of the analytical telescope) I examine four diatonic melodies and the questions

James C. Kidd is Chairman of the Hampden-Sydney College Fine Arts Department. He serves the Hampden-Sydney Music Festival as pianist and as Executive Director.

they raise about the nature of melodic tonality and how it is perceived. Is tonality a light switch, on or off, or does it convey varieties of degree? If one can speak of "degrees of tonality," as both a conception and a very real perception, how are these differing degrees manifested? I cannot help thinking here of Schoenberg's remark that "there is still much good music to be written in C major." I used to understand this gnomic remark as some sort of misplaced conservative impulse, rather than the acute statement of someone with a very deep understanding of the meaning, function, and possibilities of tonality.

Behind these questions is a concern with how a performing musician perceives, understands, intuits, and uses tonality in performance (performance being a work played under any circumstances, private or public). The musician's point of view seldom sees print, for many good reasons: a preference for playing over talking; an analytical turn of mind whose workings are primarily intuitive and whose medium is sound, not words; and a working point of view opposite (not necessarily opposed) to that of the musical analyst. Most musicians are skeptical of generalizations about morphology because their focus is always on the specific and idiosyncratic work. Performers constantly search for answers about how a work should present itself, arrived at through intuitively-guided experimentation and a heightened sensitivity to details ("God exists in the details"). These answers tend to be provisional, not final generalizations.

Finally, an event that unexpectedly contributed to the ideas here was a concert that I heard several months ago by the great Indian sarodist Ali Akbar Khan. Hearing through my Western-trained ears, I could not help asking after the fact how a music which does not modulate could have such range, power, beauty, and variety. In trying to understand some of the technical foundations of this unfamiliar and powerful art, I turned to Harold Powers's comprehensive article on "Mode" in the *New Grove Dictionary*. I found something quite unexpected: his sophisticated and highly detailed explanation of the meaning of *rāga* and mode in north Indian music eloquently expressed and articulated certain aspects of Western tonality as I had only dimly defined them to myself, based on my own experience.

Put in simple terms, if the same pitches in a scale can produce totally different *ragas*, different in both structure and emotional character, could not the same be possible in tonal melodies? In other words, are all melodies in C major simply *in* C major, or is there a range of *degrees* of "C-majorness"? I suggest that the richness of tonality can be best approached by attempting to demonstrate how it expresses itself, not as a "thing" or a "given," but as an organic process of self-creation, a process that admits of varying degrees of definition, of identity. Schoenberg's remark resonates here.

Two other useful and provocative statements, from the field of art history, entered the train of thought. The first is from E.H. Gombrich: "But any hierarchical arrangement presupposes two distinct steps, that of *framing* and that of *filling*. The one delimits the field or fields, the other organizes the resultant space."[1] What a potentially beautiful and useful model for the examination of tonal melody. Consider the visual field equivalent to some form of melodic "frame," and the "filling" as the internal relationships of the melody. Applying the concepts of "framing" and "filling" to melody is difficult, of course, because both processes occur in time. Despite these difficulties, they are very useful concepts because they reflect a reciprocity that is perceived in tonal melody—between the areas of register that form themselves (the "frame") and the activity within them (the "filling")—and they offer a way of demonstrating that melodies can and do differ in their degree of tonality.

As with visual images, one can think of melodies which are clearly delimited, clearly "framed" ("Twinkle, Twinkle, Little Star"), as well as melodies that go beyond any normal "frame" (the opening of Richard Strauss's *Don Juan*), and those that are so mobile in their motion and formation of patterns that no opportunity is given for a "frame" to form (the opening theme of J.S. Bach's D minor Concerto for Harpsichord; the roaming and unpredictable forms of the toccata and fantasy). The clearest example of "framing" is the presentation, early in a performance of Indian music, of the pitches of the *rāga*, setting the melodic stage for the "filling" to come. To this particular set of Western ears, what happens next can be anything from very tightly and intensely focused in its patterns (what can be called "strong tonality") to a fluid and free use of patterns (creating an effect of "weakened tonality" although that term does not apply stylistically). But the wide range of possibilities in tonal focus, the vivid differences in degree of concentration on particular melodic-rhythmic patterns in Indian music, raises the question whether there are examples of tonal usage in Western music that are roughly parallel.

One reads constantly of Wagner's "weakened tonality," the result of his profuse use of accidentals foreign to the key, an overloading of implied tonal functions that results in a kind of short-circuiting. The

[1]E.H. Gombrich, *The Sense of Order: A Study in the Psychology of Decorative Art* (Ithaca, 1979), p. 75.

reverse implication seems to be that a composer using only the pitches of a given diatonic key, with no additions of accidentals, is assured of producing a tonality that is stronger, clearer and more focused (though it is difficult to know with any precision what these adjectives mean) than Wagner's. Not necessarily so—there are composers whose diatonic tonality has much less "loyalty to the tonic" than Wagner's without resorting to accretions from outside the pitches of the key. I am thinking of Gabriel Fauré, who so often altered the normal tonal hierarchy without departing from diatonicism in his melodies. Gertrude Stein, in a comment on the visual arts, very beautifully describes such a condition of musical tonality:

> Everything I have done has been influenced by Flaubert and Cézanne, and this gave me a new feeling about composition. Up to that time composition had consisted of a central idea, to which everything else was an accompaniment and separate but which was not an end in itself, and Cézanne conceived the idea that in composition one thing was as important as another thing. Each part is as important as the whole, and that impressed me enormously . . .[2]

Fauré embodied this condition in much of his music, but particularly in the theme from the thirteenth Barcarolle, to be discussed shortly.

From a technical point of view, Stein's "central idea" in a composition might as easily stand for the "tonic" in a musical work, or perhaps conventionally-directed narrative in literature. The value of her comment is that she describes the condition furthest removed from Gombrich's model of "framing and filling," suggesting that just as visual composition admits a tremendous range of differences in the use and power of hierarchic patterning, the same might be true of tonality in musical terms. But whatever use is made of hierarchy, in both art and music one perceives a mode of order even in the freest and loosest usages (visual composition and musical tonality).

I must ask a chicken-and-egg question: is it not the way that the parts interact, play, cohere, resist, imply, fulfill, surprise, and otherwise disport themselves that produces the perceived "composition" in an art work and the perceived "form and tonality" in a piece of music? Do not viewers and listeners both begin with details, at the bottom of the pyramid, and gradually move to the composition and form at the top? I do not wish to raise an unanswerable philosophical question, but

[2]From *Primer;* quoted in Marjorie Perloff, *The Poetics of Indeterminacy: Rimbaud to Cage* (Princeton, 1981). p. 91.

simply to make the point that with many art-works, the viewer creates the visual composition from the ground up, working from the details, *not* beginning with the composition and moving down to the details. In a real sense, however, one is never "working toward" visual composition or tonality in music—it is these that determine and help control how one perceives and responds to the inherent pattern of details. Although a musician senses the emerging form and structure of a work in performance, there is an intense focus of attention on how the details connect, tone to tone, from beginning to end. The performer creates the tonality of the work in performance. Because tonality involves (but is not totally defined by) the emergence of one pitch as some sort of focal point, and because a fundamental question ("how does it move?") that all musicians ask themselves is answered in performance, I suggest that rhythm-and-motion is an intrinsic aspect of perceived tonality.

In everyday speech we speak prose, and we must go out of our way if we wish not to, turning to rhymed couplets, for example. But this practice would be perceived as eccentric and odd, even if temporarily refreshing; prose is inescapable. The function of tonality in music is not inescapable in quite the same way because tonality, that "loyalty to a tonic" and the many ways it is manifested, is expressed in a variety of ways that still remain recognizably "tonal." As Tovey so eloquently stated, tonality (what we call the orderly environment of musical motion and relationships) is finally impossible to define and describe fully because it is so all-inclusive.

My purpose is to describe some of the fundamental ways that a musician creates and perceives tonality, and how this sensation differs with every piece. One of the impossible things to capture precisely in words is the sensation of how tones in a melody, one to the next, relate to each other, what can be called the dynamics (not to be confused with loudness-softness) of connections. Yet it is through these that a musician senses the specific tonality of the work at the same time that it is being created and made palpable.

I have chosen four short diatonic melodies for discussion, the first three in C major and the last transposed to C for convenience in comparison. To support my point that melodies in the same key convey decided differences in their degree (flavor) of tonality, the following melodies came unbidden to mind: the opening theme from the third movement of Mozart's Piano Sonata in C major, K. 309; the opening theme of the development section of the first movement of Schubert's Piano Sonata in A major, op. posth.; the opening theme of the thirteenth Barcarolle of Gabriel Fauré; and the opening theme of "Jimbo's

Lullaby'' from Debussy's *Children's Corner,* originally in B-flat major/
G minor, here transposed to C and raised two octaves for ease of reading.

Despite their shared diatonicism and their shared tonality, and although
the first three of them begin by descending from G through a fifth to
C, from a performer's point of view each of them moves in a decidedly different way. As a consequence, each of them expresses a different
sense of tonality.

In initially trying to uncover the character and shape of a phrase, a
musician freely experiments with how the tones move from one to
another, not so much asking (consciously) ''why?'' as ''how do the
tones seem to want to connect, to relate to each other?'' (subconsciously).
The sensation one feels in this learning process, as well as in the finished
performance, can be described as sensitivity to, and response to,
resistance, degrees of momentum, inertia, attraction and repulsion, and
their fluctuations. The conventional metaphor of ''tension and release''
has always seemed insufficient in conveying the richness of connections. (In the real world, inertia and momentum are predictable
constants—in the tonal world, most often they are not.) The nature of
this perceived ''resistance'' must be well understood.

It is a perceived aspect of tonality that all melodic tones seem to exist in a state of varying tension with one another, but it is a tension
of great delicacy, not unlike the surface tension on a liquid, palpable
but easily broken. Play a series of random tones to yourself at the
keyboard to feel an absence of ''surface tension.'' Only the hope of
palpable relationships exists because any sensation of arrival or departure is lacking—only undifferentiated motion remains. The inherent surface tension of tonal melody (whose absence is the hallmark of a weak
performance) is due to the presence of some degree of predictability,
a latent sense of anticipation which is either foiled or fulfilled. But the
repertory of seven diatonic pitches does not ensure a sense of tonality
because if played randomly the sense of anticipation is blocked and
frustrated.

Motion in a tonal melody is always motion with a point of arrival
implied, whether or not it is reached immediately, delayed, or never
reached. But the quality of motion in reaching the point of arrival (in
most cases a new point of departure) takes a profusion of forms, and
it is this fact that constantly challenges, invigorates, and satisfies the
performer and listener. Again, what I call the ''quality of motion'' is
felt in terms of greater and lesser degrees of resistance: sometimes motion
from one tone to another is fluid with no sense of resistance or inhibi-

tion whatever, whereas other motion is filled with a sensation of momentum and resistance to be overcome in reaching the next tone.

The performer's experimental process of moving from tone to tone in learning, interiorizing and finally creating some kind of shape in a work occurs largely unconsciously and intuitively. It is true for most musicians that the memory of a phrase is not the shape of A-to-B, as a gestalt, but the remembered web and pattern of the ebb and flow of resistance in continuity in getting from point A to point B, remembered in their muscles, and stored away in their rhythmic consciousness (a function of the musical mind little understood). The delicate grid of correspondences between tones in a melody can never be fully described in words, but the fact of its existence invites inquiry into perhaps a deeper understanding of tonality, how it makes such correspondences possible in a dazzling array, and reciprocally how these correspondences make real the sense of tonality, "framing" and "filling" being indivisible sides of the musical coin.

Although each of the first three examples descends through a fifth from G to C, this morphological resemblance is less important than the nature of the motion in each case, and the qualitative sense of the arrival on the presumed tonic C. (I qualify the meaning of tonic because it is not given and should not be presumed; it must reveal itself in the pattern of continuity.) Each phrase has a quite distinct sense of motion, qualitatively different from the other two. One can only characterize, not fully explain, these differences, but they are felt with all the vividness of watching a stone fall, following the path of a slightly lighter-than-air balloon, or seeing a feather descend.

Example 1. Mozart, Sonata in C major K. 309, III

Mozart's phrase (ex. 1) floats down, quite directly but in a poised and unhurried manner, to its point of arrival, one that could not be more clear. At that point, what little momentum the phrase contains is dissipated—it seems to bounce on the repeated Cs. The sensation of these three Cs is nearly identical to watching a small ball bouncing on a table-top, losing energy in a mathematically-graded way with each decreasing rebound. Mozart's eighth-note upbeat is nearly passive, wanting to hold slightly before gently nudging the phrase over the edge into motion. It is difficult to imagine a more simple initiation of motion, or straight-forwardness of intention, yet there is an elegance and almost a feeling of insouciance in the descent. What is the "resistance" present? It is simply the minute resistance of momentum to be overcome in starting the phrase on its downward path, a gentle reluctance on the part of the upbeat. In two measures, Mozart creates the most elegant gesture, free of resistance (subjectively free of any concern), a musical embodiment of *noblesse oblige*.

Example 2. Schubert, Sonata in A major D. 959, I

Turning to Schubert's phrase (ex. 2), here the opening descent is a precipitous fall, a stone dropping. The first note, G, feels tightly wound, active and impatient. But why impatient? It is impatient to avoid the lower C (a tone in Mozart's phrase that is embraced, and almost relished in repetition) and to get to higher ground on the A a step above, its next point of arrival. Schubert's C is to be avoided, used only as a glancing blow, a momentary point of rebound. If Mozart's arrival on C suggests the relaxed exhalation of a sigh, Schubert's arrival on A is fraught with the tension of an even greater inhalation—the performer and listener feel the tremendous amount of energy in pushing upward but a single step against strong resistance. The "impatience" of the G in measure 2 seems even greater, the rush of the falling sixteenths increased, and the strong arrival on D even more tense and insufficent.

In but two measures Schubert has created a dramatic image of struggle, a gesture struggling and searching for some kind of release and escape. Schubert's intensification of motion, and impatient foreshortening, is the opposite extreme of Mozart's leisurely satisfaction. If Mozart's phrase contains little initial "surface tension," Schubert's phrase is highly charged with it.

If Mozart's phrase floats down, and Schubert's falls headlong, Fauré's phrase (ex. 3), with its orderly descending sequential steps, lies somewhere in between. The opening measure establishes G's position as firm and comfortable, and quite secure and stable (sensed at that moment, confirmed in retrospect), reluctant to give way. Descending motion in a melody, despite a metaphorical comparison with gravity, is not always easy or without resistance, as Fauré's phrase clearly shows. Each step down by sequential thirds (first to E and then to C) is achieved with increasing difficulty. But Fauré breaks the sequence on the arrival at C, temporarily reinforcing its sudden prominence before deceiving us by allowing the motion to continue to the real point of arrival, D in measure 5, the first actual point of repose.

Example 3. Fauré, Barcarolle no. 13 op. 116

These openings (and, as we shall see, their continuations) reveal a great deal not only about the various ways in which a phrase can move through identical musical spaces, but about the qualitative *degree of tonality* that is expressed and at work. Considered in conventional terms, each of these phrases begins in what any musician would call C major, yet the primacy of C understood as the tonic differs in each: Mozart unconcernedly embraces C as the first point of arrival; Schubert treats the C off-handedly, as if it barely existed; and Fauré uses the C as a deceptive first point of arrival, reached with a certain amount of resistance, and as if it were simply just another step in the descending sequence. "Loyalty to a tonic" must be understood as quite flexible.

Aside from the greater and lesser prominence of the tonic C in these three examples, these differences also suggest that each phrase creates a unique set of relationships among the remaining tones, that each phrase is expressing its own degree of tonality. Another major indication of this is the palpable differences among the dominant Gs, the differing functions that they play in each: Mozart's G is the most passive, and conventional, tonal dominant function; Schubert's G is a tense center of melodic motion, one that seems to want desperately to abdicate its primary and central position, anywhere but to the tonic C; and Fauré's G, the most stable and rooted, yields ground with quiet reluctance.

But the qualitative differences in the functional roles of the Cs and Gs in the three phrases are only symptomatic tips of the iceberg: the fundamental differences in the degree of tonality of the phrases are perceived through the different ways that they move, and here words can only evoke qualities of motion. I suggest that what tonality provides the composer (shared by performer and listener in performance) is a systematic ordering that makes possible a tremendous range of qualities of motion, not a system of order in itself. It is motion that a composer creates and modulates, and it is the music's inherent intentions in motion (not quite the same as the "composer's intentions") that the performer works to divine and recreate in performance and that has a life of its own embodied in the musical fibre.

Part of the beauty of Mozart's phrase is the sensation that it almost "plays itself," requiring little need for the performer's intrusion. The only detail that requires special care is the repeated-note pattern which is consistent (see mm. 1-2, 3-4, 9-10 and 11-12). Each time, the three notes must be buoyant and gradually lose energy with subtle gradation. But in measures 10 and 12 Mozart chooses to embellish the third and last note of the repetition, not simply for the sake of variety but so as to transform this note's function from passive to active. The effect of the added turn is not unlike watching the ball bounce twice, then suddenly, without warning or explanation, bounce higher on the third rebound. This last note now *leads* to the next tone, forging an active and connected leap upward where before only a passive and inactive gap had been heard. This reinterpretation creates an unexpected new sensation of connection and continuity.

The sense of ease and absence of any resistance in the opening eight measures of Mozart's phrase (the antecedent portion) is deceptively preparing the listener for unpredictable and unexpected changes in the sense of motion and continuity to come. Beginning at measure 9 we hear the same material, but the single added detail of the turn changes the anatomy of the phrase, bringing the motion to life—earlier passive upward leaps (see mm. 2 and 4) now are active, "reaching" up and connecting in a way not heard before. And it is in measure 15 that this beautifully placid melody suddenly encounters white water, dramatically opening up register in measures 16 and 17 beyond the original "frame" of the octave, moving quickly and decisively with upward leaps in each measure, sweeping to the rapid approach and arrival on the tonic C in measure 19. The entire passage gradually comes to life because Mozart takes it (and us) through three different stages of musical motion: stage 1 (mm. 1-8), regal and unruffled; stage 2 (mm. 9-15), intensification of previously passive leaps providing a new sense of connection and continuity; and stage 3 (mm. 16-19), leaping and surging motion. In microcosm, compare measures 2 and 3 with the almost abrupt arrival on the C in measures 18 and 19.

The gradation of the three stages of motion in Mozart's phrases carries us from motion that is effortless (elegantly rolling off a log) into motion that contains more tension and sense of inertia to be overcome into, finally, motion that not only is much faster but encounters unexpected resistance. In Gombrich's terms, Mozart's melody is initially beautifully "framed" by the octave, the "filling" simply reinforcing the clarity of the "frame," all motion being systematically (and easily) led down to the tonic by sequential patterns. But in the second stage, Mozart makes us aware of the tonal effort involved in reaching up an octave in measure 10 and up a third in measure 12—the floating ease of descent has been modified, having imposed on it ascending effort. One has the presentiment at this point that the initial "frame" is becoming insufficient, that the previously relaxed "filling" is now beginning to work against the "frame." In the third stage, the pattern of "filling" actually does break through the octave "frame" and at the same time produces motion of quite a different kind, dramatically leaping from register to register. The tonic C in measure 19 is now not easily achieved, but must be reached with effort that, in context, feels nearly frantic. In this general transformation, the coolness of the opening is left far behind. From acquiescence to resistance, and the consequent changes in the quality of the musical motion, is a tonal transformation without leaving the confines of C major.

Which C is the stronger and more prominent, that of measure 1 or that of measure 19? Motion flows easily to the first, but motion seems to force itself onto the second. Is a tonic clearer by acquiescence or by resistance? The question misses a fundamental point. The reality of the passage resides in the differing qualities of musical motion produced, in what I would call the differing degrees of tonality, perceived not by the tonic's role, whether inviting or resisting, but by the musical motion in relation to it.

With Mozart as a model, what can be said of the motion in the Schubert and Fauré passages, their quality of motion being the key not only to a beautiful performance but to their degree and character of tonality? Unlike the subtle transformation that occurs in Mozart's passage, Schubert's is more of a piece, happening much more quickly and in less time. Schubert's also lacks the clear sense of Mozart's "frame," giving instead an impression of tonal claustrophobia. The sense of "frame" that exists—defined by the initial tones (Gs in measures 1 and 2), the strong points of arrival which are lengthened in duration (A in measure 1 and D in measure 2), and the repeated Es in measures 3 and 4—feels restricted, preparing the search for something beyond. The motion is nearly violent in its ebb-and-flow, the first two measures searching for a crack in the tonal wall, with the increasing momentum of the repeated Es in measures 3 and 4 generating energy to break through, but to what? In conventional terms, Schubert powerfully reinforces traditionally weak degrees of the scale ($\hat{6}$, $\hat{2}$ and $\hat{3}$), while functionally bypassing what should be the actual tonic C. Although one can say that Schubert's passage is "in C major," it is an explosive and highly volatile form of it, one struggling to break free of its tonal restraints. All the potential energy that is so quickly generated in the first three measures is used to break down the tonal wall to arrive at a completely unpredictable point—F-sharp, the furthest remove from C major. (As it continues, the melody repeats itself in B major and returns for yet another statement in C major before unleashing its energy fully in the second return to B major, an outpouring that concludes a remarkable passage.)

If the Mozart phrase seems to "play itself" (the result of a fine and sensitive performance, one that finds the mid-point between mannerism and diffidence) with a spaciousness enjoyed by player and listener, Schubert's phrase demands a nervous intensity from the performer to match that quality inherent in its motion. (If played without intensity, "magisterially," it will only sound silly.) In Mozart's phrase, the descending sixteenth notes are utterly equal in length, weight and placement, with even a subtle rhythmic tendency to pull back as they approach the C, the opposite of Schubert's whose rush and implied accelerando sling us forcefully to the third beat of measures 1 and 2. Mozart fills the opening fifth with equal steps, and with equanimity; in Schubert's hands the same tones (F-E-D-C) increase the impression of *absence* in the same fifth, creating a sense of gap, by their impetuousness. In Mozart, we are aware of each step with absolute clarity, but the descent in Schubert is a single hurried gesture, a rush, nearly blurred, a powerfully functioning upbeat, one that intensifies with each repetition, becomes almost obsessive in measures 3 and 4.

The difference in the qualitative motion in these phrases is only partly due to Schubert's quicker tempo: Mozart's phrase moves with lightness and elegance, but Schubert's with considerable weight and dynamism and a general tension resulting from the absence of satisfying points of arrival. Schubert's tonality feels tightly wound, kinetic, unable to release its pent-up energy, partly because the actual ''frame'' of the melody is oddly askew compared to usual tonal usage—despite the opening descent of a fifth, the actual ''frame'' is the fifth from D to A, *not* C to G. Notice the pattern of prominent tones: G-A-G-D-E-F-sharp (!). Before the ''frame'' can be completely filled by the stepwise ascent to the upper A, it is shattered by the F-sharp, the unexpected intruder. In only four measures, Schubert produces a musical embodiment of unease, obsessiveness. The rhythmic patterning is orderly and rational in its acceleration, but when joined to the tonal insecurity, and to the struggle not to be confined in C major, the phrase nearly surges out of control, touching the border of the rational. Schubert's tonality here is not so much unstable as it is unwilling and recalcitrant. And it creates a force in the melodic connections that is visceral, going far beyond in dramatic tension anything in Mozart's phrase.

The process and shape of Fauré's phrase, as with so many of his melodies, seems quite clear and apparent both to the ear and eye, but it belies other strong underlying qualities that are present. If one applies Gombrich's model, the following generalization emerges: beginning from its starting point G, the phrase descends sequentially, with a temporary point of respose on D (following the deceptive point of arrival on C) in measure 5 before continuing the descent to the implied-but-not-structurally-reached lower G, the outer limit of the ''frame,'' from which it ascends rather quickly back to its starting point. The second phrase follows the same general pattern in measures 9-17, not reaching so low this second time around but ascending to the high, repeated A, from which motion moves back by half-steps to the G. The ''frame'' is clear, an octave bounded by the outer Gs (the upper actual, the lower clearly implied), and it is ''filled'' with sequential motion that is orderly and quite easy to follow, yet . . .

This approach is perfectly reasonable analytically, but it misses the predominant character of this passage, the uncanny equality in function of the scale steps, and the almost completely unmodulated, strongly inertial forward motion that prevails from beginning to end. Like Mozart's passage, Fauré's should sound as if it is ''playing itself,'' but in place of elegant dance steps here we have a large boulder rolling slowly, and admitting no impediments. One cannot help thinking of Gertrude Stein's remark, of which this phrase is a musical embodiment:

388 JAMES C. KIDD

". . . one thing was as important as another thing. Each part is as important as the whole . . ."

Tonality by its nature, and by patterns of usage across musical styles, encourages differentiation of function among the tones, the use of hierarchy finally to produce "loyalty" to a single tone, the tonic. Tonality in most of its manifestations is aristocratic, not democratic. Yet here is an example that serves as an exception to these patterns—Fauré has produced, as he so often did, a melody all of whose parts exist in a remarkable degree of functional equality. I suggest that his primary purpose was to create the quality of strong, undifferentiated motion, motion with an underlying forcefulness and unstoppable momentum, motion of calm intensity.

The paradox of this passage is that if "loyalty" to a specific tone exists, here the tone is not the tonic C but the dominant G, yet one would not describe the passage as non-tonal or even weakly tonal. The G remains secure and predominant with no need to be resolved—the tonic C is not avoided or evaded, it is simply a tone equal to its fellows, no more, no less. Mozart's G is willingly obeisant to its tonic C, Schubert's G is nervously suspicious of the potential gravitational pull of its tonic C, but Fauré's G has no fear of competition from its C which is just another member of the tonal proletariat.

Fauré creates this functional equality among the tones, and the powerful smoothness of their motion, by ingeniously employing sequences of thirds, sequences that even when interrupted imply their continuation. If one continues a descending sequence by thirds from G, the natural point of arrival is the starting point: G-E-C-A-F-D-B-G. It should be noted that every pitch of the diatonic scale is included in this sequence. In Fauré's phrase, two "frames" of a fifth easily form themselves, both of them containing G: G-E-C and D-B-G. Only the tones A and F are excluded. However, the first descending sequence is broken off in measure 3 by the tone A, and similarly in measure 11. A also figures prominently in measures 13 and 14. F figures prominently in two roles, as the lower neighbor of G, enhancing its stability (mm. 1 and 9), and as the lowest point reached by the melody in measure 6, emphasized by being left by leap from the F-sharp.

Although the melody gives the impression of moving primarily by stepwise motion, the underlying structure is motion by thirds: G-E-C in measures 1-3 and 9-11 (with the next step of the sequence, A, being a point of reversal); and, D-B-G-B-D in measures 5-8. By being circular, the symmetry of motion in thirds, either up or down, precludes the emergence of C as a clear tonal center unless the composer chooses to break the flow of the sequential thirds and give the tonic C special emphasis, something Fauré does only temporarily in measures 3-4 and in measure 11.

Fauré combines the sequential motion in thirds with the palindromic rhythmic motive (♩ ♪ ♪ ♩), containing a powerful tendency toward closure. It is a strange combination that yields special results. The natural tendencies of a descending melodic line are to get faster, to get softer, and to release any tension or resistance to the final point of arrival. Fauré reverses each of these tendencies in his descending phrase.

From the performer's point of view, something quite unexpected occurs on the last note in each of the first four measures, a change in rhythmic tendency on each (indicated in the diagram below, the small arrows indicating directional tendency).

m. 1   m. 2   m. 3   m. 4   m. 5

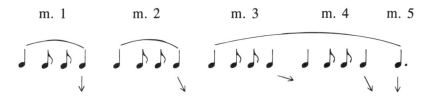

The rhythmic pattern within each measure is closed, the final note "pulling back." But in the context of the descending sequence, this last note in each measure takes on a second and contradictory function, that of an upbeat. The two functions tug at each other with the result that the last note in each measure feels psychologically longer and more charged with tension in each succeeding measure (a major reason for the "density" of the motion). The repeated C across the barline of measures 3 and 4 produces an elision and actual elongation, the point of highest tension, preparing for the cushioned and relaxed arrival on D in measure 5.

The sheer amount of implied rubato in these first five measures (which if made explicit in performance undercuts the tensile continuity) is even more remarkable in being embodied beneath the innocent and orderly façade of a simple descending sequence. In Schubert's opening phrase the struggle is apparent, but in Fauré's phrase it is more latent and tightly reined in. Schubert's phrase finds release by breaking out of the key to the F-sharp. The momentary release of tension in Fauré's phrase is purely rhythmic, the increased motion of measures 5 and 6 moving down through another fifth of range twice as fast, and much more easily, gradually slowing in measures 7 and 8 to lead back to the repetition in measure 9. The surging-and-pausing in Schubert has no place in Fauré's stylistic world whose motion, by comparison, is not quite uniform and not quite placidly reserved, but is certainly quietly relentless in the density of its progress.

Such an approach to melody has the danger of uniformity and formlessness, features that Fauré gracefully avoids. His melody is unusual in seeming always directed, never seeming to wander from its central purpose. His control of melodic direction and graded rhythmic pacing is extremely subtle, producing a wonderful fluidity and unforced momentum. Melodic motion within the tonality and the resulting shapes are so clear, with G as the anchor of their "frame," that the absence of a conventional tonic is not an issue. It is extraordinary that one can say of this passage that "each part is as important as the whole" with no sacrifice of form and shape.

These three examples of melody have been shown to move in quite different ways, with strikingly different degrees of weight, momentum, and resistance, creating environments for themselves that also differ in the amount and distribution of what I have called "surface tension." Despite these differences, they do share a fundamental feature in the most general sense: each, in its own terms, has a strong sense of direction, a sense of "getting somewhere." That feature of melody tends to be a norm that crosses major stylistic barriers. There are exceptions, however, and one of the clearest, simplest, and most eloquent examples is the opening melody of Debussy's "Jimbo's Lullaby" (ex. 4).

Example 4. Debussy, *Children's Corner*, "Jimbo's Lullaby"
(transposed)

There is nice irony in the fact that Debussy places his melody low in the bass, to reflect the character of a little stuffed elephant, but that the melody itself does not move so much as it floats—what could be less appropriate to an elephant, even a toy one? He has created a musical image that is exquisitely suspended. Movement presumes some kind of goal, but here Debussy has created simply motion, delicately balanced around two poles. The melody moves in a beautifully modulated way, but without progressing. The satisfaction that this passage gives to the perfomer is the constant ebb-and-flow of rhythmic tendency whose delicacy is that of a soap-bubble.

The opening phrase tenuously balances, or hovers, between G and E. The minor third separating them has a halo of a fifth, but the A is simply the upper neighbor to G just as the D is the lower neighbor to E. What Debussy achieves is a phrase that does not commit "loyalty" to a single tone, but rather to two tones in a condition of functional equivalence. How the first two notes are played determines whether a performance stands or falls. The G does not "move" or "fall" to the lower E so much as float down to it. The environment here is gravity-free. Not a hint of tension exists in these first two notes, nor a sense of a normal melodic "connection." Should the G feel directed or drawn toward the E, the E's instant prominence will destroy the balance within the phrase (one that cannot be restored subsequently), its beauty and its point. The eighth notes gently accelerate in bringing the line back up to G (floated onto, and softened at arrival, just as the first E). It is the most subtle balancing of rhythmic tendency and melodic implications that produces the sense of suspension, of gravity-free motion. The wings of the butterfly are apparent in a sensitive performance.

The second phrase becomes slightly more animated, increasing the distance between the poles from a third to a fourth, from A up to D (or D down to A—it does not matter because upward and downward motion balance out, neither predominating), an extension and free development of the first phrase, opening up to introduce the high E. The motion is ideally without a feeling of pulse, the eighth notes intrinsically moving ahead without being "measured," the half notes relaxed and expansive—the freedom and gentle flexibility gives the sensation of melismatic plainchant.

I do not know how to categorize this passage technically, but what I do know with utter conviction is that its quality of motion is of a very special order, not light, not slow, not soft, but totally free of any resistance or surface tension. Because almost all melody reflects in some way the sensations of bodily motion, it can with more than metaphorical accuracy be called "embodied." Debussy's melody is simply "disembodied." What a far distance from Fauré, whose melodies so often evoke for me the sensation of walking in water with its constant and fluid resistance demanding a constant pressure in response.

My discussion of these melodies indicates some of the ways that a musician understands and controls the sense of tonality in performance (in purely melodic terms), tonality being a sensation of *degrees of tension and resistance,* tonality being the individual *character* of the musical motion. Musicians learn about tonality by responding to the quality of motion inherent in the tonally-ordered tones, the hierarchic patterns of connection, sensed dynamically. Tonality is not something generalized and abstract, it is a living environment that both performer and listener recognize and respond to through sensitivity to the qualitative differences in motion. In the most real sense, it is the perceived and realized quality of motion that *is* tonality. For the musician, motion is the primary perceptual mode through which it is "sensed" and "tasted."

It may appear odd not only to associate tonality and rhythm, but to make them conceptually and perceptually indissoluble, yet that is the final and primary point that I offer from my own experience. This equivalence appears less strange if one remembers the meaning of tonality as it applies in the visual arts, the vast array of color tones, hues and values that are possible in combination. There is no question that tonality in visual terms admits of many degrees and characters, and I suggest that the same condition exists in real, perceptual terms in music, that behind the abstract Platonic notion of Tonality exists an array of tonalities. It is their degree and character by which we recognize them, and to which we respond. If we can distance ourselves from restrictive, conventional definitions of tonality (as Tovey asserts, so insufficient), a fuller understanding of tonality and its rhythmic foundation may be possible. Perhaps Schoenberg was right.

Robert G. Hopkins

When a Coda is More than a Coda: Reflections on Beethoven

It should be clear that we have not thought enough about the functions of codas in sonata-form movements. For evidence of this we need only examine the definitions commonly given for the term coda. *The New Harvard Dictionary of Music* defines coda as "a concluding section extraneous to the form as usually defined; any concluding passage that can be understood as occurring after the structural conclusion of a work and that serves as a formal closing gesture."[1] In *The New Grove Dictionary* Roger Bullivant says "The most important use of the term 'coda' is in sonata form, where it refers to anything occurring after the end of the recapitulation."[2]

Joseph Kerman points out that since we cannot identify a common function for codas in sonata-form movements, the term coda simply refers to a position rather than a musical function.[3] But viewing a coda as whatever follows the end of the recapitulation invites the attitude that the coda is always an appendage to the movement proper—that it is something of an after-thought, a superfluous attachment. Richard Norton, in his recent book *Tonality in Western Culture*, writes: "Having stated the expository material in the recapitulation in the tonic, the movement is ostensibly over, but there is the coda."[4]

[1]*The New Harvard Dictionary of Music*, s.v. "coda."
[2]*The New Grove Dictionary of Music and Musicians*, s.v. "coda."
[3]Joseph Kerman, "Notes on Beethoven's Codas," in *Beethoven Studies 3*, ed. Alan Tyson (Cambridge, 1982), p. 141.
[4]Richard Norton, *Tonality in Western Culture* (University Park, PA, 1984), p. 207.

Robert G. Hopkins is Assistant Professor of Music at Hamilton College. He is completing a book on patterns and processes of closure in the symphonic works of Gustav Mahler.

Norton's point of view may be appropriate when considering most sonata forms in music of the mid-to-late eighteenth century—pieces in which the coda generally serves merely to extend the tonic, providing conclusive cadences while at the same time expanding the work to a proper musical proportion. But is Norton's view appropriate to a consideration of sonata forms in music of the nineteenth century? Often in Beethoven's music it is not.

The problem stems from applying an eighteenth-century model of sonata form to sonata forms in nineteenth-century music. For example, applying the model of sonata form James Webster offers in *The New Grove Dictionary*: "A typical sonata-form movement consists of a two-part tonal structure, articulated in three main sections."[5] Of course, the three "main" sections are exposition, development, and recapitulation, and the two-part tonal structure is completed with the restatement of expository material in the tonic. Yet often the coda is nearly as long as or longer than one or more of the so-called "main" sections. Frequently the coda contains the climax of the movement. Why, then, is it never counted as a main section? Webster gives us an answer in his article: "Save for the functions of expansion...and 'peroration' (Tovey), the structural significance of codas is not well understood. The German expression 'second development' is applicable only to certain parts of certain Beethoven codas; and in any case the function of the development, to prepare the return, cannot be repeated."[6] If the function of preparing the return cannot be repeated, one has to wonder: what do we make of sonatas in which the development and recapitulation are repeated? And what do we make of sonata-rondo forms that have concluding *A* sections?

We should broaden our concept of sonata form beyond that based primarily on eighteenth-century views of harmonic structure and formal symmetry in order to account for the significance of codas in works of the nineteenth century. We need to increase our awareness of the functions and importance of codas in early nineteenth-century sonata forms. In short, we need to build a theory that explains the structural functions of codas and why they became necessary to the work.

Consider the finale of Beethoven's Eighth Symphony. According to most analysts, the coda to this movement lasts almost as long (236 measures) as the rest of the movement (266 measures). If coda means "tail," then here they would surely have us believe that the tail is wagging the dog. But the problem of viewing this coda as whatever occurs

[5]*The New Grove Dictionary*, s.v. "sonata form."
[6]Ibid.

after the recapitulation is obvious: it actually consists of a second development, and a second recapitulation with its own coda. Leonard Ratner
supports my conclusions about the form of this movement, which is
a type of *ABACA* rondo with coda, where *A* represents the exposition
or recapitulation of a sonata-form movement:[7]

A	B	A	C	A	CODA
1-90	91-160	161-266	267-354	355-437	438-502
P T S K	Development	P T S K	Development	P T S Br	

[P=Primary section, T=Transition, S=Secondary Section, K=Closing,
Br=Bridge]

Not only do measures 267-354 *sound* like a second development, but
the substance and structure of the section conform in many ways to that
of the first development. Both sections begin with an abbreviated return
of the movement's primary theme—a suggestion of sonata-rondo form.
(The initial eleven measures of the first development are transposed
up a perfect fourth to B-flat to begin the second development.) Both
continue with music marked pianissimo in all parts.

Much of the first development is taken up with descending and ascen-
ding scalar passages based on the ♩ ⁊ ♪ | ♩_♩ motive from
the end of the primary theme, initially with the characteristic eighth-
note triplet figure in the background (as in, for instance, ex. 1a). Note
the descending scale patterns in the low strings and the ascending scale
patterns in the violins. In the midst of the second development (as shown
in ex. 1b) we find similar material, this time without the characteristic
rhythm found in the first development, but with the triplet figures
throughout in the background. Descending scale patterns in the low
strings are countered by ascending scale patterns in the first bassoon
and first clarinet. Here, however, the scale patterns are drawn from
a new source: the melody played by the second violins near the beginning of the section, in measures 282-86 (a descending scale from A
to D followed by a descending leap E – A).

---

[7]See Leonard G. Ratner, *Classic Music: Expression, Form, and Style* (New York, 1980),
pp. 254-55, and "Key Definition—A Structural Issue in Beethoven's Music," *Journal
of the American Musicological Society* 23 (1970): pp. 482-83. Alternatively, one could
consider the second development and second recapitulation (mm. 267-437) a written-
out, varied repeat of the second half of a sonata form.

Example 1a. Beethoven, Symphony No. 8, IV.

Example 1b. Beethoven, Symphony No. 8, IV.

From Development 2:

In both developments the music builds from pianissimo to a fortissimo climax just prior to the return of the primary theme. In both a sudden decrease in dynamics and orchestration drops the dynamic level to piano and then pianissimo, when the bassoon and timpani begin playing octave F's to signal the return. (Compare measures 151-60 from the end of the first development to measures 345-54 from the end of the second development.)

When one considers the similarities between the two developments, and the fact that the beginnings of the first and second recapitulations are identical for eighteen measures (following identical statements of octave F's in the bassoon and timpani),[8] it seems clear that measures 267-354 constitute a second development section. After eighteen measures the second recapitulation continues with the well-known episode in F-minor, which helps to resolve the fortissimo C-sharp in the melody. A transition leads to a *complete* statement of the second

[8] After these eighteen measures, the second recapitulation continues with transitional material for thirty-five measures before the secondary section begins at measure 408. It is interesting to note that the transition in the first recapitulation is also thirty-five measures long.

theme in the tonic, something that does not usually occur in a Beethoven coda.⁹ In the first recapitulation the second theme is first stated in D-flat, then in F. In the second recapitulation it is stated in the tonic both times. A short bridge section leads to the real coda of the movement in measure 438, following a rest marked with a fermata in all parts. The real coda consists of an elaborate prolongation of the tonic that concludes this quite remarkable finale.

It may be that some analysts have been misled because the structure of the finale from the second development to the end typifies what Ratner calls an "extended coda," namely "a harmonic digression," "a firm return to the tonic, generally with the opening theme," and "a set of emphatic cadential gestures."¹⁰ Nevertheless, in this finale the "harmonic digression" constitutes a second development, and the "firm return to the tonic" extends to a second recapitulation. Thus, measures 267-502 are really much more than a coda. This argues that we should be more concerned about the function of the coda and that it is a mistake to assume a coda is everything that follows a recapitulation. It so happens that the actual coda to the movement (mm. 438-502), like those in numerous sonata forms of the eighteenth century, does serve to prolong the tonic and provide conclusive cadences in order to bring about final closure. But in many of Beethoven's sonata forms the coda obviously accomplishes much more than that; it is more than an appendage to the movement proper—it is more than a coda, as the term is typically defined.

There are at least three reasons why codas take on special significance. One is that, as Joseph Kerman points out, "with Beethoven a sonata-form movement is also 'the story of a theme'—the first theme—and the exciting last chapter of that story is told in the coda."¹¹ Thus, some codas serve the function of *thematic completion*, as Kerman calls it. A second reason is that there is a kind of *final recapitulation*, a final (perhaps climactic) return to the primary theme of the movement. A third reason is that the coda provides a *harmonic resolution* for the movement when the point of recapitulation or the closing of the recapitulation is harmonically inconclusive. In Beethoven's music we can distinguish codas that serve the functions of thematic completion, final

⁹Kerman, "Notes on Beethoven's Codas," p. 154.
¹⁰Ratner, *Classic Music*, p. 230.
¹¹Kerman, "Notes on Beethoven's Codas," p. 150. In a similar vein, William S. Newman writes that often Beethoven codas "exploit some of the previous thematic elements in a new light. The coda may have all the surprise and charm, then, of a punch line in a short story...." William S. Newman, *The Sonata in the Classic Era* (New York, 1972), p. 158.

recapitulation, or harmonic resolution, but citing these three types of function does not mean that some of Beethoven's codas do not serve other important functions, nor does it mean that these functions are mutually exclusive. They are not.[12] I want to argue, however, that a coda fulfilling one of these functions has far greater significance than that suggested by the common conception of the word coda, a word that needs to refer not only to a concluding section "extraneous to the form" but also, in many nineteenth-century works at least, to a concluding section essential to the form.

Let us now turn to consideration of the functions of codas in other sonata forms by Beethoven. In his article "Notes on Beethoven's Codas" Kerman has ably demonstrated how, as he puts it, "again and again there seems to be some kind of instability, discontinuity, or thrust in the first theme which is removed in the coda."[13] He finds this particularly true in works of Beethoven's second period, such as the first movement of the "Waldstein" Sonata op. 53 in which (as Tovey pointed out) the modulating sequence that begins the movement is rewritten as a tonal sequence in the coda. I should like to add that the coda provides, for the first time in the movement, a "proper" *dominant* preparation (mm. 278-83) for a complete statement of the second theme in the tonic. Previously, of course, the second theme was recapitulated beginning in VI, prepared by its dominant. The coda to this movement thereby normalizes the tonal presentation of both first and second themes. Let me add a few more examples of thematic completion to those mentioned by Kerman.[14]

In the coda to the first movement of the String Quartet in E minor op. 59 no. 2 Beethoven supplies a resolution of the Neapolitan chord and the lowered second degree of the scale which had undermined the stability of the main theme. The last part of the coda is given in example 2. In measures 245-250 the Neapolitan chord repeatedly moves to a i$^6_4$ chord, with the F-naturals in the violins resolving to E's. Previously, in both the exposition and the recapitulation, the F in the primary theme moved up to F# instead of resolving down to the tonic.[15] An extended statement of the opening thematic gesture in the coda thus completes the movement.

---

[12]For example, the coda to the String Quartet in B-flat op. 130 serves to provide both thematic completion and harmonic resolution. See David L. Brodbeck and John Platoff, "Dissociation and Integration: The First Movement of Beethoven's Opus 130," *19th Century Music* 7 (1983), pp. 160-62.

[13]Kerman, "Notes on Beethoven's Codas," p. 149.

[14]Ibid., pp. 148-51.

[15]See measures 7-9 and 147-49.

Example 2. Beethoven, String Quartet op. 59 no. 2, I.

We find another example of thematic completion in the finale to the String Quartet in E-flat op. 127 where perhaps the most striking aspect of the primary theme is the emphasis on A-natural, which leads from A-flat up to B-flat. Yet the implied continuation of this ascending line through C and D to the upper tonic is not realized until the coda. In the exposition and the recapitulation, the ascending line only reaches C.[16] In the coda, however, the implied ascent to the high tonic is explicitly stated, first in the cello in measures 265-68 (derived from the primary theme), and later in the first violin (ex. 3). The main theme returns in modified form at measure 277, but again the ascending line from A-flat only reaches C in measure 279. The ascent up to E-flat

---

[16]The A-flat in measure 5 leads through A-natural to B-flat in measure 8. The B-flat is followed by C, but the C is weak because of its rhythmic position and lack of harmonic support. In measures 187-90 of the recapitulation, the A-flat-A-B-flat-C ascent is repeated, and this time the C (in m. 190) is at the peak of a short crescendo and is supported by a C-major triad.

is finally realized in the first violin in measures 281-285, and confirmed in the closing measures.

Example 3. Beethoven, String Quartet op. 127, IV (the primary theme
begins at m. 277).

Other composers wrote codas that serve the function of thematic completion, too. For instance, in the first movement of Schubert's Sonata in A minor D. 537 (op. posth. 164) the opening theme ends on a dominant chord that is not actually resolved to the tonic (ex. 4a).[17] In the recapitulation, the theme, now transposed to the subdominant, is again open-ended.[18] In the coda, however, the opening theme in the tonic is repeated at measure 188 (ex. 4b), now modified to account for the

Example 4. Schubert, Piano Sonata D 537.

a. From the exposition:

b. From the coda:

[17]The last chord of measure 5 begins a repeat of the opening phrase, which—together with the change in register in the left-hand part—clearly establishes it as the beginning of a phrase rather than as the resolution of the preceding dominant. Though this repeat of the opening phrase could serve both as a beginning and a conclusion, there is little sense of elision, in part because of the contrast in texture.

[18]Since a dynamic accent tends to mark the beginning of a rhythmic grouping, the fortissimo entrance of the main theme at the end of measure 127 emphasizes the separation between the dominant chord in the rest of the measure and the repeat of the main idea.

subdominant statement in the recapitulation: the subdominant chords in measure 191 lead to the cadential resolution i_4^6-V_7-i, which brings harmonic and tonal closure to the theme for the first time. The cadence is repeated in measures 194-95 before two fortissimo tonic chords conclude the movement.

In addition to writing codas that fulfil the function of thematic completion, Beethoven occasionally writes a coda that serves as a final recapitulation of all or most of the primary theme. I am not speaking of codas in which a developmental section leads to a final reminiscence or reference to the theme, but rather to codas in which there is a definite sense of return. By returning to the primary theme which began the movement, Beethoven not only adds weight to the coda, but also enhances closure by symmetrically balancing the form. There is a suggestion of sonata-rondo in this procedure. In the finale of the op. 31 no. 3 Piano Sonata in E-flat, for example, the closing section of the recapitulation leads directly to an extended bridge passage which prolongs the dominant seventh chord and prepares the return to the opening theme—a procedure reminiscent of sonata-rondos.[19]

An emphatic return to the primary theme can act as the climax of the movement. At times a final, emphatic recapitulation of the primary theme follows material that recalls the development, so that we may properly call the coda a kind of peroration. In his *Traité de mélodie*, first published in 1814, Anton Reicha wrote: "Lorsque la coda finit un grand morceau, on peut la comparer à la péroraison d'un discours oratoire."[20] I suggest a definition of peroration adapted from that given in *Webster's New Twentieth Century Dictionary:* "the concluding part of a speech, in which there is a summing up and emphatic recapitulation."[21] The summarizing nature of such codas varies considerably, but generally they refer both to the development and the recapitulation, giving a more or less condensed review of the second and last part of

[19]See also the opening movement of the Piano Sonata in D op. 28. The coda (mm. 438-61) begins with a statement of the primary theme, which is harmonically anchored by a tonic pedal. The end of the theme repeats several times before a final authentic cadence concludes the movement. Thus, the quiet primary theme both begins and ends the movement. Other sonata-form movements by Beethoven that have a final recapitulation include the Piano Sonata in C op. 2 no. 3, I; the Piano Sonata in c op. 13, I; Symphony No. 1 in C op. 21, I and IV; the Piano Sonata in E-flat op. 31 no. 3, I; and the String Quartet in F op. 59 no. 1, I.

[20]Anton Reicha, *Traité de mélodie*, 2nd ed. (Paris, 1832), p. 28. Leonard Ratner cites this description as evidence for a growing recognition of the significance of the coda. See *Classic Music*, p. 231.

[21]*Webster's New Twentieth Century Dictionary*, 2d ed., s.v. "peroration."

the sonata form. Ratner describes such a procedure in his discussion of "extended" codas.[22]

The difference is that to qualify as a peroration the coda should have an emphatic recapitulation of the primary theme, as we find in the third movement of the Piano Sonata in D minor op. 31 no. 2 (ex. 5). In this movement the coda begins in the same way as the development, repeating a chromatically ascending bass line moving from F-sharp to A (mm. 323-35). After the bass reaches A in measure 335, a sixteen-measure dominant prolongation leads to a fortissimo recapitulation of the entire first theme (mm. 351-85), which had previously been stated piano.[23] A concluding passage of repeated authentic cadences fashioned from primary thematic material and a final prolongation of the tonic bring the movement to an end.

Consider, too, the coda in the first movement of the Eighth Symphony, which begins in analogous fashion to the development and moves quickly away from the tonic F major to E-flat major and D-flat major chords (mm. 302-08), thereby imitating in compressed form the C – B-flat – A harmonic succession in the first part of the development proper (mm. 105-32). The descending bass line F – E-flat – D-flat leads to C and an extended dominant (here six measures) that prepares the climactic return of the primary theme played fortissimo.[24]

Several of Mendelssohn's codas incorporate a final recapitulation. For example, in the first movement of the String Quintet No. 2 in B-flat op. 87 the coda begins in the same way as the development and continues with a development of the second theme. This developmental passage leads to a firm return to the tonic accompanied by a fortissimo affirmation of the opening theme in modified form.

In addition to the functions of thematic completion and final recapitulation, one can identify codas that provide harmonic completion or harmonic resolution. The point of recapitulation and the end of the recapitulation are places in a sonata form where a strong confirmation of the tonic is important. Occasionally, however, the tonic is not forcefully established at one of these places, leaving the required harmonic resolution to occur in the coda.

There are many different reasons why a coda might need to provide

[22]Ratner, *Classic Music*, p. 230.
[23]It is remarkable that the entire primary theme is recapitulated. It seems far more common for the primary theme to be stated in an abbreviated and modified form while still providing a definite sense of return.
[24]Other sonata-form movements by Beethoven in which the coda functions as a peroration include the Violin Sonata in c op. 30 no. 2, I; Symphony No. 3 in E-flat op. 55, I; Symphony No. 4 in B-flat op. 60, IV; and Symphony No. 9 in d op. 125, I.

Example 5. Beethoven, Piano Sonata op. 31 no.2, III (the primary theme is repeated at m. 351).

harmonic resolution. For instance, sometimes the return to the tonic at the recapitulation is weak or delayed so that a strong sense of tonic arrival is missing. In the opening movement of Beethoven's String Quartet in F op. 59 no. 1 the ambiguous harmony at the beginning of the primary theme and the general avoidance of root-position tonic chords preclude a satisfying return to the tonic at the point of recapitulation (ex. 6a). Moreover, whereas the initial presentation of the main theme ends with a perfect authentic cadence on a fortissimo tonic chord in measure 19, the restatement of the theme in the recapitulation is varied after thirteen measures and never reaches a cadence in F. Indeed, the first such cadence in the recapitulation is delayed until the beginning of the second theme at measure 307. However, the coda provides the harmonic resolution missing in the recapitulation: the first theme is fully

Example 6. Beethoven, String Quartet op. 59 no. 1, I.

a. Beginning of recapitulation (measure 254)

b. Beginning of coda (measure 348)

harmonized, beginning with root-position tonic chords, at measure 348 (ex. 6b). The crescendo from piano to fortissimo in measures 341-348 dramatizes the arrival of the first theme firmly grounded in the tonic. In some works the secondary thematic section and closing in the recapitulation do not provide adequate confirmation of the tonic, and the coda supplies the harmonic resolution required to bring the movement to a satisfying conclusion. From the standpoint of harmonic structure, then, the coda is absolutely essential, for it—instead of the closing section in the recapitulation—completes the tonal resolution which defines the second part of the tonal structure in the sonata form. In the finale to the Piano Trio in E-flat op. 70 no. 2, for instance, the secondary themes and the closing section are recapitulated in the submediant minor or major, not in the tonic. The closing section, which begins at measure 276, emphasizes the submediant before ending on the dominant in measure 302 (ex. 7). It is not surprising, then, to find a very long coda (almost one-fourth of the movement) saturated with tonic and dominant chords and including a varied restatement of the closing section in the tonic (mm. 336-55). The coda provides a weighty harmonic resolution for the movement, with its ninety-five measures (mm. 302-96) counterbalancing the ninety-five measures of unstable transitional material, and secondary and closing sections in the recapitulation (mm. 208-302).

In the finale of the op. 59 no. 3 String Quartet in C, the coda also furnishes a very necessary affirmation of the tonic, this time following the tonally inconclusive recapitulation of the secondary thematic and closing sections. As Ratner has pointed out, the second key area is never strongly defined, either in the exposition or the recapitulation.[25] Therefore, one of the functions of the huge coda is to provide a harmonic resolution and confirm the tonic by repeated cadences and various harmonic prolongations.[26]

In some instances there simply is no traditional closing section that clearly establishes or confirms a key. For example, in the second movement of the Piano Sonata in F op. 54 the second thematic area in the recapitulation is quite unstable, and there is no cadence in the tonic. The coda prolongs the tonic and provides strong authentic cadences to conclude the movement. Similarly, in the first movement of the Piano Sonata in E op. 109 there is no closing section, and the improvisatory,

[25]Ratner, "Key Definition—A Structural Issue in Beethoven's Music," p. 477.
[26]A similar example is the first movement of the op. 135 String Quartet in F, in which the key of the second key area is only weakly established. The coda (though only of moderate length) again serves to confirm the tonic.

Example 7. Beethoven, Piano Trio op. 70 no. 2, IV (the coda begins at m. 302).

unstable second key area fails to establish the tonic conclusively in the recapitulation. An extended coda based on the primary theme is thus required to confirm the tonic and thereby provide a satisfying harmonic resolution. Of course, the coda also provides an important return to the initial tempo, meter, and thematic material following the *adagio espressivo* of the secondary thematic section.[27]

Similar examples of harmonic resolution are to be found in works by Brahms, including the codas to the first movements of Symphony No. 3, the Clarinet Quintet, and the Violin Sonata in A, all of which follow closing sections that move away from the tonic.

Understanding various structural functions in the codas of Beethoven's sonata-form movements is crucial not only for our appreciation of those works but also for our understanding of the structural significance of the coda in the sonata forms of other nineteenth-century composers like Schubert, Mendelssohn, Schumann, and Brahms. Thematic completion, final recapitulation, and harmonic resolution all help to make the coda in many nineteenth-century sonata forms an essential part of the work's basic structure. Applying the eighteenth-century sonata-form model to Beethoven's sonata-form movements frequently prevents us from accounting for the structural significance and necessity of the coda. For according to the eighteenth-century model, the coda is added to an essentially complete movement, but in many of Beethoven's sonata-form movements the coda is needed to complete the basic structure of the movement. Indeed, the coda frequently becomes a fourth main section in the sonata form.[28]

The comparative length of the exposition, development, recapitulation, and coda in Beethoven's sonata forms indicates the importance of the coda; and often the brief length of the exposition compared to the rest of the movement calls into question the assumed symmetrical

[27]Other codas that serve the function of harmonic resolution in sonata-form movements are found in Beethoven's Symphony No. 1 in C op. 21, IV; Piano Sonata in E-flat op. 31 no. 3, IV; Piano Sonata in F op. 54, II; Piano Sonata in f op. 57, I; String Quartet in F op. 59 no. 1, I and IV; String Quartet in C op. 59 no. 3, IV; Symphony No. 4 in B-flat op. 60, I; *Coriolan* Overture op. 62; Piano Trio in E-flat op. 70 no. 2, IV; Piano Sonata in E op. 109, I; String Quartet in B-flat op. 130, I; and String Quartet in F op. 135, I.

[28]William Newman has suggested that some Beethoven codas (in particular the coda of the opening movement of the Piano Sonata in f op. 57) create a fourth section in a sectional form that "might be lettered A-B-A-C." See *The Sonata in the Classic Era* , p. 146. Andrzej Chodkowski also mentions that the coda became a fourth main factor in sonata form: see "Die Koda in der Sonatenform Beethovens," *Berichtüber den Internationalen Beethoven-Kongress 10.-12. Dezember 1970 in Berlin*, ed. Heinz Alfred Brockhaus and Konrad Niemann (Berlin, 1971), p. 394.

binary structure at the heart of sonata form, at least as eighteenth-century models generally define it.[29] In many movements the exposition and recapitulation are approximately the same length, and the development and coda are relatively equal in length. For instance, in the finale of the String Quartet in C, op. 59 no. 3 the exposition is ninety-one measures and the recapitulation ninety-five measures; the development is 118 measures and the coda is 125 measures. In still other movements the coda is at least as long as the smallest of the other three sections. The implications of this need to be examined further, but it should be clear that we cannot continue to view many of Beethoven's sonata forms according to eighteenth-century models.

Sonata forms changed dramatically in the nineteenth century, and the increased structural significance of the coda was an important reason for that change. As James Webster points out in his article on sonata form: "This is one aspect of the 19th-century tendency to displace towards the end the weight of every form, single movements and whole cycles alike."[30] It became characteristic for Beethoven to place the climax of the movement not at the point of recapitulation, but in the coda, which typically expresses a dramatic resolution or triumphant final statement. This is a radical departure from the classical sonata forms of Mozart and Haydn,[31] and its consequences later in the century were monumental.

[29]Indeed, in ninety-six sonata-form movements by Beethoven, the exposition—*including* any indicated repetition and introduction—constitutes at most about one-third of the total length in one-third of the movements.

[30]*The New Grove Dictionary*, s.v. "sonata form."

[31]We can only guess Beethoven's reasons for the change. Often his development sections build such tension that the point of recapitulation comes too soon to be a satisfactory resolution. Frequently his recapitulations are too long for the climactic resolution of the movement to come at the beginning of the recapitulation. As Leonard B. Meyer has pointed out to me, it is important to have a climax near the end because it is difficult to sustain interest indefinitely after the climax. Also, Beethoven may have placed the climax near the end in part to satisfy the growing, musically unsophisticated audience.

David Brodbeck

Compatibility, Coherence, and Closure in Brahms's *Liebeslieder Waltzes*

Johannes brought me, at the beginning of this month, some charming waltzes for four hands and four voices, sometimes two and two, sometimes all four together, with very pretty, mostly folklike texts. . . .They are extraordinarily attractive (charming even without the voices) and I play them with great joy.[1]

In this diary entry of 16 July 1869, Clara Schumann recorded her first impression of Brahms's *Liebeslieder Walzer* op. 52. Perhaps her thoughts fell, as she played or wrote, upon her late husband, who in a book of *Spanische Liebeslieder* op. 138, anticipated by some twenty years both the title and medium of Brahms's more familiar collection.[2] But the two works have little else in common. Though Schumann began with an instrumental prelude marked to be played "Im Bolero-Tempo," the settings that follow of Emanuel Geibel's exotic lyrics show scant traces of an Iberian idiom. By contrast, Brahms's waltzes, based on Georg Friedrich Daumer's translations of several folk poems and dancing songs from Russia, Poland, and Hungary, capture all the richness of popular

---

[1]"Johannes brachte mir im Anfang dieses Monats reizende Walzer zu vier Händen mit vier Singstimmen, abwechselnd zwei und zwei, zuweilen alle vier, nach sehr hübschen, meist volkthümlichen Texten . . . sie sind von ganz besonderem Liebreiz (auch sogar ohne den Gesang schon reizend) und spiele ich sie mit grosser Freude. . ." (Berthold Litzmann, *Clara Schumann: Ein Künstlerleben nach Tagebüchern und Briefen*, 2nd-4th eds., 3 vols. [Leipzig, 1907-10], 3:230).
[2]Schumann's cycle, along with a related *Spanisches Liederspiel*, was composed in 1849. Though the latter was issued in that year, as op. 74, the *Liebeslieder* remained unpublished until 1857, when J. Rieter-Biedermann (who was just then beginning to take on Brahms's compositions) released them as the third of the posthumous works.

David Brodbeck is Assistant Professor of Music at the University of Pittsburgh. He has published essays on Brahms, Schubert, and Beethoven and is currently working on a critical study of the sacred music of Mendelssohn.

411

musical life in Vienna, where the dance had long been flavored by the styles of the city's many Slavic and Magyar immigrants.[3]

Brahms approached the vocal waltz in steps taken over several years. On Christmas Eve 1863 he had set two Slavic folk poems for vocal quartet with piano accompaniment, shortly thereafter appending this pair to an earlier setting of Goethe's "Wechsellied zum Tanze" and publishing the little collection as op. 31. Then, in January 1865, he reworked the melody of the last number of this set, "Der Gang zum Liebchen," in the fourth of the Waltzes for Piano Duet op. 39. This cycle, Brahms's first essay in what proved to be a congenial genre, already shows a sure handling of the Viennese dialect, with many of the dances echoing the style of Schubert's Ländler, others drawing inspiration from the composer's favorite gypsy idiom. Finally, at decade's end, Brahms brought these earlier accomplishments together in a single work: the *Liebeslieder Walzer* renew the *volkstümlich* world of the op. 31 Quartets, while making unobtrusive, seemingly effortless use of both the richer duo texture and compositional techniques first worked out in op. 39.

This convergence of interests, this methodical means of winning new ground, is entirely typical of the composer's working habits. Less so is the rich trail of documentation—sketches and an autograph showing significant differences from the final text—that Brahms left behind. It is with this suggestive material that we should begin.

I

Brahms preserved sketches for two-thirds of the eighteen waltzes (table 1).[4] Little can be positively inferred about the sequence in which Brahms drafted these settings, since the seven extant leaves are neither bound nor numbered. The present arrangement of any one bifolio may not even reflect the order in which its contents were composed. On the contrary, because the sketch on fol. 6r is a continuation of the dance whose beginning was sketched on fol. 7v (number 6, "Ein kleiner, hübscher Vogel"), we may suspect that this bifolio was originally turned the other

[3]Brahms drew his poems from Daumer's *Polydora: ein weltpoetisches Liederbuch*. In this essay I have quoted from the revised edition of Gustav Ophüls, *Brahms-Texte: sämtliche von Johannes Brahms vertonten und bearbeiteten Texte*, ed. Kristian Wachinger (Langewiesche-Brandt, 1983).
[4]Vienna, Gesellschaft der Musikfreunde (shelf number 117). For a detailed description, see Margit L. McCorkle, *Johannes Brahms: Thematisch-Bibliographisches Werkverzeichnis* (Munich, 1984), pp. 217-18.

way around; needless to add, similar circumstances might pertain to others.[5] But regardless of how the leaves are manipulated, they do not suggest a coherent plan. The sketch leaves evidently contain what might be termed an "unordered set" of dances, which Brahms drafted with little regard to their ultimate arrangement.

TABLE 1
LIEBESLIEDER SKETCHES

Fol.	Contents (op. no.)[a]
1	52/10, 6, 10
	52/1
2	52/3
	52/2
3	52/18
	53; 113/9
4	52/9
	52/4; 65/14; 52/17
5	52/17
	52/12
6	52/6
	52/7; 65/5
7	52/11
	52/6

NOTE: This undated source is a miscellany found in Vienna, Gesellschaft der Musikfreunde (shelf no. A 117).

[a]op. 52 = *Liebeslieder;* op. 53 = Alto Rhapsody; op. 65 = *Neue Liebeslider;* op. 113 = Thirteen Canons.

Max Kalbeck, working from a memoir by the Viennese soprano Rosa Girzeck, concluded, in his early biography of the composer, that Brahms must have undertaken this preliminary work about a year before completing the cycle.[6] It seems that in the summer of 1868 Brahms and

[5]For example, Walter Frisch has shown that one of the other bifolios in this sketch miscellany, containing material for the Alto Rhapsody, likewise was probably folded backwards in later years; see *Johannes Brahms, Alto Rhapsody, Opus 53*, Facsimile edition of the composer's autograph manuscript in the Music Division of the New York Public Library (New York, 1983), p. 21.
[6]Max Kalbeck, *Johannes Brahms* (hereafter cited as Kalbeck), rev. eds., 4 vols. in 8, (Berlin, 1915-21; reprint ed., Tutzing, 1976), 2:270.

his friend Julius Stockhausen joined the singer in a concert at the Rhenish resort of Bad Neuenahr. In addition to accompanying the two vocalists, Brahms contributed a number of waltzes, including some from his own op. 39 collection, which he had recently arranged for piano solo. The soprano recalled that on this occasion Brahms told her he wanted to compose nothing but waltzes, among which were to be some for her to sing. Thus was born the idea for a set of vocal waltzes, an idea so intriguing, Kalbeck held, that Brahms immediately set to work composing melodies for several of the dances.

We need not concern ourselves with the veracity of Fraulein Girzeck's reminiscence; our concern is not her recollection of when Brahms conceived of the waltzes, but Kalbeck's dating of when he began to compose them. Now the sketches, which Kalbeck described at length, feature what was said to have been written in the summer of 1868: early versions of several melodies.[7] But, as George Bozarth has observed, these manuscripts are the products of a later time, being written, not in the fluid brown ink normally encountered in Brahms's autographs, but in the thick purple one found elsewhere only in sources datable to the months of May-September 1869, which the composer spent on holiday in the German resort of Lichtenthal.[8] In all likelihood, therefore, the waltzes were not begun before the summer of 1869.

Which is not to suggest that Brahms's "love songs" were inspired by the idyllic surroundings of the German countryside: since the waltz is a Viennese genre, we would do well to seek a Viennese inspiration. This might have been, as Kalbeck had it, a charming Viennese soprano. But a more immediate inspiration seems to have come from the music of one of that city's greatest composers: Schubert. Indeed, the very month of Brahms's departure from Vienna for points north (May 1869) saw the publication of a book of twenty Ländler by the earlier master, D. 366 and 814, which Brahms himself had culled from a diverse group of manuscripts in his own library, fashioned into a cohesive whole, and anonymously edited for his friend J. P. Gotthard.[9] The composer thus

---

[7]Ibid., 2:292-94 (with a facsimile of the sketch of the ninth waltz). Several of the sketches are discussed in Paul Mies, "Aus Brahms' Werkstatt: vom Entstehen und Werden der Werke bei Brahms," in *N. Simrock Jahrbuch I*, ed. Erich H. Müller (Berlin, 1928): 42-63.
[8]George S. Bozarth, "Brahms's '*Liederjahr*' of 1868," *Music Review* 44 (1983), pp. 212-13.
[9]On the *Twenty Ländler*, see my article "Brahms's Edition of Twenty Schubert Ländler: An Essay in Criticism," in *Brahms Studies, I: Papers Delivered at the International Brahms Conference, The Library of Congress, Washington, D. C., 5-8 May 1983*, ed. George S. Bozarth (London, in press).

may well have carried with him that summer a "souvenir" from the Imperial City. At all events, when it came time to try out various sequences of the eighteen *Liebeslieder Walzer*—an unordered set comparable in this way to the batch of dances from which Brahms selected the twenty Ländler—he must surely have drawn upon his recent editorial experience.

II

A certain dependence on the earlier composer is to be expected, after all: "In everything . . . I try my hand at," Brahms wrote to Clara Schumann in March 1870, "I tread on the heels of my predecessors, whom I feel in my way."[10] Indeed, as I have suggested elsewhere, Brahms had begun the op. 39 Waltzes with a dance modeled upon Schubert's "Atzenbrucker Deutscher," op. 18 number 2 (ex. 1).[11] Both pieces are in B major and tonicize the diatonic mediant at the first double bar. Moreover, each begins with the progression I-ii-V^7-I, unfolded over a tonic pedal point and supporting the structural tones $\hat{3}$ $\hat{2}$ $\hat{1}$. Even the melodies are very much alike, sharing in their third and fourth bars a striking 9-8 appoggiatura. This virtual quotation of Schubert, coming in the opening measures of Brahms's first waltz, acknowledges, in the characteristic manner described by Charles Rosen, a stylistic debt to an earlier master whose style lay at the source of the music to follow.[12] Being untried in the world of dance music (and in 1865 scarcely having veins surging with *wienerisch* blood), Brahms quite naturally looked for guidance to Schubert, native son of the Austrian capital, master of her dances, and a composer from whom he had already learned a great deal about "serious" forms, especially the sonata.

Matters were different when, in 1869, Brahms took up the waltz again. In this year the composer at last moved permanently to Vienna, taking rooms in the Hotel "Zum Kronprinzen" on the *Donaukanal*. It thus does not seem too fanciful to interpret the *Liebeslieder Walzer*, perhaps Brahms's most overtly Viennese work, as putting the seal on his significant new relationship to the city. Yet this second set—published, tell-

---

[10]"In allem Andern, was ich versuche, trete ich Vorgängern auf die Hacken, die mich geniren...." (Litzmann, *Clara Schumann*, 3:236).
[11]See my article "*Primo* Schubert, *Secondo* Schumann: Brahms's Four-Hand Waltzes, Op. 39" (forthcoming).
[12]Charles Rosen, "Influence: Plagiarism and Inspiration," *19th-Century Music* 4 (1980/81): 87-100.

Example 1. (a) Brahms, op. 39 no. 1; (b) Schubert, op. 18 no. 2.

ingly, with the marking ''Im Ländler-Tempo''—at the same time looks backward, building upon earlier references to Schubert and upon his own waltzes as well.[13]

The first dance, for example, renews and completes the quotation of the dance by Schubert begun in op. 39 (ex. 2). ''Rede, Mädchen'' not only shows a tonicization of the diatonic mediant, but, like Schubert's number, discloses a written-out repetition of the first period. The later dance, moreover, echoes the appoggiaturas prominently marking the initial cadence in the Schubertian model.

But the new waltz has the additional task of establishing a wider

---

[13]Brahms emphasized the Ländler-like quality of his dances in a letter to Ernst Rudorff: ''Ich brauche nicht zu sagen, dass das Tempo eigentlich das des Ländlers ist: mässig.'' (*Johannes Brahms Briefwechsel* [hereafter cited as *Briefwechsel*], 16 vols. [Berlin, 1907-22], vol. 3, *Johannes Brahms im Briefwechsel mit Karl Reinthaler, Max Bruch, Hermann Deiters, Friedr. Heimsoeth, Karl Reinecke, Ernst Rudorff, Bernhard und Luise Scholz*, ed. Wilhelm Altmann [1908], p.156).

Example 2. Brahms, *Liebeslieder Walzer*, op. 52 no. 1, mm. 1-18.

aesthetic framework in which to view the ensuing numbers. In op. 39 Brahms had, from time to time, taken opposing positions, assuming here a popular tone, there a more learned one. He appears to conclude in a nearly sentimental vein, with the penultimate waltz having all the earmarks of a closing number. (Indeed, one early reviewer, in a gross misreading, argued that Brahms really should have done so.)[14] Yet the composer appended to this dance a tightly woven number in strict dou-

[14]S[elmar] B[agge], ''Vierhändige Walzer von Johannes Brahms. Op. 39,'' *Leipziger allgemeine musikalische Zeitung* 1 (1866): 295.

ble counterpoint, thereby ending the set firmly on the side of high art. The *Liebeslieder*, in turn, begin where the earlier book had left off: "Rede, Mädchen" at once establishes both sides of the dialectic between popular music and art music, posed so effectively in the last two numbers of op. 39. The "oom-pah-pah" vamp in the opening bar, which immediately marks the genre, is an archetypal gambit in popular music; yet the dance proves to be highly sophisticated, consistently eschewing literal repetition—a hallmark of popular style—in favor of continual variation.

Brahms set the three strophes of Daumer's lyric in a kind of rounded binary form:

A¹	Rede, Mädchen, allzu liebes,
	Das mir in die Brust, die kühle,
A²	hat geschleudert mit dem Blicke
	diese wilden Glutgefühle!
B¹	Willst du nicht dein Herz erweichen,
	Willst du, eine Überfromme,
A³	Rasten ohne traute Wonne,
	Oder willst du, dass ich komme?
B²	Rasten ohne traute Wonne,
	Nicht so bitter will ich büssen,
A⁴	Komme nur, du schwarzes Auge,
	Komme, wenn die Sterne grussen.

[Tell me, maiden, my dearest, whose glance stirred these wild passionate feelings in my cool breast! Will you not let your heart relent? Do you, like a cloistered nun, want to forsake beloved joy! Or do you want me to draw near? Forsake beloved joy? I do not want to do such bitter penance. Do come, my darkeyed lover, come when the stars appear.]

The young man prepares his wooing in stanza 1 (see ex. 2). In the first part (A¹), he tells of the coolness that once ruled his breast, in a phrase that remains, pointedly, in the tonic. But then, in a varied repetition of this material (A²), thoughts of the passion enflamed by the maiden's gaze initiate a slip into the diatonic mediant.

The repetition of the larger second section (comprising stanzas 2 and

3) is varied texturally. Stanza 2, set as a double period B^1A^3, continues in the original vocal setting of tenor and bass, as the would be lover begins his entreaties; but the restatement, B^2A^4, beautifully eliding the cadence and coinciding with the maiden's assent in stanza 3, is sung, realistically enough, by the soprano and alto. The quartet comes together only in the last bars, when, as though the young man had not expected the maiden's invitation, the male voices interrupt, several times singing the final verse of the second stanza ("Willst du, dass ich komme?").

These tonal and textural variations, premised upon the simple story told in Daumer's lyric, are obvious. More subtle is the transfiguration of the first phrase at the outset of the restatement (cf. exs. 3a and b). The revised version not only freely inverts the opening strain, but also

Example 3. Brahms, *Liebeslieder Walzer*, op. 52 no. 1, (a) reduction of mm. 2-6; (b) reduction of mm. 26-30.

embraces material that had first been stated in the accompaniment, whose dovetailed echoes of motives in bars 3-4 and 5-6 are now, likewise in inverted form, woven into the fabric of the melody itself. Notwithstanding these twists, the new incarnation retains the descending circle of fifths (G-sharp-C-sharp-F-sharp-B-E) described by the tune during its initial presentation. At the same time, the inner voice unfolds, now ornamented and in a juggled order, the prominent ascending appoggiaturas originally divided between the outer parts (cf. the upper staves in exs. 3a and b).

The form of this dance, though striking, was not unprecedented. Several of Schubert's *Twelve Ländler*, D. 790, which Brahms had seen into print in 1864, show similar unusual realizations of the normally simple bipartite forms associated with the dance. One suggestive instance is provided by the penultimate number of the book, whose second part begins with a bold reinterpretation of salient material from the first which is strikingly akin to that seen in "Rede, Mädchen."[15] But if Brahms drew his formal principle from Schubert's *Ländler*, he did so with the added twist of inversion. Thus, despite the probable presence of a model, the subtleties of the restatement did not emerge all at once.

In the sketch, Brahms broke off the vocal line in bar 27, turning his attention instead to the revision of material slated for the accompaniment (ex. 4a). Already worked out, in bars 28 and 30, are the beautiful dissonances of the diminished octave (seen as well in the Schubert *Ländler* upon which the form of the dance was modeled); the bass line, moreover, is essentially complete, and the inner part, now carrying the ornamental appoggiaturas, in final form. But not so the melody. To be sure, Brahms ultimately retained each of the four note-pairs sketched in the right-hand part (D-natural-C-sharp, B-A, C-natural-B, and A-G-sharp); but only the first and third were worked into the tune, the other two serving, in part, as a harmonization of it in parallel thirds.

That this material was written in the piano brace and shows ungainly leaps of a seventh and a higher register than is to be found in the tenor part of any of the other waltzes implies that the line was never intended to be sung. Indeed, when, in the autograph, Brahms fleshed out the passage (ex. 4b), it was to the *primo* alone that he assigned this revised material, which had originally, in bars 2-5, been divided between the tenor voice (carrying the text and tune) and the *secondo* (in which this

[15]See my article "Dance Music as High Art: Schubert's Twelve Ländler, op. 171 (D. 790)," in *Schubert: Critical and Analytical Studies*, ed. Walter Frisch (Lincoln and London, 1986), pp. 35-37.

Example 4. *Liebeslieder Walzer*, **op. 52 no. 1: (a) transcription of mm. 26-30 of the sketch; (b) transcription of mm. 26-30 of the autograph.**

tune had been echoed). In the restatement, the tenor describes a new, continuous line, fashioned in part out of two of the note-pairs found in the sketch, but linked now by two new pairs sounding at the lower third. Perhaps suspecting that a clear rendition of the text was at risk in this arrangement, Brahms subsequently doubled the lower third in the *primo*—first, in an added layer of writing in the autograph, in bar 30 (indicated by the brackets in ex. 4b), and later, in the published version, in bar 28 as well.

III

Like the sketches, the autograph can be assigned to the summer of 1869 on the basis of its distinctive purple ink. Very likely it was completed by the beginning of July, when, as we have seen, Brahms brought the waltzes for Clara Schumann's inspection. The composer's progress, then, was rapid. The sketches had been made barely a few weeks earlier, and already the entire set had been written out in full score.[16] But though the individual numbers flowed quickly from Brahms's pen, the question of how to arrange them proved difficult to answer. Even when, at the end of August, Brahms sent the dances to his publisher Fritz Simrock, the matter remained unresolved:

> For once I have kept my word; the waltzes will arrive by 1 September. I am a little uncertain about the title and the volume ordering. You can eliminate "Liebeslieder." Do you prefer "Waltzes" for Piano Duet and in parentheses (with voices) or (voices *ad lib.*)? . . .
> Now I would like to have them published as soon as possible. . . .
> I should think two volumes with nine each?
> It also works well in one volume? Or do you want to make three volumes of six each? In that case, I would ask that numbers 7-12 be numbered as follows:
> 10, 11, 12, 7, 8, 9.[17]

The source accompanying this letter, which almost certainly served

---

[16]Vienna, Gesellschaft der Musikfreunde (shelf no. A 96). For a description, see McCorkle, *Brahms Werkverzeichnis*, p. 217. Facsimiles of the beginning of the first and ninth dances can be found, respectively, in Franz Grasberger, *Das kleine Brahmsbuch* (Salzburg, 1973), p. 86; and Otto Biba, *Johannes Brahms in Wien*, Exhibition catalogue (Vienna, 1983), p. 54. For the locations of facsimiles of a number of album leaves containing excerpts of numbers 9 and 11, see Peter Dedel, *Johannes Brahms: A Guide to His Autograph in Facsimile*, MLA Index and Bibliography Series, number 18 (Ann Arbor, Mich., 1978), pp. 40-41.

[17]"Ich halte also einmal Wort, für 1. September sind die Walzer da. Über den Titel und die Heftordnung bin ich wenig im Reinen. Sie können 'Liebeslieder' streichen. Wollen Sie lieber 'Walzer' für das Pianoforte zu 4 Händen und in Parenthese (mit Gesang) oder (und Gesang *ad lib.*)? . . .

"Nun wünschte ich, dass sie möglichst eng gedruckt würden. . . .

"Da dächte ich zwei Hefte mit je 9?

"Auch kommen sie wohl zusammen in ein Heft? Oder wollen Sie drei Hefte mit je 6 machen? Dann bäte ich Nummer 7-12 so zu ordnen:

"10, 11, 12, 7, 8, 9" (*Briefwechsel*, vols. 9-12, *Johannes Brahms: Briefe an P. J. Simrock und Fritz Simrock*, ed. Max Kalbeck [1917-19], vol. 9 [1917], p. 76).

as the engraver's model, could not have been the autograph, which differs from the first edition both in the order of dances and in a number of textual details (table 2).[18]

TABLE 2
LIEBESLIEDER AUTOGRAPH

Paper-type	Fol.	Contents (no.)	Key	Marginalia
	1	1	E	
A		1		
	2	1		
		2	a	
	3	3	Bb	
A		4	F	
	4	6	A	
		6		
	5	6		
A		6		
	6	6		
		empty		
	7	5	a	
A		5		"In G dur"
	8	8	Ab	"Nicht ausschreiben,
		8		Platz lassen"
	9	10	G	"Die 2 folgenden vorher"
B		11	c	[nos. 7 & 9?]
	10	11/12	c/Eb	
		12		
	11	7	c	
A		7/9	c/E	
	12	9		
		9		
	13	13	Ab	
A		14	Eb	
	14	15	Ab	
		15		
	15	17	Db	"Vorher 'ein dunkler Schacht"
		17		[no. 16]
	16	18 (beg.)	Db(C#)	
A		a		
	17	18 (conc.)		
B		16	f	
	18	16		
		16		

[18]For a registration of the textual differences between the autograph and the first edition, see Eusebius Mandyczewski's critical report to *Johannes Brahms Sämtliche Werke*, Edition of the Gesellschaft der Musikfreunde in Wien, 26 vols. (Leipzig, 1926-28), vol. 20, *Mehrstimmige Gesange mit Klavier oder Orgel* (1926).

NOTE: This undated manuscript is found in Vienna, Gesellschaft der Musikfreunde (shelf no. A 96). Numbers 8, 10-12, and 14-18 were published in slightly different versions.

[a]Here Brahms has set the text "Qual vergehe? Dass das herz in Qual vergehe, vergehe?"; this text is from Daumer's "Flammenauge, dunkles Haar," which Brahms later set in the *Neue Liebeslieder,* op. 65.

The engraver's model seems rather to have been a copy, one based upon the autograph, to be sure, but one that Brahms thus was required to revise in accordance with his final plans. This conclusion follows in part from one of the marginal notes in the autograph, which seems directed toward a copyist whose work was to require significant elaboration: next to the dance on folio 8 is found Brahms's command "Nicht ausschreiben, Platz lassen." A brief note from the composer to his friend Hermann Levi, music director in nearby Karlsruhe, suggests whom that copyist might have been.

> Will you be so good as to have the enclosed trifles copied and returned to me right away[?]
> Each on a separate page, thus with wasting of space and paper, just as I am showing it hereby.[19]

Could Brahms's "trifles" have been the *Liebeslieder?* On August 24th Levi rehearsed the dances, presumably in anticipation of a private performance planned to celebrate the upcoming wedding of Clara Schumann's daughter Julie to Count Victor Radicati Marmorito.[20] Since

---

[19] "Willst Du so gut sein, beifolgende Kleinigkeiten recht rasch copiren zu lassen und mir wieder zurückzuschicken.

"Jedes auf ein besonderes Blatt, also mit Raum- und Papier-Verschwendung, wie ich sie soeben durch Vorliegendes zeige" (*Briefwechsel,* vol. 7, *Johannes Brahms im Briefwechsel mit Hermann Levi, Friedrich Gernsheim sowie den Familien Hecht und Fellinger,* ed. Leopold Schmidt [1910], p. 49).

[20] On this planned performance, see Kalbeck, 2:328. Brahms may have had the young girl in mind when he composed the waltzes; at all events he described the rather more personal and moving Alto Rhapsody, written in August in the midst of a period of sullenness resulting from his displeasure with her wedding plans, as a "bridal song" (see Frisch, *Alto Rhapsody,* pp. 13-15, and the references cited there). Levi rehearsed the dances in Karlsruhe; see Litzmann, *Clara Schumann,* p. 231; and Fritjof Haas, "Johannes Brahms und Hermann Levi," in *Johannes Brahms in Baden-Baden und Karlsruhe* (Karlsruhe, 1983), p. 68. The singers were Frl. Murjahn, Herr Stolzenberg, and Herr und Frau Hauser. Brahms had promised to conduct Pauline Viardot-Garcia's operetta *Le dernier Sorcier* at her salon in Baden-Baden on the day of the rehearsal and thus could not attend. The composer mentioned this conflict and his disappointment at not being able to hear the waltzes in an undated postcard to Levi evidently written on 23 August (*Briefwechsel,* 7:51).

the dances were as yet unpublished, copies would have to have been made. The most compelling evidence pointing to the *Liebeslieder*, however, is evidence also of Brahms's continued indecision on the matter of how the dances were finally to be ordered. The composer's odd request that each piece be copied on a separate page, even at the expense of considerable wasted space and paper, reflects a practical concern. Because he was uncertain how the waltzes were to be published, it is understandable that he would want each number to appear on its own page; in such a format the dances could easily be reshuffled.

In the end, the prospective performance in honor of Julie Schumann and her fiancé did not come to pass. The wedding of the couple was postponed for a few weeks because of a death in Marmorito's family, and the idea of performing the waltzes was dropped.[21] Levi—his interest sparked—was not to be discouraged, however; he scheduled the dances for the first concert in the fall season at Karlsruhe, where on October 6th he and Frau Schumann accompanied a quartet of singers in the premiere.[22]

Brahms received a proofcopy of the score from Simrock on October 5th, in time for it to be used in the concert the following day.[23] But in a letter to Levi written some days before this event, the composer made it clear that he did not want the dances to be performed in the order and arrangement in which Simrock had decided to release them, one volume in the familiar order of numbers 1-18:

Perhaps you can number the waltzes as follows?
I. Rede Mädchen.—Am Gesteine.—O die Frauen.—Wie des Abends.—Die grüne Hopfenranke.—Ein kl. hübsch. Vogel.—O wie sanft.—Nein es ist nicht.—Schlosser auf. [nos. 1, 2, 3, 4, 5, 6, 10, 11, 12]
II. Wohl schön bewandt.—Wenn so lind.—Am Donaustrand.—Vögelein.—Sieh wie ist.—Nachtigall.—Ein dunkler Schacht.—Nicht wandle.—Es bebet. [nos. 7, 8, 9, 13, 14, 15, 16, 17, 18]

[21]According to Kalbeck, 2:328, the wedding was a rather solemn affair; yet in a diary entry dated 21 September, the night of the *Polterabend*, Clara Schumann described the party as a joyous event, during which she and Brahms played the composer's new Hungarian Dances and some Strauss waltzes (Litzmann, *Clara Schumann*, 3:232).
[22]This performance, sung by Frl. Hausmann, Fr. Hauser, Benedikt Kürner, and Herr Brouillet, was a huge success; some dances had to be repeated, and Brahms was called on stage to take a bow (see the notice of the concert in the *Allgemeine musikalische Zeitung* 4 [1869]: 359; and Litzmann, *Clara Schumann*, 3:232).
[23]*Briefwechsel*, 9:84-85. Brahms had not yet received the proofs of the parts, however, and the singers thus apparently had to read from a manuscript (see *Allgemeine musikalische Zeitung* 4 [1869]: 359).

3 volumes with 6 each would certainly be preferable, but it also works well in 2 with 9.[24]

Oddly enough, none of the arrangements mentioned in Brahms's correspondence was followed in Karlsruhe, where for some reason only ten waltzes were played. A similar truncated performance followed shortly in Vienna on 5 December 1869. It was only with Brahms's direct participation that the entire cycle was heard in public. On 5 January 1870 he joined Clara Schumann in a Viennese performance based upon

TABLE 3
LIEBESLIEDER CYCLIC PLANS

(1) Autograph		(2) Tripartite		(3) Bipartite		(4) Undivided	
No.	Key	No.	Key	No.	Key	No.	Key
1	E	1	E	1	E	1	E
2	a	2	a	2	a	2	a
3	B♭	3	B♭	3	B♭	3	B♭
4	F	4	F	4	F	4	F
6	A	5	a	5	a	5	a
5	a	6	A	6	A	6	A
8	A♭	10	G	7	c	7	c
10	G	11	c	8	A♭	8	A♭
11	c	12	E♭[a]	9	E	9	E
12	E♭[a]	7	c	10	G	10	G
7	c	8	A♭	11	c	11	c
9	E	9	E	12	E♭[a]	12	E♭[a]
13	A♭	13	A♭	13	A♭	13	A♭
14	E♭	14	E♭	14	E♭	14	E♭
15	A♭	15	A♭	15	A♭	15	A♭
17	D♭	16	f	16	f	16	f
18	D♭[b]	17	D♭	17	D♭	17	D♭
16	f	18	D♭[b]	18	D♭[b]	18	D♭[b]

NOTE: The numbers assigned to the dances correspond to those of the first edition.

[a]Begins in c. [b]Ends in C♯.

[24]"Vielleicht kannst Du die Walzer wie folgt numeriren? . . .
"3 Hefte mit je 6 wäre freilich passender, doch geht's auch wohl mit 2 à 9."
(*Briefwechsel*, 7:50-51).

the first alternative suggested to Simrock in the preceding August—subdivision of the whole into two groups of nine dances each.[25]

The autograph thus offers only a provisional sequence, one ultimately revised to yield a number of authorized arrangements (table 3). Simrock followed the simplest of these, publishing the dances in an undivided series. The composer, however, seems to have favored the plans whereby the dances are subdivided into smaller groups. To Levi he expressed a preference for a tripartite division, though in his own performance in Vienna he followed a bipartite plan. This multiplicity of arrangements raises some fascinating questions. The answers seem linked to the ideas of compatibility, coherence, and closure.

IV

I have borrowed the first of my "three C's" from Jeffrey Kallberg. In a recent study of Chopin's multipartite works—the mazurkas, nocturnes, and the like—Kallberg argues that, although Chopin sanctioned the practice of performing individual numbers from such sets, he seems to have designed his publications so that integrated performances would be aesthetically satisfying.[26] Thus the term ''compatibility'' rather than ''unity'': the constituents can be played alone or in combination with extrinsic pieces, yet appear to belong together when played in succession.

Just as Chopin would not wish to deny pianists a certain amount of discretion in the grouping of his genre pieces, the composer of the *Liebeslieder* was agreeable to a number of arrangements of his dances. As we have seen, Brahms's flexibility surfaced numerous times during the summer and fall of 1869; and it did so again in the following winter, when he orchestrated several of the waltzes and included in this suite an early version of an extrinsic piece, one to be seen again five years later in the *Neue Liebeslieder*.[27]

[25]On the Karlsruhe performance, see *Briefwechsel*, 9:81n. On the Singakademie concert, see Kalbeck, 2:310; in this performance Carl Nawratil and Hans Paumgartner accompanied Louise Dustmann, Frau Leder, Adolf Ritter von Schultner, and Ferdinand Haas. See also the *Allgemeine musikalische Zeitung* 4 [1869]: 407. Brahms's performance with Clara Schumann is mentioned in Kalbeck, 2:331-32; the singers were Louise Dustmann, Rosa Girzick, Gustav Walter, and Emil Krauss.

[26]Jeffrey Kallberg, ''Compatibility in Chopin's Multipartite Publications,'' *Journal of Musicology* 2 (1983): 391-417.

[27]See Karl Geiringer, *Brahms: His Life and Work*, 3rd ed., rev. and enl. (New York, 1983), pp. 278-79. This suite also contains an early version of the ninth of the *Neue Liebeslieder*, op. 65. The order of dances is op. 52/1, 2, 4, 6, 5; op. 65/9; and op. 52/11, 8, and 9. Brahms mentioned the possibility of orchestrating some of the waltzes in a letter to Simrock from August 1869 (*Briefwechsel*, 9:81), but work was not begun until later, at the instigation of Ernst Rudorff, who led the premiere in Berlin on 19 March 1870 (see *Briefwechsel*, 3:155-60).

But compatibility implies a "second C": coherence. Again the music of another composer comes to mind, though now it is not Chopin whom I should like to invoke, but Schubert—or, rather, the Schubert that Brahms passed off to the world in his anonymously edited collection of twenty Ländler. As I suggested earlier, Brahms's achievement in this publication was the forging of tonally and motivically coherent groups from among an "unordered" collection of dances. The authorized arrangements of Brahms's own *Liebeslieder* are marked by similar groups.

One example involves the dances published as numbers 10-12 ("O wie sanft," "Nein, es ist nicht auszukommen," and "Schlosser auf"). These pieces apparently were not conceived as a unit; they do not, at all events, appear in proximity to one another in the sketches. But early on, on folios 9 and 10 of the autograph, they were united in their published order. The state of the autograph is telling (see table 2). Most of the leaves are of what may be termed paper-type A, but a few are of what we shall term paper-type B. In examining the manuscript, we are drawn immediately to the three dances in question, for they appear together on an odd, type-B bifolium, inserted in the midst of a run of several normal bifolia of type A.

If the document draws our eye to this trio, the pieces themselves suggest to our ear something about Brahms's ordering principles. The goal seems to have been to create tonal and motivic coherence. The first two numbers, in G major and C minor, form a dominant-tonic pair; the third, in turn, sets out from C minor but concludes in its relative major, E-flat. Other relations are no less fluid. All three dances highlight the same rhythm,(♩ ♫) and each seems palpably linked to its neighbor: the chord ending number 10 is echoed at the beginning of number 11; that ending number 11 is taken over at the outset of number 12.

Similar relations connect the next three dances ("Vögelein," "Sieh, wie ist die Welle klar," and "Nachtigall"), a trio which likewise unfolds a sequence of related keys (A-flat-E-flat-A-flat). The link between numbers 14 and 15 is especially strong. Both dances show a prominent juxtaposition of E-flat and its lowered submediant (mm. 4-5 and 10-11, respectively); moreover, the beginning of the latter grows directly out of the rhythmically mobile ending of the former. But the coherence of this set also involves matters textural and textual. "Vögelein," a duo for soprano and alto, likens the longing of one heart for another to the quest of a little bird for a branch on which to rest. Then, in "Sieh, wie ist die Welle klar," a duo for tenor and bass, the scene embraces moonlit waters. The voices of the women and men, and also the imagery prevailing in their songs, come together at last in the third dance, a setting *a 4* of "Nachtigall."

Not all adjoining dances in the autograph are aptly juxtaposed, however (see table 3). "Wenn so lind dein Auge mir" and "O wie sanft" (published as nos. 8 and 10), for example, are in A-flat and G, "Wohl schön bewandt" and "Am Donaustrande" (nos. 7 and 9) in C minor and E major. Of course, Brahms could have eliminated these tonal disjuctions simply by transposing some of the pieces. He evidently once considered this approach, writing in the autograph "in G dur" next to the dance in A flat. But in the end Brahms discovered a more elegant solution. By inserting number 8 between numbers 7 and 9 he created a long-range progression by major thirds (C minor-A-flat-E) and thereby eliminated both offending appositions at once.

In addition to eliminating the tonal disjunctions, this new arrangement produced an intricate web of tonal relations. The first period of number 7 (in C minor) ends with a tonicization of A—the key of number 8 (ex. 5a). In addition, both of these dances are marked by "purple patches," to use Tovey's phrase, involving enharmonic play between the notes A-flat and G-sharp. In bars 16-17 of the seventh waltz, Brahms sidesteps an implied cadence in A major by changing the note G-sharp^1 ($\hat{7}$ in A) to A-flat^1 ($\hat{6}$ in C minor). A similar enharmonic change is important in number 8 (ex. 5b). The second period of this dance begins with tonic harmony, but the alto voice immediately reinterprets its A-flat^1 as G-sharp^1, initiating a 7-6 suspension over the A-natural in the bass and allowing a modulation from A-flat to E (mm. 18-22). The third-progression is continued an additional step, leading to a cadence in C in measure 26. This passage therefore touches upon the keys of both numbers 7 (in C minor) and 9 (in E). It duplicates, in other words, the long-range progression by major thirds unfolded by the three dances that Brahms had belatedly brought together. In the same spirit, number 9 refers back to the two pieces coming before it; in its only tonicization it moves to G-sharp minor (mm. 42-44)—the enharmonic parallel of both the tonal center of number 8 and the one tonicized key of number 7.

V

The ninth waltz brings us to our "third C": closure. There can be little doubt that Brahms thought of "Am Donaustrande" as a concluding number. He evidently voiced no objection when Levi chose to end with it in his Karlsruhe performance of ten of the pieces. He chose it as the

Example 5. Brahms, *Liebeslieder Walzer*, op. 52 (a) no. 7; (b) no. 8, mm. 18-end.

(b)

finale of the little orchestral suite he made of several of the waltzes in the winter of 1869/70. And, more to the point at hand, he placed it last in both the first group of his bipartite plan and the middle group of his tripartite plan (see table 3).

Significant in this regard is the repetition, at the end of Brahms's setting, of the first two verses of Daumer's poem (shown below in italics):

A¹   *Am Donaustrande, da steht ein Haus,*
      Da schaut ein rosiges Mädchen aus.
A²   *Das Mädchen, es ist wohl gut gehegt,*
      Zehn eiserne Riegel sind vor die Türe gelegt.
B   *Zehn eiserne Riegel das ist ein Spass;*
      Die spreng ich, als wären sie nur von Glas.
A³   *Am Donaustrande, da steht ein Haus,*
      Da schaut ein rosiges Mädchen aus.

[On the Danube's shore stands a house; there a rosy-cheeked maiden looks out. The maiden is well guarded; ten iron bolts are laid across the doors. Ten iron bolts—that is nothing. I'll break them as if they were made but of glass. *On the Danube's shore stands a house; there a rosy-cheeked maiden looks out.*]

In brief space the poem traverses a wealth of images: an initial picture of tranquillity, giving way to more than a hint of repression, which in turn yields to the posturings of a self-confident suitor. This sequence is compelling enough; yet Brahms concluded, not, as Daumer had it, with the suitor's bold declaration, but with a rehearsal of the original placid imagery.

In Brahms's version, then, the Danube River looms large. How better to conclude a series of waltzes than with one whose text focuses on the stream which cuts through Vienna, especially in light of the enormous popularity of Johann Strauss's contemporaneous "Blue Danube" Waltz?[28] At all events, both the form and content of the music make

[28]The reference to Strauss's masterpiece seems especially clear when we remember that for its first performance, on 13 February 1867, one Joseph Weyl (a police official and sometimes poet) grafted on to it insipid verses, which were sung in alternation by the tenors and basses of the *Wiener Männer-gesangverein*. These begin:

> Wiener, seid froh!
> Oho! Wieso?
> Ein Schimmer des Lichts—
> Wir seh'n noch nichts!
> Der Fasching ist da.
> Ah so, na na.
>
> [Viennese, be glad! Oho, why so? A glimmer of light. We see nothing yet! *Fasching* is here. Oh, yes—well, then.]

closural suggestions. Unlike the majority of dances in the set (most of which are simple two-part forms), "Am Donaustrande" unfolds a rounded binary form. As he had done in "Rede, Mädchen"—one of the few other examples of this type, and the only other dance in the key of E— Brahms wrote out the repetition of part 1, setting the first two lines as the opening period of the form (A¹), the second two as its repetition (A²). The soprano, significantly, remains silent during this portion of the dance: she is the "repressed" persona about whom the others sing. The four voices do come together, however, at the outset of part 2, a setting of the final two lines of the poem (B). Appropriately enough, the bass leads here, modeling his tune on the principal theme but varying it in accordance with the assertive nature of the young man whom he represents (all the while retracing the move to G-sharp minor marking the opening of "Rede, Mädchen"). This rather more agitated passage gives way at last to the restatement of the first two lines (A³), wherein, with a new countermelody, the tenor now takes the lead.

The closural implications of this return of text and music are enhanced by certain details in Brahms's setting. The strong final cadence supports a melody that descends gracefully to $\hat{1}$, and the brief codetta in the piano is marked by four "natural" signs of closure: a descending line, decrescendo, ritardando, and fermata. Moreover, the generally low level of dynamics throughout the waltz, as well as the gently rocking accompanimental figure (♩ | ♩ ♩ | ♩) not only captures the image of the peaceful river shores, but also implies that a point of repose, or closure, has been reached.

The search for effective closing numbers lay behind other changes in Brahms's numbering of the dances. The reversal in the first edition of the autograph's ordering of "Die grüne Hopfenranke" (no. 5) and "Ein kleiner, hübscher Vogel" (no. 6), for example, created a good ending for the first group in the tripartite plan (see table 3). Thus the move in the revised order from the minor mode of number 5 to the parallel major of number 6 suggests, by analogy to the long-range progression seen in countless minor-key sonata cycles, that a point of termination may be at hand. And so, too, does the new sequence of forms. By contrast to the first five waltzes, comparatively brief two-part forms ranging in length from 32 to 70 bars, number 6 is an extensive rondo form (ABACA) totaling 131 bars and embracing episodes in the mediant and flat submediant. As this huge dance unfolds, then, it accumulates weight befitting a finale. The tonal plan enhances this closural implication: the departures from the tonic in the episodes make the return of the rondo theme all the more satisfying, and thus all the more conclusive.

The decision to conclude the entire cycle with "Es bebet das Ges-
träuche" (no. 18) likewise was an inspired (and efficacious) afterthought.
In the margin of the autograph version of "Nicht wandle, mein Licht"
(no. 17) Brahms wrote "Vorher 'Ein dunkler Schacht' [no. 16]," indicating a removal of that dance from its original position in last place
to a new, antepenultimate slot, and with that leaving "Es bebet" as
the final number. The tonal scheme of the latter dance suggests one
reason for this change in plan.

A^1	Es bebet das Gesträuche,
	Gestreift hat es im Fluge
	Ein Vöglein.
B	In gleicher Art erbebet,
	Die Seele mir erschüttert
A^2	Von Liebe, Lust und Leide,
	Gedenkt sie dein.

[The bushes tremble, brushed by the flight of a little bird. In the
same way my soul quakes from love, joy, and pain, when it thinks
of you.]

In this number Brahms made use for the last time—and again with
a notable twist—of the rounded binary form seen earlier in "Rede, Mädchen" and "Am Donaustrande." The opening period (A^1) at first seems
unexceptional, moving from the key of B-flat minor to its mediant, D-
flat. Yet initial simplicity again proves illusory, as the dance concludes,
not in the apparent tonic, but in C-sharp (the enharmonic equivalent
of the "second key"). This long-range tonal progression (i → III or
vi → I) Brahms had seen in many of Schubert's dances. Yet his application of it in "Es bebet" is no mere imitation of a Schubertian mannerism. Here the large-scale tonal play is unfolded in combination with
more subtle play locally between both relative and parallel keys.

bar:	1	18	19	27	44
	:A^1	:	:B	A^2	:
	b flat	D flat	E	c sharp	C sharp
	i →	III	III/d-flat	iii →	III
	vi →	I	III	i →	I
tonal axis:	relative		relative	parallel	

The B section (mm. 19-26) sets out in E, enharmonically the relative
key of D-flat minor (which is itself the parallel key of that ending the

A section). As this phrase unfolds, it borrows from its own parallel mode (viz., the half-diminished seventh chords in mm. 21-22). In bar 27 the opening material (A²) recurs in C-sharp minor, relative key of E. The new tonic is not actually sounded straightaway. It does recur fleetingly in bars 30-31, but these appearances merely initiate a gradual evolutionary process whereby C-sharp major is asserted as tonic (see ex. 6). Thus in bar 32 the third of the minor triad is raised, and the new configuration becomes part of a secondary dominant-seventh chord. In bars 35-41 the major third is retained, but the C-sharp chord, set in second-inversion, serves to prolong the dominant. Finally, in bar 42 root-position harmony confirms the tonic major.

Example 6. Brahms, *Liebeslieder Walzer*, op. 52 no. 18 (reduction of mm. 30-42).

The enharmonic relationship between the keys ending parts 1 and 2 is matched by the passages themselves: bars 35-42 (in C sharp) are virtually identical to bars 11-18 (in D flat). In this dance, then, Brahms reverses the norms of rounded binary form. Typically the A material is restated literally at the outset of the reprise but tonally adjusted at the end. Here, by contrast, the tonal adjustment is made at the beginning of the reprise (from B-flat minor to C-sharp minor), while the endings of the two sections are enharmonically equivalent. Parts A¹ and A² end, therefore, not in a ''rhyme'' (to borrow Leonard Ratner's expression for the relation between the conclusions of the exposition and recapitulation of a sonata form), but in an ''echo.'' Thus Brahms's reading displays a ''metaphor'' which recalls that in the poem itself. By setting the words ''Vöglein'' and ''gedenkt sie dein'' to virtually the same music, the composer clinched Daumer's identification of a capricious little bird and an inconstant lover.

That the dance begins off the tonic is no less significant than the ending in C sharp. Indeed, in the first edition Brahms underscored the nontonic point of departure by including an initiatory two-bar prolongation of B-flat minor not seen in the autograph version (which has the dance beginning only at the point at which the voices enter, in bar 3 of the published score). By thus stressing the submediant region at the outset Brahms emphasized the large-scale tonal polarity, heightening the play between keys, and making the ultimate confirmation of C sharp all the more dramatic.

This explains, in part, why "Es bebet" is an effective closing number: being a key hard won, C sharp seems an appropriate one in which to end. But the suitability of the dance for this task stems also from certain other of its features. In contrast to "Ein dunkler Schacht" (the dance coming last in the autograph), whose conclusion embraces a crescendo, rising lines, and rhythmic activity through the second beat of the last bar, the ending of "Es bebet" possesses many strong signs of closure: two added bars of tonic harmony not present in the first ending (mm. 45a-46a); descending lines; quiet dynamics and a diminuendo; and a written-out ritardando of the rapid eighth-note motion in the *primo*. Significantly, the diminuendo and slowing down of the rhythmic activity coincide with a melodic progression toward $\hat{1}$, one not a little reminiscent of the final bars of opus 39 (which, in Brahms's two-hand version, also unfold in C sharp). The music at once achieves strong closure and seems to die away. With this apt passage the cycle comes to an end.

Considering the close relations between many adjoining waltzes, as well as the evident care with which the final dance in each of the various subgroups was chosen, we must reconsider the view adopted many years ago by Karl Geiringer that the *Liebeslieder* are merely "a loosely bound wreath of songs."[29] Although, as Geiringer correctly pointed out, "the separate items were only gradually given their final form and their place in the sequence," this says nothing about the criteria of compatibility, coherence, and closure that led Brahms to his three final arrangements.

Brahms was pleased with his work. When returning the corrected proofcopy to Simrock in October 1869, he commented that this examination had marked the first time he had been able to smile upon seeing one of his own compositions in print, adding, in so many words, that "I'll be a jackass if our *Liebeslieder* don't bring joy to some people."[30]

[29]Geiringer, *Brahms*, p. 278.
[30]"Ich will gestehen, dass Ich bei dieser Gelegenheit zum erstenmal gelächelt habe beim Anblick eines gedruckten Werkes—von mir! Übrigens möchte ich doch riskieren, ein Esel zu heissen, wenn unsere Liebeslieder nicht einigen Leuten Freude machen." (*Briefwechsel*, 9:85).

The "people" Brahms had in mind were amateur musicians in the home—then, as now, the main market for piano duets. On this point, the composer was explicit, writing elsewhere that he hoped the cycle would become a piece of *Hausmusik* and "soon be sung a lot."[31] Yet, characteristically, Brahms understated matters: we need not deny the dances their effortless charm and immediate attractiveness to recognize in them also the tight construction taken for granted in Brahms's "weightier" compositions.[32]

[31]"Und hoffentlich ist das ein Stück Hausmusik und wird rasch viel gesungen" (*Briefwechsel*, 9:80).
[32]This essay is an extended version of a paper read at the Annual Meeting of the American Musicological Society (Vancouver, 1985).

Janet M. Levy

About Leonard B. Meyer:
A Biographical Vignette

Leonard is fond of pointing out that "people aren't 'all of a piece.'"
A seemingly casual remark, it also reflects one of his serious skepticisms.
It is a skepticism about the reasoning that biographers and historians
sometimes use to try to show the "unity" of a person's life and creative
works. He gently pokes fun at the often contradictory hypotheses that
underlie connections implied between a work and a life. And so it is
not without trepidation that I attempt this biographical sketch of Leonard.
For of course I, too, have underlying interpretive hypotheses about connections and contrarieties, similarities and differences between Leonard's
work and his personal life—and they may not be the same as his own.
For the most part, my hypotheses govern my choices of what I write
about Leonard. But because this little essay is meant to be a surprise
for him, my choices have also been constrained by the data I have been
able only secretly to gather, especially from my primary source.
Although I have pushed my capabilities of deviousness—and, perhaps
I should add, memory—to their limits in surreptitiously interviewing
my subject, I wish I could have found ways to ask more questions without
greater risk of spoiling the surprise. My other sources have been family stories and some snooping, for which I hope I shall be forgiven.

*Janet M. Levy is a musicologist whose main interests are in theory
and criticism, especially of eighteenth- and nineteenth-century music.
Her works include* Beethoven's Compositional Choices *and, most recently, "Covert and Casual Values in Recent Writings about Music."*

Many of those who have engaged in serious dialogue with Leonard will be able to hear him asking, "What evidence do you have?" His empiricist bent seems to have surfaced in a demonstrable way early on, and before his musical one—and it seems to please him now to recognize this. As a boy of about eight he went on nature walks with one Mr. Clarence J. Hylander and several boys from his then relatively new neighborhood in Scarsdale, New York. (He had lived in New York City, where he was born, until the age of seven.) The object was to observe, study, and collect specimens of plants, rocks, and fossils, as well as to catch, and subsequently to lay out, butterflies. By the time he was ten, he and a few neighborhood friends, including "Richie" May, a good friend ever since, had founded the "Scarsdale Science Museum." They set it up in the basement of the Meyer family home on Mamaroneck Road—a large eighteenth-century house which had served as head-quarters for General Howe's army during the Battle of White Plains. And Leonard was the Head. Legend has it that everything in their museum was meticulously labelled according to Latin species names and carefully and neatly displayed. (Was his later concern with pattern-ing and the nature of relationships already manifest?) The nascent publishing scholar issued a mimeographed newsletter of the Museum, while the budding administrator established life-time memberships for something like fifteen cents. There was also the young boys' Scarsdale Hunting and Fishing Club: he and his friends went out to look for and collect turtles, salamanders, et al. No stray forays, these; all the ac-tivities were in some way certified—and lent an air of profession-alism—by their institutionalization. Now *Science* magazine seems near or at the top of the list of his favorite regular reading; indeed it seems to be more regular and important for him than journals in the field of music. His early empiricist bent was never superseded, only rechanneled.

Leonard's earliest formal training in music was not particularly unusual. From about the age of eight there were music lessons of some sort. First, piano with Mrs. Eugenie Newman, who included basic musi-cianship skills. At that time Leonard was apparently better at imitation or playing by ear than at reading music, for he tells with a certain devilish pride (still) of having pretended to read for Mrs. Newman when really he had memorized what she had played for him. Piano lessons lasted for only a few years. After a brief interlude with the clarinet he began to study the violin (about age twelve). This study, for approximately seven to eight years, was central and sustained. Initially his violin teacher was James Levy, the first violinist of the London String Quartet, and Leonard commuted to New York City for his lessons. When commuting proved inconvenient, he switched to John King Roosa in Scarsdale. Roosa was Leonard's main teacher and an important figure in his overall musical development. With Roosa he worked on pieces like Nardini's E minor concerto, Vivaldi's famous one in A minor, Mozart's violin concerti in E-flat and A major, and Mozart and Handel sonatas. And he spent two high-school summers at Roosa's summer music camp in Glenora, New York (on Lake Seneca in the Finger Lakes region), playing in the orchestra and doing a little work in musicianship.

Although his early formal training in music was not remarkable, his early listening experiences do seem to have been so—and to have left a traceably strong imprint in some of the music that to this day entrances him most, music that he continues to seek to understand and explain. (He himself ruminates from time to time on what the effects of his repeated listenings in childhood may have been on his subsequent musical development and interests.) While still a little boy on West 71st Street in New York City, he would wind up the Victrola to play the family's recordings of Caruso singing Verdi—"Di quella pira," "Celeste Aida," and others—and of Louise Homer singing "Che farò" from Gluck's *Orfeo*. Leonard's parents' collection of recordings seems to have been heavily weighted in the area of operatic excerpts (excerpts, of course, because these were 78s—"Celeste Aida" covered an entire side). Exactly what Leonard listened to, when, is hard to reconstruct precisely, but fairly early on in his life there were also the Quartet from *Rigoletto*, the Sextet from *Lucia di Lammermoor*, "Ai nostri monti" from *Il Trovatore*, "Solenne in quest'ora" from *La Forza del Destino*, the duet between Aida and Amonasro in the third act of *Aida,* and excerpts from *Lohengrin, Parsifal,* and *Die Walküre,* Acts 1 and 3, with legendary casts.

Leonard's long affair with Gilbert and Sullivan began in youth, too. It is likely that before the age of seven he was listening to "gems" from *H.M.S. Pinafore* and *The Mikado* and, after the family's move to Scarsdale and the acquisition of an electric phonograph, to *Iolanthe, Patience, The Pirates of Penzance,* and *Trial by Jury* (none had spoken dialogue). He and his older brother, Daniel, played these records all through their teens. They, especially, but also their mother, Marion, and younger sister, Carolyn, still communicate in Gilbert and Sullivan-ese whenever they see the opportunity; Leonard has a few fluent friends, as well. All of a sudden one of them will break into some lines from Gilbert and Sullivan and the other(s) will join in unison-duet or compete in rapid continuation. Gilbert and Sullivan paraphrases are still the order of the day as offerings for birthdays of family and friends and other special occasions.

Before he ever had a formal course in harmony—first at Bard College with Ernest White, the college organist—Leonard had begun to compose. Around 1935 he wrote a violin sonata which, along with assorted other late high-school efforts in composition, apparently found its way to the wastebasket. (There are no traces. Leonard is, on the whole, maddeningly unsentimental—especially for present purposes—about keeping things.) He continued to play the violin at Bard—he played in the college orchestra and took lessons with Elias Dann—but composition was superseding his other musical interests. And when, in his junior year, he transferred to Columbia University (1938), he took his first composition lessons privately with Karl Weigl. Mostly those lessons were exercises in species counterpoint. (He once told me that he chose to study composition privately rather than with Seth Bingham, a composer then on the faculty of Columbia, because he was dismayed when, in response to lyric piano pieces Leonard had brought him as a sample of his composition, Bingham said "Piano music should be percussive.")

Stefan Wolpe was Leonard's next—and primary—teacher of composition. He studied with Wolpe in the years 1939-41, which straddled his senior year at Columbia and the year and a half or so after graduation and before he went into the Army. While his father took a dim view of Leonard's being a composer (the reasoning went that, after all, were Leonard in the league of geniuses, like Mozart, he would have shown his compositional talents at an early age; a non-genius should not compose . . .), Wolpe took him seriously. Leonard became part of a very close-knit group of students and other musicians around Wolpe—a clique—and part of the entourage that followed Wolpe to Port Clyde and Blue Hill, Maine, in the summers of 1940 and 1941. The "inner circle" included what Leonard, with a certain proprietary air, once referred to as "the original triumvirate": Josef Marx, oboist, Isaac Nemiroff and Leonard Meyer, composers. (Somewhat later on, Wolpe's circle included people like Ralph Shapey, Netty Simon, Elmer Bernstein). For the first time in his life Leonard felt that he was in the midst of a group of musicians rather than humanists and philosophers—about which more anon. And during those summers in Maine, the story goes, they all composed or practiced all day. (One of Leonard's vivid memories is hearing Robert Mann, later the first violinist of the Juilliard String Quartet, practicing Prokofiev's Second Violin Concerto all summer for the upcoming Naumberg competition.) When a very pale Leonard returned home, his mother asked him if he ever went outdoors in Maine.

"Only at night" was the answer. Wolpe's own intensity about hard work was infectious and Leonard felt compelled to follow his example.* (Leonard's Quartet for Oboe, Viola, Bassoon, and Piano—one of two works he submitted to the Prix de Rome committee—is inscribed: "To my dear master, Stefan Wolpe.") He *had* to tell Wolpe he was working hard all the time—even if, as was seldom the case, he wasn't. Wolpe's influence on Leonard's future work in music may have transcended his role as composition teacher. One of the things Leonard remembers Wolpe's remarking during composition lessons is something like "that's an empty interval; it needs to be filled in," and Leonard has occasionally reflected on the possibility that such remarks, together with his own subsequent reading in Gestalt psychology, may have influenced his formulations about "gap-fill melodies."

He devoted himself fairly exclusively to composing in the period between graduation from Columbia (1940) and entering the Army (1942). (During part of that time he lived in Greenwich Village and frequented the Village Vanguard in the evenings. It was probably the closest Leonard ever came to having a "Bohemian period.") Indeed, during that time a festival of American music on radio station WNYC focused an entire program on Leonard's compositions. And before entering the Army he submitted two compositions in the competition for the Prix de Rome: a cantata, *John Henry,* and his Quartet for Oboe, Viola, Bassoon, and Piano. From Camp Livingston in Louisiana, Leonard wrote his parents in May 1942: "I just heard over an international hook-up of CBS that your son, Leonard B. Meyer of Scarsdale, N.Y., was awarded one of the $25 prizes for excellency in musical composition by the American Academy in Rome. I hoped you were listening." (It was one of several second prizes.) Aaron Copland was a member of the jury and subsequently tracked Leonard down at Camp Livingston where, in a letter dated June 16, 1942, he wrote him about the "excellent impression" he had of Leonard's *John Henry* piece:

> We all thought the technical resourcefulness was quite remarkable for so young a composer. . . . Despite the complex texture, I think you managed very well to preserve the folk spirit of the tune—or, at any rate, to blow it up in a way that didn't seem out of key with the John Henry subject matter. We all agreed that it would be interesting to hear the piece tried over.

*I should add, however, that he did not lack for role-models—in hard work—at home.

But even with this as a spur there was no opportunity—no peace and quiet—to compose while Leonard was in the Army.

Before continuing—in the Army—there is another strand to be picked up in the knit of Leonard's early life. It might be called "the atmosphere at 31 Mamaroneck Road." Although his parents read him some of the usual children's books (*Winnie the Pooh, Doctor Doolittle*, etc.), from the time Leonard was a boy his father, Arthur, would also read aloud to the children* short stories of O. Henry and R.L. Stevenson, plays of Molière (in English translation) like *Les Fourberies de Scapin* (an amusing favorite of Leonard's) and *Le Bourgeois Gentilhomme,* and, as time went on, of G.B. Shaw—*Pygmalion, Major Barbara,* and *Man and Superman*—and Barrie's *Admirable Crichton;* the complete novels *David Copperfield* and *Nicholas Nickelby* of Charles Dickens, and *Vanity Fair* of Thackeray. Above all, there was Shakespeare. Arthur read many of the plays, from the histories of *Henry IV* and *Richard* to *Hamlet* and *Twelfth Night.* Leonard quotes readily and in sizable chunks from these. Originally Arthur read—performed—these plays aloud for the family alone but in time the readings became the focus and raison d'être of soirées for neighbors and friends, as well. According to Daniel, the children were sometimes so jealous of the "outsiders" who came to the house for Arthur's readings, that they would say with disdain, "Those people come only for the food."

It was not merely Arthur's arresting performances that characterized "the atmosphere at 31 Mamaroneck Road." It was also the "crowd" at the house on many a Sunday afternoon while Leonard was growing up. These virtually weekly gatherings of family and friends included people like Morris R. Cohen, philosopher and close family friend, whose writings Leonard frequently quotes; Osmond Fraenkel, a noted civil liberties lawyer; and professors from Columbia Law School where Leonard's uncle, Jerome Michael, taught. There were lively and, evidently, high-powered discussions of religion, politics, Zionism, legal issues. When Leonard decided to take a year "off" between high-school graduation and college in order to read philosophy and literature, he did so under the tutelage of one Ned Rubin who was a graduate student of Morris Cohen.

It wasn't until shortly before graduating from Columbia that Leonard became aware that he was doing so with honors in philosophy. That is, he had in fact majored in philosophy, but he thinks he hadn't con-

---

*Arthur S. Meyer was a successful businessman and a distinguished labor mediator, and the children three in all: Daniel, three years older than Leonard; Leonard, the middle child; Carolyn, five years younger than Leonard.

sciously chosen. He had simply gravitated toward courses in philosophy with Irwin Edman (aesthetics), Ernest Nagel (philosophy of science), and John H. Randall, and toward courses in biology and zoology, as well. With a happy smile, he recalls doing experiments on sea urchins with H. Burr Steinbach, apparently a memorable teacher. He also took courses in history (with Jacques Barzun among others), economics, and Columbia's famous "Contemporary Civilization."

Just how heady Leonard's humanistic background must have been comes through vividly and movingly in letters he wrote home from the Army (and which, fortunately, his mother kept). He enlisted—because he knew he'd be called—and entered in March 1942: Company L, part of the 28th Division of the 109th Infantry.* Right after landing in England in October 1943 (age 25), while "billeted at an old castle-manor estate," he wrote:

> For the second time I am in England and it is still, even under such questionable circumstances, a thrill to be here.** For England is to me more than just another countryside—and another monetary system—a new taste to beer. The countryside is the green forest of Arden—fields through which Tom Jones so unceremoniously scampered—money with which Jack Falstaff drank "sack"—and but a "penny worth of bread for all that deal of sack."—And ale at the Mermaid Tavern. And when I pass an old inn it is not just another slightly weatherbeaten building—like one anywhere in the world—it is perhaps a tavern of Doll Tearsheet—or one where Goldsmith, Blake, or Johnson had good talk over their ale—All this added pleasure—you have given me background and insight to enjoy and experience.

And from the dusty (or miserably muddy, when it rained), often hot and humid, camps of Louisiana and Florida, where he trained in 1942 and part of 1943, he wrote not only of long forced marches with heavy loads, of rifle-squad and maneuvers, but also about his reading of poetry and essays, short stories—from K.A. Porter to H.G. Wells, of mysteries, of John Dos Passos's *USA,* Virginia Woolf's *Mrs. Dalloway,* Thomas

*Leonard was first a Private, then a Corporal, later a Technical Sergeant and, finally, commissioned in the field to Second Lieutenant (March 1945). For a considerable time before he was commissioned an officer he was a Forward Observer with the Cannon Company of his division—something he does not let me forget when we go hiking! He participated in many of the famous battles of World War II, including The Battle of the Bulge and the Battle of the Hurtgin Forest. He was also with the outfit that took Colmar, and he is proud of having "liberated Paris."
**He had been before, at age fifteen, with a cousin and an older boy who acted as chaperone.

Wolfe's *Look Homeward, Angel,* and a biography of G.B. Shaw (the last two sent him at his request by his parents); and he wrote probingly and at considerable length of his reactions to *The Federalist* and Veblen's *Theory of the Leisure Class.* From "somewhere in England" on Christmas Eve 1943 a poignantly lonely Leonard began writing of his reading of George Santayana's *The Life of Reason.* His detailed comments on the various parts, especially on "Reason in Common Sense," "Reason in Society," and "Reason in Religion" continued in successive letters throughout much of January 1944.* On January 19 of that year he wrote, "And it is in such desperate loneliness for a like viewpoint, that I have turned to Santayana—and found him a friend with a warm heart and an understanding spirit."

And all the time he was on active duty he thought about and wrote home about the nature of things in the Army. At one point, from Germany in 1945, he wryly referred to his own remarks as " 'De Rerum Natura' (Revised Trench Edition, 1945)." He speculated on the nature of human beings at war. He wrote like both a political philosopher and an anthropologist of Army behavior. Apparently irritated by an article in an autumn issue of the *Saturday Review* he wrote a long Letter to the Editor, dated 4 February 1945 and published in the issue of March 10, from which I excerpt:

> I doubt that war matures men. It is a strictly regulated life in which most of one's thinking is done by 'higher headquarters.' Seldom does a 'doughboy' know what he is attacking, what the plan of attack is, or why he is fighting. . . . Most of a soldier's time is spent trying to get warm, dry, and heat his cold rations. . . . The suffering . . . is *not* mental suffering. . . . The *real* suffering is *physical.*

The conviction about the importance of understanding "why" is present in some of his very first letters from training camp in Louisiana. He wrote then of the poor spirit of his outfit, the lack of pride in the 28th division: "These men do not want to fight—they don't think there is anything in the war to fight for and they don't understand the implications of the whole war." He tried to explain the poor spirit (among other things: "They [the officers] coerce the men instead of leading them.") and complained that the officers were not good teachers for they didn't show "why," only "how."

---

*He especially liked the sections on "Mythology" and "Love." He carried his little Modern Library Edition of Santayana all through Europe during the war. It is that beat-up, rain-stained copy that sits on his bookshelf now.

During the summer of 1943 he had written home: "I must write music again after the war—if there is such a thing as 'after' . . . .I must . . . just learn to live all over again." That same summer he invited Lee Malakoff, whom he had met while he was stationed in Florida where she was a college student, to join him at his home in Scarsdale on his leave from the Army. They married in August 1945, a few months before his Army discharge. He enrolled at Columbia University for the Spring Semester 1946 to begin work on a Master's degree in composition.

This time at Columbia he took many music courses. Otto Luening was his composition teacher while he worked on the M.A., and was the dedicatee of Leonard's "Music for Orchestra" (1948), his only twelve-tone piece. (About this, he told me that he tried to make sure it wouldn't sound twelve-tone!) He took other courses in music with William Mitchell, Curt Sachs ("wonderful"), Paul Henry Lang, and Erich Hertzmann. During his first post-war summer (1946) he went to Tanglewood to study composition with Aaron Copland. Not long after his return to New York from Tanglewood, Leonard was sitting in the Chock Full O' Nuts at 116th Street and Broadway when Copland walked in and asked how he would like a job teaching music at the University of Chicago. That was the serendipitous if, Leonard claims, somewhat nervous beginning of a twenty-nine-year-long relationship with the University of Chicago. He began teaching there on October 1, 1946, the very day his first child, Muffie (Marion), was born.

From then on, his work on the M.A. at Columbia (1949) was sand-wiched into summers and one semester of leave from teaching. During this period he composed, in addition to the "Music for Orchestra," "Three Songs" for mixed chorus, flute, clarinet, horn and harp (1948) on texts by the symbolist poet H.D. (Hilda Doolittle), and dedicated to his colleague Siegmund Levarie and to the Collegium Musicum of the University of Chicago who premiered the work in April 1948; a Trio for Piano, Clarinet, and Viola (1947), dedicated to Cecil Smith, Leonard's first chairman at the University of Chicago; and a Violin and Piano Sonata (1948), which was his M.A. thesis.* The Trio was premiered as a concert piece in October 1947 at a much-reviewed

---

*This was performed at least once, in January 1949. He is usually negative about his own compositions, but about this one he confessed that he liked the finale and described the slow movement as "juicy and tonal." There are several other compositions I know of that I have not mentioned. Of these I have found only one, "Three Pieces for Piano," composed in 1941. The first and last pieces in the group are dedicated to Elmer Bernstein who performed the set in Chicago in May 1948. Apparently there was also a Duo for Violin and Violoncello and an unfinished cantata for men's chorus and two pianos, based on the last speech of Vanzetti to the court.

University of Chicago concert; there were additional scattered performances of it as late as 1956 (at an ISCM concert in New York). In somewhat altered form, the Trio also became the music Leonard was commissioned to provide for a ballet, "Wind of Torment," choreographed and danced by Jerome Andrews. The subject of the choreography was temperamentally unsuited to Leonard: the tortured conflict of the Id, Ego, and Super-Ego of an individual personality. (The ballet was performed at least several times in the winter of 1948, in both Chicago and New York.)

For his father's seventieth birthday in 1950 Leonard composed a set of piano variations on "Happy Birthday," in Arthur's favorite musical styles. After that there seems to have been little composition. One possible reason may be that his then Dean at the University of Chicago had told him that "he'd better get a Ph.D." since no one at the University was being promoted to tenure without it. And so, in 1950 and 1951, he began work on his Ph.D., not in the Music Department—since he was teaching there—but, rather, in the Committee on the History of Culture. The nature of that program worked well for him; it allowed him to read and talk with faculty people in different disciplines. There was Otto Gombosi in music, and Grosvenor Cooper after Gombosi left Chicago; Charles Morris in philosophy (one should perhaps say philosophy/psychology); Joachim Wach in the sociology of religion; and others. Leonard's primary interest gradually shifted from composition to the aesthetics, theory, and psychology of music that, very broadly speaking, became the subject of his Ph.D. dissertation, which became his first book, *Emotion and Meaning in Music*. The degree was awarded in 1954; the book was published in 1956. And the first review, by Winthrop Sargeant, in *The New Yorker* magazine of January 5, 1957, was laudatory beyond wildest dreams. Leonard likes to think that the ensuing avalanche of reviews and attention had something to do with that first "lucky" one by Sargeant. Indeed, Leonard not infrequently says "I was lucky"—and he seems really to think this way about his life.

With the Ph.D. and, particularly, the publication of *Emotion and Meaning* had come tenure (1956). There was time now for some respite from the intensity of those first ten years in Academe—years which had seen not only teaching, lecturing, and writing but also a major shift in professional orientation from composition to music theory/analysis/aesthetics/psychology, the completion of two advanced degrees, and, last but not least, the birth of two more daughters, Carlin in 1948, Erica in 1953. The entire family spent from March to December of 1957 in Europe.

When Leonard returned to the University of Chicago in 1958, he began a more administrative phase of his career as Head of the Humanities Section of the College (1958-60). Even now, perhaps wryly—because of mild embarrassment at the indelibility of that teaching?—but never cynically, he refers to things he and others taught in "Hum I," as they called it. (There was also a "Hum II" and a "Hum III," but it is "Hum I" that he refers to most often and with stories that affectionately caricature some of the teaching.) It was, in his own words,

> concerned with the materials and the structural principles of literature, music, and the visual arts. In many ways it . . . was a 'skills' course; that is, its goal was to make students competent and perceptive readers, listeners, and viewers. In general, the 'Socratic method' was used . . . . Hum I was not organized chronologically. Instead, works, often radically different in style or character, were chosen because they exemplified particular techniques, kinds of relationships, or structural principles. . . . Nor was the course designed to be cross-disciplinary. . . . Within each art, however, works studied early in the year were often reconsidered in the light of later learning or of a new context.*

Hum I's fundamental principles continue to be basic to Leonard's beliefs about the way the arts should be taught at an introductory level.

The kind of thinking that characterized the Humanities program in the College was highly congenial to Leonard's own style of working—both intra- and inter-opus, so to speak. In remarks made preliminary to his detailed description (1974) of the "Hutchins College" at the University of Chicago, he used a "shovel metaphor" to describe his own preferred mode of intellectual "digging" as follows:

> . . . take an unprepossessing shovel and begin to dig in what seems an attractive spot. . . . The deeper down you go the wider the perimeter at the top of the hole becomes. And, as the perimeter widens, it will even- tually touch upon and overlap those of other, related disciplines. . . . Breadth and depth are inextricably joined.

During the late fifties he continued to pursue in greater depth—to read and think about, lecture and write about—some of the subjects he had touched upon in *Emotion and Meaning*—especially "meaning in music

---

*This description is quoted from a newspaper, "Seminar Reports" I/8 (Columbia University, May 15, 1974), pp. 6-7. It is the text of a talk that Leonard gave on "General Education at the University of Chicago" at a Seminar on General and Continuing Education, held at Columbia in the academic year 1973-74.

and information theory," "value and greatness in music," and "universalism and relativism in the study of ethnic music." He had begun to work seriously on rhythm even before the publication of *Emotion and Meaning:* as early as 1955, he gave a talk, "Toward an Understanding of Rhythmic Process in Music," at a midwest-chapter meeting of the American Musicological Society. Of course his major work of the late fifties was *The Rhythmic Structure of Music,* co-authored with Grosvenor Cooper, and published in 1960. During this same period he also wrote a piece on music therapy and he had begun thinking about matters that led first to the essay "Art by Accident" (which he likes to call by its original title, "Chance, Art, and Value") and, later, to many pages in *Music, the Arts, and Ideas* (1967). It was—and is—characteristic that his projects dovetail: writing one while, in more leisurely fashion, reading, thinking and making notes about another, usually quite different, subject.

While a Fellow at the Center for Advanced Studies at Wesleyan University for the academic year 1960-61, Leonard's special breed of intellectual pluralism had a field day. John Cage was there, too; his office was just down the hall and he and Leonard had numerous dialogues. Leonard also enjoyed provocative talks with Fellows in the biological sciences, as well as with Faculty and Fellows in history, art, and ethnomusicology. It was, he said, "an enormously enriching year." An immediately tangible "product" was one of his most widely read pieces, "Forgery and the Anthropology of Art." It was during this year, too, that he worked on a comparative study of style in Baroque and Classic minuets—an empirical study that was never brought to completion. Before returning to Chicago from the year at Wesleyan, the family spent the summer of 1961 at Woods Hole, Massachusetts in company with people at the Marine Biological Laboratory. One might speculate that Leonard's alter ego was asserting itself again, but it seems equally probable that a confluence of pragmatic considerations led the family to Woods Hole that summer.

Part II of Leonard's "administrative phase" was his nine-year chairmanship of the Music Department at the University of Chicago, from 1961 to 1970. His strong belief in the importance of faculty—people—over buildings in shaping and distinguishing a department is demonstrated by the outstanding group of people that the department hired while he was chairman: the musicologists Lawrence Bernstein, Howard Brofsky, Howard Brown, Philip Gossett, Robert Marshall, and Leo Treitler; and the composers William T. McKinley, Ralph Shapey, and Richard Wernick. Through his efforts, too, the University of Chicago's Contemporary

Chamber Players flourished under the direction of Ralph Shapey. Leonard must have taken the chairmanship in stride, for he managed at the same time to write most of *Music, the Arts, and Ideas* and began to work on *Explaining Music* (1973)—much of which was first presented as five public lectures when he was Ernest Bloch Professor at the University of California at Berkeley in the winter and spring of 1971.

Three pivotal changes occurred in Leonard's life in 1975: first, after twenty-nine years at the University of Chicago* he accepted an appointment as Benjamin Franklin Professor of Music and Humanities at the University of Pennsylvania (when he left Chicago he had been Phyllis Fay Horton Professor from 1972); second, his first marriage ended; finally, in November of that year he and I were married.

At the University of Pennsylvania he taught not only in the Music Department—where he was also a mentor for students/scholars who came from places as distant as Japan, China, and Australia to talk with him and, when feasible, to sit in on his classes—but in the Psychology Department, as well. There he co-taught courses on "Emotion" and "The Evolution of Culture." And, with people he met in the Psychology Department, his empirical leanings found new outlets. Principal among his collaborators was Burton Rosner with whom Leonard worked on, and published, two empirical studies of melodic perception.**

---

*During those twenty-nine years he was also a visiting professor at a number of other schools, sometimes in the summers, sometimes during leaves from Chicago: the Universities of British Columbia, Michigan, California (at Los Angeles and Berkeley); while at Penn he was also a visiting professor at Oklahoma. The places he has lectured are far too numerous to list; they range from Saskatchewan to Texas, from Massachusetts to California, and even to the Far East. He has addressed professional meetings of music educators, ethnomusicologists, aestheticians, and psychologists, as well as those of musicologists and music theorists.

**Rosner is now at Oxford University in England. With Harriet Oster, formerly in the Psychology Department at the University of Pennsylvania, Leonard worked on a very different sort of empirical study on "Facial Expression and Musical Performance"; this project has not yet been completed. There is one other area of empirical investigation in which Leonard has twice begun to work: attempting to measure and assess the relation of notational determinants to the performance of particular rhythmic groupings. The interest is in what performers in fact do when confronted with certain kinds of notation—for example, slurs and phrase-marks. He first—and basically unsuccessfully—tried to study performances from this point of view with the aid of a melograph, during the summer he spent at UCLA. He worked together with Robert McMahan who was a graduate student at the University of Chicago. Interest in this project surfaced again in a somewhat different form when Leonard tried to do experiments on the subject, together with Robert Hopkins who was, at the time, a graduate student at the University of Pennsylvania.

That Leonard is something of a "workaholic" seems self-evident. That, for him, work is a form of play—in the best sense of *homo ludens*— may be less so. And his pleasure in, his relish for, reasoned argument (both of his own and that of others) permeate not only his work-life but his everyday life as well. He likes to think of himself as "an eighteenth-century person." Indeed, his idea of "fun-reading" on the beach in the Caribbean is Alexander Pope and Samuel Johnson—from whom he cannot resist reading passages aloud, *con espressione*. Anyone who knows Leonard personally will be familiar with those other aspects of his *homo ludens* spirit that are continually manifest in his puns and bons mots, in his delight in (hearing and telling) good jokes and (reciting and composing) limericks.

Perhaps it is because for him work is always serious play that Leonard seems never to have had a fallow period. Habitually he has several irons of inquiry in the proverbial fire. As suggested earlier, he often begins to work in a new area as a way of relaxing from the rigors of ongoing hard work in another one. And as soon as he begins to think and read about a subject Leonard begins to make notes. He carries a little notebook at all times. Clearly there is nothing too wild, too "far-out," no self-censorship in the realm of note-making; "everything" goes; and the note-making seems to come at any time—in waiting rooms, in line at the bank, on mountain tops, in the middle of the night.

As I complete this vignette, Leonard has recently finished the manuscript of his new book on style, tentatively titled *Style and Music: Theory, History, and Ideology*. At the moment, along with his usual periodicals, he is reading *The Dialectical Biologist* by Richard Levins and Richard Lewontin. He has just told me a new idea he has for work on melodic schemata in relation to musical *topoi*. And there are file-folders labelled "Sociobiology" (on which he has already been working for a while) and "Motor Behavior," into which, typically, will go notes from his notebooks and xeroxes of relevant articles. By the time this is in print I expect those folders will be much, much fuller.

Writings by Leonard B. Meyer

In 1988, Leonard B. Meyer retires as Benjamin Franklin Professor of Music and Humanities at the University of Pennsylvania. His distinguished career has been recognized by honorary degrees from Grinnell and Bard Colleges and Loyola University, and by his election as a fellow of the American Academy of Arts and Sciences and the American Association for the Advancement of Science. He has been invited to serve as resident scholar at the Bellagio Study and Conference Center and as a senior fellow of the School of Criticism and Theory, and to deliver several prestigious series of lectures, including the Ernest Bloch Lectures at the University of California, Berkeley, the Tanner Lectures on Human Values at Stanford University, and as Patten Lecturer at Indiana University. For his published work, Professor Meyer has received the Gordon Laing Book Award and has twice been nominated for a National Book Award.

BOOKS

Emotion and Meaning in Music (Chicago, 1956). Translated into Polish and Serbo-Croatian; a Chinese translation is in preparation. Excerpts have been included in a number of books on aesthetics and the humanities.

The Rhythmic Structure of Music, with Grosvenor W. Cooper (Chicago, 1960). Translated into Japanese by Yoshihiko Tokumaru.

Music, the Arts, and Ideas: Patterns and Predictions in Twentieth-Century Culture (Chicago, 1967). Translated into Korean.

Explaining Music: Essays and Explorations (Berkeley and Los Angeles, 1973). Paperback edition Chicago, 1978.

Style and Music: Theory, History, and Ideology (Philadelphia, forthcoming).

ARTICLES

"A History of Musical Instruments in Slides" (catalogue published by Dr. Julius Rosenthal, 1952).

"Learning, Belief and Music Therapy," *Music Therapy* 5 (1956): 27-35.

"Meaning in Music and Information Theory," *Journal of Aesthetics and Art Criticism* 15 (1957): 412-424.
  Reprinted in *Music, the Arts, and Ideas.*
  Translated as "Vyznam v hudbe a teorie informace," in *Nove cesty hudby* (Prague, 1970), pp. 37-49; "Musiilin merkitys ja informaatioteoria," in *Nykyestetiikan ongelmia* (Helsinki, 1971), pp. 155-171; "Mening i Musik och Informationstheori," in *Musikestetisk Antologi,* ed. T. Anderberg and B. Edlund (Sweden, 1985), pp. 178-196.

"Some Remarks on Value and Greatness in Music," *Journal of Aesthetics and Art Criticism* 17 (1959): 486-500.
  Reprinted in *Music, the Arts, and Ideas* and in:
  Aesthetic Inquiry, ed. Monroe C. Beardsley and Herbert M. Schueller (Belmont, CA, 1967), pp. 260-273.
  Aesthetics Today, ed. Morris H. Philipson (New York, 1961), pp. 169-187.
  Graduate Comment 8 (1965): 194-206.
  Mirrors of Man, ed. Paul C. Obler (New York, 1962), pp. 156-184.
  Perspectives in Music Education, Source Book III, ed. Bonnie C. Kowall (Washington, DC, 1966), pp. 83-99.
  Translated as "Nagra kommentarer om varde och storhet i musiken," in *Musikestetisk Antologi,* ed. T. Anderberg and B. Edlund (Sweden, 1985), pp. 178-196.

"Universalism and Relativism in the Study of Ethnic Music," *Ethnomusicology* 4 (1960): 49-54.
  Reprinted in: *Readings in Ethnomusicology,* ed. David P. McAllester (New York, 1971), pp. 269-276.

"Art by Accident," *Horizon* 3 (1960): 30 ff.

"On Rehearing Music," *Journal of the American Musicological Society* 14 (1961): 257-267.
  Reprinted in *Music, the Arts, and Ideas* and in:
  Problems in Aesthetics, ed. Morris Weitz (New York, 1970), pp. 520-531.

"Forgery and the Anthropology of Art," *Yale Review* 52 (1962): 220-233. Reprinted in *Music, the Arts, and Ideas* and in: *Academic Discourse*, ed. John Jacob Enck (New York, 1964), pp. 285-295.
Culture and Art, ed. Lars Aagaard-Mogensen (Atlantic Highlands, NJ, 1976), pp. 53-66.
Translated as "Fakszerstwo—I Antropologia Sztuki," *Tematy* 3 (1964): 36-51.

"The End of the Renaissance?" *Hudson Review* 16 (1963): 169-186. Reprinted in *Music, the Arts, and Ideas* and in: *Innovations*, ed. Bernard Bergonzi (London, 1968), pp. 46-65. Translated as: "El fin del renacimiento?" *Sur* 285 (1963): 24-41.

"The Arts Today and Tomorrow," University Lectures, No. 21 (University of Saskatchewan, 1969).

"Critical Analysis and Performance: The Theme of Mozart's A Major Piano Sonata," *New Literary History* 2 (1971): 461-476. Included in part in *Explaining Music: Essays and Explorations*. Translated into Japanese.

"The Dilemma of Choosing: Speculations about Contemporary Culture," in *Value and Values in Evolution*, ed. Edward A. Maziarz (New York, 1979), pp. 117-141.

"Reply to Rudolph Arnheim," *Yearbook of Comparative and General Literature* 25 (1976): 15-18.

"Concerning the Sciences, the Arts—AND the Humanities," *Critical Inquiry* 1 (1974): 163-217.

"Grammatical Simplicity and Relational Richness: The Trio of Mozart's G Minor Symphony," *Critical Inquiry* 2 (1976): 693-761. Reprinted in *The Garland Library of the History of Western Music*, ed. Ellen Rosand: vol. 14, *Approaches to Tonal Analysis* (New York and London, 1985), pp. 91-159.

"Toward a Theory of Style," in *The Concept of Style*, ed. Berel Lang (Philadelphia, 1979), pp. 3-44. Paperback edition (Ithaca, 1987), pp. 21-71.

"Exploiting Limits: Creation, Archetypes and Change," *Daedalus* 109 (1980): 177-205. Reprinted in *The Garland Library of the History of Western Music*, ed. Ellen Rosand: vol. 13, *Criticism and Analysis* (New York and London, 1985), pp. 141-169.

"Process and Morphology in Mozart's Music," *The Journal of Musicology* 1 (1982): 67-94.

"Melodic Processes and the Perception of Music," with Burton S.Rosner, in *The Psychology of Music,* ed. Diana Deutsch (Orlando, FL, 1982), pp. 317-341.

"Innovation, Choice, and the History of Music," *Critical Inquiry* 9 (1983): 517-544.

"Music and Ideology in the Nineteenth Century," in *The Tanner Lectures on Human Value* VI, ed. S. M. McMurrin (Salt Lake City, 1985), pp. 21-52.

"The Perceptual Roles of Melodic Process, Contour, and Form," with Burton S. Rosner, *Music Perception* 4 (1986): 1-39.

REVIEWS

Donald N. Ferguson, *Music as Metaphor,* in *Journal of the American Musicological Society* 15 (1962): 234-236.

E. H. Gombrich, "In Search of Cultural History," in *History and Theory* 9 (1970): 397-399.

UNPUBLISHED ESSAYS

"Formal Ambiguity in the First Movement of Beethoven's String Quartet in A Minor" (ca. 1960).

"Thoughts about Unity in Music," paper for meeting of American Society for Aesthetics (1962).

"Contemporary Analytic Procedures," paper given at Indiana University (ca. 1963).

"McLuhan's Message: Monism and Models," lecture given at The University of Chicago (ca. 1968).

"The Creative Dimension: The Fine Arts and the Art of Healing," paper given at Kent State University (1975).

Index